"Radnar!" cried Nibulus, then hurled himself towards the beast.

But at that precise moment the same screech that had sounded earlier was uttered again, only this time much closer. Everybody, the Afanc included, looked up towards the doorway.

There now stood Bolldhe, the fingers of his left hand enmeshed inextricably in the thick tresses of Nym-Cadog's hair as she convulsed at his feet. His axe, in his other hand, was poised above her neck.

"Kill it, Nibulus!" he cried frantically.

"Kill them, Afanc!" Nym-Cadog sobbed with equal desperation.

Then Bolldhe's axe swept down, at exactly the same moment as did Unferth.

From the top of the stairs came the obscene sounds of chopping, choking, and gristle separating, till nearby the steps and walls streamed with blood. From the Afanc, however, came only a single wet grunt, followed by a squelching impact as it landed on the cold, hard flagstones, its head split neatly in two.

Silence...

The last lingering light from the jade walls glowed red through the blood that ran down them, traced the trickle of the Afanc's life-force as it coursed down the sluice and into the well, flickered one final time...and died.

"*The Wanderer's Tale* plunges readers into a rich, vividly realized world, exploring it alongside fascinating characters."   —Ed Greenwood

The

Wanderer's

Tale

ANNALS OF LINDORMYN: I

David Bilsborough

TOR®

A TOM DOHERTY ASSOCIATES BOOK
NEW YORK

THE WANDERER'S TALE

Copyright © 2007 by David Bilsborough

Printed in the United States of America by special arrangement with Pan Macmillan.

Published simultaneously in the United Kingdom by Tor UK, an imprint of Pan Macmillan.

North American edition edited by James Frenkel

A Tor Book
Published by Tom Doherty Associates, LLC
175 Fifth Avenue
New York, NY 10010

www.tor-forge.com

Tor® is a registered trademark of Tom Doherty Associates, LLC.

Library of Congress Cataloging-in-Publication Data

Bilsborough, David.
    The wanderer's tale / David Bilsborough.
        p. cm.
    "A Tom Doherty Associates book."
    ISBN-13: 978-0-7653-2100-8
    ISBN-10: 0-7653-2100-9
    I. Title.
PR6102.I47W36 2007
823'.92—dc22

                                                                    2007009536

First Hardcover Edition: July 2007
First Trade Paperback Edition: May 2008

Printed in the United States of America

0 9 8 7 6 5 4 3 2 1

To black sheep, herd-strayers, wanderers, gaps, and cunnans the world over; to all those who know a lie when they hear it. To anyone, in fact, who has taken the king's shilling and shoved it right back down the king's throat. Let the gods, senators, and ministers fight their own useless bloody wars.

Acknowledgments

Paul Frater
Jonathan Greenwood
Robert Hale
Paul Harding
Ian Hutchinson
Paul Waggot
Nigel Winters
and
James Shallow
(Fifth year)

And, for all those years of blind faith and encouragement,
special thanks to John Parker and Guy Tomlinson.

Thanks also to my parents, and to all at Pan Macmillan, especially Peter Lavery,
for the careful pruning, the judicious trimming, and not least, the swabbing out
of the most feculent bits.

Vaagenfjord
Maw

Wyrld's
Point   Jagt Straits

Wrythe

Dragon   FR
Coast   Seter   O
Heights   N

Fram Point   Eotunlandt

Fram Peninsula   Ghoulem   Blue Mountains

Herdlands   Old
of the   Kingdom
Friy   Tusse
Hawdan
Gothla   Valley

Nail   Blighted
Hrefna Forest   Mountains   Heathlands
Tyvenborg
Bhergallia
Venna
Rhelma-   Crimson
Find   Sea
Moel   Grendalin
Bryn
PENDONIUM   Crouagh
Forest
Ymla-Eligiad
QUIRAVIA

Drachrastaland

Lazhor

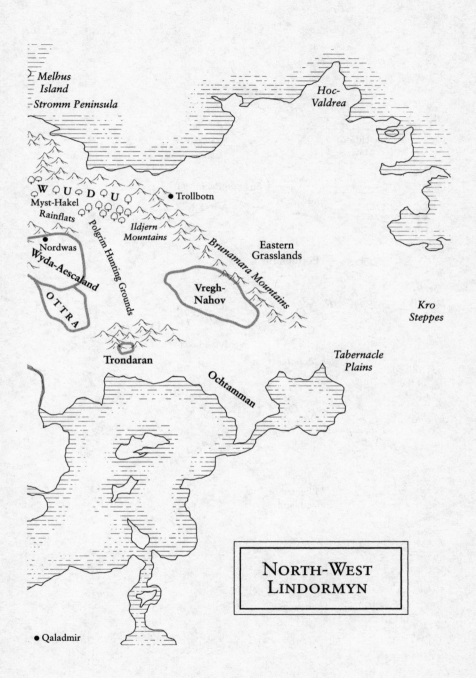

Melhus
Island

Stromm Peninsula

Hoc-
Valdrea

W U D U • Trollbotn

Myst-Hakel
Rainflats

Ildjern
Mountains

Brunamara Mountains

Eastern
Grasslands

Polgrim Hunting Grounds

• Nordwas

Wyda-Aescaland

O T T R A

Vregh-
Nahov

Kro
Steppes

Trondaran

Ochtamman

Tabernacle
Plains

• Qaladmir

NORTH-WEST
LINDORMYN

Vaagenfjord
Maw

Melhus
Island

Stromm Peninsula

Wyrld's
Point

Jagt Straits

Wrythe

Eotunlandt

Seter
Heights

F R O N - W U D U

Myst-Hakel

Blue Mountains

Rainflats

Herdlands
of the
Tusse

Old
Kingdom

Nordwas

Wyda-Aescaland

Polgrim Hunting Grounds

Hawdan
Valley

Blighted
Heathlands

O T T R A

The

Wanderer's

Tale

Vade-Mecum

Vaagenfjord Maw. Tower of Darkness. Throne of Evil. Undercroft of the direst Rawgr ever unleashed from the vile hands of Olchor.

> . . . *Unholy Trinity of Darke Angels, Archangels*
> *of Olchor, from Hell have been hurl'd;*
> *Scathur the Herald, the Wolf from the Sea, has ris'n,*
> *now releas'd from his frozen prison,*
> *and walkes now upon the wyrld.*
> *Gruddna, the Fyr-Draikke, Engine of Destruction, has from the Pit*
>   *crawllen.*
> *And Drauglir, greatest of them all, from blacken'd sky has fallen,*
> *Darke Angel descends where the wyrld ends . . .*

Verge of the world, the northernmost rim of the continent, and beyond that, the island of Melhus. A land of turmoil, of fire and ice, where the four elements wage constant war with each other. Winds filled with shards of ice scream like a host of rapacious demons from the very heart of Eisholm, terrible enough to flay the skin. Volcanoes there are too, mephitic behemoths of incandescent fury that cough great pyroclastic clouds upon the seething ice fields below.

> . . . *For Evil has forg'd its Avatars, and rais'd itself a tower, a kingdom*
> *of pestilence, a domain of resplendour, and woulde reache oute its claws*
> *o'er this wyrld, Lyndormyn (whose carapace yet be so perniciously in-*
> *fest'd), rain in blood o'er lesser orders, and besmear its illimitable dark-*
> *ness o'er all . . .*

Vainglorious in their darksome apotheosis, the unholy trinity judge that heaven will suffer them to go unchallenged:

> *. . . But the clash o' firmaments resounds, like the baying of Heaven's Houndes, o'er the beshiver'd ice of the Wyrld's Bounds, continent's jagged rim. For we came, warriors grim, Pel-Adan's finest, in numbers undream't of in this age or the last . . .*

Vanguard of Unferth-wielder, banners held high, horns blaring in defiance, the multitude of knights valiant journey to the land of fire and ice in ships beyond counting. Relentless, they storm the Maw, thrust on through the Moghol, and arrive at last unto Smaulka-Degernerth, the Hall of Fire:

> *. . . Then, earth-shaken, Gruddna did awaken, its coils unfurl'd, and haul'd its scaly bulk from the Underwyrld. Its head uprear'd thru the ebon smog, eyes flash'd like bescarletted stars thru fog, unfolded its wings, wall to wall, o'er the Hall o' Fyre . . .*

"Valor! Valor! We can do this. Just keep your eyes peeled for its weak spot, then shoot without hesitation. Don't hang about!"

> *. . . Thru visor'd helm 'gainst the awful glare did we stare, and the hostages we now saw, hung spiked upon pinions' claw, the Oghain-Yddiaw, eyelids peel'd bare to afforde them no shield 'gainst the light so bright, blinding them of sight, steaming eyes milky-white . . .*

"Vizards down! It's coming in for another sweep . . . *Oh Hell!*"

> *. . . With a roar that splinter'd this glassy hole, and laid our legions low as a field of hay, upon us the fiery juggernaut did roll. In a rush of beating wings that drove befor it the blackness of Hell's bowel, the nectar of its maw disgorg'd 'pon our ranks an ichor so foul, which then did kindle from the river of fyre to engulf us all . . .*

Victims now, some have time to scream then die, some to melt into mire, others merely to vanish into vapor.

Oaths, though, have been taken, votive entreaty that can be broken only upon most terrible retribution.

> *. . . In that hall in multitudes did we fall, building a wall of blacken'd flesh, crisp'd meat, a dike of dead, insufferable heat. Yet thru befouing waftings of opiate smoke, tho reel we might, and scream and choke, our*

crossbows were let fly, loud as tempest's cry, and the air did sigh with the breath of God . . .

Volley after volley of quarrels discharge, over the molten river, igniting in the air as they fly, a rain of fire upon Fyr.

Veiled in sleeting, gouting crimson, trailing its own bowels along pinnacles of glass, Gruddna goes down for the last time.

There at the mouth of Lubang-Nagar, like a soul plummeting down to Hell can be heard the fall of the Fyr-Draikke. Of Scathur and Drauglir, though, not a sign is to be seen.

. . . And when the smoke it lifted, there stood we, the shining soldiers of the Purging Sword, Peladanes of the One True Lord . . .

VICTORY . . .

G

Prologue

Well, that *didn't go so well,* Scathur reflected as he made his way to his master's throne room.

No, that hadn't worked out so well at all. Gruddna the Fyr-Draikke was destroyed, and though both Scathur and Drauglir yet lived, there was something deeply, fundamentally displeasing about an Unholy Trinity made up now of just two.

They made jokes about Scathur, his lowliest foot soldiers did. "Old Sca'-Face," they would call him. Impersonate the grandiosity of his walk, the grandiloquence of his talk. Satirize his risible attempts at poetry. Smirk at the vainglory of his vair-and-ermine attire, and moreover his refusal to wear black. And then one day they would find themselves, for the first time in their lives, actually within but a few yards of him, and all of a sudden the smiles faded and the jokes did not seem so funny after all.

And when they felt the rumor of his approach, smelled the soured air that went before him, and then at last laid eyes upon him close at hand, it was then they knew they would never laugh at anything ever again.

True fear, now, lurked in their eyes as Scathur approached. Their bearing might remain proud, their jaws firmly set, but there were indications in their manner that belied such apparent soldierly fearlessness. The steady gaze of the hunter tracking his quarry was now replaced by a franticness in the way their eyes darted about in their sockets, accompanied by the dilation of nostrils, the irregular catch of breath in fear-dried throats. All such symptoms spoke of a terror scarcely concealed in the depths of their eyes, a terror that increased with each approaching footfall.

To others, these barely perceptible signs would have gone unnoticed, but Scathur had lived through many such conflicts, and knew well the measure of a man. Even at this distance he could read these telltale minutiae, assessing the extent of a man's endurance, as worry became fear, as fear descended into panic, and the point at which panic waxed into blind terror.

The hollow thud of his boots echoing down the stony passageway was like a fanfare of fear heralding his arrival to all in his path. And the mere sight of that swiftly approaching sinister figure, silhouetted against the smoky orange light of the sputtering wall cressets, was enough to buckle many a man's knees beneath him.

As Scathur strode up to the throng of men who crowded the corridor, they instantly drew back to let him pass unhindered. He needed no godlike perspicacity now to sense their terror. There was, Scathur mused, even at a time like this, something immensely gratifying in the haste with which all living creatures got out of his way, *recoiled,* as if dreading even the touch of the bone-pale cloak that fluttered around his tall frame. Such fear was deep-rooted and instinctive: the primeval dread of the unknown.

Redoubtable, untouchable, himself without fear, Scathur was the ideal commander for his overlord's forces. Unswervingly loyal to his master, he carried out his every command with unquestioning obedience, and had done so for longer than anyone could remember. Many generations of men had lived out their lives on this turbulent island in the frigid northern seas, and yet Scathur had always been there, unchanged, unchallenged. Few could guess at the extent of the powers that lay hidden beneath his blank mantle of secrecy, or read the thoughts concealed behind his great-helm's impenetrable visor. Scathur confided in no man.

Yet for once his appearance of untouchable calm was deceptive. Had his men beheld his face, they would have seen the fear in their own eyes mirrored there. For the first time in his centuries of untarnished service, the unthinkable had happened: Scathur had failed. And he alone could guess the terrible punishment that awaited him.

Even now the distant, muffled rumor of the siege way below had changed into the clearly definable clamor of clashing iron, screaming men, and the searing pyrotechnic spells of the magic-users getting closer. The siege hammers employed by the Peladanes from the South had finished their devastation of the outer defenses, the wide moat of white-hot magma had been traversed, Gruddna the Fyr-Draikke was thrown down, and Scathur's men-at-arms were swiftly being forced to retreat from the lower levels up to the less effective defenses of the intermediate ones. The necromancers' dark arts had failed to instill their usual terror into the legions of Northerners, the *Oghain-Yddiaw,* whose morale was now fired by the new comradeship of the Southern Peladanes, and whose frenzied fury was multiplied tenfold by so many years of yearned-for vengeance. They were relentless, as irresistible as the tide that lashed the island's jagged coast. Scathur had done his utmost, but this combination was beyond even him.

The destruction of Vaagenfjord Maw was at hand.

These feeble, sweating mortals before him, striving so uselessly to appear calm, knew only of *physical* pain. In the next few minutes such agony would become bad enough, but they had never beheld the Master, never known the awe-filled terror that arose from merely being in his presence. Only Scathur possessed the inhuman strength that enabled him to converse with his over-lord, but on this occasion he wondered if even this was enough to help him tell this unearthly deity what he now had to reveal. And as soon as the Master beheld Scathur, he would know of his fear.

Yet there was no getting away from it: he was totally bound to his master and powerless without him. So Scathur slowly began to ascend the smooth, black-and-violet marble steps that led to the forbidden chamber, leaving the confused rabble of frightened soldiers behind him to await whatever Fate had in store for them. They were beyond help anyway, the worthless creatures.

As the dull rhythm of Scathur's boots on the steps quickly faded, the last guardians of Vaagenfjord Maw gripped their battle-axes and faced the in-evitable.

"My Lord Drauglir . . ." Scathur began, each word of confession nauseating him. "I bring you the latest report . . ."

Scathur stood all alone in the sudden quietness of the Chamber of Drauglir. Many times he had been here, and he knew it well, but this time was different. Upon entering the huge, echoing hall, he normally felt as if he were intruding on another world, even another time, some terrible plane of existence trapped in the mind of an ancient god. The blood-hued floor of polished marble seemed to mirror the ghastliness of the ceiling high above, with its grisly latticework of severed human heads spiked into every available gap and gaping down lifelessly at their tormentor below. And somehow the scarlet drapes that hung from the walls never ceased stirring, even without any movement of air in this vast room, as evidenced by the unwavering columns of acrid smoke that rose from the tall black candles all around. Even the ziggurat dominating the center of the hall radiated an evil intent like some silent watcher. In its hellish vastness this whole chamber, glowing like magma and reeking of death, felt more animated now than the master who dwelled within it. Soundless still, he sat upon the altar atop the ziggurat, like an icon of Death incarnate.

Today all seemed changed: there was no power in this place. The awe that Scathur usually felt had evaporated. As he stood by the doorway through which he had just entered, it was as though he had just arrived into void, the burnt-out shell of a place that had once known greatness. He felt all alone within the hugeness of this ancient, whispering hall. Still he received no answer to his announcement, which echoed and then died. The place was as still as a crypt.

If he had possessed the ability to sweat, he would have done so as profusely as those feeble wretches outside. For an unaccustomed sensation of fear rose inside him with each passing second of this awful silence. He dared to raise his eyes to the altar atop the lofty pyramid, trying to see beyond the great hooded reredos that presented itself to him like a blank wall. Why wasn't his master answering him? Had he fled? Could he be dead? Was Scathur now an unholy trinity of one?

Doubt added itself to his fear.

Suddenly the insidious hiss of Drauglir's voice cut through the silence, startling the captain out of his ponderings.

"A most enlightening report, Scathur. Whatever would I do without you?"

The sarcasm stung Scathur like a whiplash.

"Forgive my hesitation, Lord. I shall now come to the point."

"Please do."

"We have lost Gruddna, Your Dire Eminence, and our situation appears beyond hope. The entire fjord festers with the warships of the Peladanes, abetted by the xebecs of the Oghain. The cliff defenses have meanwhile succumbed to the overland assault of the Nahovians and their mercenary captains. The united front of this coalition is quite unprecedented, O Lord of the Night, quite total. All escape routes are blocked. The efforts of our necromancers have been ineffective in allaying this. . . . In fact, if I dare say it, our own men seem the only ones to be terrified. And now that the Hall of Fire has been breached, and the Draikke cast down, and Lubang-Nagar penetrated, there seems no way of holding the foe back. The lower floors are taken, and their forces are rising through the mid-levels like a flood. Your army, O highest and most revered Icon of Darkness, cannot I fear hold them back for much longer."

"So, nothing too bad, then," sneered the voice from on high.

Stop playing with me Drauglir, please . . . the dark commander entreated silently. The whole island was taken, and now that the Cult of Olchor had been forced underground by the Peladanes and this other new religion from the South, there was no further hope of outside help.

Judging by the death screams from dangerously close by, it seemed now to be only a matter of minutes before the High Warlord of Pel-Adan would be hacking asunder the door to this very chamber with his Holy Greatsword.

Yet Drauglir sat here calmly awaiting the end of all his designs with seeming unconcern.

"What would you have me do, Lord?" Scathur pleaded.

Still the Rawgr held his calm. "What *would* you do?" he asked.

"Attempt escape, perhaps?"

Instantly the whole hall flared up in a burning glow of scarlet, as Drauglir at last chose to reveal himself, standing up in full view atop his altar. Scathur immediately averted his eyes.

"Brilliant!" his master exclaimed sardonically. "I just knew you'd think of something clever."

But there the sarcasm ceased. The deep-throated bellowing of the battle-maddened Northmen, heralded by a screeching blast of their silver war horns, now reached a triumphant note, and was quickly followed by the thunderous ascent of a multitude of hard-booted feet up the stairs leading to the door by which Scathur still stood.

"Sounds like the last of your puny humans are being wiped out," Drauglir spat in contempt.

A horribly unfamiliar feeling of panic now rose in Scathur's throat as the enemy surged relentlessly up the steps outside.

"Escape? Yes, Scathur, escape indeed—that's all that remains now. Listen carefully, my most trusted servant, for there are scant moments left to us."

The change in his master's voice caused Scathur to look up sharply. Just ere the avenging army poured into the chamber, Drauglir was talking as if there might be some hope, some last plan to save them from the nemesis that awaited them.

Drauglir continued; "Any hopes of I myself escaping this island were dashed long ago, I realize."

—*What's this?!*

"Were I even to try the secret way up to the ice field, our enemy would still find me before long, as the whole island is theirs now. They will not stop till they see me dead."

—*No!*

"You, though, mean little to them. Were you to lie low in the hidden place of Ravenscairn, you might be safe there."

". . . But what of yourself, my lord?" Scathur implored. Why was his master suddenly talking like this? What was he, Scathur, worth without him?

But a new tone now crept into Drauglir's voice. "Forget it, Scathur, my time has come. Bring me the Sword now. . . ."

And so Scathur, unable to disobey this command even now, fixed his mind upon this, his final task. On the other side of the door could be heard the death screams of the last of his troops. Time was when he might have tarried to listen with relish, enraptured by those alluring sounds of torment and despair. But this was the end of everything, and Scathur was now oblivious of such distractions.

Solemnly, he approached with the Sword.

The door that separated Scathur from the marauders outside was strong. Forged by the fire giants from adamantine steel in the depths of their deepest, most hallowed smithies, strengthened by the ichor of unspeakable under-world deities, and embellished with silver images—of the fires of the infernal abyss—which framed its broad surface, it was able to withstand even the mightiest of the Peladanes' siege engines.

But *they* had magic too. For the worshippers of Pel-Adan had come prepared this time. Even now the Jutul-wrought portal that stood between them and victory was buckling under the power of their magic-users' spells. The silver tongues of flame bordering the door now glowed fiercely red from the heat of the magic that was beginning to consume them, resembling now more closely the legendary fires that they imitated. A few moments more, and the door would explode.

In the huge but crowded passageway outside the Chamber of Drauglir, Arturus Bloodnose stood fidgeting behind the vanguard of his men. As smoke gradually filled the air, and the fountain of blue sparks struck from the yielding steel increased in brilliance, so the sweat trickled increasingly down the High Warlord's fleshy face. All the while, a continuous stream of arcane power poured from the magic-users' fingertips, relentlessly wearing down the resistance of the giant-built portal. In seconds it would be down, and nothing would stand between Drauglir and his fate. Then those long years of meticulous planning, rigorous training, and endless diplomatic exchanges between the Peladanes and the other armies of the Fasces league would soon be vindicated. And Arturus Bloodnose, High Warlord of Pel-Adan, bearer of the Holy Greatsword, was the one ordained to wield that fatal stroke.

As he gripped the hilt of this ancient blade, clamping and unclamping his fingers around its sweat-sodden leather grip, his men could sense the panic that threatened to snap their leader's nerve in this overcrowded place. Yet they also knew perfectly well that he would not be the first to enter the chamber, for that glorious duty was the lot of others. Not the Elite, those fanatics of his bodyguard who had trained for years just for this final assault, protected throughout the siege itself by lesser fighters so they could be here for the coup de grâce. Instead this honor fell to the Anointed, that special corps who had been granted the privilege of providing the first wave of the Soldiers of God to finally come to grips with the Evil One.

Arturus glanced over at them briefly as they were hustled up from the rear. Pressed tightly together, the hundred and fifty Anointed were soon assembled immediately behind the magic-users. Though future sagas would never dwell on this, the Anointed were a mixture of old men who had seen better days and young boys who might never get that chance.

A good combination of wise experience and youthful vigor, Arturus assured himself as he stepped farther out of the way.

The old men were trembling in anticipation, tears and death in their eyes; the boys, some looking as young as eight, merely gaped around themselves in puzzlement. All bore whatever scraps of armor and weaponry they had managed to scrounge from their families.

The seconds ticked down, and the magic-users were coming to the end of their task. Everyone was braced ready. One hundred and fifty pairs of eyes now fixed themselves on the Warlord's, but somehow he found he was not able to meet theirs. They were waiting for a few encouraging words from him, but none were forthcoming. As soon as these Anointed had been blasted into bubbling jelly by Drauglir's infernal power, the Warlord would still be safely at the rear, ordering the Elite next into the hall of death. Only when all real danger had passed would he enter the hall to claim his victory.

Then, with a sudden deafening thunderclap that stole a heartbeat from all there, the door finally gave way. The power that had held it shut was at last overcome by the concerted battering of the magic-users' spells. A split second of dazzling blue light was followed by the heavy crunch of the door slamming against the inside wall. A thick plume of smoke billowed out, but not a second was wasted. Though choking and half-blinded, the Anointed hurled themselves through the doorway . . . and into whatever lay beyond.

"Spread yourselves out! Don't bunch together!" came the hoarse cry of the Warlord, just in case any of them were still alive. He paused for a moment, then with a wave of his sword sent the Elite through the smoke next.

Getting ready to send the third wave in, Arturus paused to reflect that something was clearly wrong. Despite a frenzy of angry shouting and a furious gale of missile-throwing, there was no roar of immolating flames, there were no death screams, there was no hint of Rawgr-generated carnage. It almost sounded as if his advance troops were somehow prevailing. . . .

Through the wall of smoke that yet hung around the blasted doorway, Arturus could see nothing. But it sounded as if his own men were moving farther in, pursuing something. . . .

The sweat was oozing from every clammy pore, and his already-labored heart had begun pounding like the drums of war. *What was happening in there?*

Suddenly he almost leapt for joy as he heard the voice of Gwyllch, his chief bodyguard, bellowing above the din.

"Lord Bloodnose, he's dead!"

His world now safe again, Arturus boldly strode through the pall of smoke and into the Chamber of Drauglir.

To his surprise, not a single one of his own men was dead. The room, in fact, seemed completely devoid of enemy. No dark knights, no necromancers, not even the dreaded stained-glass demons. The only remnant of the evil of Vaagenfjord Maw now lay unmoving at the top of the ziggurat. Inert, prostrate, with a long sword buried in its heart.

The Evil One? Could it really be . . . ?

Then his disbelieving stare was wrenched off to the right, where the main body of his forces was still engaged in some kind of pursuit. Standing with the

Anointed, who seemed at a loss as to what to do next, Bloodnose peered at the obscure scene and realized that the Elite had discarded most of their weapons and were now in full cry after a single fleeing figure that was now disappearing into the darkness of the far end of the hall. There followed a flurry of useless activity and much shouting in cheated fury and frustration.

Minutes later, Gwyllch came bounding back to the Warlord with a look of indignant wrath upon his ruddy features.

"My lord," he breathed hoarsely, "the Rawgr Scathur seems to have eluded us, for the moment. But behold, Drauglir is *dead*!"

Bloodnose was lost for words. He could hardly believe his good fortune.

"Thank you, my man," he managed at last, and turned toward the ziggurat. "You're absolutely sure that thing's dead, aren't you?"

"Absolutely, my lord," Gwyllch replied, "I climbed up myself and checked."

"Well done, then." Arturus nodded. "You can leave this to me now." And, clutching his Holy Greatsword, he began to ascend.

"Actually," he called back as an afterthought, "you can go first, if you like."

With Gwyllch several paces behind him, the Warlord began ascending the ziggurat. The closer he got to the altar, the more reassurance he felt that the still form atop it was, as Gwyllch claimed, truly dead. And when he cautiously gained the topmost step, and gazed down at the lifeless hulk of the once-terrible Rawgr lying motionless upon the cold stone, Arturus knew he need fear no more.

"Drauglir is dead!" he cried out in triumph.

He savored these words that he and generations of forebears had dreamed of uttering for so long, but that none had yet dared believe would ever actually be said.

Yet despite his relief, here at the end of all his exertions and tribulations, there lurked a cutting shard of disappointment, a bitterness that began to saw its way through his elation, and would remain eternally buried in his heart, tainting his long-coveted victory.

For *he* was the one meant to slay the bringer of all their woes, cutting this cancer of corruption from the world and ending forever the threat of a dark and terrible future. *He* was the one who should look forward to being celebrated for centuries to come, as the Hero of the Age immortalized in the songs of the skalds and akynns.

Yet the enemy lay here already dead, his destruction snatched from Bloodnose's outstretched fingers by the hands of another. Just who had plunged that sword into the Rawgr's heart, Arturus did not yet know or even care right now. He felt, inexplicably, that it had been planted in his own.

Grasping it firmly by the hilt, Bloodnose wrenched the offending weapon out of the corpse and hurled it all the way down to the floor below, using all the strength that his fat arms were capable of. Those of his followers not vainly engaged in the hunt for Scathur (which meant mainly the young boys, who were now laughing and busy playing tag) flinched as the steel rang loudly upon cut marble and clattered into silence in some dark corner of the huge room.

Now the sacking of Vaagenfjord Maw could commence. Every item of worth or unworth would be destroyed. Any statue or idol small enough to be brought down from its plinth would be smashed into powder. All icons or standards would be burnt. All books, tomes, librams, scrolls, and any other record of dark arts practiced here would be utterly eradicated. The whole place must be purged of Evil from top to bottom, erasing any chance of even a small remnant of Drauglir's influence remaining on this benighted island.

At least, that is what history would later recall.

And, amid the noise of destruction, no one would notice the frail, mail-clad hand of an old man reach into a dark recess, withdraw the blade that had slain the Rawgr, and slip it quietly beneath his tunic.

The destruction of Vaagenfjord Maw was a thorough yet hurried process. For although nearly every living thing that had dwelled in the den of the Rawgr perished in the siege, and nearly everything else in it was either destroyed or removed, it had been the original intention to raze the entire place down to its very foundations. Instead the actual fortress survived almost intact. Carved as it was into the very mountainside, and massive beyond the reckoning of the Peladanes, not even the most ardent efforts of the most skillful artisans could make much of a dent in it. How could it be brought down to its foundations when its foundations stemmed from the very earth itself? And the Peladanes, however well supplied, could not survive for too long on that remote arctic island.

So they had to content themselves with destroying or illicitly appropriating whatever they could lay their hands on, otherwise leaving the whole place as an empty memorial to all that had transpired there.

Many grumbled that their search had not been thorough enough, and that there must still be hidden places storing great treasures. Others feared that it would attract new evil to it were it left open, so the entire complex was sealed and entrusted to the guardianship of the Oghain, whose homeland lay but a few days away over the water.

But in time, as often happens, original priorities are forgotten, and even the sentinels eventually drifted away. Vaagenfjord Maw came to be just a name, a place of ill omen that lay safely remote somewhere far, far away to the north. Out of both sight and mind, it became nothing more than a kind of bogeyman, a byword for evil.

Despite the strict decree that all items found there were to be destroyed on pain of death, most Peladanes felt that the vanquished Rawgr owed them something, and they resorted to the time-honored rule of war that plunder was the right of the conqueror. As a result, many innocuous souvenirs managed to find themselves resting upon the mantelpieces of returning veterans, or hanging from their parlor walls gathering dust. Many, in time, were lost, broken, or discarded, and not a few eventually reached the marketplaces of the South to be sold as relics of the glorious campaign. They represented a profitable source of income for those soldiers who bargained wisely.

Eventually, centuries later, at a time when the names of Drauglir and Vaagenfjord Maw had passed into the ignominy of folklore, and nearly all the relics of that place had disappeared or disintegrated one way or another, one such item found itself again heading for the bargaining table. Wrapped up in a thick layer of oily sackcloth, a long and curiously shaped sword was being brought to market. Dumped carelessly atop a small pile of millet sacks, it was bounced about in the back of a large camel cart with every bump in the road.

Among the rest of the payload in the cart on this day were several kegs of dried ox meat, a cartwheel being taken to town for repair, and two dark-skinned men dressed in rough camel-hair cloaks. Their heads wrapped in grubby cheches to keep out the dust, they were jolted up and down uncomfortably as they slumped awkwardly against the millet sacks. One had on a tether a small brown and black goat that crouched wretchedly between a huge basket of green lemons and a tobacco bale. Now and then its owner would stretch out his leg lazily and kick it for daring to pass its droppings, thus confusing the cringing, bleating animal even more. A third man, lighter-skinned with blond hair and an untidy red beard (clearly a traveler from the North), sat upon a large pile of rugs, wondering if he could jump unnoticed from the cart and avoid paying his fare.

A large iron-bound chest was tucked unobtrusively but carefully between two crates of dates. This was heavily padlocked, as it contained some unusual items that might just make this whole dusty, sweaty journey worth all the bother. The driver of the cart hated this particular route. Snaking up by the banks of the Qaladr and through the desert, the road was open to all sorts of danger: wild animals, thieves, and, worst disaster of all, the very real possibility that any one of the vital water holes along the way might have dried up. Was it all worth it just to sell the pathetic selection of wares he now carried in the back?

Still, at least he had those little bottles of smelly stuff in the chest there. Those and the carefully wrapped bars of metal, those strange "scholarly instruments"—whatever they might be—and the jars of powders. They should fetch a good price, just so long as the alchemist was still in business.

A strange man, that one, he had been in Qaladmir for years now. Never could tell how he made a living, but he always had a stack of cash at hand, ready to buy funny items that no one else had any use for. Sometimes you'd bring him bits and bobs worth a gold piece or two, and he'd just laugh in your face; other times he'd spot something you'd swear was useless, and pay a fortune for it.

Odd, definitely not normal—but at least it meant money.

With great relief the carter at last beheld the unmistakable sight of the Qal-admir mountain looming up ahead, with its city of sparkling fountains, sway-ing palms, and gleaming palaces of turquoise and gold high up on its slopes. A most wonderful sight indeed after the long days of grueling travel. And be-fore long he was driving his dromedary-hauled cart triumphantly through the massive, arched gateway that breached the towering city wall. Here at last was succor from thirst, hunger, and weariness, and a chance to indulge in those pri-vate pleasures that were so difficult when traveling with only three men, two camels, and a goat.

But before any of that came the wearisome but exigent need to acquire some hard cash, the only key that opened any doors in *this* place. First he must negotiate streets ankle-deep in filth and lined with the worst cases of poverty, disease, and corruption in the whole of the Qalad basin. To eventually reach the upper terraces where wealth, luxury, and beauty resided, he had to push his way through this throng of beggars, drug peddlers, and assorted opportunistic ne'er-do-wells and get to the alchemist's place.

"Pashta? Good day to you!" rasped the peddler through the open doorway of the alchemist's hovel.

Flicking away a large bluebottle that seemed determined to force its way in between his honey-smeared lips, Pashta-Maeva the alchemist looked up from his book and sighed.

"Oh no . . . *please* not now," he muttered in a voice heavy with bored resig-nation. "Not that dusty-faced, red-eyed little nosebleed again! Right now, I think I'd rather push hatpins into my eyes than talk to him."

Glancing at the figure silhouetted in the doorway against the searing white sunlight of the hot afternoon, Pashta reflected upon the luxurious coolness here inside his house. Though only on the second level of this five-tiered city, therefore still in the poorer quarters, his abode possessed the clean simplicity of a monastic temple, austere but comfortable, a refuge from the noise, heat, and dust of the street outside. Here he could practice his arts, write his theses, and dream his dreams, undisturbed by the smelly denizens of the streets out-side. And thereby still retain the anonymity that protected him from the un-welcome attention of any of the powerful cults controlling this city. For his work was, to say the least, "uncommon," and there were many out there who distrusted such deviance from the norm.

"Ah well, business is business, and he may have something of vague use in his magpie's hoard of trinkets this time. See to him will you, Nipah. Keep him talking while I finish this . . . sun-dried lizard slop you call dinner."

He went back to picking distastefully at the meal before him, while the lanky youth sitting opposite him got sulkily to his feet and went to meet the peddler, scuffing his sandaled feet noisily on the stone-tiled floor as he went.

"Hello, I'm Nipah Glemp," the boy announced to the dust-caked stranger who stood before him; then he added politely, "Did you have a nice journey?"

A choking splutter of a laugh from Pashta behind him made Nipah realize that this probably wasn't the best way to greet someone who has just spent the last few days toiling through one of the worst regions of the desert. Nipah Glemp was often described as being "alone with his thoughts," conversation having never been one of his strong points.

"Hello yourself, young sir," the peddler replied with a fixed smile. "I've got a few little items in my cart which might interest your master. Perhaps you'd both like to take a gander, eh?"

Nipah smiled nervously, wondering just what to say next.

"Look, just bloody ask him in, will you, and stop dithering," Pashta chided from within.

Nipah stepped back and bade their visitor enter.

"Well, Xhasha," said Pashta, holding a jug of cool black beer to his lips, without offering any to his guest, "what valuable little gems to extend the frontiers of human knowledge do you have for me today? Something worthy, I trust? Scorpions' legs, perhaps, or camels' teeth? Maybe even (and let us not get our hopes up too high) some strangely colored pebbles you found whilst rooting around in the latrine of High Priest Brethed's Temple of Correction?"

Insulting simple folk like Xhasha the peddler, who came from a part of the country where irony was not readily grasped, was one of Pashta's less endearing pleasures in life. Xhasha replied: "Well, I did have a box of dried fragrant weasel, but I lost that when I threw it after some passenger who ran off without paying me."

"A box of dried fragrant weasel!" exclaimed the alchemist, clasping his hands to his face in simulated delight. "What a boon! What a treasure! What a veritable catalytic cornerstone in the development of alchemical science! My heart has not soared so since the time you brought me some powdered seaweed!"

"What's seaweed?" Nipah interposed unguardedly.

"Weed that comes from the sea, dear boy. Hence: 'sea,' 'weed.' It looks uncannily like the stuff you served up for dinner."

"I'm here as an apprentice alchemist," he retorted, "not a scullion!"

"I'm glad you're aware of that fact," Pashta replied, "though I've seen precious little evidence of your development under my tutelage. Fifteen years old and still can't translate Quiravian! Anyway, Xhasha, let's have a look at your hoard of treasures, shall we?"

They all moved from the cool, dark room and out into the fierce heat of the day. There the peddler dragged the heavy chest to the rear edge of the cart, unlocked it, and threw open the lid. Pashta was already feigning lack of interest before even beginning to peruse its contents.

"Hmm, not much here, I'm afraid. . . . No, got that already, and one of those . . . and I wouldn't touch *that* with a billhook. Nothing here I could use, really, unless . . ."

And so the well-practiced warm-up to their haggling began.

Nipah Glemp, tall for his age and strikingly handsome, did not at first sight appear to be the obvious candidate for the role of alchemist's apprentice. The "science" of alchemy was still very new to this part of the world, and most people (at least those who had any idea that it existed at all) regarded it with extreme suspicion. Educated and uneducated parents alike forbade their children to go anywhere near Pashta's house after nightfall. Thus the only folk who had any dealings at all with this strange man tended to be rather strange themselves: oddballs, underworld-dwellers, and nocturnal wanderers. The ideal apprentice, in most people's eyes, should have been a slightly hunched, saucer-eyed, bandy-legged youth who mumbled to himself and twitched a lot.

So it was met with much interest when Pashta decided to accept the comely presence of Nipah Glemp into his practice. The boy's mother, for one, had been surprised and disappointed by his choice of career. But now, five months into his apprenticeship, he was already showing signs of becoming a success at his trade; he was becoming increasingly withdrawn, his face was acquiring a disturbingly wan pallor, and his grooming had taken a sharp turn downhill. Nevertheless he remained highly intelligent, studious, and above all *absorbed* in his work.

Totally so. He would spend hours poring over the strange, leather-bound librams in Pashta's study, learning the history of far-off lands as well as more relevant subjects. He had assembled his own collection of ancient relics, which he liked to rummage through, trying to imagine what kind of people their previous owners had been. Inevitably he would see them as heroes, and assumed he could become just like them if he honored the possessions that had once been theirs.

Already he had acquired a great knowledge of how substances worked. At a surprisingly early stage in his schooling he had learned, and been impressed by, the energy and strange powers that could be unleashed when certain combinations of elements reacted together. A bit like people, he mused. And he was ever keen to try out different substances and experiment with new magicks.

Thus it was always with great interest that he would examine the wares offered by peddlers from afar. Today, however, there did indeed appear to be nothing in Xhasha's trunks that Nipah wanted to get his hands on; just the standard items that any self-respecting alchemist would already possess. Most disappointing.

The two men were by now arguing quite vehemently; it was midafternoon and the blistering heat was doing nothing to cool their tempers. Pashta was as disappointed as his assistant, but Xhasha was livid. His one chance of making this trip worthwhile was unavoidably slipping out of his grasp with every dismissive gesture of the alchemist's hand. Nipah looked longingly over his shoulder at the welcoming sight of the shady doorway that promised relief from the heat.

As he did so, his gaze fell upon the strange bundle of oily rags perched atop the millet sacks on the cart. Immediately an odd sensation came over him, flashing into his mind and then out again so quickly that it was almost imperceptible. As his regard lingered upon the bundle, the noises of the street faded. He suddenly felt alone in the world, just himself and that oily bundle, and he did not like this sensation at all. A soft, persuasive voice, compelling yet sinister, seemed to call out to him, not from the cart but from far, far beneath the ground. He wanted to cry out, but something in his mind told him to wait and see what would happen.

Suddenly he snapped out of his reverie as Pashta began yelling at the traveler. Taking a deep breath, the youth gazed around at the comfortable familiarity of the street, relieved that his "daydream" was over but still feeling puzzled. The bargaining seemed to be over, and his master was striding indoors, leaving the frustrated Xhasha, penniless still, glaring at the alchemist's back as he disappeared into the dark.

"I came all the way from Ben-Attan for you, mister! Why don't you buy something?"

Nipah smirked. This had happened before with other peddlers, but such incidents never seemed to bother Pashta. One day, the boy mused, his master's blunt and mocking dismissiveness would work against him, and his eloquence would not then be able to save him. Still, the wily old goat had managed his affairs shrewdly up till now; he knew what he wanted, and what he did not.

But Nipah was not sure this time. These peddlers traveled all over, acquiring goods that had been transported along trade routes extending right across the world. They often got hold of items that interested the impressionable youth greatly. So what *was* wrapped up in that bundle of rags that had drawn his attention so strangely?

Glancing around to see if anyone was watching, he quietly lifted himself onto the back of the cart, picked his way through the millet sacks, and, still without thinking, grasped hold of the greasy bundle. The sackcloth felt gritty, the oil having become encrusted with a layer of windblown sand, and whatever it contained was surprisingly heavy. Almost certainly metal, Nipah decided, and wondered excitedly what could be inside. Fumbling in his haste, and hoping that Xhasha would continue to be distracted by his ranting for a little longer, he unpeeled the mysterious object from its crude coverings, layer by layer, until its shape became more clearly defined. Surely it must be a weapon, maybe even a sword?

Just then, the sound of the peddler's voice drew nearer, still spewing oaths. Within seconds now, Nipah realized, he would be discovered. Why had he not simply asked what the object was, without all this furtiveness? But he *had* to find out now, so without further thought he leapt over the side of the cart, landed lightly on the dusty earth, and stole away out of sight.

Breathing heavily from sheer nervousness, for he was unused to thieving, he rounded the corner of the house, leapt up the notched log leaning against the wall which served as a ladder, and gained the sanctuary of the flat roof above. A trapdoor led down to his room below, and now he could examine his prize undisturbed, secure in his little bedchamber and surrounded by his collection of other relics. His heart was pounding like an engine, not from physical exertion but from the anticipation of discovering just what it was he had purloined. He tore away the last remaining rag as if it were wrapping paper, and stared wide-eyed at his latest acquisition.

He had handled swords before, but nothing like the one that lay before him now. Long and curiously fashioned, it possessed a distinct aura of antiquity. There was something rather ominous about it, in the shape, the smell, the feel of it . . . Nipah did not know for sure, but . . .

Actually he did not know anything, where it came from, how old it was, and its shape was totally unfamiliar to him. But he sensed that it was worth more than all his other relics put together. As he stared uncomprehendingly at this magnificent blade, a thousand thoughts raced through his mind, while the sweat dripped from his body onto the grubby blanket he perched upon.

"Nipah, where are you?" came the irate tones of his teacher from below. The youth only vaguely heard his master complaining, but half-consciously thought: *Old fool, see what you missed. . . .*

And the heavy length of steel, lying across his knees, seemed almost to laugh with him.

"We're going to have to find out a little bit about you, aren't we, sword?" the boy whispered, and placed it carefully in the storage box beneath his bed.

Fifteen years later, on a high, lonely hilltop, thousands of miles to the north, in the deadest part of the night, a small man knelt in prayer. It was a strange place to be praying, so lonesome and desolate, illumined only by the pale gleam of a half-moon. The town of Nordwas lay at the foot of the hill some way off, too remote to be of any comfort to this solitary figure. The only company he had—or knew of—was the rustling gorse bushes all around, draped in a ghostly, moon-silvered mantle of windblown loosestrife-beard, whistling in time with the sudden, irregular gusts of wind that spiraled over the bleak hilltop and cascaded down the other side, then over the moaning pine forest below. A strange place to be praying indeed.

But in most people's eyes, old Appa was himself rather strange. He had to be, to struggle up the steep hillside at his age, alone in the middle of the night, with only a staff to protect him. Many times he had cursed under his labored breath as he stumbled over the rocks and stones strewn about the desolate slope, remnants of an ancient temple destroyed long before Drauglir's time. The breath wheezed and rattled in Appa's elderly windpipe as he perservered upward, but his resolve never wavered. Such was the great need that drove him.

However strange he might seem, he was not weird or dangerous, though he managed to discomfit almost everyone he came in contact with. He was usually harmless enough when silent and alone with his inscrutable thoughts; whenever he did give voice it was always with a shrill and fiery *rat-a-tat-tat* making little or no sense to most people.

His face was small and lean, like his body, and scored with the deep lines of age and hardship. But, unlike those of most folk his age, his small, bright eyes showed no hint of sorrow or regret for times past.

Tonight, as ever, Appa was alone, for no one else ever frequented this place, by night or even by day. It was a place of ill omen, shunned by the local people, and avoided even by beasts and birds. But when Appa had finally reached the hilltop and paused to gaze down into the shallow depression where once the temple had stood, he felt no fear, only relief. There in front of him rose the last stones still intact of the crumbled shrine, pointing like black fingers toward the heavens.

Appa stood and shivered for a minute, before drawing tightly about him his grey, woollen robe; then he picked his way carefully down the treacherous side of the gorse-covered depression.

In the shelter of the hollow it suddenly became quiet, and Appa had dropped to his knees upon a low, flat prayer stone the size of a hearth rug. The stars were obscured by gigantic, lowering storm clouds that now blew steadily from the north, and the cool night air was soon filled with the familiar smell of moist turf.

Whenever he had something important to brood on, Appa always came here to this ancient holy place of his cult. Alone and undisturbed in the cold, quiet night, he found he could always think much more clearly. And on this night, in particular, he knew he would need both the strength of his own conviction and the wisdom of his deity to guide him through the momentous days to come.

Lord, he prayed, *I am old and I am weak. The vigor of my youth has departed me, not just of my body but also of my mind, and doubts gnaw at my resolve like some rotting disease. For seventy years have I dwelt upon this world, seventy long years of toil in your service. I know that whatever days are left to me are few, yet I also know that those soon to come will determine the fate of many, perhaps the whole of Lindormyn! But yet I am confused, for what Finwald is now*

*preaching has troubled me greatly. He serves our cult well, but surely this cam-
paign he advocates against the forces of Evil will jeopardize the future of us all.
Please, I beg of you, Lord, tell me more.*

He did not even notice the figure now standing on the rim of the hollow,
looking down at him. It was tall and broad-backed, and from a powerful pair
of shoulders hung a long sleeveless tunic of yak skin. In one hand it gripped a
staff with an unlit lantern atop it, and from this hung a string of glistening orbs.
Stretched over its head was a coif of satin-soft hide so silvery-white it seemed to
absorb the moonglow, while upon his forehead rested a chaplet of translucent
stones, lending the appearance of some kind of wizard.

Although the wind up on the height raced past him like a frenzied beast,
clawing at his coat and at the long black hair emerging from under the coif, he
himself did not move a muscle. As motionless as the standing stones all around,
he stared at the kneeling figure below with eyes burning red as glowing
embers.

Though the figure stood in full view, silhouetted against the silver-black of
the lunar sky, the old priest remained unaware of his presence. Finally, Appa
did sense something and looked up sharply. Though the figure remained, all
the old man could see were the clouds, the half-moon, and the sky.

"Well, you heard him," intoned the stranger. "Is that too much to ask?"

All Appa could hear was the wind in the rushes, and the shrill call of a distant night bird.

The stranger continued: "All he asks for is a clue, a mere hint of what is
afoot. That isn't much, surely?" This time there was a hint of pleading in his
voice, but it was devoid of any subservience.

There was no answer from the night, save for the sound of the waxing wind,
though these words were directed to a ridge on the other side of the hollow.
Even if Appa had turned to look behind him, in the same direction, he would
have seen nothing. But there they were, all of them.

Standing in a line, facing back over the ruined temple, were several figures where moments earlier only the ancient standing stones had been. It
was difficult to tell exactly how many of them there were, as they manifested
as shadows that shifted in form between megalith and man, merging among
each other and also with the shifting shapes of the night. Their robes were
grey, a vapid neutral grey, the color of ash that has long forgotten the heat of
fire. These garments covered their figures so completely that not even the
red-eyed one opposite could guess what lay beneath those enveloping
hoods.

Like him, they stood motionless except for their wind-whipped raiment,
which flew about them in tatters like a mad frenzy of bats. The whole night
now seemed to join in a frantic, violent dance as the wind increased to gale
force, bending the long grasses first one way then another, and sending spirals

of dead leaves flying through the darkness in vortices of madness. The storm clouds raced on across the sky, a rolling mass of turbulence gathering momentum with each minute that passed. Appa peered about himself in alarm, and futilely drew his woollen cloak tighter about his sticklike frame.

All the while, the grey-robed watchers stood silent and unmoving.

Then the middle one spoke at last.

Its voice was hollow, without a trace of emotion, like the slam of a judge's hammer when sentence has been passed.

"You are playing a game with us, Lord. When Finwald first announced his intention of essaying this quest, we were well within our bounds in letting you to suggest to Appa here that he should go too. And when you then insisted he take Bolldhe along with him, again we made no objection. Even when you pleaded with us to give Appa a hint that there was some treachery afoot, yet again we found it in our hearts to comply. But what we cannot do is to continue with this game any further, for perhaps you will only be satisfied when we have revealed each and every secret of your enemy. Have we not already conceded you enough?"

"No you haven't, as well you know! These fragments of hints are like mere needles in a pine forest. How can any mortal be expected to make sense out of them?" The lantern-holder's eyes glowed even hotter, as he protested.

"But," the other argued, "that is more than I have allowed to your enemy. For I have given him leave to grant no information at all; not even the sliver of a needle in a pine forest."

"That is because my enemy has no need to learn more! The dice were loaded in his favor from the start, so he has almost won the game before it begins. I was under the impression that you and your brothers are here to ensure that neither of us gains an unfair advantage." His voice rankled with the unfairness of it all, and he ground the tip of his staff into the turf, rattling the lantern and the string of orbs attached to it.

But the hooded ones remained unmoving, unmoved. "Let us not be naive," their leader replied. "We all know that the game does not start here. It began five hundred years ago, when Scathur ended his master's life. And even that game began long before the construction of Vaagenfjord Maw. These battles between you and your enemy have been going on ever since the world began. Whoever wins one round passes on the advantage to the other for the next round. And thus will it go on forever, if we have anything to do with it."

Though there was still no feeling in the words of the hooded one, the tone was a little more relaxed. Perhaps colored by a tiny hint of ironic intimacy, as though the speaker had become well accustomed to the persuasive machinations of his opponent? They had clearly had this argument before.

The red-eyed entity began again. "You and I are old combatants, Time. Always I seek to build, but always you have the final say, and thwart me. You and your fellows stand there like statues, as if imagining that by your rigidity you can keep the world just as you like it. Yes, we are old combatants; and I know which, out of myself and my enemy, you lean towards. But think not of politics or power games; just look at the man now before us. . . ."

They dropped their gaze to where Appa knelt shivering in the cold, his aged frame bent under the burdens of a lifetime. Here, all alone and praying so earnestly, he was a pathetic sight, his face shriveled up like an old potato left to go bad at the bottom of a sack, all screwed up with such anxiety.

"Are you without pity?" The tall one's burning eyes tried to bore through the heavy grey cloth of Time's hood, tried to catch any glimpse of an expression. But, as usual, he was wasting his time, for the hood was completely impenetrable.

He went on: "It is but a simple request. He does not ask for secret powers, or vast armies. All he asks for is a little knowledge . . . call it an omen, if you like."

"Omen, indeed," his opponent laughed. "Omens are games, baits, illusions set to trap the simpleminded. Omens can be misread, with disastrous results. Would you risk the life of your old servant here in such deceptions?"

"Well, yes, frankly," the other replied with a shrug.

"Then who is without pity now?"

"Do not dare to speak to me that way! Remember that you too are a servant, though I must yield to you sometimes."

More deferential now, but still unwavering, the grey figure replied, "Well, such things as pity are not for me or my brothers to discuss. Besides, it is you and your adversary who play the games, not us. We merely ensure that the rules are kept, leaning towards neither side. The rules have been set, the pieces are now in play, and the game is in your hands. We shall involve ourselves no further."

And, on that final note, the audience was over.

Appa was unaware of the strangers, even though they had been standing within yards of him, but his old prescience told him he would get no answer tonight. With bent shoulders and a deeply furrowed brow, the old priest rose wearily to his feet and brushed the clinging lichen from his robe. As he shuffled away, deeply troubled, he resigned his fate, and indeed that of the whole world, to the whim of Chance in the days to come. Perhaps he and this man Bolldhe would find the answers in time.

The silent figures watched the old man depart. The gale still blew, tearing at the ragged robes of Time and his brothers, as the red-eyed one addressed them.

"So, he is leaving the outcome to you, Time—you and the fellow by your side," he sneered. "Not much of a pair to put your faith in: Time and Chance?"

The second figure in grey said not a word at this mention of its name, but there was a third figure standing on Chance's other side. It was this one, wearing an engraved stone tablet suspended on a heavy chain around its neck, which responded with a small sound. Red-Eye wondered if it was a laugh.

"And only *you* will have any idea of the outcome, eh, Fate?"

Only when Appa was finally swallowed up by the dark forest below did Time speak: "They are bound for the Far North, the realm of Fate, it is true. Though he puts his faith not in us but in you. Or rather in this Bolldhe of yours—though why in such a faithless, unreliable, wandering old rogue is beyond me."

"He is not 'my' Bolldhe," the lantern-bearer retorted. "He has no allegiance to me at all. Not yet, anyway."

"Quite," Time replied.

"Or to you either, come to that," Red-Eye snarled.

Time continued his needling: "And it is a mortal so unreliable that you expect to thwart your enemy, by following yon priest into hardship and darkness, maybe even laying down his life for something he does not believe in? Is that not a little optimistic?"

The lantern-bearer turned his gaze directly on his questioner. "That is all you have allowed me, as you have been at pains to point out."

There was a pause, and then Time persisted: "True, but we did not specify Bolldhe. He was *your* choice, though you could have chosen anyone: an elder, a high priest, even a warrior hero. . . . What is it about this vagrant that makes you select him, above all others, as the one to now champion your cause?"

Red-Eye gave a smile: cunning and without joy, but a smile nevertheless, for clearly he knew something he was not about to reveal. Yet it was a smile without substance, for if the fate of the world did indeed rest upon a "faithless, unreliable, wandering old rogue," Red-Eye did not rate their chances too highly.

"I know his past, his mettle, and his mind. He is unique. He may betray my will as often as he likes on the journey, but I believe he can be guided and molded, so that by the end he *will* know exactly what to do. That is why I send my devoted servant along with him. And as for the outcome, only time will tell."

"Don't count on it," Time murmured.

No one else knew of their presence there, nor did anyone care. The night held secret terrors enough for the good folk of Nordwas without their venturing up into the dark hills. The rumors circulating throughout the region were beginning to trouble people, till sleep became the only sure escape from nighttime's shadow of fear. For the Darktime has claws, and they can reach out even from your dreams to grasp your soul and wrench it from you in peals of quivering laughter. . . .

But as the pale gleam of early dawn began to wax in the eastern sky, the

birds one by one began their song while night began to fade, yielding inevitably to the bright warmth of another day. And finally, as the birdsong had
grown from that single voice to a tumultuous chorus of delight, the tired,
lonely figure of a little grey man at last reached the wooden gates breaching the
stockade wall of Nordwas.

1

The Moot at Wintus Hall

There was an air of mounting excitement as the market hall began to fill. Each passing minute would see more people pass through the heavy oaken doors to enter the echoing vaults beneath Wintus Hall, swelling the throng that waited in anticipation there. Although these vaults were cavernous, built to accommodate the entire household of Wintus Hall in the event of siege, those newly arriving had to push their way through the crowd just to find somewhere to stand. And with each minute the noise grew more tumultuous, as all waited impatiently for the proceedings to commence.

Master Gapp Radnar sat toward one end of the dais, squinting at the crowd through his spectacles and occasionally rubbing his reddened eyes. A thick haze of tobacco smoke hung in the air, its obnoxious fumes tainted further by the caustic odor of various other herbs being smoked throughout the hall. No one else even seemed to notice this pollution, but Gapp was suffering badly as his eyes smarted incessantly.

Occasionally he scratched the back of his neck in discomfort, where the thongs holding his lenses in place kept itching behind his ears. Despite his fifteen years, he felt very small and vulnerable sitting there, flanked by men who were all bigger and much more important. He was confronted by the largest crowd of onlookers he had ever seen in his life. All of them seemed to be staring right back at him, and he felt nervous, intimidated and so self-conscious that it was all he could do to stop himself burying his face in his hands.

Steepling his fingers before him in an effort to look self-collected and important, he covertly studied the men arrayed before him in the body of the hall.

What a bunch of blackguards, he thought. *I wouldn't trust one of them to run an errand, let alone embark upon a sacred quest.*

Ordinarily used as a meeting place of the Peladanes alone, it would normally have been a sea of green, that being the predominant color worn by their order. Peladane society observed strict rules of hierarchy, one's rank determining the number of colors one could wear, but each and every member, from highest to lowest, wore a long green robe called the Ulleanh. Today, however, the vaults of Wintus Hall were liberally sprinkled with the alternative shades favored by a wide variety of mercenaries.

Just look at the ditch-born scum, Gapp's thoughts went on. *Dented armor, notched axes, dirty clothes, filthy faces, and hair that looks as if it's served to clean out the grease tray under the pork spit . . .*

Of course, he knew, many of them had endured days, possibly weeks, of hard travel to get here. The boy ran a finger through the shock of clean, well-combed brown hair that crowned the top of his own head, and wondered briefly if he too might look as they did in the weeks to come.

There was one in particular to whom Gapp had taken a dislike right from the moment he had first clapped eyes on him. That one there, right in the front row, the one who was staring at him even now. Though Gapp kept trying to avoid eye contact, their eyes constantly seemed to meet. The boy would casually survey the back of the hall or rest his gaze on the middle distance, but always there would be the old rogue staring, *glaring,* straight back at him. This time Gapp hurriedly averted his gaze and studied the tabletop instead, nervously scratching at its surface with his fingernails.

"Will you cut that out, you little prat!" snarled a hungover voice at his side. "It's like demons scraping their claws on the inside of my skull . . ."

Gapp muttered an apology, keeping his eyes lowered. Stufi and Bhormann, seated right next to him, might be his master's closest drinking mates but they certainly were not Gapp's favorite comapany. As full-fledged Peladanes they were entitled to wear a white surplice over the Ulleanh, and in the case of Bhormann adorned with the black hem denoting a sergeant. But the cleanness of these outer garments could not hide the filthiness of the chain-mail hauberks beneath, which were permanently soiled with old blood and flakes of dried skin, causing the pair to stink permanently of rotten flesh. In his eyes they were as crass and decadent as the worst of the drunken oafs holding forth in the Peladanes' favorite taverns in Nordwas. Gapp decided he would almost prefer the company of the mercenaries.

The Order of Peladanes, Gapp reflected, *how could you sum them up?* They were charismatic and lordly and magnificent, of course, and he could not help but look up to them in awe, but, Jugg's Udders, they made a lot of noise. In fact they shouted all the time; they woke up shouting, shouted all through the day, then went to bed shouting. Some even shouted in their sleep.

A voice rose above the noise, striving to be heard.

"Could we have a little less noise, please. The council will commence shortly."

Those who even heard this request either glared at the speaker in contempt or openly jeered. Gapp glanced to his left to see who had dared make this announcement, and saw that it was Finwald. The young man stood hesitant for a while, then sat down abruptly. As he glanced in Gapp's direction, he gave him a smile as one might to an ally.

Which in a way they were, neither of them being held in any regard whatsoever by the assembled throng: Gapp because of his youth and lowly status as an esquire, and Finwald because he was neither a Peladane nor even a soldier. Civilians were barely welcome here at Wintus Hall; even the warlike mercenaries were accorded little regard. But the presence of a Lightbearer curdled the atmosphere right from the start. Those gathered here today were all *soldiers,* who had nothing but the deepest loathing for Lightbearers, especially their hated mage-priests.

Even the charismatic Finwald, the instigator of this whole quest, was seen by these hardened fighters as belonging to the lowest vermin on the face of Lindormyn. Gapp felt sorry him, as he surely did not deserve such treatment. Finwald was one of the most popular men in Nordwas, and that said a lot in this town where the glorious Peladanes enjoyed the status of demigods. But these jealous knights were not used to sharing popularity with others not of their narrow beliefs. Yet even among their own ranks there were some that would occasionally welcome Finwald into their homes with a loaf of bread and a tilted jug. He was friendly, supportive, and caring to everyone, unlike the majority of mage-priests in Nordwas.

The boy had taken notice of him ever since Finwald had come to Nordwas. Handsome, elegantly attired, and possessing a distinctly "foreign" look, he invariably turned heads on the occasions he set foot outside the temple. Now and again he would even sit with Gapp and answer patiently his many eager questions about life down South, among deserts, exotic peoples, fabulous beasts, and the famously decadent city of Qaladmir. For Gapp he provided a welcome distraction from the humdrum daily existence of this small, isolated town.

With his piercing dark eyes and long, straight dark-brown hair falling to his shoulders, the young priest's pallor contrasted sharply with the rest of his dramatic appearance: the wide-brimmed hat, the sweeping cloak, and the thigh-length boots all of jet black. The only hint of color about him was a large, ornate silver amulet of Cuna, the torch-shaped symbol of his cult that hung proudly upon his chest.

Yes, Finwald had come a long way from his early days in Qaladmir. He had matured so thoroughly in body and mind that perhaps only his modesty and lack of worldly ambition prevented him from achieving worldly greatness. Gone now was the shyness of youth, to be replaced by a cool confidence and strength of purpose and a firm belief in all he did.

It was after first meeting Appa, when the old priest visited Qaladmir twelve years earlier, that Finwald became disillusioned with the corruption of his native city. Embracing the Word of Cuna with a glad and joyous heart, he had finally persuaded Appa to take him back home with him to Nordwas. Here, in this northern frontier town, Finwald had made his new home. Accepted into the cult of Cuna as a Lightbearer, in a surprisingly short time he was ordained as a mage-priest. A few years later he won the heart of the daughter of a Peladane, an entrancing beauty named Aluine who could have taken her pick of Nordwas's finest. Inevitably their betrothal had caused much resentment among the Peladanes, and still did.

Undeterred by his reception from their audience, he was soon smiling and chatting with the Warlord's son seated beside him, a familiarity that aggravated the warriors even further.

Nibulus Wintus also liked Finwald, though as followers of different cults they might normally have kept their distance. And although the cult of Cuna was counter to the warrior ideals of Pel-Adan, they were not openly hostile. The Lightbearers, devotees of Cuna, had moved up from the South many centuries earlier, while the Peladanes were relative newcomers to Nordwas, having arrived only in the last hundred years or so to swell the population and fortify the place against their common enemies. Both cults had since managed to co-exist in an uneasy but mutually respectful truce, if not in close harmony.

Unlike his friend Finwald, Nibulus could never really take any religion seriously, even his own cult, which was not, by most people's standards, particularly spiritual in its demands. Though regularly observing temple rituals, *true* worship for the Peladanes was through combat and conquest, and their "collection plate" was a cart of harvested heads. Their holy water was hot and red, their incense charnel-scented, and their choir music provided by the screams of dying enemies. Magic and meditation were forbidden by their Warlords, for, as Finwald put it, "they want to hold the keys to Heaven in their own hands."

Nibulus was son and heir to the Warlord Artibulus, the leader of all the Northern Peladanes, and Nibulus himself was considered the mightiest warrior in Nordwas. Having, over the years, enthusiastically accompanied his father on many campaigns down in the South, he reveled in the glory and excitement of battle and had often proved himself a true follower of the Holy Order of Peladanes.

At six foot four and built like a siege engine, Nibulus was a formidable adversary and had trained all his life as a swordsman. When he was fully armored and wielding his greatsword, few could stand up to him. Yet the fierce posturing and well-rehearsed snarling that were the custom with so many of his kind were not for Nibulus. He had long ago learned that with his bulk he had no need of such artifice. In any case, his chubby, good-looking, personable features just did not seem intended for looking mean. Eschewing the long, flowing locks that were the fashion among his comrades, he kept his black hair modestly short and let the stubble grow freely on his jaw.

Today he had donned all four colors of his elevated rank: green, white, and black, burnished with the gold braiding of a Thegne. But he wore this uniform loosely, casually, one might even say untidily. The colors may have designated his eminence, but the way he wore them definitely befitted his disposition.

Nibulus had everything going for him that a warrior could hope for, and at only twenty-five years of age he still had much to look forward to. He cared little for the disapproval that some of his kind felt toward him, that being due mainly to his unpardonable closeness to Finwald. It was one thing to employ a Lightbearer as a flunky but quite another to actually become *friends* with one. Where would it all end? Getting married to horses?

The aged cleric Appa was also sitting at the table, looking frailer than usual after his night out in the hills. His eyes were cast down, his head resting upon one hand, and he looked as if he bore the troubles of the whole world on his back. The fingers of his other hand were clutched in his thick-cropped grey hair. Nobody else at the table talked to him, or even acknowledged his existence. They preferred, like most others, to avoid this mad old priest who incessantly mumbled mantras while rapping his ring against the Cuna symbol on his chest, and who smelled permanently of the ewe's butter that the priests used to mold their candles. And he, for his part, seemed completely oblivious of the present company.

"Looks as if your brother priest's had a good night on the town," Nibulus commented to Finwald without bothering to lower his voice. "Didn't know he had it in him."

Finwald smiled uncomfortably. "I know he seems a bit odd, but he really is a good man. We often disagree on things. . . ." He broke off to scan the room again.

The chamber had now filled to total capacity, with still no sign of the Warlord, and most of the warriors and mercenaries were becoming visibly impatient. The waiting was even worse for Gapp, though, as his discomfort over being stared at increased.

Armpits, he realized, *he's still doing it!*

Gapp had never seen anyone so grim-looking in all his life, not even among all these other murderous ruffians here today. The staring one seemed to have something very wrong with his face, exactly what Gapp could not say, for it was shaded by a great, charcoal-grey hood with two long crow's feathers sticking out to the left side. Maybe he was trying to hide his features because he was wanted by the local militia? Not impossible, Gapp considered, since there had been reports of Tyvenborg thieves operating in the area recently. Even the soldiers sitting on either side of the hooded man seemed to regard him with distaste, judging by the way they kept edging away from him on the crowded bench. All Gapp could definitely make out was a single eye staring back at him, pale and deathly.

He shivered involuntarily. These mercenaries were definitely not to his liking. Nibulus might feel easy in their company, but Gapp quailed at the thought of traveling with men such as these.

As the tumult of impatience increased, he glanced nervously down the length of the head table. There were eleven places in all, and the council would commence only once all of these were occupied. But at present there were only seven men here, the three remaining places being for Warlord Artibulus himself and his household officials. Those already present were himself, Nibulus and his two uncouth friends, Finwald, Appa . . .

. . . And that weird-looking foreigner who had entered earlier with the old priest. Who exactly he was, Gapp could not guess. He did not look anything special, at first sight just a balding, red-faced bloke in his thirties, with bloodshot, bulging eyes and a bit of a strange leer.

Gapp appraised him for a moment longer, and then was suddenly struck by a profound sense of melancholy. This emotion startled the boy considerably, for he could think of no reason for feeling this way. Unlike most of the mercenaries, this one looked neither brutal nor psychotic, nor did he seem to evince any of the arrogance and superiority that were the natural disposition of the typical Peladane. Could it be possible this was no warrior?

But there was nevertheless something about him that frightened the boy. There was something bleak and unsettling in his bloodshot eyes, in the way he kept himself very much to himself, not even conversing with Appa. It was all very suspicious, a mage-priest of Cuna associating with one such as this, and Gapp had an ominous feeling that this man was a harbinger of deep, dark secrets. The thought stirred up all the sadness, fear, and loneliness in Gapp that he would rather forget. Particularly the loneliness.

He shook his head to clear it of such nonsense. This newcomer, he remembered now, was just that fellow Bolldhe who had something significant to do with the quest; the one whom Appa had insisted must come along for the good of them all.

But exactly what did Appa mean? So far he had not given a single hint as to why this stranger was so important. And it did seem a tad suspicious that the cleric should be hatching secret plans with a foreigner—

Suddenly there was a fresh disturbance at the front of the throng. Someone new was pushing through to the head table, gesticulating and calling out urgently. It was yet another foreigner—*really* foreign this time—with dark skin, billowing robes, and (of more immediate concern) a vicious, five-foot length of shining steel gripped tightly in both hands. In one dexterous bound he was suddenly clear of the crowd, and he landed noiselessly upon the table right in front of Nibulus.

"Death to the Green Ones!" he cried, sword held high above Nibulus's head.

Gapp and the others at the table gaped in horror, but Nibulus himself remained motionless. Then the huge blade sliced downward . . .

. . . And stopped less than an inch from the Peladane's skull.

"Hi, Methuselech," Nibulus said cheerily, "would you like a drop of wine?"

The desert warrior lowered his sword gently and, all in one movement, he sheathed the weapon in its scabbard, then jumped to the floor and clasped his old friend in a joyous embrace.

"Xilva!" Nibulus laughed. "Glad you could make it, old pal."

Gapp's eyes were wide with wonder. Though he had heard stories of the famous Methuselech, as had everyone in Nordwas, until now he had never set eyes on him. And what a sight he was, with that huge curved sword, the ornate hood with its tassels of braided wool hanging down his back; the two fine golden chains that ran from each pierced ear to a pierced nostril. Incredible! Who here in the drab Northlands would have the audacity to dress like that? This tall, lithe, handsome soldier of fortune evoked all the mystery of the legendary Southlands that had fascinated Gapp so much since early childhood. This was about as exotic as it came, and Gapp's heart surged with a giddy excitement at the thought of the days to come. In that one brief moment, his soul was filled with a bottomless yearning for Adventure.

"Fatman," the newcomer beamed, his open smile mirroring the happiness evident in Nibulus's face, "it's great to see you."

The man's olive complexion and long, jet-black hair, kept out of his eyes by a scarlet headband, identified him as a member of one of the tribes of desert folk who dwelt in the Asyphe Mountains, impossibly far away.

"Well, well, well! I always hoped you'd turn up," Nibulus went on. "How's Phalopaeia?"

"Oh, still alive. Still spending all my money."

"And the kids?"

"Same as ever: rank, sweaty, and covered in jam."

"Come, have some wine. Or some porter? In fact, let's get pissed!"

He turned to the others at the table. "Everyone, meet Methuselech Xilvafloese, a trusty friend from way back. We used to ride together on my old man's holy wars against the warriors of Frea-Vilyana." He gestured for Methuselech to take a seat in one of the vacant places, then went on with his introductions.

"Uh . . . hullo," Gapp replied when it came to his turn. He wanted to say so much more, but this was the best he could manage in the presence of such sublime godliness. *Just look at him!* The gold of his boots and cummerbund shone like the flames on the highest temple altar, bringing with it the reflected warmth of hotter climes; the color of his cloak's lining was not merely red, but the scarlet of the blood of the gods themselves; while the dazzling white of his baggy shirt and trousers shone with a brilliance that surely no mortal bleacher anywhere on Lindormyn could match.

The black of his cloak, however . . . well, that wasn't any superior to the "local" black. No, Aescals, he had to concede, were good at all things black.

Why did everything have to be so drab up North? Gapp's own varicolored tunic seemed to him so washed out, faded, and dull—even the hues meant to be showy.

The desert man merely scanned the boy up and down without a word. Gapp was summoning up courage to address the newcomer further but just then, with a strident fanfare, the Warlord Artibulus Wintus finally arrived. Flanked by two personal bodyguards, his scribe, his steward, and his accountant, all arrayed in their finest livery, he strode toward them with a solemnity and pomp normally associated with royalty. Resplendent in green, white, black, and gold, Artibulus bore upon his chest the xiphoid purple badge of Unferth, which represented the Sword of Pel-Adan himself and which could be worn only by a general. Armor that shone with the luster of chrome glittered beneath every gap in his raiment, and his hair and even his face gleamed with a special radiance, as if he had just plunged his head into a tub of syrup.

Many immediately leapt up from their seats and began to cheer and clap, adding their throaty voices to the general cacophony of the ear splitting fanfare. Others, however, just sat where they were with their fingers in their ears. Those at the head table rose as one, in greeting. Even Bolldhe tiredly got to his feet and expressionlessly imitated their salute.

"My most noble warriors of Pel-Adan, and honored guests from afar," announced the herald, though few could hear his words, "I present to you, the most High and Excellent, Splendid and Magnificent, the preeminent Peladane of the North, the Warlord Artibulus Wintus!"

The cheering waxed into an uproar as the Warlord grandly paraded through them. Holding his head high, he nodded left and right in gracious acknowledgment. A thousand heads strained forward to better view this near-god who now walked among them, almost swooning from the opiate charisma that emanated from his transcendent majesty. Even those who had suffered at his hands over the years now roared in jubilation, eyes moist with fervor. The heady aroma of herd instinct could be smelled for miles around.

Mounting the dais, Artibulus took his seat in the center of the long table. Gapp, now that he saw him close at hand for the first time in his life, could not help feeling that the man looked more like a wealthy merchant or banker than a warrior.

Though Methuselech hastily faded into the throng, Artibulus noticed him immediately. His noble mien lightened for a moment as he smiled in surprise at his trusted comrade-in-arms. Meanwhile, the crowd began to quieten, and waited expectantly. All eleven places at the head table were now occupied, so the council could commence.

Then the herald rose. "Most honored guests and companions of the Warlord Artibulus, I present to you his son and heir, Thegne Nibulus Wintus."

"At last," murmured Nibulus, rising excitedly to his feet. This was the first time that his father had allowed him to take full charge of the proceedings, and make his first address to a council. And moreover this was to be *his* campaign, and he would not let the old man forget that. With one last glance toward his father, he faced the throng.

Now that Nibulus was facing ahead, the Warlord's syrupy eyes studied his son unblinkingly. Artibulus, like many a Peladane, had never considered it particularly important to get to know his son, and he could not help but speculate about his performance now. The lad seemed worthy enough, the sort you could depend on in a tight spot. But what about his oratory and leadership skills? How would he handle them? What demands could he make of his men that would still sound like promises?

Nibulus cleared his throat. "Right, first I would like to thank my father for hosting this gathering today," he began, "and also thank you all for attending on this, my first . . . *campaign.*" He savored the word, drawing it out luxuriously.

Pel's Bells! Artibulus rolled his eyes and his gaze rose up to the vaulted ceiling.

"I shall come to the point," Nibulus went on. "I realize that many of you are under the impression that, following our triumph over the Villans of Frea-Vilyana three years ago, we are here to raise another army to repeat such a victory."

There was a general buzz of approval from the throng, many of whom were veterans of the Villan crusades and, having spent most of their spoils already, were keen to have another crack at the enemy. For many, too, the sacking of cities and general harrying of the South was their only escape from a life of relentless boredom.

Nibulus changed tack: "However, since our last victory over them three years ago, those Southern upstarts are of little concern to us now. . . ."

The first murmurings of surprise and disappointment began to be heard, and Nibulus resisted the temptation to look at his father, though well imagining the expression on the old man's face. Still, there was no avoiding the subject now, so best to get it out of the way the soonest.

"No," he affirmed authoritatively, "there are far more important matters to concern us now, my friends. The force of elite warriors I intend to raise today will be granted the honor of defeating an even older, greater enemy, a threat that is now poised to engulf us all. For an ancient terror is once again stirring across the land." He paused for effect, as his father had taught him. "I lead you against the vile forces of Olchor and his minions!"

There was a buzz of surprise at this announcement, but one of interest too. Olchor, the "Evil God of Death," was not only recognized as one of the most powerful deities in existence but as the common enemy of all others, immortal and mortal alike. His cult was one of the oldest in the world, and his worshippers were many. His temples lurked in many places, some veiled, shadowy, and primordial, others bold, shining, and new. And their priests, the necromancers, were feared by all; some of them were reputedly so ancient that they hardly

resembled any other race that dwelled upon the face of Lindormyn, either because of inconceivable decrepitude or, in the case of those with the greatest
powers, because they were born in an era so far distant in the past that
mankind then simply did not look as he did nowadays. In some cases their true
age transcended the count of years, for their beginning occurred before numbers had even been conceived. And there were other necromancers barely out
of their childhood, proud acolytes given to saturated excess and sanguine ostentation.

If there was one sacred cause that could unite the different religions and
bickering factions of this world, it would be a crusade against Olchor. So the
crowd now listened attentively as Nibulus continued, the very air becoming
dark with anxiety.

Well, Nibulus considered cheerfully, *that wasn't too painful, was it?*

"As you know," he went on, "Peladanes have always stood uncompromis-
ingly against the devilish schemes of Olchor, and it is because of this noble tradition that my father has agreed to fund this quest . . ."

There was a snort from Bolldhe, who swiftly clamped a hand over his
mouth, but said nothing.

". . . but it is only right that I now hand you over to the instigator of this
holy quest. My friends, I give you Finwald."

It was not often that Artibulus's face registered expression, but on this occasion it bore one of quiet astonishment. *That's it? A few mumbled mewlings
and you're going to pass the scepter to a* civilian?

Finwald rose dutifully, amid a general hum of irritation, contempt, and hostility from the crowd. This priest was absolutely not welcome here in the hall of
warriors. Finwald glanced nervously down at the Warlord's son, but Nibulus
merely motioned him to get on with it before any catcalls started.

The priest cleared his throat, and began, "Brave fighting men," then immediately realized how feeble he sounded in this cavernous hall. He quickly raised
his voice, though in doing so found that it now quavered like a boy's.

Nibulus joined his father in staring ceilingward.

"Undoubtedly you are all aware of the many forms and guises that evil entity has assumed in the past," Finwald continued bravely. "Ever and anon will
the Father of Lies send out his minions to corrupt our world, and it has always
fallen to men such as yourselves to stand in their way. Indeed every page of history is written with such strife. Some of these servants of Evil are well known
to us, others less so, but it is of one pernicious above all that I now speak,
namely the Rawgr lord, Drauglir."

The hostility from the throng instantly faded, but the contempt multiplied
tenfold. Drauglir was infamous as one of the most dangerous Rawgrs ever to
have existed, but that was half a millennium ago. So what was this string boy
doing, telling them all this rubbish?

"Over five hundred years ago," Finwald hastened on, "this same terrible demigod held sway over the whole of the Far North, threatening to infect our entire world with the plague of his evil. It was only a timely and unprecedented league of Peladanes, Oghain-Yddiaw, mercenaries of Vregh-Nahov, and others that finally cut out that abominable cyst and hurled it onto the triumphal bonfires of Justice. His land was invaded, his fortress besieged, and he, together with all his vile minions, was thrown down. Not one soldier or necromancer of the Maw was left alive, and the entire accursed place was purged of evil."

He paused for breath, then continued quickly. "However, the sword of Arturus Bloodnose did not eliminate forever the name of Drauglir. Such dire entities have a knack of hanging on, and even now there persists the legend that one day Drauglir would rise again, after five hundred years. Just about now, in fact."

Another nervous pause. "As anyone in Nordwas can tell you, I myself possess an exceptional skill in theurgy—meaning I can contact the spirits to request their advice. I do not boast in saying this; I simply tell the truth, as many will gladly verify. Over recent months I have been in contact with my deity, and he has revealed many things. So it is my woeful duty to vaticinate to you all today, my friends, that the legends concerning Drauglir's second coming are true. He will be among us again *before the year is out!*"

There was a moment's silence; then the entire hall erupted in raucous laughter. There were also angry shouts, and at one point a throwing axe thudded into the table in front of Finwald. The offender was swiftly removed and (as Finwald learned later that day) his fingers ceremonially fed into the gear mechanism of the nearest watermill, but the whole reaction was totally unexpected by those sitting at the head table.

Finwald the priest looked over to Nibulus and his father for support, but they too seemed to be in some confusion. Even Methuselech shrugged in bewilderment. What was so funny or provocative? Everyone was familiar with the legend of Drauglir's second coming. It was true that nobody knew how this legend began, but there were now persistent rumors circulating the markets and taverns of Wyda-Aescaland regarding a resurgence of terrible evil in the Maw. And for many years now, it seemed, various groups of reckless "adventurers" had actually been journeying there.

They had their reasons, these people, some not as virtuous as others. Off to the North they would go, and often that was the last ever seen or heard of them. These disappearances had piqued the imagination of the skalds and gossipmongers, for filling in the blanks with creative fantasy is ever the job of the storyteller, and that which is not known is the blankest page of all. But what had really caused excitement during the last few years were reports of the few groups of travelers that had actually *returned*. Tales of "soured" people in the Far North, dead men walking, and unspeakable horrors that stalked in dark places all now added authenticity to the burblings of the skalds.

So what was the problem here?

One man stood up and shouted above the din: "Horse manure! Have you brought us all the way here just to tell us bedtime stories? Come off it! We all know Drauglir died that day, burned into a heap of bubbling jelly!"

"Yeah!" cried another. "Even if he *were* to come back, what danger would we be in from that?"

Then Appa stood up. He was not a natural speaker, not with a voice so weak and croaky, but it was the surprise of seeing him dare to stand up at all that stilled the crowd.

"I can endorse my brother Finwald's claim, for I too am a Lightbearer and have known this man beside me for many years. I can assure you therefore that he *does* possess 'powers'—as do all true followers of Cuna."

Unfortunately, such confirmation from just another Cuna priest, and a senile one too, proved less than helpful in convincing them. But eventually there did arise support of a kind from unexpected quarters. For a number of Peladanes from the most northerly regions now made themselves heard, and it seemed that there were indeed stories rife in their villages about the "escape of the hellhound Drauglir from his icy fastness."

One such soldier, from the village of Wrache on the northern fringes of Wyda-Aescaland, began. "There came from the North one night a storm o' such violence and fury that the whole village fled to the temple, for within its stony fortitude we did hope to find sanctuary. And there, as the tempest scream'd outside carrying upon it diabolic voices that no wind nor rain should ever make, we came to realize that this was no storm born o' the heavens, but rather from the reeking mouth o' Hell itself. The smashing o' slates, the felling o' trees, the ripping-up o' fences, all could be heard as the tempest went about its destructive task.

"But within the House o' Pel-Adan we was safe . . . or so we'd believ'd. For anon rose, above the havoc o' the winds, an utterance that brought a terror into our hearts such as none gather'd there had ever thought possible; 'twas the clamor o' demons, like as the baying o' the Black Dog itself, and round and round the shaking building it tore in its ire. Great rending sounds as of some terrible talon could we hear upon the door, and a hammering upon all the shutters so strong it was only Faith that held them from splintering asunder.

"Course it could not get in as long as our faith held fast. But there was those in our company what were going mad with fear, and 'twould not be long 'fore their minds departed forever, such was the horror o' the Beast that raged without. And when finally the steeple came crashing down in ruination, Thegne Toktoson took up his greatsword and went out to meet it. He slid back the bars, wrench'd open the door, and in that second all the fury o' the Black Place burst into the temple. Thrice round the sanctuary this pack o' fiends tore, as we curl'd in an agony o' fear upon the flagstones.

"And then, suddenly as it'd enter'd, it was gone . . . just not there. The tempestuous manifestation died, the trees ceased their tumult, and we all stagger'd to our feet. What'd befallen, we never found out, but 'twas Thegne Toktoson what saved the day. And there he was, upon the floor by the portal, his head ripped clean off by the hellhound.

" 'Twas Drauglir, I tell you. O' that there's no doubt in my mind."

Those at the head table relaxed a little; the words of the Peladanes of Wrache, a place too far to be considered "in the pay" of the Wintus household, did more to quieten the assembly than the words of any priest. They were a hardy and honest lot, less given to the excesses of their more southerly peers, and were held in a kind of grudging respect by other Peladanes.

One soldier, the leader of a band of archers from Rhelma-Find, then spoke up: "Holy man here zsay Drauglir will rize, and man of Wrache say he already riz. Either way, far as we concerned you *all* talking manure: Arturuz Bloodnoze zstuck hiz zsword into Rawgr'z heart, then dezstroyed corpse with fire! *That* the way it alwayz done with Hell-thingz. Zso *that* an end to it; how can Drauglir pozsibly rize again?"

There was a general buzz of agreement. Like beez.

But Finwald was unflustered: "To start with, Arturus never so much as laid hands on the Rawgr. It's a well-documented fact that it was by the hands of one of Drauglir's *own* servants that the demon's heart was pierced."

This much at least was not too shocking a revelation to those listening, as there had always been doubt as to who had actually thrust the blade in.

"And are you really such an authority on the subject of Rawgr-slaying that you can assure us all, and the good men of Wrache here, that burning the body would be enough to destroy one? Can you truly gainsay the word of those who have spent their lives studying this legend? Are we to risk the entire world on just the theories of an archer from . . . wherever it is you come from? I venture to suggest that you are suffering from the same delusional overconfidence that afflicted the Peladanes five hundred years ago. You see, their great error was in mistaking the correct way of slaying the Rawgr . . ."

Immediately there was an uproar. All the Peladanes in the hall surged forward and bayed their outrage, and it did not look as if they could be placated this time.

"What was that you were saying about delusional overconfidence?" Nibulus hissed at the priest, as the Peladanes began a war chant denouncing magepriests, Lightbearers, and all things civilian.

All the Peladanes, that is, except the Warlord and his son, who had already endured this same argument with Finwald earlier. After a few ugly minutes, their intervention calmed the crowd down enough to hear Finwald further.

"I know how galling it must be for you to stand around listening to some follower of Cuna tell you what is and what isn't right. Believe me, I'm not enjoying this, but it is of the utmost importance that we sort out this problem right here and now. If not, we will still be arguing when the skies are red with fire creeping down from the North, and while the leprous serpents of Hell come slithering into our children's cots!"

He paused, struggling to keep the shrillness from his voice. He had never been the preaching type. "There is however a correct way to slay a Rawgr lord—"

"And that iz to immolate the body in fire," persisted the archer, to whoops of triumph from others nearby.

But Finwald would not be deflected: "Wrong! According to every de-monology I have found, and which I have shared with my honorable associates here at the table"—there was a nod of assent from the Warlord—"the only way to destroy a Rawgr lord of Olchor is to pierce the heart *and* the brain with a magical blade. Failing that, a weapon of silver-plated iron will do. Any other method will most decidedly *not* do. That is a fact."

There followed a heated debate on sundry ways of killing a Rawgr lord, which raged on for nearly an hour. Most stuck firmly to the popular belief that burning was adequate. A few, mainly foreign mercenaries, had also heard tell that silver-plated iron would work, and sided with Finwald. But no matter how eloquently he argued, the priest could not convince them that a sword through both heart and brain was the surest solution. Finally, in frustration, he said, "Then if you are right about immolation by fire, how come it failed the last time?"

As soon as the words had left his mouth he cursed himself for his own stu-pidity. He knew what was coming next.

"How do you know it *did* fail?" was the reply from a hundred throats. "It is only you who claims otherwise. For all we know, Drauglir was slain there and then."

Finwald took a deep breath and, truly believing his conviction would save the day, proclaimed: "It is not *I* that claim this truth; it is my god."

Straight away the very air of the sweaty chamber turned even sourer, as close on a thousand voices bawled out their disdain. It sounded like feeding time at the hyena house. Finwald closed his eyes in despair, while Nibulus cov-ered his face with one hand, not sure whether to groan at his dwindling hopes of raising an expeditionary force, or to laugh at Finwald's stupidity. Gapp merely looked away; he simply was not here in this hall anymore.

The derision continued until Appa once more rose to his feet.

"I'm afraid you'll just have to trust us on this," he croaked in irritation. "If you refuse to believe that it is Cuna who has revealed this message to him, then just believe that it is your own deity too who warns you. If there are any here who simply cannot accept the possibility that Drauglir yet lives, they may as well leave right now, for we have no need of them!"

Many took up this challenge and immediately departed. They had heard enough. With a third of the assembly now walking out the door, and those remaining only doing so because of the presence of the Warlord himself, Finwald had to try a different approach—his last-ditch attempt to win them over.

"Is not your god Pel-Adan considered the greatest enemy of Olchor?" he inveigled. "Is it not Pel-Adan and his loyal followers who have always been the foremost stumbling block to Olchor's malign machinations? So does it really seem so improbable to you that the Sword of Pel-Adan—the very talisman of your cult—is the key to Olchor's downfall?" He studied them closely and then added carefully, "Do you not believe in the power of your own god?"

Well, that just about did it for the council at Wintus Hall. The Warlord had entirely misjudged the mood and reactions of both the Peladanes and the mercenaries. The ensuing uproar denouncing the mage-priests and their blasphemy was visibly apparent to those at the head table in a sea of furious red faces, slobbering tongues, and glaring eyes:

"Insolence!"

"Get him out!"

"Stand down, preacher man!"

"Shove off, beanpole!"

"Out! Out! Out!"

Finwald looked down in despair. The visions he had of raising a vast army of highly trained soldiers were fading from his mind with every chant of outrage.

"You're not handling this very well, are you?" Nibulus stated mildly.

This at least could not be denied; the hall was emptying so fast it looked as if someone had pulled a plug from the floor of Wintus Hall. Within just ten minutes the company were staring at an audience of no more than thirty men. As the last Peladane stormed out of the hall, he yelled back at the Warlord: "How can you allow this infidel to speak thus?" Artibulus stared expressionlessly at the man, who quickly continued his exit. Soon, all that could be heard of the departing Peladanes were his echoing footfalls, and then were all gone. Finwald's grandiose plans went out of the door with them.

The remainder sat uncomfortably on the desolate benches, each with an embarrassingly large empty space to either side of him. Gapp noted with displeasure that the grim-faced mercenary with the crow's feathers sticking out of his hood still showed no signs of leaving.

There was a profound silence in the chamber, interrupted only by the occasional cough from one of the diminished audience. Nibulus began drumming his fingers on the tabletop; Gapp wanted to bury his head in his hands.

"Well," announced Finwald, "as I was saying—"

"I wouldn't say anything," Nibulus interrupted. "We've lost enough of them as it is."

Finwald frowned and lowered the brim of his hat to cover his eyes.

Then Appa spoke up coldly. "Well, what are you lot waiting for? If none of you believes this is any more than fairy-tale nonsense, why don't you just leave too?" There was a distinct note of challenge above the defeat in his voice.

Methuselech, perhaps feeling sorry for his friends at the table, stood up and replied simply: "Because we don't believe this is nonsense."

"No," interjected another. "The Wintus family has too great a reputation to risk throwing it away on the dreamed-up fantasy of some upstart mage-priest." He then stood down, happy with himself for managing to insult both Finwald and the Wintuses in one statement. But at least it seemed their scanty audience was willing to hear more.

Nibulus stood up and tried a different tack, one that he knew was more likely to win them over than any sense of obligation, and that was *pay*! Warlord Artibulus did, after all, control exceedingly large amounts of money.

Ah, now *you're talking.* Artibulus nodded in approval.

Terms and conditions of service, estimated duration, individual precedence, all these Nibulus outlined as briefly as possible, and left till the end the thorny subject of finally destroying the Rawgr lord Drauglir, assuming he was even still alive. But before he could expand on that, he was interrupted by one of the remaining soldiers.

"We don't know if that thing is still alive, and to be honest I couldn't give a damn anymore. So long as we get properly paid, that's all I'm bothered about, but we still have to work out how to kill him before we get there. If he's still about, there's no way that I'm going to stand around while you lot are still bickering about how to destroy him."

Nibulus sighed. "Look, if it pleases you, we can use *every* method suggested to us: pierce the heart and brain with silver, and also with a magical blade; set the bugger alight, drown him in gravy, stick a billhook up his backside, whatever . . . I can pass round a sheet of parchment right now and you can all write down any method you want. That way everyone should be satisfied, so long as we're properly equipped beforehand. Finwald . . . ?"

"My method," Finwald replied, holding up a silver shortsword. "I possess no magical blade, so have had this one made."

"This is all very well," butted in the last soldier irritably, "but according to my count we've listed no less than eleven different ways to kill the bastard. Exactly how long is it going to take to complete all of those, and just what is Drauglir going to be up to while we're doing all this to him?"

"Twelve ways," corrected Appa, and all heads turned toward him.

"Oh yes," Nibulus said, "I was wondering when we'd get round to Bolldhe."

The balding, red-faced foreigner did not show any reaction. He knew the ways of men better than most, and clearly was not about to waste his time trying to convince anyone of anything. Remaining seated, he merely nodded and returned his gaze to the tabletop in front of him.

So, instead, the old priest Appa rose to address the prospective campaigners.

"Brave enemies of Olchor, a while ago I had a vision. In that vision my lord Cuna told me—"

"Oh no, here we go again," said a bored voice from the rear.

"He told me that I too must accompany my colleague Finwald upon his quest."

This was met with a burst of cruel but predictable laughter. Though none of them had actually been there, the Far North was well known to be one of the harshest and most inhospitable regions of the known world. Appa, however, did not exactly look the hardy sort.

But the old priest was undeterred: "Yes, I, Appa the worn-out old cleric, was told I must also make the journey to Vaagenfjord Maw. And there was one destined to go with me, one who has already traveled the world. This man, Cuna revealed, would arrive unexpectedly from the East, going by the name of Bolldhe. And though not a follower of Cuna, he would be sent with Cuna's blessing. For he is the one destined to destroy forever the Evil of Drauglir. Yet he would have no understanding of his mission, or even how to accomplish this sacred task."

At this Bolldhe simply smiled and nodded.

"But at the end," Appa went on, "he would know, and it would be up to me to help enlighten him. That's how my vision ended—but a week later the very man arrived amongst us."

All eyes were now on the traveler. He certainly did not look anything special. Judging from the weird array of clothing and accouterments, he could hail from just about anywhere on the face of Lindormyn. Apart from the rawhide trousers, deerskin tunic, and stoatskin cloak, which might have been purchased from any trader right here in Nordwas, nothing else he wore looked familiar. Everything else was alien to them: the garnet-studded leather belt from which hung a lizard-hide waterskin; the necklace of bizarrely shaped teeth sporting a large and opaque, pale-blue gem in the center; those heavy jade bracelets covered in exotic runes; the scimitar-shaped brooch-pin . . . And what about the strange tattoos on the backs of his hands: some kind of horned serpent, or dragon perhaps? Clearly this was a well-traveled man.

But why was this ordinary-looking man attired so extraordinarily? Though obviously no warrior, he did at least look fit in a wiry sort of way; a man who could look after himself. He had about him the ragged, "unsleek" look of a wild hare: that constant watchfulness in his eyes and the careful way he held himself. While Peladanes and mercenaries *lounged,* this man seemed taut and ready to spring away at the first sign of danger, a man canny enough to dodge any opponent, or double back with a speed that would throw off any predator.

In short a loner, and a survivor.

All eyes remained on the traveler, but if they expected him to say anything, they were in for a long wait. Bolldhe just gazed back at them with an expression that seemed to say: *Yes, can I help you?*

Finally one soldier called out impatiently: "Let me get this straight, cleric; you want us to accompany some old priest across near-impassable country, by a route you won't disclose, to an old ruin inhabited by the burnt ashes of a five-hundred-year-old corpse, then to stick all manner of sharp things into it, burn it *again*. And then, if it looks like rising to life again before the year's out, to let this chatty foreigner destroy it by some means not even *he* knows of?"

"He *will* know by the end of it," replied Appa. "That's a promise."

"A promise made by *your* god—the one who appeared to you in a vision. You expect *us* to believe that?"

"I know it sounds a tad unlikely, but it is true. That's all I can say."

"Nice talking t' you," said the mercenary, and calmly walked out of the room too. Those at the head table then had to look on helplessly as most of the rest rose to their feet and, without a word, followed his example. As the last man disappeared through the door, the company found themselves staring at a gathering of just two. These were the flamboyant Methuselech Xilvafloese and the grim mercenary with the disturbing stare.

"Armholes!" Gapp swore under his breath.

To either side of Nibulus there was a squeak of chair legs across the stone floor. "I'm sorry, old man," Bhormann muttered as both he and Stufi got to their feet.

"You too?" Nibulus exclaimed incredulously.

"Well, you know how it is. . . ." Stufi replied awkwardly, and the pair of them shuffled on out of the hall.

Words could not describe the absolute despair and bitterness that descended on those remaining at the table. Crushed and defeated before they even set off, they buried their heads in their hands.

"How incredibly embarrassing!" Nibulus breathed. This was not how he had expected his first campaign to begin. Or end.

Then he became aware of other eyes fixed upon him, and looked up to see Methuselech and the mercenary eyeing him, patiently, waiting for him to say something more. Nibulus merely stared in silence at the swirling spirals of dust dancing in a beam of light slanting through the window, and listened idly to the scratching of a mouse somewhere nearby.

"Well?" he said eventually, with a hint of vexation in his voice. "What are you waiting for? Council's over. No point in hanging around here."

He felt a little guilty at treating his old friend Methuselech thus, especially after all the miles the man had traveled just to get here. But there was also a feeling of resentment that Methuselech should be dragging his humiliation out like this.

But the Southerner, with pride in his bearing, loyalty in his eyes, sympathy in his smile and warmth in his voice, replied simply: "We await your orders, my lord."

"Come again?" Nibulus gasped, wondering if the man were serious or if this was just another example of incomprehensible Asyphe humor. Then he turned his gaze to the other man who had stayed on. Though he could not make out the mercenary's eyes beneath the shadow of the dark grey hood, a silent nod bespoke sufficiently of the man's willingness to join their party.

"So," Finwald announced quietly in his ear, "it looks like we've got our army."

Nibulus just stared in front with a glazed look in his eyes, and muttered, "Oh, Shogg's Arse!"

2

The Dream Sorcerer

Between Nordwas and the high, bleak hills where Appa had prayed the previous night, the well-ordered fields and meadows gave ground to a large wood. Many small tracks threaded their uncertain way through it, parting the dense, thorny undergrowth of bramble, nettle, and fern, crossing stony streams of cold, clear water, and winding through the irregular ranks of knurled trees. The folk of Nordwas depended on these woods for much of their livelihood; fuel for their fires, timber for their buildings and furniture, and nuts, fruit, and game for their tables.

But despite the bounty that these woods—the remnant of a much vaster forest in ancient days—had to offer, the good people of Nordwas were loath to pass beneath its murmuring boughs. For the Aescals—the predominant race of Wyda-Aescaland—were not forest people. They regarded such places as "uncivilized," and for the people of Nordwas these woods were a reminder of wilder, more savage times, times when strange forest cults held sway; an era of shamans, sacrifices, and primeval, night-born terrors. In short, they were seen as places of fear, and only the outer reaches were trod by them.

Aescals, though, were not the only people who lived in these parts. It was just in the last few centuries or so that they had moved up from the south, dispersing an older race—one that had been here since before records began—to the fringes; banishing them to the drear hills, the cave-ridden gullies, and here to the wild woods.

But there were some places in the shadowed depths of this primordial forest where not even the older race walked. Some, even, which had never been visited by Man since the world began. It was not that they were *all* guarded by terrible beasts or shades—though some were, to be sure. But they were sacred, hidden, and fey, and there was something about them that forbade any disturbance by the wasteful plundering of these two-legged upstarts. The only sounds to be heard in these gloomy yet beautiful places were the moaning of the treetops in the breeze, the creaking of ancient boughs, the dull thud of falling cones upon mossy ground, the furtive rustle of unseen creatures through the fallen leaves, and the scraping of beetles in rotten tree bark. Now and again the cawing of a crow would filter down through the leafy roof of these woods, but even this was rare.

Today, however, there *was* something—or someone—in the hallowed depths of the forest. Whether man or beast, it was impossible to tell, for though it walked upright, it was covered in shaggy grey-brown fur, and moved with a stealth not seen in even the wildest, wiliest hunter. There was something in its footfall, causing neither sound nor any disturbance of the leaf mold, which told of an instinctive oneness with its natural surroundings. Not one twig was snapped, not a blade of grass bent, nor even the fragile, dew-hung threads of a spider's web shaken, as this unseen, unheard, and unsmelled prowler stalked through the closely intertwining foliage.

Then it stopped. Crouching upon all fours, it began to crawl forward, more bestial than human now. Padding silently over the ground, it took in everything with its quick eyes: the red and white toadstools that forced their way up through the moist, worm-broken soil; the pale, fungal remains of a burst puffball, its cloud of brown dust spiraling up through the one pale beam of light that illumined the glade; even the hair-thin legs of a harvest spider that carefully tested its weight on a blade of grass. Not one thing went unnoticed.

But it was neither fungus nor invertebrate that this lurker sought on this day. There was something terrible in these woods that it desired; something more dangerous than the quick-tempered boar with his ripping tusks, or the ferocious Hikuma-Bear whose arms might crush a man just for sport; something more terrible even than the solitary Monoceros, whose single horn could pierce any material known, or the "flying" Jaculus, that evil serpent who could launch herself from trees to deliver a bite poisonous enough to dissolve both flesh and bone.

This silent prowler was looking for the deadly spirit known as the Bucca.

The Bucca? Its reputation and legend were known well by the men of the North, and they avoided it at all costs. By the superstitious Aescals, mumbling sterile prayers in their stony temples, it was feared even more than the Ferishers that would at times rise in packs from their rivers in the Old Kingdom to plague the northwest marches with their disgusting practices. As for the Peladanes, those braying men of the West with their shining iron implements, they refused even to believe in it. But the Torca, the original men of this realm, they alone of all the peoples of Wyda-Aescaland knew its true nature; and it was for exactly this reason that they, too, avoided it.

Few had ever seen a Bucca, and would not have recognized one even if they did. But it was believed that they dwelled somewhere in the pathless depths of these woods, for every now and then some poor fool who had strayed too deep would come running back to town, screaming insanely, clutching his bleeding ears, and covered in a horrid slime, only to die within hours.

The Bucca's secret glades were also said to be guarded by wood demons and wraiths. But the figure that hunted it on this day knew far more about it, and its dire companions, than did anyone. And, though this hunter knew the full extent of the Bucca's powers—and was thus the only being in these parts that had real cause to be afraid—it also knew its weaknesses, and how it could be snared.

Raising its head, the seeker sniffed. Yes, this was the place; the only glade in the woods where hawthorn, oak, and ash would grow together, and thus a place of fey. The hunter did not have to see these trees to know their kind; their smell, the sound their leaves made in the air, their very aura, these things told it all it needed to know.

Protected by a garland of blessed bay leaves to ward off evil spirits, it had stalked through the dense foliage and clammy undergrowth quite undetected, heading into this night-shrouded circle of bare earth where only the three sacred trees grew: the domain of the Bucca. The hunter could not be touched by the creature's guardians now; only by the Bucca itself.

Crawling out of the cover of the undergrowth, it could now be seen that this hunter was, indeed, a man. A man on all fours, clad in a great, shaggy pelt of wolf skin, tattered at the edges, but uncanny in the way it truly bestowed upon its wearer the semblance of a live wolf. This pelt had the animal's head still attached, which served as a grisly, snarling hood that stared ahead with unseeing, cold grey eyes. The eyes of the wearer himself were green, leaf-green with earth-brown flecks, and stared out from under a straggle of wild red hair beneath the covering of the wolf mask. The intruder's ruddy face bore an expression of the utmost concentration, for he knew well that he now needed a focusing of all his mind and instinct for the task ahead. His breath came out steaming in barely perceptible swirls in the dank air of that forever-sunless glade.

This hunter was not of the same race as the folk of Nordwas. He was a Torca, whose kind had dwelt here for thousands of years before the present-day occupants of these lands invaded from the south or west, bringing with them their new religions. Very few Torca there were now, pushed out as they had been by the bright, purging sword of Pel-Adan and his proud followers, driven north toward the Blue Mountains, or west to the Old Kingdom where forest, river, and the old ways still held sway. Here, in what was now called Wyda-Aescaland, many Torca had turned to hard drink, and their religion had all but vanished except in this untrod fastness of the forest's heart where it still hung on. They did not properly understand, those degenerate outlanders, the language of the trees, the music of the roots, or the whisperings of the wind. They ran in fear whenever they heard the song of the forest wolf, or felt the silent watching eye of the snake or the lizard upon them.

He could see the Bucca now, alone in its circle of mossy earth, unaware—as yet—of the intruder's presence. Long he stared at it, and marvel was evident in his face. But he was not beguiled, for he had earlier rubbed his eyes with an ointment of vervain, and was thus protected against every sort of fey glammer.

To the gaze of the common man, the Bucca appeared as nothing more than a tiny, delicate flower, similar to a daisy but smaller, and with an inky-violet disk that was surrounded by a ray of thin, pale-mauve petals. Actually, had a man the opportunity to study it for any length of time, he would realize that its color was unsure, swimming before his eyes until it confused his brain. For these were the unique colors of fey, and only the Torca shaman had eyes able to discern this particular shade of the spectrum.

And once the color was seen, so too was the true form behind it; the Bucca was in fact not a flower but a tiny, tiny little man. A stem-thin, androgynous body of untouchable delicacy, with shifting hues of translucent violet and the smoothness of gypsum, was crowned by the disproportionately large and incongruously grotesque head resembling a wizened old man's. Above the high forehead, a thin straggle of pale mauve hair stuck out around its otherwise bald pate. As it stood still, swaying slightly like a man in a trance, or a flower in a breeze, its bulbous eyes remained closed under heavy, veiny lids like those of a newly hatched chick. The creature's nose was tiny and sharp, its ears long and pointed, and its mean little mouth turned down at the corners in a perpetual grimace framed by a long, wispy beard that stank of stale carrion.

Hardly causing a stir in the air, the hunter reached into one of the many little folds of his clothing, and carefully, delicately, scratched an itchy patch at the top of his thigh that had been growing more distracting by the second. Thus prepared, he waited, having already made the incantations that would ensure him the self-discipline to carry out this task. All he needed to do now was pause a while to summon up his courage, awaiting just the right moment.

Though he tried to concentrate, a hundred thoughts and images flashed through the wolf-man's head as he stared at the manikin in front of him. That very morning, he had been foraging in the woods for some hemlock to make a poultice for one of Warlord Artibulus's servants who was suffering from rheumatism. And then, while still searching for this rare plant, the shaman had noticed something lying on the ground. It was a sprig of hazel, the holy tree of his cult. Strange, he thought, since there were no hazel trees around here, the soil not being chalky enough.

He picked it up and noticed that hanging from the smooth brown skin were eight catkins: eight soft "lambtails" of bright red, as though they had been dipped in the blood of the Earth Spirit himself. He had looked up to see where the sprig had fallen from, and smiled in recognition at the black shape peering down at him from a lofty branch.

It was a raven, known to those who revered him as one of Erce's messengers. It was the raven that had dropped the hazel sprig: an omen if ever there was one. He had not hesitated then, for this portent meant something really important was up. And exactly what it signified could be discovered only by casting the runes. For each catkin on the sprig, one rune should be cast, and eight runes indicated things must be extremely urgent. He would have need of powers greater than his own to divine the intention of Erce the Earth Spirit. . . .

And what better powers than those of the Bucca?

That is how Wodeman, the sorcerer of the ancient cult of Erce, came to be here in this sacred, terrible glade.

Suddenly he knew the time had come. If he were to do it at all, he must do it now. Deftly he drew out ten foxgloves from a pouch, and slipped them one on each finger. Immediately the Bucca was aware of the proximity of the "fairy thimbles" but (so Wodeman prayed) not yet aware of who wore them. Its purple eyelids snapped open, revealing two huge, featureless orbs of clear green, and a thin whine escaped its mouth. Slowly, still undulating like a flower in a breeze, it drew nearer, unable to prevent itself.

Closer, Wodeman entreated. *Closer . . .*

Then with lynxlike agility, he suddenly leapt out of cover and dived straight into the glade. Immediately, the game was up and he had to work fast, for the Bucca knew what had happened as soon as the predator made his move—and Wodeman's life was now in danger. He could see, hear, and feel pandemonium breaking loose all around him. Before he had even grabbed the tiny body, the Bucca began screaming, its deathly keening searing the very air, sending shudders of pain and protest through each fiber of every plant and animal within half a mile. As Wodeman sprawled belly-down upon the vibrating earth, trying to get a good hold on its slippery body, he saw the ugly, bulbous head of the Bucca suddenly expand to the size of a pumpkin, its now-cavernous mouth opening so wide it threatened to engulf the sorcerer's head. The diminutive captive shrieked with a fury so diabolical it sent the trees and bushes all around swaying violently back and forth, their branches whipping the air in frenzied anguish and silently screaming in their agony.

Wodeman desperately fought with the hideous Huldre, and finally gained a viselike hold upon it. While it writhed, screeched, blew vile little raspberries, and near turned itself inside out in its efforts to break free, the sorcerer continued howling out the occult incantations that would complete his spell. Though he had "harvested" Buccas before now, he still gasped in amazement at the awful power the little creature could release in its madness to free itself of its assassin. It even managed to prize Wodeman's great hands apart just enough to shoot, from the vicinity of its navel, a spray of the most revolting, vile, and sickening emission straight at the sorcerer's chest. It felt as if he had been hit by an entire cauldron of this bile, and he beseeched Erce that his spell would be complete ere he was forced to draw breath once more.

Still he persisted, bawling out the last words of the spell, while wrestling with the squirmy little monstrosity with all the strength his wiry muscles could summon. Even the lifeless wolf skin he was wearing seemed reanimated under the arcane power of the Bucca, its fur bristling and jaws snarling unnaturally as it tugged and quivered upon the sorcerer's back.

But Wodeman fought on and, with one last effort of mind and muscle, he finally ripped the minuscule body away from its massive head, the sinews tearing apart like the snapped roots of a flower being pulled from the soil. Immediately the howling of the Bucca ceased, and the woods all around, released from the power of the Huldre, at last settled back into an uneasy stillness.

Nature red in tooth and claw—there was little of subtlety in the Way of Erce.

Tightly gripping the decapitated, wormlike body between finger and thumb, Wodeman booted the rapidly deflating head into the undergrowth, then ripped his own clothing off in a spasm of disgust. Still inhaling through his mouth, he writhed about on the earth to rid his body of the worst of the Bucca's slime.

He collapsed finally onto his back, and let out a deep sigh. For a long while he lay there, resting his shuddering body and silently offering a prayer of thanks to the Earth Spirit for protecting him. Then he got back to his feet, wiped his grimy brow, and studied the tiny strand of violet jelly that lay motionless in his palm.

It was customary at this point for a sorcerer to draw a little of his own blood and squeeze it onto the soil where the Bucca had dwelled, a small sign of respect for the slain creature, and a hope that a new one would soon "sprout" in its place.

But Wodeman simply shoved the body into his pouch and stormed out of the glade.

"Little bastard!" he swore. *"I hope that hurt like hell."*

Squatting beneath the cover of a low, overhanging rock by a stream, Wodeman began chanting his next spell. Now he had harvested the Bucca, he was attempting to tap its power. Here, surrounded by hazel trees in this secret corner of the wood, he had ritually boiled the elverlike strand of Bucca flesh in water drawn from the sacred spring using a simple wooden bowl of alderwood.

As a nature-priest of Erce, Wodeman was well aware of the exigency of ritual in these matters. Just as Man needs ritual in the special moments of his life, so too did the sorcerer at times like these. He admitted, in the back of his mind, that most glyphs, incantations, and magical ingredients had little or no power in themselves. But the power of Symbol was absolute; it spoke to the mind's eye and could focus the psyche far better, as it encapsulated in one simple image any logical thought process or wordy explanation.

Take for example the tree, the sacred symbol of his religion; not just the hazel that grew all around this part of the wood, but all trees. They were the symbol of the interconnectedness of all things: their roots were in the earth, yet their crowns reached up into the sky farther than anything else living. The elements—earth, water, and the fire of the sun—fed them, while the air carried their seeds. Creatures lived in them, and were fed by them. And the hazel grove, the most sacred place of all, was just what he needed for his most powerful spells.

As for the alder, which provided shelter to the water sprites and whose leaf they used to dye their clothes, what better wood to use in this spell than that? What better way of demonstrating the sorcerer's reverence for the world of the Hidden People, and for the Bucca he had taken from them?

At least, that was what he had been taught. *Mash, mash, mash,* went his pestle as the vengeful shaman ground the sticky Bucca flesh into a horrendous-smelling pulp. *Crunch, chomp, grind,* went his teeth as they masticated the paste before letting it slip down his gullet. Slowly he consumed it, chanting the spell between chews. The narcotic steam from the alder bowl wafted up his nostrils, till already he was beginning to feel light-headed.

He did not have to look up or even open his eyes to know that the night-hued raven was back. Just as it had to be, to receive that part of the sorcerer's soul which he was now lending it.

"Raven," he intoned hoarsely, the astringency of the concoction stinging his throat, "take this, my spirit, into your eyes. Go now, and show me your master's intent."

With the help of the Bucca's flesh, Wodeman had become a medium. The ignorant folk of Nordwas would never believe that a wild man of the woods could do this; they assumed that mediums only communicated with the dead. And for their own priests maybe that was true. But for a nature-priest such as Wodeman, a medium was a conduit, a path that allowed the Earth Spirit's divinity to flow into the mind of Man. Thus had he now become, like the tree, a thing that joined heaven to earth.

He seemed now to be rising, leaving his cage of flesh behind and ascending into the highest branches of the trees. Up there he found himself looking through the eyes of the raven, seeing all that it saw. Delaying not an instant, it and he took off from this lofty perch and soared above the treetops, witnessing a thousand shades of green in the mellow, late-spring sunlight. They glided on over the open pastures beyond, everything looking so sharply defined from up here, and Wodeman's soul thrilled with the exhilaration of it all. Soon they were flying over the rippling, cream-colored fields outside Nordwas, and above farm buildings that looked like little wooden toys. The people who worked there were like ants running around on a path.

Then the raven turned, and Wodeman could see that they were approaching the town itself. In particular they seemed to be heading for one lofty tower that Wodeman recognized as part of Wintus Hall. The raven glided closer and closer, until finally it flapped down to perch upon a windowsill.

Suddenly, Wodeman felt troubled. This vision was beginning to fade long before it should do. Something was trying to intervene, to interrupt the vision before it could tell him anything meaningful. Erce, no, not after all he had just been through!

He had to work fast. On an impulse, Wodeman sent the raven into the room beyond, in a last desperate effort to glean as much information as possible.

There was not much to see there: just a stranger sitting on the edge of his bed, intent on honing an axe. He had thinning, curly brown hair, and the definite look of a foreigner. The man looked up sharply, but made no attempt to disturb the raven.

It was only a glimpse he received, but Wodeman knew he would remember this man; the premature lines of a hard life etched into his face, the troubled look in the eyes—and those odd images of dragons tattooed on his hands.

Then the dream faded, and he was back in the hazel grove by the stream.

"Oh, come on!" he called out in frustration to the trees. "Is that all I get for risking my life with a Bucca?"

But no answer was forthcoming, and he felt cheated. All he could assume was that the Skela, they who governed even the gods themselves, including Erce, had for some reason of their own interfered.

"This must be serious indeed," he muttered to himself.

Wodeman bit his lip in anxiety. Clearly much was now expected of him, but as yet he had not the slightest clue what that was. All he knew was that the man seen in his vision was the key. Of course, he could march into the tower and simply ask the stranger, but what would he say to him? "Excuse me, but I believe you are very important to my god. Now, please tell me how." No, that would not do. The folk of Nordwas already considered Wodeman some sort of lunatic, and this would merely confirm that belief.

For now, he would just have to cast the man's runes, and hope to discover more later.

The magician proceeded to do just this, kneeling down upon a patch of dry soil by the bank of the stream. His knotted fingers with their sharp, strong nails slipped under the wolf pelt and drew out a small leather bag that contained something that rattled. He untied the thong, placed the bag on the ground between his knees, then lifted up his arms. Then he raised his face to the sun and let out a long sigh.

All about him became still. The birds ceased their chattering, the breeze died down, and the leaves rustled no more. Into this sudden quiet, Wodeman began to chant. At first his voice sounded like the warning growl of a great cat, bestial and threatening, almost evil. Then this gave way to a low moaning from the pit of his stomach, issuing from his mouth like the breath of a phantom. Gradually it began to grow sonorous, and hypnotizing in its constancy. No man of Nordwas would have guessed there were words contained in this dirge, but words there were, words of power from an ancient and secret tongue known only to the Torca.

Wodeman stopped, and the chant was over. He opened his eyes and blinked against the sunlight that dappled his face. Looking down at the bare, cracked earth of the stream bank, he suddenly had a vision that all around him was black, and only a small circle of earth could now be seen. But it was not earth—rather it looked to the sorcerer like cracked flagstones glowing under a sputtering orange torchlight. He could smell the warm fug of a horse, and hear a strange kind of whimpering, like that of a woman . . . and the air was *freezing*.

This new vision faded.

Odd, he thought. *I haven't even cast the runes yet.*

He shrugged, and plunged his hand into the leather bag, rummaging about. Eight runes he needed, one for each of the catkins on the hazel sprig the raven had brought him. As he did so, he asked his first question.

Who is the foreigner with the axe, residing with the Peladanes?

Averting his eyes, he then withdrew his hand from the bag, and cast its contents upon the earth.

"Only one?" he murmured. "Not much to go on. . . ."

Only a single rune tile had been given. He had expected at least three. Nevertheless, he turned over the hazel-wood tile, rubbing his fingers over its smooth, age-worn surface, and peered at the blood-marked symbol engraved upon it:

The Road.

On its own this told him little; it could signify a journey, a traveler, even a long distance. But, regarding the man in his vision, it was easy enough to assume he was a traveler from afar just from his appearance—and Erce would not waste a valuable rune in telling him that. No, in this case it had to signify a *quest*. The man must be traveling to seek something, something of great importance.

Still with seven runes remaining, Wodeman did not hesitate. Pausing only long enough to put back the *Road* rune, he asked his second question.

Where does this quest lead to?

This time there were two runes. The sorcerer picked them up, and frowned. This did not look good:

The Rawgr—and *Ignorance.*

Very ambiguous indeed. *The Rawgr* could stand for literally that, a Rawgr; or it could mean some disaster of another kind was imminent. To even begin to know which, he would have to ask that man who appeared in his vision. *Ignorance,* though, was a different matter. Did it mean the man was unaware of *The Rawgr* (or disaster), or was he on his way to avert some great calamity, but did not know how?

Worse still, was he on his way to *cause* a disaster, and did not know it?

Working on all three possibilities, Wodeman asked his third question, choosing it and phrasing it with care.

Which god causes the stranger's ignorance?

This was presuming a lot, but if he had guessed the first three runes correctly, it was still a shrewd question. By asking this he was determining which "cause" the stranger would be working against, and thus whether he, Wodeman, was to help or hinder him.

He threw again:

The Rawgr again, and *The Shield*!

This was good: it told him much. By equating *The Rawgr* with a god, it was clear that it was indeed a Rawgr—and not merely some other disaster—that was the object of the traveler's journey. And Wodeman was automatically *against* the destructive power of all Rawgrs. Now he could well guess where he stood; if the man appearing in his vision was ignorant, and the Rawgr stood to gain by this ignorance, then Wodeman's role was to be present as a messenger of the Earth Spirit to enlighten him.

But what of the *Shield* rune? It stood for the Skela, the "guardians," but what did they have to do with the Rawgr? He went over in his mind all that he knew of the Skela and their relationship with the gods. Soon he came to a conclusion: Though it was clear that the Rawgr stood to benefit from the mystery traveler's ignorance, the chances were that it was actually the Skela who were responsible for this ignorance. For ignorance, the sorcerer knew in his strange way, was nearly always due to the Skela. They did not allow the gods to tell their adherents too much; a vision here, an omen there, perhaps the odd bit of rune-casting; nothing too obvious, just enough to keep them guessing.

In this case, owing to the intervention of the Skela, the god that was the enemy of the Rawgr had failed to get a message through to his servant. Exactly which god that was would be difficult to say at this point, for until he talked to the traveler himself he would not know which deity he served. Cuna the Light-giver was the prime choice, for he was directly opposed to everything involving

Olchor the Lord of Evil. But it could be his own god, Erce the Lord of Nature. After all, Olchor had never shown any regard for the land or anything that dwelled on it.

Yet the man he had seen through the raven's eyes had looked nothing like a typical follower of either cult. Maybe he followed one of the lesser gods, or even a false one. . . .

He then asked his fourth question. He had to know how he, and the traveler, could find out whatever it was the Skela were keeping from them.

How can we know that of which we are ignorant?

He looked down, surprised. Three runes lay upon the earth at his feet, all the last three runes of the hazel sprig

The Wyrm of Erce. The Tree of Knowledge. The Moon.

These last three told Wodeman everything. The traveler was not a worshipper of the Earth Spirit, but of some other deity. This same deity was being prevented by the Skela from granting the traveler the knowledge he needed to defeat the Rawgr. But Wodeman's god had found a way past the Skela; and Erce was slipping this tiny sliver of knowledge to the traveler behind the Skela's backs! This knowledge, then, was to come—as the *Moon* rune, or rune of the night, signified—in the form of dreams.

It was not much, but to get past the Skela, of course, it could not be much. Dreams and visions could be misread, often with disastrous consequences, even by one such as Wodeman who had dealt in them all his life. But it was all they had, and that just might be enough to tip the balance. . . .

Wodeman the wolf-man, Wodeman the Torca, Wodeman the Dream-Sorcerer, was to accompany this poor, confused traveler on his quest—and through his servant Erce would pass on to the man his moon knowledge.

In a sudden burst of energy, he leapt high in the air, like an insane frog. Armed only with his Spirit's dreams, he was to be the guardian of the entire world of Lindormyn.

Not wanting to waste any time, he set off immediately for Wintus Hall. He bounded through the trees, chattering excitedly to himself, running as swiftly as a deer. On crude sheepskin boots he made hardly a sound, and his wolf skin flapped behind him with a wildness that was mirrored in his eyes. Before long he had left behind the sanctuary of the woods, and relinquished its dark whispering depths to all those that dwelled in it.

And watching him go, its black, emotionless eyes blinking in the sunlight, was the raven perched high on a branch, a sprig of hazel in its beak.

3

The Wanderer

There was still much open country between Wodeman and the town. A dirt track raised high on an ancient dyke ran through rolling meadows of rich green grass thick with wildflowers; on and on until open pasture became fields protected by hedgerows blossoming with the fresh light hues of late spring. Fields gave way to livestock enclosures, then a muddy cattle market, and finally the untidy, smoky straggle of wattle-and-daub hovels that huddled against the stockade wall. Beyond this protective barrier awaited the pungent and colorful streets of the town proper, Nordwas itself.

"Pungent" was how the few cultured visitors described this frontier town. And it was as if, during the last couple of weeks, it had positively embraced this reputation, growing more pungent with each passing day, as more and more travelers arrived.

This always happened when word of the Peladanes' latest campaign got out. The town would fill up with all sorts: mercenaries and merchants, actors and acrobats, artisans and partisans, souvenir-sellers, storytellers, oracles and seers, purveyors of beers, dodgy puppeteers, slavers and freemen, jongleurs and gleemen; freaks, quacks, tregetours and preachers, bearwards and show-men with all sorts of creatures . . .

And any other sort of moneymaker one could think of. The town would become gripped by a kind of "gold rush" excitement that was self-propagating and very hard not to get caught up in. Wherever one went one would en-counter ordinarily decent and shrewd townsfolk walking around with that faintly glazed look of the terminally beguiled, pink of face and open of mouth, desperately trying to sell anything from a chair leg to their grandmother, then tearing around trying to spend their newly acquired coppers on the sort of things too worthless even for a Yuletide cracker.

Here in Nordwas every kind of currency became legal tender, everything from zlats to zibelines and all in between. There were other coins, of course, which were essentially thin offcuts of the embossed copper, silver, or gold cylinders used elsewhere in Lindormyn, but these were rare in such northerly parts. Here, being more practically inclined, the folk of Nordwas preferred zlats: squares of copper or silver or gold cut from a single large sheet—much easier to make, and no waste. Merchants from far countries would bring rare stones of enormous value, but in this region sardonyx, topaz, and amethyst were still preferred as currency, being more abundant in the local geology, and their value easier to gauge.

But perhaps the most unusual form of currency in Nordwas was the zibeline. Made from the fine but tough leather of the sable, these "bills" were branded with an ornate crest that was difficult to counterfeit, and the higher denominations were even signed by all six officers of the mint. In Lower Kettle Bazaar today, the zibelines were passing from hand to hand so quickly one might be forgiven for thinking they were red-hot embers.

The smells of badly cooked meat and onions, and the stupefying array of unknown spices; amid the braying of pack animals, the clanging of hammer on iron, the shrill histrionics of the medicine vendors, the shrieking laughter of the children watching puppet shows, and everywhere a dizzying furor of voices, music, chimes, rattles, whistles and any other means of attracting customers' attention, all of this drifted up from Lower Kettle Bazaar, up, up, and up, and in through the ivy-grown window of the little room at the top of the tower at Wintus Hall.

And was completely ignored by the man who lodged within.

Bolldhe lay upon the bed, staring up at the ceiling. It was not that he was tired, but this was what he always preferred when he found himself in the temporary haven of civilization. It was impossible to recall all the towns and settlements he had visited in his eighteen long years of traveling around the world. But whenever he arrived in such a place, and allowed himself the luxury of a cheap boardinghouse, he would lie on his bed for several hours, making the most of whatever privacy was afforded him, and staring up at the ceiling.

One hand idly picked at the notches along the haft of his broadaxe as he thought back over time. Exactly how many ceilings he had stared up at these past eighteen years, Bolldhe did not care to contemplate. But each time he did so, he was reminded of past ceilings, past beds, past hostelries . . . past towns, past realms, past *continents*. Pel-Adan's holy self, he must have stared up at more ceilings than . . . well, how depressing.

Most of Bolldhe's nights were spent sleeping rough, which he had long since grown used to. On backstreets that smelled of rubbish and sour milk; in filthy cattle byres; in wet leafy hop fields; on crowded decks of riverboats; in cemeteries and refuse tips that stank of rotting carcasses; on needle-covered forest floors; high in the trees of rank, mosquito-infested jungles; in the deep cool sands of sighing deserts; on horse wagons jolting their way through the night; upon precarious rock ledges; in ruined temples; under stone bridges—he sought anywhere in fact where he could avoid the relentless, merciless attention of curious but unwelcoming people.

They were the worst thing he had to face. Rain, though dismal, he had little problem with after all this time on the road. Night-borne insects, though annoying, he could put up with. Even the danger of predators he could sleep through. But people, they were something else again: "Eh, mister! Where from? Why here? What want? Bed? Guide? Weed? Other men here not good, but I from mountains—I honest. Eh friend! Where go? Why not talk? Why you like this? Yeah, well, to hell with you, then!"

Always prying, pestering, grinning, fawning, trotting out the same old lines, same old lies, same old tricks; hanging around seaports, ferry docks, horse dealers lounging about trying to make a fast one; thieves, guides, creeps, black marketeers, cultists, never leaving him alone, following him, asking, asking, asking, until he thought he would go *mad*. . . .

Faces staring, teeth grinning, beggars begging; surly looks, sidelong glances, blades loosed in their scabbards, furtive hands beneath cloaks with knuckles whitening around hilts. Bolldhe seethed in silent bitterness, still staring at the ceiling, his body stiff with remembered injustices. Sometimes he would carry on right through such a town and not stop till he had left it and its diminishing ranks of inquisitive inhabitants behind him, denying himself the temporary surcease from hunger and hardship that such a place could offer. Anything rather than face that leering throng.

Why could they not just all shove off and leave him alone?

In his more paranoid moments he would allow himself to believe that they were punishing him on purpose because they were jealous of his freedom. But deep down he knew it was a hard, merciless world, and those who dwelled in it had to be just as hard and merciless. He was no different himself.

Sometimes he would become so ill he did not even have the strength to be angry—and he would be pushed to his very limits just to stay alive.

"Why do I carry on?" he suddenly blurted out from his bed, only now realizing how he had been muttering to himself all this time.

It was not even as if he enjoyed the traveling. After just a year or so of it, he had found that one place—no matter how exotic—began to look much the same as any other. Once you've seen one mountain or desert, you've seen them all. The lure and romance of the road he had felt so strongly as a boy, living at home with his mother in far-off Moel-Bryn, had long since vanished. And the freedom he had craved all those long years ago now felt more like a cage than his dull little boyhood home had ever done.

At least in those days he could still dream. . . .

Bolldhe turned onto his side, and his eyes fell on the cloth pouch in which he kept his charms and baubles. And that was another thing, he reflected bitterly; it was not even as if all his travels amounted to anything. What had he achieved in all these years? That little purple and blue bag contained almost the sum total of his years on the road. Trinkets of little intrinsic value, ones that had simply caught his eye here and there in some bazaar. Shiny, quirky, dangly novelties he had taken a fancy to. Nothing more to show for a lifetime of great adventure.

He let out a long sigh. Many a time he had been tempted to give it all up and settle down to a normal life. But he had never found anywhere in all his wanderings that really appealed to him; not one single place with enough attraction to keep him from the endless road that ever beckoned him leading out the other side of town. The open road he hated but could not relinquish.

"Not one place," he reflected, "and not one . . ."

He broke off the sentence, but could not so easily break off the thought: *Not one place, not one person*. There, he had admitted it.

Bolldhe knew he possessed unique qualities; his self-reliance and fierce independence could not be equaled. But for all his uniqueness, he still lacked many of the attributes that would make him more "human." For one, he lacked the basic capacity to love. It simply was not there and, whether it ever had been, in his youth perhaps, he was unsure. But, if it had, he had somehow been cut off from that warm sun of affection at such an early stage in his emotional growth that the seeds of love had simply withered.

Bolldhe might occasionally tell himself that it was his traveling lifestyle that denied him the opportunity of finding that special person who might give him peace, but it was not just that. He reached over to the pack he always kept close at hand, and drew out a small mirror made from glass laid over a square of highly polished silver. In its perfect surface he now studied his not-so-perfect visage. True, he had never been a looker by anyone's standards.

There had been moments in his earlier travels when he had found some kind of "friendship." While traveling over vast stretches of uninhabited desert or steppe, he had been forced to team up with others, usually merchants or drovers with their accompanying guards, who were undertaking yearlong journeys along the overland trade routes with hundreds of camels, horses, and bison. At first he would remain aloof, for he was Bolldhe the Wanderer and knew more than they did about traveling. But as the journey progressed there would invariably be times when everyone, including himself, would have to pull together—call it teamwork if not friendship. It did at least free him from the shackles of his loneliness for a while, and allow him once again to feel the thrill of adventure, to enjoy the sun and wind on his face, to enjoy in company the romance of watching the pinky-orange sun go down over some strange, exotic horizon.

Though he could never admit it, those were the best times he had ever known.

But for the rest of the time he was like a ghost drifting among humanity but unable to join in. Like an outside observer at some festival or wedding, he could only watch and listen, knowing it was nothing to do with him.

"Loneliness," he pronounced aloud, "the Great Soul-Eater."

A sudden knock at the door aroused Bolldhe from his daydreaming. Irritated at this invasion of privacy, he swung his legs to the floor, walked briskly to the door, and yanked it open.

"Oh, it's you," he said. "What you want?"

Finwald, taken aback both by Bolldhe's unfamiliar accent and his brevity, replied, "I just wondered if I could have a word. It won't take long."

Bolldhe sighed. "We already are," he said. He could still do with more time to sort out his thoughts on his permanent loneliness, so the last thing he needed right now was company.

"I have to talk with you," his unwanted guest persisted.

Bolldhe held the door open for him, and let him make his way to a seat.

"Well, what is it you want to say to me?"

Finwald realized that small talk was not the order of the day here, so he cleared his throat and began.

"I know there exists a great difference of opinion on how to slay the Rawgr, so I don't want to go over the same ground again."

"Good," Bolldhe interrupted, stretching himself out on his bed again. "So don't."

Finwald continued, "We all know where we stand on that point, and Appa seems to be content to leave the whole problem in your capable hands." He paused for the traveler to reply, but Bolldhe continued to stare up at the ceiling.

"Only I've asked him several times now," Finwald went on, perching uncomfortably on his hard stool, "what exactly this other method is, involving you, and why he puts such great faith in it. Do you really know how to do the job?"

Bolldhe turned to him and said simply, "No. Why? Should I?"

Finwald was, to say the least, a little surprised, and more than a little irked, by Bolldhe's apparent unconcern. "Well, yes, to be quite honest, I think you *should* know."

"*You* know," replied Bolldhe. "You said so at the council. So what's your problem? Starting to have doubts already?"

"*I* know, yes, but I'm very concerned about Appa. His mind isn't as sharp as it used to be, and his ideas are getting more and more fanciful with each year that passes."

"How old is he, then?"

"Seventy, I'm told."

"Really? He looks older."

"I agree. And I also agree with Nibulus that it's far too old to be setting off on quests. Especially to the Far North. He's got twenty-two sheep to think about, and that cow of his that he dotes on so much. He ought to content himself with looking after his flock. . . . I'm seriously worried for him, you know."

"He seemed enough happy to come along," Bolldhe replied blandly.

"But why should he?" Finwald persisted. "It's ridiculous! I tell you, Bolldhe, he's sinking into his dotage, and . . . and if we're to go trolling off into the worst of the wildlands, the last thing we need is a millstone like Appa around our necks. All because he has this mad idea that he alone can guide you in killing Drauglir. . . . Look, I'm not putting him down or anything. What I'm saying is he means well, but anyone can see that concepts like 'goodwill' and 'truth' aren't going to be enough on this quest."

"Aren't those the same things your cult is all about?"

"I think you're missing the point—"

"I think *you're* missing the point." Bolldhe said. "Your friend Appa thinks he must come and that without him, or me, this whole adventure is in vain. There's not any telling him otherwise."

Finwald rose stiffly and paced around the room. He gazed momentarily out of the window, then turned back to Bolldhe.

"How *did* you come to meet Appa?" he asked.

Get lost, Bolldhe thought, for the manner of their meeting was still a sore point with him.

A few days ago Bolldhe had ridden into town from the southeast. It was a dark and windy night, heavy with the threat of a storm, and Bolldhe was feeling in a dark and dangerous mood himself. As he crested the hill that looked down on the warm, orange lights of Nordwas, that old disdain for "civilians" began to stir in him again. He coaxed his horse into a canter, just fast enough to cause his cloak to billow, yet slow enough to make him look menacing in his approach. Despite the weather, there was a crowd of revelers in the marketplace as he rode through, but no one much seemed to notice his intimidating arrival.

So he stabled his horse and went into the nearby inn. Any attempt to play the part of the cloaked and hooded stranger who sat smoking a pipe by himself in a dark corner was thwarted because all the dark corners were already occupied by other enigmatic strangers. So he had to content himself with sitting at a brightly lit table in the middle of the room, being chatted to by a group of hop farmers from Ottra, who did not find him particularly unnerving.

It was then that Appa arrived, as if somehow expecting him. Once he spotted Bolldhe, he walked straight over to him as though he knew him, and sat down at the table. That was how it happened.

Bolldhe now looked away from Finwald and replied, "Oh, I just came into town a few days ago, and Appa got talking to me at that inn down Pump Street."

"The Chase, you mean?" Finwald looked puzzled. "Appa doesn't normally go into places like that."

"Ask him yourself if you don't believe me."

"No, I don't doubt you . . ." The priest was still frowning. "So, what happened next?"

"He bought me a pint, then asked me if I could help him."

"You two had met previously?"

"Never seen him before in my life. As I said, I'm new in town."

"So what did he say to you, exactly."

"Something mad about him having a dream in which his god told him that unless I go with him to Melhus Island the whole world will come to an end. That sort of thing."

"Oh, is that all?" Finwald replied. "And what did you think about that?"

"Sounded fair enough to me."

"Really. So you decided to come along with us?"

"Looks like it," Bolldhe finished, yawning languidly. Normally he hated people asking him questions, but on this occasion he was partly enjoying it.

"I don't believe it!" Finwald exclaimed, throwing his hands in the air. "Some old priest—a total stranger—just comes up to you in a tavern and demands that you accompany him to one of the worst hellholes in all Lindormyn, and all because he's had some crazy dream, and you *believe* him?"

"I don't know why," Bolldhe confessed, "but I just do."

That much was true, because Bolldhe never went along with anyone unless he had some reason of his own for doing so. His only "vocation" was himself, therefore it was an essential part of his nature that he would do things purely on whim. Nearly every journey he had taken, he had done so on a whim. He was a wanderer. *So why not?* he had thought at the time; he had never seen the Far North and it might be exciting and different. It was a hard land, of course, but who better than he to explore such a place? And it was not as if he expected any real danger there. Just as well, as Bolldhe was no warrior.

But there had also been something about Appa himself that had helped persuade him. There was definitely something about the old priest and *beyond* him, some urge, a feeling, that called out to Bolldhe.

This feeling was not new, either. For the past few years Bolldhe had been wending his meandering way westward again, through the Kro Steppes, Tabernacle Plains, and Vregh-Nahov, as if guided by Fate. He had no particular desire to return to his native Pendonium, lying farther in the west, he assured himself, yet somehow his feet seemed, by ways however circuitous, to inexorably draw him back there. Now in this room, this tiny dorter above the chapter house of Wintus Hall, he sensed his thoughts being tugged back once more to the land of his childhood.

Whether he liked to admit it or not, Bolldhe was coming home. Already he was close enough, back in a country where at long last they spoke his native language. But he did not tell Finwald any of this. He had not even told Appa. They were his private thoughts, and were going to remain so.

Finwald sat back down, and inquired, "You must have a great deal of faith in Cuna, so are you a Lightbearer?"

Bolldhe snorted. "No, I am bloody not!"

"Then what are you?"

"Nothing," Bolldhe said sullenly. "I don't worship any of your deities."

"But you do believe in gods?" Finwald persisted.

"Oh, I believe in them, yes," Bolldhe answered. "I seen too much sign of the gods to believe other: temples, villages, whole towns razed; nations enslaved; countries going to war over some petty 'god' squabble . . . Some gods exist, some don't; but it makes no difference to me, because if they exist or not, no way they're getting any worship out of *me*."

Another unique characteristic of Bolldhe's independence was that he did not possess that singular mental quality of humans that enables them to deny utterly in their minds that which they must secretly realize to be true, or conversely. He could not therefore make a choice of his beliefs depending on whether they might advantage him or not.

"I was brought up Peladane," he continued reflectively, almost to himself. "But I soon recognized *that* creed for what it is. . . ."

Bolldhe broke off and silently rebuked himself. He had not meant to give anything at all away about his past.

Finwald was having much difficulty in taking in the enormity of what Bolldhe was telling him; that a man, any man, could exist without faith or creed seemed simply too abhorrent to believe. Bolldhe, however, was used to this reaction, having encountered similar all over the world, and it often amused him to witness such exasperation.

Realizing that he had come up against a brick wall, Finwald decided to leave it at that. He tried another approach: "Well, why are you here in Nordwas?"

Bolldhe smirked mischievously. "I'm an oracle," he replied.

In a way it was true. Bolldhe was indeed an oracle. He told people's fortunes for a living. If you could call it a living.

It was an odd career for someone brought up to become a warrior. In the small town of Moel-Bryn, in the country of Pendonium far to the west, he was the son of a Peladane; therefore he and his brothers had been brought up as such. His earliest memories were dim, but he did remember always hating the strictures and indoctrination he had been subjected to from an early age. At some time during Bolldhe's childhood, his father had been killed in a far-off land, and later still, when he was about fourteen, something in the boy had just snapped. Without any warning, he had snatched up his sword, grabbed a few provisions, and left home never to return. He still to this day did not know what had prompted this move; it had just happened without warning, like a bough breaking suddenly under too much snow.

It was fortunate for the youth that Moel-Bryn lay at a crossroads located

along an important trade route. He gained employ at first as aide to a mercenary guarding a caravan on its way to the Crimson Sea. But the company was
not to his liking, and after six months Bolldhe had struck out on his own. At
first, rather naively, he had wandered from village to village in search of work as
a casual laborer, but the sort of money he made from such toil hardly enabled
him to survive, let alone put something aside for his continuing travels. What
he needed was a trade, something that would earn him plenty of money over a
short period of time.

But what sort of trade, he wondered. Armorer? Certainly he knew the rudi-
ments of that from his military upbringing; but it might prove a little impracti-
cal carrying a forge around on his back wherever he traveled. And, in any case,
he was trying to leave all that sort of thing behind him.

Healer, then? People would pay good money for that skill; and again he
knew a fair bit about it, and could pick up the rest as he went along. But, no,
healers frequently had to deal with amputations and open wounds, and for
some reason Bolldhe was nauseated by the sight of too much blood.

Then, one day, he was struck with the idea of becoming a fortune-teller—an
oracle. It sounded easy: all he had to do was to buy a few cheap charms as
props, then in distant lands, with his foreign appearance, the punters, especially women, would readily believe he could tell them the future. And just to
make sure they paid him well, he would always make sure to tell them what
they wanted to hear.

"Yes," Bolldhe smiled, "so we're not that different after all, us. The main
difference is that people pay for my predictions."

Finwald was speechless.

"That's the trouble with you religious oracles," Bolldhe went on. "You're always forecasting terrible times ahead."

"But it's the truth!" Finwald blurted out.

"I thought you yourself said earlier that truth and goodwill aren't going
to be enough on this quest?" Bolldhe scoffed. "Anyway, no difference; most
people despise the truth. You'd be a lot more successful if you told a few lies;
people much prefer being deceived."

Finwald's black eyes burned even blacker. "Bolldhe," he said in a voice
quavering with ire, "nobody here in Nordwas even knows who you are, so
you'll forgive me if we question your motives for joining us on this venture."

"There *is* the money to consider," Bolldhe pointed out. "And you *are* taking
on mercenaries, right?"

Finwald shook his head wistfully. "It's not *just* the money," he stated.
"We're going to Melhus, remember. It's quite likely the journey alone will kill
us, and surely no money is worth that risk."

"Oh, come off it," Bolldhe sneered. "How dangerous can it be?"

"Do you have any idea how terrible that land can be?" the priest demanded, looming over Bolldhe on his bed.

"Not a clue," the wanderer replied lackadaisically. "What do you think I am, some kind of oracle? *You're* the one should . . ."

He trailed off. He had quite enjoyed the banter up till now, but now the look in Finwald's burning, coal-black eyes made him wonder if the mage-priest was about to turn him into a pillar of salt.

The tense moment passed, however, and Finwald simply stormed out of the room.

Bolldhe got up and closed the door, then went over to the window to breathe in the bouquet of raw fish, dung, and spicy aromas on offer.

No holy man is going to get to me, he told himself with a forced smile.

"There's someone waiting outside to see you."

Appa was roused with a start from his concentration. Even in the graveyard quiet of the dark temple he had not heard the approach of the Lightbearer who now stood at his side. While the stone amulet of Cuna hanging from a cord around his neck dangled forgotten in midair, the old cleric had been praying fervently to his red-eyed god. He did not speak his words aloud, as others did; the thoughts he passed to his god were secret and could be revealed to no one. He had been immersed in a meditation of such profundity that when his fellow Lightbearer approached and shook him roughly by the shoulder, it was a shock to be catapulted from the depths of his reverie into the daylight world of man.

"Who's that?" he spluttered, his weak eyes blinking rapidly as he tried to focus them on the grey-robed figure who stood looking down at him.

"Oh, it's you, Tommas. . . ." He quickly fumbled the amulet back into its hiding place beneath his robe, then glanced around.

The temple was so quiet, dark, and cold. As if seeing them for the first time, he took in the great wooden columns supporting the lofty roof, the bulrush-strewn flagstones, the simple altar bedecked with a clutter of cobweb-hung icons and artifacts, and the untidy ranks of ewe's-butter candles that glimmered palely. For a moment, the familiarity of this sanctuary in which he had prayed so frequently over the years was gone. It felt as if he were in another world altogether.

"Whatever is the time, Tommas?" he muttered. "I must have been here for hours."

"It's only two hours after midday," Tommas replied, studying the ancient mage-priest's face with uncertain interest, though unwilling to be drawn into a lengthy conversation with him.

"Oh, right. . . . What's that you said before?" Appa asked.

"Someone to see you," Tommas repeated. "A man is waiting outside."

Despite his confused state of mind, Appa was still sharp enough to notice a hint of awkwardness in the voice of his brother-in-faith.

"Someone to see me?" he asked, perplexed. "Why didn't you bring him in, then?"

"He refuses to enter the temple, Appa. It's Wodeman."

"Wodeman? To see *me*? Whatever for?"

"He . . . would not say. He just told me to fetch you. He seemed a little agitated."

"That's strange. I wonder what he wants me for. Well, you'd better tell him I'll be out in a minute. Thank you . . . er, Tommas."

The Lightbearer was already making a rapid exit as Appa straightened his robe, then followed.

Wodeman? he thought. *What's going on here?*

Though a distinctive figure and well known about in the town, the Torca was rarely seen in Nordwas itself. He would occasionally put in an unexpected appearance, on some business of his own said to involve hidden mysteries, and which invariably concluded with a lengthy ale-drinking session at the Chase. But for the most part he appeared to spend his time wandering about in the woods outside.

Appa did not need to wonder why his visitor would not enter the temple. As a "priest" of that pagan nature cult that embodied all the local superstitions and fears that Cunaism had tried to erase, Wodeman would not even consider entering the sacred house of Cuna, a god whom the old sorcerer inevitably considered to be a knife in the back of the "old ways."

As Appa approached the open doorway of the temple, he could see Wodeman waiting for him as a black silhouette against the bright daylight outside. With that great, bristling wolf skin around his broad shoulders, the sorcerer appeared more like a were-creature than a man. Appa shuddered inside his own fleece-hemmed cloak and, despite his contempt for the old religion, he could not suppress a shiver that crept up his spine.

He stepped out into the daylight, leaving the door open behind him. The first thing Appa noticed was the smell of the man: it was worse than cattle's business. Beneath the wolf skin he wore a filthy tunic of some unidentifiable animal skin, which fell almost to his knees; it was tied around his waist with a length of hemp rope that was hung with an assortment of bone amulets. For Appa it was quite hard to discern where the garments stopped and the man began.

Their eyes met: the beady, watery eyes of the cleric, blurred by temple darkness and smoke, and the sharp, feral eyes of the man-of-the-woods. Both priests regarded each other in silence, the defiance and hostility of their bearing tempered only by mutual curiosity.

"The f-first time we have met, I believe," Appa began, unsure how to address the sorcerer.

Wodeman stared back at his rival, and wondered how these pathetic grey little men could possibly have won over the hearts and minds of the stalwart people of the North. He sighed deeply, a curiously sad note of inevitability lingering on his breath.

"Greetings, Southerner," he replied at last. "I am the medium of the Earth Spirit in these parts. My name is hidden—my real name, at least—but you may call me Wodeman. No doubt you'll have heard of me by many other names, too."

"Oh, indeed," Appa laughed uncertainly, remembering some of the less than complimentary ones invented by the townsfolk.

Wodeman did not share his mirth, and Appa cleared his throat.

"So, Wodeman, what can I do for you?"

"You seem, Southerner, to assume that I would only come to you if I needed your help," Wodeman replied. "On the contrary, I am here to help *you*."

"Really," Appa replied doubtfully.

"I have read the runes—" Wodeman began, only to be cut short by the cleric.

"Ah, no thank you, no rune-reading here today, thank you very much. Perhaps you might try next door."

"Priest!" Wodeman growled. "I come to offer my help. I ask for nothing in return."

"Sorry," Appa condescended. "Please continue."

"Earlier today," Wodeman began, "I received a message from my god, a message . . . What are you staring at?"

Appa's eyes snapped back up to meet those of the shaman.

"Sorry," he said awkwardly. "Do go on." In truth he had been peering at the man's ankles, trying to see through the gaps in his thong-bound leggings in order to find out if it really was true that the Torca shaman's feet were furry and clawed.

"A message," Wodeman continued, "that instructed me to go and seek out the man whom I now know to be called Bolldhe."

"Bolldhe?" repeated Appa suspiciously. "What have *you* got to do with Bolldhe?"

Wodeman grinned. "A great deal, it would seem. In this instruction I was told how, during the next few weeks, this man is to become the decider of all that will befall. How he shall embark upon a quest that will determine the fate of the whole world."

Appa relaxed a little. *The little tinker!* he thought. *Probably overheard one of those mercenaries bragging about the quest in some tavern, and now he's trying to cash in.* But all he actually said was "This is common knowledge."

"Indeed," Wodeman continued, "but as I was saying to Bolldhe himself earlier today—"

"You've been to see Bolldhe?" Appa snapped, his bulging eyes and jutting jaw making him look more terrierlike than ever. "What gives you the right to go interfering in matters that don't concern you?"

"Don't *concern* me?" Wodeman burst out. "The fate of the world does not concern me? *Of all the arrogance . . .* It concerns us all, cleric, not only those who hunger for power."

"I don't know what you mean!"

"No, you don't, do you. There's a great deal you don't know. Perhaps if you left your stony barrows now and then . . ." Wodeman sneered. Then a curious look narrowed his eyes, and he craned his neck, trying to see around Appa and into the temple.

"What is it you do in these places, anyway?" he asked, genuine curiosity in his voice. "Is this where you breed your moths?"

"Moths?" replied Appa. "I breed only sheep, but certainly not in here."

"My ex-wife told me you breed moths," the shaman affirmed.

Appa shifted uncomfortably, smoothing down his holey robes. "Well—not intentionally," he answered.

Wodeman shrugged, and went back to conversation. "I don't suppose you know bout the Skela, do you?"

Appa paused. "Skela?" he echoed, and thought: *So, the Skela, is it? This forest person could have his uses after all. . . .*

Wodeman chuckled. "Indeeed. I have read the runes; it is the Skela that are denying Bolldhe the knowledge he needs."

"And this knowledge?" Appa pried, hardly daring to hope, yet trembling with anticipation nonetheless.

"Don't know for sure yet, sorry, but we will. So, you see, I have been delegated to be Bolldhe's . . . guide and companion. I shall be the Giver of Dreams to him and, as the journey progresses and we near our goal, that which he seeks will be revealed to him through *me.*"

"Now, wait, hold on a minute! Let me get this straight . . . are you seriously suggesting that *you* are to be his counselor? *You?*"

"Not counselor—but his dream-giver."

Appa laughed openly. "Absolutely not! Do you honestly think I'm going to let the superstitious lies of your hedge cult poison Bolldhe's mind? Pervert him from the one true path that is our only hope? It is in *me,* if anyone, that he will find guidance."

Wodeman's eyes suddenly flared with cold green malice. Appa backed away, afraid now, and his hand unconsciously groped for the reassuring iron handle of the temple door behind him. The wolf-man's eyes bore into his, and he saw in them a challenge, the challenge of a forest creature whose right of territory has been violated.

And in Appa's own eyes, there was a vague hint of guilt; for the first time in his life, he began to understand the primeval instinct of this strange pagan cult that had been dealt a near-fatal blow by the arrival of foreign religions such as he represented.

"Sorry," he managed. "Do go on."

Wodeman grunted. "As I said, I'm offering my help. Remember, you are heading up into lands you know little of, the ancient lands of my forefathers as we are told. *Wild* lands where a man such as me would be invaluable. Also, I ask for no payment, nor any reward; only the chance to accompany you. I have already seen Bolldhe about this, and the Peladane Wintus—and they have no objection. All I need now is the consent of at least one of the Lightbearers in the party."

Appa was carefully turning over the possibilities in his head. *Dream-giver, eh?* Maybe he ought to take the risk. If Wodeman had any way of securing information that he himself was not privy to, that could only work to his eventual advantage.

Despite Wodeman's aggressive tone, Appa realized how galling it must be for the sorcerer to humble himself thus to an "invader." He had shown great strength in this, and it was Appa's turn to do likewise.

He was also increasingly aware of Wodeman's potential usefulness.

"Well," he said tentatively, "as long as you don't mind the company of us 'Southerners,' I suppose you could tag along."

As he returned to reenter the temple, he added, "We leave in three days."

———

". . . Thru darkness and pain Gwyllch trampl'd the slain,
Upon devilry and fire his ire did he rain,
To his left he slew fifty, to his right clove thru sixty,
As the horde met the sword of the glorious Thegne.

Then came to his ear lamentations of fear
As the foe were brought low, pierced by arrow and spear.
His men sang as they slew, voices valiant and true,
For the graves of those braves, Gwyllch swore, they'd pay dear . . ."

Cheers of proud jubilation and approval almost drowned out the complex vocal melodies and subtle, intertwining harmonies of lyre and flute, as from the dais the troubadours sang their lays of triumph to the enthusiastic Peladanes gathered in Wintus Hall.

The air was rank with smoke that hung in dirty brown clouds above the head of each man there, sweet and vinegary with the reek of the spilled ale that stiffened the rugs on the floor. Mead flowed freely down the gullets and chins of the "Defenders of Virtue." Servant girls bounced gaily upon the laps of those "Gallants of Goodness, Protectors of Probity, and Warriors of Worth, ev'ry one, ev'ry one . . ." Heroes from the illustrious past of Pel-Adan glared from woodcut and arras, down upon the present generation of his Holy Knights; and one could only speculate what they might have thought of the scene below.

"Boy!" Bhormann bawled, his face red with passionate self-indulgence as he berated the esquire. "Your master's cup runneth dry. What d'you think he pays you for?"

Gapp Radnar's lips thinned in indignation, but he dutifully served up the beverage demanded, and Nibulus slapped him hard on the shoulder by way of thanks.

How Gapp longed for "the off." He had been counting down the days, hours, and minutes to their departure ever since he had been informed he was to accompany his master on this noble quest, so he was now almost hopping from one leg to the other in ill-suppressed impatience. He had no problem with his master, but he just could not stand his friends. On a clear, sunny day like this he would much rather have been in the company of his own friends, joining in their near-obsessive pastime of stone-skimming. Gapp also loved stone-skimming.

"Now, Gwyllch," Bhormann spluttered between mouthfuls, "there's a man you could do with on your quest."

Yes, right, Gapp thought as he resumed his place standing behind his master, *Only one problem there: He's been dead for five hundred years. Mind you, even dead he'd be more use than you, you sweaty tub of lard.*

"But we've got him," Nibulus informed his crony, "at least in spirit. I'm taking along *The Chronicle of Gwyllch* as our guide. It contains lots of useful tips on the terrain between here and there, and it'll make provide good storytelling for the civilians amongst us, too."

"Why not just bring along these troubadours?" Stufi pushed in. "They know those lays word for word, and have better voices than you."

Nibulus became suddenly serious and perhaps slightly pompous amid the revelry. "We do not pay for the services of mere minstrels upon our holy errantry."

Gapp reflected on what Finwald had told him the previous day. "If you would learn about Peladanes," he had complained, after the treatment he had received at the council, "you have only to look at the stalwarts of Wintus Hall. They are given, and fully embrace, a whole set of rules on what is right and what is wrong, but above all else, how to criticize others; how to see fault in everyone and anyone. Their world is submerged in ten thousand petty, picky censures of the common man, yet they have not the slightest ability to recognize their own transgressions of the laws they so fervently preach at all around them. They are for the most part fat, drunken, and immoral, but for them these are failings found among 'civilians' rather than themselves. The trouble is, it would never, *could* never, even occur to them that their rules might actually apply to themselves too. It's as if each Peladane considers himself to be the hub of the universe, so the rest of the world are a mere corollary of 'Not-Me' that surrounds them and follows them dutifully wherever they go. They are the center of all things, and anything else in the world only pops into existence whenever they encounter it."

By this stage the vomiting had started, so Gapp left the room to fetch a pail of water and a good supply of rags, brushing past a red-robed newcomer who had just entered.

A moment later, from behind Nibulus's head, two brown hands reached out and cupped themselves firmly over the startled Peladane's eyes.

"Death to the Green Ones," a thickly accented voice hissed.

"Xilva!" Nibulus laughed. "Can't you ever be normal and just say hello?"

Methuselech vaulted over his friend's knees to land in front of him. "Afraid not, porky," he laughed. "We of the Asyphe dance through life with a jest ever in our hearts. If you could but—"

A sudden blade at his throat pressed Xilvafloese's head back, and the joviality of the scene was instantly vaporized under the sheer intimidation radiating from the tip of the knife pressed at the mercenary's neck. It was wielded by Stufi, who leaned so close to Nibulus's guest that the spectators thought he was about to slip his tongue into his ear.

"If you *ever* try something like that again," the Peladane said softly, "you'll be dancing through your own entrails with your bollocks in your mouth . . . *foreigner*!"

"All right lads, that'll do," said Nibulus nervously. "Myself and Xilva have got an appointment right now. Can't keep Kuw waiting, can we?"

"Where were those two miserable oafs during the charge of the Ouanif lancers, anyway?" Methuselech muttered irritably as he and Nibulus strode through the cloisters of Wintus Abbey. "Celebrating *our* imminent victory in the palace wine cellars, no doubt."

"No doubt," Nibulus agreed as he steered his friend out of the shade of the cloisters and over the garth. "That's about all they're good for, these days—but thanks for not killing them both, anyway."

"Anytime, my friend."

Nibulus led Xilvafloese on through a troop of Peladane novices who were practicing on the garth—clearly novices, for they wore only a single green tunic as they wielded mace, spear, and bow—and on through a heavy door, between two lounging sentinels. Down a winding staircase they continued, and into the noisiest, busiest vault in the whole town.

"Ah, Master Nibulus," came a voice over the metallic clamor of the chamber. "Almost on time. Come in, come in! Oh . . . you've brought your foreign friend with you, I see. . . ."

Kuw Dachs was a retired but highly respected veteran of the Felari Wars, fought many years past, and the Grand Arsenal here was his domain. He did not disclose its secrets lightly.

"Methuselech Xilvafloese is no foreigner in Wintus Hall," Nibulus replied, masking his embarrassment with a stiff smile. "Come, show me what you've got for me this time."

The two warriors were guided through the armory by Kuw himself, while all around them men hammered and beat, folded and forged, cut and trimmed, and generally made a lot of noise with bits of metal. There were armorers, fletchers, blacksmiths, carpenters, tanners, and seamstresses, all working as diligently as possible whenever Kuw walked past. Expert and apprentice alike were busy enmeshing the fine links on chain-mail habergeons, layering bands of iron over closely fitting cuirasses and gorgets, fitting feather to arrow, stirrup to crossbow, engraving scrollwork onto pommels and blades; every process, in fact, from the initial smelting of iron for weapons and armor to the fine detailed sewing of insignia onto lordly tabards. The place was heavy with the smell of a hundred different materials.

But it was past all these that Nibulus and his friend were led, to a smaller chamber in which lay Mr. Dachs's "special stuff."

"Your arms and armor await, Master Nibulus," Kuw announced with relish. "Let us first start with your new sword here, Unferth."

The aged retainer ceremoniously lifted the six-foot-long greatsword from its bracket on the wall and presented it to the Peladane. "We've rebound the leather grip," he explained as Nibulus gazed in rapture at his father's sword, "and honed the blade to a sharpness never before achieved."

Nibulus was astonished. This weapon had been forged thirty years ago for his father and, as was the fashion among latter-day Peladanes, the blade of the current Warlord was named after the legendary sword of Pel-Adan himself. Now, for this his first campaign, it had been handed down to him! He hefted it, amazed at the lightness of such a huge weapon.

"Crafted in tengriite for lightness and strength, alloyed with iron for use against you-know-what," explained the armorer.

Nibulus gave it a few practice sweeps, and was no less than dumbfounded at its lightness.

"Now pay attention, Master Nibulus. Let me show you this next item. . . ."

Kuw handed what looked like a leather mare's-milk flask to the Peladane. "Looks perfectly innocuous, doesn't it? But just watch what happens when I press this little catch *here.* . . ." There was a soft *snik,* and a veritable forest of razor-sharp spikes sprang out of slits in the leather casing, making it resemble a metal hedgehog. "Then all we do is . . ." Kuw twisted off the "stopper," which turned out to be the handle, on the end of a retractable chain. ". . . *this* and, as you will no doubt agree, you have a formidable swinging morning star!"

"Hmm . . ." Nibulus said, raising a sidelong eyebrow at Methuselech. "Not sure what the point of this is, exactly. Why not just carry a normal morning star?"

"As you will," snapped Kuw, openly irritable, snatching it back without any further persusasion. "Perhaps you could find a use for this, then. I call it the Thresher."

It was a chain, light and strong, made of tiny linked blades, with a specially made hook at one end. "For those times in a busy Peladane's life when he finds himself surrounded by many enemies, and conventional weapons just aren't enough," Kuw explained. "You snap your sword onto this hook like so, grasp the other end of the chain, then swing the bugger round your head for all your worth! Cuts down all and everything within a fifteen-foot radius . . . so long as they're not armored. Made up a pair of these for my kids for their last birthday."

Both Nibulus and Methuselech gaped.

"I think you could do with getting out a bit more," Nibulus suggested.

"You don't like it?"

"On the contrary," Nibulus said, folding the chain carefully into its toughened leather bag, "I can't wait to try it out!"

"Though perhaps not just now, with all that mead in you," his friend suggested.

"And this . . ." Kuw announced with the greatest of pleasure, ". . . I am particularly fond of. It's your new suit of armor."

If the Thresher had caused him to gape, this latest item caused Nibulus's jaw to almost dislocate and drop on the floor. There before him, arranged upon a rack and illuminated on either side by torches specially treated with a resin that caused their flame to burn with a particularly dramatic effervescence, stood the most unbelievable suit of armor the young Peladane had ever beheld.

Of all the peoples in the world, the Peladanes had perfected the technology of armoring. The elite of their number wore a specially forged, superheated metal called tengriite, the same substance that Unferth was wrought from. Through the heating process, it could turn either a burnt-copper color, a varnished redwood, or an igneous blue. The eventual color depended on the quality, with blue being esteemed the highest grade. All grades were strong and very, very light in weight, but the blue had the added distinction of being able to produce an electric shock when struck by metal weapons. This would not penetrate the special padding beneath, but would as often as not give the attacker a jolt, usually causing him to drop his own weapon.

But it was not just the blue tengriite of this suit of armor that caused the onlookers to drool like victims of a debilitating disease; it was the sheer magnificence of design. The hauberk was of the finest, most exquisite chain mail reinforced by overlapping shell-shaped scales down the sides, and a burnished red tengriite plastron over the chest, embossed with the grim visage of Pel-Adan himself. The fluted pauldrons, vambraces, and greaves all bore fierce spikes that would be useful in the kind of brutal, close combat that their wearer was so often forced to employ.

To grip Unferth's mighty hilt a pair of unfeasibly large gauntlets of black chain mail was provided, with overlapping silver fish scales, spikes protruding from each knuckle, and a wide, fishtail-shaped guard covering the wrists.

These were of simple iron, for heftiness was needed here, as also with the great iron-capped boots of toughened leather.

And finally, to crown all this, a majestic dragon-crested helm with a sallet shaped like a fierce boar's head, behind which only the wearer's eyes could be seen, anonymous and menacing.

" 'Tis the finest and most extravagantly expensive suit of armor in the whole of the North," Kuw Dachs intoned solemnly, "the culmination of centuries of knowledge, craftsmanship, and experience. Wear it nobly, young Peladane."

Nibulus merely nodded, still awestruck.

"Don't suppose you've got one in lilac, have you?"

"Oh, do grow up, Master Nibulus!"

Out on the tourney fields, it was a fine evening. The sky was a deep, rich blue, its clarity tainted only by a scatter of clouds in the red glow of sunset, and a soft, golden glow from the dwindling rays of the westering sun bathed the green lawns and yellow battlements of Wintus Hall. High up on the walls where the red, white, and black flag of the Wintus clan rippled in a stiff breeze, a single sentry patrolled. The roseate light of the setting sun reflected off his bright helmet and shining spear tip as he lethargically watched the fighters practicing below.

Nibulus was feeling on top of the world. The fragrance of newly cut grass on the cooling breeze filled his nostrils as he inhaled deeply, and above him swallows soared in the sky. This was surely his favorite time of year, when the trees were bright with fresh green leaves, the headier spring fragrances filled the air, and no matter how strongly the sun shone, always there was a fresh breeze to brace the soul. He felt a thrill of excitement and anticipation each time he heard the swish of a blade, the ring of metal upon metal, or the sharp yelp of pain as iron bit into flesh. These sounds and others on the tourney field today reminded him of every other occasion on which he had practiced before undertaking a campaign, and it sent a surge of electricity through his body.

This occasion was, if anything, even more stimulating than previous times, for he now had strode out wearing his new suit of armor, and carrying the greatsword. He was thrilled at the way he looked and felt like nothing short of a god.

With him walked Methuselech, who, in his loosely flowing desert garb, contrasted as sharply as was possible with the hulking man-of-iron at his side. He too bore a two-handed sword, a great, curved length of rune-engraved sharpness called a shamsheer, almost as long as the Peladane's own. Also strapped across his back was a great ivory longbow and a soft leather quiver adorned with feldspar, lapis lazuli, and turquoise, and studded with beryl.

"You're not seriously intending to bring that metal suit along with you, are you?" Methuselech asked.

"And why not?" replied the Peladane haughtily.

"Because it's enormous, and it's metal, and we're going to be traveling for weeks or months, up to the coldest place in the world. And this time there'll be no wagons to carry things in. . . ."

"This armor is the most wonderful thing that has ever happened to me," Nibulus explained slowly and deliberately, as though in a daze of rapture, "and if you believe that I am going to leave it behind on my very first campaign, you really must be a bloody foreigner like everyone else says. I am going to wear it *every* day, all the way there and all the way back, and probably even sleep in it. I'm not going to take it off even once . . . in fact come to think of it, I might even have myself sealed into it forever."

"That's just the mead talking."

"No, that's the true Peladane talking."

They continued out onto the field, and there began to practice. No sooner had they begun than they were joined by the eighth member of the party due to set out, the silent watcher from the front row at the council. The sun did not actually darken at his approach, but it certainly seemed as if it might have.

"Hello, Odf," Nibulus stiffly addressed the newcomer. "Come to practice?"

He was hoping the fellow was here merely to watch, but unfortunately he was intending to practice too.

He introduced them: "Odf, this is Methuselech Xilvafloese, warrior of the Asyphe. Xilva, this is Odf Uglekort, mercenary of Vregh-Nahov."

"Paulus," the man corrected.

"Of course; Paulus is the name he has adopted when he works with Peladanes," Nibulus explained.

Methuselech was painfully aware of just how blatantly he was staring at the Nahovian, yet found he was quite unable to stop himself. The forest land of Vregh-Nahov did not enjoy a favorable reputation. Situated to the east of the Polgrim Hunting Grounds, it was a harsh and wild region. Apart from frequent and bloody raids by the hillfolk of the Brunamara Mountains to their northeast, invasions by the greedy Polgs from the west, and the regular winter incursions by the terrible eighteen-foot-tall, two-headed Ettins from the Ildjern Mountains to the northwest, there was also the fierce rivalry between the various tribes of their own race to contend with. These tribes, or Chlans, had little interaction with each other unless it was fighting, and there was consequently much bloodshed between them.

As a result, this dark, tree-covered land bred fierce and bitter men, hostile to outsiders and distrustful of each other. They were notoriously cruel, but also noted for their efficient deadliness and their willingness to hire themselves out as mercenaries.

Judging by this one's appearance, he was no different. In all Methuselech's years of fighting, he had never met anyone who looked so dark and grim as the man in front of him now, gauntly dressed in black, and standing seven feet tall. The mere sight of Odf—or Paulus—was enough to impose caution, discomfort, even fear in most observers. There was an air of death about him, in the very way he walked and moved, so calmly, carefully.

Some likened him to a raven, the Peladanes' symbol for death, but it would be perhaps more accurate to compare him to a crow, with his square-cut black hair, his sharp and pointed face with its beaky nose, and his bitterly keen hand-and-a-half sword ever at the ready. Like a carrion bird he stalked about Nord-was on his high, blue-black boots, ever alone, as if patiently waiting for a kill. A charcoal-grey coat that almost reached down to the ankles concealed most of his black leather tunic and trousers. He bore no shield or other armor, save for a long, black, brass-studded cape that covered his shoulders almost like a pair of folded wings. Concealing most of his head was a slate-grey hood decorated with two long, black feathers that stuck up on the left side.

Despite this hood, the more Methuselech studied him, the more a sense of discomfort crept over him. Whatever was the matter with the man's face?

The Nahovian squared up to the Peladane.

"Go easy on him, Nibb," Methuselech said with a smile. "He might turn ugly."

The practice commenced. Even as a practice, by the Peladane's standards this was a tough one. As the two fighters faced up to each other, it appeared to be a blatant mismatch: the magnificently accoutered Warlord's heir, with his haughty demeanor and intimidating bulk, against some ragged scarecrow who looked too elongated to even stand up straight. Yet, as soon as the steward had given the signal to begin, Nibulus felt the tip of his adversary's sword pressed to his throat.

There did not seem to have been even the slightest split second between the starting signal and the blade already grazing his neck.

"One to you," Nibulus conceded, his voice faint with awe. It was clearly going to take a lot more than his flashy armor to score against *this* one.

As round two began, Nibulus immediately closed in on his opponent, only to find him not there, and himself sprawling on his face with a mouthful of grass.

Yet Nibulus Wintus was considered one of Nordwas's finest, so round three commenced. This time he leapt back sharply, hoping to buy at least a second of time in which to react. As he did so he swept the greatsword around in a wide arc, to keep the mercenary at bay. Unferth, for all its size, was easy to handle, and the armor hardly hindered him at all. Maybe he could win this one round at least.

And so their practice began in earnest. Nibulus had heard something of the Nahovian's reputation, but he had never competed against him, and it seemed now that this was probably the way it should have remained. Indeed, it seemed he was fighting for his very life. . . .

Methuselech looked on with growing fascination. At one point Paulus's hood flipped back, and at last his entire face was revealed. Pallid, bony, and deformed, it was not a pretty sight; below the thick eyebrows that met in the middle, there was only one sound eye, pale and grey. The other was no more than a white, featureless orb and even the skin around it was encrusted with livid sores.

"What an unholy mess!" Methuselech gagged. *"How did he ever get like that?"*

"I yield!" Nibulus's voice boomed as he lay upon his back, with Paulus's sword less than an inch from his right eyeball. The Nahovian smiled knowingly, and with the tip of his sword tried to flip his foe's boar-shaped sallet up. But an especially good charge had built up in the tengriite helm, and with a loud crack the ensuing electric shock almost knocked Paulus from his feet and caused him to cry out in surprise and pain, dropping his weapon.

"It does work, then." Nibulus smirked, and got to his feet.

Paulus was outraged. Where he came from, defeat meant only death, and in that country there was no concept of a fair and honorable tournament. But he was especially outraged at being defeated by this Warlord's son. Jerkily he rose to his feet, picked up his sword, and in increasingly spasmodic movements, turned to walk away.

"Oh no," Nibulus muttered. "Here we go again. . . ."

As he went, the whey-faced warrior slowed, trying desperately to regain control of his movements; then his whole frame began to shake in spasms. Through gritted teeth a deep, strangled cry forced its way out, and he fumed with anger and frustration. The electric shock had triggered his "condition," and robbed him of control and dignity. All he could do now was to retire from the tourney field, stumbling and jerking like a puppet.

The two men watched him go with a mixture of pity and disgust.

"So what's *his* problem?" asked Methuselech.

"He's never told us," Nibulus replied. "He gets these fits . . . I don't know if it's connected with his hideous deformity or not. He never talks about it, always keeps himself to himself. I doubt if even his own countrymen know much about him. All he's ever told me is that his father was both an undertaker *and* a tanner—"

"Probably never had a shortage of fresh skin to cure, then," Methuselech commented darkly.

"True. Anyway, we've been hiring his services for years now, and he's one of the best fighters in this part of the world. A right vicious bastard, I can tell you. Did you hear what he wrote on his application letter this time?"

"No, what?"

"In the section where on hobbies and interests he put 'Tampering with the dead.' "

"I can believe it, from what little I've heard about his kind," Methuselech commented, "Is it true Nahovians kill their old folk with mallets?"

"Only if they're too weak to throw themselves into the family quicksand,"

Nibulus replied. "Anyway, we've had no trouble with him yet, and he does his job well. I don't think his appearance and typically Nahovian temperament have endeared him to prospective employers, so he's had a pretty lean time of it over the years. Anyway he seems happy to throw in his lot with us—and even if I wouldn't say I trust him that much, he is extremely good at killing."

"Poor sod," Methuselech murmured as they headed back to the hall.

"Come on, let's get some beer."

"We leave in three days!" Wodeman recalled the words of the mage-priest, still ringing in his ears as he strode away from the temple. Just three.

It was so little time to prepare, Wodeman realized. The commotion of this town was seriously befuddling his brain, so he headed off to the Chase. The sorcerer needed to sit down, to think, to plan.

"No holy man is going to get to me!" Bolldhe repeated inwardly, as he marched away from Wintus Hall. He too needed to think and plan, but most importantly, to drink. And he knew just the place to do that.

"Bolldhe!" came a familiar voice through the barred window of the Chase as he approached. "Come in and join me. I'll buy you a drink."

Bolldhe looked up sharply, half in shock. It was not often he heard *those* words.

"Oh, Wodeman," he registered, nonplussed, but decided to join him anyway, more out of a sense of novelty at this rarest of opportunities than any desire to converse with the shaman. He patiently maneuvered his way through the excitable throng of gin-swigging farmers and mead-quaffing foreigners with their amusing voices and interesting smells, and sat down heavily next to his new "companion."

"Two pints of ale and a packet of pork crackling," the wolf-man bellowed, above the din of the assembled carousers.

"You have money?" Bolldhe asked the woodland shaman, trying not to sound astounded.

"I'm not a healer for nought," Wodeman replied as he tendered a silver zlat for ale and pork rind. "They pay me enough for my simple needs. . . . Here, to *your* good health and *their* bad. Cheers!"

Bolldhe resisted the temptation to sneak a look at the shaman's feet to see if they were hairy and the rumors were true. He also carefully ignored the curious bone amulets that jangled about on the man's waist; as an "augur" himself, he recognized them for what they were, and did not wish to be drawn into any conversation along *those* lines.

Instead he kept his eyes on Wodeman's face as the shaman downed the ale in one long, blissful slug. His eyes closed with what could only be described as utter ecstasy; he savored the blend of warm, malty hoppiness with a rapture that only one possessed of Wodeman's heightened senses could attain.

He finished the mug, slammed it down on the greasy tabletop, and almost

shuddered in euphoria. Then, after a pause in which he seemed to forget everything in the world save the dizzy glow now spreading up from his feet, he
turned to Bolldhe.

"We don't spend *all* our time in the woods, you know," he informed his bewildered new acquaintance. "There are certain pleasures even in this smoke-
hole that I might as well partake of, since it's available."

Bolldhe shrugged, and tipped a quantity of ale into his own mouth. He
swilled it around, relishing both taste and texture, as the nut-brown liquid left
its oily deposit upon tongue and gums.

"All the other, er, 'forest magicians' I've met keep themselves to themselves,
as it were," he explained.

Wodeman spat in contempt, "Not much good as sorcerers, then, if they act
like that. We Torca are not hermits. Keeping yourself to yourself is as damaging
to the world as it is to you. Take this pork rind, for example; if you cut it off the
living pig's back, it rots . . . and the pig itself is that much worse off too. We
consider ourselves, all of us, an essential part of the world."

Bolldhe just blinked, dumbfounded. Wodeman had been sitting with him
for less than a minute, and already the bloody man was trying to *enlighten* him.

"Thank you, mentor," he replied, not sure of his nuances in this foreign
tongue, "but that's the sort of horse shite *I* normally talk myself—and get paid
for."

Wodeman laughed, without a hint of rancor, at Bolldhe's bluntness. "Well,
that lesson was for free. As will be all the others in our weeks to come."

"I can hardly wait," Bolldhe sighed, and wondered again if he had made the
right decision about joining this enterprise.

Wodeman, in Bolldhe's mind, had now become a disembodied, floating mouth
that just would not stop talking.

"Dreamers, *real* dreamers," the sorcerer was explaining to his glazy-eyed
guest, "do not run away from reality; they dream in order to change the world.
In dreams we're able to think freely, to release the imagination. And from this
release, comes *creation*."

"Really."

"Those mage-priests can never dream properly, because their minds have
become too bogged down with their dogma. They cling to the affirmations of
their faith like a drowning rat to a lily pad. If only they would simply allow
themselves to *feel,* but they prefer the stagnant reek of their smoky halls to the
sun and the air, so cut themselves off from Life itself."

"Is that so."

"Only openness to everything snaps the fetters of misunderstanding—and
allows the soul to go forward. Therefore do not believe or disbelieve. Just stay
open-minded! Life is a series of questions and nothing is certain."

"Certain, right—Oh look, here comes Nibulus. Nibulus, over here! Quick!" Bolldhe yelled through the open window.

Most of the punters in the Chase became aware of the presence of the War-lord's son before he even arrived in the square, for a large and rapidly growing crowd was forming. Gasps of amazement waxed into cheers of jubilation as Nibulus, still clad in his magnificent armor, swaggered down Pump Street with Methuselech. Men clapped, women swooned, and even the yellow dogs seemed to have a smile on their faces.

"Bolldhe!" Nibulus cried, all smiles and lofty gestures to those around him, relishing this new, heightened adulation he was receiving on this most excellent of days.

"We're heading down Neph Lane to watch the players there," he explained. "Fancy tagging along?"

Normally Bolldhe would have declined the invitation, but at the moment would have accompanied Nibulus to a leper colony rather than spend another minute with the droning shaman.

"Sounds great," he enthused.

"I'll come too," agreed Wodeman.

So, within minutes, all four of them had piled into a pair of passenger-carrying cyclo-tumbrels. The two drivers cackled inanely, and excitedly repeated the destination, before hurtling off through the throng lining Pump Street, gleefully running down anyone who got in their way. As tumbrel drivers tend to do.

While his three companions whooped with joy, and pedestrians flattened themselves against the walls to let them past, Bolldhe reflected on the uncanny uniformity of certain aspects of life around the world. One might assume, considering the vastness of Lindormyn, and therefore the isolation of so many settlements, that each town or village would be fairly unique. But as far as tumbrel drivers were concerned, they were a constant: uniformly horse-toothed, grimy, and ignorant, they seemed to like nothing better than hanging about their patch with their own kind, squatting around a game of cards, smoking mystery substances, and boasting about their latest fares, however meager.

Amid the clatter of rickety wheels and flapping sandals, the constantly yammering drivers charged ahead. Along increasingly narrow streets they hurtled, herding all before them like the Wild Hunt. Men, women, children, animals, none were spared by the tumbrel drivers from hell. Dogs barked savagely but were too craven to attack. Drovers and tradesmen yelled with indignation, but their fat-mouthed grimaces soon turned to smiles when they saw who it was seated in the lead tumbrel. No one else would have got away with it, but Nord-was truly was notable for the zeal with which its poorest inhabitants would always champion the cause of the richest and most privileged.

The streets were now so narrow that Nibulus could almost touch the walls either side with his outstretched hands. Soon the beating of timbals and the crack of staff upon staff could be heard. Within moments they had arrived at the six-way junction of Neph Lane, Sump Road, and Ueno Parade, and ventured unto the jovial pandemonium that was the Levansy Theater.

The place was packed, on this glorious sunny day, with what must have been half the population of Nordwas. Everyone from beggars to barons, far-flung foreigners to indigenous inhabitants, one-year-olds to one-hundred-year-olds, had gathered in this turgid spot. Even the rats had turned out, and were chattering animatedly with each other from their elevated position on the spital-house windowsills, or hurling down morsels of corn or verbal insults at the people below, excitedly awaiting the performance.

An impromptu stage made of two carts had been erected by the water troughs that stood in the center of this junction. Hanging above it was a silken banner of bilious purple and gold. Embroidered upon it were the words LEVANSY THEATER CO. PRESENTS: THE AMAZING PAULUS FATUUS AND HIS TWISTED IMPS!

On stage stood a man dressed in a huge, dirty brown, multipocketed coat that hung loosely over his naked, heavily tattooed torso. He had skintight leggings with bright orange, white, and green stripes, and was wearing a hat that looked like an upturned barley riddle. His face was daubed thickly with a virulent ink-blue "greasepaint" intended to give him the appearance of some kind of demon, while he appeared to be performing in quick succession just about every type of act that a minstrel could fall back on, and more besides.

Meanwhile, a forlorn Boggart was perched atop the tallest water pump (chained to it, of course), playing a three-stringed komuz with more skill than would seem possible for one of his species. And all the while among the crowd, an indeterminate number of Haugers of indeterminate gender kept howling and beating upon crude but brightly ribboned timbals, whipping the onlookers into a paroxysm of drunken but for the most part good-natured revelry.

The pair of tumbrels plowed their way straight into the crowd, whereupon their four occupants leapt out, looking around them. Immediately a small group of children gathered around their knees with palms upturned. Bolldhe's face turned sour, and he shooed them away with a few copper zlats pressed into their grubby mitts; the other three looked disapprovingly at him, smiled merrily at the children, but just shooed them away.

Brass beakers of sticky mint tea were purchased from sallow-faced vendors with long black mustaches, stools were hastily assembled, and soon Nibulus and his three companions were seated in respectfully comfortable isolation to watch the entertainment.

The blue-faced minstrel capered around the stage like a lunatic, singing, cavorting, and puppeteering in between, playing an assortment of bizarre musical instruments, and telling jokes that few there could understand (not because of the man's thick, foreign accent but because it was a type of humor that ap-peared to say one thing but at the same time mean something completely dif-ferent, a refinement that was met with the same kind of easygoing bewilderment that the rest of his act induced in the simple folk of Nordwas).

The minstrel then, for some inexplicable reason, turned around, swept up his coat, tore down his breeches, and flatulated a passable rendition of the Wintus war anthem. The crowd roared with laughter, while those nearest Nibulus and his crew nonchalantly edged away.

Methuselech and Bolldhe glanced at the Peladane. To their relief, his fixed smile eventually softened, and he shrugged. "Sounds better than the trouba-dours, anyway."

The wandering minstrels—crude, provocative, and about as foreign as you could get—were despised by lords and gentry, but better received by the com-moners. They had no bonds or loyalties to any but themselves, and roamed the land freely, entertaining any who would listen, for whatever coppers they could cajole.

"Bolldhe, my man," said Nibulus, suddenly turning to him, "Appa tells me you're really a Peladane."

"Was a long time ago," Bolldhe corrected him.

"Still are, then," Nibulus insisted with a dismissive smile. "So you're famil-iar with *The Chronicle of Gwyllch*, I take it."

"I heard mention of it," Bolldhe replied, staring distractedly at an acrobat performing right in front of him, who seemed to have twisted either her head or her feet completely back to front. Either way, he could not decide which way round she was.

"You'll have the chance to catch up on it during our journey," Nibulus con-tinued, "since I'll be bringing it along with us. Apart from being the most stir-ring story in history, it's the only real guide we have in written form of this journey we're undertaking. Old Gwyllch was a cultured man as well as a sol-dier, and he kept a detailed journal of his march northwards with the Nordwas contingent, to meet up with Lord Bloodnose's fleet. Since those days, hardly anyone has needed to consult it, but I tell you, Bolldhe, it must be fate that prompted him to write down his experiences. We'd be so much the worse off otherwise."

Bolldhe was suddenly uncomfortable. "Your book is the only guide we take?" he repeated. "No actual *people* what know the land? Just a diary writ half a cen-, milleni-, five hundred year ago?"

"Not *just* a diary. *The Chronicle of Gwyllch*!" Nibulus huffed.

Bolldhe stared at him in disbelief, but Nibulus was no longer even aware of him; his attention was fixed upon the acrobat who was now brazenly peeling off her clothing.

Bolldhe did not press the matter, preferring, as did most of the crowd, to look away from the whole disturbing spectacle. The Warlord's son, however,

seemed totally engrossed; not by the woman's nakedness—she had a face like a
sea lion's, and a body to match—but at the sheer impudence of the way she was
staring at him with not the slightest hint of subservience, or even deference. He
was not used to this at all, and felt a little unnerved.

Just then, Methuselech drew their attention to Paulus. The Nahovian was
standing just twenty or so paces away, glaring at all around him with a look of
open hostility on his face, while his hand rested on the pommel of his sword.

"Why doesn't he come over and join us?" asked Methuselech, clearly puzzled.

"Does he look like the sort of man who wants company?" Wodeman commented, looking at the man appraisingly as he glared at the female acrobat who
was now writhing in front of him.

"Then why doesn't he just sod off?" snapped Nibulus, clearly having had
enough of his raucus surroundings by now. "If he hates company so much, why
come to a place like this?"

"I can see we're going to have to watch that one." Methuselech frowned.
"Maybe we should get him a job with the Levansy Theater Company instead.
He'd be more at home with this freak show. . . ."

"People certainly do seem to stare at him," Bolldhe noted, not without a
small measure of sympathy.

"He's even got the same first name as the minstrel," Nibulus laughed.

"Your mercenary's called Paulus Fatuus too?" Bolldhe asked doubtfully.

"Just Paulus."

At precisely that moment, as if on cue, the blue-faced minstrel plunged his
rear end into the water trough, and the whole surface began to seethe like a
bubbling cauldron. The audience gasped with admiration, then roared their
approval.

"Paulus Flatulus, more like," joked Nibulus.

It was destiny, of course; a new name had been created. The grim but proud
mercenary from the forests of Vregh-Nahov, he who had fought lethally alongside the Peladanes and proved his excellence at arms, would now and forever
after be thought of as Paulus Flatulus.

Well, anything was better than Odf Uglekort.

At last the long-awaited day of departure dawned.

A pale, bleary sun crawled out of the ground-hugging mists in the east, its
paltry rays barely warming the chill of a crisp, dewy dawn. The birds were in
full song, almost drowning out the other sounds of morning that were gradually growing in volume: the irritable clattering of shutters, the occasional slam
of a door, and the hacking cough of some old man as he walked up a lane in the
distance.

Through squinting eyes, Gapp peered out of the single window in the loft room. People were rising, the day was beginning, and it felt good to be alive. He breathed in deeply to clear his sleepy head. The air smelled good, so fresh and vibrant with the fragrances of early morning—sweet, bedewed grass, newly baked bread, and freshly passed pig dung—providing Heaven-sent relief from the stuffy fetor of the loft's confines. In a sudden twitch of exuberance, Gapp leapt over the huddled forms of his recumbent brothers to reach where his clothes lay, and quickly got dressed.

While he fumbled with his clothing, his heart pounded with excitement. He could barely control his fingers as he laced up his heavy green shirt, pulled on his tan trousers, and thrust his feet into the soft grey leather boots his mother had bought him specially the previous day.

I can't wait! I can't wait! I can't wait! he buzzed to himself, his whole body tingling with agitation.

"I'll show you . . ." came a voice from behind him.

Gapp froze. It sounded like his brother Ottar, the eldest of seven boys in his family.

". . . get it away from me . . ." the voice murmured again, this time quieter but loaded with venom. Yes, definitely Ottar.

Gapp turned, and stared across the line of blanketed brotherhood that lined one side of the loft. He located the hulking mound wherein lay—somewhere—the source of that disturbing voice.

Sleep-talking! Gapp breathed in relief, and, in absolute silence now, picked up his little white belt, lowered himself through the trapdoor, and slunk away from the stuffy dormitory to the lower story.

When he had safely reached the stone floor of the cottage, he hurriedly donned his belt, making sure all its accessories were secured: his simple sling and its missiles, four little throwing knives, the small leather pouch that contained his boxwood reed pipes, and, most important, the scabbard that held his hand weapon—a shortsword with the badge of the Wintus clan embossed in the center of its hilt. Then, pausing only long enough to take one last look at the bittersweet familiarity of the hovel that had been his cottage for the past fifteen years, Gapp slipped outside.

He lowered the latch noiselessly behind him, then sprinted away.

Done it! he screamed within his soul as he tore off down the lane toward Wintus Hall and, with an uncaring hardness that can only be excused by youthfulness, did not care if he ever saw that house or its occupants again.

Being the youngest of seven brothers had never been easy. All his life he had lived as the underdog within those walls, derided by his merciless brothers and virtually ignored by his parents. His folks did the best they could, of course, their hide being only just big enough to raise the food necessary to support a family of nine. But having no prospect of earning the dowry that a daughter would have secured them was ever a disappointment to his parents, and as the youngest, and last attempt, Gapp was somehow the most resented for this.

Ash-boy, they called him, and had given him the most menial of tasks. So it had been the greatest relief to Gapp when he had finally caught the eye of a noble Peladane in need of a squire, none other than Master Nibulus Wintus himself.

Not that this had gained him any more respect from his family, of course. To his parents he was still, and forever would be, a silly little boy, and to his brothers a complete prat.

"You'll see," he had muttered defiantly against their indifference to his new status, and now he had informed them he was being taken along on the "Finwald Quest." "You'll see."

But they didn't. So now he left without even a good-bye from them.

Gapp was the first to arrive at their rendezvous in the stables of Wintus Hall, while the others of the company were still being levered from their beds by big-fingered servants. The farewell banquet, to which everyone save Gapp had been invited, had been so lavish that it would be weeks before they would get all the gravy off the ceiling. He therefore set to, helping the stable boys ready the horses. He started with his own pony, Bogey, then proceeded to his master's magnificent warhorse, Hammerhoof.

There was a lot of work to be done before their departure, and the stables were soon a wasp's nest of activity. Gapp had soon worked up a good sweat, so when a large platter of bread and goat's cheese was brought to him, he enthusiastically dug in, grateful for the chance to sit down.

It was only while he was munching away that he noticed for the first time the odd looks the other servants were giving him. Normally he was treated as just another employee. But on this particular morning he began to feel their eyes lingering on him. Such attention was a new experience for him, and he risked returning their glances. There was an odd mixture of pity, jealousy, and even goodwill in their eyes.

A few of his friends presently wandered in and sat themselves down next to him. They too seemed unsure how to behave on this unprecedented occasion. Every apprentice in town had been allowed the morning off work to watch the grand departure, with the joyous prospect of getting in at least two hours of hard-core stone-skimming before they must return to their labors. But eventually finding nothing further to say, after a brief mumbling of farewells, they sloped off.

The bread and cheese suddenly tasted dry and hard in his mouth, and it was as much as he could do to force it down past the sudden lump in his throat. Up until now, he had only felt excitement at this, his first adventure, his first time out in the real world. But now, having said his last good-byes, a sudden crushing sadness sprang up from nowhere and settled in the pit of his stomach.

Aware of a moistness around his eyes, he breathed in deeply, straightened himself up, and tried to smile.

Stupid, he cursed himself, and got straight back to work, the last crusts of his breakfast forgotten.

Meanwhile, Appa trudged up the country lane, leading his cow Marla over to Tommas's father's place. In his right hand he gripped her halter, in his left a sprig—no, more like a bouquet—of her favorite herb grass, weba. In his eyes, he held back—but only just—a well of tears.

His sheep he could bear to part with easily, but Marla . . . she seemed to sense that they would never be seeing each other again.

Ah, bitter was their parting. . . .

And finally, after two agonizingly slow hours of waiting around, did the party finally set out for Vaagenfjord Maw. A single bugle sounded a shrill fanfare to alert all who might be standing along their route leading through the streets of Nordwas, and to cue the commencement of the Quest.

With a mighty bellow from Nibulus's throat, the fully-armored Peladane waved one gauntleted fist in the air for all to see, then brought it down as though signaling the start of a race. For him it might as well have been, as he spurred his huge warhorse forward in a headlong gallop that scattered the suddenly panicked but nevertheless grateful crowd like rats in a barrel.

Methuselech followed on Whitehorse, gleaming in red, white, and gold, and matched in splendor only by the superb beast upon which he rode, the golden bells on its reins jingling merrily.

Behind these two leaders came Paulus, looking like a grey and black shadow upon the brown mare he had purchased three days earlier; Bolldhe was, as ever, on his faithful slough horse, the broadaxe slung at its side, while Finwald rode his black steed Quintessa, whose trailing mane strikingly resembled the long black hair flying out from beneath its rider's priestly hat.

And finally, not even trying to keep up, came Gapp on Bogey and Appa on a pony his temple had managed to scratch up for him.

Wodeman, surprisingly or not, was nowhere to be seen.

Onward the company rode, surrounded by cheering. There was a brief anticlimactic pause near the main gates, as a young woman of arresting comeliness, yet with marked firmness of jaw, stepped out right in front of the Peladane's horse and brought him to an ignominious halt. Nibulus cussed, rummaging about in his saddlebags, and brought forth a small clutch of zibelines, which he hastily shoved into her outstretched hand. With a final, slightly embarrassed nod to her, he recommenced his heroic progress toward the town gates.

Through the gap in the stockade wall they galloped, kicking up great sods of mud into the faces of the last of the crowd of well-wishers. Up the road beyond, winding its way through hedged enclosures, they thundered on and on until they resembled mere motes moving slowly toward the distant hills. Then, with the Peladane's last cry of uncontrollable elation drifting back to the smiling crowd upon the breeze, the magnificent seven dwindled into the distance, and were at last swallowed up by the North.

4

The Blue Mountains

Gapp shivered, and pulled his cloak tightly around him, shielding himself against the elements. Though soaked heavy with rain, and caked with mud around the hem, at least the garment did something to keep the weather off him as he huddled beneath the partial shelter of an overhanging rock. Freezing droplets dripped from the matted strands of hair clinging to his forehead, trickling through eyebrows and his stinging eyes behind his steamed-up spectacles. Elsewhere they trickled down his neck and into the diminishing warmth beneath his shirt, like an army of frigid insects seeking drier places to hide in. He was wet and miserable, and even his clothes smelled of damp.

He was not the only sufferer; even his master's proud green Ulleanh clung dejectedly around his armor, and all seven of them now crouched under the overhang beside the mountain path, equally smelly, silent, and miserable.

As he gazed down at the foggy valley below, beyond the line of horses that waited gloomily but patiently in the rain, Gapp wondered how many miles now lay between them and Nordwas. They had been traveling for two weeks solidly, and in all that time had passed through only half a dozen hamlets. In each one they had traded for food using copper and silver coins, or small amounts of scrap iron, medicines, spices, and other luxuries that so rarely passed that way.

In between these settlements they would sometimes spend the night in abandoned posthouses. In the old days, when Nordwas boasted an important caravanserai on a great trade route, such makeshift posthouses had been set up at regular intervals between the villages to accommodate the king's messengers and passing merchants. Since then they had fallen into dereliction, but their musty and forlorn shells still offered partial shelter for the weary travelers.

"Welcome to the Darklands, young man," Nibulus had muttered to his esquire after leaving the first of such primitive villages. "Feeling more at home, *ha-ha?*"

"Not all that dark, really," Gapp had replied, not sure what his master was going on about.

Nibulus chortled. "We're now beyond the borders of Pel-Adan's own realm and these people here are all of *your* own stock, Aescals every one of them. As I said, welcome home to the Darklands."

To be honest, most of the group were so far feeling fairly good about the whole enterprise. As visitors, they were accorded great respect and treated with friendliness, hospitality, and much curiosity. At each village they would be invited in to share large earthenware bowls of heady, fermented gortleberry, and offered baskets of sweet black bread for their journey.

In all that time Wodeman had not yet been seen. It appeared he would not be joining them on the quest after all—and nobody was in any hurry to go and look for him. Till, on approaching the latest hamlet, down a rutted path wending tiredly through the woods, the sorcerer had suddenly dropped from a tree to land in front of them. He had said not a word, just regarded them in turn, then gestured for them to follow him.

Nibulus had already guessed the reason for this unexpected appearance. The settlement they were about to enter was too northerly even for the Aescals. A tiny cluster of miserable dwellings right on the very edge of civilization, it was inhabited entirely by Wodeman's own race.

"Be on your guard," Paulus warned them, uncaring that Wodeman walked right by him. "These people are Huldre—fey—and not to be trusted."

"Fey?" Nibulus snorted.

"Fey," the Nahovian affirmed. "But they will not come near if we bear iron, for it is anathema to them."

The company glanced at Wodeman. "It's true," the Torca confirmed. "If you attack us with iron weapons, we can die."

Nibulus laughed along with the others. "Whose idea was it to bring him along anyway?"

That's the trouble with the Torca, Nibulus considered. *No respect for their betters.* Like all Peladanes, he was half-amused and half-irritated by the Torca's complete inability to kowtow respectfully.

As they rode into the village, their first sight of the inhabitants they came across caused more than a stir among the riders from the South.

"Is that *green* skin they have?" Nibulus inquired, making no effort to disguise his distaste.

The men who were gathered in a small group in the road to watch the arrival of the strangers were attired only in ragged kilts and a kind of fleece wrapped about their shoulders. The jewelry hanging round their necks was heavy, crude, and wrought exclusively of bronze, in strangely disturbing designs, while numerous strings of brightly colored seashells were suspended garishly from their kilts. But it was the sickly green pallor of their skin that drew the eye so arrestingly, and it was only when the company got closer that they realized their men were actually covered in runes tattooed in long spirals encircling both torso and limbs.

As Nibulus rode past, he leaned over to inspect one more closely, peering as unself-consciously as the old man who stared back.

The Peladane marveled, "Are those the names of all his girlfriends? The de-generate old goat!"

"I'd have a care how you speak," the shaman warned. "Those are the names of enemies he's slain."

Nibulus's unvoiced admiration was doubled.

This was a time of great activity for the Torca, for they were reaping the first *orrnba*-seed harvest of the year. They wailed crack-voiced incantations as they slashed with bronze sickles, accompanied by their shamans, who flicked sacred water from their ring-elongated fingers onto the crop as it was cut. And at night the village really came alive, for it was then that the threshing took place. The Torca believed that seed which was threshed under the silver light of the waning moon would be blessed by the spirits.

This village actually had a hostelry, of sorts: the Grey Dog Inn. Here the company stayed the night, and made the most of the occasion by draining an ancient firkin of Rynsaka, the only cask of ale found in the place. On the urging of Wodeman, they stayed locked in their loft during the darkest hours of the night, while he himself joined his people in celebrating their secret pagan rites.

As the travelers lay abed in their stalls, they listened fearfully to the other-worldly sounds of the final stage of the harvest, the winnowing, being per-formed outside. This was left to the care of Erce; the crop was laid out upon reed mats on the village green and, while hedgehogs screamed like Mandragora and danced like Trows in the woods nearby, a twisting wind swept through the village and whisked the husks away. Candles were immediately afterward placed in wooden shrine huts beneath the deodars, by way of thanks, and then the *real* celebrations commenced.

Wodeman had explained to them that they were particularly fortunate to pass through at that time of year for, during the harvest, violence and ill man-ners were forbidden, in order to appease the spirits. The only hints of excess were the frenetic dancing of the villagers, the savage carousing of the hedge-hogs nearby, and of course the ritual sacrifice of a couple of enemy marauders who were strung up on tree boles and pierced through all over with long, thin rods of sharpened hazel. These last were inserted so as to avoid rupturing any vital organ, and to come out intact the other side.

"A skilled priest might manage to implant as many as fifty hazel rods one by one into a victim ere he dies," Wodeman had assured them, "or just one long rod running from bottom to top, like a spitting roast. In fact, in times past, in the Seter Heights where my people originated, they would even eat them alive off the sacrificial pole! Anyway, enjoy your rest."

The night had continued heavy with blood, savagery, and all sorts of weirdness, and to the wayfarers who lay curled in their bedrolls in the Grey Dog it seemed as though they had strayed into another time and another world.

But that had been a week ago. Four days later they had begun to climb the Blue Mountains, and the change of terrain had been complete as field and pasture gave way to wild upland, across which only a single ancient and ill-kept track snaked its way.

Since their departure from the hamlet, they had seen no evidence of humankind at all save for the rough and rocky path upon which they traveled. Gapp could not imagine who had constructed it, or why; there seemed to be no people in these mountains. Were they really, as Nibulus claimed, using the same road Gwyllch's Peladanes had taken all those years past? If so, it looked as if no one else had used it in all the intervening years. The only creatures that dwelled here were elusive mountain goats that could be heard clattering among the stony slopes above, or occasionally seen peering down at them from inaccessible rocky heights.

He had never known anywhere as lonely and remote as this, and it was certainly not what he had imagined before they set off. Gapp had always pictured the Blue Mountains as a wild region of lofty crags and snowcapped peaks, where adventurers stood atop high ridges with their swords raised to salute the dawn; where sorcerers practiced their arts in stony castles perched at crazy angles on the tops of crags; and where gryphons leapt out of the inky blackness of their caves to attack and devour fair maidens.

Well, it was wild, that was for sure, but now, as he sat here in the wet with no hope of dry shelter for weeks ahead, the magic of the wild had wholly lost its allure for Gapp Radnar. The young traveler was saddle-sore, aching all over, soaked through, and had begun to shiver violently. He was sick of the blandness of their rations every day, sick of the rain that drove straight into his face no matter what direction they took, and sick of the way the meager pauses they took never seemed to provide him with any comfort or relaxation until the very minute just before they had to resume their journey.

He was beginning to realize just how much he loved his humble home, his parents, even his brothers; how he yearned for warm, dry clothes, soft blankets, and hot food. Before setting out, he had imagined himself gloriously as a brave adventurer, but now all he felt like was a pathetically ordinary human.

Many a time he was tempted to complain, but the silent grimness of his companions always quelled this impulse. Bolldhe and Wodeman were clearly not men to appear weak in front of, and even his master and Finwald, with whom he was better acquainted, seemed to have changed. Gapp was beginning to see how hardship robbed men of their usual warmth and turned them into sullen, quick-tempered bullies.

This was becoming the most depressing thing about this whole enterprise. All his life Gapp had been treated as just his name suggested: a gap. If standing in a crowd or a queue, and someone wished to get through, it would always be *him* they chose to push past. Even when there were other smaller, younger kids nearby. Almost as though he had a large sign on his head saying THIS SPACE VACANT. That seemed to be his role in life: a gap in the ranks of humanity. But now he was embarking upon this Quest, naturally all that should change. Surely?

Alas, this lot were now treating him with about as much respect as a stray dog. Less, in fact, for at least they would have avoided stepping on one of those.

Paulus, that grim mercenary, still never smiled, never whistled, only ever spoke when necessary, always walked alone. Continually he was stretching, flexing, clenching and unclenching his muscles, his fingers; like a machine, a killing machine, constantly priming itself.

The only ray of sunshine among the whole group was Bolldhe's mount, a sturdy, spirited little horse that answered to the name of Zhang. To use the Aescals' own term, it was a slough horse, that small, tough breed that was native to the Tabernacle Plains. Their habitat was one of open steppe and rocky, ravine-scored hillsides, where grass was lean and winters extremely harsh. This ungiving country bred a horse with an abundance of tightly packed body fat and a "donkey tuft" coat in order to survive, giving it a rather comical and inelegant appearance. However, the slough horse was also extremely tough, with an easygoing and almost philosophical attitude toward hardship. The nomads of the Plains called them Adt-T'man, which meant "friend horse," and to the company now it did indeed seem as if Zhang possessed a fine sense of humor. Quite at home in these mountains, he remained untroubled by the constant rain and the general dark mood, and playfully butted the rump of whichever horse was ahead of him, or tried to overtake it on the outside curve of the narrow cliff path, unconcerned with the two-hundred-foot drop that lay mere inches to one side.

The only beast that did seem to bother him was the Peladane's horse, Hammerhoof, which was (typically) arrayed almost as sumptuously as his master. Fully barded in leather and tengriite armor that was exquisitely wrought and engraved, here was a true knight's charger. Bolldhe himself scorned such ostentation, preferring instead to accouter his own mount with the bare minimum of equipment, for he believed this preserved Zhang's essential nobility, by honoring the "wild and free" barbarian tradition. If he had bothered to consult Zhang on the matter, however, he would have discovered that the slough horse actually was very jealous of Hammerhoof and would love to be similarly caparisoned. Occasionally, to make up, he would sidle up to Hammerhoof and "accidentally" kick him or give him a "friendly" bite.

Of the humans, Wodeman had retained his good humor the longest. They did not see him often—but on these occasions Gapp had never seen him become angry, no matter what the adverse situation. The man seemed equally at home in a dry cave or standing outside in the rain. Even when so bedraggled that his wolf skin stank worse than it had ever done when its owner was still alive, Wodeman would just carry on, fetching them edible plants or freshly killed animals, sitting with them for a while before disappearing again.

But since they had left the lowlands far below them, the climate had undergone something of a change. Down there they were still enjoying late spring, but up here it seemed early winter. It was so much colder, with chilling fog, even the occasional patch of snow. Even the shaman, who had never ventured far from his woods, was finding all this extremely difficult to comprehend. He did not care for it at all, since his whole natural world no longer made sense to him.

Yes, the initial zest Gapp felt on those first few days of riding and laughing in the sun really did seem like a sad joke now.

The rest of the afternoon dragged by miserably, the rain never really letting up. Appa had resumed that most annoying habit of incessantly chanting mantras while rapping his prayer ring against the torch amulet in a way that looked as if he was continually patting his heart. He would do this for hours upon end, and at times of heightened stress would accelerate the chanting until one or more of the company would scream at him to shut up. It was, to say the least, annoying, and it was only the occasional intervention of the other mage-priest in the party—who seemed unbothered by the older one's eccentricities—that prevented Appa from being hurled off the side of the cliff.

"Poor old Marla," he would mumble, "I wonder what she's doing right now? Probably about time for her to return home from the pasture. I'd always let her out of her stall at dawn and she'd take herself up to the hills, then return before dusk, same time every day; never had to be led. . . ."

The company filed along a path which had by now deteriorated into little more than a rocky sheep trod. Any doubts lingering as to whether this track was ever used these days were now confirmed. It was difficult to say which was the biggest cause of irritation, Appa's ceaseless chanting or Nibulus's rock-solid but apparently ill-founded faith in that damn book of his. At the moment it was taking them northwest, threading gradually upward and ever deeper into the mountains, and it was only on the assurance of their redoubtable leader that they could believe they would, in about a week's time, be descending the final foothills of this upland and into the moors beyond.

Today, though, their destination was only as far as Estrielle's Stair, a waterfall fed by a small stream that cut a narrow, high-sided cleft through the grey granite, though a fair way above the pass through which they now rode. Over this stream, at the very point where it cascaded over the cliff, ran a small stone bridge, and beyond that, if the book was to be trusted, they might find a series of caves, to provide shelter for the night.

It was late evening by the time they came in sight of the Stair, and the fading light was darkened further by the thickening clouds of fog that filled every valley and ravine. All that could be heard now was the clatter of their horses as they tramped along the rock-strewn path, and the crunching of slate breaking under their hooves.

Have to get us all into some kind of shelter soon, Nibulus fretted, scanning the ridge looming high above them. *Before it gets too dark to go on.* The path, he could see, snaked a very meandering way up to the ridge. It was only after many laborious twists and turns that they would reach the top where the caves marked on the sketch map in Gwyllch's book were supposed to be. Sometimes the path would turn back on itself just to gain a few extra feet upward, so it was clearly going to take a very long time. Nibulus raised his hand to halt his company, then stopped to think.

In the sudden quiet of their welcome pause, they were all struck by the eerie silence of the place. Whether it was the dampening effect of the fog, or just the sheer absence of any life in this grey, stony world, they could not tell. But as they tarried, listening hard, all of them experienced a disturbing feeling of complete loneliness, nakedness even, stuck way up here in the mountains. Gapp shivered, and not just with the cold. No wind blew, no crows cawed, not even the clouds moved. All was still, save for the occasional slithering rattle of a slate as it slid down the slope. Or the single bleat of a distant goat.

"What are we waiting for, Nibulus?" asked Finwald softly.

"I don't know," replied their leader. "Just listening for . . ."

A second bleat sounded from somewhere high above them, its lonely echo trailing off into silence.

"Peladane," Wodeman said, suddenly appearing at his side, "if we are to make camp tonight, we'd better do it soon, and make sure we are secure. There's something in this valley other than goats. They're scared of it, can't you hear?"

Gapp was chilled by the darkness of the sorcerer's words. He felt close to panic, and longed to turn and gallop as fast as possible back the way they had come. But he would not dare to be alone up here in the darkling mountains, so he kept still, though fretting at the thought they were riding into some terrible, unknown peril.

Their leader, Nibulus, did not miss Wodeman's tone either, but he himself was well accustomed to danger, little likely to be intimidated by words of a "wizardly type" from the woodlands back home. He paused a moment to run his eye over the crags rising about them. Immediately to their right, the mountainside plunged down steeply into unknown depths, into an impenetrable fog that filled the whole valley like soup in a bowl. To their left rose the steep slope of a mountain spur.

He considered for a moment. That spur looked likely to lead them up to the little stone bridge spanning the waterfall. It would be a difficult ascent, so steep and through loose scree, but if they could goad their steeds up that way he was sure they could reach the bridge in less than half an hour. And have just enough time to find one of Gwyllch's promised caves before the dark really settled in.

"Follow me!" he called out. "We're going up."

The ascent proved to be even more difficult than he had anticipated, and Nibulus rode a Knostus, the most highly esteemed warhorse that a Peladane's money could buy. These steeds were heavy and strong, fierce in battle, and unswervingly obedient to their masters' whim—but completely hopeless at mountain trekking, being too heavy for high altitudes, and far too cumbersome for climbing difficult slopes.

The most notable thing about the Knostus—a Pendonian word that meant "Faithful"—was its devotion to its master, or herd leader. This was extremely useful on long missions for, unlike most horses, it could be left alone, untethered and unhobbled, to look after itself without wandering off. Its master could ride it up as far as he could go, then dismount to climb the steeper slopes on foot. When he returned, days or even weeks later, the Knostus would still be there, exactly where he had left it. Furthermore, it was in the nature of this breed to bunch together and fight off predators (whether bears or snow hyenas) even in the absence of the humans.

But Hammerhoof was the only Knostus in this group, and Nibulus was loath to abandon him here alone during the night. Secretly, he also recoiled at the indignity of scrambling his way up that slope on hand and foot, especially in his armor.

Hammerhoof was already having a very bad time of it, and so were the other horses. For every three steps forward he slid two back, and even when Nibulus made him side-wind, the animal's bulk made the sharp turns next to impossible. Meanwhile, Appa and Gapp had to dismount and lead their ponies up the spur, whereas Finwald was forced to physically drag the whinnying Quintessa upward, digging his heels into the scree and hauling on the reins with one hand while using the other to maintain his balance.

Of all of them, only Bolldhe's mount had no difficulty. The agile little Adt-T'man's hooves were delicate and trowel-shaped (useful for scraping away snow and ice from the grass needed as fodder), so he picked his way up the slope with contemptuous ease. Given a free rein he could have set off ahead by himself, but Bolldhe was reluctant to leave the security of the group.

Sweating despite the cold, and mentally exhausted with the unrelenting concentration of the climb, the worn-out group gradually ascended higher and higher. It was growing darker by the minute, and soon they feared they would not have any light to see by.

Gapp peered down into the gloom of the fog to either side of him, and shuddered. Down there through the foggy depths, he could not even guess how far one would fall before reaching the bottom. To his consternation, Bogey kept slipping on the treacherous slate, sending loose stones rattling down the mountainside. Clearly the animal was losing its concentration, and Gapp did not have to be a nature-priest to know that this was due to fear, not of the dangerous climb but of something that only the horses, Wodeman, and the now-vanished mountain goats could sense.

There was something up there on the path ahead waiting for them.

The same fear was felt by all of them now, and it tightened its grip the farther they ascended. One would spin around quickly, only to see nothing behind him; and they began to fancy stony faces grimacing from the rocks about them. With the sound of their hearts beating loudly in their ears, they looked up and saw now the beckoning outline of the small stone bridge, like an open, hungry mouth that called to them.

At last they reached the top. They had rejoined the main path at its highest level, and stood panting, wheezing and dripping, about thirty yards from the bridge. Apart from the stream and the bridge itself, there was nothing to be seen but rock. No evil presence awaited them after all.

Gapp peered down at Estrielle's Stair, and noted with surprise how strangely quiet it was for a waterfall; the water slithered, rather than cascaded, down the first few yards of steep slope, before disappearing totally into the all-enveloping blanket of fog below. He looked away from the fall, and glanced at the bridge.

It was then that he saw the face.

The shock hit him as if he had been struck full in the chest by a battering ram, stiffening his whole body and rooting him to the spot. Then came the surge of fear, a deep-rooted, primal horror that seemed to drain every drop of blood from his veins and replace it with ice.

Bolldhe noticed it too. He had seen that face several times before: a huge, brutish, granite-hued visage that glared at them fixedly from the bridge. Two angry orange eyes smote him with a sickening terror that arose from deep within his ancestral memory. An iron fist seemed to clamp itself around his windpipe, silencing the scream that threatened to burst forth. But when it did emerge, releasing him from his momentary paralysis, his fear turned into anger as the scream became a roar.

"Ogre!" he yelled in warning, and snatched up his broadaxe.

Gapp was still gaping with terror when Paulus brushed him aside, knocking him onto the ground as the mercenary leapt toward the Ogre. Within almost the same second another figure sprang over Gapp while he lay sprawled upon the path, his head spinning in confusion amid the battle cries of his comrades and the roaring of the Ogre.

Axe at the ready, Bolldhe stood his ground, but did not advance.

"My lance!" someone bellowed. "Get off the ground and hand me my bloody lance!"

"Get back from there!" another was shouting. "It won't attack if we leave it alone!"

But if there had been any chance of avoiding a fight, it was gone now. Paulus had charged headlong into battle, and was now upon the chasm-spanning bridge, confronting the Ogre. Armed with a massive stone club, this hill giant stood fully two feet taller than the Nahovian. Ducking with surprisingly dexterity for one so tall himself, Paulus avoided the terrible sweep of the club as it whistled through an unstoppable arc scant inches above his head. In almost the same instant he brought his razor-sharp sword up in a vicious swipe across the Ogre's stomach. The giant roared in pain as the blade scored a bloody gash across its rock-hued hide. It twisted its yellow fangs in a spittle-flecked snarl.

But as Paulus hopped back and reversed the sword in his grasp with a lightning-quick flick of the wrist to parry the next blow, the Ogre's elephantine foot came up and caught him unexpectedly in the chest, hurtling him backward with a winded gasp of surprise.

At the same moment Methuselech also reached the bridge. He veered deftly to one side to avoid Paulus's semiconscious body as it crashed against the rampart; then, his shamsheer gripped tightly in both hands, he swung its huge length of curved steel at the Ogre's unprotected flank. Gapp gagged in wild-eyed horror as he saw the blade bite deep into the creature's flesh, with the sickening sound of a butcher's cleaver hacking up a haunch of beef.

Some of the horses were rearing in terror, whinnying and stamping their hooves wildly, and it was all their riders could do to restrain them from bolting. For Hammerhoof, though, this situation was all too familiar. He sensed that his master was intending a lance charge, but could not now understand what he was waiting for.

"Radnar!" Nibulus bellowed. "Hand me my damned lance!"

Bolldhe shot a glance over toward the esquire, who was up on his feet now, but seemed wholly unable to get his thoughts together. Straightaway Bolldhe leapt over to the squire's pony, and yanked the Peladane's lance out of its rest.

"It's all right!" shouted Finwald, grabbing for the lance simultaneously. "I'll do that. You go help Xilvafloese!"

"Just give it here!" cried Nibulus, his face purple with rage.

Bolldhe turned back to look at the bridge. Methuselech, after his initial lunge, was now in trouble. Incredibly the Ogre's wound had not proved fatal; it had a hide as tough as saddle leather, and though the monster had taken the sword in fairly deep, it had still not penetrated any of the vital organs. And now, with the weapon still wedged into its flank, the Ogre twisted violently sideways and wrenched the shamsheer out of Methuselech's grasp. In the same

movement it brought its club down in a swift blow towards the warrior's unprotected head.

Nibulus froze, Finwald stared openmouthed, Gapp screamed "No!," and
Appa closed his eyes.

If it had not been for Paulus, Methuselech would certainly have died right
then. But, as the shamsheer was yanked from his hands, he stepped back,
caught his heel on Paulus's prostrate form, lost his footing, and fell over backward. The boulder-heavy bludgeon just missed him and crashed against the
rampart. Splinters of granite flew through the air as both club and rampart disintegrated and tumbled down the waterfall and into the fog below.

"Help him, damn you!" roared Nibulus to the unwilling traveler, and Bolldhe
finally released his hold on the lance, snatched up his own axe, and charged toward the Ogre. Finwald, meanwhile, ran over and handed the lance to Nibulus.

Unarmed but still dangerous, the wounded Ogre towered over the two
fallen mercenaries, the shamsheer still protruding from its side. Methuselech
stared up into its eyes, at last taking in the enormity of this adversary, and realized now exactly what they were up against. He rolled backward over his own
head, like an acrobat, to leave only Paulus in the creature's path. The Ogre
reached down for the tall mercenary's leg, and yanked him off the ground as
easily as picking up a rabbit. Conscious again, Paulus screamed in fear at the
terrible face right in front of his, and instinctively lashed out with his free foot
as hard as he could into that hideous visage.

The Ogre howled in surprise as its nose crunched beneath the force of the
well-aimed blow; not for nothing did the mercenary wear hobnailed boots. But
this only fired its wrath further, and the struggling Paulus was held up, dangling, ready to be thrown down into the gully.

Suddenly the Ogre's leg buckled, as Bolldhe's broadaxe sheared through
the tendons of its calf. Hamstrung, the hill giant crumpled heavily to the
ground, with Paulus trapped beneath it.

Again Bolldhe brought down his weapon, and this time the stricken Ogre
caught the axe head in its outstretched hand as it tried to defend itself. Maimed
from the wounds dealt by its three attackers, the howling Ogre struggled uselessly as Bolldhe's axe hacked mercilessly into its mangled flesh; up, down, up,
down, up, down. Its roars rose to a high-pitched shrieking, then died into a
gurgle, and finally stopped.

Sickened by his first sight of bloody battle, Gapp sank to his knees and
wept convulsively. This was not the adventure, glory, or even courage he had
imagined; it was nothing more than simple butchery. Retching in horror, the
tortured boy finally threw up into the gorge.

His deerskin tunic splashed with hot blood, and the gleam of berserk madness now fading from his eyes, Bolldhe stepped away from the bridge. He
glared defiantly at the Peladane, as if daring him to utter one word of repri-
mand for Bolldhe's initial hesitation.

But Nibulus merely sat astride his horse, his face still red with fury and frustration. How he yearned to howl at Bolldhe angrily, but he could hardly do so when the man had saved the life of the Nahovian, and possibly Methuselech too.

Instead, he handed the unused lance back to Finwald, and silently dismounted. He walked briskly up to his esquire, and kicked the crouching youth hard in the ribs. Sprawling across the path, Gapp squealed in pain and stared up with frightened eyes at the metal-clad warrior standing over him.

"You *EVER* do anything like that again," the Peladane spat, "I'll stick your head on a spike. Next time I order you to do something, you *do it bloody sharpish*! Xilva here could've died because of you!"

Suddenly a voice cut in harshly: "Don't take it out on him, Peladane, just because your own sport was thwarted!"

They all turned to see Wodeman glaring at Nibulus angrily. Gapp stared in surprise at this unexpected support. "Blame your lanky mercenary, instead," he went on. "Ogres never attack against the odds." He pointed an accusing finger at their leader. "Just remember that," he said.

Then before Nibulus could answer, he turned to Gapp. "Come on, Greyboots," he said in a gentler tone. "Get up off the ground."

Gapp still eyed Bolldhe with disgust. To witness that obscene screaming and hacking was like a waking nightmare, and he was still trembling with revulsion over it. But worse by far was that look in Bolldhe's eyes as he had set about his prey. Gapp could understand that fear might have motivated such a frenzied attack, but what made him shudder was seeing the mad glint of satisfaction still in the man's eyes.

And he isn't even a warrior!

Gapp turned to stare at the mangled corpse of the Ogre, steam rising in wreaths from the gaping wounds in its flesh. Paulus, still dazed, was pulled out from beneath its weight, and then several of them heaved the bloody carcass through the newly made breach in the rampart. The Ogre's remains slithered off the little bridge and disappeared into the foggy oblivion below, swallowed up by the night that had finally descended in full.

That night, none of them managed to get much sleep. After crossing the bridge, they had found a suitable cave, but the events of the evening had cast a cloud of gloom over their heads. The travelers were still too fired up with adrenaline to relax, and although none of them was seriously injured, the effort of battle had taken its toll.

Cautiously approaching the cave, they could see a fire burning within. Its warm glow drew them toward it as though they were under a glammer, and when they entered, they found Wodeman waiting for them. No one had even noticed him go on up ahead.

Gapp could get no sleep at all. He lay awake all night, going over in his head every detail of the shocking conflict, reliving each gory moment until he felt he would go mad. These waking nightmares haunted him through the hours of miserable darkness, cheating him of the sleep that both his body and mind desperately needed. By the time dawn broke over a colorless, craggy landscape, he felt more drained than he had felt before settling down for the night.

The next day passed by uneasily, a black cloud of tension hanging over the company throughout, silencing every attempt at conversation. There was a bad feeling among them. Nibulus rode alone at the head of the line, silent, sullen, his face set grimly against the wind that constantly buffeted them from the north. His esquire kept his distance, and even Nibulus's friends were reluctant to approach him.

He sighed inwardly, his face feeling uncomfortable with the frown it had worn since the battle on the bridge, for his was the sort of face upon which frowning sits ill.

Well, that was a lousy start, he reflected bitterly. *I only manage to get seven men to command, and I can't control even them!*

It had never been like this on his father's campaigns. He was a Thegne, and as such had the command of an entire Manass-Uilloch, a company of two and a half thousand soldiers. Two thousand five hundred well-trained Peladanes, brave and strong, every fifty—or Oloch—under the command of a sergeant. . . .

This lot were more like a gaggle of fishwives, and even the two mercenaries had managed to piss him off. It was definitely high time to sort out who was in control here, and to get his head around exactly how one goes about commanding civilians.

He could learn maybe from Schwei Dautchang, the seventeenth sultan of Qaladmir, who had listened to even the lowliest of men, asked their opinions, made out he was interested in them and their lives, and thus gained the love and devotion of a whole nation.

Or he could be like Stag-Headed Ichtatlus, the legendary Dragoon-Lord of Rhelma-Find, who had ruled by barbarous cruelty and slaughter inconceivable. *His* methods appealed to the pack mentality in humans; in other words, if you can raise the level of your clan's strength and cruelty above that of your rivals, your men see themselves as the elite and will follow your orders fanatically, even knowing how wrong it is, taking pleasure in its sheer extremeness. . . .

Wondering which style of leadership he should aim for, he again sighed, for Nibulus Wintus really did not possess the disposition for either.

Bolldhe rode at the rear, staring up at the lammergeyers that soared overhead, their huge wings filtering air with a sound like tearing silk. He remained as taciturn and unapproachable as ever. And as weary. So very weary. Far more than any of the others. They had been traveling for just over two weeks now, whereas he had been on the road for eighteen years. Eighteen long years of pointless traveling, wandering aimlessly from one place to another, without ultimately any real reason for doing so. Maybe there had been cause to travel years ago, when he had first set off, but not now. Now he only journeyed because there did not seem to be any good reason to stop.

Seven days after the fight with the hill giant, while riding along at possibly the highest point of the track so far, the party happened upon another cave. It was only late afternoon, but the horses were exhausted from this most arduous day's travel, so it was decided to make camp early. Their path, after all, was little likely to improve for some time yet.

All that day, and for three days before, they had stumbled along at a snail's pace. Steep rises, broken bridges, stretches of track that had fallen away down the mountainside decades or even centuries ago, boulders and scree-fall in their way, everything possible seemed to have conspired to hinder their route. The ancient and little-used path was deteriorating with every mile and, to make matters worse, it was still climbing.

That afternoon, while negotiating the fifth cliffside stretch that day, it had been so narrow and slippery that Finwald had nearly lost his horse. It took four of them—Nibulus, Methuselech, Wodeman, and himself—to haul the terrified Quintessa back onto the ledge. Contemplating this incident and others, their worsening and unavoidable situation was becoming a considerable strain.

On exploring the cave, they discovered that it was not so small as at first sight. Several recesses lined the main cavern, one of which turned out to be a narrow crack leading to a larger space than the outer cave itself. The dirt floor was strewn with dried grass and a gnawed bone or two, and was rank with the musk of some wild creature.

But for the present at least it was uninhabited. Bolldhe, being well used to spending nights in animals' lairs, recommended that they line the cave mouth with dry firewood, and keep a torch burning at all times to ignite if necessary. This suggestion was gladly (and hurriedly) taken up.

After such an arduous day's travel, no one might have felt bothered to prepare a meal. But they were all famished and cold, and soon their efforts had produced a good-sized fire and plenty of warm food. Though bland and uninteresting, their rations did manage to coax some spirit into the weary travelers, and it was not long before some of them were even in the mood for conversation.

"Well!" Methuselech began. "I don't know about you lot, but I feel much better for that!"

No response.

"What with good, warm food in me, and all," he continued, trying hard to sustain the levity in his voice.

Someone muttered something sarcastic about the weather being good for the time of year, but apart from this, nobody bothered to join in.

Methuselech persevered: "I feel almost fit enough to take on whatever revenge Skaane may inflict on us now for killing his pet . . . mmm."

His voice trailed away as a ruby-tailed wasp buzzed in through the cave
mouth, snooped around halfheartedly, then wandered off. The travelers watched
its every movement, in silence.

Then a small voice piped up from the back of the cave: "Who's Skaane?"
Gapp, in spite of himself, was still awake enough to be inquisitive.

"Skaane?" The desert mercenary brightened up again. "You've never heard
of the Great Ogre himself?"

Gapp inquired fearfully, "He doesn't live around here, does he?"

"No, no, no!" Methuselech laughed. "You've no need to worry on that
score, young Radnar. No, Skaane doesn't live *anywhere*. He never has. He's just
a story: Skaane the Great Hill Giant, fiercest of all mountain spirits—the Ogre
God himself. They worship him, in their strange way, offering sacrifices and
suchlike. Keeps them happy, I suppose. Like all pagan religions, just a bit of
harmless fun."

Crouching on the floor at the cave mouth, Wodeman laughed hoarsely.
"You've changed your tune. *'Harmless fun'!* According to what a little bird
told me, you were wetting yourself at the Grey Dog during the winnowing."

"Only because of those bloody hedgehogs." Methuselech smiled. "Tell me,
do *you* believe in Skaane? If you do, how come you're sitting so close to the
mouth of the cave? Aren't you worried he might suddenly appear and grab
you?"

The sorcerer chuckled strangely. "I don't believe any giant Ogre God
would want to harm *me*. And even if I did, I doubt this cave would be much
protection against it. No, I question Skaane's existence, but that is still no reason to mock. Hill giants may have a barbarous reputation, but they are all, like
us, children of Erce."

"You have to understand that Erce exists in countless forms," Finwald
joined in, enthusiastic all of a sudden, "depending on how the primitives interpret it. For some tribes it is a bison, a wolf, a tree, or even the sun. It all hinges
on the environment or needs of the tribe concerned. For your people, Methuselech, Erce is Uassise, Bringer of Gardens, and Shirraq, the Great Sand Elemental who leads the traveler—"

"Ordure."

"Ordure notwithstanding," Finwald insisted, "I have read much on the
subject."

"And you believe in it?"

"Of course not; it is a load of ordure. Cuna is the only way."

A snort from the cave mouth drew their attention. Wodeman glared toward
them, looking Finwald straight in the eye.

"You put too much faith in your bits of paper, priest. Whatever Erce is, he certainly cannot be imprisoned by leather-bound parchment. Erce can only be perceived by those close to him, those who live *in* him, those whose senses have not become fogged by ritual incense and darkness. You and your brethren are so inward-looking you have even less perception of the real world than a bunch of Aescal farmers."

"That was a bit cheap, wasn't it?" Nibulus put in, unexpectedly.

Surprisingly, Wodeman backed down a little. Aescal farmers were, indeed, a little "fogged," but it could be due to all the gin they drank. Because Nord-was a divided community, this had bred disillusionment and malaise in its citizens. Some followed the way of the Peladane, others inclined toward Cuna, but there was more than a hint of the old ways in many of the population still. Hence their age-old veneration of a kind of hefty venus figure: a lumpen female deity of bygone days, whose living embodiment could still be seen in just about every wide-buttocked fifteen-year-old farmer's daughter in Wyda-Aescaland.

As the sorcerer squatted upon his haunches on the floor of a stony cave high up in these lonely mountains, Gapp saw how his eyes glimmered like blood in the flickering firelight.

"You know what *we* call those fine horses of yours, Peladane?" he suddenly asked.

"Loef," Nibulus replied without hesitation. "It means 'Faithful.'" This much of Torca at least he did know, and he sat back, rather proud of himself.

"It means 'congregation,'" Wodeman corrected him, "or, to put it another way, 'faithful idiots.' We use the same word to describe their owners, too, *and* also the Lightbearers; you're all one in the same to us, herded into your stablelike temples like cattle, faithfully awaiting salvation like idiots . . ."

He trailed off, knowing by their quiet indignation that he had now gone too far.

Yet it seemed to Gapp that he did not talk of his religion with the fiery fanaticism of a zealot. Instead his was a quiet, confident faith that needed no ardor; a faith that came to him as naturally as water fed a spring, air stirred a breeze, or heat sprang from a flame.

Appa leaned closer to the fire, staring into the red tongues of flame gradu-ally consuming the crackling wood. He spoke up in a trancelike voice, as if see-ing things far away in time and space. Gapp could not be sure whether he was talking to them, to himself, or to some "other."

"Cuna has a purpose for each of us," he said, "and it is up to the individual to decide which path to follow. Freedom and Law are honored side by side; without the first, a man has no mind of his own; and without the second, coex-istence is impossible. Chance and Fate too must be honored. So our way is also one of Balance. But the way of Cuna is not the easiest; it may be beset by an un-ending succession of tests, distractions, or terrible hardships, even death. But one cannot follow Cuna only in times of peace, and set him aside when some other code seems preferable. Believe me, the true Lightbearer is the strongest one of all."

Even before Wodeman had the chance to sniff in disdain, Nibulus erupted in a snort of contempt: "Everything is Wrong unless *I* do it, you mean." Appa growled low, but did not make eye contact.

Bolldhe meanwhile had cocooned himself in his bedroll against the night, his back to them all. He seemed about as interested in their reflection as a cow would be in the buzzing of a bluebottle.

Deep within his bedroll, however, he was fully awake, and deep in thought. There was truth and fallacy in the dogmas of all three priests here. Finwald was right about Erce; he himself had witnessed so many aspects of the Earth Spirit, far more than were contained in the pages of the mage-priest's librams or tomes. But there were so many other religions, too, the countless cults and innumerable ideologies. How could even the wisest man make any sense out of it all?

Often he had tried to relate his life in some way to these various beliefs, but exactly where did he himself stand in relation to Good or Evil? Somehow the neutrality of Wodeman's "Erce" seemed more likely to him. He had, after all, always considered himself the eternal lone wolf. Was he, then, as Wodeman had hinted, a child of the Earth Spirit? Looking at the man, he somehow doubted it, but there was something about his words that rang true.

His gave up thinking about it. He was physically and mentally exhausted, and could no longer think straight. He put it down to traveling so closely with all these religious fanatics, each one of them trying to control his mind. He would have to watch them closely in the days to come.

But for now he just wanted to sleep. . . .

It was the dead of night, and a blanket of total silence had descended upon the mountains. There was no wind, no rattle of slithering slate fragments, not the remotest cry of beast or bird. The clouds that cloaked the mountain heights had both deadened any sound there might be and obscured the scant light radiating from the stars and crescent moon above.

Gapp sat alone at the mouth of the cave, staring out into the night in silent contemplation. He had been sitting thus, unmoving and hardly breathing, ever since he had been shaken awake by Paulus, nearly an hour ago, to take over the watch. The silence was so deep he could even hear his own heartbeat, and the darkness so complete he felt as if he might have gone blind. In fact he had been staring into this nothingness for so long now that he was beginning to forget what his companions, and friends back home, looked like, his tired and numbed mind failing to evoke any images of their faces. It was as if he had become all that was left in the universe, everything else having disappeared into the void.

It was a strange feeling, to be sure, just sitting here all alone, high up in a silent world of mountains in the depths of a timeless night, with mountain spirits crowding the edge of his mind, the beat of his heart counting out the seconds of his life, beat after beat after beat. He could not even see the outline of the cave mouth, the only assurance of facing the right way being the occasional, almost imperceptible stirring of air against his face.

He glanced behind him into the depths of the cave, seeing two glowing points of orange, the last embers of the dying campfire. He turned back toward the cave mouth, and was somewhat surprised that he could still see the same glowing points of fire, as if their images had engraved themselves upon the back of his eyes. They would gradually fade, of course, and again he would have nothing to focus on.

Suddenly he stiffened, the hairs on the back of his neck prickling. Those points of light were not fading, but were now moving about in front of him. A cold fear rose in him, and he blinked hard. When he opened his eyes again, the lights were gone.

He eased his stiff frame carefully and silently over to the dying fire and blew softly on its embers. He was suddenly very afraid of the night now, stuck up here in this alien cave on the roof of the world. As he coaxed the glowing embers, he assured himself that those two points of light were merely a trick his tired mind was playing on him. Either that or they were eyes belonging to some unnamable horror prowling just outside the cave mouth. The thought frightened him so much that he blew even more urgently on the brightening embers.

He even considered waking up one or two of his companions, but as quickly as this thought occurred to him, he rejected it. What would he tell them—that he had imagined a pair of eyes staring at him, and wanted someone to hold his hand? No, that would definitely not do, so in the meantime he continued to rebuild the fire, carefully and skillfully encouraging the whitening embers until before long his eyes were greeted by the welcome sight of dancing tongues of flame.

All the while he pushed from his mind the prickling sensation that ran continually from the nape of his neck to the base of his spine, warning him how exposed he was.

Once the fire was alight again and burning merrily, the esquire paused and breathed a sigh of relief. Ten minutes more and he would awaken Methuselech to take over the watch. Then maybe Gapp could sleep peacefully until morning. This night had lasted too long already.

All of a sudden, Gapp went cold. It was not a sensation felt externally, but rather from deep inside him, spreading outward from his heart to his extremities, as if his soul had been plunged into a pool of icy water. His neck hairs bristled like the hackles of a dog, and the odor of his own sweat wafted up into his dilated nostrils, as panic threatened to overtake him, though still he knew not why.

Then came the growl, so low it was more like an unspoken thought deep inside his mind than a vocal sound. Hardly daring to look, the boy slowly turned and forced himself to behold what lay behind him.

His heart stopped, and his whole body froze. For there, just outside the cave mouth, a whole pack of dark, wolflike forms now stalked backward and forward.

It was like a scene from his darkest nightmare manifesting itself into reality. There were at least a dozen large and shaggy forms out there, with lips curled back to reveal horrendous snarling fangs, and featureless eyes that smoldered like the burning coals of hell. They prowled barely within range of the firelight, like a melee of bestial mountain spirits whose thick fur, reflected in the flickering flames, took on the hue of running blood.

And beyond them stalked a larger, more evil shape, a creature that was not of wolf-kind, but one that must occasionally seek out their company. This monstrous hunchback form seemed to be covered in poisonous bristles, and in its massive head a pair of glowing eyes fixed on the stricken lowlander with such malevolence that he nearly passed out from fear.

But the paralysis evaporated as soon as he noticed these horrors were eyeing his sleeping companions, as if picking out their targets with cold calculation. He hurled himself at the nearest mound of blankets and frantically tore at the man's bedroll.

"WAKE UP! WAKE UP! WE'RE BEING ATTACKED!" he cried, though his shrill warning was nearly drowned by the sudden ferocious snarling from without. *Pel-Adan,* he prayed, *deliver me from this night!*

Immediately there was movement from the back of the cave as Bolldhe flung himself from his bedroll, leapt to his feet, and grabbed his axe in one swift, fluid movement, before even he was fully awake.

The next moment Nibulus, Paulus, Methuselech, and Wodeman were on their feet, reaching about in bleary-eyed confusion for their weapons. It was only as Gapp leapt to his master's side to hand him his greatsword, then scuttle to the back of the cave, that the two mage-priests stirred.

By now the night was filled with noise and fear. The cave echoed with the confusion of men shouting, horses screaming from the side chamber where they had been secured, metal ringing upon stone, and above it all the snarling of their assailants rose in volume and ferocity. A stench of such sickening corruption that it might have come from an overflowing cemetery now wafted in from the humpbacked, abominable monstrosity that ran with the wolves on this night. It stood now on its hind legs, and cackled insanely as the frightened humans stumbled over themselves in panic inside the cave.

The other beasts were advancing now, poised to attack, their eyes slitted with malice, powerful shoulders hunched, and hind legs tensed like coiled springs. With a suddenness and a speed that none would have believed possible, they launched themselves into the cave. Claws extended and jaws snapping, they piled headlong into the startled company, hurling them backward or bowling the slower ones over. A chorus of panic went up as someone trampled through the fire, scattering the burning faggots across the floor in a shower of sparks that lit up the cave in a sudden frenzy of dancing light, and illuminated the walls in a furious, moving pattern of orange and black.

The battle lasted only a few moments, but exactly what happened during that time was anybody's guess. Of all the company Gapp probably had the clearest idea, as he cowered at the back of the cave.

Bolldhe, who retained his sharp wits even after sudden arousal from sleep, met the initial onslaught with the instinctive, swift reactions born of years of experience of sudden nighttime raids. He stood his ground until the last moment, then sidestepped with the speed of an adder, and in the same movement brought the blunt edge of his axe head up in a sweep that hurled his startled and yelping adversary back out through the cave mouth.

Nibulus, Paulus, and Methuselech, bearing the brunt of the attack, were now all on the ground in a confused tangle of flailing limbs. Nibulus hurled two assailants from him in one mighty lunge, then, free of his armor, scrambled agilely to his feet and brought his blade fully to bear. A fierce light burned in his eyes and, wholly possessed by the thrill of combat, he would not be denied the change to vent his pent-up anger now after the fiasco of Estrielle's Stair.

Then the night grew even darker and more evil as the huge humped leader battered its way in. It was massive and deformed, with a mottled and ragged pelt that was riddled with maggots and hung in tatters about its ravaged frame; in its eyes burned the fires of the Abyss of Pandemonium.

It was Paulus, already beset by a particularly large wolf, who was singled out by this night horror. It swept the wolf aside, and leapt upon the grounded mercenary with its jaws opened ridiculously wide. Almost unbelievably, Paulus showed no panic, seeming almost to take everything in his stride. He seized a firm grip on the beast's windpipe, and while he held the snapping jaws away from his face, he delivered several savage kicks to its underside.

Of the three, only the desert man was foundering. Two of the wolves had him pinned on his back, with no chance to get to his feet, and had inflicted several deep and nasty wounds to his hands and forearms as he desperately tried to fend them off.

Over against the cavern wall Finwald and Appa stood side by side, striking back at their attackers from the comparative shelter of an arched opening leading into another section of the cave. Finwald brandished his sword cane, already bloodied from the deep gash he had scored on one attacker's shoulder, while Appa now felled his own opponent with one sharp blow of his crow's-beak staff to its skull. Clearly he had some experience in dealing with wild animals, and, with his cloak thrown back to reveal skinny but wiry arms, he suddenly did not appear quite so frail.

Amid their struggle to stay alive, Wodeman was leaping about like a mad thing, his arms flailing above his head, his hair flying wild. He chanted and

snarled, whooped and whistled, as if caught in the throes of demonic posses-
sion. Wolves would hurl themselves at this lunatic, only to stop dead before
him and cower back, snapping, snarling and whining in confusion, unable to
break past the strange spell that warded them off.

But more of the beasts still came loping into the cave, while yet more yam-
mered hysterically outside. The situation was becoming desperate, and
Methuselech was in the direst straits of all. With his neck, arms, and chest lacerated, his shirt torn and blood-soaked, he was rapidly weakening and crying
out in fear.

Bolldhe, too, was in trouble, beset now by three adversaries lunging and
feinting on all sides, waiting for him to tire and his defenses to weaken. His
back against the wall, the traveler was growing more desperate with each
wasted effort.

Only Paulus seemed unharried, as yet. Still on the ground with the monster
atop him so that no other beast could reach him, the Nahovian was slowly
strangling the life out of the wide-eyed, gurgling monster he held scrabbling
helplessly in a viselike grip.

Gapp stared in disbelief, too terrified to move. His companions were
locked in mortal combat, while all he could do was cower there and watch
them being gradually torn to pieces . . .

. . . At which point he would be alone.

It was this thought that finally goaded him into action. His hand slipped
down to the hilt of one of his throwing knives, and he felt the smoothness and
firmness of its grip. Drawing upon the seed of courage that swelled within him,
he yanked the little blade free, aimed it at the nearest wolf, gathered every
ounce of fierceness he could muster, and *threw.* . . .

It was a desperate shot, but the boy was well practiced, and the deadly pro-
jectile buried itself in the shoulder of one of Methuselech's attackers.

Howling in rage and pain, the wolf broke away from the bloodied desert
man, then spotted Gapp and, with a snarl of pure hatred, leapt toward the
wide-eyed squire.

Before he even realized what he was doing, Gapp whipped out the shortsword and aimed it before him. A deep, liquid cry broke from the wolf's throat
as it bore him to the ground; then the beast fell away from him lifelessly, the
blade thrust into its gullet up to the hilt.

Gapp stared at the quivering animal at his feet in dumb surprise. He had
made his first kill!

Suddenly there was a terrific roar as of a mighty wind, and a blinding explosion of golden-red light banished the darkness of the night utterly. A great
wall of fire had sprouted from the floor where the barrier of dry firewood had
been placed only hours earlier. The sulfurous flames blazed like a beacon, seal-
ing off the cave mouth with a searing sheet of fire. All turned as one to stare at
this terrifying spectacle in shock.

All, that is, except Finwald, whose eyes glittered fiercely in the reflected light his spell had ignited.

Immediately the fight drained out of the wolves. They broke off their attack and ran panic-stricken about the cave, snapping at whichever men threatened them, snapping at the flames that held them here, even snapping at each other in their frenzy. Paulus momentarily loosened his grip and the monster tore itself free.

Their assault gone to pieces, they were now easy prey for the humans. Paulus, his deformed features livid with bloodlust, wasted no time in springing over to retrieve his black sword, then falling upon the two panicked beasts nearest him. . . .

Nibulus, following the Nahovian's lead, kicked away the remaining wolf savaging Methuselech so hard that the snapping of its spine was audible. Bolldhe succeeded in ridding himself of his three assailants by cleaving the head of one of them, which sent the other two bolting away from him in such terror that they hurled right through the wall of fire, and ran smoldering and howling off into the night.

The remaining predators followed their example, for the choice was clear. Stay here and die or endure the discomfort of a singed pelt for the next few weeks. Even their choking, staggering leader managed to collect its wits enough to hurl itself through the flames.

Screams of agony and rage rose into the night, echoing horribly throughout the gullies and crevices of the Blue Mountains, as the fleeing wolf pack sprinted madly down the path, or toppled over the precipice to plunge, burning, like shooting stars in the night sky.

For the next few minutes the cave rang with disorder. The sudden attack had left them all shaken, and in Methuselech's case only half-conscious. To be awoken to such a vicious attack was bad enough; to be subjected to a display of such arcane magic from one of their own number was downright unnerving. A strange look, almost of sadness, or nostalgia, shone in Finwald's eyes as he peered out from under the straggling mane of hair that had fallen across his face. He was back in Qaladmir now, the acrid smell of chemicals filling his brain. It would be a while before he was fully back among them.

Dazed they were, to be sure, but not overconfused. No one argued as the Peladane barked out a torrent of orders. Paulus hurriedly built a new line of firewood across the cave mouth, in case of a fresh attack. Bolldhe was put on guard just outside the entrance, for clearly he was far more suited to this task than the boy, who remained skulking in the deeper recesses, "tending to the horses." Had he not felled one of Methuselech's attackers and possibly saved his life, Nibulus might have thrown him out of the cave along with the dead wolves. As it was, he was keeping well out of everybody's way.

It was a pity, for if he *had* dared to look up at his master he might have noticed a grudging respect in the man's eyes. Gapp had, after all, notched up his first kill, but Nibulus was not about to let him off too easily. The esquire had seriously failed them, and would therefore strive all the harder to earn his master's respect. That was just how the Peladane liked it.

But first there was the more pressing matter of Methuselech. Of all the party, only he had received serious injury. Appa and Wodeman busily cleaned his lacerations and applied sutures and bandages, while Methuselech himself lay back, groaning, with his eyes shut fast and teeth clenched stoically. After Appa finished bandaging him, he spread his outstretched hands over the man's wounds. A faint, orange-yellow glow shone from his palms, and Methuselech sighed comfortably as he drifted into sleep.

"Maybe you should try this sort of thing occasionally, Finwald," the irate priest admonished darkly, "instead of dabbling in your firework displays—I thought you grew out of that sort of thing twelve years ago. I've warned you before, it's not right, especially for a follower of Cuna. You play with fire, and fire will end up playing with you. . . ."

Finwald responded by dismissing his elder with a wave of his hand. (Some of the others flinched in case some new burst of magic should accidentally fly from his fingertips.) He grinned, and did not retaliate. He did, however, give Bolldhe a long, meaningful look, as if to say: "Remember! We're not going to get very far by *healing* our way to Drauglir."

Nobody noticed the cloaked figures staring down at them.

High up on the ridge on the other side of the gully they stood, a line of watchers, most dressed in grey, and one in yak skin. Elemental forces surrounded them, tugging frantically at their impenetrable cloaks, and danced around them in a howling discord shrill with the sounds of night. Silent and unmoving, the watchers stared down at the cave and its inhabitants. Had anyone ventured nearby they would have still gone unnoticed, for these were a part of the night itself, intangible, imperceptible. Save perhaps for the two glimmerings of reddish light that glowed from deep within the yak-kirtled one's eyes.

He turned to gaze at the line of watchers alongside him, still and silent as standing stones.

"Eight weeks old is the game now, Lord." Finally came a voice that cut effortlessly through the shrieking wind. "Two moons since those pieces were set in motion."

"Yes, eight weeks," he replied. "Eight weeks, eight moons, eight years . . .'tis of the meagerest importance so early in the quest. It is what befalls them at the very end that matters. Mistakes made now can only be for the good, for they serve as lessons for the final resolution."

"But surely it is at the beginning that the direction of all journeys is set. Have you not heard the maxim 'A river cannot flow back on itself'?"

"A *river* has no choice whither it flows. Bolldhe, however, is a man of the *road,* so can backtrack at will."

The line of watchers did not waver. "Let us hope for your sake he can, for so far he shows little sign of taking the path you set for him."

"He is being led astray," Red-Eye protested hotly. "Other forces are interfering which I had not envisioned. These are ills I had not foreseen!"

A hiss almost like laughter issued from the vocal watcher's hood. "You mean the sorcerer?" it whispered gratingly. "Indeed, sundry factions have come into play, it would seem. And what does Bolldhe himself make of it? Erce-sent and armed with potent reveries, the Torca comes to lure Bolldhe to the Way of the Earth Spirit, and already fertile seeds have been sown in his mind. Your man even wonders if he is indeed a tool of Erce. And, look you, his dreams have not yet even commenced!"

But Red-Eye refused to manifest his frustration on hearing the Syr's galling words. He knew the entity to be totally impassive, yet that hint of mockery in its tones could be sometimes *so . . .* He often wondered if the Skela had been granted a sense of humor by the One that came before.

Refusing to be drawn, he continued: "The treachery that lies within the company is as a mormal upon a shinne, and it engenders a humor most adverse in him. He is being lured along as though by a serpent with many heads. Were the mage-priests united to their aims, things might develop as I had planned. But now we have the sorcerer to contend with, and *that* was totally unforeseen."

"A mormal upon a shinne," the Syr echoed. "An unusual metaphor; but who exactly is the mormal? Who is the treacher? Is it the sorcerer, or one of your priests? Or it could be any other of the sundry members of this band of perfidious churls? Indeed, are you so even sure that there is but *one* treacher here? You say he is waylaid by a many-headed serpent, but it seems more that he is torn apart like a stag between a pack of wolves. Maybe you will even discover Bolldhe himself is the quisling."

Finally Time spoke out. "The game is but eight weeks old, an insufficient period of testing from which to draw a meaningful conclusion, as you say, but sufficient to reveal to us enough of the psyche of your man Bolldhe. He walls himself off from his fellows, he is violently unpredictable; he knows not what to believe, flitting from one notion to another as a fledgling plays amongst the boughs of springtime. The divide between your priests confuses him, though in truth he does incline towards the reasoning of Finwald. But the Dream-Sorcerer manages to befuddle him, and it is within himself that the most significant problem lies. We know now your true reasoning in choosing this man as your tool, but we fear your judgment is awry. This man clearly cannot find *himself,* and thus cannot hope to succeed."

Red-Eye turned away to gaze at the cave wherein lay his last slim thread of hope, fraying with each day that passed. Though he said nothing to the Skela, he silently agreed.

There was a movement at his side, and he turned to see that the wolves had returned. Their leader at their head, they padded gingerly toward him upon singed paws, and one by one collapsed at his feet. Though they did not perceive him in any real sense, yet there was a feeling of comfort and sanctuary where he stood. That was reason enough for the dispirited beasts to tarry awhile.

As they licked their wounds, they occasionally glanced in the direction of the warm, fire-lit cave, listening to the dim sound of human voices from within. The leader's pale eyes were bright with intelligence, and now smoldered with a deep hatred. The sound of its enemies' voices drew forth a half-audible growl of bitterness. The hunt was far from over, and the new day scant hours away.

5

The Valley of Sluagh

"We should be in sight of the Northlands by tonight, I think."

Wodeman was perched high on a rocky outcrop above their path, his face lifted to the sky, sniffing the air. Ahead, the path wound away for a short distance before disappearing up into a narrow cleft, and was then lost from view. To their right, a scree-covered slope rose up to a distant ridge. Behind them, somewhat obscured by the dust of their passing, the path fell away down the steep pass that had brought them here, so high up among the Blue Mountains' highest peaks. And to their left the ground simply dropped away down a sheer cliff face, affording them the most stunning, panoramic view of purple and blue mountain peaks, of pale, sun-flecked bluffs down which cascaded countless waterfalls, and steep, pine-forested slopes sweeping down toward dark shrouded gullies, all stretching from one end of the horizon to the other in one wide sweep of breathtaking, wild beauty.

All day they had traveled up here along the highest level of the path. Here, their route was at its steepest and most dangerous, often deteriorated to such a state that it was almost undetectable, whereupon they had to trust to their own instinct to find their way forward. Sometimes broader, sometimes narrower, but always covered in loose rocks or blocked by falls of boulders, the path wound its arcane way northward, along knife-edge ridges that fell away steeply on either side, up funnel-shaped passes that echoed eerily the sharp crack of stone impacting on stone, halfway up cliffs upon ledges that were so narrow as to be almost nonexistent, and through dark gullies that rose sheer on either side, their confining darkness softened only dimly by the band of daylight from high above.

A strange silence pervaded the whole region. The air was thin and unnourishing. Up here they had come to a place that was too high even for the mountain goats. It was as if they had ventured into a world so elevated and so removed from the rest of the world that life and movement, even sound, just did not occur here, were things alien and unwanted. Every rock and crag seemed to be listening, glaring down at the puny little invaders in stony silence. Every clattering, clumsy step they took was magnified tenfold in this unfriendly place, and the company was feeling very ill-at-ease. They did not talk. They slowed their breathing. They picked their way with deliberation and care. But still their subdued racket went on, filling the void of stillness to mark their passage more conspicuously than any beacon.

Occasionally they would spy dark cave mouths high above them, where no path could run, out of which thin lines of smoke wound lazily into the sky. Pillars of rocks placed crudely one upon another stood by like sentinels, pagan and ancient. The place smelled of dragons, gryphons, and Ogres. All conversation ceased, and they wasted no time in going on their way.

The attack the previous night had shaken all of them badly. An assault by wolves outside winter was unnerving enough in its strangeness, but it was the creature leading them that had scared them most of all.

"Leucrota," Paulus had explained. "They prowl around our villages at night, attracted by the smell of our tree-hung corpses. But our dead are not for *their* sort, and if we catch them, we purge their innards with hot coals."

Leucrota were a legend Bolldhe had already heard of in northern lands. Normally solitary creatures that could be found skulking among the headstones of graveyards, hungrily digging up newly or not so newly interred corpses. He had hoped he would go to his own grave without ever encountering one and, remembering Paulus's deft handling of the monster, he made a mental note never to antagonize the Nahovian.

Wodeman scrambled down from his vantage point to land lightly upon the track below. "Yes," he said, "unless my nose deceives me, we should get to look upon the lowlands before sunset—but only if we get a move on."

This announcement was met with tired but grateful smiles of relief from all. The Blue Mountains were undeniably beautiful in their way, but right now it was a beauty they would rather appreciate from lower down.

Nibulus regarded the sorcerer quizzically. "You can smell the lowlands from here?"

"Of course!" Wodeman chuckled. "The smell of the marshlands is unmistakable. If you and your ancestors had spent less time shut away in your smoky halls and stony castles, and more out in the *real* world, you might be able to smell the lowlands too."

Nibulus laughed. "Remind me to berate my ancestors when I meet them in the next world, and may you be standing there with me when I do so!" He clapped the sorcerer roughly on the shoulder, almost knocking the wind out of him.

Everyone was noticeably happier; their mood up until now had been very tense and uncommunicative. The thought of further attacks from wolves or Ogres remained uppermost in their mind, with scant cover, up here among the peaks, from any dreadful winged beast that might swoop on them from above.

And if that were not enough, the problem of Methuselech's injuries was becoming crucial. He had received some serious lacerations the previous night and, had it not been for the combined healing powers of Appa and Wodeman, he might well have died. While Appa had knelt over the groaning man and poured out his most heart-wrung and brow-sweating petitions to his deity, Wodeman had enlisted the young esquire to help in his herb-searching.

"Greyboots," he had urged, "do you know of the plant *athelsfut*?"

Gapp had stared at the shaman blankly.

"It is a small, dandelion-like species, to you maybe just a weed, with a thin, wispy ginger growth of seeds that can easily blow away on the wind."

"Oh yes," Gapp replied excitedly. "In Nordwas we call it young-man's-beard."

"See if you can find some," Wodeman urged. "It may help to slow Xilva's bleeding."

The herb had been found, the infusion prepared, and the monotonous praying continued. Yet still, a day later, Methuselech remained doubled over in pain as his wounds healed over, and the forced ride through the mountains was cheating him of the proper convalescence he so urgently needed. His normally healthy, brown face was now a sickly grey, and he spent most of the time slumped listlessly over his mount, allowing the horse to pick its own way after the others.

But now Wodeman's news at least made him smile. The priests, too, forgot their differences of the past day, and beamed at each other in friendship and solidarity. Even the taciturn Paulus temporarily put away his disagreeable aspect, and chuckled in anticipation.

Only Bolldhe was unmoved. He remained apart from the company at their rear, gripping the haft of his broadaxe anxiously, while rueing such eagerness to consider their mountain trek as good as over. They could still be several days away from actually *leaving* the uplands, and anything could happen to them between now and then. He himself had traveled through more mountain ranges than he could remember and, despite what the others believed, he realized they had been lucky to encounter so little trouble so far.

As they mounted their horses again to set off through the cleft, Bolldhe nervously glanced behind him. He could not be sure, but he thought he had caught sight of something moving back there. With a shake of his head, he spurred his horse on to rejoin the company.

About two-thirds of the way up a sheer cliff that must have been over a thousand feet high, the path took them in a series of twists, turns, rises, and falls toward the final ridge that curtained their view of the lowlands beyond. The craggy line of purple rock, hazy in the midafternoon heat, looked tantalizingly close, but they were all aware of the dangerous drop to their left. And the path ahead looked dangerous; they had needed to pick their way carefully over its unsure surface for the last mile or so, and from what they could make out ahead, it did not look as if it was about to improve for a long way. Soberly the company continued, well aware that this would not be a good place to get caught in.

Suddenly a cry of alarm went up at the rear from the ever-vigilant Bolldhe. "The wolves! They're right behind us."

There was an instant of stunned silence, then a flurry of activity. Nibulus squeezed his bulky horse past the other steeds to get nearer to Bolldhe, while the rest of them twisted around on their mounts to stare back down the track.

"Not possible!" Finwald breathed. "After last night, they would not dare. . . ."

"*Very* possible," Bolldhe corrected him. "These are mountain wolves, and have been known to track and pull down a Rock Dragon. And the Leucrota won't have forgot its defeat; it won't leave us until we are dead."

Sure enough, the distant shapes of fleeting wolves could now be made out behind them, occasionally flitting out of the shadows of the cliff into the evening's softened light. They were about a mile away, but moving fast.

"Xhite," Nibulus cursed softly. "That's all we need. . . ."

His veteran's eyes swiftly and expertly surveyed their position. The path they followed was narrow indeed, and forced them to ride single-file. This would have suited the big warrior fine if the cliff that rose up to their right were sheer, for he could have held the wolves back single-handedly, going one-on-one. But the cliff was not sheer, though too steep for their horses to climb, and also too steep to allow him to try out his Thresher. It was not too steep for wolves, however, and while the men and horses were strung out in a line, the wolves would be able to approach and attack them broadside, driving them against the edge of the path and the awful drop below.

Lacking the maneuverability, speed, and numbers of their pursuers, they would be overwhelmed. If he were to do anything to prevent that, the Peladane would have to act fast.

"Xilva!" he called out to his friend at the other end of the line. "Lead everyone further on, as fast as you can, and don't stop till I catch up with you. But Paulus and Wodeman, I'll need you two here."

It was the best he could think of under such duress.

"Good luck, Fatman," Methuselech called back, spurring Whitehorse unsteadily forward along the rocky path. Zhang, bearing Bolldhe, did not wait to be told and, on his nimble, trowel-shaped hooves, scrambled along the steep bank of scree to overtake all the other horses that were now hastening after Methuselech. The slough horse felt no remorse whatsoever at leaving the Peladane's hated, fancy warhorse to the mercy of the rapidly approaching wolf pack.

In the same instant, Paulus and Wodeman were ranged with Nibulus. Paulus dismounted now and crouched a few feet up the bank, covering Nibulus's flank, his sword drawn and waiting eagerly. Though normally unwilling to risk his life on behalf of others, he was nevertheless gratified to have been acknowledged as the most skillful fighter among them. He and the Peladane had fought side by side on previous occasions, and though there was not much love between them, there was at least mutual respect; they were both expert killers, and together, they could be deadly.

And, apart from all that, the mercenary was just itching to choke the life out of the wolf-pack leader. He still had a score to settle there.

Wodeman had already anticipated how his services would be required, and positioned himself just in front of the two warriors, facing back the way they had come.

"Take your time, Wodeman," Nimbus instructed. "We're right behind you. Why not do something scary, like that fire-wall thing Finwald did earlier?"

Wodeman glanced back at him sharply. "I don't know anything about such 'fire-wall' stuff," he protested. "I'm a *sorcerer*!"

Nibulus leaned forward menacingly on his saddle. "It's all just magic, isn't it? What's the difference? If you can't do something decent like that, then what bloody use *are* you to us?"

Wodeman let out a slightly mad whimper of a laugh, unable to decide which appalled him more: the vengeful pack in front of him or the stupidity of the Peladane behind him. He had always known the man's sort were ignorant, but *this* . . . ?

"I will do the best I can," he replied. "Watch, and stay absolutely still."

The two warriors patiently did as they were bidden, and Wodeman slowly drew himself up to his full height. With eyes closed, he breathed in the cool mountain air, held his breath for a few seconds, then gradually released it from his lungs.

Nibulus and Paulus looked at each other doubtfully as the wolves drew closer. Yet the sorcerer did not appear to be doing anything much to avert them.

. . . the inward contemplation of silence . . .

Then a slight wind began to stir from the path before them, carrying with it the snarling rumor of the nearing pack, hungry with the promise of blood. Wodeman yet remained as still as a tree, the only movement about him being the wind-ruffled stirring of his wolf's-head cloak, and the slight flickering of his eyelids.

. . . the stilling of the soul . . .

The pack was now dangerously close. As the warriors readied their swords they could count at least a dozen of the beasts leaping nimbly toward them, with many more visible in the distance. Still the sorcerer stood ramrod-straight against the increasing breeze that swept through the gully.

Paulus, his coat snapping in the wind, cast a black look at the mounted warrior at his side. "I truly hope that your faith in this shaman is well founded, because he seems to be cutting it a bit fine for my liking."

Nibulus ignored him, biting his lip.

. . . the submergence of the consciousness, all essential for the evocation of magic . . .

Then, just as the first of the wolves, led by the Leucrota, bounded into clear view, Wodeman held out one hand and began to rotate his extended index finger rapidly before his face. A low, whistling moan rose from deep within his throat, blending perfectly with the sound of the wind that had nearly turned into a gale.

All that could be heard now was its sudden shrieking as it whipped up dust and billowed out their cloaks. The air gradually became alive with inhuman voices that drowned out all other sounds. Nibulus held an arm up to his face, as Wodeman concluded his somatic entreaty to the elements.

Suddenly, with only scant seconds before the pack reached them, a dark shape appeared between the men and their adversaries—a conical vortex of dust that manifested itself out of the very air to block the path.

Just then the Leucrota leaped straight for Wodeman's throat. . . .

Up ahead, Appa and Gapp were desperately coaxing their ponies on with promises, threats, and copious amounts of cursing. Far beyond rode Finwald on the fleeter-footed Quintessa, following Bolldhe, whose impatient mount Zhang kept trying to squeeze itself past Methuselech, still in front.

Through slitted, wind-moist eyes the Southern mercenary tried to focus on the path ahead, but with each jolt of his stumbling horse, pain was clouding his vision. Trying to control the jittery Whitehorse was becoming an increasingly impossible task, and he felt he was slipping into a dream world in which time slows down almost to the point of stopping, its passing marked only by each heart-jolting scare as both horse and rider nearly slid over the edge.

Bolldhe, however, was intent on saving his own skin, one thing in his life he knew he was an expert at.

Zhang needed no coaxing and indeed was given free rein by his rider, who trusted his mount completely to get them both out of this one. The slough horse was bred to this sort of landscape, and knew far better what he was capable of than did his rider. Enthusiastically, and of one mind, both man and beast set about putting as much ground as possible between them and their doomed companions, unhindered by any scruples of guilt.

That was till they spotted about a score of ravening wolves massing *ahead* of them also, leaping down the path toward them.

At about the same time that Bolldhe realized the whole company was trapped Methuselech went stumbling blindly onward, oblivious of Bolldhe's shouted warnings. Nibulus and the rear guard meanwhile were still fighting for their lives.

Wodeman had successfully invited the Air Elemental among them, but from then on his control of the situation began to slide. Before it had time to comprehend its rashness, the Leucrota had launched itself headfirst into the very midst of the whirlwind.

Instantly the babbling monstrosity disappeared from sight, and then, amid the cyclonic howling of the vortex, a terrified screeching and cracking of bones could be heard. A second later the blurred shape of the broken Leucrota was catapulted, like a rock from a trebuchet, off the path to disappear, spiraling into the yawning gorge below.

"Bastard!" cried Paulus indignantly. "That one was mine!"

Unable to halt their headlong momentum, the three wolves immediately following the Leucrota into the fight also followed it into the outer currents of the Elemental, and were similarly whipped up in the same spinning, yelping, bone-cracking frenzy as their leader.

While the expectant wayfarers looked on with excited but fearful eyes, the first wolf reemerged from the spinning cone. Flung in the opposite direction from its leader, it crunched against the rocky slope with bone-shattering impact, then whimpered briefly, and died.

"Such power!" Nibulus whispered, in awe, despite himself.

The second to be ejected was hurled back into the path of the oncoming pack, crashing right into their midst. The impact felled one of them, and knocked another over the edge and into the hungry abyss below.

The third beast, unexpectedly and with stunning velocity, was slung directly into the sorcerer himself. With the full weight of a mountain wolf cannoning straight into his body, Wodeman was knocked back with such force that he slammed into Paulus behind him. Hammerhoof reared up, staggering backward a few paces on his hind legs; then all three defenders went down like skittles.

Immediately the Air Elemental slowed, shrank, and then stopped. With a sigh it departed. The spell was instantly over.

Moments later, Nibulus looked up dazedly, to find himself pinned beneath the dead weight of his own warhorse. His greatsword was lying on the path several feet away. Wodeman lay just beyond, while Paulus's mare was nonchalantly trotting off up the path. Paulus himself appeared to have slid right over the edge.

And then there were the wolves, a whole pack of them still, just a few yards away, approaching slowly.

"Methuselech!" Bolldhe yelled as loud as he could. "Come back! It's a trap!"

Methuselech, however, was clearly in another world now as Whitehorse continued lurching headlong toward the waiting wolf pack.

Bolldhe reined Zhang to a standstill, scratched the back of his neck thoughtfully, then without too much agonizing, turned back. He fancied his chances now far better with the two warriors and the sorcerer than with any of the others in their group.

A perplexed and extremely fretful Finwald was the first of them he encountered.

"Bolldhe," he demanded, "what's going on?"

"We've just fallen for the oldest trick in the book," Bolldhe replied hurriedly. "The wolf pack's split up—other half's just up ahead."

Finwald gasped in disbelief, his faded brown complexion losing what little color it had to start with. "But—"

"No time for buts," Bolldhe snapped as Zhang squeezed on past, almost forcing Finwald's Quintessa over the cliff. "We must get back to the Peladane if we're going to get out of this."

"But where's Xilvafloese?" the priest demanded. Against all rules of his race's pigmentation, his face was now pure white.

"I don't know," snarled Bolldhe, riding full-tilt back down the path. "What's his religion?"

"Oh, Cuna save us all!" Finwald breathed heavily, and straightaway turned the whinnying Quintessa to follow Bolldhe. The pure white of his skin had now developed faint traces of blue.

By the time they had rejoined Appa and Gapp, and herded them, too, back down the path, Methuselech was already forgotten. He was barely conscious now, with his face buried in the horse's mane; only instinct kept his hands gripped on the reins. His mount was now picking its own way.

Whitehorse snorted in sudden fear and stopped dead in his tracks, stamping his hooves on the dusty ground. The way ahead was blocked by a whole new pack of wolves, and they were less than half a minute away. The horse screamed in alarm; the track here was so narrow he could not hope to turn around, and even if he could, he would never outrun the sprinting wolves. And his master was no help at all, slumped across his back and oblivious of the danger they were in.

It was just then that a gust of damp-smelling air wafted out of the cliffside just in front of his nose. Nostrils dilated and ears pricking forward, the horse turned his head to one side and saw a split in the rock face. It was the narrowest of clefts, and had he not paused here he would have simply passed it by. The cleft, however, was just wide enough for a horse to squeeze through, and the moist air that issued from it smelled as if it came from a long way down.

The horse could now hear menacing growls from the wolves as they sensed that their quarry was attempting to escape. As they increased their pace along the stony path, without further hesitation Whitehorse maneuvered his ungainly bulk into the gap, and entered farther into the cleft.

At once, he was brought up sharp. There was something about the smell of this new place that roused fear in his dull, equine brain, and warned him to stay well clear. Whether it was the way in which the currents of cold, damp air clung to him with their clammy embrace, or the scent of something ancient and long-forgotten down below, Whitehorse could not discern. But there was definitely a "presence" here that caused his instinct to scream at him to flee, and take his chances outside in the open.

Whitehorse was not accustomed to making decisions for himself, but a terrible snarl, sounding alarmingly close, made his mind up in an instant. With one last look behind him at the world of light, he threw caution to the wind, and disappeared deeper into the cleft.

Immediately he was engulfed in a chilling darkness that surrounded him like the black hand of death. The vestigial warmth of the late afternoon was gone as quickly as if it had never been, but the vicious clamor of the thwarted wolves, now reaching the mouth of the cleft, propelled him on farther into the darkness.

Behind him the pack went berserk with fury at losing their prey, snapping at the entrance to the cleft in frustration. But they knew all too well about the dark places of the Blue Mountains, and nothing would get them to follow the horse down *there*.

But Whitehorse knew nothing of these fears, and plunged on and on into the darkness. He could hardly see a thing ahead, but was goaded on by the shuddering howls from behind. In his panic he did not realize they had already given up the chase; and, as long they were still within earshot, he was not even going to think about stopping.

There followed a nightmare for the terrified beast, racing through a chilling, cobwebby dankness that tore the breath from his lungs as if he had plunged into the waters of an icy black lake. His choice, such as it was, having been made, he kept galloping onward over the slippery wet rocks to whatever awaited below.

Nibulus had to think hard and fast. In fact he probably thought harder and faster than he had ever thought in his life. But as he lay there, his legs pinned beneath the dead weight of Hammerhoof, and stared fixedly into the hypnotic eyes of the predators just yards away, the sum total of all this hard cogitation merely amounted to a frenzied: *Oh hell, I'm going to die!*

He tried to haul his numbed legs out from under the horse, but the animal, clearly not about to get up for some time, was far too heavy to shift. He tried to stretch one arm back far enough to grab his sword, but it was just too far away, and in any case he would not have been able to wield it from this supine position. He roared for help as loudly as he could, but the only voice that responded was the echo of his own.

Nibulus arched his head back, desperately scanning his surroundings for anything that might help him. It was then that he spotted Paulus's bastard sword lying upon the path where the mercenary had dropped it as he fell. It was a sword of renowned sharpness, he knew, and could be used in a pinch. . . .

He stretched his arm over as far as it would go. If he could only reach it, he might be able to convince the wolves that this was one prey better left alone. Or at the very least, he might go down with some dignity befitting a Peladane, instead of being torn apart like a snared badger back home, set upon by a pack of hunting dogs and their turnip-brained, beetroot-faced Aescal "masters."

But the straps of his armor constricted his movement, snagging painfully at his arm so that he could not hope to reach the blade.

As yet the wolves seemed unsure as to what to do. The complete and swift removal of their leader had changed things, for clearly the Leucrota had been their guiding influence. Some merely crouched there, ready to make a run for it should any further display of magic threaten. Others had already decided not to risk finding out and these scampered off.

But it was the third group that was most worrying, for they kept slinking forward tentatively on their bellies, undecided if their target was capable of magic.

If only I could convince them that I can, thought Nibulus desperately, and instinctively raised his gauntleted hand before him and began rotating his index finger in the same way he had seen Wodeman do. It was a bluff that would use up his lifetime's supply of luck, if it worked, but it was all he could think of at this time.

Some of the undecided ones promptly made up their minds, and hurried away back down the path. The rest froze, but still remained uncertain.

To add emphasis, Nibulus now began imitating the sonorous chanting of the sorcerer. He did not know the precise words to the spell, as it was of some strange, archaic woodland tongue he could not hope to comprehend, but then he doubted very much that the wolves did either. He improvised as best he could, and chanted so loudly and earnestly that he began to feel himself being transported along with the magic of the spell. He even started to believe in it himself.

To his utter amazement, it actually appeared to be working. Those last few wolves finally turned and slunk off with their tails between their legs, and were soon gone.

Nibulus stared after them in incredulity, hardly daring to believe what he had just accomplished. "If only *you* could have seen that," he declared to the unconscious shaman sprawled out on the path up ahead.

The smile of satisfaction suddenly vanished from his florid face when he heard a stifled grunt nearby. He snapped his head around to scan the edge of the path, but saw nothing.

"Who's there?" he demanded, confused.

"Who the . . . bloody hell do you think?" came the voice again, more clearly. "It's me, Paulus! I'm here . . . just below the ledge and I . . . don't think I can hold on . . . much longer. . . ."

But there was nothing Nibulus could do to help him, stuck as he was under the crushing weight of his fallen horse. Nothing, that is, except bawl at the top of his voice and just hope that one of the rest of the company was still within earshot.

"Xilva!" he bellowed as loud as he could. "Finwald!"

Nothing. He tried again: "Bolldhe!"

He lay back, panting, his face beaded with sweat.

A few seconds later, he heard the welcome sound of approaching hooves. . . .

It did not take long for Bolldhe, Gapp, and the two priests to arrive and haul the gasping and cursing Paulus back up onto the safety of the path. There he lay, pouring with sweat, and already shaking spasmodically in the first stages of a fit. They nervously left him to it, and concentrated on dragging Nibulus out from under his fallen horse.

Luckily the Peladane had not suffered any broken bones, while Hammer-hoof, though still unable to get up, did not appear to have any injuries other than a nasty gash to the side of his head after his fall. Wodeman, too, was still breathing but would clearly remain comatose for quite some time.

The newcomers glanced about themselves in confusion. "Where're the wolves?" Gapp asked finally.

"Gone," gasped Nibulus, struggling with difficulty to his feet. "Either gone back the way they came or down there." He jerked a thumb down toward the gully.

They looked at their leader in astonishment and awe, wondering how, even with his redoubtable skills, he had managed to drive off their terrible pursuers while he was still trapped beneath his warhorse. But Nibulus kept his silence; this was the stuff legends were made of, and he was not about to cheat the skalds of their chance to sing his praises.

Appa set about trying to retrieve the shaman through his magic, while Finwald went over to the Peladane.

"Nibulus," he said urgently, "we've got to get going. Bolldhe says that Methuselech was heading straight into another pack of wolves up ahead."

"*Another* pack?"

"Yes," Bolldhe interjected. "They must have split up earlier—"

By now Nibulus was already limping along the path toward Paulus's mare, grabbing his greatsword as he went. "Come on, you lot," he shouted. "We've got work to do! Appa, bring Wodeman with you as soon as he's ready, and Flatulus, stop messing about and get your backside over here!"

But Paulus was not going anywhere for the time being. Already his one good eye was bulging feverishly. This was going to be a bad one. . . .

Leaving Appa, Wodeman, and Paulus behind, they came upon the second pack almost immediately, trotting down the path toward them. Without a second's delay, Nibulus charged straight at them. Now released from the influence of the Leucrota, the wolves did not seem quite so bold, and when they saw the howling warrior charging toward them, they simply turned round and scarpered the way they had come. This had been a bad couple of days, and quite frankly they had had enough.

"Ha!" cried Nibulus, reining his horse in. He cast a look back at his followers as if to say, "See, told you I was good."

At first they all feared the worst for Methuselech, expecting to come upon a pool of blood and their companion torn apart. But as they searched frantically, it became obvious that there had been no such encounter. Had the horse and rider careered over the edge? Had Methuselech managed somehow to scramble his horse up some high place the wolves could not follow? They searched and they searched, and called out his name.

Then a shout from Finwald brought them running. The priest was now concentrating on a part of the cliff with a worried look on his brow. There a dark and narrow cleft broke the rock face, a corridor deep down into the mountains, out of which whistled a dank, evil-smelling wind. As the others crowded round, he held up a finger to quieten them.

"Listen," he said softly. "Can you hear it?"

They listened intently, and, faint now but growing louder, there could be heard the approaching sound of stumbling hoofbeats echoing out of the darkness, like some form of horse-riding wraith coming out of the earth itself, maybe from a time long past and best forgotten. And then, carried on the eerie currents of air, rose a terrified whinnying.

Far down into the cleft had Whitehorse gone, the frightened and confused animal descending ever deeper into the very core of the mountain. Far above, a thin ribbon of daylight filtered down, but only enough to hint at shapes, and to play tricks on the mind.

Whitehorse stumbled on down the rocky slide while his rider seemed totally unaware of anything around him. There had never been a time that the poor horse could remember feeling so completely alone, so utterly beyond the reassuring guidance of his master's hands. Where was that warm safety and control he had known all his life?

He snorted in alarm, and stared wild-eyed into the darkness ahead. There were *things* around him now; things that his dull horse brain did not understand but that his instincts detected. They floated toward him, forming out of the frigid, eddying mist to weave cobwebs of fear about him. Nasty, evil, sharp-pointed things that wanted not him but his master.

He wished his master would wake up.

But Methuselech *had* awoken, though he did not yet realize it.

Moments earlier his tormented conscience had risen out of its insensibility into the new world about him. He had been dreaming of great, black, loping hellhounds with teeth that glowed and gaping jaws that belched fire.

And those *hideous eyes*!

They were chasing him, and he was running for his life through a bewildering maze of rocks that spewed magma and turned into the faces of his companions, grisly, leering faces that spat at him as he passed. There was Finwald, wrapped in a cocoon of leathery bat wings, his black hair flying about him in the frenzied demon wind that howled around him, with hollow black eyes piercing into Methuselech's brain. There was Appa, a brittle skeleton covered with tight-stretched, yellowing skin, a horrible dead thing that should have withered away long ago. There was Radnar, a despicable little imp holding a pair of sharp, gleaming blades that dripped Methuselech's own lifeblood. There was Wodeman, a snarling werewolf from the darkest recesses of night, ready to leap out and tear his heart from its shattered rib cage. There was Paulus, a howling, gibbering obscenity, melting in his fury. There was even Nibulus, his own friend, now a stone giant in rusted iron armor, who reached down for him with massive hands, taloned fingers twitching uncontrollably in anticipation.

Then he saw Bolldhe, who looked back at him and smiled wickedly. Bolldhe turned, and beckoned a second figure, who moved over to stand directly in Methuselech's path.

Methuselech stared at this newcomer. It shimmered like a white shroud, and he could see right through it. He looked back imploringly at Bolldhe, but the traveler had now vanished. All that remained was the shade directly in his path. When it raised its hood, Methuselech gasped. The face of the ghost was his own.

"Methuselech Xilvafloese"—its voice resonated like a funeral bell being tolled deep underground—"I am Sluagh. I am your death."

Then he awoke with a start to find himself lying facedown on something warm and familiar. Was he in bed? Yes, surely, for it was dark enough. . . .

But, no, he could not be awake. In his mind he was still riding Whitehorse, riding him down a narrow, stony passage . . . and why was it so . . . *terrible* here? So dreamlike?

No, he must still be asleep.

Still not aware of it, Methuselech was fully awake, yet in this place, for all he could tell, he was still trapped in his nightmare. Had he known for sure that this was reality, he might have sat up and reined his steed about, headed back to find the others.

Instead he just lay there across the horse's neck and waited for the nightmare to run its course.

Run its course it did. Right to the end.

Sounds that were only half-heard, half-imagined, drifted up through the cleft on the poisonous air. They were like the voices of the dead, voices from the past, voices full of a brooding hatred fueled by the passing of centuries. Methuselech kept his head down and tried to hold on to his courage; surely the night would soon be over and he would awake from this evil reverie.

The voices, however, seemed so real that eventually Methuselech looked up through reddened eyes. Every slimy, dripping rock surface seemed to take on the shape of a snarling muzzle, flesh-ripping and dire. Every wispy growth of vegetation trailed lazily in the air currents like a dead man's beard. And where pale patches of slime-encrusted rock showed through the ancient layers of moss that clung to it, Methuselech could see only the bones of mangled warriors.

A denser mist crawled out to meet him from somewhere down below, where the passage ended. Spilling up out of the shadows ahead it approached him like some primordial phantom of terror till he felt he was traveling down into the darkest, most fearful pit of his subconscious.

Ah, if only it were just that!

He could sense it now rolling toward him in a tidal wave of blackness. Something down there was waiting for him, lurking like a malignant, bloated spider. But still he could not turn back, even through he knew it would always claim its victim in the end.

For it was Death that lurked down there: Sluagh, the final truth; the baring of his soul.

Then, even through the fear that numbed his senses, Methuselech suddenly realized that he had ridden out of the confines of the cleft, and they were now out in an open space. His horse finally stopped, as if unable to continue, and the cold wrapped itself around them like a moist cadaver's glove.

He looked about. On all sides rose great cliffs of jagged black rock, trickling with water and hung with glistening cobwebs, which soared up hundreds of feet to the distant sky above. Below them, scant inches to their left, the ground fell away into some kind of vast pit. Methuselech rubbed droplets of condensing mist from his eyes, and peered over the edge.

It was from here the mist emerged. He could see it slowly curling out of the pit like steam from a cauldron, washing past him on either side to disappear up the narrow cleft that led to the outside world. Beyond that he could see absolutely nothing, for whatever scant vestiges of light fell from above were simply swallowed up.

He shuddered, in a sudden chilling spasm. It did not seem quite so dreamlike anymore. The thought that this might be real after all began to intrude into his mind.

He leaned farther over the edge, straining to hear. There was something else down there. In some distant place in his mind, he could detect a strange sound.

It was like a chorus of lamenting voices singing a dirge for the dead—for themselves maybe, a last soliloquy for the Lost. He heard it not with his ears, but in the silence he could feel it, reverberating in his mind, reaching down into his soul. To his surprise, he found himself sobbing.

What *was* down there?

Then he gasped, for he now knew beyond all doubt that this truly was not a dream. He really was here, Hell only knew how, and his companions were nowhere to be seen. He did not even know how long he had been separated from them. He felt more alone now than he had ever thought possible, so alone that he might as well be standing on the remotest planet in the universe, beyond even the distant stars. And still the cries of the Lost ringing in his mind.

Then there was a change in the air that caused Methuselech to shudder. The pathos of those cries had transformed into malice, as if something down there, something not of this world, was hungry for him and wanted to steal his mind. He could sense it rising out of the pit to claim him, rising with the mist that shrouded it. Panic gripped him, but he could not move. Whitehorse sensed it too, and stamped about the ledge in terror.

Then came the cry: an ululating wailing of such demonic insanity and diabolic evil that every drop of blood was frozen inside Methuselech's veins.

It was the keening of Sluagh.

Whitehorse screamed in response, and reared up high. With a cry of total despair, Methuselech was launched off the saddle. Arms flailing uselessly, he plunged into the blackness of the pit that gaped open to swallow him up.

The horse, no more use now, bolted in a frenzy as fast as he could gallop, with Methuselech's final cry echoing in his ears.

When they had finally managed to calm down the terrified animal, Bolldhe and the others wasted no time in entering the cleft themselves. Whitehorse would not be dragged back inside for anything, so was left stamping and whinnying on the cliff path outside.

"Just what *happened* down there to scare the horse so much?" said Finwald.

"And what's happened to Methuselech?" Nibulus wondered.

None of them actually heard the keening, but just before Whitehorse reemerged an inexplicable disquiet had suddenly settled on them all.

Nibulus led the way, the only one among them who really wanted to venture down into this place. Though extremely wary, he led them down without hesitation in his urge to reach Xilva.

What they all felt in the damp and gloomy rock fissure perturbed them but it was nothing to what they felt as they drew near the pit itself, and heard the keening from close up.

As one they all froze, faces blanching in horror. As that terrible cry hung in the air, there was not one among them who would not have turned and fled all the way back to Nordwas, had their horses not also been rooted to the spot. No one now spared a thought for Methuselech or the quest. The fear they felt transcended anything they would ever have believed possible in this world.

Then the howl ended, trailing off into a forlorn sob of such devastation that the travelers felt as if their life force was going with it, drifting into eternity upon a black wind of endless despair.

Finwald gaped ahead of him with his face prematurely old. In a voice numbed with death-fear he gasped: "What in hell was that!?"

"I don't know," stammered Nibulus, "and I've no intention of finding out."

All of them turned tail and fled for their lives back up through the cleft. If Methuselech was down in that pit, then there was nothing they or any other power in the world of Man could do to help him.

With his own last wail of utter despair still ringing in his ears, Methuselech lay, gasping for breath, in a crumpled heap at the bottom of the pit. Broken and bleeding, he was not so much fighting for life as fighting for death.

His eyes were open, but he could see nothing in this pitch blackness, could not see what place this was in which he had finally met his end, could not even see the carnage that had been wrought upon his flesh.

It was a mercy, for had he been able to behold the travesty that his body had become, he would have been reminded of all those tortured and mutilated corpses he had witnessed during the sacking of the cities of the South. He was coughing gouts of blood from his smashed torso, and his right leg stuck out at an insane angle, he could tell without being able to see, the splintered bone protruding in several places.

As for the rest of him . . . He was dying, that much he was certain. Already the coldness of death was creeping over him. How much more of this agony must he endure before his life winked out?

Now he lay, far beyond the help of his lost companions, and totally at the mercy of whatever agent of darkness it was that had made that dreadful keening noise. Tears welled in his eyes, at the devastating loneliness he felt now that he had fallen away from the world.

Moments later, the air all around him crystallized into shards of ice. Methuselech stiffened, not breathing, not moving, his pain almost forgotten. The silence closed in, and the whole world stopped to listen. Something was watching him. The suspense seemed to last for hours, yet only for one heartbeat.

Then he heard the watcher approach. . . .

The company did not stop. By the time they had emerged from the cleft to where Whitehorse awaited them, Appa, Paulus, and a still-dazed Wodeman had caught up, having ridden up on the recently recovered Hammerhoof. Thus reunited, they continued their flight to the northern ridge as fast as the poor light allowed them. And when it became so dark that the path became impossible to see, still they did not stop; each member of the company dismounted, and with torches lit to see the ground at their feet, led their horses on by the rein.

For the first time since he had joined this quest, Bolldhe brought out his bull's-eye lantern. Unlike most of the company's equipment, this had not been provided by Wintus Hall; it was his own, and was possibly one of his most prized possessions. None of the others could make out what he was handling, had never seen this item before now. All they could hear was a rapid "sawing" sound, and then suddenly a powerful beam of light sprang out into the night, the like of which none there had ever seen before.

But despite their wonder at Bolldhe's "little magic," they wasted no time in idle talk. At the head of the line now, Bolldhe shone the lantern's beam ahead to light their way, and thus they continued. On they marched, over the ridge behind which, had it been lighter, they had been expecting to see their first view of the Northlands.

It was a journey full of anxiety, with many a backward glance, and a fear of what might lie ahead around each corner. They were now going inexorably downward, plunging down narrow ravines and steep slopes into the dark, twisting passages of the mountains' hidden valleys.

Eventually, exhaustion and mental strain overtook their fear, and Nibulus was forced to call a halt. They had arrived at a cirque, a hollow hemmed in by high, sloping walls that gave them some protection from the cold wind that was blowing from the north.

"You've all done well to make it this far," Nibulus commended them as he listened to the lonely wind buffeting through the unseen passes and clefts around them. "We may as well camp where we are; I can't see it getting any better."

"I don't fancy camping *here*," Finwald muttered in spite of his exhaustion. "It feels like Death; just listen. . . ."

They paused. Though the wind passed over them, it brought with it odd sounds that could never quite be discerned. There seemed to be voices, high and screaming, or bestial and muttering. The very air was alive with the uncanny cries of phantoms that flew through the secret places of this region. These mountains were unfriendly at the best of times, and had little mercy for outsiders; but here on the very threshold of the Northlands, they were no place to be at all.

Appa wagged his head madly in agreement. " 'Tis an evil place still, I can sense, not a place any man should have to walk at all, at all. . . ."

Let alone spend the night! Gapp thought, choking down his fear as stoically as he could.

But they had little choice. Bolldhe, being more used to camping out alone in similar (if less disturbing) places, did not wait for the others, but unsaddled Zhang, spread out his bedroll on the levelest piece of ground in the hollow, and set about preparing his and his horse's rations.

Seeing no alternative, the others followed, and within half an hour they had all settled down for the night.

Bolldhe and Paulus took the first watch.

Nibulus forced down the knot that was forming in his throat. During their race along the mountain path he had not had time for any thoughts other than flight. But now that they had put some distance between themselves and the horror back there, grief stole over him fully. He shook his head, dumbfounded, and cursed the ill chance that had claimed the life of the best man he had ever known. It was just so stupid! He should not, *could not* have been taken. It served no purpose that he could see, no purpose whatsoever. *Xilva*, he cried in some place deep in his soul, *you stupid, foreign toerag, what am I supposed to do now, with you gone? And what the hell am I going to tell Phalopaeia?*

Now as he pulled his bedroll over his head, a strange sound began to escape from him, one that no one had ever heard the Thegne make before now. It was a strangulated sound, one of constriction, of anguish—a sound that did not want to be made. But it was one that was escaping from him nevertheless.

The company chose not to hear it.

In the hooded light of the bull's-eye lantern, Bolldhe and the mercenary sat staring with wide eyes into the blackness that lurked just beyond the radius of illumination. At each sound emerging from the dark, their heads would snap round to investigate. But not one word passed between them.

Then Paulus said softly, "It's a strange and wondrous device you bring with you."

Bolldhe turned in surprise to stare at the hooded figure sitting just a few yards away. In the light from the lantern, only the sharp, beaky nose could be seen protruding from under the cowl. The mutilated eyes were hidden in shadow, for which Bolldhe was thankful; this night contained enough horrors as it was.

Paulus said no more, continuing to stare out into the night, but Bolldhe noticed the mercenary's hands flexing constantly on the pommel of his bastard sword, a nifty weapon that could be wielded one- or two-handed. He realized he did not really know this taciturn Nahovian at all. Since the commencement of their quest, Paulus had kept his distance from the rest, more so even than had Bolldhe himself.

Bolldhe had to admit to himself he was intrigued. That was probably the first time the grim mercenary had spoken to anyone in the company without its being necessary, and it seemed odd that he should choose Bolldhe.

"Wondrous device?" he replied. "You mean the lantern?"

For nigh on five years he had carried it everywhere with him, and for Bolldhe, ever the pragmatist, it had proved more useful than any weapon. Small and lightweight but very tough, the bull's-eye lantern had been wrought in Trondaran, the tiny, isolated mountain kingdom of Jyblitt the Hauger King, and was consequently of a craftsmanship unequaled in all of Lindormyn.

Its cylindrical brass frame held a long thin rod of "xienne"—a light, yellow metal that burned with a fierce light when shaved—that could be plunged up and down into the top of the cylinder to whittle it and at the same time ignite the shavings through friction. The flame was shielded by specially treated silk stretched over the brass frame, and this lamp itself nestled inside a slightly larger leather sleeve attached into an intricately carved ivory handle. This sleeve was lined on the inside with highly polished silver mirrors that would, once the brass frame was snapped up into the sleeve, reflect and focus the flame's light through just one hooded aperture, thus concentrating a powerful beam. Thus, this flexible artifact could either be suspended sleeveless by its fine silver chain, lighting all around it, or sheathed in the sleeve so as to project a bright beam straight ahead.

Like so many other rare minerals found only in Trondaran, the source of xienne metal was a secret jealously guarded by Jyblitt's subjects, and how Bolldhe had come by such a precious object was a traveler's tale in itself.

But in answer to Paulus's unexpected interest, Bolldhe simply replied, "Yes, it is rather handy, I suppose."

Paulus did not make any immediate response. Minutes later, however, he spoke up again.

"In the land I come from, we call such spirits Vardogr."

"I beg your pardon?"

"That shade that cried out earlier," Paulus explained, "we call it Vardogr."

"I have heard the word," Bolldhe replied, "though fully I do not understand the meaning."

Paulus glanced quickly at Bolldhe, his one sound eye reflecting as a single point of gold in the lantern's light. "You *know* of this word? How so?"

Bolldhe shrugged, not wishing to prolong this conversation any longer than need be. "I heard rumors of such a shade when I was passing through your territory earlier this year."

"You have passed beneath the boughs of Vregh-Nahov?" Paulus asked, surprised. Then he relapsed into silence once more.

At further length, and to Bolldhe's surprise, the mercenary began to chant. It was a deep and sonorous incantation, almost discordant, yet rising and falling in such a way that made it difficult to judge whether it was a song or a poem. But the descant seemed to Bolldhe as mournful and haunting as the cry of gulls on the Shore of Death.

And it went like this:

"Into darkest reverie,
We sink, and dream, and see,
Dark thoughts like phosphorescent sea draugrs float by.

Vardogr dances before our eyes like Ellyldan above the quagmire,
Floats by, out of reach,
Its laughter echoing through the lightless deep.

The man, he knows his death awaits him,
'Neath benighted windowsill Vardogr lurks,
Keening his death knell.
No morning shall come for him.
Lych-light shines, the siren sings,
Stronger now by far,
But Marmennil chains bind the hands that might have turned those voices
*   away.*

Utrost is hidden in the fog
That swirls around the mast,
Dark sea laps against the hull,
Whispering the Ancestors' voices.

The Wyrm of our world's ending tightens its coils,
Draws round full circle,
For Sluagh sweeps through the mind,
Rake and broom in hand."

Bolldhe did not comment and, after an awkward silence, Paulus muttered, "It is composed in the ancient tongue of my people, sung by our bards, the *akyns,* and maybe loses something in the translation."

"Yes," Bolldhe agreed dismissively. "Quite a lot, by the sound of it. I've never heard such rubbish in all my life."

Paulus visibly flinched. A strange expression clouded his face, and he uttered not one further word that night.

6

Wasteland

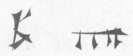

So they continued doggedly, pacing out the most painful steps upon that darkest stretch of their road so far. The Peladane's mood was black and leaden, and emanated from him like a cloud of necrotizing spores to the others of the company, infecting them with its bane. Few words were uttered, the name of Methuselech mentioned not once, and only Whitehorse—lightened of his burden but darkened of heart—dared glance back toward those evil heights wherein still lay his master.

The next few days saw the bedraggled company's slow but steady progress out of the Blue Mountains. Despite their expectations, they could not, yet, see the Northlands from here. The first day was spent leaping one by one over deep crevices and narrow fissures that fell away sheer into blackness below, and from which surged freezing currents of air and the distant echoes of rushing streams and the forlorn bleating of goats.

On the second day they traveled northward along a narrow, knife-edged ridge of uneven rock that was split by frost and shaped by the wind of a thousand centuries. It felt like traveling along the chipped blade of a timber saw. The gales howling up at them threatened at any moment to pick them up and toss them down the slope. They all ensured their mounts trod very carefully, for once they started sliding down a slope like *that,* they would not stop till they reached the very bottom—however far that was.

In all that time their only company were the lammergeyers that wheeled high above against the deep blue sky, or the occasional line of saiga antelopes that clattered below along almost sheer rock faces.

On and on they traveled, the next day hauling their reluctant steeds over great slabs of jagged granite or picking their way gingerly around wide patches of ice. All the time the raging wind sang in their ears and lashed their burning faces. But toward the end of the final day, after an hour of arduous scrambling up the shoulder of a particularly hazardous peak, they finally gained the summit and stared in wonder at their first, and now unexpected, view of the great, wild Northlands.

"Ha!" cried a jubilant Wodeman above the shrieking wind. "I told you we'd be seeing the Northlands by tonight."

Nibulus steadied himself against the wind, clutching Hammerhoof's reins for support, and shouted back: "I seem to recall you saying that four days ago." Nevertheless, he slapped Wodeman heartily on the back.

It was the most stunning view any of them had seen yet in all their time traversing the Blue Mountains. Below the peak on which they stood, the mountain dropped away gradually in a long, unbroken slope until it reached the green, wooded foothills miles away. And beyond that extended the beautiful magnificence of the Northlands. Below those hills marking the boundary of the uplands sprawled the grey-green emptiness known as the Rainflats: mile after mile of moorland where a few solitary hillocks poked through an enshrouding blanket of mist like islands drowning in a cold, grey sea. This greyness stretched all the way to a darker patch that lay almost on the horizon, and which, they guessed, was the great forest of Fron-Wudu, beneath whose boughs they were destined eventually to pass.

Beyond that—though they could not be sure—the keener-sighted among them believed they could discern distant peaks of white shining right on the very limit of their vision. Those must be the fabled Giant Mountains, compared with which the Blue Mountains were little more than a ragged collection of knolls.

"Take a good look now," said the Peladane, drawing his great Ulleanh around him against the chill, "for this is the last view we will enjoy of where we are bound."

Gapp shivered violently, not from his sudden exposure to the wind after their sweaty ascent, but from the thought that all that vast, dark expanse of land (more extensive than he had ever seen in his life), with all its unknown dangers, was but a journey leading to an even worse place, a place where the cold would cut right through his body without bothering to go around it. All that land to cross, all those weeks of hard travel, with scarce sign of civilization, and nothing at the end but a hollow castle which—if they were lucky—would still be empty. He glanced at Appa, and briefly their eyes met: the young and the old sharing a mutual bond of intimidation and dread.

Bolldhe on the other hand felt more elevated in spirit than during the whole of this quest so far. He gazed down the slopes and breathed in deeply. The scents from below reminded him acutely of the land in the West he had forsaken, and brought back vivid memories of his beloved and forsaken Moel-Bryn. As they began their descent, he walked alone in his mind, treading again the familiar pathways of his youth as the smells of pine forest, damp needle-strewn earth, and whispering moorland filled his head.

For the rest of that day, his heart ached with a profound happiness.

During the next week, progress was tediously slow. As the company descended the foothills of the Blue Mountains to the lowlands beyond, the "path" that had grudgingly and somewhat unreliably led them through the mountains now, to their dismay, disappeared altogether. *The Chronicle of Gwyllch* told of "a gradely highway used by many trayders and marchaunts, bilt upon a dyke they name *Enta-Clawdd,* that dothe run strayte and trewe unto the town of Myst-Hakel, that we calle Edgemarshe."

"Trade's obviously dried up somewhat in the last five hundred years," Bolldhe commented dryly to their leader. "I don't suppose you've got a more up-to-date guidebook, have you?"

There was also a growing sense among the men that they were now descending into unfriendly, alien lands. Ever since leaving the mountains, they had the distinct feeling of being "spied upon," and both Wodeman and Paulus were fairly confident they knew by what.

"Spriggans," Paulus whispered. "It is an evil land we come to."

"How so?" asked Wodeman.

"We approach the marshlands," Paulus explained, "neither earth nor water but something between. Such places are the dominion of Huldre, treacherous and evil."

"Among *my* people the marsh is considered a sacred burial ground," the Torca countered, "for it is there that our dead are most easily dragged down to the next world below. *We do not fear it.*"

"Treacherous and evil," Paulus repeated. "We will not even eat the creatures inhabiting such places, newt and toad, for they too are neither one thing nor the other, but unclean and detestable. I tell you, we are entering an evil place."

Wodeman might have argued further, except that the previous night he had had a dream that disturbed him greatly. In it he found himself standing alone upon a desolate wasteland, while a woman with hair as black as her aura had floated toward him over the tussocks, her feet not touching the ground.

Nibulus, at least, was concerned with more practical things, for the journey through the mountains had taken longer than anticipated, and their rations were dwindling. This would not present too much of a problem if they could find their way to the town of Myst-Hakel fairly soon. But the lack of any clear road and virtually no information about the town itself, save that it lay to the north of the mountain path they had emerged from, meant that they now had to spend much of the day foraging. Much like nomads, they started living off the land, setting traps at night and subsisting on meager victuals.

Wodeman came into his own at this time, and proved himself invaluable in finding things edible. Second nature to him was the art of smoking wasps' nests to plunder their delicately flavored baby grubs, locating wild roots, herbs, and edible fungi, and coaxing amphibious creatures out of their hideaways. His knowledge of such lore of the wild seemed without limit, and he came up with a thousand and one natural recipes to please all tastes.

By night their camp would be plagued by velvet ants that would drive the sleepers mad with irritation, leaving painful bites all over their skin by morning. Only Wodeman was untroubled: he would sing to the ants, entreating them not to touch his rations or disturb his sleep and, to the exasperation of the others, they obeyed him.

"The secret," he informed them, "lies in rewarding them beforehand; a little of the food you don't finish yourself, and they soon go away."

This angered Paulus greatly, for to him it was the surest sign of capitulation to the "treacherous filth-dwellers." Whenever the velvet ants filed away with the shaman's offerings, he would secretly crush them into the mud with his great boots.

The following morning Bolldhe abandoned the quest. He simply mounted his horse and rode off into the West, leaving the company behind forever.

The company stared helplessly after the swiftly departing horseman as he grew smaller in the distance, and was then lost from sight. Only Appa made any attempt to call him back; but the pathetically comic gait of his pony was no match for the speed of Zhang, the Adt-T'man from the Tabernacle Plains, and the priest's attempt proved no more than an act of desperation.

Now, a quarter of an hour later, as the company stared westward at the sight of the aged rider slowly returning without his quarry, feelings of apathy and futility stole the last of their good humor away.

It had not been a promising day to start with. All night it had been chilly, with a determined wind blowing unhindered across the Rainflats, and then during the early hours it had started to rain. At first this was just a cold spattering of raindrops, but it soon grew into a steady drizzle, soaking into their bedrolls and even into their clothing. Their first attempts to make another fire had proved futile, but when one was finally kindled through the craft of Wodeman, all it achieved was to attract hordes of biting midges and fierce little black flies that bit and stung them for the remainder of the predawn sleeping hours. All that could be heard was the incessant downpour, the high-pitched buzzing of insect life, and the constant bad-tempered curses of the travelers as they vainly slapped the winged tormentors away from their itching faces.

By the morning they had all been cheated of any strength that sleep might have restored. They arose, half-awake and bleary-eyed, to one of the most cheerless days imaginable, and seemingly in the middle of nowhere. A grey fog had now settled about them, so it was impossible to tell in which direction they should be headed.

Even Wodeman's "expertly set" traps had yielded nothing all night, except for one aged and rather poisonous-looking Weal-toad, which squatted in the middle of the camp, gazing at them balefully before lumbering off into the tall grass.

It really looked as though it was going to be one of those days.

With ration packs now empty, and still no sign of a road, their frustration quickly led to bitter arguments, accusations flying and general foul-tempered bickering, with everybody determined to have his say.

"At times like this," Paulus spoke up suddenly, "my people look to the lammergeyer for inspiration. It will not blanch at any carrion, no matter how foul the beast, how old the meat, nor how ravaged by other scavengers. And when it eats," he went on, with a faraway look in his eye, "it simply thrusts its head in, right in up to its shoulders! Encased in meat, breathing blood, gorging till it is sated! How I would now love to be a lammergeyer."

Nobody cared to discuss this further with him.

With an inward sigh, Nibulus was forced to admit to himself that he had failed abysmally in the first test of a Thegne: He had not managed to form his company into a cohesive and cooperative expeditionary unit.

To add to the general air of discontent, a certain member of the group appeared to have something else on his mind that was making him even grumpier than might be reasonably expected.

It had caused Bolldhe long hours of wakefulness. What exactly was he doing here out in the wild Northlands, thousands of miles from his homeland, among a motley group of characters he hardly knew? Certainly none of the others knew the answer to this crucial question, not just the old priest who had persuaded Bolldhe to join them.

All night he had debated with himself, endlessly, futilely, his exhausted mind mulling over the reasons time and again, until that little seed of doubt which had been with him from the very beginning now hung over him like a black cloud, quietly insisting: *Why are you here?*

So, by the time he rose from his nonexistent slumber to the news that their rations had totally run out, Bolldhe felt tired, bad-tempered, and ready to quit.

"Bloody quests!" he muttered irately. "Who needs them?"

He had not necessarily meant anyone to hear this, and in the general hum of swearing, had certainly not expected anyone to have paid him any attention. But on hearing this, Finwald, who had been preoccupied with scratching his armpits and yawning, suddenly spun around upon Bolldhe and snarled:

"You don't need quests? Good! Then we don't need you either. Go pack your bags and piss off home!"

The whole camp went dead silent. Finwald never spoke like this, not to anyone. The atmosphere darkened with violence and thickened with anger, and there was the feeling that something had started here that had to be seen right to the bitter end; there was no avoiding it now.

In the awkward silence they all stared at Bolldhe and waited to see what he would do.

Bolldhe stared straight back into the tar-black eyes of the mage-priest, whose open anger was matched by his own silent, smoldering fury.

His hand involuntarily traveled down to the hilt of his axe.

Everyone waited.

Then Nibulus stepped forward. He had never taken to Bolldhe, never seen the point of him.

"Finwald's right," he said now. "You're not needed here anymore, Bolldhe. Or wanted. You'd better leave."

Bolldhe stared at him without a word, unblinking, his astonishment at this sudden turn of events shared by the other five in the group. Seconds passed that felt like hours. Bolldhe found his thoughts going back to a time last year when he had found himself in the mountain country of Trondaran, and had been watching a player in a traveling theater being pelted with rancid aubergines by the raucous crowd. He recalled the embarrassment and pity he had felt for the luckless thespian as he stood there on stage all alone, hot tears of rage and self-consciousness clearly visible in his eyes.

So, without a word of explanation, he jammed his gear into his saddlebags, slung his axe over his shoulder, leaped onto his horse's back, spurred Zhang to a headlong gallop over the plains, and was gone.

So Appa returned from pursuing the departing traveler, his voice hoarse from uttering weak cries of desperation.

With despondency, the others watched the exhausted priest's pony stumble back into camp again. He was clearly in a bad way, coughing fitfully and wiping the cold sweat from his pallid, febrile face with one grimy sleeve. As he drew nearer, they could hear him curse the uncooperative wanderer to hell, then disgustedly announce that they had lost their sole chance of defeating the Rawgr.

All their options had disappeared with the fleeing Bolldhe, so no point in going on now. Drauglir, curse his foul existence to hell, would rise again unopposed, and there was nothing either they or anyone else could do about it. Nothing left for them now except to return home and prepare for approaching darkness, despair, and death.

"Lord Cuna!" he wailed tearfully. "Can it really be true that we're beaten?"

As the others looked on with mixed pity and surprise, Appa fell to his knees in the muddied earth and trembled like a dying creature. His hands were clasped tightly around something and he was squeezing it fitfully till blood trickled between his fingers.

Suddenly he pitched forward and buried his face in the mud. Finwald leapt forward to raise him back to his feet. He unclasped his fellow priest's hand, and stared sadly at what lay therein.

"Appa," he said softly, "it isn't as bad as that, surely? Nothing can be that bad. . . ."

The words were spoken poignantly, and with great feeling. It was the Torch that Appa held, the little stone amulet of Cuna, symbol of his faith, and he had been wringing the life out of it.

Finwald turned from the frail figure to face the others.

The two warriors remained impassive, unmoved, not one of them having ever understood why it was necessary for that wandering trickster to have come along in the first place.

Even Wodeman stood there without expression, continuing to stare westward to the point where Bolldhe had disappeared from sight. Finwald could not guess at the thoughts that might lie hidden behind that inscrutable Torca mask, for Wodeman's very existence seemed a strange anachronism to the learned mage-priest.

But the set expression of the shaman belied the intensity of feeling within him. Like Appa, Wodeman had been entrusted with a divine mission to ensure that Bolldhe destroyed the Rawgr Drauglir before he could rise again. But unlike the priest of Cuna, Wodeman was remaining calm. Worried but calm. Nobody could deny that things had definitely taken a turn for the worse; maybe, as Appa now believed, there really *was* no hope. Yet he could not bring himself to accept that mankind's luck had run out completely. He could not believe that everything, the forests, the hills, the rivers and all that dwelled therein, were now doomed to blackness and despoliation just on the whim of one man.

Anything could happen to turn things around, he reflected consolingly. So often the strands of the web of fate would be disturbed by an ill wind, becoming entangled, confused, and turned back upon themselves. *Something* would happen. Things had a way of sorting themselves out. If Bolldhe did not return to them, it could simply be that they themselves were not destined to be with him any longer. Possibly it was that, in some inexplicable way, the company had already played its part in the unfolding drama. Maybe Bolldhe needed them no more now than a fledgling deserting the nest when it is time to do so. Maybe Bolldhe would eventually turn North again to continue his appointed mission by himself. Or perhaps he would find others who would pick up where his old companions had left off.

That Gapp was thoroughly despondent at the turn of events was clearly evident from the scowl on his face. He had looked up to the silent Bolldhe as an embodiment of all the heroism, romance, and adventure of travel that he had yearned for himself, and now that the man had simply given up, under no visible threat, his disappointment quickly turned to bitterness.

So much for heroes. . . .

So they continued as if nothing significant had happened. Their objective was still the same, their immediate problems unaltered. Even in his inconsolable frame of mind, Appa readily resumed the journey along with them. After all, being seventy years old, he could not hope to return to Nordwas alone, even if he could find the road back.

"But I'm only going as far as the next town," he insisted. "There I shall make myself comfortable for my last remaining days, and prepare in solace for the End of Days that befall us all ere long."

By nightfall Bolldhe had reached the lonely road that would take him south and west, and away from the Northlands. He had ridden long and hard, pushing himself and his horse to exhaustion in his anger, and now as he pitched camp, he reflected upon the turn of events that had brought him to this desolate place, and to one of the loneliest situations he had ever found himself in during all his years of wandering.

When he had been a child, at home, he had imagined the joy of being a free spirit, so he had been surprised when, on his first wanderings, he had so often felt sad, lonely, even heartbroken. Even after he had long grown accustomed to this rootless lifestyle, though he did often feel every bit the legendary lone hero, at other times it was good to feel the warmth and security of company.

It was inevitable, right from the start, that it would end this way. After all, had not all his brief companionships ended thus? No matter how free and easy the traveling relationship, no matter how long the journey shared, no matter what bonds of camaraderie were forged, it would always end up with something snapping in Bolldhe, followed by his sudden disappearance.

"Always without a backward glance," he mumbled to himself, with a perverse sense of the aloof. Yes, that had almost become a matter of pride.

See now, he had spent the last week in the company of a group of would-be adventurers, and in all that time they had hardly managed to catch themselves enough for even one decent meal. Yet, within hours of leaving them behind he had succeeded in snaring two gorse hares and three fen-skippers and picked enough gortleberries to last him for three days. Feeling well fed, he was now warming himself over a cheerful campfire, relaxed in the knowledge that he was safely on his way without any other people cluttering up his life. Mercifully alone at last, save for the myrmidonic Zhang, the only friend he needed. Yes, he was much better off without that pack of religious maniacs.

Pleasantly tired, he kicked the dying fire gently to life with his brown wolf-skin boots and savored the brief glow that radiated from it. He considered his journey ahead—moving back into more familiar regions: places he was familiar with from maps he had studied over the years.

A journey continuing westward would inevitably take him through the Herdlands of the Tusse. He had encountered them many times before, the Tusse, those nomadic herd giants who could be encountered just about anywhere in the world that was flat enough to accommodate their vast herds of bison, camel, horse, or yak. Most ordinary humans avoided the Tusse, but through ignorance and xenophobia. Bolldhe, however, knew them well enough to ensure his safe passage through their ranks, "just so long as I respect their customs and keep myself to myself."

Once past the Herdlands, he was offered three choices: either head south over the eastern foothills of the Nail Mountains and into the great cosmopolitan country of Quiravia; or northeast into the Fram Peninsula and board a ship heading for Fram Point at the capital city of Aalesfleot; or he could risk the many dangers of traveling southwest through the river country that separated the Nail Mountains from the Speinstieth—thence heading into Venna, Bhergallia, Rhelma-Find, or any of the other nations bordering the Crimson Sea. Whichever route he chose, he would be getting closer to approaching his homeland. . . .

Ah, the choices were endless to a free man such as he, he reflected as he stamped the dying embers of the fire into ashes and curled himself up in his bedroll. He needed no one; he was the Lone Wolf. Where the herd craved the security of others of their kind, he needed to rely only on his own resourceful-ness. He would never succumb to their pathetic weakness, he thought con-temptuously, because . . .

Bolldhe let out a deep sigh into the cold night air. His mind was tired from too much thinking, too much embittered self-esteem. And, besides, it was not entirely true. He always felt more resentful of his acquaintances after he had left them than when he was actually with them. Silently his surly mind gnawed upon itself in the darkness and solitude of yet another lonely night.

Far away, many miles to the east, daylight faded, relinquishing its unsteady and unwelcome hold upon the Rainflats. The evening's shadows—such as they were—lengthened over the marshes till they finally faded into the greyness that surrounded them, yielding to the black hand of darkness that descended upon the land. It was a land of tall reeds and wind-whipped, sighing grasses between solitary hillocks; pools of weed-covered quicksand opened up before the un-wary traveler. But very few trod this land nowadays.

Long ago, in an age when the Torca ruled the North, this same terrain was covered by trees. But the rivers widened, gradually losing track of their courses altogether, and they slowly flooded the vast woodlands until most of the trees had drowned. Now only a few remained, sad remnants of the great forest that had died centuries ago. Alone they stood, grey, stunted, and diseased, dying remnants clinging on to a doomed life. Their branches were raised futilely to the sky like skeletal fingers gripping the cold, uncaring air, holding back—for a while—from the glaucous, sucking death that awaited them.

Many were already sinking, their slimy boles half-submerged in the mud that was now incapable of supporting them. They tilted sharply, their lower branches even now submitting to the embrace of the livid green weeds that reached up to entwine them, ensnare them, strangle the life out of them, then pull them down into the mud to feed upon them.

It was a dead land, a land unwilling to sustain any but the most creeping, parasitic, fungoid life. A land shunned by people, hateful of any life-form that stood upright; a land of rank, stinking flora, of slithering, crawling fauna, and of clammy grey mist that enshrouded everything.

Into this dismal, drowning, dying land, the six came. Still they had not gained the road they so urgently sought, the "gradely highway . . . bilt upon a dyke . . . that dothe run strayte and trewe" through the marshes. And although at one point Nibulus was sure he had seen the solitary figure of a man some distance away, they had not yet made contact with a living soul.

Slowly they rode in single file, only daring tread ground already tested by the wolf-skin-clad sorcerer who paced ahead of them. They could all sense the vast stretches of fey ground ("neither earth nor water, but something in between") that surrounded them, waiting eagerly for them to take just one step in the wrong direction, waiting to swallow them up. All eyes strained blearily into the gloom ahead, and no one spoke. Only the troubled whicker of horses and their muffled hoofbeats disturbed the barrowlike silence that hemmed them in.

Solitary trees loomed out of the darkness to either side. The esquire stared wide-eyed at them, believing them at first to be the silent, still-standing forms of barbaric Tusse intent upon slaughtering them. Only when Gapp drew closer could he identify them properly, the mist that had wrapped itself around them forming cold beads of moisture on their bark, which dripped steadily into the murky pools below like putrescence from a skeleton. Now and then, half-drowned boughs rose out of the mud, slime-covered and rotten, like tombstones of long-dead trees.

This land is swallowing us, Gapp thought in rising panic. *The mist has covered us up, a-and we're going to perish here!*

He could not shake off the feeling of dread that this loathsome land engendered on him. But he had to go on, did not have any choice. It was like wandering alone through one of his own nightmares, the swirling mist lending the experience a dreamlike ambience. He held tightly on to Bogey's reins with his left hand, and gripped the reassuring haft of his master's lance with his right, forever casting fearful glances into the gloom all around. He expected at any moment that something bestial and evil would suddenly leap out at them and devour his companions one by one, before turning to chase him out over the hungry marshlands all alone.

Suddenly his fearful train of thought was broken by a sharp hiss from Wodeman:

"Look, over there! There's somebody out there!"

Instantly the company drew together, weapons at the ready, eyes straining against the gloom.

"What is it?" came the excited voice of Finwald, followed by an expectant "Is it Bolldhe?" from Appa.

The sorcerer motioned them to silence with an irate wave of his hand, then slowly pointed off to their right. Following his finger, they saw, just within their limited range of sight, a lone figure standing atop a knoll of tufted grass. Appearing briefly between wreaths of rolling fog, it was silhouetted against the last, faint, silver-grey light of evening. It appeared to be motionless, but in the dismal twilight it was difficult to be sure. It was even hard to gauge the distance, or even if it was human.

"Is it the same one you saw earlier, Nibulus?" someone asked.

"It could be," the Peladane replied vaguely, "but it certainly doesn't seem to mind us knowing it's there."

Finwald agreed. "It's definitely making no attempt to conceal itself, up there. Do you think it's a trap?"

Nibulus was a seasoned warrior, and reluctant to jump to conclusions. He peered through the tendrils of marsh gas and clammy mist that snaked between them, then admitted, "I haven't got the foggiest."

"Has it seen us yet, Nibulus?" asked Appa.

"And is it human," interjected Gapp worriedly, "or Tusse?"

They continued to stare at the figure, even though it was now a mere wraithlike shade among deeper shadows.

"No, not a Tusse," Wodeman reassured them.

"Right," agreed the Peladane. "The herdgiants seldom venture this far east. Especially not alone, and at night."

Gapp breathed a sigh of relief. His memories of the Ogre were still too fresh to permit him any ease in the presence of any giant, even the relatively "civilized" Tusse.

Then Wodeman's low voice cut in again. "It knows we're here," he said cryptically, "and it isn't afraid of us."

The others stared at him, but none questioned his words, acknowledging that his power of perception was far greater than theirs.

"See!" he whispered sharply. "It moves off. . . ."

As they all peered, the figure disappeared. Whether the smoky pall between them had thickened, or whether it had indeed slipped away, they could not tell. Either way, it was no longer visible.

"Quick!" urged Finwald. "We don't want to lose him."

"What!" cried Gapp, forgetting himself in his panic. "Go after that thing? You jest, surely?"

"It'll almost certainly be from some nearby village," Finwald persisted. "No one would travel alone in this place."

"Aye," agreed Appa, "this might be our only chance of finding the road. Another day and we'll starve—or I will, at any rate."

"Have a care, Aescals," Wodeman warned them. "It does not pay to be hasty in the marshes. There is something fey about yonder wight. It wasn't walking on firm ground, and it smelt of Huldre."

"Huldre" was a Torca word, adopted by the southern Aescals, meaning "those that are hidden." It was the name given to all those spirit creatures that dwelled on the very edge of daylight, in the strange, veiled world of fey, which was always there, but could never be discerned by mortal men—unless the Huldre themselves desired it. To the men of Wyda-Aescaland it was a name associated with many things not of this world, things that were evil, unholy, troublesome, and malicious—meddling little bastards who sniggered at honest people on the very edge of hearing, slipping in and out of their world to cause mischief, turn milk sour, cause horses to be already sweaty in the morning, corrupt the innocent in unholy unions betwixt ill sheets, steal babies and replace them with their own malformed little brats. They were not to be trusted, not to be sought out, not to be acknowledged. Not even to be believed in.

But to Wodeman's race, a people much closer to their roots in the earth, the Huldre meant something very real. *They* did not need to question their existence, for the Huldre had been here long before men, before any of the various races that dwelt on the earth today. Only the Rawgrs were older in origin.

But Nibulus, leader of men, basically a pragmatic and unfanciful person, was not Torca. He could feel the firmness of his greatsword hilt through the leather of his Gauntlets, and made his decision.

"We are enough against one," he solemnly declared, "be it man or devil. Put trust in your iron, my men, and follow me. For hunger is one enemy no sword can defeat."

In pursuit of the vague figure they went, the going becoming increasingly difficult with each passing step. Darkness had descended in full by now, and they walked in a dreamlike limbo world of mist, all now sharing Gapp's earlier apprehensions. The constant sucking of mud that hindered each and every step was gradually getting to them, draining their will as if sucking their very life essence from them.

Every now and then one or other would cry out, "There it is!," and they would all head off in a new direction, their pace temporarily quickened by renewed hope. Yet their elusive quarry seemed always a step farther ahead, and would not stop or turn at their urgent calling. Ever alert lest they were being led into a trap, they anxiously persevered on their progress through the mist. Suddenly a wall of darkness loomed up ahead. At first they could not tell what it was, but as they cautiously approached, they discovered it to be a thicket of trees.

"There," came the sudden whisper from Wodeman through the stillness. "Off to the left, just before the trees—see it? Our slippery friend."

They followed the direction of his finger, but had to concentrate hard for a few moments before they saw it. Something was moving about twenty or thirty yards away. It was that same figure again, just about to enter the thicket. But before any of them could call out, it disappeared into the darkness of the woods.

Hurriedly they rode on, closing the gap, and within seconds were following their quarry into the thicket.

If it had seemed strange and fearful terrain out in the swamp, then it was doubly so here in these woods. With the mist now as thick as soup, and even the vestigial light of late evening lost to them, visibility was reduced to almost nothing. There was no clear path to be found, so they had to force their way through a dense undergrowth of thorns and roots that clawed at their cloaks and snagged their feet. Their pace slowed almost to a standstill as they hacked their way through the entangling foliage, while every so often branches dripping with moisture suddenly reached out and raked their faces.

Though exhaustion dulled their instincts, all they could think about was finding the stranger and somehow putting an end to this day's futile journeying. But into their overtired and overstretched minds stole thoughts of great unease; foremost among these was that anyone else passing through these woods must have had as much difficulty in finding their way as they did, for they had entered at the same point, and yet had found no path. Yet there was no sight or sound of anyone or anything. Was it waiting for them, hidden in the dark? Was it alone? Was it human? It was above all a mystery why anyone should be out in the marshes on a night like this, so far from human habitation.

They now realized that they had completely lost all sense of direction—even Wodeman, to whom this had never happened before. They had also lost their quarry, and were just wandering around in this tangled thicket with no idea of where to go next. A decision as to whether they press on or go back was no longer relevant, for they did not have any clue where they were.

And now they began to hear, some way off yet all around them, a low bubbling sound that carried within it the rumor of drowning. One thing was for certain: None of them was prepared to stop and make camp for the night. Not in this place.

Then all at once they felt themselves descending a slope, and before long the trees began to thin out a little. They perceived that they had descended into a hollow, and, filling this entire depression ahead and illuminated by a dim, unknown source of light, was a bog of thick black quicksand. It was a morass of such blackness, such life-swallowing awfulness that they felt as if their souls were draining out of their bodies and into its bottomless embrace. It was as if countless millions of things had died here, decaying into a stinking miasma. Here and there, sticking up out of the putrescent slime, the travelers shuddered to see the pale and fleshless bones of those that must have fallen prey to this dreadful place. Above the constantly sucking ooze floated a grey-green haze that lit up the entire hollow, looking noxious to the touch and repulsive to behold.

The travelers did not utter a word, but simply stared. Huge strands of pale cobweb hung from tree to tree, bough to bough, hemming the hollow in like a tent, while above them, even larger sheets of gossamer hung like a canopy, crawling with great black spiders and poisonous-looking red-and-green insects that scuttled about silently. Ravens resembling reanimated gibbet-hangings stalked about stiffly amid the branches even higher up.

As they gazed out across this awful glade, their hearts sank and fear flowed into them.

No one human had come this way tonight. No *living* person, at least.

Not this or any other night, for this was not a place for the living, and death permeated the very air. It was not a natural place. It had the air of dreams about it. Even Wodeman wrinkled his nose in distaste, sensing the darker side of fey here. It felt like a place where lost souls wandered, drifting off into a walking sleep through a somnambulant world of creeping numbness and disturbing, dreamlike pseudorealities.

This marsh was where it all came from: the fear, the dread, the swampy stench of death and decay, drifting out toward them in wreaths of whispering vapor. All sound was deadened: the susurration of hushed voices, the muffled clump of hooves, the eerie squeal of dead twigs scraping over armor plate. And from the rotting world before them only the sounds of dripping, sucking, whispering, and scurrying.

They could feel a sense of suffocation that squeezed the life out of everything just as they could feel numberless eyes upon them, watching malevolently from the shadowed trees and undergrowth.

"Where to now, boss?" asked Finwald, his fear prompting him to say something, anything.

Nibulus thought for a minute. "He didn't come this way," he said at last, "so we'd better turn back. . . . Come, follow me."

Without a moment's hesitation, the company wheeled about to depart this hateful spot. As he too made to turn about, Gapp's gaze was held by a sudden movement in the pool of slime. Curious little amphibians were popping their heads up through its clammy surface to regard him with unknowable intent. He did not wish to tarry a moment longer, but still he looked on, transfixed.

It seemed to him that, as he watched, other small, pale shapes materialized out of the murk. What it was he was looking at he could not at first tell, feeling confused. Little shapes now hung from the trees, hanging limp or swaying slightly. Paper? Old clothes, like laundry that had been hung up to get damp and filthy? But as he stared, it became apparent that they were too tenuous and ragged to be human clothing.

A darker level of fear now leaked into his soul. These were not clothes; they were skins, hairless skins hanging upon every twig.

Human skins. The flayed hides of infants. Baby skins all around.

Then, with a great, belching suck of mud, the elusive figure for whom they had earlier been searching rose out of the swampy depths and loomed before them all, its all-encompassing robe dripping with slime from surely the rankest corpse-filled drainage ditch in Hell's lowermost level. Its blackness seemed to fill the entire hollow, and any doubts they had had before about this place were now replaced by an absolute certainty. For one second they all froze, then they turned and bolted out of the clearing.

Behind them a shrill howling rose from the gaping mouth of the swamp thing, sending shudders through the earth that seemed to bring the whole hollow alive. The trees shook violently as an unearthly wind raged through them, their limbs thrashing about like claws intent on cutting off the petrified men from any retreat. Beneath them the ground began to crawl and seethe, while the undergrowth whipped toward them, curling tendrils around their horses' legs. Into this chaos rose the human and animal cries of bewilderment, fear, frustration, and sheer panic, as all twelve victims flailed about helplessly to escape such manifestations.

Then, below them, the pool began to swell.

It all happened so suddenly. The firm ground beneath was transformed into a sucking morass that began to swallow them up, while behind them the baying horror in the swamp rose up and up, till it hovered over them.

As they felt their mounts sinking fast despite the beasts' terrified attempts to lunge free of the clutching mire, it soon became clear that they were going nowhere but down. For the riders, too, as the trees and bushes continued to lash their unprotected faces, escape seemed increasingly impossible.

While the fey creature of darkness continued to wail like a satanic choir, Gapp leapt from Bogey's back to try and drag him by the curb rein out of the death pool. But the boy landed in the mud and immediately sank up to his knees, while before him Bogey reared up this way and that, screaming horribly and eyes rolling in fear. Gapp still tugged desperately at the rein, but as his eyes met those of his pony, now up to its chest in mud, he saw defeat there. Bogey knew he was about to be swallowed up completely, and his screaming reached a new pitch of terror. It was much the worst sound Gapp had ever heard in his life and he knew, one way or another, he would take the memory of it with him to the grave.

Close by the fully-barded Hammerhoof had sunk in up to its withers, and continued to sink further. Nibulus had already lost his balance and tumbled out of the saddle, landing with a great squelch in the quicksand, his armor also dragging him down.

"Radnar!" he cried. "Come! Loosen my armor—I'm sinking!"

But amid all the howling, thrashing pandemonium, Gapp was no longer thinking of his master. As Bogey disappeared up to his neck, the boy tried one last time to haul the doomed animal out of the pit. Then, sobbing like a child and blinded by tears of remorse, he drew his shortsword and, as Bogey craned his neck up in one last attempt to breathe, Gapp leant over and cut short the poor beast's agony.

The shadow that hung over them swelled in size and malignancy, and seconds later, amid further curses and promises of a vengeance from his master,

Hammerhoof the faithful Knostus disappeared beneath the bubbling surface, hauled under by the weight of his tengriite barding.

More swelling from the Huldre, as if it fed upon the life forces of the dying.

Desperately casting about for any last chance for himself, the rapidly vanishing Nibulus cried out to the three holy men.

"Finwald, Wodeman, Appa—*do* something!"

It was the undeniable voice of command and it sliced through the chaos instantly. A dazzling pulse of blue-white lightning crackled forth from Finwald's outstretched palm, and smote the marsh phantom straight in the spot where its heart should have been. A second later, a deep throbbing dirge from Wodeman rose above the wailing cry of their enemy—which, undulating sickeningly and still smoking from the power Finwald had sent against it, began to diminish slowly. So too did the flailing plant life, recoiling from this shamanistic invocation.

In spite of his predicament, Nibulus's eyes smiled broadly. *Not so bad after all*.

Then Gapp at last remembered his duty to his master. He leapt toward the sinking warrior and grasped his gauntleted hand in a futile attempt to hold him back from the all-consuming swamp. For a brief moment their eyes met, and Gapp recognized what he saw there. Unlike Bogey's eyes, filled with terror and despair, in Nibulus's there shone only *life*—courageous life full of vitality and scornful of death. In his uniquely stubborn way, Nibulus was almost smiling, and Gapp felt sure then that it would take a whole lot more than this disaster to put an end to the son of Artibulus. In that brief moment both were joined as one, a new understanding of each other breaking down all barriers of age, status, and innate character.

Both of them held on for grim life, and waited.

And through the screeching, the throbbing, the screaming, cutting through the entire cacophony that raged about the hollow, a gentle voice now sounded. Though dulcet and placid in tone, it echoed throughout the woodland with a quiet power harmonious and irrefusable. Both Gapp and his master swiveled their heads about in wonder, unable to locate the source.

It came from Appa. Up to his midriff in the fetid, undulating quagmire, the mage-priest yet maintained a countenance of deepest tranquillity. A golden-white halo radiated from him as he spoke his prayer, and peace was in his eyes.

With a gibbering wail of vexation and despair, the thing from the pool shrank away from the priest, recoiling from the elemental power of his god. In rasping ululations it sank back into its pool, still smoking from Finwald's thunderbolt, and was gone.

The limits of the death pool receded, the baby skins slowly vanished, the trees calmed their fury—and they were in darkness once more.

Stunned by the sudden quiet, the men just sat there, shaking violently. Then a hoarse cry from Nibulus snapped them back to their immediate reality, and they jumped up and rushed over to haul him out of the quicksand.

They were all grateful to be alive, and could think of nothing else for several more minutes. Not the fey terror of that unholy apparition nor its abysmal lair, nor the deaths of their beloved horses, nor the ruination they felt in their bodies, nor the starvation that yet faced them, nor the loss of their baggage to the sucking slime. They *had survived,* and every minute from now on would be a gift.

Then they heard something moving toward them through the woods.

No one moved, no one breathed. But also no one felt fear, for there simply was none left in them after their ordeal.

The sound of footsteps drew nearer, and a light, bobbing uncertainly.

Then, just at the opposite side of the clearing, a head poked through the tangled curtain of foliage and cobwebs.

It belonged to a plump, red-faced, middle-aged woman, holding a staff in one hand and a lantern in the other.

"'Scuse me," she said (in *Aescalandian,* they noted; and never before had their own tongue sounded so welcome), "but 'ave you young men got any idea what time it is? I can 'ardly getta wink o' sleep wi' all this racket goin' on!"

7

Nym

They stared across the dismal swamp in bewilderment.

After the dreadful ordeal that had left Paulus, Wodeman, and Appa unconscious, and deprived them of four of their mounts, those remaining knew they had nothing left in them. Any further hostile encounter now would be the finish of them.

So it was with immense relief (and no small amount of confusion) that they beheld the woman who stood before them. Wearing neither furs nor skins, and apparently unarmed save for the knobbly stick she clutched in one hand, she was obviously not of barbarian stock. A drab, russet-colored gown snagged with bits of twig clothed her plump form, over which was draped a grey cloak that had seen better days, and a woollen shawl with a faded pattern. She could have been a traveler, as her unkempt appearance suggested, yet there was something too rustic, too homely, about her. She looked more like a simple Aescalandian villager—and entirely out of place in this terrible wilderness.

"Wha's goin' on, Nym?" came a muted voice indistinctly from somewhere behind her. The exhausted Southerners' eyes immediately narrowed as they began to perceive shapes moving about in the darkness beyond.

"Grockles," the woman replied, "caught inna bog."

Her companions—several of them by the sound of it—seemed reluctant to come any closer, and continued shuffling about hesitantly under the cover of the trees. She, alone of them, drew closer and stood over the men who still lay panting on the ground. But though she faced them squarely and glared irately, they could sense she was nervous and still clutched her knobbly stick tightly.

"You a'right? Don' look too well to me. . . . You boys bin inna fight?"

An ironic laugh escaped the Peladane's lips as he gazed thankfully up at her. It was a plump, florid face lined with the creases of late middle age, but the

eyes held, within their earthy brownness, a clarity hinting at a vitality that was
forever young.

Nibulus rose to his feet with difficulty, bowed slightly to her, and said,
"Good evening, old lady, I am thankful to—"

"Wha's him sayin', Nym?" came a disembodied voice from the trees again.

"Bletherin'," Nym replied, not taking her disapproving eyes off the
strangers. Then, waving her stick at them, she motioned them to make haste
and follow her out of the hollow.

"Come on, come on!" she scolded them. "Don' do to hang about here,
you'm."

As quickly as they could, the travelers hauled their still senseless companions onto the remaining horses and hastened after her, leaving behind them
forever the bubbling pool that had claimed four of their mounts.

"Myst-Hakel?" Nibulus cried out after her, as she disappeared ahead of
them. "How far?"

"Just yonder." She gestured without stopping. It seemed clear that she did
not like this place any more than they did. The sounds of her companions—
family, fellow villagers, or whatever they were—could also be heard up ahead,
then also others on either side of them, and before long even some behind
them.

On through the lightless woods they were led, wondering what fate could
befall them next.

Her name, it seemed, was Nym-Cadog, and she lived alone in a small cottage
not twenty minutes' walk away from the hollow. Whether she was reluctant
to linger near the stinking pool for any longer than was necessary, she certainly was not hanging about there. Not for anyone, nor anything. Not on
this night.

'Struth, can she shift herself! Gapp marveled, as he and the others tried to
keep up with her. She may well have been on more familiar ground here than
they, but it seemed to the gasping travelers, as they plunged through the trackless woods, that the old girl was positively streaking ahead.

All the while the other villagers continued to escort them unseen. In truth,
it began to get a little unsettling, for though they kept pace with Nym and her
charges, they also kept their distance, as if refusing to allow the wayfarers to
come too close. They could be spotted only as occasional dark figures out there
in the woods, or heard only as the odd sniggering or strange fluttering.

It was a long twenty minutes, and when, eventually, they came to the edge
of the woods and arrived at her house, the other villagers had disappeared.
Gone off to their own homes, no doubt—in any case, they were not here now.
In the gloom all Nibulus and his men could make out was the vague shape of a
cottage, a simple peasant's hovel, set in a clearing, and surrounded by a small

picket fence. It had one door, two windows, one on either side, and there in front of the gate waited Nym.

They drew up sharply. She was stood there like a featureless moon shadow, silent, absolutely motionless, staring straight back at them.

"Nym?" Nibulus inquired.

The shadow stirred to motion them forward.

"Through here," they heard her say at length, leading the way through the gate and into her cottage.

Having tethered Quintessa and Paulus's mare to the gateposts, and bit by bit hauled all their baggage—human and otherwise—through the door, inside they found themselves in a small room dimly lit by four or five tallow candles that sputtered smokily in little niches set in the walls. In this murky light it was difficult to see much, beyond a dirt floor carpeted with dried rushes that gave off the dusty pungency of late summer. In the middle of the room a large and ancient cauldron hung from a tripod, its gridiron, spit, and trivet all layered with a thick black grease that exuded the same odor as late nights at the Pig and Gristle in Lower Kettle Bazaar.

Next to it was a crudely constructed yet comfortable-looking rocking chair that had worn two deep lines into the dried grease on the floor, with a small, vinegary-smelling jug and a massive water pitcher by its side. There was also a large table of solid oak set against the far wall, and a simple bench that consisted of a plank laid atop two squat logs.

Apart from this, there was little to see save two doors in the opposite wall, one on the left and one on the right.

"I'll just be a minute. Make y'selves at home," Nym said, indicating the floor.

Looking doubtfully about themselves, the guests remained standing while their hostess disappeared through the right-hand door. A moment later she returned with a huge pile of blankets, rugs, and fleeces, dumped them heavily on the floor, and quickly set about building a fire. Within a surprisingly short time she had kindled a sizable blaze, and hefting the pitcher in her stocky arms, she poured all its contents into the cauldron.

Nibulus cleared his throat. "We really are most grateful for your hospitality, my good woman," he said as graciously as he could, "and rest assured you will be rewarded most handsomely for your kindnesses. I still have not introduced myself. My name is Nibb, a soldier of fortune from the South, and these are my companions. We travel to Godtha, far away beyond the Herdlands of the Tusse, and we were passing this way when we were waylaid in these woods by some foul shade of Evil."

Neither acting nor lying came easily to the Peladane, for it was not something that one such as he had much need or desire of. But he had no intention of giving anything away about his identity or purposes until he felt surer about this Nym-Cadog and her kind. In any case, whether the woman saw through

his mendacity or not, she did not let on. Neither did she show any particular
interest in what he had just said, or give any indication that she even knew
what a soldier of fortune was. She simply went about her obligations as a hostess, and said nothing.

When she had finished building the fire, she retreated into the shadows,
and the company eagerly gathered around it. Leaving the recumbent forms of
their companions still upon the floor for a while, they warmed their hands and
stared deep into the hungry red flames that danced and crackled before their
eyes. Ignoring Nym, who kept coming and going, they savored the warmth that
gradually permeated their damp, chilled bodies, welcoming it back like an old
friend. As the fire grew apace and sent a column of smoke and sparks billowing
up through the hole in the roof, light began to fill the room.

The insensible ones were tended, the remainder of their baggage sorted,
and at last the four men were able to relax a little, and take stock of their surroundings.

To be frank, this was not the sort of lodging any of them was used to. The
main reason was the fetor: apart from the wood smoke that had impregnated
the soot-caked timbers of the low ceiling, and the mustiness that rose in curling
tendrils of steam from their sodden clothing, there was the lingering odor of
thousands of meals that had been cooked in this stuffy, badly ventilated hovel
over the years.

It was a graveyard of fragrances, a memorial garden of scents, a Grand Hall
of Remembrance for unsavory, undying fumes.

But (and this was all that really mattered right now) it was *indoors*—a situation they had not found themselves in for nearly a month—and it was warm
and dry. There was even a large tin bathtub in one corner waiting to be filled,
and most welcome of all the saliva-inducing aroma of food being prepared.

Lots of food for a bunch of adventurers who had not eaten properly in
weeks! Somehow, Nym-Cadog's cottage did not seem too inhospitable a place
after all.

One by one, during their lengthy repast, the exhausted and filthy travelers
availed themselves of the bathtub. Both table and cauldron were kept topped
up by Nym, who brought in a seemingly unending supply of food and fresh
water from the next room, but who seemed otherwise content to leave her
guests to themselves. Old clothes were discarded in a great, sodden heap in
one corner, and after each one of them had washed most of the muck off them,
new garments were donned.

After an hour waiting his turn, Gapp—the last one, of course—finally lowered himself into the slightly murky but warm embrace of the bathtub. He had
already eaten well, gorging himself on black bread and mutton, and four bowls
of a thick soup made from various root vegetables, edible toadstools, tree bark,
and spicy forest herbs. He had also drunk deeply of a full-bodied elderberry

mead that Nym kept in apparently limitless supply in the back room; and even now the kettle was whistling shrilly as the after-dinner harebell and fungus tea was being prepared. As the tub's last, slow wisps of steam exhaled through the thin scum that layered the water and adhered wetly to his face, and the comforting warmth of the water permeated every pore in his skin, Gapp felt his whole body relax: every chill, cramp, and ache floated away and was forgotten. Bloated with food, half-drunk on mead, all he needed do now was let his troubled mind drift away into sensuous semiconsciousness.

Barely aware of the others' existence, Gapp could hear the distant drone of their conversation, the muted, contented hum of their talk only occasionally punctuated by sudden bursts of his master's raucous laughter. But he was heedless of whatever was being said as he languished in blissful unawareness.

". . . bit odd, don't you think? Didn't show their face once. . . . Where're they all now? I mean, does she live here on her own?"

Finwald's voice was quickly interrupted by that of the Peladane:

"Who cares?" he said, just before thrusting yet another hunk of gravy-soaked bread into his staggeringly capacious mouth. "She's got food."

Clearly their leader was fully aware of their present situation regarding rations, and was taking full advantage of this unexpected opportunity to feed himself with as much as he could cram in without causing himself internal bleeding.

"We'll not come by such fare as this again till Myst-Hakel," he explained between mouthfuls.

"Myst-Hakel's just up the road," Finwald exclaimed. "Didn't you hear what she said earlier?"

The voices faded again as Gapp's mind wandered away. After what seemed hours, but may have been only minutes, he awoke again to the sound of Nibulus's laughter. The bathwater was still warmish, the fire still lit.

". . . that thing in the pool . . ."

"Just forget it, Finwald, it's gone. In any case, these are the wildlands; you have to expect things like that."

"But to just appear then disappear like that? I tell you, Nibulus, I don't like it at all. We're still too close, and this place . . ."

"Finwald; you always were a worrier."

"But—"

"But nothing. It's gone. I have decreed it. You three priests dispelled it or 'turned' it, or whatever the word is. Trust me, it's gone."

There followed a short pause in which Gapp's bathwater seemed to become notably cooler; then Wodeman's voice cut through clearly.

". . . can't believe you didn't even *try* to rouse me! What's the matter with you people? Can't you *smell* it? Euch! The whole place *reeks* of aberration. . . ."

Eyelids like lead, the boy finally fell asleep.

———

As he slept, he dreamed. He dreamt he was walking the high, bleak hills north of Nordwas with his brothers Ottar, Snori, and the rest. They were chattering endlessly, but whenever he tried to join in they would merely laugh and ignore him. After a while he became aware that somebody else was walking alongside him, but something prevented him from seeing who it was. He tried asking his brothers about this newcomer, but now they had transformed into Nibulus and the rest, and *still* would not speak to him.

The unseen walker emanated a distinctly macabre aura, smelling of dead crows nailed to a wooden post on a stifling summer's evening. The newcomer suddenly whispered to him in a female voice: "Look o'er there at yonder horseman. . . ."

Gapp looked, and saw that it was Bolldhe, galloping hard toward a cliff edge.

He called out warnings, and called and called, but it was no use. In desperation he turned round to face the stranger at his side, and saw at last that it was Nym-Cadog. But younger, slimmer, and infinitely more alluring than he remembered her. She was laughing at him wickedly and then he became the rider, the one galloping hard toward the rim of the cliff.

With a sickening lurch the ground gave way below him, and he was falling, falling into a blackness so dire, floating down a long, black tunnel of freezing water . . .

. . . With a violent kick, Gapp awoke. This time, he knew for certain, he was genuinely awake. He breathed a sigh of relief.

Then he realized that it really *was* dark, totally lightless, and he *was* floating in cold water. And there was a rank, *marshy* smell now that had not been here before.

In blind panic he lunged out of the chilly water and tumbled unceremoniously from the tub. He stifled a grunt, some inner voice warning him not to call out. With shaking, desperate hands he felt about on the floor for his spectacles, then his clothes, and managed to pull them on. Then, just as he was about to try to grope his way to the door, he heard a kind of fluttering, snuffling noise right behind him. . . .

Something enormously heavy smote him on the back of the head, and Gapp was propelled back into unconsciousness.

After what might have been days or even weeks, Bolldhe awoke. He jerked upright in panic. Confusion and disorientation combined to cloud his sleepy mind. The night was without any light whatsoever, and all he could hear was the gentle whisper of a night breeze through the tall reeds.

It was a cool breeze, which Bolldhe breathed in deeply, gratefully, in an effort to rouse himself. A few yards off to his left, Zhang wheezed. Then Bolldhe, smelling the familiar moor grass in the air, recalled where he was.

Not quite so obvious was why he had woken up, or rather what had woken him. There was something very disturbing about this night, a distinct sense of menace. He searched his thoughts, and had a vague recollection of a stranger, a tall, ragged man approaching him in the dark across the moors. He had held a ruel-bone scroll case in his hand, but as soon as he had proffered it to Bolldhe, the figure, its scroll case and all, had been snatched away. . . .

And then, well, Bolldhe had woken up, he presumed. . . .

Yet even now, not all was as it should be; the night seemed just that shade too dark, that little bit too still. And there was a feeling of . . . *expectancy* in the air. It was like the lull before the thunderstorm, yet Bolldhe could smell no such weather in the air this night.

Silently, he waited . . . and waited.

Eventually, still a little perturbed, the Wanderer fell asleep.

At that same moment, many miles to the east, Gapp awoke again.

At first, vague thoughts and images came and went, floating randomly through his brain. Then they became more insistent, pressing in on his mind and demanding attention. But he did not really want to wake up, for already a dull sensation of throbbing pain at the back of his head was giving him the impression that, if he were to acknowledge it in any way, it would not be pleasant. So waking up, he concluded, would be an even greater folly.

A droning hum, deep and sonorous, invaded his senses. At the moment it was still far away, a dull frequency that was felt rather than heard, just on the edge of his perception. But gradually it drew nearer, its pitch occasionally rising and falling as it grew clearer.

Now voices . . .

Finally, reluctantly, he awoke.

"W-Wass 'apnin'?" he mumbled, drawing dank air sharply into his lungs. "Where am I?"

He sat up, slid his index fingers under his spectacle lenses, and rubbed his eyes. Still the hum droned on, and the voices muttered quietly. He stared about himself but, though he knew his eyes were wide open, still it was pitch black in here. He was confused.

The voices stopped, and then one called out: "Radnar? Is that you?"

Gapp continued to stare into the darkness, fighting the urge to panic. Why was it so dark? What time was it? What was he doing sitting on a cold, gritty flagstone floor? What was that awful smell? And where were those voices coming from?

"Who's that?" he called back, a little hesitantly. "Master Wintus?"

"Yes. Are you all right?" replied the voice, a little off to his right. It sounded dead and flat, as if they were confined to a burial barrow underground.

"I'm . . . all right," he claimed, even though in truth his head now felt as though someone had bored a hole in the back of it, inserted a red-hot pipe, and was unrelentingly sucking his brains out. Purple-green lights swam before his eyes, and he felt nauseated to the point of being sick.

On top of that, he could hardly breathe for the foul stench from some unknown source.

Still the droning continued.

"Keep calm, then, Gapp," Nibulus said, in an uncharacteristically responsible, measured tone. (Gapp's pain and sickness were instantly forgotten, and a chill immediately cleared his head; Nibulus *never* talked like that. Gapp was anything but calm, now.) "We could be in a spot of trouble, here."

"Why, what's happened?"

"It seems we may have put a little too much faith in Nym-Cadog. She is obviously not what she would have us believe. Apparently we all fell asleep without posting a guard. At any rate, we now appear to be somewhat . . . incarcerated. Now, if you can manage to stand, get up and have a search around you. Tell me what you feel."

Gapp dutifully did as he was told, and crawled uncertainly about the floor with one hand waving in the dark before his face. His fingers soon came up against a stone wall, which he used to help him stand up. Then methodically he ran his hands over the whole of its smooth, almost glassy surface. Above him, no more than two inches above his head when he was standing upright, he could feel the ceiling. The walls on either side were just the same but the fourth contained a row of thick metal prison bars running from floor to ceiling, as immovable as the stone into which they were set.

Gapp sat down heavily, and his chest began to constrict in panic. The truth of the situation was that he was trapped in a tiny dark cell.

He called out to his master in a shaky voice, "D'you think you can get me out of here, please?"

" 'Fraid not, Gapp," Nibulus replied in that same calm tone. "We're all of us in the same position. We think that woman Nym must have sold us to some lord or other to hold for ransom here in his donjon, or wherever we are."

There was a general buzz of agreement from different directions.

"Everyone else here too?" asked Gapp, feeling close to despair.

"All here," Nibulus confirmed. "All awake, all unhurt, and all hopelessly trapped in separate cells, I'm afraid. Except Finwald, who's been squashed into an animal cage so small he can't even stand."

Gapp, despite everything, began to feel vaguely irritated at his master's apparent composure. Peladanes were *always* so calm and unflappable in situations like this. Why couldn't they just panic like everyone else?

"The walls are solid, the bars immovable, and all our weapons have been taken from us. So it looks like we're going to have to sit this one out and see what happens."

"What about our magic-users?" Gapp persisted, as though he were the first one to think of it. "Can't they do—?"

"Not me, unfortunately," came the feeble voice of Finwald from another direction. "I overspent my powers back there at the swamp—it'll take me some days to build up my resources."

"And Appa's even worse depleted," Nibulus continued. "He can't seem to stop falling asleep."

"Not that he'd be much use to us even if he were fit enough," Finwald added, "Not really up his street, this sort of thing."

"According to Wodeman, not up anyone's street," Nibulus pointed out. "He claims we're trapped in 'another world,' locked away by Huldre magic, and if that's true, it means none of our own magic will work."

The rapid breathing audible from the cell to Gapp's left began to accelerate, and the stench became suffocating.

"Not that it's stopped him trying," Finwald remarked. "Hear that thrumming? That's him trying to find out what's going on."

Gapp turned his attention to the noise he mentioned, which seemed to be continuing without even the slightest pause, a constant drone reminding him somewhat of the mage-priests' plainsong he had so often heard echoing through the stony temples back home. He shivered. This closeness, this darkness, it was not to his liking at all, and the sorcerer's incantations were not reassuring him one bit.

He began to frisk himself in the vain hope of finding something that might prove useful, but partly to keep his sanity from fragmenting. He was still wearing his spectacles, thankfully, and the clean set of clothes he had put on after emerging from the bath, but all his other gear—cloak, belt and pouches, baggage and weapons—was missing.

However, there might still be a few articles that he had concealed in various items of his clothing. Before setting out from Nordwas, the youngster had considered the possibility of being robbed, so had sewn a number of small items into the lining of some of his garments, for just such an emergency as this. He ran his fingers along the hems of his clothes, trying not to hope too hard that it was into these same clothes that he had hidden these precious objects.

"They're here," he whispered in relief, and grinned at his own resourcefulness.

"What?" hissed a voice in the dark. It was the voice of the stinking individual who had been breathing so hard next door to him.

"My survival kit," Gapp whispered back, conspiratorially.

"Survival?" came the voice again. It was, of course, Paulus—who else could smell like that? It was only now that Gapp began to appreciate the Nahovian's efforts up until now to sleep downwind of them whenever they pitched camp.

Everyone was listening attentively now, hopes rekindled by this unexpected foresight from the least one among them.

"Let me feel what's here," Gapp said. "A length of wire, a small lodestone . . . several pinches of *Khetann-Hittam* pick-me-up . . . and some string."

"Yes?" Nibulus prompted.

"That's it."

"That's it?"

"Yes, I think so . . . yes, that's it," Gapp concluded.

"You call that a survival kit?" hissed Paulus, now sounding on the verge of hysteria, "You stupid little maggot! I'll twist your soggy little head off when I get my hands on you. What were you hoping to survive? A head cold? Your boot laces snapping?"

"There're many situations," the slightly abashed esquire began defensively, "in which my personal survival kit could be—"

"*Name* one!"

"The lodestone can tell you the direction—"

"Brilliant! So now we know which direction is north: through a set of inch-thick bars or fifteen feet of solid rock! . . . Have you *nothing* useful?"

Gapp flushed. "No," he replied coldly. "Have you?"

"You little bastard, I'll—"

"Shhh," hissed Finwald. "You'll disturb Wodeman. I think he's trancing."

They considered this for a moment, then simultaneously came to the conclusion that Wodeman's trancing was probably even less use than Gapp's survival kit. It was fortunate for the boy, therefore, when he suddenly announced: "Oh, here's my flint and steel, too . . . and my tinderbox."

He tore off a length of his shirt, tied it around with the wire, doused it with tinder, and struck sparks over it with his flint and steel. The tinder caught almost immediately, and though the cloth sputtered a little at first, before long it was burning happily. The flames growing, fed by Gapp's careful breath, he took it over to the cell's bars and placed it upon the floor.

The cloth was not perfectly dry, which meant it burned slowly, and also meant it hardly burned at all. The flame was not much, then, but to eyes that had become accustomed to the darkness it shone like a beacon.

Gasps of wonder mixed with distaste breathed around the prison as the company looked for the first time upon their surroundings. They were confined in a long narrow chamber with a line of cells down each side, and a wide passage running between them. Near one end was a freestanding cage that held the dejected, cross-legged form of Finwald, and right in front of this was a hole in the floor that could have been a well or latrine, and out of which issued a sound very faint and indistinct. At the opposite end of the long cellar a short staircase ran up to a single door, apparently the only way out of this place.

But it was the color, the shapes, and the *grain* of the place that was so alien and unsettling to their eyes. The smooth, glassy walls were composed of something that resembled jade, a translucent, soapy green stone shot through with weird swirls of gold that seemed to absorb the light of the paltry flame and reflect it back in bright pulses; while the bars of the cells looked deceptively like gleaming copper, and on the walls intervening between each cell door hung

velvety, crimson drapes. The entire place was unlike anything that any of the
company had ever experienced before, and suited perfectly the dizzying aroma
from the diseased Nahovian.

"Maybe Wodeman wasn't so far from the truth in talking about 'another
world,'" Nibulus muttered. Appa opened one eye and groaned, and Paulus's
breathing redoubled in pace.

"That's it," Gapp moaned. "We've got to get out of here. . . . Master Nibulus, does the *Chronicle* make any mention of this place?"

"Oh, I hadn't thought about that," the Peladane replied, "Let's see . . . ah yes:

"Inne the marshes wer we captored by a foulle
wich, who didde trobell us with vile prisonment.
But a tunel we didde bild, and thence cam oute
To yonder marshland—"

"A tunnel!" Gapp croaked. "Does it say where?"

". . . inne the last sell but one, behinde a sette
of loose stones."

"Last cell but one?" That meant his own cell. Gapp spun round and began
searching the shadowy walls. "Does it say where, exactly?"

"Just behind yew, to yor left."

"What, here?"

"No, there, yew halfwitte!"

Gapp paused, then quietly sat down in one corner.

For want of anything better to do, he peered at Wodeman, who was still
droning on.

The shaman knelt motionless upon the floor of his cell, his head slumped
upon his chest. His intoning was fainter now. But Gapp also noticed something else: In the unsure light of this otherworldly place it was difficult to tell,
but it looked as if Wodeman crouched in the middle of a chalked circle, with
arcane sigils bordering its outside rim. Gapp stared in genuine curiosity now,
his previous disquiet forgotten.

After several minutes, his patience was rewarded. Without any forewarning,
Wodeman's plainsong ceased and he collapsed upon the floor. One moment he
was kneeling in rigid concentration, the next his body went slack and he crumpled like a rag doll. He now lay spreadeagled on his back in the middle of the
chalk circle, his face deathly pale, his body as inert as a corpse.

"What's he doing?"

"Is he all right, d'you reckon?"

"Quiet, everyone! It's just his magic."

Straining their eyes to see better, the company watched the still form of

Wodeman in perplexity. They all realized his lore was ancient and bizarre, part of an alien tradition that preceded conventional wizardry and alchemy by many centuries. But in that dark gaol, with its flickering shadows and half-heard echoes, it was not so easy to curb the imagination.

Then out of Wodeman's open mouth appeared a pygmy shrew.

The watchers gasped in fear and awe. Something was happening here of which they had no comprehension.

The shrew, a tiny, black creature with a silky sheen, sniffed the air nervously, its whiskers all atwitch. One tiny paw pressed down upon Wodeman's lower lip, then out it popped. It darted away from his face and landed lightly on the damp straw covering the floor. It plowed its way through the stinking, wet stalks until it reached a drier patch. Here it hesitated. It stood up on its hind legs and sniffed the air again, as if to determine its next direction. Then it moved off, slower now, nosing its way through this cleaner straw.

"It's trying to find something," Finwald commented, his eyes bright with fascination.

The shrew made as if to exit Wodeman's cell, but as it reached the bars, instead of slipping straight through, it wove in and out of them as if doing a slalom, before continuing on its way. Thereupon it changed direction and skittered across the floor toward the row of cells opposite.

In doing so it virtually fell into a drainage channel that ran the length of the passage toward the well at the far end. Far from taking fright, it set off at a greater pace down this course. Pausing only twice, once at a blockage of sludge and once to savage a worm it encountered, it continued along the runnel until it reached the lip of the dark well.

There it stopped, and stared intently down into the gaping black hole.

"Weird," remarked Nibulus.

"Without doubt," Finwald agreed.

All of a sudden the shrew began squeaking urgently, far louder than one would expect from such a minuscule creature. The men gawked in astonishment. It was as if the creature was calling out to something down below there.

Then abruptly, it fell silent. Without a moment's delay it pelted back up the length of the runnel, across the floor into Wodeman's cell, and dived straight back into the shaman's wide-open mouth.

Wodeman's whole body jerked violently, then he sat bolt upright, looking about himself in bleary confusion, till he focused on his watching companions.

"Oh, there you are," he said limply. "I've just been talking to Bolldhe."

With a choking cry, Bolldhe awoke. Sweat had broken out all over his body, and he was trembling violently with cold and with fear. He sat up straight, and stared out into the dead blackness of a night filled with portentous dread. The last vestiges of sleep still fuddled his mind, and with them the dreams, dreams that felt more real than waking.

"What a—!" he gasped, drawing his bedroll up around himself. "What a dream that was."

As his visions quickly faded away into the recesses of his subconscious, so the thunder receded into the distance.

The thunder! Had that been a part of his dream, too? Bolldhe listened hard. There was not the slightest hint of it now. He assumed that was what had awoken him, but there was a chance that it, too, might have been solely in his head.

Yes, now that he concentrated he *could* still hear thunder echoing, right on the very outer rim of perception. But it was in his head, not outside.

With a shiver he hurriedly fumbled for the dry kindling in the saddlebag at his side, to build up the fire again. There were still a few glowing embers, so it did not take the traveler long to rekindle a small but reassuring blaze to chase away the demons of the night.

"What the hell goes on inside my head?" he breathed as he hunched over the crackling flames.

As he thought about it more, some of his dream did come back to him. It had started, he seemed to remember, much like any other: a nonsensical collection of random images and feelings, recollections of the previous day's events. It had rambled on at a comfortable pace, and was just about to lull him into the deeper sleep of dreamlessness when all of a sudden something stepped right into it, and shouted: "LISTEN!" There followed a terrific peal of thunder, and Wodeman strode out of his dream and stood there before him with fire in his eyes.

Bolldhe had stared back at him blankly. "Can I help?" he piped.

"Bolldhe," the sorcerer had urged, "you must listen carefully. Time is short." His voice had a strangely hollow ring to it, almost as if shouting down from the top of a deep well. "The Lady of the Mounds has taken us and we cannot get out. You must come back for us, Bolldhe. You must. . . ."

Without warning Wodeman had disappeared, as though he had been suddenly cut off. Bolldhe then had the briefest vision of a great circle of menhirs exploding up out of the rock like ancient sepulchres on the Last Day. High on a mountain they were, lashed by a ferocious black rain. Between gusts of shrieking wind, voices were shouting frantically to be heard: strange voices crying out in despair, warped by the frenzied gale into demonic howls.

Then, as a spear of lightning had lanced down upon the mountaintop and lit up the entire scene for an instant, it seemed to Bolldhe that he was no longer looking at standing stones but tall figures, giants, shrouded from head to toe in long grey robes, and it was their power that had called up the tempest that carried the sound of the imploring voices away.

Then they had vanished.

Bolldhe was now standing atop a high hill. It was daytime, and on a warm, gentle breeze came to him the pleasant scents of day-old cut grass, and of green plants growing by a brook. They brought with them long-forgotten feelings, and memories of so many years ago. Ah, the passing of time! Was it possible that he had ever been that young, so full of a youth that he himself had killed off so long ago?

He realized that he was back at home in Moel-Bryn. He could see the town clearly, below him at the foot of the hill; stockaded, fortified, and well patrolled, but a peaceful and prosperous town for all that. Joyfully he began running down toward it, descending through the sheepfolds, along the terraces, between the fenced-in hides, scattering sheep and geese as he ran.

But then he came upon two diverging paths. One of them, a broad and well-trodden lane lined with blackberry-laden hedgerows and shaded by gently swaying beeches, swept smoothly, and without meandering, toward the town; it looked pleasant, inviting, and safe. But just as it drew near to the town's outer protective dyke, he could discern that it veered sharply away and carried on past Moel-Bryn, on and on and on, toward the far horizon, all the way to the Crimson Sea and beyond.

Despairingly, for he had taken that road once before, and indeed was still on it now, he gazed along the other path. This one, instead, led directly away from Moel-Bryn, winding through jagged mountains, marshes, and forests, and then over a strange and terrible country of fire and ice, a turbulent land where the elements constantly fused and separated in violent eruptions. However, as he strained to see farther, Bolldhe realized that eventually this path turned back on itself, and headed straight back into the town.

He noticed then a wolf padding along it, which turned to him as if to say, "Come on, Wanderer, this way."

Suddenly a huge and savage peal of thunder shook the very ground upon which he stood. It split the air in its fury . . .

. . . And Bolldhe had awoken.

He now gazed into the multicolored flames of the campfire that seemed to purr their protest against the gentle wind that stirred them. He had experienced strange dreams before, but none so *symbolic,* none so heavily laden with meaning. Bolldhe shivered in the predawn coldness, as it reminded him of another time, years ago now, when he had likewise shivered in the dark upon cold, open grassland. On that occasion he had been taken captive by a renegade tribe of horsewomen out beyond the Kro Steppes, and had picked up only enough words of their barbarian tongue to understand that he, like most of the other prisoners, was held on the heinous charge of "Being a Man."

During his mercifully brief spell as their prisoner, he had found himself shackled next to an old pilgrim from some country far to the south who, in addition to the crime of "Being a Man," was also due to undergo torture on the further charge of "Having a Beard." This same pilgrim—Habyib, his name was, Bolldhe recalled—turned out to be what the Peladanes back home would call a witch doctor.

This witch doctor, it seemed, lived his whole life under the guidance of dreams. Every decision of his was made by the cold sands of the desert that whispered to him in his sleep; even the decision to embark upon this long journey that would lead to his being captured and tortured. Bolldhe, on successfully escaping, had decided to experiment with this principle. The reason he gave himself was for research in his capacity as an oracle—for the more authentic he could appear to the herd, the more money he was likely to be able to fleece from them. But there was more than a hint of genuine curiosity, too, for he had been troubled by very strange dreams ever since he was a young child.

However, all he had received at that stage was an earful of sand.

But last night's dream had meant something, he was sure. He *felt* the truth of it as surely as he had felt his destiny tied up in this adventure, right at the very start.

His destiny! That was it. The two paths, his search all these years . . . And then Wodeman begging him to come back, to rejoin them on the long and arduous path through fire, forest, and ice . . .

And if he chose the other path, the easy way, but one that would never end?

Or was this just the sand getting in his ear again?

For two hours he pondered and, as the sun materialized out of the saffron-tinted mists in the east, he let his mind wander wherever it would.

Then, with a sigh from the deepest place within his soul, he rose, saddled up Zhang, and took to the road again, changing direction. With the light of the jacinth sun inflaming his face, he muttered darkly: "You'd better be right about this, Habyib—and you, Wodeman."

The light from Gapp's makeshift torch was scarcely brighter than the glow of a pipe now, yet in this strange world of jade, copper, and crimson that seemed to magnify light, still it was enough to see by.

"So . . . what's up, Wodeman?" the Peladane inquired, chary, circumspect. "You all right?"

"We thought you'd died," Gapp added.

"In a way I did die, Greyboots," Wodeman replied, wincing at the shrillness of the boy's voice like a man with a hangover, "in that my soul departed from my body . . . but I'm all right now, it's back."

"*Are* you all right, though?" Nibulus persisted. "I mean, this business of tampering with your soul . . . ?" He trailed off darkly.

Wodeman peered at the Peladane curiously. He was surprised at this seeming concern for his soul, especially from a crass and insensitive killer such as Wintus.

"Tampering with my soul," he echoed. "But what is magic if not a means to transform oneself?"

Nibulus was always at a loss when confronted by the cryptic riddling of magic-users. He was far more concerned with the well-being of one of his party than with cosmic discussions on the nature of magic.

Finwald on the other hand was intensely interested in Wodeman's spell. "What did you *do,* then?" he asked, "Neither me nor Appa could summon up the slightest power down here."

"That is because you have not been brought up with magic from birth," Wodeman replied, "and because you still use your brain too much. Remember, your thinking mind is only the servant and messenger of your soul, not its master. Bring it under control! But . . . I'm afraid you are a true Cunnan, Finwald, and always will be."

"A what?" Finwald replied guardedly.

"It's our word for a 'knowing one.'"

"I see," Finwald replied, somewhat relieved. "That doesn't sound too bad to me."

"And that is exactly your trouble," Wodeman sighed. "You and your sort *think* too much, and refuse to *feel.* Cunnans of Cuna, the brain god."

"Aptly named," Nibulus cut in. "It is said that Cuna gained his knowledge from the Brain of Ayame, whom he slew, and there it hangs on his belt to this day, encased in its skull box."

"Well, if we ever get out of this mess and make it as far as the Maw," Nibulus commented, "it might just happen that you find your heart's desire there, Finwald—if it *is* knowledge you seek. There are documents in Wintus Hall, records of actual firsthand accounts by some of the Peladanes at the siege five hundred years ago, that tell of a hidden place deep within the Maw. They claimed to have found a 'vast and dredfulle pit' that they believed to be a gateway to Hell itself. Above this pit the flow of souls can be heard as a torrent, a raging, screaming cascade that, were any living man to hear it, would drain his very sanity. Here, so they say, time, space, even reality itself have little meaning, and were a man to brave this terrible place, to merely stand at this gateway, he might reach in and draw forth a treasure beyond price. I mean *knowledge*—an entire world of knowledge the like of which no one can imagine. And the *power* that goes with it; power to reshape the world!"

Finwald stared in the Peladane's direction, but did not say a word.

"But what use is knowledge that has been taken, not learned?" Wodeman demanded. He turned to Finwald: "You want to share in the Torca's knowledge," he said, "to extract the bits you have use for, yet disregard the tradition that lies behind it. But how can you ever do so? Your magic is self-taught; you are first-generation. Mine is part of a tradition handed down word-of-mouth for *countless* generations. I've been raised a Torca, so it is my life, as much a part of me as my arms, legs, or head. My magic is as everyday a function as eating, not just some add-on, some acquired skill, as it is with you."

"We share our knowledge freely, gladly, with any who ask for it," Finwald protested. "We keep nothing to ourselves."

"Books, lengthy recitations, all that stuff you dabble in," Wodeman persisted, trying to explain, "they're just the scraps we threw away, the bastardized remnants of a much older, greater way, one you will never understand. And you know why? It's because what you seek, what you really seek underneath it all is not knowledge but *power.* Power without the learning. Power to get whatever you want. *Evil* power, as often as not. But know this, Finwald: You can't do evil magic without ultimately harming yourself. That is why we never try to share our way with *magicians* like you."

"I think what we all want right now," Finwald insisted patiently, "is to get out of here. And for that we'll need magic. Any magic."

"Then transform yourself," Wodeman said. "That is what magic is, as I said earlier. Use it to find out what it is you are *not,* so you may know what it is you may *become....*" The sorcerer broke off and waved his hand impatiently. He was wasting his breath on the mage-priest. He would much rather have been telling this to Bolldhe. There were more pressing matters at hand.

"What did you see, then?" He turned to the others.

They told him all that they had witnessed: the shrew, the complex journey it had made, the well. While they talked, Wodeman nodded attentively. Finally he took a deep breath and explained:

"I dreamt that my soul rose from my body, and passed out of the confines of this place, this dimension. Long days through the awful morass did I travel, struggling to find my way. But eventually I came out upon drier land, where the going was easier. Though at one point I became lost in the trackless deeps of a wood, I soon regained my bearing, and after only another day and a night I finally reached a flat plain. Swiftly now I marched, and thence arrived at a road. This was a boon I had not dared to hope for, and from there the miles fair flew by. There was a delay when I reached a fallen bridge, and later on I was attacked by a Jaculus that tried to feed upon my spirit, but other than that the road took me straight on. And sometime during the night, I came upon Bolldhe.

"He was lost to me, however, and no amount of shouting would rouse him.

"In the end I was forced to use a dream on him. It was a sore choice, for I had wanted to save my Erce-sent dreams for when he and I were closer together—but I had no other option. Nevertheless, despite the intervention of the Skela, I *think* he got my message. All we can do now is hope."

There was a thoughtful pause.

"Fascinating," whispered Finwald. "The soul as a pygmy shrew. What a concept!"

"It's not a spell I'd ever undertake lightly," the sorcerer admitted, "for once I project my soul, I have no control over it. It's like a tame dove; I can send it out, and hope that it'll return, but if it decides to fly away, well, that's it. . . . Like the houseless souls that wander the wastelands, my soul would roam forever."

"Yet to send your soul on a journey so *far.* . . ." Finwald breathed in open admiration.

"And at the end, the well?" added Appa, who had woken up a few minutes earlier.

"Bolldhe's mind," Wodeman explained, "as deep and dark as a real well." He sounded disturbed.

"So what now?" Nibulus demanded. "Is Bolldhe aware of our predicament?"

"And more to the point," Paulus added, his fey-induced fear now held in check, "does he care?"

"I can't answer that question," Wodeman replied. "All I can say is that he'd *better* care, or none of us is getting out of here. I've now done all that I can. I'm afraid, Finwald, that my magic has more to do with questioning answers than answering questions. Like your own religion, it is a search for truth, and truths change as constantly as do people."

"So our lives depend solely upon the whim of that wanderer," Finwald exclaimed. "Cuna help us all!"

"Was it ever otherwise?" Appa asked provocatively, and he of all of them seemed the least worried. "For that is the very nature of this Quest. Always was. . . . But don't be too quick to judge Bolldhe; people change as constantly as the truth, eh, Wodeman?"

"They transform," agreed the nature-priest, "and with any luck, that's just what I've helped do with Bolldhe."

"Don't you dare meddle with my charge!" Appa suddenly barked. "If there's any transforming to be done with him, I'll do it myself."

Finwald laughed placatingly. "Don't worry about him," he said as quietly as possible to Wodeman. "What I want to know is, how could you effect that spell—your transformation, if you will—when you are unable to work any other spell in this wretched place?"

"Yes," agreed Paulus, "like getting us out of here?"

"Because it is simply not possible," Wodeman protested. "My magic comes from tapping into the universal mind of the world, but here we are not *in* the world, not in *our* world. We are totally cut off from it." He hesitated a second. "I can't be certain, but I believe that it was by a Ganferd, a waylaying spirit of fey, that we were led into this realm; and so in the realm of fey we are now trapped. I can change nothing in here, neither the bars, nor locks . . . nothing. I can only change my own soul. Our only hope, I'm afraid, now lies in help from outside."

———

There was one further attempt at escape, despite what Wodeman had said. The soul journey of their shaman had greatly inspired Finwald, and he decided it was time to try out something of his own.

"Vocal, somatic, and material," he explained to his audience, "are the components of any good spell. Hear the vibrations of my incantation, see the movements that tap into the power of my body's median points, know the chemicals and fluids that course through my system. . . ."

Thereupon he began to clench his stomach, wriggling and grunting, whilst simultaneously chewing upon a foul-smelling leaf he had extracted from some inner pocket. The others looked on with interest, but were not much surprised when all this produced was a sudden eructation from the magician's backside.

Undeterred, he continued, and after a time, to everyone's amazement, he actually seemed to be getting somewhere. There was an undeniable feeling of pressure coming from the cage he sat in, and a manifest aura of power, crackling and spitting, like a coiled serpent of fire writhing around the bars on all sides, about to strike. Sweat exuded from the priest's forehead like blood, and his face became a twitching, contorted mask of relentless concentration. The buildup of energy was massive, awesome, even frightening.

Then with a silent explosion of arcane power, all four sides of his cage suddenly burst outward, and slammed with a resounding clangor against the walls of their gaol.

And the roof of the cage, unsupported now, came crashing down upon Finwald's head and knocked him out cold.

The watchers slumped back in their cells dejectedly.

A long time passed. It might have been hours, it might have been days. None of them was yet dying of thirst, so it could not have been too long. But the waiting, it felt that there would be no end to it. And all the while Finwald remained unconscious upon the floor, breathing shallowly but never stirring.

Gapp was reminded of that long night in the Blue Mountains, before the wolves attacked.

Throughout it all, the company neither saw nor heard any sign of their captors. No food or water was brought to them. There were no sounds from outside the dungeon. It began to feel as if they had been abandoned in this hole to die. They could only talk, they *had* to talk, to distract themselves from the crippling numbness and cramp increasingly afflicting their caged bodies. At times even this diversion was not enough to quell the feeling that they would go mad.

And they would sleep. Fitfully. Never enough to give them rest, but enough to give them dreams. Disturbing dreams.

Eventually their confinement began to affect them so badly that it was as if the very bars of their cells were closing in upon them. There was then not a single one among them who would not risk his life for just one minute of freedom, one brief moment of running as fast as he could, stretching his giddy limbs and feeling the wind and the rain upon his face.

Finally, they did hear something.

There was someone just on the other side of the door. Right on the very edge of silence, so quiet that they could not even be sure it was there, they thought they could hear a chilling sound, a laugh perhaps, or a whisper, like myrrh smoke trailing through the strings of an untuned violin. It was a sound that held within it the soft sibilance and assured patience of a spider's chuckle, coupled with the wraithlike tread and hidden malice of an assassin's footfall. It was the kind of sound to associate with trails of oozing silver on cabbage leaves.

A *click*—sharp and jolting to the heart.

Wheels and cogs, well-oiled in their casing, levering to.

A *snap!*

And the door creaked open. A feel of new air, oily and warm, wafted in through the portal. With it came a sweet, cloying smell, the scent of Huldre-Home. Paulus's breathing accelerated hoarsely.

Then a voice as mellifluous as it was terrible:

"My Spriggans inform me that you are on the way to the island at the top of the world, bent on awakening the Hellhound. . . ."

Fumbling in panic for weapons that were no longer there, the men stared at the darkness at the top of the steps from where the voice sounded.

"And I, Nym-Cadog, am to do nothing? Then shall my dormancy be rewarded in full."

The speaker stepped from the shadows, and stood before them.

". . . Nym?" Nibulus whispered, too stunned to be any more eloquent. His throat felt blocked, an entire throng of words, it seemed, piled up behind, waiting to be spoken.

The figure before them was not Nym-Cadog—at least, not the plump, rustic little old lady who had invited them in for dinner the other day. About twenty-five years (and at least that many pounds in weight) had fallen away from her, revealing a vision of such stunning and unearthly beauty that even Appa was transfixed. Her skin, milk-white and flawless, now radiated a faint inner light that, like the moon's reflection upon a still crystal lake, would surely vanish in ripples if mortal hands were to touch it. Her eyes were large, black and sparkling, all-enveloping pools of ancient knowledge and fey magic. To look into them was like gazing up at the vast firmament of space upon a clear night, causing the beholder to feel utterly small and insignificant. In her sharp features could be recognized a perfect blend of ephemeral yet timeless beauty, spritish mischief, animal cunning, and backstabbing cruelty. Black hair, bramble-spiked and lengthy as a willow's fronds, tumbled around her shoulders and plunged on down to her thighs, while covering her sylphlike body was a close-fitting one-piece garment of such blackness that it swallowed up all light that came near.

She appraised them as a scientist might study a collection of insects.

"Well?" she continued as she moved down the steps. "What do you have to say for yourselves?"

At this point the prisoners became aware of two figures looming behind her. They did not remember them following her down the stairs, though the beauty standing before them was without doubt a sufficient distraction. In any case, there they were now, two great, hulking bastards of such odious and brutish ugliness that it was a marvel how such a vision as Nym-Cadog could suffer to be seen with them.

Of basically human form, they stood over eight feet tall, but were so grotesquely muscled that their arms appeared almost as separate creatures, hanging down to the ground and terminating in spasmodically twitching fingers each the size of a cucumber. Each sprouted a bristling mop of ankle-length ginger hair, under which a large red nose stuck out like a marrow. Eyes that were no more than pink slits and a cavernous, slobbering mouth added the final touches to their comeliness, while yellow drool dripped from a jungle of misshapen fangs.

With a celerity the eye could not follow, Nym-Cadog thrust one hand into the nearest cell and grabbed its occupant by the arm. Nibulus did not resist, but could not help gasping at her remarkable strength.

"A big man . . ." she said, licking her lips hungrily, then drew his arm out between the bars to sniff it properly. ". . . whose opulence smells unmistakably of the elite. I'll warrant you are the leader of more than just this pack of curs that trail at your feet . . . ?"

"Who—*what* are you?" the warrior replied evenly, not attempting to retract his arm.

"I am a lady of great estate . . ." she replied with a knowing smile, then suddenly bit his arm, drawing blood. ". . . and taste."

"I am the laughter, spell-weaving, you might hear in the dark,
The rapist, soul-reaving, that lurks in the park,
A cobweb-spinner of pernicious lies,
An original sinner with malicious eyes
But delicious guise, to hold your attention,
The Siren of the Marsh, that you're too scared to mention.
In some worlds they name me a vile seducer,
In others my fame is as a poison Medusa;
In this world, Chailleag Bheur, the Hag of Blue,
But I think that a trifle unfair, don't you?"

She looked deep into the Peladane's eyes, but he did not even flinch.

"Civilian!" he spat at her. "You may have us at your mercy, might torture or kill us, even damn our souls, but do we really have to put up with this poetry crap?"

"Ha!" she replied, pointing at him girlishly. "The leader."

She still held on to the arm, and in one sybaritic stroke of her tongue, rasped his blood into her mouth.

She finally let go of him, and turned instead to Finwald, awake now, but huddled with his back against the far wall. His expression was difficult to gauge.

"I am the stab in the back," she spoke at him, swallowing him with her gaze, "the wind in the woods, the walker without rest—"

"I am the pain in the backside," Finwald mimicked suddenly, "the whinger in the woods, the talker without rest."

Nym hesitated a second. Then she simply said, "Your death, priest, will be *unbelievable.*"

"Quite possibly," Finwald replied, "but at least you won't be around to see it."

She looked down then, and noticed the remains of the cage he had blown apart.

"Look what you've done . . ." she said, like a weary parent, and at a glance from her, one of her creatures approached the priest. The next moment Finwald found himself prostrate upon the floor of Wodeman's cell, moaning slightly.

She turned away, leaving him to his pain. Walking on, she caught sight next of Appa, crouched at the back of his cage with a look of dread on his face. She began softly stroking the bars of his cell. The look of horror on his face redoubled when he noticed the length of her talons, and his eyes almost popped out of their watery sockets. As she glared at him, he groped for his amulet.

"You don't like me, do you?"

She waited for an answer, but none was forthcoming.

"Cat got your tongue, old man?" she laughed, then became serious. "We always were in your way, weren't we?" She looked from Appa to Finwald, then back again. "Two priests of the White Light," she went on, "two flambeaux of the Great Purger, and such finely arrayed lackeys. I am truly honored to have you as guests. Have you come to cleanse me also?

"*Swift is my right hand in greeting, bearing a gift beyond price,*" she quoted from a famous Northlander prayer, "but swifter still my left, the one behind my back that holds a dagger. Your gift shall be returned to you, priests. The only question is, by whom? Hellhound or Huldre?"

"We have no quarrel with you, Blue Hag," Finwald spoke up from his dark corner. "We are bound for Melhus on business that does not concern you or your kind. We would have passed by your 'realm' if your Ganferd had not led us here."

Far from flaring up in anger, Nym-Cadog merely laughed.

"You need not tell me of your task, pale one. My Spriggans have been with you ever since you came down from the mountains, and brought to me dispatch of your every utterance. I know what it is you intend to do, and, believe me, it has a great deal to do with my kind. Ever since you first emerged from the South you have encroached on our land; you have built over our holy places, destroyed our sacred woods and groves with your farms, and desecrated our barrows—"

"Yes, sorry about that," Finwald muttered sarcastically.

"—and with this you bring your lies, your sweating confessions, your puny, weak-eyed austerity. For countless ages we had lived in these lands, enjoying the wild, free life that burns like fire through our veins. Now even this our last haven of wilderness is threatened, for you go to stir up an evil long dead, and bring him down upon us all. But I will *not* be harried by a hellhound! Seen off by a sea wolf! Flung out by a fiend! Driven away by a daemon! And definitely not ridden down by a Rawgr—he of the fetid breath, the flaming eyes, the noisome stench, and the black finger—"

"Your shoelaces are undone, did you know?" Wodeman commented.

"And *you* should know better!" she spat, spinning round to face the Torca. "Would you dig up an evil that others once had stilled? Exhume a cadaver just to see if it yet stinks?"

She turned back to them all, and her ranging expression was now one of pondering with a hint of sadness. "Could I not just have anointed you with the fairy ointment, to take away all knowledge of this place, and of Nym, of your *mis*adventure to the North? Sent you back home with nothing but bemused smiles on your soggy faces, nothing in your cabbage heads but vague memories of pretty ladies?"

She hesitated but briefly. "Only to be reminded of your quest as soon as you spoke again with your masters? No, I have thought on it; and my thoughts are this. Any that can overcome yon Ganferd in the swamp are too dangerous to be set free. You must face the Afanc, one by one."

"The Afanc!" Wodeman hissed. His face blanched in disbelief.

"Trollmollet! Trollapluck!" Nym turned to her massive henchmen. "Bring the boy; we'll start with him first."

Leering dementedly, the two Huldre creatures wrenched open the cell door and plucked Gapp out. Between them the pathetic jabbering bundle of rags and bones was carried, kicking and screaming, up the steps and out of the room. Amid seething cries of vengeance from his companions, he disappeared through the door leaving nothing behind but a last echoing wail of utter despair.

As Nym-Cadog reached the top of the steps, she turned and faced her clamoring prisoners.

"I should save your strength, if I were you," she said, then glared steely-eyed at the mage-priests. "Especially you two, vile purgers! You will need it if you are to stand any chance against my two Kobolds. Trollmollet and Trollapluck are no friends of the White Priests, having been driven into the hills by the raucous and unhallowed din of your steeple bells. The boy's fate, bad as it may be, will be merciful compared to yours."

And with that, she disappeared into the darkness whence she had come.

The dungeon door thudded hollowly, sounding as though it had shut upon their lives.

With a shuddering cry of anguish, Gapp was flung through the portal to sprawl upon the floor.

For a while he just lay there, too terrified to move, his face pressed against the floor. It felt like cold sand, but had the color of charcoal, and smelled of rotten jasmine. There was also a strong animal smell in here, blending unpleasantly with fragrances reminiscent of the leafy green vegetation that grows over quicksand.

Gapp could hear the Kobolds close behind him, hear their ragged breath and the irregular patter and hiss of their saliva hitting the floor. The witch was there, too: he could sense her, though she made no sound. All three of them were just standing there, waiting.

Slowly he raised himself up on all fours. He shook his head in an attempt at clearing it of the dizzying effect of the sickly smell. With a nauseating knotting-up of his innards, he slowly raised his head to look about the room.

It was small, and reminded him of those little chapels of the Lightbearers back home. Indeed, it did have a certain air of sacredness about it: the austerity, the simplicity, and sanctity. Tallow candles burned in each corner.

Yet somehow it seemed all the wrong way round: perverted, desecrated, brooding; like being on the wrong side of a mirror. The black candle smoke stung his eyes, and the very air was infused with darkness, sickness, and a hidden primal dread . . .

. . . And then there was the Thing that emerged from the shadows.

Gapp's face froze, his chest became tight. His throat closed in on itself, almost strangling him. He stared in wide-eyed horror as the figure began to reveal itself, a great shape clothed in a robe with both the smell and hue of rain-sodden ashes, and his gagging sobs became ugly, heaving rasps.

Slowly, savoring the torment it could see in its victim's face, the thing approached. Claws like jagged shards of steel reached up and drew back the hood as it came on, and finally Gapp cried out aloud as if he had been speared through the head.

It was like a creature that had stalked from the dark places in his mind but that he had never suffered himself to acknowledge before.

The abomination stood proudly before its prey, relishing the effect it was having. Through wide nostrils composed of bone and slimy black gristle, it breathed in deeply the hot waftings of the boy's sweat. Thick, dirt-encrusted horns struck out from its domed skull to curl round behind its head, and hide like set wax stretched glistening and livid over its cranium. Hunched over it stood, with arms trembling in weird excitement, as featureless black eyes fixed Gapp with their malefic intent.

Slowly, but eagerly, it advanced.

"... And then there were five," the Peladane breathed heavily.

In all his years of campaigning, he had never known the like of it. At his father's side he had faced hordes of enemies, vast battalions of the infidel, and still come out victorious. Whether as a sergeant in charge of fifty, Thegne in charge of two and a half thousand, or as part of an entire Toloch of fifty thousand, he had never yet tasted defeat. He, *they,* had been invincible! There had been casualties, there had been madness and confusion, and Death was ever present; but courage, strength, and determination had always seen them through.

Nothing, however, had prepared Nibulus for this. He was only now realizing that up till now all his battle experience had ever taught him was how to succeed. And now began the next stage of his education: how to fail. Clearly, however, it was not as easy as it seemed.

His failure gnawed at him, gnawed away so quickly he felt himself being consumed by the second. But Nibulus Wintus silently swore to himself, and to his god, that if Pel-Adan would grant him but a chance, no matter how desperate, he would do *everything* in his power to help his men. Even if it meant making the supreme sacrifice.

But at the moment it appeared he would not get even this opportunity. He almost *deserved* to die.

He looked around. Gapp's torch—that pathetic little twist of damp rag—had at last burnt out. But still its dim illumination was retained, for a while at least, in the gold-flecked jade of the walls in this strange place. In its fading light he could see the dejection of his companions, but he was strangely warmed to note that they, too, had not totally given up yet.

Finwald, Appa, and Wodeman sat in concentration, trying against all odds to summon up what little priestly power they had left in them. It had been agreed that any magic they might invoke would not be wasted on trying to release them from their cells; they would be out of them soon enough anyway, once Nym returned. Instead they had opted for making an attempt on the lives of the Kobolds. Those monsters seemed to be the main obstacle in their path, once they were out of their cells.

Nibulus, in an attempt to forget the sickening cries of his esquire that still echoed in his head, called out to the others:

"Do you have any idea what we're up against here? What *are* these things?"

"Chailleag Bheur," Paulus mused, "the Hag of Blue, the Siren ... these are names I have heard of from the old times of the North. Children's tales. To be honest, I don't believe she knows who she is."

A voice interrupted them. "Old stories that were once just that are now reaching out of the darkness to engulf us," Wodeman said, breaking his own concentration. "It's a strange journey we're taking, this one."

Nibulus was becoming a little annoyed at the pair of them; they both appeared to know things he did not. "Well, what is she—are they—then? If there's anything I should know, tell me. It might help."

"We have met up with a Huldre," Wodeman explained, "as I warned you we might, now that we are beyond the lands of men. And a rather potent one, too, to exert dominion over all these others."

"*They're* all Huldre, too?"

"Oh yes," Paulus confirmed. "Those Spriggans she talked of—Nym herself must be a particularly potent one to hold sway over *those* willful little devils, all the way from here to the foothills of the Blue Mountains. I'd guess those 'villagers' we heard back in the woods were they."

Paulus was now shuddering almost uncontrollably, and his customary fetor had taken on a new piquancy. "They must have been spying on us all the time," he whispered shakily, "walking amongst us without our knowing. My people say that the Hidden Ones are everywhere, always ready to snatch away mortal souls for their deviant purposes. Not even our beasts are immune from their tampering. Oft have I opened the stable door of a morning to see our horses literally besodden with sweat. We slay them whenever we can."

Nibulus thought about this for a second, but failed to grasp the Nahovian's meaning.

"Making horses sweat doesn't sound *that* terrible to me," he remarked.

"It means the Huldre have been riding them hard all night long at their disgusting carousals," Paulus explained in spittle-flecked loathing.

"Like that young shepherd you got rid of?" Appa suddenly asked of the Peladane. "The one who used to make sheep limp?"

"No, that was something entirely different," Nibulus replied, vexed at being sidetracked. "Tell me about the wanderer on the moor."

"A Ganferd, as Finwald guessed," Wodeman explained.

"Ellyldan," Paulus agreed in his own tongue. "They are lamentable souls, pitiable to behold, Huldres that fill the hearts of mortals with sorrow and darkness. But troublesome, drawing folk wherever they will, and usually to a sticky end. The Blue Hag must have sent it out deliberately to lure us to her domain."

"And the Afanc thing she mentioned?"

"Odd," Wodeman admitted. "For Afanc is not just one of her world, but also of ours. I do not understand why she would have such a creature in her employ . . . still less how she could control it."

"Perhaps she rewards it in ways we dare not think about," Paulus suggested darkly.

"Hmn, possibly," Wodeman pondered. "I certainly wouldn't blame the Afanc for *that*. Yet Afanc is not something to be controlled. Kobolds are one thing, slow, unbelievably dull-witted clods that can be led by any Huldre worth her salt, but the Afanc is a creature of great power, a thing of Chaos." He paused as if listening. "I'm sorry, but I very much doubt there's much left of your esquire now, Nibulus."

At exactly that moment Gapp burst through the door, threw an armful of their weapons down on the ground, and began fumbling with a ring of keys. He had his own small pack upon his back, and his shortsword safely in its scabbard at his belt.

"Bolldhe's back!" he shouted in elation as they all sprang up from the floor. Then finally he found the key to his master's cell, and freed him.

"That thing . . ." the boy stammered as Nibulus burst out of his cell and swept up his greatsword.

"The Afanc, yes," the Peladane replied, savoring the feel of Unferth in his hands at last.

"Whatever it is," the esquire went on breathlessly, "it was up there in her room. It came at me with its fangs and all, but—there you go, Paulus, your sword's down there—but then I heard the witch screaming and looked round, and there was Bolldhe holding a shortsword—mine, I might add—at her throat. . . . Oh fiddlesticks, this isn't the right key. . . . And then, and then . . . oh yes, and then he tells her to call off her lackeys or he'll kill her, so he sticks my sword into her neck a bit, only a bit but it draws blood, and she screams and he goes on threatening her, so, um, so yes so she snaps her fingers and the two hairy buggers, they just scream and start smoking and shriveling and leg it out the door, and I can see them shrinking still and smoking as they dash out the house and are gone. . . ."

Nibulus and Paulus were now distributing the weapons, hurling them through the bars of the appropriate cell doors as well as they could in the scant light, while Gapp still struggled with Appa's lock.

"Got it!" he cried, still suffused with excitement after his harrowing experience. His voice had climbed to a new level of shrill hysteria, but for once this was the least of the others' worries. With Appa now also free, he leapt over to the next cage, and continued his story to any who might be listening:

"But the thingy, the Afanc, it wouldn't go away, just ranted and steamed and tried to get at Bolldhe. But it knew it daren't get too close 'cos of the sword at Her Ladyship's neck—and she screams to Bolldhe that she can't do anything so he pushes the sword in deeper and it—that Af-thing—it cowers away 'cos of her screaming much worse, and it holds its head like so—"

"Gimme some of those keys!" Paulus snapped, and ripped a few from the ring.

"Then Bolldhe chucks me my sword," Gapp continued, "and the monster suddenly jumps at him really quick but Bolldhe's already got his axe in his hands, and he HACKS it one of the best hacks I've ever seen in my life, *right in the face*—"

"So it's dead?" Nibulus cried.

"But that didn't have much effect, and it comes back for more, but Bolldhe's got her by the hair now and there's all this stuff coming out of her mouth and . . . and, and he holds his axe right above her head! That stops the monster, and Bolldhe yells at me to get our weapons and the keys he's found, and to get you all out of here, so I did but I don't know if he can hold it off for long, what with it being so mad and all—"

A ghastly screech echoed down the passageway beyond the door, and after four or five footsteps that approached with impossible swiftness, the Afanc burst into the chamber. The last glimmers of light in the gold-flecked jade walls now sprang into life again, and the gaol was lit up with sick light.

The Afanc had clearly decided that Nym was too precious to risk, but the *other* enemies in this place held no axe over her head. It surveyed them now appraisingly: the boy with the keys; another one, much taller, also struggling to unlock cell doors; a puny old one backed up against the far wall, beyond the well; and the big, royal warrior in the middle of the room. Drool gouted from its mandible; it would *decorate the walls* with their remains!

As Nibulus gazed upon his latest enemy, there was a part of his mind registering the fact that the Afanc was, quite simply, the most dreadful and loathsome adversary he had ever faced in his life. There was another a part of his brain that reminded him he wore no armor, and that of the four of them who were already out of their cells, only he was likely to engage straightaway.

But none of this made a blind bit of difference; he had made his vow to his god, his prayer had been answered, and he was a Thegne of Pel-Adan—and more to the point, a right hard bastard.

The Peladane in him kicked in immediately, and, hefting his sword, Nibulus charged screaming at the beast.

The Afanc's face split wide in a horrible grin, and it hurled itself down the steps toward him. The Peladane's challenge would not go unanswered; many more fearsomely accoutered than this one had it slain in the halls of kings ere now. . . .

Nibulus flung himself out of the way of the onrushing monster, and at the same time used the weight of the greatsword to spin himself around in a full circle, the blade fully extended, all in one smooth, well-practiced motion. Unable to swerve in time, the Afanc found itself flying into the path of the weapon as it scythed through the air. With a sickening thud the beast caught the six-foot-long blade full in its stomach.

The impact caused the walls to shudder and the copper-hued bars to sing, its echo reverberating down the well like the moan of a fleeing phantom. Gapp's gut lurched and he reeled with sudden nausea. Unferth had struck so hard and bitten so deep it was almost wrenched from the Peladane's grasp. It was a blow that would have cut any normal man in half, and the air throughout the gaol was immediately tainted with a stench like rotten fish mixed with oily acid.

Nibulus recovered his balance and looked. His mouth sagged; the monster was still standing!

Three thoughts flashed through his brain simultaneously: The Afanc was *not* a normal man, the others had *not* joined in yet, and he *was* going to die.

Then a blow he had not even seen sent him crashing with a gasp against the wall nearby.

He sprawled on the ground as many-hued patterns like lightning bolts and exploding flowers filled his vision. Wodeman's voice kept screaming something he could not understand, and just in time he realized that the Afanc was coming for him again. Instinctively he brought up his right foot and kicked the brute savagely in the face. His enemy roared in muffled fury as the big man's boot crunched hide and bone into one painful substance.

But still it came on. Nibulus had a vivid image, one that he knew would stay with him for the rest of his life—however long that might be—of a leering, fang-filled mouth flowing with blood-reddened saliva, and two tiny, hell-black eyes staring straight into his own. He was only just aware of the frantic gibbering of Gapp as he still scrabbled with the ring of keys.

Then, just as a huge taloned hand caught the Peladane by the throat, Paulus finally plunged his blade deep in between the beast's shoulder blades, scraping noisily in between two vertebrae. Screeching in agony the Afanc lurched upright, its back arched and wet with blood, but in the next second the Nahovian's blade swept back again and caught it a vicious swipe across the neck.

Unbelievably, the monster still did not fall. This time it lashed out at Paulus. There was a strange sound as all the wind was knocked right out of the stricken mercenary, and he was flung right across the dungeon to fall right beside the well.

On the other side of this aperture, Appa stared down in shock at the fallen warrior lying on the floor. He himself cowered against the wall, gripping his crow's-beak staff tightly and refusing to move. All he could do now was stare.

Gapp, fingers quivering uncontrollably, bounded over toward the cell in which Wodeman and Finwald were still confined, leaping up and down like caged monkeys. And, within the chaos of his fury, Wodeman finally managed to find his Aescalandian tongue and scream at Appa, "Help Paulus, you useless bastard!"

The Afanc was now free to come after the two little people fiddling around at the far end of the subterranean gaol.

Yelping in alarm, Gapp gave up on the final cell door and drew his shortsword to face the beast. In the cage right beside him Wodeman crouched with his quarterstaff brandished horizontally, while Finwald stood back against the rear wall, with sword cane drawn. Outside, even Nibulus was trying to get to his feet, but they all knew he could not reach them in time.

Suddenly there came a shrill scream from somewhere outside the prison chamber. The Afanc halted its advance momentarily and cocked its head.

Then it returned to its grisly purpose. It was coughing blood and bleeding abundantly. Nevertheless it now lunged at the boy with the limping gait of a wounded primate, and Gapp, stricken with horror, dropped his sword upon the floor and stumbled backward.

At exactly that moment, Wodeman thrust his staff out between the bars of his cell, between the feet of the oncoming monster, and, already unbalanced, the Afanc tripped. Howling, it pitched forward, and swept savagely at the boy as it went down. Gapp instinctively flinched away, and the blow missed him by inches. But as he did so, his feet caught against the still prone form of Paulus, stretched across the aisle, and he lost his balance.

For one awful moment he teetered, as he sought desperately to right himself. Then, with one final wail of despair, Gapp pitched over backward and disappeared down the well.

"Radnar!" cried Nibulus, then hurled himself toward the beast.

But at that precise moment the same screech that had sounded earlier was uttered again, only this time much closer. Everybody, the Afanc included, looked up toward the doorway.

There now stood Bolldhe, the fingers of his left hand enmeshed inextricably in the thick tresses of Nym-Cadog's hair as she convulsed at his feet. His axe, in his other hand, was poised above her neck.

"Kill it, Nibulus!" he cried frantically.

"Kill them, Afanc!" Nym-Cadog sobbed with equal desperation.

Then Bolldhe's axe swept down, at exactly the same moment as did Unferth.

From the top of the stairs came the obscene sounds of chopping, choking, and gristle separating, till nearby the steps and walls streamed with blood. From the Afanc, however, came only a single wet grunt, followed by a squelching impact as it landed on the cold, hard flagstones, its head split neatly in two.

Silence . . .

The last lingering light from the jade walls glowed red through the blood that ran down them . . .

. . . traced the trickle of the Afanc's life force as it coursed down the sluice and into the well . . .

. . . flickered one final time . . .

. . . and died.

There came from the darkness that familiar rasping noise again. Like the sawing of bones with a trepan. But it was only the xienne rod of Bolldhe's lantern, and seconds later a spark leapt out of the dark at them, and blossomed into a bright flame that stung their eyes.

They looked around themselves, hardly daring to breathe.

"For Nokk's sake, where *are* we?" cursed Nibulus.

They were no longer in the dungeon, that was for sure. The chamber that only seconds ago had surrounded them was now gone, and they were standing instead in what looked like a derelict mine shaft. Gone were the smooth flagstones, evaporated now to a rough, pitted earth floor bestrewn with rusted mattocks, fallen wooden support beams, and grimy puddles of freezing water. Gone, too, were the walls of jade, the crimson drapes and the copper bars, now transformed into nothing more than creaking pit props. And gone was the well, replaced by a shaft that plummeted down vertically to unknowable depths— and presumably down to Gapp Radnar's corpse.

The Afanc, however, was still with them, just a pathetic heap of carnage steaming in the sudden chill. But of Nym-Cadog herself there was not a trace.

The smells of decay and stagnant air, never mind the dripping of icy water from the sagging roof above, told them that this mine shaft had not been used for decades at least. It all had an undeniably creaky feel to it, and to this unease was suddenly added a deep rumbling beneath their feet.

"I really don't think you should have killed that Huldre bitch while we were still in her dimension," Finwald reproached Bolldhe.

"Shut your blabbering, you lot. It's time to leave," the Peladane snarled. "Bolldhe, take the priests with you to wherever it is you left our gear, and get it and yourselves out of here fast. Wodeman, help me with Flatulus. We'll rejoin them at the top." He paused. "Oh, and Bolldhe, thanks. I couldn't have done it without you."

Bolldhe hesitated in midstride, and turned briefly to stare at the big warrior. He shook his head in disbelief. "Really? Well, I'm glad to have been able to assist," he muttered in his own unfamiliar tongue.

Just then the rumbling increased to an alarming shudder, and the entire passage began to shake.

"Get out!" Nibulus hissed.

Nobody stopped to argue. Without even a backward glance, Bolldhe sprinted away along the mine shaft. Lantern held out in front of him, he leapt over debris strewn on the floor, in the direction where he assumed the exit lay. Finwald and Appa reeled after him, calling out for him to slow down as they tried desperately to keep up with the bobbing lamplight fast disappearing ahead of them.

Behind them, stumbling at each convulsion of the heaving earth, Nibulus and Wodeman had to almost drag along the coughing and swaying Paulus, his arms draped awkwardly about their shoulders.

"Nibulus," begged Wodeman, as parts of the ceiling began to disintegrate above them, "I don't think I can carry . . . this . . . Oh hell, he's too lanky and awkward and . . . Wouldn't he manage better without us?"

Unnoticed in the dark, the Paladane's face turned red with anger. He knew exactly what the shaman really meant. Barely able to keep even himself upright, Nibulus gave his silent response by propelling all three of them onward with such a violent wrench that it almost tore Wodeman's supporting arm from its socket.

We are not going to lose a third, he swore to himself, and Wodeman did not argue further.

Not even when the noise of destruction rose to a roar that filled the air with blinding dust, and the ground beneath them buckled and split open.

8

A Flame from the Pit

They got out only just in time. Stumbling through the pitch blackness of the mine, they had been guided by Wodeman's instinct alone. The light from Bolldhe's lantern had disappeared altogether, and they had been forced to grope their way after the fleeing men in total darkness. (Orders were orders, Nibulus realized, but did they have to obey them with such zeal?) Moments later, however, the Peladane found that his senses too had become "heightened."

Through all the creaking, snapping, crashing din, he yet managed to discern the sounds of running and shouting from ahead and, together with the shaman, fair propelled the wounded Nahovian up the steep gradient that opened before him now.

A moment later he could feel the chill swamp mist upon his face, and within seconds they were out in the open, out on the moors again, *above* ground at last, and back among the rest.

There was one final, tremendous groan, and a second later the entire shaft caved in with a thunderous crash. Thick clouds of dust and debris billowed out like a giant's phlegmy cough; then all settled into a troubled silence. The mine was sealed forever.

It was about an hour before dawn, and they were back out on the Rainflats again. The faintest hint of silver glimmered above the dark eastern horizon, and the first tentative chirping of birdsong heralded the beginning of a new day. Nibulus filled his lungs with the euphoric sweetness of clean, fresh air, the first he had breathed for nearly thirty hours. It smelled of wetlands, rain, and sedge. A few miles off to the north, low clouds grumbled.

. . . Thank You, Lord, for granting me the occasion to deliver these men, Your servants, from the Underworld.

For one brief moment, one meanest sliver of time, Nibulus fancied he saw, formed in the shifting wreaths of mist before him, the dumb, bespectacled face of his esquire; the boy was lost and alone, drifting through a morass of damnation, carried along in an icy, ethereal current, down and down. Then, just as he was swept out of sight, he turned, caught sight of his master, and with one glance, punched an auger of guilt straight through the Peladane's armor and into his soul.

Nibulus instantly looked away, shook himself in the cold predawn air, and wrenched his mind away from such thoughts.

. . . *Pity it couldn't have been* all *of them.*

None of them felt like saying a word. Paulus lay moaning upon the damp ground, and shivered convulsively. In all the furor he had forgotten about his condition, but now it was coming back to him, and he shook spasmodically in the first stages of a monster fit. Wodeman was squatting beside him, weary and even more bedraggled than usual, dispirited at losing his "Greyboots." And the two priests lay flat out, coughing and wheezing and spitting out gobbets of black and yellow slime. Only Bolldhe was still on his feet, but even he looked fatigued enough to drop. Their baggage was scattered all around and appeared to have been lying there for some time, for it was soaked through. It was as though Nym had hurled it all out of her underground realm as soon as she had the men safely in her clutches. The tengriite armor, Nibulus noted with pride, had been hurled the farthest.

"Bolldhe!" Nibulus breathed. He never thought he would be so pleased to see the old wanderer again. "What can I say? I don't know how or even *why* you came back to us, but thank you . . . *thank you.* We all owe you a debt we'll probably never get the chance to square up with you, but I for one am going to make sure I repay you one way or another."

He grasped the traveler's hand tightly, and looked deeply into his eyes. Bolldhe returned the handshake uncomfortably, but without reluctance. "Don't thank me," he replied. "Just decided to stop wasting time and get on with this job. If you really want to pay me back, make sure I get an extra slice when we return."

Nibulus smiled fondly at the Wanderer's request. But, for now, more words would have to wait. They still had a fair way to go before they reached Myst-Hakel, and their rations were every bit as depleted as they had been two nights ago.

Nibulus kept the fixed smile on his face as he turned away. That smile was all that was keeping him together.

Oh Gapp, he lamented, *whatever am I going to tell your mother?*

An hour later, they started off. They had only one beast of burden now. Quintessa and Paulus's mare had disappeared sometime during their incarceration, leaving no tracks or any clues as to where they had gone. Presumably they had

been scared off by all the *not-naturalness,* as Bolldhe put it. Only Zhang remained, who currently stood with his backside to them, letting fall a veritable
landslide of excrement in their direction (he had deliberately been holding it in
for hours for just this occasion) and steadfastly refusing to look at any of those
who had so rudely banished him and his rider two days previously.

So, after Wodeman had bandaged up their wounds with spider's web and
strips of sable, and after all the remaining gear—Nibulus's armor included—
had been loaded onto a sulky slough horse, the company set off on foot. There
were still miles of trackless marsh ahead of them, but for the first time in days
as they tramped the lonely wilderness, their way lit by a golden, crisp light from
the east, they marched as a team, united—at least for the present—by the ordeal they had somehow contrived to come through.

A full day's traveling was all it took for the company to leave the worst of the
marshes behind them. Though chill and misty to begin with, the day soon
warmed up, and as they left the lower ground, with its hollows, depressions,
and mires, they found themselves staring about themselves at a land of unique,
unexpected beauty, its very remoteness rendering it a strange tranquility. As far
as they could discern there was not the slightest hint of habitation here—
human or otherwise. All that could be seen were the gentle undulations of the
land: the small and oddly shaped knolls clad in broom and capped with solitary hawthorns, and the hollows and dells filled with a dense, white, low-lying
mist.

At times they were forced to enter these hollows, an experience not unlike
journeying into a giant's cauldron. But for the most part they kept to the higher
ground. Above, the sky was a pleasant, hazy blue, and swirling about their feet
was a knee-high blanket of white mist, out of which the taller grasses poked
like rushes in water.

At other times, when the sun shone out clearly, they witnessed a most unusual weather phenomenon, one that none of them had ever experienced, or
even heard of, before: all of a sudden the pale mist, lit up by the sun, seemed to
"ignite" somehow, shining out a pure white that obscured everything else in
the world, as if the entirety of existence had ceased. The resulting glare was of
such brilliance they would be forced to stop exactly where they were, and entirely cover their eyes lest they be blinded. Such moments happened several
times that day, usually lasting less than a minute, but once or twice continuing
for nearly a quarter of an hour. At first it was unnerving, but eventually they
began to adjust to it.

In weary silence the six men traveled on through this land, all of them in an
odd, dreamlike torpor. Save for Nibulus, they felt their hearts eased in a way,
their minds displaced from the horrors of the past few days, but it was still a
strange land they had come unto, and through it they traveled in a disquieted
wonder. No birds could they see, yet from all around them came a continuous

chorus of bizarre calls unknown even to Wodeman: high descending whistles, a rapid chattering, a plaintive *eep-eep,* trilling barks, a deep honking, low rasps . . .

Sinkholes suddenly opened before them, partly concealed by their fringes of thick vegetation; tree roots and trailing plants reached right down into their black, freezing depths, from which came the eerie, stony echo of running water and the occasional flurry of monstrous, squealing bats. Small pools of black water they found, too, at which they sometimes refreshed themselves; the water was surprisingly icy and black, and rippled with currents that suggested they were bottomless. Through his divining, Wodeman informed them that these pools and caves were all connected by deep subterranean streams, and could run for hundreds of miles.

During the afternoon they finally came upon the dyke of Enta-Clawdd that Gwyllch had promised ran "strayte and trewe" to the town of Myst-Hakel. There was little evidence of a highway upon it now, the old trade route having long since dried up, but it was the first sign of civilization they had encountered for far too long, and it injected a definite spring into their step.

Striding along it, the company now began to notice other evidence that the wilderness was falling behind them. At first they could just see the occasional standing stone or ancient tumulus, with weird petroglyphs from forgotten, primordial civilizations, or indecipherable graffiti from more recent ones, etched rudely upon their mossy surfaces. But by late afternoon, as the flies and midges began to bite and foreheads began to run freely with sweat, they would come across small, square patches of bare earth, and the little paths that the peat-cutters made, winding through fields of bulrushes and along the banks of wide streams. Here, where the kingfishers darted from their earthy holes, the company passed several mooring posts, and even the occasional flat-bottomed boat.

Soon the dyke all but disappeared, and they found themselves again in lower, wetter country. Here, even the bird life was more familiar to them: the grey heron flying overhead with ponderous wingbeats; the egret, lanky, white, and with crest a-bobbing; dancing cranes; barking crakes; the sedge warbler, the marsh harrier, the merlin, the godwit, and the teal; all coming out to feed now that the heat of the day was waning.

At one point they passed a wooden signpost. Standing over seven feet high it was plainly visible in this flat riverland they were now traversing. There was a large, black, evil-looking stork perched atop it, which made no move to fly away at their approach, but eyed them steadily in a sinister way. The signpost was very old and partly rotted, but its inscription was just legible.

"*Bac . . . Bermak* . . . It's in a dialect similar to Grassland Polg," Finwald informed them, "one I've come across in my studies. Though I'm not sure . . ."

"What's it say?" asked Nibulus.

"All I can make out is 'silver,' and some word like 'hole,' " Finwald replied, "though it seems unlikely there'd be any mines of *any* description round these parts."

The sign pointed along a narrow track, away from the burn they now walked beside; they decided to ignore it, and its ill-favored occupant, and continued along their current path.

As they progressed along the winding course of the stream, they noticed other channels joining it. It began to widen, and its color turned from a dark but clear peaty-brown to a milky, muddy grey. There were so many other tributaries, new channels, and interlinking waterways now that it became impossible to discern which was the main flow, if indeed there was one at all. The stream eventually became a network of clogged and swampy channels, none appearing to flow in any particular direction. There was a stagnant smell, and the biting of midges intensified.

Dusk approached, while the travelers trudged wearily, mechanically, onward, urged on by the necessity of finding Myst-Hakel before nightfall.

Suddenly Finwald spoke. "You're the traveled one, Nibulus. What do you know of this Myst-Hakel?"

All day they had traveled with hardly a word between them, and the mage-priest's conversational tone offered a welcome distraction from the constant squelch of trudging feet. Nibulus himself was not in high spirits at all; he had walked ahead in silence all through the day's march, refusing to let the others see his face, and ceaselessly brooding on the deaths of his friend Methuselech and his esquire Gapp. Nevertheless, after the day's hard slog, the worst of his bitterness had died down, and he was finally willing to get his mind off this gloomy treadmill.

"None of my clan has ventured this way for decades," he began, "because there's no real reason to now, at least not since the old trade route moved on. Even in those days Myst-Hakel was fairly isolated, because it so often got cut off by floods or outbreaks of swamp fever. But since the visiting merchants died down to a trickle, so did the town; and it really went to the dogs. All the locals who couldn't get out just stayed and stagnated. It's a place you end up in, not go to, and there's nothing here to attract people, unless they're on the run, and even then they'd have to be pretty desperate. . . ."

"What about the silver mine back there?" asked Finwald. "That's got to be worth something, surely?"

"You saw how old the sign was," Nibulus reminded him. "They probably scraped the last of the lode years ago. Anyway, as far as I know, Myst-Hakel's just a small town—a village, really—about a day's march south of the fringes of Fron-Wudu. I think it's built on stilts, or something, I'm not sure. But the inhabitants are said to be a real mixed bag: humans, Haugers, a few Polgrim and their Boggarts, even the occasional giant. And half-breeds, too—plenty of mongrels. Pretty much a law unto themselves, really; since nobody comes to them, they've sort of gone their own way, independent of any sovereign lord or city-state. They've even got their own homegrown religion, a sort of fire cult, from what I can gather."

He continued, encouraged by their interest. "Last time we heard from the place, there was just fishing, trapping, and wet-farming. Humans and Haugers do the fishing and farming, Polgs do the trapping."

"Ungodly, degenerate scum!" Paulus spat. He was clearly back to his usual xenophobic self.

"So they can't mind strangers too much then," suggested Finwald, "if they allow just anyone to settle?"

"They ought to be glad of us, then," Appa suggested. "I bet they'd welcome some news from the South."

"They sort of accept them, eventually," Nibulus replied to Finwald's question. "I suppose their sort just let people move in and stay because it's easier than the effort of defending themselves against them. Typical of uncivilized, leaderless barbarians the world over. I doubt we'll get any trouble from them, anyway."

"Not with a group as few as us," Bolldhe put in, though as a man used to traveling alone, he felt no threat whatsoever at the thought of arriving in any town, however outlandish. As far as he was concerned, all Myst-Hakel meant to him was warm food, rest, and a roof over his head for a while. After four weeks of wandering about in the wilds he was greatly looking forward to that, even if it did mean yet another ceiling to stare up at.

They continued in silence again, until they met the giant.

The first one to hear the singing was Wodeman.

"Be still!" he hushed them. "There's someone up ahead."

At once they stopped in their tracks, and listened. There was a note in Wodeman's voice that put them on their guard, and they had learned to trust the sorcerer's instincts by now. Even the bitterns in the reeds nearby ceased their croaking and froze still, their tiny, arrow-shaped heads pointing upward.

Then they too heard it. At first it was impossible to tell what it was. A deep and warbling drone that rose and fell strangely, it was similar to a song, but no song any human might make. It could almost have been the moan of the wind through the rushes, except that there was no breeze to be felt. It could have been a wading bird or some other swamp creature, but there was a melody to it that was far too complex for that. It could even have been another marsh-dwelling wraith, for the song was weird and haunting enough, but none of the company felt any presage of evil.

A gasp from Paulus drew them around, and the bitterns legged it as fast as they could over the water.

"Look at that!" he breathed, pointing over to the left. There came a chorus of hushed exclamations as they followed Paulus's finger, and saw the giant approach. The scrub and swamp grass over that side of the water must have risen at least ten feet tall, yet it barely came up to the newcomer's shoulders. Wide-eyed and silent, the company watched it float gracefully along, gradually drawing nearer.

Then, without warning or any sign of surprise, it ceased its song and turned to look at them. Nibulus and Paulus gripped their weapons in alarm, but no one made a move. The giant continued to stare solemnly at them, not moving a muscle, floating on. Within moments it had glided out of its cover of tall grasses, and was revealed to them in full, standing possibly twelve feet tall, upon a large wherry. On it drifted, and they were just about to lose sight of it when the raft abruptly stopped.

"Gjoeger," whispered Wodeman as the figure continued to stare at them.

"Come again?" said Nibulus uncertainly.

"Swamp giant," Bolldhe translated in hushed tones. "One of the rarest of all giants. Hardly anyone has ever seen one, so make the most of it now. . . . I myself have only seen three in my whole lifetime, this one included." He could not help smiling at this last little boast. "Don't worry—they never interfere in other people's lives unless they are provoked."

"Where've *you* ever seen swamp giants?" Nibulus asked skeptically.

"Usually in swamps. . . ."

"Why's it staring at us like that?" growled Paulus in agitation. "Why doesn't it do something?"

"Probably because it don't know quite what to make of us," Bolldhe suggested. "As the Peladane said earlier, you don't get many visitors to these parts."

"Or maybe it wonders why *we're* staring at *it*," Wodeman commented. "Come on, let's make contact."

Despite a look of alarm from Paulus and the mage-priests, Nibulus nodded his assent.

"Ho, Gjoeger!" Wodeman called out confidently. "Over here!"

At first the swamp giant continued to peer at them dumbly, but presently it began to approach, propelling itself along powerfully but gracefully by means of a great barge pole.

"Be careful what you say," Bolldhe cautioned them as it drew near. "They look far more simple than they actually are."

I'll be ready for it if it tries anything, Nibulus thought bullishly.

"Yes," added Wodeman, "they're the only giants to use magic."

Magic?

The Gjoeger drew up to them. It was built to the general proportions of a man, except for its arms, which hung down past its knees. The pole was held in great hands the size of paddles, with long fingers slightly webbed, that ended in short talons. Long hair the color of marsh weed hung in matted clusters around the broad shoulders, and it was dressed in a single, loose-hanging garment of strange design, the same glistening, dark-brownish grey as its hair. In contrast its face glimmered palely in the fading evening light, like the cleanly picked bones of the dead that lie just beneath the surface of ponds. Deep-green, liquid eyes regarded them inscrutably from its almost batrachian yet highly intelligent face.

"Hail!" Nibulus cheerfully greeted the giant. "Fair be the weather upon your most honorable aquatic trade. I trust the currents are in your favor, the wind at your back, and the mud not too"—he sought for words—"deep. May your floats be forever buoyant, your hands without cramp . . . and not too clogging the weeds upon your pole."

He stopped there. The Gjoeger was not responding at all. But, then, what exactly was one supposed to say to a twelve-foot, magical, amphibious wherry-man? What did they talk about? And what, now that it came down to it, did Nibulus actually want?

"They do speak Aescalandian, don't they?" he demanded.

"Ssenh M'bngo lihd-sna Mnorbn-Mlud na' frhornm," the giant commented.

"I doubt it," Bolldhe hazarded, to the astonished vexation of the Peladane.

It was Wodeman who hit upon the idea of trying to communicate with runes. He brought out his little leather pouch, squatted on the muddy path, and spread the little hazel-wood tiles out before him. The giant leaned closer and peered at them, then nodded his head hesitantly.

"Think he understands those things?" Nibulus asked.

"These runes have been used throughout the North for thousands of years," Wodeman replied. "By all races, too. They bypass language, and go straight for the mind's eye."

He placed the runes of *The Road, Water,* and *Gold* before him. The Gjoeger squinted a moment, then smiled.

"Hrn-Mnon'fa Drzkh-thula!" he enthused, and motioned for them to come aboard.

"I guess he does, then," Nibulus said, shaking his head in wonderment. They all boarded the raft, letting Zhang eagerly go first, his hoofs clattering noisily upon the boards.

"Drrgn'm du'adh Nno'marmn-niobh, Mnsenh da fforrim'mdh?" the giant asked politely when they were all aboard.

They looked at each other dubiously.

"Myst-Hakel?" Bolldhe ventured.

The Gjoeger cocked his head as if considering this destination for a moment, then simply shrugged and pushed them out into midstream.

———

Hemmed in by the tall swamp grass that rose about them on all sides, the company's view of their surroundings was limited. Now and then during their half-hour journey with the wherryman they would glide among the grassy, floating islands of the moorhens, their occupants blinking at them beadily as they passed. Snipes there were too, probing the silt with their long, needle-like bills, and storks aplenty, unafraid of the boat and its strange company. Huge nets they would pass, that were suspended either just above or below the water level by great, long beams of pliable wood; and, appearing more frequently the farther they went, there were low, humpbacked bridges of a single log with a rope handrail, and maybe the odd skinny mongrel nervously nosing its way along its awkward wooden surface.

Such bridges obliged the passengers to crouch down whenever they passed beneath them. But, strangely enough, they noticed this never seemed to apply to the Gjoeger, who would remain perfectly upright even though he loomed a few feet above these bridges, and would then simply pass *through* them.

So far they had not seen any local inhabitants, but it was not long before they caught their first glimpse of some buildings, at the moment just the tops of towers off in the distance, that could be seen poking above the screen of tall grass. Gradually they drew nearer to these towers, and soon they could see them clearly. A great temple built of light-colored, sunbaked clay rose up out of the swamp. With turrets of weird and intricate design, and walls with rounded, "undulating" crenelations, this was clearly the work of a more ancient and civilized culture than that which inhabited the town currently. Presumably this temple was dedicated to the fire god Nibulus had mentioned earlier. Standing well over sixty feet above the water level, it served as a marker post for any who might become lost in those jungle-like marshes with their maze of weed-choked channels.

As the company was ferried closer to this anomalous edifice, they finally caught their first sightings of the locals. Nibulus hadn't been wrong; most were human or Hauger, but some were Polg. All were on boats of one type or another, and every one of them immediately stopped whatever they were doing upon spotting what the Gjoeger had brought in his wherry. They stared silently, motionlessly, expressionlessly as the newcomers drifted past.

"Hands on money belts, men," Bolldhe warned his companions quietly, "and have your weapons ready. If anyone tries to talk, keep going. Don't talk unless you must, don't look them in the eye, and above all try not to look wealthy."

"How exactly does one go about not looking wealthy?" Nibulus demanded.

"Well, don't stride, for one thing; try shuffling."

Through the gawping fishermen and trappers they continued, trying not to stare back, but trying at the same time to sneak the odd sidelong glance at these unfamiliar people. The humans and Haugers were dressed in light, loose clothes of drab greys, greens, and browns, while the Polgrim favored deep, richer colors and also wore furs and skins.

Ahead there were yet more boaters, fishing, weed-cutting, or seeing to their traps, and soon the first dwellings came into view. In sharp contrast to the grand temple that towered over everything, these were much humbler, more transient structures. Supported on stout poles, these ramshackle huts were made out of flimsy planks of wood nailed and lashed together crudely to provide shelter cheap and easy to build. They appeared every bit as damp and miserable as the people that dwelled within them. Pale, half-seen faces peered out at the travelers from gloomy interiors; dour-faced men in woollen hats and wizened old Haugers smoking weed lounged in doorways, and these too stared at the uninvited newcomers. In fact there was not a single inhabitant that did not stop and stare.

The six men began to feel increasingly uncomfortable as the swamp giant propelled them into the midst of this silent audience, and late summer evening seemed a little too sticky. Looking behind them, they noted with consternation that the boaters they had passed earlier were now following them, muttering quietly among themselves and pointing, though still at a respectful distance.

Soon the tall swamp grass petered out, and the whole of the town rose before them in plain view. From an Aescalandian point of view, Myst-Hakel was, to say the least, highly unusual. Gapp, had he been there, would have described it as "exotic." This was true insofar as it was bizarre and foreign-looking, but it was noticeably lacking in that certain romance, color, and beauty which the word tends to imply.

Centred around a broad knoll, the town rose out of the wetland like an island. The low knoll itself supported the larger houses, which were built from the same clay mud as the temple, and to a similar, if simpler, design. The houses that encircled this knoll, however, were completely different; like the outlying shacks the company had already passed, these seemed no more than a collection of shabby little huts, built upon stilts, all interconnected by a crisscross jumble of shackleboard walkways. They huddled together in a disorderly manner, clinging to the periphery of the knoll in much the same way the floating moorhen nests they had seen earlier anchored themselves to the riverbanks—or, perhaps more aptly, like drowning men clinging around a life raft.

The group on the wherry sailed on into the shantytown, in among its maze of poles, cabins, and walkways. The first boats composing the floating night market were beginning to arrive, laden with an assortment of dubious and unpleasant-smelling wares. Here also were found larger vessels that served as houseboats, strung with washing lines and milling with children. Some were setting out bowls on the flat roofs for the evening meal, while their mothers toiled in the smoky interiors below. All such vessels looked to be in serious need of repair.

Lining their route, more people had gathered to watch the newcomers, for word had already spread fast. Noisy children scuttled along the shackleboards, grinning and pointing at the wherryman and his charges. Some threw sticks and stones, screeching in wild, uncontrollable excitement. They looked the sort of kids who might live in the worst part of town, the low-rent housing zones where every hovel seems to have a broken-down cart parked outside, supported on stacks of bricks and with its wheels removed.

Paulus eyed them intently, and began sharpening his blade.

They passed under an arch, and approached a wide docking area. One of the broader walkways appeared to serve as the main jetty, and it was toward this that the giant now punted them. A larger crowd had gathered here to have a gander at these outlandish foreigners who had come among them, but unlike the previous gawpers who had kept their distance, these ones physically blocked their way.

The Gjoeger, however, was apparently treated with a considerable amount of reverence, for a loud bellow and a wave of his pole soon dispersed the crowd sufficiently to enable his passengers to finally climb up onto the jetty. A plank was brought out by the wharfinger specially for Zhang, who nimbly trotted up it to stand with his companions.

"Well," announced Nibulus cheerfully, but with a slightly mocking undertone, "Myst-Hakel."

The others nodded uncertainly.

"Hot bath, huge steaming meal, then a dry place to kip for the night," Nibulus promised to his men—as if they needed this encouragement—and stretched his big arms wide. "Come on, lads, let's find an inn."

He handed the swamp giant a golden zlat for his services, then, with one last look at their taciturn boatman, gave a wave and set off into town. The others followed their buoyant leader as he marched off along one of the wider platforms, apparently oblivious of the large throng he was striding through. The half-rotted boards creaked alarmingly as he went, but this did not seem to bother him. Finwald followed him closely, wrapping himself up in his black cloak and pulling his wide-brimmed hat low over his eyes. Wodeman came next, staring around at their spectators in open curiosity. Then Appa, blowing mucus from his nostrils with his pinched fingers, Paulus with bastard sword held at the ready, and finally Bolldhe, leading his horse noisily over the sagging planking.

Sometimes they would have to step aside, dangerously close to the edge, as surly fishermen lumbered by. Past gangs of sag-jawed net-menders they went, too, who would uniformly stop in their tasks to stare up at them; also gap-toothed old Haug-crones, peering out ignorantly from darkened doorways; packs of insolent brats of indeterminate race, sitting upon barrels of nails, pitch, quicklime, and hemp, smoking pipes and making rude gestures at the arrivals; while down below, where the barges were laid out like floating planks, slime-coated Boggarts, waist-deep in water as they caulked the hulls with oakum, risked the wrath of their Polgrim overseers by pausing in their toil to glance up at the strangers above.

All around them was evidence of poverty and decay. Marsh birds and vermin stalked or scuttled everywhere, gathering in raucous or squeaking melees
whenever a bucket of slop was thrown into the filthy water or tipped across the
planking. An old man squatted unself-consciously over the edge of a walkway
doing his business onto the children playing in the mud below. A crying puppy
was having its eyes pecked at by crows, and at one point Nibulus tripped over
a dead, rat-gnawed baby abandoned at the wayside. At least, he *assumed* it was
rats that had gnawed it. He stared at it fixedly, until Paulus irritably booted it
into the water. No one made any comment.

Mobs of diminutive Polgs could be seen hanging around. They had short,
thick, black hair, long mustaches, and squat legs. Their skin ranged from sal-
low to light brown, the complexion of leather, and their beady eyes were of the
palest grey. Many wore brightly colored shirts, but mostly their raiment was either deep green, rich earth brown, or night blue. Most had long knives slung at
the waist; some bore spears. None addressed the newcomers.

But there was one person who smiled openly at them. As Bolldhe often noticed, in any crowd of inhospitable, staring locals there is nearly always one
who welcomes the stranger in. Usually young, poor, as often as not without a
family, and *always* male, they come up to the stranger smilingly, and assume the
position of guide. Though money is expected, it is rarely asked for, and even
the meagerest of sums will buy help, guidance, and unswerving loyalty.

Here in Myst-Hakel, Job Ash was that one.

"Wealh!" came his shrill voice. "Wealh! Need frend, need frend."

Aware of Bolldhe's advice, the travelers paused briefly but did not stop.
Nibulus called over his shoulder to Bolldhe. "One of your parasites, I imagine?"

The Wanderer glanced sideways at the approaching boy but did not allow
his pace to slow either. "Maybe not this one," he replied. "There's always one
who can be trusted to go along with. What do you reckon, Nibulus? Think we
could do with a guide? Could save us time."

The Peladane slowed a little, and studied directly the boy hurrying down a
side walkway toward them. "He's on his own . . . and limping. Could be all
right? Yes, I don't see why not. Hey, boy!"

The lad caught up with them, panting heavily but still smiling. They could
not help but notice now one leg dragged behind him, the ankle twisted at an
angle. His clothes were, if anything, even drabber and dirtier than his fellow
citizens', but his demeanor lacked their dourness. His hair was a grubby blond
matted into several greasy spikes, his flat, squint-eyed face dirt-brown, and the
smile he wore so big that the corners of his mouth almost met at the back of his
head.

"Good wealh," he trilled at the six men. "You frendamyne? Need bedt?
Yut? I for you good bedt, good yut. You frendamyne, wealh, yes?"

He shifted his weight nervously as the six tall strangers stared down at him,
the boards squeaking under his bare feet.

"Speaks a little Aescalandian," Nibulus observed. "Could be useful, that. What's your name, boy?"

The boy hopped about eagerly. "Yes, yes," he said, "I name Job Ash. I helf you something. Nice horse, nice horse. Come me, get bedt. Not from here, you. I guide all wealh."

"Wealh? Waylanders, maybe?" asked Finwald.

"Dry rooms, clean beds, lots of food, and beer," Nibulus asked, "you can do?"

Job did not seem to understand a word he was saying, and laughed with a slight hint of desperation in his voice. "Yes, yes! Good wealh, cyneherjar. Nice horse. Come me," he replied, his eyes continually drawn to the slough horse.

"Cyneherjar?" exclaimed Finwald in an amused tone. "That's a word from the old Polg legends. He thinks we're 'royal warriors.'"

"What century's he living in?" laughed Nibulus.

"The same century as this whole town, by the look of it," Finwald commented, looking around. "Sounds as if they haven't seen Peladanes, or horses either, around here for many years. Look at the boy and the way he's eyeing Zhang."

"Yes, yes, nice horse," Job picked up, glancing at the mage-priest as he shuffled past him to take the lead. "You follow. Stroda not helf you, think bad, but I you to house. Yut, bedt. Come, come. Nice horse, too."

Hesitantly, they allowed themselves to be led. Bolldhe kept a tight hold on Zhang's reins. "If that little bastard gets too fond of 'nice horse,'" he muttered, "I'll see he limps on the other leg too."

Putting up with their unexpected guide for just as long as it suited them, the company allowed themselves to be led deeper into the town. Job Ash, despite his lameness, progressed as sprightly as the best of them along the confusing web of walkways. He guided them through a dingy collection of ramshackle huts, until they had all lost any sense of direction. On every side now the huts hemmed them in, and below them was the ever-present threat of the stagnant, oozing water that smelled like one vast latrine. Now and then they might pass over humpbacked bridges that spanned one of the wider channels, and could then see up long lines of huts all perched upon their forest of stilts. One or two of these waterways were little more than sluices of mud, with only the meagerest runnel of water trickling down the middle, and maybe a grounded barge listing forlornly to one side.

Dogs backed away at their approach, then growled cravenly as they passed by. All looked flea-ridden and stinking, and scratched despairingly at the hairless, scabby skin that patched their sides, driven mad by whatever itchy condition would doubtless eventually kill them.

Soon they emerged from the suffocating labyrinth of the shantytown, and found themselves upon a broad dyke. This earthwork, probably as old as the inner town itself, ran around the knoll on which it extended. A wide road (wide by Myst-Hakelian standards, at least, meaning three people could stand abreast) ran along the summit of this dyke, and several rickety old bridges, and one large covered bridge, spanned the moat lying between it and the knoll. The ditch itself was a channel of unspeakably abhorrent effluence, a thick black soup interspersed with islands of crust with livid red and green fungi growing on them. "Things" floated (or, rather, *sat*) in it: dead things, bits of dead things, and things that fed on dead things. There was an audible hum that rose from it which caused the six strangers to head straight for the covered bridge beyond instead of the smaller one Job had led them to.

Once inside the covered bridge, they marveled at just how spacious in extent it was. Stalls and kiosks were set up along either side of the central walkway, just like in a marketplace, and at this time of the evening it was heavily crowded with all sorts of people. The wayfarers had to push their way through a throng of shouting, haggling, sometimes fighting vendors and customers, though they themselves gladly seized the opportunity to avail themselves of some of the produce on sale. There were heaps of every sort of fruit and vegetable imaginable, and many more besides. There were large baskets of cheeping, yellow chickens, and glass tanks containing adult pike that were too big to even turn around. There was an entire menagerie of rodents, reptiles, and birds, kept in unbelievably tiny cages, and squealing and hissing for all they were worth. And there were stalls that served up highly animated bowls or kebabs of *live* food, also squealing, hissing, and shitting for all they were worth. The entire edifice trembled and groaned alarmingly and sometimes even lurched under the weight of so many.

Several silver zlats lighter and loaded with a veritable festoon of provender, the travelers emerged red-faced and sweating from the covered bridge, and into the cooler air and relative calm of the "upper" town.

"Heathen bastards!" Nibulus exclaimed. "I swear if I'd spent a second longer in there I'd have killed someone!"

"Yes yes," Job assured them as he led them cheerfully up a narrow dirt lane. "These Stroda are very bastards. But here good. Stroda not bother you here. Not steal horse."

"Stroda?" asked Nibulus. "You mean Polgrim?"

"No no Stroda . . . We! Men of Marsh. Polga no Stroda. Polga new. From East. Trap, get meat, but bad men. Say we beasts!"

Sure enough, the Polgs did appear to wear an air of superiority about them. They hung about lazily, and glared at any humans and Haugers who passed near to them. Racially, though, they were similar to the Haugers, roughly the same height and of similar build, and it was said they were distant relatives. But culturally they were worlds apart, for Haugers lived in highly civilized, settled communities, usually located in high places or escarpment villages, and they would rarely travel more than two miles from their homes. Polgs, however, were a barbarian race, nomads who roamed the vast, flat grasslands to the east, hunting the plains herds. They were fleet of foot, and said to be unsurpassed among all the races of Lindormyn in fortitude and endurance, doing their hunting entirely on foot. Their chiefs might ride upon stags occasionally, and some of their more powerful warlords even rode the dreaded Sailam horse, but for the most part, it was not their custom to use steeds.

Along with them, the Polgs had brought their slaves, the hairy, degenerate, subhuman Boggarts, whom they kept on leashes. Here, by the outlet of the covered bridge, a series of small treadmills had been set up to turn the spits of roasting game that the Polgs inside were selling, and it was in these that the Boggarts were patiently and uncomplainingly toiling.

Finwald paused a moment to regard them with sympathy. "I often get the feeling they know something we don't," he said to Nibulus. "Why else would they be so calm under all the ordure we pile on them?"

On encountering any Polg, Bolldhe would return their haughty stare. He was reminded of the Leqather hunter-nomads of the forest hills of Rynsaker, way back east. Every so often they would come down from their rainy highlands to trade meat and pelts for the iron arrow tips and farm produce of the settled communities, and would parade down the streets half-naked and proud, as if they owned the place. The settlers detested them, calling them animals behind their backs, but Bolldhe found out that in the Leqather tongue the words for "settler" and "cattle" were one and the same. Such appeared to be the case with these Polgs, and few communities would tolerate them for any length of time. But an already racially mixed town might not be so quick to expel them, and meanwhile they did as they pleased.

On a whim, Bolldhe suddenly decided that he wanted to make closer contact with these locals. He kicked one of the lounging Polgs hard as he passed, then immediately hefted his axe threateningly as the Polg and his companions flared up. Bolldhe loomed over them, looking down from on high, and sneered as they bitterly backed down.

Job Ash led them farther up the narrow, earthen lanes of the old town. Here the ground was drier, and the air was cleaner. Even houses were larger and built to last, yet the place appeared much more sparsely inhabited.

"I can't understand how those people can live down there in all that filth and noise," said Appa, "when it's so much more pleasant up here."

"Probably they prefer to be on top of their work," Nibulus suggested.

But Bolldhe guessed the truth of the matter: This old town was now the domain of the craftsmen, who were principally Haugers. Racial segregation was apparent in Myst-Hakel, and, though the different races looked as if they got on reasonably well together, it was clear that the humans had been handed the swampy end of the stick.

They soon arrived at the temple. Standing below its soaring walls and

strangely shaped crenelations the six Southlanders were awed. It looked so utterly out of place here in the Rainflats. The baked-mud walls, glowing a faint
red in the last of the sun's light, still radiated heat.

Job urged them to follow, and led them through the open gateway of the
temple's west wall. There were no actual gates left, just a high, arched opening,
but the rusty old hinges could still be seen.

The whole courtyard inside had been taken over by Hauger craftsmen.
Cloisters, casemates, and small antechambers lined all four inner walls, each
with a separate artisan plying his trade within. There were furriers, coopers,
tanners, numerous tailors, and at one end even an artificer. The whole of the
north wall must have once been devoted to the altar, for there upon its surface
could still be seen a large bas-relief of a blaze of flames. But the stonework was
now chipped and the old decoration faded or blackened by soot, for this area
was now, suitably enough for a fire god, the property of the town's one and
only blacksmith.

As they looked on, the party realized that he was at least eight feet tall, and
concluded that he must be a Tusse.

"Must be at least one member of every race inhabited the Northlands gathered in here," Nibulus concluded. "I'm amazed they aren't at each other's
throats half the time."

"Mongrels, deviants, and scum," Paulus sneered. "Crossbred bastard outcasts of civilization. Let's buy what we can afford, take what we can't, and leave
them to their foul, swamp-dwelling squalor."

Despite the distrustful Nahovian's vehement antipathy to their present situation, the company allowed themselves to be ushered into a large room just off
the main courtyard. There were dry straw mattresses, a long table, several
stools, and amphorae full of relatively clean water standing in each corner.
Three large windows gave them a good view of most of the town below them,
and it looked a light, airy place to lodge in.

"Job Ash," Nibulus called over to their bustling host, "does your family
rent out this room?"

The boy looked up in smiling incomprehension.

"You. Father. Mother. Here?"

Job grinned. "This all Stroda own. Parents dead now."

"Ah, I see."

That night they made themselves as comfortable as they could in their new
dormitory, recovering from their ordeal in the marshes. Now that they were
washed and reclining upon mats, waiting for Job to finish cooking their meal, it
seemed incredible that that very same day had seen them still imprisoned in
Nym-Cadog's dungeons waiting to be fed in turn to the Afanc.

There had been moments down there in the "wooden" part of town, and
especially in the covered bridge, where, after so long in the wilderness, the

noise, commotion, and closeness of this town had almost brought the travelers to blows. But up here within the thick walls of the temple, with the sturdy door of their room shut and firmly bolted, they found they could relax in a way they had not been able to since Wyda-Aescaland.

Apart from the boy, the only locals in here at the moment were a party of rats that had dropped by to check out the newcomers they had obviously heard about. They seemed affable creatures, which surprised the Aescals, for back in Nordwas, despite a certain level of coexistence, the rats generally had little to do with the human population as they did not want to risk catching anything off them. Here, though, they appeared to get on fine together.

The muffled noises of hammering and sawing from behind the door, the more distant sounds drifting through the windows from the town below, and the gentle sizzle of cooking nearby induced in each of the company a feeling of safety and well-being that they had all but forgotten even existed.

They did not know what half the items purchased at the bridge market were exactly, but there was certainly no lack of variety. When Job was finally ready to serve up their banquet, he proudly went through the list of succulent dishes that he had prepared for them. There may have been some misunderstanding with the translation, but apparently they were about to feast on head and neck of sandpiper served in blue marsh weed, skinned mouse rolled in multicolored pulses, dog's legs marinated in Riverhaug medicine, tentacles from . . . something or other, deep-fried arachnid, and (this was Bolldhe's favorite) fragrant weasel served as a false frog-meat dish.

Actually there was a lot Job said that they did not or could not understand. The boy's grasp of Aescalandian was somewhat rudimentary, and wherever he did not know a word, he would automatically substitute it with one from his own language. Myst-Hakelian was an idiosyncratic tongue that had developed to suit the needs solely of its inhabitants: for instance, there was no generic word for "toad," but eighty words for the different species of it; many words for types of mud; similarly, no verb just for "fishing," but instead, the various methods of fishing, such as "fishing with a pole," "with a net," "with a bludgeon," "by night," and so on.

And an entire nomenclature devoted to "idling."

But no words were needed after the company beheld the spread that Job laid out before them. Indeed, none would have been heard above the tearing, crunching, slurping, choking, belching, whimpering, and heaving that filled the air for the next half-hour or so.

It was only when Nibulus suddenly paused in his eating—something the others had never witnessed before—that this engorgement was interrupted as they stared at him in surprise.

"Did any of you boys hear stories about Myst-Hakel women eating their own dead babies?" he inquired, peering curiously into his bowl.

They paused.

"No. Why?"

"Oh, it's probably nothing," he replied, and went back to his meal with a resigned shrug. After a dubious interval, they did likewise.

Bolldhe was already tired of staring up at the ceiling. Things kept dropping from it onto his face, and scurrying away. Instead he contented himself with staring out of one of the windows at the benighted town below.

It was a peaceful night, warm and fragrant. The evening breeze brought to Bolldhe's nose a distinctly Myst-Hakelian blend of odors: marsh weed, cool, green and leafy; fish, fresh, cured, and rotten; latrines, overflowing, crusty, and disease-ridden. It was not the most pleasant of aromas, but after weeks in the wilds it was more welcome to the wanderer's nostrils than a hundred garlands of jasmine.

A low mist enshrouded the marshes, tendrils of which drifted up through the streets toward the temple. But right up here it was still clear enough to see the heavens, and the waning, gibbous moon whose light reflected off the mist like a silver blanket.

There were still people about, even at this hour, he saw. Far out in the marsh, fishermen called out to one another in the darkness, and closer by the more distinct sounds of conversations and artisans' tools could be heard. Even the rats below his window sounded contented, getting ready for their night shift of running messages for the townsfolk, or just idly grazing for morsels. These all mingled together to produce a soothing hubbub of settled existence that the traveler found unusually comforting.

Maybe tomorrow night he would go out and mix with strangers again. Maybe Bolldhe had spent too long in the enforced company of the Aescals.

Bolldhe turned from the window and walked over to his mattress. At that moment, in walked Job Ash. Like every good host, he had waited to make sure that his investments were comfortable and wanted for nothing. Bolldhe glanced involuntarily at the makeshift stall he himself had constructed for Zhang, but the horse was still safely there.

"Where you from, cyneherjar?" the boy inquired with obvious interest. He had already given up on trying to find out their destination, so contented himself with trying to discover where they had come from. That might at least provide a hint at the direction in which they were headed.

"Shut up and get out of here, you little sod," Paulus snarled.

Most of the company were tired of the boy and his constant, incomprehensible, and high-pitched chattering. But Finwald did not mind humoring him. The little wretch reminded him so much of the esquire they had lost.

"We come from the great mountains in the South," he explained slowly, and with gestures. "Many days' travel."

"From south?" Job's eyes widened in apprehension. "Travel through fairy haunt?"

At that, the others, sitting or reclining upon their mats, propped themselves up and regarded the boy, attentively.

"Where is this 'fairy haunt,' Job Ash?" Finwald asked. "Does it lie in the woods south of here?"

"Yes yes yes!" Job stammered excitedly. "One day, two day away. Grandt Beorh of Old Thaine. Only dead live there. Then Huldres. Bad place, very bad. She come. Huldre-she. Live in beorh like house. Monster keep in water to shoo Stroda away."

Finwald stared through the window away into the distance, to where he guessed lay Nym-Cadog's place. "It's the barrow of some old chieftain," he murmured, either as known fact or merely speculation. "They do say the Huldre folk like to live with the dead."

"And . . ." Job went on, but was having difficulty with the words. He made a series of two-handed, downward, chopping movements.

"Miners?"

Job shrugged. "Minas," he repeated, nodding. "Wealh go in hole . . . dig . . . take—no, *thief*—thief house of dead. Belleal! No good wealh."

"Interesting," Finwald said to the company. "The barrow seems to have been desecrated by grave-robbers. Made it ideal for the Huldres."

"Job, who were these miners? Same as ones who made . . ." He paused, trying to recall the words written on the signpost they had passed earlier that day, "*Bac-Bermak*?"

Job hesitated, then nodded his head vigorously.

"You're just confusing the lad," Nibulus objected, "leading him on. Miners don't go breaking into barrows. He probably doesn't see any difference, men going down below ground to dig for precious metals. Miners, grave-robbers, they're all the same to him."

"But the mine—Bac-Bermak?" Finwald went on. "Long time not used, yes? No?"

The boy stared dumbly at the black-robed priest. Then he said, "Long, long time no Stroda in Bac-Bermak."

"Interesting," Finwald repeated, this time to himself, and stared out of the window again.

The following day was a day of rest for them. The company arose separately, as they pleased, went down into town to find their breakfast, and then either wandered about the shantytown watching the fishermen at work, or explored the old town with its alleys and strange, ancient buildings. They had agreed to meet at noon, and then again convene every second hour back at the temple, just to make sure that if anyone went missing, he would not be missing for too long unnoticed. It was an arrangement that suited everyone, as they were glad of the chance to be free of each other for the day.

However, it was also agreed that a celebration would be held at the town's only pub that night. Hauger ale was served there, they were informed, a brew the secret of which lived and died in the heads of the few Haugers who brewed it. It was one of that diminutive race's closest-kept secrets, and one that had ensured their welcome among any non-Haug community for centuries. It was an opportunity not to be missed, one that Nibulus hoped would bond the company together a little, and perhaps even lead to cooperation once or twice in the hazardous days that lay ahead.

Also it was a good chance for him to blow his brains out on one of the pokiest ales known to Man.

Generally the day went well, and proved very relaxing. The company went their separate ways, and re-met only every two hours as agreed. Nibulus spent most of his time sunning himself upon the flat roof of one of the temple towers, looking up into the blue sky or gazing half-interestedly down at the busy town, while listening to the happy whistling of Job Ash as he polished the Peladane's tengriite armor down below in the courtyard.

The view from there was excellent. One could see the Blue Mountains dominating the whole of the southern horizon, stretching away on either side to disappear into the curve of the earth. To the east and west the land stretched away into infinity, an unending sweep of drab, featureless plains. As for the north, he did not care to look that way just yet. He would get plenty of opportunity to appraise *that* view in the days to come.

But Nibulus was not really taking any of this in. For no matter how hard he tried to focus on what lay around him, in his mind all he could see was his dead friend's face. That open, affectionate smile he recalled from the good times they had shared; that clumsy attempt at a serious mien when he was trying to go along with the Peladanes dignity. . . .

Nibulus took a deep, shaky breath, and thrust the latter image of Methuselech from his mind, preferring to dwell solely upon the man's smile. *Because that's the way he was,* he pondered gloomily, *his entire face would smile—not just the mouth, but the eyes, the cheeks . . . even his nostrils. Smiling nostrils! Who else in this world could do that?*

Appa rarely strayed from the confines of the temple. He had suffered more than any of them, far more than he would admit, and he had to conserve his strength. Up till now, they had had it easy; he shuddered to think what Fron-Wudu, the Far North, and, worst of all, Melhus Island would be like. So he wandered about the temple precinct, looking at the various wares of the craftsmen, and studying the remnants of the religious imagery that, like the bygone religion itself, still clung on to Myst-Hakel like mold on a plastered wall.

"A sort of fire cult," Nibulus had described it. Appa peered closely at the faded icons and reliefs that were all that remained. From what he could make out, the fire goddess—if that was what he was looking at—was a rather unremarkable female whose heavenly sanctuary bore a striking resemblance to a household hearth. In her right hand she held a poker, in her left a coal scuttle, and there were bundles of twigs and kindling strewn about her feet. In other pictures, however, she was depicted in her more wrathful aspect, spitting out burning knots of wood and embers onto the bulrushes that served as floor mats.

"Myst-Hakel . . ." he muttered, shaking his head.

Paulus lay abed all day. His wounds, though dressed, were still giving him problems. Nevertheless, even he seemed lighthearted compared with his usual demeanor.

Wodeman spent most of his time wandering about the jetties, searching for odds and ends that he might be able to turn to good use: herbs, molds, various stones and crystals, all meaningless junk to anyone but a sorcerer.

Bolldhe just ate, drank, slept, and scratched; he at least knew exactly what days off were for.

Only Finwald remained unaccounted for. Though he had reappeared on time at noon, he only just made it. And at six o'clock he turned up half an hour late. The company had then set out to look for him, and Bolldhe had eventually found him hurrying up from the jetties, panting heavily. His clothes were stained with mud, and when Bolldhe asked him where he had been, he snapped a curt reply that he had been trying to get some solitude, "away from you lot," and refused to discuss the matter further.

"Five pints of Old Ropey and a packet of salted nuts, please, stout yeoman," Nibulus ordered in a loud voice at the bar, "and two each for my friends."

The bartender of the Kjellermann Inn turned around and regarded the boorish warrior icily. Nevertheless, he began drawing the beer Nibulus was indicating from a huge puncheon behind the bar. These outlandish newcomers to town had caused quite a stir in Myst-Hakel these past twenty-four hours, and it appeared that the eager townsfolk would at last be rewarded for their patience, and could observe how such foreigners behaved.

"And tonight we'll show these miserable stick-in-the-mud Stroda peasants exactly how Aescals have a good time," Nimbus trumpeted.

He grabbed the first tackerde of ale from the bartender's hand and held it up to his nose.

"This, I have waited for *far* too long."

He inhaled the potent vapor of the lukewarm ale deep into his lungs as though attempting to *inhale* himself drunk. Gasping with red-eyed exasperation, he endured the gaseous assault in his cranium with as much stoicism as he could muster, then grinned like a child as he felt a strange numbness spread into every nerve ending in his body. The ale smelled sweet, sickly and piquant, and fizzed beneath his nose. Hauger ale had a barrel life of about two days, and was meant to ferment in the stomach. And Old Ropey, here, one of the strongest and vilest of all Hauger ales, was if anything even more fleeting, at its peak.

The Peladane paused, reluctant to rush the moment, unwilling to miss out on even one sensation that this longed-for pleasure could render him. The whole pub, had he cared enough to notice it, had gone absolutely quiet as the locals stared on in fascination. Now finally they would get to see which hole foreigners drank from. Then slowly, ceremonially, Nibulus poured the ale down his throat.

It took about five seconds for the tackerde to be drained; then he slammed it down, entirely missing the bar top, and heaved fresh air into his lungs like a drowning man.

"It . . . burns! Ocht, how it . . . burns!" he rasped in incredulity. "Beautiful . . . !"

He did not die on the spot; the locals went back to their own drinking, muttering and nodding with approval.

"Come on, Bolldhe," Nibulus proclaimed. "You look like you could do with some of this too. I'm buying this round—least I can do for you after rescuing us back in the woods."

Bolldhe could not suppress a smile, and gratefully accepted the big warrior's token of friendship. He had not tasted Hauger ale before, and now seemed the perfect opportunity.

"Your health." He gestured to the Peladane at his side. "Wodeman, how about you?"

The shaman had also decided to join in the spirit of the occasion. There were several reasons for this, among them the need, as he saw it, to draw Bolldhe into the camaraderie of the group, and thus draw him out of his silent shell. He was also anxious to prove that the Torca's reputation for drinking themselves insensible was an unfair slander.

"I never touch a drop of the hard stuff," he assured them, and to prove it spent the whole evening touching only ale.

And went on proving it until the early hours, just to make sure.

Finwald and Appa kept themselves to a table by the fire. They too felt in need of a relaxing drink, but preferred a more sensible brew. Finwald sparingly poured a clear, sticky liquid into his glass, which went by the unlikely appellation of Xambadabuubaa, while the old priest contented himself with nursing a steaming, spicy, and fruity wassailing cup.

Only Paulus isolated himself from the company. He could not stand the thought of sitting all alone in that empty temple-dormitory while his companions were busy enjoying themselves downtown, so he decided to sit all alone here instead. In truth, he had at first refused the Peladane's invitation to join them, preferring to wander about the docking areas, his black sword at the ready to take on any of these locals who might dare to so much as scowl at him. He knew the others had asked him to join them only because they felt they had to. Out of embarrassment, more than anything, he thought bitterly.

But in the end his innate acrimony had spent itself, and he had wandered in an hour after they had. Now he sat with his back to them all, in another part of the tavern, ignoring them completely.

No sooner had he sat down than the table's other occupants got up and left. Not a word was said in any language, but the deformed mercenary did not need to ask to know why they had departed so abruptly. This kind of thing was happening to him all the time, and in part explained his discomfort in joining in. Now he silently ignored the bar's laughing punters, and sat all alone drinking.

The sound of his companions' revelries (or rather, the Peladane's) rose above the general hubbub of the throng. Once Paulus was sure he heard his name mentioned, his *second* name, followed by a burst of laughter. He grimaced and turned away, only to find himself facing the group of young couples sitting around the next table. The lads looked relaxed and healthy, and the girls surprisingly pretty for this town. They were laughing and fondling each other excitedly, apparently without a care in the world. Occasionally the girls' sparkling eyes would stray in his direction, narrow in disgust, and turn back to their handsome swains.

Paulus winced in almost physical pain: this hurt him more than anything the world could throw at him. He felt sick with the emptiness inside him, and breathed deeply to suppress the first tremors of a fit. As usual he sought refuge from the cruelties of the world in another glass of ale, as hurt and bitterness turned into hatred once again.

A group of players had set up in one corner of the Kjellermann, and the whole place now resounded to the pounding beat of timbal and bodhrán, and the wail of the lur. Even the rats were dancing on the windowsills, and on every side the good folk of Myst-Hakel were joining in. Through this press of dancing revelers, Bolldhe pushed his way over to stand next to the shaman.

"Wodeman," he began, trying not to be overheard by his other companions, "how many dreams have you given me so far?"

The sorcerer sobered up immediately, and the whole room suddenly seemed very quiet to him. Caught unawares, he wiped the ale from his mustache and stared up at the Wanderer. This man certainly did not beat about the bush.

"What makes you ask such a question now?" he asked quietly.

"What do you mean?"

"I mean," Wodeman replied, "that this is the first time you have ever come to me over such matters. Till now it's always been the other way round."

Bolldhe acknowledged this with a nod, but held his tongue until he could find the right words. He felt more on his guard now than at any other moment during their journey together, but knew that sooner or later he would have to bring the matter up.

"I've had plenty dreams so far on this little escapade, but for all I know they got nothing to do with you. . . ."

Wodeman's face foliage barely hid the artful smile that tweaked the corners of his mouth. "Until what . . . ?"

Bolldhe now knew, or could guess well enough, the answer to his pressing question: Wodeman *had* been behind his vision three nights earlier. He turned away, somber and sulky. He *hated* having to confide in anyone.

Then he heard Wodeman say, "That night, all I wanted to do was to contact you, and get help. We had to do *something* to escape—"

Bolldhe cut in, "It really *was* you, then." His eyes moistened, and he had to clear his throat before going on. "All those miles I'd traveled, and you still managed to get inside my head. I'd wondered if it was, well, just male intuition."

"Mailing tuition?" Wodeman queried. "Well, in a way it was, I mean, it was a message—"

"Male—intuition," Bolldhe corrected him. "Like female intuition, only it works."

Wodeman could sense the feeling of intrusion that Bolldhe was now experiencing, but had to strike while the iron was hot.

"You too have felt a closeness to the Earth Spirit, have you not?" he questioned. Bolldhe looked at him without expression, waiting for him to go on.

"That night in the cave two weeks ago, before the Leucrota attacked, you opened your mind to Erce. I know, I could feel the searching of your soul."

Bolldhe looked down and studied the dregs in his tackerde. The hedge wizard was perceptive, if nothing else. While they had discussed religion, Bolldhe *had* indeed opened his mind; opened it to questions he had secretly been asking himself for years and years. But there had never yet been any answer.

"But I was interrupted," Wodeman continued. "The Skela would not allow it. Always they seek to hide things from us. I don't think they can stand the truth. The rune of *Ignorance* seems fated to play a heavy hand in this game we play, right up to the end. But your dream, Bolldhe, the *real* dream, the one I sent you after that . . . Would you tell me about it?"

"My . . . dream?" Bolldhe replied absently.

"Yes, it is important for me to know."

"Forget it," Bolldhe replied.

"What?"

"I said forget it. Don't go poking around in my head again. If anything need doing, *I'll* do it. Just leave me alone."

It was said quietly, without menace, but the message was clear. And Wodeman left it at that.

Just then a dark shadow fell across Bolldhe, and the earthy odors of Wodeman were replaced by an earthy smell of a more gravelike origin.

"We hang our dead from trees," came the accompanying voice.

Bolldhe turned around, and found himself face-to-chest with the Nahovian. He had cast his hood back, despite the crowds, and wore an expression that Bolldhe had never seen before. A thin line of ale trickled down his chin, turning the black stubble white as it went, and he appeared to have something on his mind.

"You what?"

"From trees," Paulus repeated. "When we die, we of Vregh-Nahov are hung from the lower branches of the trees, in the deeps of the woods. The beasts then decide which chapter of the Chlan the dead's next of kin will be initiated into. The first beast that eats of the flesh of the cadaver, *that* is the chapter selected. My own father was first pecked at by crows. . . ."

Bolldhe had not the slightest clue what was going on here. He now wished he had stuck with the sorcerer. What had this got to do with *anything*?

"That's all very interesting, Paulus," he stammered, "but I'm drinking, here."

"Don't you see?" Paulus suddenly moaned, and Bolldhe recognized now the *pleading* in the mercenary's eyes. The man was trying to reach out to him. "Who would ever bear me a son? And even if I had one, he would have no chapter. For what wild creature would be desperate enough to partake of my rotting flesh!?"

Paulus registered the utter blankness in Bolldhe's face, and turned away. What was the point?

Just then a loud bellowing laugh burst in upon Bolldhe's bemusement. Nibulus, a young woman in hand, staggered over to the table and went crashing over it. Mugs and plates went flying, and those sitting nearest held their hands up protectively in front of their faces. Both Nibulus and his voluptuous new friend crumpled in a laughing heap upon the floor.

Everyone was staring, and Bolldhe went red. Appa wiped beer off himself in disgust, and would have nothing to do with his leader at all. Nibulus, meanwhile, made no attempt to get up; he simply lay there on the floor laughing hysterically.

"*Imbecile!*" he heard Appa hiss vehemently.

Finwald, smiling, heaved the big man off the floor and settled him on a low stool.

"You going to diddle her up, then?" He nodded toward the fleshy wench.

Nibulus looked over to her, smiling inanely, then suddenly snapped back to reality.

"No!" he roared, "Are you joking? My wife would kill me."

At this, Bolldhe pushed his tackerde away. This was all becoming too surreal to cope with.

"Your *wife*?" he exclaimed in astonishment.

Finwald grinned again. "Remember that woman who waylaid him just before we rode out of Nordwas?"

"What, you mean the one demanding money?"

"That's her!" Nibulus beamed.

"You sound surprised, Bolldhe," Finwald commented.

"Well, it's just . . . *money* . . . not the sort of thing I myself would expect at a last farewell," Bolldhe explained, clearly in virgin territory here.

"You've obviously not had much experience with women, son." Nibulus smiled.

Finwald turned back to Bolldhe and whispered, matter-of-factly, "Anyway, don't believe any of that rubbish Wodeman was telling you earlier; he's had too much beer. Just put your trust in your sword." And with that, he got up to leave the pub. As he walked out of the door, he was swallowed up by swamp mist and darkness.

Bolldhe wished he had never traveled to Nordwas in the first place. What the hell was wrong with these people? But just as he was about to order another huge tackerde of Old Ropey, he suddenly thought to himself: *Funny thing for a mage-priest to suggest. . . . Anyway, I haven't even got a sword.*

Later that evening, as Bolldhe left the pub, his head was still buzzing loudly with the music, the noise, and the dizzying effects of potent Hauger ale. After tripping over several times, he eventually reached the temple gate. But just as he was about to enter, he turned back and gazed at the midnight blackness of the swamp. He could not see a thing there.

And into his mind came the words of Wodeman:

"The rune of Ignorance *seems fated to play a heavy hand in this game, right up to the end."*

These words were still racing around his confused and inebriated brain when he noticed the dark shape slip out through one of the windows of their dormitory and race away into the darkened alleys beyond. It was clutching a sack—and a large broadaxe.

"Oy, that's mine!" Bolldhe cried in amazement. "Come back here, you bloody thief!"

Incensed, he plunged after the burglar. It was a chase that saw him fall flat on his face more than once, slam into walls and snag his garments at every turn. The thief was quick, but Bolldhe was determined not to lose sight of him. He had owned that broadaxe for more years than he cared to remember, and though he bore no particular love for the weapon itself, he did bear a deep-seated loathing for thieves. He chased the fleeing figure down through the streets of the old town, off the knoll via one of the alarmingly springy footbridges, and onto the encircling dyke. The thief sprinted along the path running along the top of the dyke, looking back at the panting and spluttering pursuer.

All of a sudden it leapt off the dyke and headed sure-footedly for a lengthy walkway leading out into the marshes.

"Howzat!" Bolldhe exclaimed, confidently believing those shackleboards led out onto a jetty or some other dead end.

But the thief was on home ground here. With Bolldhe clattering noisily along the loose planks in hot pursuit, the thief leapt off the end of the walkway, and landed not in water, but on firm ground. Straightaway the dark shape sprinted off into the night.

Bolldhe snarled in drunken rage, but did not hesitate. He followed the barely visible shade of his quarry over muddy but reasonably firm ground, never once thinking of giving up. He was confident that he could outrun any thief that was carrying a sack in one hand and a heavy axe in the other.

For long minutes they ran. Uphill, always uphill. And the higher they progressed, the firmer became the ground. But just as Bolldhe seemed about to catch up, the thief suddenly vanished.

"Wha'! Where . . . ?" Bolldhe cursed between wheezing gasps. He was by this time almost completely sober. "Come out, ya . . . ya bastar'!"

It was only then that he realized he was now right out on the moors, a long way from town.

Nothing stirred out here on the dark moors, save perhaps for a light summer breeze that ruffled his hair. Not a sound could be heard. It truly was profoundly dark and lonely out here.

His leg brushed a stand of reeds, and immediately a tremendous cacophony of brain-penetrating squeals, wails, grunts, and groans burst into the night, right by his side.

Half a dozen yards away, Bolldhe picked himself up where he had landed, and breathed deeply. "Rails!" he cursed, damning all marsh birds to hell, then took some time to regain his composure.

What was that? A chink of stone, off to the left! Bolldhe stalked silently over to where he thought the sound had come from, and almost fell down a hole.

He patted himself up and down, but to his dismay found his bull's-eye lantern was not in its usual place; he must have left it back at the temple. *Cuna-on-a-kebab!* That thief hadn't taken it, surely? *No!* Of all the things!

He ceased his useless worrying; he did not know yet if it *was* gone. He investigated his clothing further, and was consoled to find his flint and steel. Moments later his probing hands alighted upon a length of dry timber among a pile of debris, near the hole's entrance. Minutes later, he held a dim and flickering torch in his hand.

A long mine shaft sloped away into the dark before him. Barely hesitating, Bolldhe descended into its subterranean levels.

Almost immediately his foot slipped on the loose, wet scree of the shaft, and he fell flat on his backside. He cried out in pain, and swore vehemently. But far from taking greater care, he sprang back up onto his feet and plunged farther into the darkness. Anger and self-reproach at his foolishness spurred him on ever more determinedly, till, barely a dozen paces later, he slipped again, lost his balance completely, and pitched forward into the darkness.

When he came to, Bolldhe's head was throbbing painfully, and he felt horribly queasy. At first he could see nothing, but after a while he sensed light before his eyes, and it was gradually growing brighter. Soon its piercing glare shot needles of pain through his bleary eyes and into his bruised and jellied brain. With an odd sense of detachedness he watched the light as it pulsated luridly. All the while, sharp stones pressed painfully into his cheek.

Torch! he suddenly remembered, and heaved himself groggily to his feet. He picked up the makeshift torch just as it was about to go out, and breathed life back into it. Slowly the flames grew, and he held the stick of flickering wood out before him.

With a sudden rush of blood to his head, he felt violently sick. He lurched sideways, and collided with the wall of the shaft. Extending his free hand against its surface, he managed to steady himself and his spinning world. Then he began breathing slowly, deeply, steadily.

Can't have been out for long, then, he thought as he looked down at his torch. He tried not to think what could have happened to him down here, and instead concentrated his thoughts on images of cool, leafy forests and sparkling waterfalls. That usually worked. Soon he noticed that ice-cold water was running down the wall and trickling soothingly between his fingers. The buzzing in his head gradually subsided.

Hauger ale! he cursed. *They can stick it right up their secretive, closely guarded little backsides!*

A few moments and several lungfuls of air later, Bolldhe's legs finally stopped shaking, and he could stand upright on his own. He peered into the darkness around him, and decided to get this over with as soon as possible. The torch, if it could be called that, cast little light; he would have to rely on his ears more than anything.

"Stupid!" he muttered as he explored the mine shaft. That was the trouble with traveling for too long with others. He hated getting drunk; hated the sickness; hated the befuddlement and incapacitation; he hated the way it made one act so stupid, like a kid at his first grown-up party.

And he especially *loathed* the way it opened your mouth so wide that anybody within earshot could see right the way down into your soul.

That was the trouble, really. He was just so unused to company that whenever he did mix with others he ran the risk of making a real tit of himself. But he was sober again, and now he meant business.

Bolldhe soon discovered that the torch was next to useless in these dark passages. The little light it provided, as he held it directly before him, only managed to dazzle him, and there was not enough room above his head for him to hold it up higher. He tried holding it a little behind his head and to one side, but that was too awkward; and when he held it behind his back it nearly set light to his deerskin tunic. Bolldhe swore in frustration, and groped his way ahead.

These passages smelled awful. The reek of refuse tips, stale cellars, and urine made Bolldhe wrinkle his nose in disgust. He was used to scummy back-streets, but at least they were out in the open, not fifty feet underground. This smelled like the lowest level of the five-tiered city of Qaladmir, where even the lepers wore masks to filter the stench. . . .

Fifty feet underground! The thought alone was enough to clamp a steely hand of terror around Bolldhe's heart. He hated caves at the best of times—to be trapped so deep underground with only bare stone all around you! He fancied he could hear the screams of men and children, and the washing of the sea . . . and something so much worse. . . .

This had happened before. There had been times in his life when this cave-fear had taken him. He did not understand it, and furthermore he did not want to admit to it.

More deep breaths, more mind-stuff, more control. He was Bolldhe, remember. He was Bolldhe. . . .

Again, he forced himself to concentrate upon the search. He studied the walls, the roof, the floor. The floor, what a mess! It was strewn with a hundred different types of debris and filth. Apart from the rusty and moldering remains of mining tools, there were also slides of fallen rock, collapsed timbers that half-blocked his way, household refuse from the people who lived above, and, rising up out of all this, the occasional skeletal hand, skull, or rib cage. Whether these originated from humans, beasts, or something more sinister, Bolldhe did not care to ponder. And between it all were pools of that same stinking, oily water he had noticed in the mine just after Nym-Cadog had vanished.

Bolldhe picked his way forward extremely carefully. He guessed that this part of the mine, closer to the surface, would serve as a refuge for the odd outlaw, drunken vagrant, or other scabrous lowlife that might pass this way from time to time. He wondered whether the thief who had stolen his axe was one such.

After five minutes he came to a dead end. The passageway abruptly finished with an immovable pile of fallen rock. Bolldhe held his glowing stick inches away from the bank of rock and studied it carefully. His probing eyes could discern no sign of recent disturbance. It was impossible to be sure, but as far as he could tell, in this almost nonexistent light, it looked as if none of this had been touched for years.

He sighed; maybe his quarry had not come down here at all. Then, he reflected, it was possible that he had missed a side passage on the way. Not very likely, but possible. He would have to check. . . .

Bolldhe instantly turned around, and instinctively grabbed for the axe that was not there. He stared intently into the darkness ahead, heart suddenly pounding madly.

What in the name of the wee man . . . ? Why had he started like that? He had not heard anything, nothing at all . . . yet he had *felt* something. Something evil, right behind him. His eyes strained to pierce the darkness beyond the glowing brand he held, almost willing his sight to extend farther than its pitiful radiance.

The hair at the back of his head prickled like a living animal. He could still see no sign of anything, but *something* had made him start, something right behind him. . . .

Bolldhe rubbed the nape of his neck with a wet hand. This spooky old pit was getting to him. It must have been his imagination. Yes, he was scared, still very scared, though now managing to push his fear to the back of his mind. But in any case, he was not going to hang around here a moment longer; the makeshift torch was on the point of sputtering out for good, and he had no intention of finding himself stuck down this damnable pit without any light at all. If there were indeed any side passages he had missed, maybe he would find them on the way back out.

As swiftly as he could while resisting the urge to panic and bolt, he started making his way back. He had almost reached the place where the passage met the shaft leading up to the surface when he did spot another opening. It was a small side passage, barely four feet high, that plunged down steeply into utter blackness. The stench from this hole was worse than the rest of the mine, and hinted at "something" lurking down there. Not so much a presence, more like an aura, it almost shouted at him to retreat.

Bolldhe, however, had not got where he was today by listening to his feelings. If he had been the sort who was easily constrained by his fears, he would never have even left Moel-Bryn. Perversely, he decided to check this new way out.

He bent down, and entered.

Straightaway he knew this was not the right decision. Every particle of his being screamed at him to turn back and run, to get out of this godforsaken tunnel immediately. He could sense that he was entering a place that contained within its heart a great evil, and a deeper shade of darkness that had no tolerance for the living.

The shaft led down to all this horror, and bit by bit Bolldhe lowered himself down toward it.

He had to stoop and choose his footing carefully. Whatever lay down there, he did not want to tumble into it. One hand clasped the wall to brace himself; his eyes were as wide as lantern lenses.

As he made his slow progress downward, he began to hear his careful footsteps echoing back to him. Each measured pace he took repeated itself dully like a gritty *chink,* off in the distance. He listened with growing concern, and thought it odd that, in such a confined space as this, where all sound fell dead, there should be any echo at all. But as he continued, he soon realized that these reverberations were not emulating his footfalls with very much accuracy. His tread was careful and regular; the echoes were decidedly not.

He abruptly stopped, and listened hard. The sound of his footsteps ceased at once—but the echoes, carried on—*chink, chink, chink* . . . Bolldhe's heartbeat doubled in speed, and his head felt thick with pumping blood.

Then he heard them, the voices so quiet he was not sure at first that they were not merely the slight eruptions of his own restrained breathing.

No, voices—tiny, chilling, macabre voices, squeaking in laughter and eerie song, only just audible above the tapping of their tools. From all around the traveler they came, yet sounded so distant they might originate from deep within the rock itself. Either that or they were just memories, vestiges of sound from a distant past.

Then the name came to Bolldhe as clearly as if it had just been spoken: *Knockers.* The Huldre miners. More tales from his childhood, come back to haunt him.

Little bastards, he cursed fearfully, *they're mocking me!*

He had to go on. This he knew for sure. Knockers were not considered to be dangerous unless one crossed them, or returned their mockery. If he gave in to his fear now, he would likely spend the final few hours of his miserable life hurtling round these lightless passages in blind, screaming terror. Furthermore, Bolldhe realized with unexpected insight, if he were to turn back from this now, he would never be able to confront the horror that surely awaited him on Melhus Island. As it had always been in his life, Bolldhe had to conquer his own fears.

But there was also a feeling in him that he could not shake off: that, in some inexplicable way, this old silver mine had something to do with his destiny.

He continued down. Soon he sensed new passages branching off to either side of him. He held the torch, now little more than a candle taper, out into the left-hand opening, shielded his eyes, and peered in. There must have been some residual gas in here that he could not smell, for the torch's flame suddenly turned a greenish yellow, bloating and undulating strangely like a thick syrup. By its garish light he could see old wooden rails reaching back along the length of the passage, wherever they were not covered with heaps of fallen earth. There was also an old derailed mine cart, overturned, broken and decayed, its wooden wheels smashed and its brass bindings green with age.

Bolldhe backed out of this passage, and turned around to investigate the other. This one was darker, reflecting back none of the torch's light at all, despite the fact that the additional gas here was causing it to burn even brighter. He peered into the strangely dense darkness in fascination. It was so totally lightless in there that when he extended his hand into it, torch and all, it simply disappeared, and he was back in darkness once again. It was as if he had immersed his arm in a pool of tar.

In his bemusement, he failed to notice that even the Knockers had gone silent.

Then a white hand lunged out at him from the wall of darkness and slapped him hard across the face. Bolldhe screamed in terror, and an entire chorus of high-pitched laughter errupted throughout the mine. He struck out instinctively, lost his balance, and the torch fell from his hands and bounced away down the incline. In its sudden flare he caught a glimpse of a dark figure leaping out of the side passage and scrambling away from him up the steep shaft.

Despite the bells of panic that were clanging in his reeling mind, Bolldhe knew that any danger from his attacker was now over. It was just the thief, still on the run from him. But this consoled him little, for he now found himself tumbling head over heels into the pit below—down into the very source of the fear.

With a jarring impact that drove the wind out of him, he landed in the chamber underneath. He rolled over painfully on the jagged, splintering surface of the floor, leapt back onto his feet in the same movement, and stumbled in blind hysteria over to his fallen torch. He snatched it up in violently shaking hands, and stared around himself.

The chamber—or whatever it was—fell away from the pool of torchlight into darkness; its size could not be guessed. All that could be seen was a large, empty wooden chest with a smashed lock and its lid open.

But there *was* something else in this room. Just on the very edge of darkness. The fount of all the instinctive fear assailing Bolldhe all this time, that fear that he had been so determined to overcome. This had nothing to do with the thief or even the Knockers, but was something *entirely* different. He could sense an overpowering aura of evil down here with him, could feel its age-old malignancy boring into his mind. It was so potent he could almost smell it.

There was the briefest of movements, like the fluttering of a departing soul, and Bolldhe was gone.

"So basically," Nibulus stated patiently, "what you're telling us is: You've lost your axe."

Bolldhe glowered, and turned away from the big man in contempt. He should have known better than to try telling this lot. As far as they were concerned, the drunken idiot had simply allowed his axe to be stolen, failed to recover it, and now wanted them to provide a new one. All this talk of hidden mines was about as relevant to them as yesterday's weather forecast.

It had taken Bolldhe less than half an hour to reach Myst-Hakel. Gasping for breath and dripping with sweat in the humidity of the night, he had finally reached the sanctuary of the temple. All the others awoke blearily from their inebriation and stared up at him in alarm. But he had merely waved a dismissive hand at them, and staggered over to his mattress. Within minutes, he was fast asleep.

In the morning they were woken early by Job Ash. He had brought them a breakfast of raw tentacled mollusc in fish oil (which the green-faced diners had picked their way through with a kind of stunned disbelief) and cheerfully asked them if they had enjoyed their night out. None of them had been inclined to enlighten him but, later on, Bolldhe drew the boy aside and asked him what he knew of the mines.

But Job's dumbly smiling expression did not waver.

Stupid bloody savages! Bolldhe snorted irritably.

Finwald suddenly called out from his vantage point at the window. "You're not going to find out anything from that boy. He probably knows as much about those mines as I know about peat-cutting. I've been talking with some of the locals here, and I don't think anyone goes near the various mines or holes around here. Remember those deep sinkholes we passed on the way here? And all the bottomless pools? From what I can gather, this whole area's dotted with them, and apparently they're considered taboo. Something to do with those huge bats, I think; the locals see them emerging at dusk, as if they're flying straight out of the underworld itself."

It was clear that Bolldhe would discover nothing of the mines—or more specifically the evil down there—from the locals.

"If you like, I'll go with you," Finwald suddenly offered.

"What?"

"To the mine. You need to get your axe back, remember?"

"My . . . The thief's got that," Bolldhe replied, puzzled by Finwald's offer. "What d'you care, anyway?"

"It just sounds interesting, that's all," Finwald protested. "Mazes and hidden chests . . ."

"Empty, I said, not hidden," Bolldhe corrected him, surprised that anyone had actually been listening to his story earlier that morning sufficiently to actually remember that bit. . . .

He paused. Finwald was staring at him rather intensely all of a sudden. The mage-priest's hands had balled into fists, and it looked as if he were not breathing.

Suddenly he leapt up.

"Come!" he urged as he strode across the room. "There's something not right about all this. I think we should take a look at this mine of yours, right now."

"What are you talking about?" Bolldhe stammered.

"A feeling," Finwald said, "a presentiment. I do have them, remember?"

He wrenched the door open and shouted out to the others, "Nibulus, get your armor on. And you, Paulus. We're going hunting."

Without so much as a backward glance, Finwald marched off into the clammy heat of the morning.

The others stared at each other in bewilderment. What was all this?

But obviously Finwald had "seen something" again, just as he had "seen something" two and a half months ago, which had induced them along on this mad adventure in the first place.

Out of curiosity more than anything else, they helped Nibulus on with his armor, and hurried after their precious augur, wherever he had got to by now.

A while later, they all stood at the bottom of the mine's entry shaft, glancing around uncertainly. Each one of them now carried a flambeau that had been steeped in pitch so that it burned with a strong, oily heat, giving off a steady emission of black, acrid smoke. All except Bolldhe, who held the bull's-eye lantern that he had been much relieved to find safe in the temple-dormitory. Nibulus, rather eccentrically to Bolldhe's mind, had strapped his torch to one side of his helm, in the way of the adventurers depicted in the woodcuts back home in the Wintus hall of trophies. He led the way boldly, filling the whole passageway with his tengriite-clad bulk.

"You certainly do pick the most charming places for your late-night wanderings, Bolldhe," Appa snapped as he extricated one of his shoes from a patch of sucking muck.

"Not my choice, old man," Bolldhe replied tartly, training his lantern's beam suspiciously on every bump and niche in sight. "Beats me why any thief would choose it, either."

Even in company this time, the constantly shifting shadows were making him so jumpy that after barely two minutes he was almost a nervous wreck.

"Look to your back, Paulus," he warned the man at the tail end of the line. "You don't know what might be lurking down here."

Paulus, however, merely paused to adjust the weight of his bestudded leather cape upon his shoulders. He maintained his silence, and continued with his black sword waving before him like a cockroach's antenna.

Of all of them, Finwald looked the most serious. His face was set in concentration, his brow furrowed like those leathery old farmers he drank with at the Chase, and his black eyes stared intently ahead into the path of the lanternlight. He uttered not a word.

The party splashed along the freezing tunnel slowly, carefully picking their way.

"Down here," Bolldhe said quietly, pointing to the hole that opened up to their left. His heart raced madly.

"You went down there on your own?" Nibulus wrinkled his nose in distaste. "You've got guts, I'll give you that."

Bolldhe was by now too scared to register the compliment. He was hearing those screams in his head again, and with them the far-off rumbling of the sea.

He directed the lantern's beam down into the shaft, and the others crowded around to look.

The Peladane stroked his blade, weighing the sword in his hands. Bolldhe studied his face and tried to gauge the temper of their leader, and whether or not he was taking this escapade seriously. But the Peladane's features remained impassive. After a quick readjustment of his armor, he said, "All right, Bolldhe, keep close behind me, and keep that lamp directed ahead of us at all times. The rest of you, keep your wits about you, and be ready to act swiftly and precisely; I don't want you crowding any more than—"

He never even finished the sentence. All eyes were now staring fixedly at the horror rising out of the shaft toward them.

"*Shit!*" cried Nibulus in alarm, and leapt back from the hole.

Immediately panic gripped the company. Torches swept about wildly or were dropped to the floor, weapons swung, men screamed, and bodies writhed in a melee. Exactly what happened in those brief moments none of them would ever know, but afterward all they could remember was the panic, the insanely dancing flambeaux, and the sound of the Beast. Deep and liquid, it snarled its way up out of the darkness in savage, shuddering breaths, as terrible as the Rawgr itself.

Nibulus truly came into his own that day. Deprived of space and bereft of the light Bolldhe should have been providing, the Peladane nevertheless somehow managed to keep his head while all around him turned into pandemonium. Channeling every scrap of his training and experience, his great strength and a barrelful of fear-induced fury, he threw himself at the Beast and brought his greatsword to bear in a series of vicious, well-placed blows. He never caught sight of the nightmare clearly, only brief flashes of some terrible apparition in the frantic light: great fangs, huge, blood-hued talons, a mane of black hair flailing about behind it. It was probably fortunate that Bolldhe had dropped the lantern.

Then the clash of metal—green sparks flying into his face and smoldering in his stubble—a sword being wielded with great strength but little skill—the crackle of magic from behind—moans of terror and despair—hastily babbled prayers—the stench of sweaty terror . . .

Then Bolldhe, screaming something in his own language, hurling a flask of torch oil full into the face of the monster—the arc of a flaming torch flying overhead—a flash of fire—a hideous howl of agony—the smell of boiling oil, singeing skin, ignited hair that thrashed about in a whirlwind of smog-belching flame—

And the horror was gone.

Gone in an echoing, gibbering wail; gone in a trail of smoke as its bristling mane trailed fire behind it. Down into the depths of its lair. Sobbing in misery and defeat.

Silence . . .

Then a voice, straining to hold itself steady:

"Just grab that sword, and let's get the hell out of here!"

Finwald's voice. No one disagreed.

Three days later, Bolldhe was still feeling sick. The day after their ordeal in the mine he had woken up in a state of deep malaise, which during the course of that day had waxed into a black depression. The following day had seen no improvement, and by the third it had developed into a physical illness. No efforts on the part of the healers made any difference.

His companions, by contrast, exuded vitality: they were positively twitching with energy and vigor. The sudden excitement of the conflict—though it had terrified them at the time—had both thrilled and animated them, and by the time they had arrived back at the temple, they were suffused with the kind of dynamism none of them expected in this torpid little swamp town.

Shouting and chattering excitedly in the safety of their dormitory, the first thing they had done was to allot the monster's sword to Nibulus, in recognition of his valiant deed. But the Peladane had insisted that it should be Bolldhe—who had inflicted the only real injury upon the Beast with his flask of oil—who should receive this trophy.

This had surprised everybody, not least Bolldhe, for it was not like their leader to be so self-effacing. But then there was also the suspicion that Nibulus was merely being practical; he would not give up his beloved Unferth for anything, and the already encumbered warrior was not about to further weigh himself down with another burden.

Finwald had at first seemed a little put out by this. As far as he was concerned, the sword was too good for the likes of Bolldhe. But he could see this decision was out of his hands, and did not raise any serious objection.

Bolldhe, though, had wanted nothing to do with the weapon at all, and had regarded it with a distrust that bordered on loathing. But in the end, he had relented. This was not because of Nibulus's persuasions, nor any sense of pride in his prize. It was simply for the pragmatic reason that he had clearly lost his broadaxe for good, and this finely crafted weapon was the best he was likely to come across in these uncivilized lands.

All three magic-users had cast spells over it, and all three were in no doubt that it was in some way enchanted. It was only Finwald, however, who was convinced that it was just the sort of magic weapon that they needed against Drauglir. He was very excited about the whole affair, even going so far as to claim that with such a sword their battle might already be won.

They had all studied the weapon with great curiosity. It was strange indeed. None of them could put an age to it, or hazard a guess at its origin, for the style was totally bizarre. The hilt, large and heavy, was wire-bound and blackened with age. The cross guard was straight and unadorned, much in the manner of the ancient swords of the Northmen before their decline. And the blade was like none any of the company had ever seen before: snaking out from the cross guard, it was razor-sharp, double-edged, and undulated like the backbone of a serpent. It was almost beautiful in its craftsmanship.

"It looks like the kind of sword we used to call flamberge," Nibulus had announced. "A firebrand—a tongue of fire."

"Yes," Finwald had added enthusiastically, "a flame to fight the fires of Hell! You could even name it Flametongue. . . ."

Bolldhe stared at the object doubtfully as it lay on the table where the mage-priest had placed it for him. But he took it up anyway and, as he held it in his hands for the first time, a clear image had suddenly popped into his head. No, stronger than an image; this was more like a vision:

It involved a heath, a desolate and forsaken place of sparse, yellowing tussocks of grass that bent in an unquiet wind. Beneath a grey sky it lay, a sky heavy with storm clouds. At the far end of this heath, a great drop—a cliff that looked out over a troubled sea. And standing right at the edge of this cliff, a figure. This figure was too distant for any precise details to be made out, but there was a familiarity about it that Bolldhe could not quite put his finger on. . . .

Puzzled, Bolldhe carefully laid the flamberge back on the table. Perhaps he was turning into a genuine oracle after all.

It was probably from that moment that his depression had set in. He was increasingly troubled by a nagging feeling that would not leave him, and it grew worse with every hour that passed. Maybe it was caused by the Beast? None of them had any clear idea what had attacked them, though an Ogre, a Jutul, and even a Kobold like the ones they had seen in Nym-Cadog's realm were suggested. But whatever it was, it did seem very strange to Bolldhe that a monster like that should wield any weapon at all. That creature had been one of tooth and talon, and surely a savage beast like that had no need of any man-made weapon. The sword had slowed it down, made it clumsy, and in the end, perhaps lost it the fight. Had it not been thus encumbered, it would have doubtless made short work of Nibulus and the rest of them, yet it had held on tight to the flamberge like an old friend—or a new toy.

Bolldhe wondered. Again, that nagging thought at the back of his mind . . .

Each time he studied Flametongue, his depression grew worse. A bitter taste clung in his mouth, and a gripe had settled in his stomach. Each night he lay awake for hours that seemed to have no end, and each morning the warm sunlight mocked him in his melancholy.

Whatever the Beast had been, it had brought home to Bolldhe his own fragility and mortality, far more than any other encounter he had suffered on this journey so far. The road ahead now seemed a never-ending, futile folly, fraught with dangers along its entire length.

And at the end of that road, if he arrived there at all, waited only Death.

Bolldhe had taken to brooding all day over such black, morbid thoughts. He shunned his companions, and they in turn shunned him.

In the days leading up to the company's departure from Myst-Hakel, it was not only Bolldhe who was in a black mood. Paulus, too, appeared to have something on his mind, something that was turning his customary dourness into something even more acerbic. He looked constantly haggard and drawn, and while the others in the party were trying to complete all the final preparations before they set off, the Nahovian spent his days wandering about like a zombie.

On the eve of setting off, he lay awake all night in the temple hall, staring up at the ceiling. A chill mist had crept in through the windows, and his companions slept fitfully, huddled under the warmth of their furs. But Paulus had cast his covers aside, long ago having given up the idea of sleep. His one good eye wide open, he gazed up into the darkness above him, and ruminated.

Sleep had similarly abandoned him for the past few nights. Always he would lie there awake while his mind buzzed with thoughts; each night dragged endlessly as he tossed and turned, grumbling irritably and constantly readjusting his covers. His body yearned for the sleep he so badly needed, but his brain would not allow it. Then, after an eternity of fidgeting restlessly, the sound of birdsong would filter through the windows, followed by the first hints of dawn's cold, grey light. Outside, early risers would shuffle past, coughing and mumbling as they carried their tin basins and slabs of soap down to the jetties. Whereupon Paulus would curse and fidget some more, but still sleep would not come to him. It was only when the temple hall was lit by the brighter glare of early morning and the townspeople were all up and about their daily business that he would finally feel a merciful heaviness descend on his surviving eyelid, and sleep would soon follow.

In this way the mercenary had managed perhaps two or three hours of sleep each morning, and later he would wander about looking pale, drained and lethargic, only half-alive. This night—their last in Myst-Hakel—was no better. In fact if anything, it was worse. They had to be up early the following morning, and Paulus knew that this would cheat him of even this brief chance of sleep. The thought of the coming day's hard trek across the remainder of the Rainflats to Fron-Wudu, in his current state of exhaustion, agitated him even more.

He lay awake in the damp, marsh-scented mist that rolled in from outside, and pondered the reason for his recent insomnia. It was due to the incident at the mine, of course. But it had nothing to do with the Beast itself. No, he had seen nothing whatsoever of that terrible adversary, having been too far back down the passage when it was encountered.

Being rear guard had its advantages. It meant he could unobtrusively hang back a little, and explore the tunnel much more thoroughly than his companions, just in case there were any discarded valuables they had overlooked.

So while they had gone ahead in search of Bolldhe's axe, Paulus had lagged behind to do some searching around of his own.

But it was not treasure that he had found. No silver, no precious uncut stones, no interesting baubles. Nothing valuable at all, in fact. But he *had* found something that had interested him.

It was a little shutter set in the wall, about head height—old and rusted, but not so rusted that his powerful fingers could not prize it open.

And out of that open shutter emerged a cold blast of air from what had to be a vast empty space behind; an icy wind that chilled his face and stung his eye, and brought with it rumors of far-off, running water. Rumors of a splashing, gurgling, thundering current . . .

. . . And, barely audible above the rush of water, the forlorn wailing of a voice.

Is anyone there?—Please, let there be somebody there!—I'm so cold. . . .

Paulus had promptly snapped the shutter closed, cutting off both the icy blast and the ghostly voice it had carried.

But it was not fear that had made him do so. It was gratification. For there was a certain grim satisfaction in ignoring that voice and its desperate, hopeless plea for salvation. He *relished* the thought that he had sealed its owner's fate forever. It somehow assuaged all the bitterness he had felt at the Kjellermann, the dire loathing he had felt that night for all those happy, pretty people who had laughed at him as he sat there on his own.

Now that voice, with all its lamentable pitifulness, its terror, and its despair, repeated itself over and over in his mind.

Gapp Radnar's voice.

Days later, out on the moors, a low sobbing rose into the night. Deep and bestial, it echoed long and far from its pit, reaching out across the swamp waters, through the tall reeds and bulrushes that whispered among themselves in nocturnal secrecy, and drifting over the creaking shackleboards toward the sleeping shantytown. By the time it filtered through the shuttered windows and barred doors of the stilt huts, it could hardly be heard, sounding no more than a low wind that moans from afar. Scant heed was paid to it by the townsfolk, huddled within their gritty and mist-dampened blankets against the terrors that rose from the swamp and into their dreams.

Again the lament rose, forlorn as the crake's cry, distant as the last glimpse of the waning moon that lay reflected upon the wind-rippled surface of the marsh pools, and as hopeless as the hearts of the moonrakers who dredged their waters.

Then the Beast emerged from the mine shaft and revealed itself. A gigantic, lumbering monstrosity with swinging arms, curving fangs, and filthy black hair that had grown uncontrollably from the mean little topknot it had possessed when first the company had encountered it many miles to the south.

Wodeman had guessed right; this whole region was indeed riddled with caves, a vast subterranean network of water-carved and interconnected tunnels that honeycombed the rock beneath the Rainflats. And it was by negotiationg these troglodyte paths that the Beast had arrived at the silver mine, escaping the entombment of Nym-Cadog's collapsed barrow. All that way it had forced a passage, howling its madness, pain, and hatred in the dark confines of the earth, driven by an unholy lust for vengeance, and swelling in size as its wounds worked their abhorrent transmutations.

For such was the way of the Afanc. Bastard child of Incubus and priestess of Yeggeth-Dziggetai, it was neither Huldre nor human, belonging to neither world yet forever trapped between. Though terrible had been its injuries sustained at the hands of the company from Nordwas, it could not be so easily destroyed. Not even the stroke of Unferth that had cloven its head could put this hybrid beneath the turf. For with every wound it received, the Afanc was not diminished but *enlarged*—after a period of dormancy—its body distending from within as foul fluids pulsed through it to swell its stricken organs.

Swell, not heal, for the Afanc bore with it forever any hurts it might receive, now engorged with poison, and befouled beyond belief. What with the hacking it had received during the battle at Nym's, and the burning from Bolldhe's oil flask just days earlier, its charred and gashed hide now appeared like a blackened landscape of gorge-riven magma crust, weeping rivers of pus.

Never was there one so hideous as the Afanc. Despised by all for its repulsiveness, the Beast had funds of hatred and stupidity untrammeled by mortal limitations. Beheld openly by torchlight, it could strike terror deep into the very essence of a man's soul, so much so that forever after he would question Life itself, and wonder how this world could suffer such a blasphemous abomination to walk upon its surface. Beheld by the light of the full moon, just a sight of this apparition from the darker regions of Man's most awful nightmare was sufficient to kill on the spot. By day, fortunately, it must perforce remain within the earth, lest it perish in the cleansing light of the sun.

And yet, mere yards from the Barguest stood a dark figure that might have been a man. His kirtle hung from broad shoulders, and twin fires burned from behind the veil of hair surrounding his face. Though it could not see the stranger, the Afanc sensed his presence. It sniffed the night air through its clogged-up, funnel-like nostrils, and swung its great head this way and that, but it could not locate him. With its rakelike claws it then thrashed the invisible aura that surrounded the stranger, and gurgled in malice like a cauldron of boiling blood.

Eventually it stopped and whimpered in defeat. There was nothing in the world that this fey-spawned obscenity feared, but the presence it now sensed was not of this world. Still whimpering, it retreated back down into its lair.

"Ah, loathely Denizen of Darkness," the red-eyed stranger whispered, "you alone who can perceive my presence, need you arise from your pit to trouble an already darkening world with your malodorous being? Go back to your lair.

This game has no role for you. The Flame has already risen to take *its* part, and even now my servant walks blindly with it to his doom—our Doom."

But despite the power evident in that sibilant voice, there was pleading, and sadness. Pleading for the Beast he knew could not obey him, and sadness for a race that was almost lost.

9

Dripping Wet

Several hours after he had fallen down the well, Gapp began to wake up, but consciousness did not come easily.

Out of the blackness of nonexistence, the occasional fleeting thought would appear, mere sparks in the void of his senselessness. Eventually, these tiny pulses of mind-stuff began to increase both in frequency and in duration. Before long they had joined up, strung together into a dream, a horrendous nightmare of nausea, pain, and mortality; human, *living* feelings that, in a vague, removed part of his mind, he had considered mercifully behind him.

No, no, not that world again, not again PLEASE! Just let me stay dead. . . .

Numbness. Freezing cold numbness. A chill that had turned him to ice.

I'm dead. I'm buried. I'm under the cold, cold earth. Don't let me wake up now!

Rocking, undulating, swirling. Enclosed in the womblike envelopment of death.

Oh, my head! My head! How is it possible to feel such pain when I'm dead?

A surging rush of consciousness. A dazzle of green and purple lights in his brain. A flooding of blood to the head. Sickening dizziness, like lying in bed when very drunk, eyes closed but feeling the entire world spin faster and faster until it seems the body is turning inside out. Then the sensation of being carried down a long, dark tunnel, out of the womb of death and into whatever awfulness lay beyond.

I don't want this! I can really do without all this. . . .

Then Gapp felt a sudden jerk that pulled him fully around, and he moaned again with the nausea sweeping through him. He was fully awake now, though he did not know it, and he was hating every second of it.

Where the heck . . . ?

He floundered wildly, and gulped in a quantity of freezing water. Instantly he sank, and thrashed his limbs about in wild panic. Another mouthful of water, this time into his lungs. He did not even know which way was up or down. Kicking in frenzy, he had the dull sense of his foot striking against something solid, and he pushed away from it hard.

Instinct took over. In his present position, it had to.

Coughing and heaving, Gapp surfaced, and flailed about hysterically. His entire existence became one mad struggle. But after a while the recognition came to him that he was clinging to a hard surface, and on to this he held fast like a barnacle.

It took Gapp several minutes to cough up the residue of water from his lungs. At that moment, all he could be concerned about was the luxury of being able to breathe again. The rest could wait.

So he gripped the rock tightly with his numb fingers, and resisted the current that threatened at any moment to tear him from his precarious hold on life and sweep him away. He had no idea where he could be, for it was utterly lightless; and the only sound in his present world was the hollow thundering of what might possibly be an underground stream.

Things, as usual, were *really* bad.

Gapp's painful return to consciousness marked a turning point in his life. For on this occasion, for the first time in all his fifteen years, he was totally on his own. He did not have a clue where he was, how he had got there, or what he had been doing beforehand. And he had no one to advise him on what to do now. All he knew was that he was floating in some kind of narrow tunnel, and that he felt cold and sick almost to the point of death.

If he was going to survive, he was going to have to do it all by himself; there would be nobody to help him out of this one.

With an unprecedented effort of will, Gapp forced himself to take action. In such dire straits as this, the animal instinct in him had to take over. A side of his mind that had not up until now played much of a part in his life, it now cut through the haze of disorientation, suffering, and fear, till one single urge drove him on. *Survival.*

It was something that had never happened to him previously, but something that afterward, however long his future might be, would occur all too frequently. And before long he would be able to call on that instinct at will.

Still holding himself as close to the wall as possible, he forced his unfeeling fingers to find a better handhold on the lumpy rock. He grunted through gritted teeth as he put all that remained of his strength into heaving his sodden weight upward. His arms were pathetically feeble, to be sure, but the thought of giving up did not even on a subconscious level occur to him. All his being was now channeled into surviving. Several handholds later he was largely free of the pull of the stream, with only his lower legs still submerged.

He halted briefly to gasp a few deep lungfuls of air, then resumed the climb.

Gapp had no way of knowing what lay ahead. For all he knew the wall might curve back over on itself like a pipe, and he would be forced soon enough to drop back into the water. But such details were irrelevant at that moment; all he could think of now was to get away from that freezing water.

He continued. Soon he found himself clinging onto the sheer wall with no footholds at all. Still in their saturated, slimy boots, his feet kept slipping on the slick surface of the rock, and more than once he came close to losing his hold altogether. But raw and bleeding though they were, he still had fingers and nails and his new survival instinct gave strength to his tenacity. He managed to find tiny crevices down into which he could just about wedge his unfeeling fingertips, and then larger outcrops began to appear.

In what was probably just a few minutes, he grew aware that the wall was becoming not quite so sheer. It might even be leveling out!

He desperately scrambled further up the rock face before his strength ran out completely, and at last found himself just under a narrow ledge. With a final heave, he was over.

For how long he remained that way, drenched, curled up, and quaking, Gapp had no way of guessing. He felt worse than ever before in his life. He shivered uncontrollably, his head was pounding like a war drum, and sickness ran through his whole body. Unable to rise from his prone position, he languished in torment upon the ledge while the sharp rock surface dug deeply into his side and shoulder.

Eventually, with a supreme effort of will, he managed to push himself up into a sitting position. A fresh coughing fit overtook him with such violence that it felt as if his ribs were dislocated. Gapp was not sure if it were even possible to dislocate ribs, but it was a worrying thought. Worrying too was the wheezing sound of his lungs, which hinted strongly at pneumonia.

But he did not dwell upon this. Instead, he began chafing his limbs to try and restore their circulation, and hopefully get some warmth into him. At first this was a painfully slow process, for his hands and arms were so stiff he could hardly move them. But he doggedly persevered, and eventually his body began to remember what it was to be alive.

Gradually, awkwardly, he worked his sodden clothes off (after removing the little pack that was still miraculously strapped to his back) and wrung as much water from them as he could. He then put them back on. They felt repellently clammy against his skin, and he immediately broke into another fit of coughing.

I'm ill, he thought darkly, *I might even be dying. But I've got to get out of here—there is absolutely not a chance that I'm going to end my life in a place like this.*

Underneath, he knew how slim his chances were, but the front part of his mind refused to acknowledge this. So bit by bit he began carefully feeling the walls around him.

At first there was nothing to suggest any way out. The wall continued upward, only with an even smoother surface, and when he risked jumping up to feel what lay above, he was shattered to discover that the roof was only a couple of feet higher. The ledge itself dropped sharply away on either side of him. He was stuck on a tiny outcrop of rock protruding from the tunnel wall, with *Pel-only-knew* how much solid rock directly above him, and a freezing stream below that probably only led farther down into the deeps of the earth.

He was trapped as surely as he had been in the Huldre woman's dungeon dimension, only this time his situation seemed far, far worse. A sodden scrap of freezing wretchedness washed down the drain of life into the underworld like an old dead leaf. No sooner had he confronted these thoughts than he broke down in great, heaving sobs of black despair, and stayed like that for quite some time.

A while later, Gapp suddenly thought of something.

The pack!

He still could hardly believe that this saturated lump of leather had survived all this way with him, and thanked his foresight in strapping it on so securely. He had never kept very much in it; for the bulk of his baggage was carried by poor old Bogey. He doubted he would find much left in it now, but at least it was something.

Indeed there was not much, from what his frozen fingers could determine: a mush of indeterminate foodstuff he had stowed away from Nym's table; a thin roll of bachame he always kept to hand while traveling, for use either as an extra layer in his bedroll, or as an undergarment, or a small groundsheet; and—ah, here was something at least—one of his precious throwing knives. It was the one whose blade had snapped, which he had put into his bag ages ago, hoping to get it fixed later.

Before anything else, the boy scooped all of the mush of waterlogged food into his mouth, and missed not a smear from his fingers. Then his hands went down to his belt and rummaged through the pouches attached to it. In one of them his hands closed over the familiar and reassuring little box that contained his tinder, flint, and steel.

"Light," he announced, his voice no more than a harsh croak, and prized the lid open. Inside were still the tiny packets of wax-sealed tinder—unbroken.

Now, what can I burn?

The bachame, he remembered, was special Peladane-issue; tightly rolled in a thin oil-skin wrapper, it was fashioned to be proof against even the most torrential downpour. But how effective would it be against the soaking Gapp had endured?

To his growing dejection, it did at first appear to be completely saturated; but as he continued unraveling it, he discovered to his delight that there was enough of it in the middle of the roll that was still dry. Not hesitating for a second, he set to work on it with his fire-making gear.

Thank You, Pel-Adan, he prayed, *for granting your followers such foresight.*

It crossed his mind that he ought to keep aside most of the bachame to use for lighting, but he was still so frozen that he could not resist using more than he should have there and then to make a fire. He kept it burning low so it would last for as long as possible, and then crouched over the flames to make sure that not one tiny waft of heat would go to waste. As it warmed his body, feeling came back to him, and his blood began to flow properly again. That was painful, very painful, but he did not mind. He meanwhile carefully held each one of his clothes over the flames to dry them.

Eventually they were just about dry enough to put back on and, still steaming slightly, he hunched over the meager flames and stared about him. From what little he could see, he was still in what appeared to be a narrow tunnel, the course of a subterranean stream, with a low ceiling and no immediate means of escape.

The warmth and the light were meager, but sitting there, with almost-dry clothes and a little food inside him, Gapp Radnar now felt like a king. Using instinct alone, he had crawled out from under the very clutches of his own extinction, then used his own resourcefulness to get to a position where he could now start to plan his way out of here. How many other esquires could have managed that on their own? How many people in this whole world could float maybe for days down an underground stream, and then climb out and build themselves a fire halfway up a tunnel wall?

"Not ruddy many, I'll bet!" he croaked in self-esteem.

There was always a way, so long as you were prepared to look for it. On a whim, he dipped his hand into one of his trouser pockets, and withdrew his old set of reed pipes. He rubbed their lacquered wooden surface fondly, and placed them to his lips. He would have music in this despicable hole, music such as there had never been heard in the depths of the underworld ere now! And when he got out of this place and returned to Nordwas, he would play this same tune to all the townsfolk, to the elite of the Wintus household, to his stone-skimming friends, even to his rotten family; and they would marvel! Songs celebrating his adventure would be sung by the troubadours and wandering minstrels, and his fame would ne'er die. . . .

So he began to blow. But the only sound that came forth from the pipes was a bubbling semiwhistle, like a toad, boiling in a pot.

"Armholes!" he swore, and shoved them back into his pocket.

Still as trapped as he had been an hour ago, with his eyes he now searched the wall opposite for any sign of escape. After a while he could just about make out a shadow indicating there was another ledge like this one on the other side. He could not see how far it extended, but at least it was something to investigate. Fired with sudden excitement, he made preparations in the last flickering light of his fire.

In one of the belt pouches he had a few small packets of pitch gel, a viscous, foul-smelling, oily substance that was intended for certain emergencies. He tore one of them open and smeared its contents on the end of the throwing knife's hilt, wrapped a good quantity of bachame around this, bound it tightly, then wiped off the inside of the pitch-gel packet onto this. He held it to the fire. With a small *pffss* it ignited, and he held it aloft. It was probably the most pathetic torch ever made, but it was all he had available.

Gapp clamped firmly in his teeth the remainder of the blade, still attached to the hilt, and steeled himself. With the flames singeing his cheeks, and his braced limbs shaking badly, without further hesitation he sprang.

Over the churning stream he flew and, with an impact that nearly knocked him back down into the water, he landed upon the opposite ledge. Madly he grabbed for handholds as he felt himself topple.

He found none, a gasp erupted from his throat, and he toppled backward.

But at the last second, he managed to twist himself around and kick away hard. He sailed back across the gap, and with incredible luck was back again, where he had started from.

He panted heavily, his heart pounding in his chest. "Not again!" he breathed. "Never again! If you want me, you'll have to try harder than that."

He glared with loathing at the icy stream below, then, on a mad impulse, suddenly leapt across the gap again, grunting in defiance.

This time he was successful, and landed perfectly upon the ledge. Straightaway he clamped his fingers onto the rock face like a gecko.

"Ysss!" he snarled with the knife hilt still wedged between his teeth.

Carefully and steadily he inched his way across this new ledge. It was hardly a hand's span wide in places. It rose and fell unevenly, and was always slippery, and before long he saw with dismay that it finally came to an end. His feeble torch did not show him if it carried on farther beyond the gap, so he desperately stretched his foot out to test it. Whereupon he at once lost his balance and pitched forward.

As he fell, he reached with outstretched arms to grab at something, anything. Luckily they came into contact with a further section of ledge, as it continued on the other side of the gap.

So there he was, like a human bridge stretched across the divide, the icy torrent a few feet below him, and the flames of his makeshift torch burning the skin of his face. Again, survival instinct took over, and he scrambled like a mad thing up onto this new ledge.

He finally spat out the torch onto the stone surface ahead of him, and lay panting in great, shuddering gasps.

"Too close," he blurted into the darkness. "That was far too close!"

Gapp was a nervous wreck by now, after two close shaves in less than three minutes, and he could feel his whole body quivering like jelly. The torch was flickering with only a faint blue glow now, so as he lay on his belly, he occupied himself for the next few minutes with fastening on a little more bachame and relighting it.

Here the ledge was only a foot or so below the tunnel roof, so Gapp was forced to proceed by crawling on his elbows. This was the closest he had ever come to understanding what it felt like to be an earthworm. On occasions he had to squeeze through gaps of no more than a few inches leeway, where he could feel the rock scraping him both at front and back.

Long minutes passed in such torturous progress.

At length, he came to a wider section of the tunnel, and there he beheld something rather interesting. Just visible in the light of the flame was a fall of tiny droplets of water, sprinkling in a fine, bloodred haze from a hole in the middle of the tunnel roof. Gapp peered up at it in wonderment. The hole was fairly large, but without much water coming through. Could it be that there was another stream up there somewhere?

A trickle that size did not necessarily mean that there was a tunnel large enough for him to crawl through. It might be tiny, just a crack in the rock. And if he became stuck there . . .

He peered at the ledge ahead of him, and thought about the narrow gaps already that had nearly been the death of him. *Gap the Gapp-Slayer. Ha!* That was not funny. . . . Again he glanced up at this new hole, which, now he came to think about it, might be just big enough to haul himself up through. It then occurred to him that if he were to continue following the stream along its course ahead of him, it was bound at some time to lead him *down*. No, what he needed was to find a way *up*.

On an impulse he leapt for the hole. He grabbed the edge of it, and panicked when he felt how slick it was. But he held on doggedly, and hung dangling above the lethal current. He braced himself for a second, then heaved himself up through the hole—and scrambled onto the floor of the new cavern he was in.

He had succeeded in leaving the tunnel behind him.

He hardly dared to hope as he looked about himself at his new surroundings. After adding a little more pitch gel to his torch, Gapp held it up and stared around at this subterranean wonderland he had come to.

To his utter bewilderment, he found that he could see quite far. The feeble flames of his little knife torch were reflected back by a million points of glittering light, all of them the most marvelous and varied colors, that reached back a dizzying distance that hurt his eyes and confused his brain. From the near-lightless wormhole he had just emerged from, he was now in a cavern so vast the range of his sight seemed to simply fall away, and beyond that he could feel by the air that a vast space waited for him out there in the darkness. This cavern was absolutely huge.

His still unsteady senses caused him to lurch suddenly, and he had to close his eyes to regain his balance. Deeply he breathed in the fresher air. In contrast to the tunnel below, it now felt that he was out in the open once more.

It was also, he noticed, so quiet in here. Below, he had grown used to the constant roar of water, but it was just a dull rumor now, more like the echo of a bad dream that was gradually fading in his head. Then, as his ears adjusted to the welcome stillness of the cavern, he began to hear the gentle, musical ringing of a hundred tiny trickles of water dripping into deep pools.

Gapp wiped the steam from his spectacles, and gazed spellbound at the weird and wonderful rock formations that protruded from all directions. He had never in his life seen anything like these stalagmites, stalactites, and other strange shapes, nor even heard tell of their like, before, not even in the wildest and most fanciful boastings of the bards. He marveled at what they might actually be, whether they were plant, animal, or some other life-form unique to this world he had entered. He even wondered if the cavern had been created by some mad troglodyte artist or wizard.

Some outcrops were a pure, brilliant white, while others were orange, gold, blue, purple, green, or deep red. Some undulated smoothly, bumpily, or curvaceously, others stuck out sharply in a bouquet of crystalline, needle-like spines.

Other tunnels he could now make out, branching off in all directions, leading out of the main cavern. Some were filled with clusters of rainbow-hued limestone icicles, and resembled gaping, fang-filled mouths. The floor and the roof rose and plummeted to a score of different levels. The whole place had a chaotic randomness to it that defied both reason and gravity.

Gapp exhaled as a sudden spasm of shivering overtook him, and watched with fascination as his breath turned to sparkling motes of ice. It was freezing in here, but it was a cold that seemed to Gapp somehow pristine and wholesome. Soft currents of air wafted in from the various tunnels and brushed past his face like tendrils of dew-spangled cobweb.

This cavern had an air of undefiled sanctity about it, and Gapp felt like an alien intruder. He was seeing things that men from the world above were not meant to see—probably never had seen. Perhaps he was the first human to witness it. His heart accelerated at the thought.

Tentatively, he began exploring.

The next few hours saw the young Aescal going from one cave to another. Each tunnel, each cave, each tiny hole he found himself crawling through provided a new wonder. He now wore most of the bachame wrapped round him under his shirt, partly because of the cold but also to dry it with the heat of his body. This provided a constant supply of material for his torch, so he was never deprived of seeing the alien beauty of this underworld.

He was surprised to find that he was still able to appreciate such things, considering that he was hopelessly lost hundreds or even thousands of feet underground, unlikely to ever see daylight again. Despite his mad struggle for life when caught in the stream, despite his channeling every last fiber of his mind, body, and spirit into the struggle to survive, a certain resignation to his fate had settled into him now. He was ready to take every minute as it came, and not concern himself too much with what might happen next. Something in him kept nagging at him, to admit that he was in all probability lost beyond redemption, that his supply of bachame would not last very long, and that soon he would be blundering around this cold, sharp, alien world in total dark, and eventually, after long miserable days of starvation, he would simply wink out of existence as if he had never been.

But his ordeal in the tunnel had brought out something in him that would not go away now, something as hard and icy as the stalagmites he wandered among. And so he continued, and was calm.

Hour after hour, still the boy journeyed on. Ever exploring, forging ahead, eager to see what lay around the next corner. Gapp grew weak with hunger, but that only seemed to drive him on ever farther.

In any case, there really was not anything else for him to do.

Time dragged by, measured only by the tightening coils of pain that gripped his empty stomach, and by the dwindling supply of his bachame. He slept only once, curling up in a ball of shivering misery beneath a shelf of overhanging rock. The constant dripping of limestone from above disturbed his slumber, and filled it with troubled dreams. When he awoke and ignited a fresh pitch-smeared rag, he was horrified to see that this "stone-bleeding" had deposited upon him a thin, crystalline coating that made him believe at first that the rocks themselves were trying to turn him into one of themselves, and draw him eternally into their world.

Could it be that they resented his movement, his warmth, his light?

Strange things began appearing around him now. He was not sure what they were, and to begin with he did not care, but as time went by they became more apparent. At first just vague images on the periphery of his vision, it was possible they were shadows cast by the uncertain flickering of his burning knife hilt, but before long they began darting about in front of him, crisscrossing his path, sometimes even stopping as if to stare at him before fleeing back into the shadows. But whenever he strained his bleary eyes for a closer look—for they remained always just beyond the halo of his torchlight—he would see nothing at all.

He dimly wondered whether he was hallucinating through hunger, or illness.

But eventually they did come fleetingly within the range of his light, just long enough for him to see that they were definitely figures.

Figures of short, misshapen people, with long, skinny arms, big ears, and twitching claws. They emerged from the walls, appearing out of solid rock, dancing and cackling in tiny, shrill voices, then disappearing again, through either wall, roof, or floor. They seemed two-dimensional like shadows, and as lacking in substance as air. But they were there nevertheless.

Gapp half-ran, half-staggered onward in a cloudy haze of fear. He was still hoping that this was a dream, but they gathered around him more closely now, seeming to feed off his draining life force. They hissed like spiders, snatched at his clothing as he blundered past them, growled, spat acid, and glared at him hatefully with their huge, luminous eyes.

Gapp glanced behind him, and saw with horror that the whole tunnel was now filled with them. He spun away and plunged on ahead. But now his legs no longer seemed to move; it was like a dream of running, of escaping, in which each step seems to last forever. His whole body felt weighed down like lead.

Suddenly his mind exploded with blinding color, as he smashed his head into a wooden crossbeam. At once full consciousness returned to him in a searing flash of pain, and immediately the apparitions vanished. Fragments of old, rotting wood went flying, and he realized that he had crashed through some sort of barricade. He fell flat on his face and his torch went out.

Reality had returned.

Groggily, the lost traveler picked himself up off the ground.

Kinayda! he wondered in utter perplexity. *Where am I now?*

Man-made barricades in a natural cave network did little to sort out his confusion. Nevertheless, he could not restrain the sudden surge of excitement at finding himself possibly in the realms of real people again. For a short while, hope rekindled itself in his heart. And with the return of hope came the ending of his sense of resignation, and inevitably the recommencement of his anxiety.

Fear stole over him again, and he fumbled in the dark for his fire-making equipment. Those horrible little imps had chilled him to the marrow, and he knew he had only minutes before the pitch darkness finally drove him completely out of his mind. This time he did not bother to take off his bachame undershirt—what was left of it—but instead simply tore at the fraying material in panic while he still wore it, until a clump of it came off in his hand. Hurriedly he smeared the last of his pitch gel over it, and set about striking sparks.

Eventually he had kindled a new flame, and held the burning rag up to see around.

Hope leapt up anew; the unmistakable sight of neatly excavated rock walls was the first thing to greet his eyes. He was now in a tunnel that had been fashioned by *people.* There on the ground lay the broken knife hilt he had been using as a torch, but more importantly, scattered about were several lengths of wood. Probably from the barricade. On closer inspection, they were satisfactorily *dry!*

Within minutes, Gapp brandished aloft a two-foot length of brightly burning timber. Compared with the measly tufts of bachame cloth he had been using, this new faggot blazed like a beacon in the darkness. His fear subsided, and he almost sobbed with relief.

"Now," he said to himself grimly, "let's get this over with."

His illness and hunger now forgotten, Gapp wasted no time in further surveying his surroundings. He shielded his eyes from the glare of his new torch, and peered down the dilapidated passage that stretched ahead of him. It was littered with collapsed pit-props and other debris, and so cramped he had to stoop low to avoid cracking his head.

Whoever mined these tunnels must have been small indeed, he considered. Haugers, he guessed at first, but reminded himself that the Haugrim rarely resorted to mining. Still, that scarcely mattered now, and without further tarry, he plunged on up the shaft.

Long minutes passed, and still the passage continued. So far he had not seen any other shafts or side passages. Soon he found it becoming difficult to breathe properly, and he longed to stand up straight and stretch his backbone.

Eventually however, he did come to a side passage. He took it without the slightest hesitation, and pressed on eagerly. So eagerly, in fact, he did not think to mark the turning.

As he progressed, more passages now opened out to either side of him. Excitedly he took whichever looked most promising, and never once paused to leave a marker. He just kept lurching onward with head bent low, and persevered in this random exploration with what little wit still remained to him.

New passages came and went with increasing frequency. Nearly all he tried led to a dead end, either an abandoned pit face or a collapsed shaft. But this deterred the half-crazed youth little. Tunnels opened this way, turned that, branched off and twisted almost back around upon themselves. There was little logic or pattern to them, yet Gapp felt at home within their random chaos. None, however, led upward.

Within an hour, Gapp was hopelessly lost in a labyrinth of tunnels. In one brief moment of lucidity, the boy realized just how lost he was; he had a brief vision of himself running like a rat down each new passage, wearing a grin of such stupidity and not appearing to have the slightest notion or care where he was going.

He halted straightaway, and the old fears and the panic began to rise in him again like vomit. He was lost and nearing the point of total exhaustion. Never before had he felt so tired. Fighting against the despair that threatened to overwhelm him once more, he leaned back against the wall and slid down to land heavily on his backside.

As he sat there in misery, tears welling up in his eyes, the dancing shadows began to return. He could hear their horrible little voices whispering malevolently, somewhere nearby. He looked up fearfully and, to his surprise and bewilderment, found he could see all the way back to the natural caverns! It was from there that they came, a swarm of weaving, leaping, dancing shapes that poured in through the broken barricade. As they swiftly drew nearer, the boy could only stare in horror, too paralyzed by fear to make any move.

Within seconds, they were all about him; they pounced toward him, flitted away, twisted and span, cavorted and writhed; and all the while they pointed their sharp little fingers in mockery, and laughed in those disgusting, shrill little voices.

"GET OUT! GET OUT! GET OUT!" Gapp cried in anguish.

Suddenly they were gone, vanished as though they had never existed. There was nothing to be heard but the sound of his own voice, as it echoed away down the dark, labyrinthine passages.

Wearily he staggered to his feet, and plodded on. Though the shadow figures were gone, he still saw faces now and then. They stared up at him from the ground in a silent scream of death, devoid of flesh and half-buried by loose scree and soil. They did not appear human, and he did not even know if they were really there at all, or existed only in his mind. But as long as he could not hear them, he did not particularly care. He did, however, allow himself the satisfaction of hearing those stony faces crunching into granules beneath his feet.

He did not know how long he went on for after that. But once he heard his voice wailing:

"Is anyone there? Please, let there be someone there! I'm so cold!"

Suddenly he heard a sharp click. It was like the snapping of a catch, or something; and he was sure he could hear voices—shouting even. It sounded as if it came from . . .

. . . That passage there!

No. It was the voices in his head again, he knew. He pulled himself together again, and moved quickly on.

It was a pity, he reflected as he trudged on, because that was the only shaft that had actually led upward. But no; that way led only to madness.

It was another two days before Gapp finally saw daylight.

Starvation and the mental strain of his entombment (to say nothing of his debilitating fever) had taken almost their full toll on him, and his mind had retracted into a world of darkness and disturbing half-dreams. But finally, as if rewarding his mindless perseverance, the palest hint of light far ahead began to dimly register in his withdrawn consciousness.

Had he been in a fit enough mental state to register such things, Gapp might have noticed that this part of the mines was much different from that of two days previously. Tunneled by another race, it was far older, roomier, danker.

He squinted at the faint glimmer uncertainly. Yes, there was no doubt about it; that was *natural* light up ahead!

He lurched ahead shakily, and his cracked mouth opened in an attempt to cry out exuberantly. The pale shaft of light grew steadily brighter the closer he came to it. He even fancied he could smell fresh air!

Daylight! his mind sang.

As he approached, he saw that the light came from around a turn in the passage.

Probably a side shaft, he thought optimistically, already imagining himself striding proudly up the gently sloping tunnel toward the world of daylight above. But he could not still a nagging little voice at the back of his mind that warned him it might be a long vertical shaft with no way of scaling it.

Nevertheless, without further hesitation he stumbled around the corner— then skidded to a halt as he saw what lay before him.

There was a pool, a large, square pool that almost entirely filled the chamber he had arrived in. A narrow, crumbling, and partly decayed ledge ran along one side of it, and continued on to an upward-leading shaft; it was from this that the daylight dimly filtered into the mine. Yet this was little source of joy for Gapp, as his attention became riveted upon the pool it illuminated.

It was like a vast and bubbling cauldron of poisonous, phosphorescent green acid. It churned around slowly and unnaturally in a whirlpool, and had every appearance of possessing a life of its own. There seemed to be things moving about just below its surface, and as the boy stared, he realized these were huge bubbles. They would swell below the glistening surface, then pop like a ripe pustule, releasing a foul vapor like the breath of a halitotic cadaver, and spit luminescent globules of viscous slime all over the hissing, melting walls. A noxious cloud arose from it in sickening waves, and the entire cavern reeked of plague and mutation.

It assaulted the boy's every sense, and he gagged in nausea. Even the fresh, clean daylight that had the misfortune to fall into this den of disease was corrupted into something perverted and evil by these gases.

Then to Gapp's horror and revulsion, he saw a huge, quivering tongue, glistening with blood and mucus, rise out of the eye of the whirlpool. He understood then that the entire pool was itself a creature.

As he stared through his fogged lenses at this unholy manifestation of utter grossness, he beheld great, long tentacles break through the scummy surface to wave menacingly—searchingly—in the air. These extrusions were covered in hideously bristling filaments of virulent yellow and purple, and each terminated in what looked like . . . *no, it could not be!* . . . a living, manlike head!

Gapp's gut heaved uncontrollably. Each head was composed of lumps of festering matter that had begun to distort and run together, until they loosely formed the image of a face. Some had distinctly humanlike features, others were more like the other races that must have worked these mines over the long years. But each one bore an expression of such tormented agony that it was as if they were dissolving and re-forming eternally in the very vats of Hell.

The paralyzed boy's knees suddenly buckled, and he had to lean heavily against the wall to keep himself from collapsing forward into the seething chamber.

My . . . final test, he realized in a fog of hysteria, *the final obstacle in my path! . . . If I can get past this one, nothing else can stop me any longer. I'll be free of these abysmal tunnels. . . .*

But he reckoned without the Stalker.

Gapp backed up a little, and wrenched the tinderbox from his pouch; using one of the tattered old drapes of sacking that hung sadly in the entrance to the chamber, he wasted not a second in striking flames, and was surprised when it blazed up as though it had been steeped in oil. The venomous gases in this place did have a use after all. But as the cavern was suddenly illuminated by the flare, Gapp heard a terrible hiss from right behind him. He span around in shock—only to find himself face-to-face with the *real* final test.

In the sudden glare of the burning drape, the half-blinded Gapp now found himself facing a new atrocity, whose nodule-encrusted head split wide open in a grin of the most ghastly, Hell-disgorged malevolence. To think that this must have been following him through the dark tunnels all along. . . .

Instinct took action where his thoughts could not lead. He hurled the burning drape over the creature's head, then kicked viciously deep into the yielding softness of its belly, before springing back into the pool cavern.

Instantly an earsplitting howl of inhuman rage and agony followed him, but he hardly even noticed it. Along the crumbling ledge he scurried, oblivious of all but that shaft of daylight ahead of him. He did not even notice the seething mass of tentacles and filaments that erupted from the pool and surged toward him.

One of the pseudoheads shot across like a lizard's tongue and knocked him hard against the wall. But it neither slowed his determined progress nor dislodged him from the ledge. It only succeeded in leaving upon his tunic a squelchy scum that stank of putrefied oysters.

That beam of sunlight, so beautiful to Gapp's eyes, was mere yards away when he suddenly felt the agony of ten long talons thrusting into his back. He shrieked loudly and pitched forward onto the rim of the ledge, only narrowly avoiding a fall into the living slime below.

With the full weight of the troglodyte horror now pinning him to the floor, Gapp was powerless to protect himself. Bony knees dug painfully into his back, and he heaved in desperation. Just above him the monster seethed in fury, and began trying to throttle its helpless victim. It was only the distraction of trying to spit away last remaining tatters of burning cloth from its burnt lips that prevented the Stalker from bringing its teeth to bear. Even so, Gapp knew with awful certainty that it was only a matter of seconds before the life was squeezed out of him.

His vision clouded, and his mind began to slip away.

All of a sudden there was a horrible cry, and he was free of the weight that bore down on him. In dumbfounded shock he twisted round, looked up, and through a red haze saw what had befallen.

The Stalker had been lifted into the air, where it screamed and flailed about helplessly, in the coils of numerous tentacles. Still writhing, it was dragged over and down toward the palpitating tongue in the middle of the pool.

Gapp's instinct for escape resumed. He found himself flying farther along the narrow ledge, spinning around a corner, and haring as fast as he could up the shaft. He did not even slow down when he was blinded by the dazzling light of day. A thrashing, rending, and useless screeching echoed up the tunnel behind him.

Back within the mucus chamber, there was a loud belching sound, a sinister bubbling, a protracted hiss, then silence. The mines were still once more.

10

In the Wake of a Snake

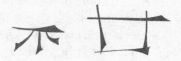

In this way did Gapp Radnar finally deliver himself from the corridors of the Underworld, and emerge once again into the bedazzlement and warmth of the world above.

His native Aescalandian was entirely inadequate in giving voice to the medley of ecstatic emotions that surged through him during the next hour or so. The blessed sunlight upon his face was alone enough to make him weep, but the resinous perfume of the huge deodars—those colossal behemoths that spanned the gap between earth and heaven—and the spongy cushion of old needles and leaves beneath his feet, not to mention the exultant chorus of birdsong all around, nor the insane palette of living color everywhere he looked, all simply made him want to sprint through the trees like a lunatic, leap high in the air and cavort for the sheer joy of being alive.

A tidal wave of relief steadily flooded through him. It felt as though he had fought his way out of the steely Keep of Hell and back into the Land of the Living above. Still not fully able to believe his sudden liberation, never before had he felt such exuberance tingling through every nerve from his toenails to his teeth. He simply ran and ran like a hunted deer, caring nothing for the direction he was headed in, just enjoying the gift of life to its fullest.

For the next hour, the forest rang with the echoing whoops of the lone madman as he crashed through the undergrowth and disappeared into the depths of Fron-Wudu.

Of course it did not take long before his hunger, fever, and exhaustion finally caught up with him. One minute he was leaping over fallen tree trunks and bounding through the ferns, the next his legs simply gave way beneath him and he collapsed onto the ground. He had not eaten for three days, had drunk only what foul floor-lickings he could stomach, and in this severely debilitated state his fever had regained a firm hold over him. Within minutes he was unconscious, sprawled facedown upon the leafy forest floor.

About an hour later, he awoke with an abrupt start, and found that he could not see a thing. His first thought was that he must have slept right through until nightfall. But he soon realized, with mounting confusion, that this could not be the case, for he could hear the song of a hundred birds in the trees above him, and feel the warm sun on his face. It could only be early evening at the latest.

"Ah," he said to himself rather stupidly, "I've gone blind. . . ."

He lurched up out of his bed of bracken and staggered to his feet, but his legs would not support him. Immediately he crashed to the ground again in a crumpled heap, and bleated in alarm.

The first oh-so-familiar mangle-turns of panic began to twist his insides. He realized only now just how starving and feverish he was. He had to eat and drink immediately, and must find some way of sheltering himself before nightfall. If he permitted himself to slacken his self-control for even a moment, he might drift off into a sleep from which he would never awaken.

Maybe if he managed to find some stream water and some leaves or berries, perhaps even some edible fungus, then that might just be enough for the present. Then he would be safe to sleep, which might assuage his sickness. It might even give his eyes a chance to recover.

"Yes, that's it! Whoever heard of anyone going permanently blind just from hunger?" he laughed almost hysterically. After all, he knew of several magepriests who regularly fasted for a month or more. This had to be just a passing symptom of his current physical state. All he needed to do was to forage for food. . . .

But how could he do that, when he was blind? How could he possibly even begin to find food when he was like this? Foraging was not one of the skills regularly taught to esquires. His only practice at it had been during their trek through the Rainflats, and he had not then met with much success. Now he was blind, he would have to crawl about on hands and knees and *sniff* out his food like an animal!

Where were his companions now that he needed them? Above all, where was Master Wintus?

Were they all dead? Was he truly alone here in the Wild?

And how far had he gone? Which direction had he gone in? What was going to . . . ?

His mind stalled. He was as doomed now as he had been in the mines.

. . . The mines! He suddenly thought of them again, and it seemed to him that the mouth of the tunnel he had fled from earlier was now racing toward him over the forest, turning the trees black as it came on, and was bearing down upon him like a hungry leviathan, about to engulf him in its lightless deeps yet again!

No, he was not in the mines anymore. He would never be in the mines again. No matter how bad things might be, they could never be as awful as that. They were the worst time, the ultimate test. They had been his training ground, his apprenticeship, his tutorial, for whatever now lay ahead. In just a few days they had taught him more about survival than could an entire term spent at Wintus Hall. And now, at least, he was back in his own world again.

Gapp grew calmer. He inhaled deeply, as was his habit now, breathed in the humid air heavy with resin and the creamy yet sour fragrances of unknown woodland flowers. He noticed also smells that told him it had rained recently, and these brought back to him vague snatches of his early childhood, memories that he had up till now completely forgotten. His thumping heart quieted, for these were good smells.

He then concentrated on the warmth of the late-summer sun upon his skin, the softness of the bracken underfoot and the leaves that caressed his face, the occasional whisper of air, and the soothing noises of the forest in the evening.

Now, *that* was something he could not have experienced in the dankness of the mines. This was a good place he had come to, wherever it was, and for that he could never cease to be grateful.

The panic receded, and finally disappeared.

Gapp was surprised at himself. That had been easy.

"Now for some dinner," he muttered, and shakily but determinedly set off on his hands and knees to find sustenance.

His first priority was water. This did not prove as difficult as he had expected, for after the rain there was no shortage of wet leaves to lick. This did little other than whet his thirst, but it was a start. Later on, he found a tiny pool of rainwater at the bottom of a natural recess in a fallen tree trunk. It tasted of wood lice and peat, and had fragments of decaying wood in it, but it was just about potable. This was adequate to moisten his swollen lips and tongue, though they stung considerably for the next few minutes.

A while later, his expanded hearing picked up the musical sound of sweet, trickling water. There was a stream nearby!

Hastily he crawled toward it, pausing frequently to listen and get his bearings. He might have got up and walked had he thought about it, but in his state this did not even occur to him. Soon his nettle-stung and thorn-scratched hands felt the cool, blissful rush of water flowing over them, and the fine sandy grit of the streambed beneath them. It was only the meagerest of rillets, but to the diminishing boy it was as good as a river. He pressed his lips slowly to the water's surface, and drank deeply.

Eventually he was sated. He had been careful not to gulp too greedily; a mouthful here, followed by a long pause, then a mouthful there, and so on. In spite of his febrile condition, he was well aware of the dangers of drinking too speedily after a long period of dehydration.

Task number one completed, he thought with quiet self-esteem. *Next: food . . .*

He wasted no time in retracing his trail through the trodden-down under-growth to the fallen tree bole he had drunk from earlier. When he finally bumped into it, headfirst, he began carefully running his fingers over it. He had a beginner's knowledge of the feel and the smell of the many varieties of edible fungi. (For that, he had Wodeman to thank, bless his pagan heart!) And there were numerous little grubs and insects lurking deep within the rotten wood that provided easy pickings.

He did not need to pace himself on the food, as he had done with the water, for each tiny morsel had to be worked hard for: and by the time he was satisfied that there was no more to be found, he could smell and feel that it had got dark.

Though the pickings of food had left him feeling rather sick and shaky, it had undoubtably reduced the worst of his hunger. He pulled up several hand-fuls of fern and made a comfortable mattress for himself beneath the partial shelter of the tree bole. It was not much, but compared with the stony floors of the mines, it was heavenly. For he could now feel *life* all around him.

He inhaled the scented air of the forest in the early night, and only then knew just how exhausted he was.

Seconds later, he was fast asleep.

Gapp awoke with a start. He raised himself up sharply, only to crack his head painfully against the overturned tree trunk. Instinctively he stifled a cry, and lowered his splitting head carefully back to the ground. He then stared out into the night. Something had awoken him.

He stared for several minutes, hardly daring to breathe. The frigid early-dawn air made him shiver almost uncontrollably. He was sure there was some-thing out there; he could almost smell it. But he could not hear or see anything that might presage danger. The only sounds were the muted songs of the early birds echoing throughout the stillness of the forest, while all he could see were the numerous dew-heavy cobwebs hung out on the bushes like little silver fish-ing nets, and the grey-green mist that entwined itself about the black silhouet-ted trunks of—

He could *see* again! Pel's Ribs, he could see! For a moment all his fears van-ished. He could see again! His sight may be a little fuzzy and his eyes sore, even in this dim light, but at least he was no longer blind. He could hardly believe it. He blessed any gods that might happen to be listening at this early hour, and chuckled. *He could see!*

Luck was definitely with him on this wonderful new day!

But he soon got over this most pleasant early-morning surprise, and re-membered just why it was that he was peering out into the twilit forest. Some-thing out there had caused a sound. Something furtive? Gapp had the impression that, whatever it was, it was a long way off still. In fact, he had *felt* it rather than heard it.

Instinct again, he chided himself. *It's getting so's I can hardly keep it quiet anymore.*

So he listened long and listened hard, but heard nothing else except the tiny, furtive sounds of the forest's awakening.

Perhaps it had not come from "out there" at all, he mused, but instead from within his mind. Maybe to do with that vague sense of unease, that vestigial anxiety that still clung to the inside of his head.

Muttering wearily to himself, he decided to snatch a few more hours of sleep. He pulled the fronds of fern back around himself, and settled down in the warmth of his nest. It was still night out there, and he shivered.

Just then, a pack of huge, slavering hounds burst into the clearing and bounded straight toward him.

The ten animals came to a halt just feet away from him, and growled menacingly. Their teeth were huge and white, their coats sleek and black, and the muscles rippled beneath their skin. They all stood at least three and a half feet high at the shoulder, with eyes like cold slits of yellow-green chrysoprase. The whole pack stood so close that Gapp could feel and smell their fishy breath upon his face, but none made any move to advance further. They just stood there ringing him in against the tree trunk. Squeezing himself painfully against the knobbled bark until he could retreat no further, Gapp stared out at ten panting red tongues.

Then, without warning, they ceased snarling, and settled back upon their haunches, all except one. Gapp frowned at the way they had all acted in perfect unison, as if on command, yet he had heard no voice.

The biggest of the pack, however, a hairy monstrosity in silver-flecked brown, still crouched upon all fours and continued to snarl as it fixed its yellow-green eyes upon the quaking boy.

"Schnorbitz!" came a sudden gruff command from the edge of the clearing, and this last hound grudgingly lowered its rear quarters to the ground. Gapp heard the swift approach of heavy feet, and peered out of his shelter to see who the newcomer might be.

After his ordeal underground, Gapp believed himself to be inured to surprises, but nothing could have prepared him for the sight of the creature that strode into the clearing now. From behind the semicircle of waiting hounds stepped the tallest figure the boy had ever encountered. He quailed at its approach, wondering whether he was seeing it wrong from a distorted angle. It would even tower over the Ogre of the Blue Mountains.

At least twelve feet tall, but of basically human appearance, it was so skinny it looked like a collection of long sticks joined together loosely. Despite that, this lanky figure looked as tough as ironwood, with *massive* leverage in those elongated arms. Long bloodred hair, entwined with ivylike tendrils, was tied back from its domed forehead, and trailed in a horsetail behind. Around its neck was a torc of twisted green stems that looked as if still living, and its weathered skin was of a pale, creamy yellow, except where a blue-black stubble covered the lower jaw.

It was not just the intruder's size that caused the Southlander to gape. For the giant looked as if it had fallen straight from the pages of a history book. It was dressed in simple raiment of forest green and earth brown, all leather and oiled hessian, just like in those pictures of the legendary trapper-barons of Grendalin that hung in the galleries of Wintus Hall. The tabard was cinched about its waist with an enormous, age-worn leather belt, clasped with an ancient, tarnished buckle that was nearly as wide as the giant's narrow torso. Loose-fitting leggings were tucked into great bucket boots. It carried a lengthy wooden spear, a great bow with a bag of arrows, and a hunting knife long enough to serve as a sword for any normal human.

All this gear was clearly utilitarian, and as such should enable its wearer to blend in with his surrounding, but to Gapp it looked like a costume from a stage play of a Hero Saga.

Whether this giant would play the part of hero or villain, however, was yet to be revealed.

The wood wight returned the boy's stare with equal curiosity, but for the time being it did not advance any closer. His bearing appeared neither threatening nor welcoming, merely *interested*. Gapp tried to mentally list all the various types of giants he had heard of, and in each case whether they were considered friendly to humans or not. But he could not force himself to think clearly, and the great beanpole that stood in front of him did not seem to fit immediately into any of the categories that came to mind. Nevertheless, Gapp did not feel himself in any immediate danger. He permitted himself to relax a little, though continuing to regard the giant warily.

It was intriguing, but there was something about this giant that told Gapp he could be respected and trusted. He had no idea why. Perhaps it lay in the eyes? They were colored the rich brown of newly tilled soil in the evening sunlight, and seemed to hold within them a secret tie with the ways of the forest, much like Wodeman's. There was also a sadness there that reminded him of Bolldhe, and at the same time an openness that was definitely Nibulus.

Eventually, the giant seemed satisfied that the miniature person under the log was not enemy, or even "game." He stepped over the line of hounds, and held out a hand to Gapp.

"B'kundha Un-laf Haethenna hirnoest-A?" he asked.

Gapp blinked uncertainly. "I'm sorry?" he replied.

They both grinned foolishly, and then the giant helped the stray youth to his feet. Gapp was no longer on his own. He had found a friend at last.

Gyger—that was his name. That was the only thing Gapp knew about his new companion as he was led deeper and deeper into the forest. Even this was an assumption, for that was the single word the giant had used, while pointing to himself as they shook hands. For all Gapp knew, "Gyger" might be the name of his race.

But for now, it was enough. There were no other words between them as Gapp followed Gyger into the darker reaches of the forest. He had no idea where he was being led, and no way of knowing how far they had to travel. He was still feeling extremely weak, and hoped it would not be far; but really he had no choice but to keep up with this new lot he had fallen in with.

They went by trails that the inexperienced townsman would not have noticed even existed, so invisible were they. Hardly even ranking as pheasant runs, to Gapp's eyes. He could not seem to stop tripping up on uneven ground and snagging his feet on the concealed roots that strung themselves like snares across their path. Soon he began to lag behind, and was sweating like a Peladane. He was meanwhile astounded at the grace and silence with which the twelve-foot-tall forest man moved through the undergrowth, almost suggesting a total lack of any real physical presence. The hounds too were endowed with an almost ghostly noiselessness.

The woods now seemed very dark, and very dense. The sounds of the awakening day were left behind them, to be replaced only by the croaking of bullfrogs, strange furtive whisperings, and the sudden scampering of unseen beasts off to either side. Long strands of cobweb hung like dead skin from every tree, some even crisscrossing their path, having been fabricated in the short time since Gyger had passed that way earlier. Once, having unwittingly strayed, Gapp almost walked straight into one such web that blocked the way like a giant flyscreen. He drew to a halt just inches short of it, and found himself facing the biggest, most bulbous spider he had ever encountered in his life. Pink and hairless, it pulsated evilly, then slowly unfolded its great legs before Gapp's petrified nose. He remained there frozen, until Gyger realized he was no longer following, and came back in search of him.

From then on, Gapp kept close to his guide, and stumbled on resolutely until, not very long after, they emerged into a clearing. Directly before them was a stockade wall, similar to—if a little more rustic and less ambitious than—the one that surrounded Nordwas. Out here the morning sun shone down from a clear blue sky, lighting up Gyger's stronghold in the bright, russet colors of a hundred varieties of wood. Here the only cobwebs to be seen were small, and glistened delicately between the great logs composing the wall.

For an instant Gapp was reminded of home, but he quickly brushed the thought away, and followed the giant up to the gate.

Both Gyger and his hounds became visibly more relaxed in the vicinity of this residence. The hounds barked almost as if with laughter and cavorted about in horseplay.

Suddenly there was a furious rattling of locks and chains from within that broke the stillness of the morning, and after a few seconds the huge gate swung outward to admit them. Gapp looked up questioningly at his large companion, but the giant merely strode on through and into his compound.

Gapp followed the hounds in and gazed about uncertainly. There were a large central structure, several outhouses, and a well. Nothing out of the ordinary, except that the dimensions were approximately double those he was used to. The main house was built from huge, carefully fashioned boulders that glistened and sparkled softly in the sunlight with a score of different colors, for they contained seams of crystal and quartz, and had obviously been hauled here by the giant himself. Perhaps, Gapp guessed, all the way from the very mines he himself had recently escaped from.

But the most puzzling thing was, when the boy turned to look behind him at the opened gates, he saw no one nearby. No door ward nor servant. Nobody.

Again Gapp glanced at the giant quizzically, but his host just smiled, waved a hand vaguely all around, and said, by way of explanation, "Heldered."

Heldered, right, thought Gapp as the giant approached the main house. *That's supposed to explain everything, I suppose.... What have I got myself into this time?*

He followed the giant, and behind him the door in the stockade wall swung shut, and was locked.

Inside the main house, Gapp had to seriously adjust his initial impressions of his host, whatever they had been. He had always thought of giants as being just, well, giants; it had never really occurred to him that there might be as many different social divisions within the general scope of "giantity" as there were in humanity itself. What he was stepping into now, the boy realized, was not simply a giant's home, it was a *bachelor giant's* home.

This was going to be a truly enlightening experience.

To begin with, as soon as he entered the porch he almost put his foot directly upon the spring-plate of the most enormous bear trap he had ever seen in his life. It was purely his newly honed reactions that saved him from having one leg amputated at the thigh. Heart pounding madly, he allowed himself to be led along with the hounds, farther into the smoky gloom of the house.

If he had been alarmed at the trap left so carelessly by the threshold, he was doubly so when he gazed around at the cluttered interior. Apart from the fact that everything was twice the size, everything seemed twice as *odd,* too.

For a start, that coffer there on the floor. It was obviously very old, and clearly of great value; its entire surface was covered in beautifully finished snakeskin, banded with well-polished gold, lined with red crushed velvet, and filled with dirty underwear. Gapp could not help feeling that somewhere along the line his host had missed the point.

Also in the room he noticed the hugest bat imaginable hanging from one of the beams. It was cocooned in aged, leathery wings covered in dust, and seemed completely oblivious of their arrival. The boy again looked up at the muttering giant, half-expecting him to say something along the lines of "Who's been hanging from *my* ceiling, then?" before swatting the intruder out of the window. But it seemed he had not even noticed it and, when Gapp pointed it out to him, merely replied with a muffled oath that seemed to say: "Ugh! How did that get there?"

Seconds later, the intruder was as forgotten as the strata of bread crusts and dust piled up beneath all the tables and chairs. On top of one side table, nestled between two great earthenware jars of vinegar, was a skull, so terrifying to behold that the young Aescal did not even want to know what monster it had come from. The awesome effect of it, however, was somewhat diminished when he noticed that this trophy of the giant's hunting prowess was currently being used as a paperweight for his book-bound collection of pressed wild herbs.

They pushed their way under a clothesline hung with the most un-giant-like garments and headed over to a side room. The floor of this room had been tiled with wonderfully engraved flagstones—presumably a skilled craft known to Gyger—but it was only half-completed, the rest of the floor being still bare earth. By the look of it, this giant was more apt at starting things than finishing them, for these tiles had been laid down years ago.

Continuing down a short passage lined with an assortment of hooks, cressets, dangling ropes, midge-coils that smelled strongly of soap and pitch, and dozens of roughly cut planks that leaned against the wall, they soon came to another place that Gapp guessed must be the utility room.

The giant did a quick mime that indicated this was his own bedroom. Before moving on, Gapp stared in at the pile of old sacks that looked to be the nearest thing to a bed, at the random collection of shelves (some of them still fixed to the wall), and at the clutter of jugs, vases, mousetraps, kitchenware, and candles strewn everywhere. There was also a large sandpit for the hounds to use whenever they were taken short in the night. Yet the sand therein was probably the cleanest surface in the room.

Good grief, Gapp thought. *Even the dogs haven't got it right.*

He joined his host in the next room, where the giant seemed ill-at-ease. He clearly was not accustomed to having guests, and did not remember what one was supposed to do with them once they had entered one's home. He looked around uncertainly, till his gaze fell upon the teapot on the hob. Gapp studied the teapot adorned with various colorful growths of vegetation, and his anxiety was immediately justified when Gyger offered him a cup of tea.

Desperately he tried to think of any religion he could lay claim to which forbade tea-drinking, but was reluctantly forced to assent to his host's hospitality with as much grace as he could muster.

"Tohte!" The giant beamed as he picked his way dexterously through the clutter and over to the hob, at the same time motioning for his guest to sit down and make himself comfortable. Gapp looked around at the rubbish-strewn floor, and wondered if this were at all possible.

While Gyger busied himself with making the tea, Gapp turned to study the rest of his surroundings. On one wall hung a map of some country he could not guess at; there was also a score of spears (some with fishing lines still attached) amid several knives, arrows, and a scythe with an eight-foot blade, all mounted on another wall.

Then his attention was caught by a crudely assembled pipe rack resting upon the floor. It must have contained near-on two dozen pipes of varying shapes, colors, and styles. Using hand signs, he inquired if the giant smoked, and was strangely not at all surprised when Gyger shook his head with a grimace.

A minute later, Gapp was relieved to hear the ancient teapot split asunder, and its contents shoot up to the ceiling in a great hiss of brown steam. The giant cursed under his breath, paused in thought for a moment, then shrugged and bade Gapp follow him into another room, pointing to his mouth and patting his stomach.

Gapp followed reluctantly with a panicky sense of foreboding, dreading what lay therein that he might be forced to behold (or worse still, be forced to eat). However, he was surprised to find it a relatively tidy room, one that smelled unbelievably good.

Food? Real, cooked, edible food! How long had it been? His stomach ached with the thought of it, and he salivated like a rabid dog.

This new chamber was sparsely furnished, but comfortably so. There was none of the filth or haphazard jumbles of neglected paraphernalia that he had encountered in the preceding rooms and passages. Here, the floor was recently bestrewn with sweet smelling dried rushes, and the furnishings, though simple, were freshly dusted and uncluttered by any discarded equipment. There were beeswax-polished shelves ranged along all the walls too, displaying an impressive collection of neatly stacked crockery and cutlery.

This struck Gapp as odd, that there should be so many plates and things here when he had assumed the giant lived alone. But he could not think how to ask about it.

In any case, he was far more immediately concerned with what was spread upon the table. Before his bulging eyes, upon the expansive board was laid enough breakfast to feed him and his entire family for a week, back in Nordwas. A great bronze pot with ornate handles and a silver ladle sat in the middle of the table, and steam rose from it in serpentine wreaths. It contained a stew that Gapp was soon to discover consisted of venison, edible fungus, sundry herbs, wild barley, and even a hint of peppered wine. Three long loaves lay on the table next to it, steaming slightly as if they had just been baked. A freshly opened amphora, containing at least a gallon of elderberry wine, stood next to this, and all about were bowls and plates of thick cream, raspberry jam, and an array of cheeses.

This was clearly breakfast for the giant. But he must have been out hunting for hours. Yet all this had been recently prepared. If this servant of his—who had presumably opened the gate for them—had arranged all this so quickly, then he must be good indeed. For Gapp guessed that the giant had not intended to return home for at least another couple of hours, nor would have done had he not chanced upon the little human under the tree.

There was even a place set at the table for the boy himself.

He glanced up at his host with that now habitual questioning look on his face.

But the giant was already feeding his own face noisily, his guest clearly forgotten, and Gapp decided to do the same.

Gapp was still seated high up on an oversize chair of straw-filled cushions, his stomach churning dangerously and his legs dangling over the edge, when Gyger brought in to him from another room a rather familiar object.

It was a meditation wheel, a small, ornately engraved, thick-rimmed wooden disk with a short handle through the middle and a small brass ball attached to the rim by a fine chain—exactly the same as used by the Lightbearers back home. The giant handed the instrument—tiny in his hands—to the boy, who noticed that it had engraved upon its handle the crest of the Chapter of Missionaries.

Before Gapp had time to wonder further, the giant nodded for him to use it. Decidedly baffled at this completely incongruous item, the lad nonetheless did as he was bidden.

Holding the handle firmly, he began spinning the wheel upon it by means of the brass ball, as he had so often watched the Lightbearers in Nordwas doing. He did not know the ritual words they chanted, and in any case was not sure he wanted to. But almost as soon as he had set the wheel in motion, it began to make a strange humming sound. That was something he had never heard from the meditation wheels back home.

No. It was more than just sound, for with the hum came a very peculiar feeling in his head. It felt as though a slight pressure was building up inside the front of his skull, accompanied by a queasy, "unbalancing" sensation.

Behind the strange noise he became aware of the voice of the giant droning on and on, in that unintelligible language of his. It sounded like the same word repeated over and over. He glanced up to check, but Gyger motioned him to keep his eyes on the wheel. As he dutifully did so, he saw that in the blur of speed, the thick outer rim of the disk had turned white.

Then his eyes widened as he saw letters begin to appear there.

Gapp stared in almost hypnotized fascination. Whether it was something to do with the motion of the wheel—some trick that its spinning played on the mind—or a spell being cast by the droning giant, he had no clue. But there were definitely letters appearing upon the disk, like writing upon a blank page from an invisible quill held in an invisible hand.

Vijneh: the script of the Aescals! It was in his own people's writing.

Not only that but, as he squinted closely, he saw that it was in his language, too; he could understand what was written—was *being* written:

"*. . . testing . . . testing . . . testing . . . testing . . .*" it said.

Gapp looked back to the giant, who paused from chanting his mantra, for a second to signal to the boy to keep looking at the wheel. On doing so, he noticed that the former writing had now faded and was being replaced by new words:

"*. . . testing . . . testing . . . R U reading this yet?*"

Gapp again glanced up at Gyger, only to be once more motioned to keep his eyes on the wheel.

"*. . . doesn't work unless U read the words as they R being said. Now, wave at me if U understand.*"

What's this? Gapp thought in alarm. He did not like this at all.

"*. . . Go on, don't B Mbarrassed . . .*"

The boy awkwardly and unenthusiastically raised his hand and, feeling like a complete prat, gave a little wave. He straightaway lowered it again when he heard the giant burst out laughing.

"*. . . wasn't so bad, was it?*"

"Actually, it was, rather," Gapp muttered to himself, but did not look up.

"*. . . It was given 2 me by a man from the South, a U-man like yourself, my glazen-eyed little friend—*"

Either the translation is a bit off, Gapp thought tersely, *or giants are a cheeky bunch; "glazen-eyed," indeed!*

"*. . . So let me introduce myself. My name is Yulfric, and I am a Gyger.*"

"Gyger!" Gapp repeated in a cry of revelation, chiding himself for his erstwhile stupidity. He should have guessed the moment he set eyes on the fellow. He *had* heard that word after all. It was not one often used in his country, as there, with typically Aescalandian lack of imagination, the term "forest giant" was preferred.

He knew little of this race, though he had heard tell they were a civilized people who lived together in small, close-knit settlements not unlike those of humans. Though distantly related to the Gjoeger, they lacked the magical abilities of their aquatic cousins. Gapp had heard of only one Gyger homeland, and that lay many months' travel southwest of Wyda-Aescaland, in the deep and unexplored forest of Crouagh in far-off Grendalin.

Grendalin. Of course. That was probably the country depicted in the map hung on the wall in the other room. But what was Yulfric doing here in Fron-Wudu? All alone, with only his hounds and that as yet unseen servant for company? This did not seem to fit at all the description of the gregarious forest giants he had heard of.

The humming of the meditation heel altered in pitch slightly, now developing an unpleasant whine to it. He looked back at the instrument:

"... *dzon't nmind dhe hounz, zey wn't hrm yoo ff n yoo lijvm erlone* ..."

Something was wrong; his head began to throb, and the spelling had become even worse than Nibulus's. He peered closer at the spinning object, inclining as he did so.

"... *dd#jntu*guss dn gfun!m fjhe?wps f~uxv@axh* ..."

The whine rose to a scream that lanced through Gapp's brain like a red-hot skewer, and he felt horribly sick. Yulfric grasped him by the wrist, and gently eased his hand back so the wheel was upright again.

"... *U have 2 keep it verTcal or the magic doesn't work. Sorry, I should have said earlier, but as U can imagine I haven't had much oppor2nity 2 use it, out here in the wilds and all.*"

"So what *are* you doing out here," Gapp asked, "and who gave you that thing? I've never seen anything like it in my life."

Yulfric shook his head, and took the wheel from Gapp's grasp. He began spinning it himself, and indicated that the boy should speak.

"... *Uh ... Hello ... That is ... My name is Gapp, Gapp Radnar ... Uh, I'm from ... I say, can you understand what I'm saying?*"

Yulfric nodded enthusiastically, a wide grin spreading across his face as he continued to stare at the wheel. He was clearly enjoying every second of this.

It was without doubt the most bizarre conversation Gapp had ever had in his life. As the humming and the spinning went on, both human and Gyger gradually introduced themselves. Yulfric would talk in his strange tongue while Gapp read his words being printed out in translation on the meditation wheel. Then they would swap over, and Gapp would do the talking.

He noticed that the hum was always deeper while Yulfric was reading, and that he could see a deep red light reflected in the Gyger's eyes, as opposed to the white light that must be reflected in *his* own; presumably, different languages produced different color effects. It was a fascinating toy, and neither was in any hurry to stop communicating.

It had been a present, so the boy learned, given to Yulfric by a passing Lightbearer missionary from Wyda-Aescaland, in gratitude for Yulfric's hospitality. It was the ideal "tool of the trade" for anyone requiring the necessary translation skills for converting the heathen of distant, foreign lands, but Gapp wondered just how keen the Lightbearer in question had been to simply *give* away such a marvelous treasure, or had the twelve-foot forest giant with the pack of ravening hellhounds perhaps been a little more assertive in this matter than he was letting on? He also vaguely wondered why Yulfric set such store by it, living alone out here in the forest with nobody else to use it on. The poor giant had probably been waiting all this time for the opportunity to try it out.

But perhaps the *real* magic was altogether simpler, for how else could two quiet, rather withdrawn individuals such as Gapp and the Gyger be suddenly transformed into the world's most enthusiastic conversationalists?

There had been one incident, however, which had intruded upon their congenial chinwag. Gapp, ever the inquisitive one, had at one point decided to spin the wheel in the *opposite* direction, just to see what happened. The white "page" had all of a sudden turned black, and as a deep, horribly demonic GROWL replaced the humming, he saw glowing red letters in an ancient and occult script:

"Skin the giant alive! Go on, you know U want 2 . . ."

Gapp rapidly reverted to spinning it in the right direction, and did his best to ignore the red steam that curled briefly from the wheel.

Yulfric was a natural recluse. He said little about his reasons for leaving his own folk and settling here in these strange and reputedly terrible woods, so many thousands of miles away. He preferred to talk about his current life rather than his past, and sensing this reluctance, Gapp did not press the matter. The only company Yulfric saw was his devoted hounds, and his only visitors (apart from the Lightbearer missionary of two years ago) the occasional band of "forest-hoppers" that might happen to pass through once in a blue moon.

These forest-hoppers, Gapp was fascinated to discover, were like the legendary trapper-barons of Grendalin, who were the heroes of some of the boy's favorite adventure stories. Usually Polg, but occasionally human, Tusse, or even Hauger, they were a phenomenally hardy—not to say brutally mercenary—amalgamation of explorer, soldier, furrier, and prospector, who would penetrate deep into the wildlands by river as far as they could, hauling their boats overland whenever necessary from stream to stream, and sleep outdoors at all times, even during winter. Exactly what relations Yulfric had with them, the Gyger would not say, but from what Gapp could gather about them, if the giant could hold his own with such people, he must be a pretty formidable sort himself.

The boy felt extremely small in comparison. In fact *was* extremely small. As he perched there on the edge of the gigantic chair, he reflected how fortunate it was that studying the meditation wheel meant he did not have to make eye contact with this giant while they were conversing.

"So, the meal we ate back then?" Gapp asked, as the two of them sipped the tea that had suddenly appeared behind them on the low table. "Was that Heldered?"

He had been longing to ask about the unseen servant who had opened the gate in the stockade wall earlier . . . then laid on the meal that had probably saved Gapp's life. He now almost snatched the wheel back from Yulfric in his eagerness to read the reply.

"*. . . No, that was breakfast. We don't eat Heldered . . .*"

Gapp studied Yulfric through narrowed eyes. Again he wondered if this was a fault in the translation, or merely the Gyger's somewhat provocative sense of humor.

"*. . . Heldered is here if you want him. He is all around, but you will never see him . . .*"

That did not really answer his question, but before he had a chance to persist regarding Heldered, Yulfric demanded that Gapp tell the whole story of how he came to be here like this.

Gapp waited for Yulfric to start spinning the wheel. But no sooner had he started his narration, than he paused.

What was he to say?

Up until now, his thoughts had been focused entirely upon survival: hunting down the basics of life—light, heat, food, drink—and avoiding being torn limb from limb by subterranean creatures of chaos. It was only now as he sat here warm, dry, and well fed within two-foot-thick walls of stone in the cluttered domestication of the forest giant's home, that he even thought about his former companions, and the quest they had been pursuing.

Where were they now? Had they all fallen victim to the Huldre and her horrendous henchmen? Or had they by some miracle contrived to escape? And if so, what had become of them subsequently? This was, after all, the wilderness. . . .

A terrible weight of loneliness and isolation bore down upon him; everything had gone wrong after he had become separated from the company. Great tears, as unexpected as they were unwelcome, flooded his eyes. He lowered his head, pretending to adjust his sitting position, before commencing his story; at all costs he must not let this wild woodsman detect any weakness in him.

Gapp's head reeled all of a sudden. He felt sick to the marrow, light-headed and trembling.

It was obviously the fever, the exhaustion, and the huge meal after so long without any food, all brought to a head by thoughts of his fellow questers. The forest giant was regarding him strangely, expecting a stirring tale but seeing only this puny little creature swaying lackadaisically atop his armchair.

But it was no good; Gapp was beyond any thoughts of bravado or even self-preservation. With his world humming and spinning more vertiginously than the meditation wheel, he lay back on his chair and was gone.

Though he did not know it, Gapp slept solidly for two whole days. He lay curled up on that same chair exactly where he had slumped, sleeping off his remaining sickness and exhaustion undisturbed, for in all that time the Gyger did not look in on him once. He was left alone, and eventually forgotten, as completely as the bat hanging in the other room.

On awaking, he found that he was clean—actually *clean*—for the first time in heaven knew how long. Even his clothes had been laundered, dried and slipped back on him while he had slept, though there was a distinct mustiness and a sprinkling of dog hairs on them from where Schnorbitz had used him as a cushion earlier.

There was also a bowl of some dark purple, *medicinal*-smelling, steaming hot broth waiting for him on the nearby table.

"Heldered!" he breathed, and almost plunged headfirst into the bowl.

When he finally met up with Yulfric again, the forest giant at first just stared at him in utter perplexity, as if he had no idea what this little human was doing here in his house. Then he appeared to remember, gradually, and spent the next few moments dithering about while he decided what he was supposed to do with him.

Eventually they were seated together once more, and Gapp, under pressure, got back to telling his story, though he did not want to. Everything in him wanted to forget about the whole thing, and just get back home, somehow. The countless miles between this place and there made him feel sick, and talking about it could only make things worse.

But he felt an obligation to this strange creature who had saved his life; and in any case, it did not look as if he had much choice. Yulfric seemed to lead an uncompromising life, and did not look the sort to tolerate any weakness. Payment would be expected, and Gapp, just like any wandering minstrel back home, had to sing for his supper.

Don't tell him about the quest, he told himself as the giant began rotating the wheel. *Finwald would kill me—if he were still alive.*

So he began, but he immediately realized it was difficult to say anything at all about his reasons for being here without referring to the quest. He would rather have avoided the subject entirely, but he just could not dream up any plausible reason why an Aescal youth should be traveling alone in these wild woods. In the end, after much vacillation and several false starts (causing a furrow-browed Yulfric to shake the wheel impatiently and rap it sharply upon his armrest), he decided to tell it exactly as it was. Besides, Gapp did not relish the thought of lying to someone who had just saved his life.

But when it came down to it, the truth sounded so completely absurd. Here he was, telling tales of portents, priests, and Peladanes, and a Rawgr lord of whom the giant seemed never to have heard, and a quest undertaken to destroy it when it was already dead. And the incident at Nym-Cadog's, well, that was just about believable, but it did not even begin to explain how it had led him here, all these miles away in the forest of Fron-Wudu. How could it, when Gapp himself did not know how all that had come to pass?

By the time he had finished this part of the story—a tale of such epic proportions that it would have shamed the greatest of the skalds back in Nordwas (mainly because it was all true)—Gapp felt that he might as well have stuck to lying in the first place. At least then he might have been believed.

People, when they bothered to listen to Gapp Radnar at all—which was not often—always assumed the boy was either telling tall tales or simply wittering on without a clue what he was talking about. In his more vexed moments, he had often wondered what would happen if he stood up in front of an audience of the world's greatest doctors of mathematics, and declared that one plus one equals two. It would probably result in a furor, with said doctors scrambling around in panic trying to understand why the very basis of mathematics had been swiped out from under their feet.

But to his surprise, Yulfric apparently did not disbelieve a word of his account. He simply sat there in his armchair, reading the wheel as casually as if reading a novel, and nodding now and then. In fact, he seemed at times almost bored by it all, and would occasionally glance about himself distractedly.

The only bit which appeared to galvanize his interest was mention of the mine shaft deep in the forest. Clearly Yulfric knew of it, and was interested by the boy's description of its contents. When Gapp got as far as his encounter with the animated pool of slime, Yulfric nodded sagely and handed him back the wheel.

"... *The Nycra* ..." explained the giant, staring into space. "... *A living eczema ... a coagulation of liquefied, dead tissues ... an evil discharge of Hell-spawned mucoid waste from the dark places of the Evil One herself* ..."

"Yes, I suppose it was, really," Gapp continued hesitantly, rather taken aback. He was not too sure which impressed him most, the giant or the wheel. He handed the device back to Yulfric, only to have it pushed toward him again.

"... *A Nightmare of Nausea* ..." he went on, really getting into his stride now. "... *A Feast of Foulness ... A Veritable Vesicle of Venomous Vitriol ... indeed, a glistening, dripping puddle of pus* ..."

Yulfric sat back and smiled in satisfaction—only the second time Gapp had seen him do so—and allowed his guest to continue. The handle of the wheel felt rather hot now, Gapp noticed, as he handed it back and went on with his story.

He now told of how he had escaped the mines, how he ran through the forest, his fever, his blindness, his hunger, right up until he had met up with the Gyger himself.

The wheel spun to a stop. Yulfric said nothing. Gapp shifted awkwardly in his seat, and lowered his eyes. It was a worthy tale, to be sure, and one that he could see had entertained his host. But if the boy had expected any commendation, he was to be disappointed; Yulfric looked pensive, but clearly was not so easily impressed.

The Gyger scratched the crisp, wiry hairs of his left armpit, and again proffered the wheel. He came straight to the point.

"... *So. You are now alone, hopelessly lost, and don't know what to do, yes? And you want me to help, yes?* ..."

Two nods from Gapp. This giant certainly did not mince his words.

". . . The question is, do you want to try and find your friends, carry on with your business alone, or go back home?"

Gapp stared blankly ahead of him. His head, he now noticed, was feeling blocked and numb, and his insides starting to feel the return of fever. But he did not let any of this show. All he could see now were those final words of the Gyger, those scribbly little Vijneh characters appearing in the white blur of the meditation wheel. They filled his vision like a testament written across the sky.

What the hell *was* he supposed to do now?

Until now he had not concentrated on anything other than staying alive. In truth, he had not wanted to. But the giant was not going to let him off: he wanted a decision now.

Continue the quest on his own? Ha bloody ha! Maybe Yulfric could manage that, but Gapp? And find his friends? For Jugg's sake, they were *dead,* surely. . . . And even if not, how could he hope to meet up with them? He had never been privy to details of the route they were going to take. All he had known was that they were headed for Myst-Hakel—a town in the Rainflats— and from his very limited knowledge of the lands they had been traveling through, he realized that, here in Fron-Wudu, he must be somewhere north of the Rainflats. But northeast? Northwest? Due north? Even if he could somehow contrive to make his way to that little town from here, would they still be there?

No, they were dead, Gapp had decided. Even if they were not, they must have gone on without him. *The quest had gone on without him.* The decision was now made: He would go home.

Relief coursed through him, and an almost overwhelming sweetness of euphoria buzzed in his head. He was *free* of it! At last, he could go home. Gapp's renewed fever quickly subsided, and he felt happier now than at any other time during this whole sorry misadventure.

But, what to do next? Despite this sudden freedom, he still had to get home somehow. Had to regain his strength, had to find the best route, had to stock up on rations. This would take planning, and time.

Clearly he could not stay with the Gyger for too long. Yulfric might allow him to tarry long enough to fully recover his health, and might even send him on his way with a pack of rations, but even then he might expect some sort of payment, that was clear.

"Problem," he admitted to himself sheepishly.

Yulfric, guessing from his tone what he was thinking, agreed; he sat back and began chewing the dirt under his thumbnail, thoughtfully studying the little human.

After a while, he spoke:

". . . Well, this isn't the first time such a thing has happened to me; a human wanderer stumbling through the forest, scaring the game away and drawing off

my hounds. Hungry, sick, needing guidance. And only Yulfric there to guide him . . . So . . . these things happen . . ."

Gapp flushed and nodded. But he did not meet the giant's gaze.

". . . You do not have forests where you come from, then? . . ."

Gapp did look up at that, thinking he was being got at.

". . . It's just that the last human I took in was an Aescal, too . . ."

Gapp pointed to the wheel questioningly.

". . . The Lightbearer missionary, yes. He hadn't got a clue what he was doing . . ."

"I don't know," Gapp said. "I really don't. Just a coincidence, I suppose. Wyda-Aescaland *is* the nearest civili—no, *settled* country to here. Maybe we just have more travelers . . . or more idiots, perhaps." He trailed off, feeling more pathetic than ever next to this knurled ironwood figure before him. "We do have forests, I suppose, but hardly anyone ever goes into them anymore," he added, in a hopeless attempt to justify his people's feebleness.

Yulfric rubbed the end of his nose, plucked some nasal hairs out, then scratched his eyebrows for so long they let loose a snowfall of flaky skin and white mites onto his tabard. He appeared to be trying to remember something.

After a while, he stood up and beckoned Gapp to follow him.

". . . Come. He left something behind. I show you . . ."

They went into another room, the "guest room," as the wheel translated it, which went some way to explaining why he had so few guests. There was a crudely built bed filled with loose straw (actually it looked more like a byre) and next to it a stool with only two legs. The third leg had been eaten away by some pernicious fungus, and the stool was now supported upon a pile of books. Grimy and damp, they had obviously seen better days.

". . . Behold, the library . . ."

Yulfric was having difficulty disguising the pride in his voice. And there was no doubting that, this far north, six books all together in one room probably did constitute a library. But looking at this sad heap of weathered old tomes, with their surrounding cloud of spores, only made Gapp wonder if Yulfric had again missed the point.

The Gyger went over to his prized collection of literary masterpieces, and pulled them out one by one. Gapp joined him, and together, they studied their near-illegible covers. Two of them were so damaged the titles could not be read, and one of these could not even be opened, so pulped together were its pages. The third book was written in a tongue neither boy nor Gyger could understand, but the fourth and fifth were written in Aescalandian. Of these one (currently being used to nest a family of field mice) was entitled *Morio and the Gleemen from Friy,* the other *The Bumper Book of Nahovian War Atrocities.*

The sixth volume (perhaps the least decrepit and certainly the smallest, being only a pocket book) was written in a script Gapp recognized as deriving from the territory of Qaladmir. The cover bore symbols that looked distinctly alchemical, and it was this one that Yulfric took hold of. He thumbed through the pages nostalgically, the book tiny in his massive hands, then turned to the inside cover, and showed it to Gapp.

To his surprise, there was a handwritten message there; some of this, again, was in the unintelligible tongue of Qaladmir, but right at the end, added almost as an afterthought, the young Aescal recognized words in his own language:

"To Yulfric," he read out loud. "So long, and thanks for all the venison: Finwald."

Gapp's jaw dropped so low it almost hit his chest.

Finwald?

Yulfric regarded the boy inquiringly. He had never seen such an expression on a human before.

Finwald? Gapp thought incredulously, and bade Yulfric start spinning the wheel.

"The missionary?" he demanded, pointing to the signature. Yulfric nodded.

What's Finwald doing in all this? Gapp puzzled. *It can't possibly be the same . . . but how many Finwalds can there be in Wyda-Aescaland? And possessing a book on alchemy, to boot?*

"Slim build, indoor complexion, long black hair, black eyes?" Gapp described, "And wearing a medallion shaped like this . . . ?" (He outlined the shape of the Torch of Cuna with his hands.)

Yulfric nodded enthusiastically.

". . . Made of silver . . ."

"Silver, indeed," Gapp confirmed. That was it, then. It had to be Finwald. Gapp had not mentioned any of the names of his companions upon the quest, nor even the name of the town they started from; he saw no necessity in giving such specific details.

". . . You know him, then . . ." Yulfric responded with a shrug. To him there was little coincidence in his two visitors happening to know each other, since they did, after all, come from the same country.

But it was not the coincidence that astounded Gapp, for coincidences are bound to happen once in a while. What he could not get his head around was why Finwald had ever been here in the first place.

"Yes, I know him," Gapp replied thoughtfully, "or rather, I *did* know him. Finwald is—was—the mage-priest I told you about earlier, the one whose idea it was to journey to Vaagenfjord Maw in the first place. It was he who experienced the vision of Drauglir's reawakening." *And he who got me into all this trouble in the first place.*

". . . Interesting. He must be a man driven by great need, to be sure. When first I happened upon him, he was much as you are now—starving, frightened, exhausted, feverish; blundering about the forest with no idea of what he was doing. I took him in, as I have with you, and let him stay till he was fit enough to go

on his way. After a week, he was ready, and he departed, vowing never to return to the North again in his life. Ha! I don't think he expected the wilds to be quite so wild!

"And yet, two years later, here is a friend of his who tells me he has set forth intending to travel through the Great Forest once again! Even in the company of warriors, this new mission of his must be exigent indeed if it means he is to journey where once he nearly perished. Do you yourself believe that the Rawgr is truly arisen once more?"

Gapp did not reply at once. He chewed his lower lip and stared absently at the damp patches on the floor by Yulfric's feet. Then he said, "Two years ago, you say? Did Finwald tell you exactly what he was doing out in the forest all by himself?"

". . . Yes, he told me he was a missionary sent by the elders of his land to teach the pagans of Wrythe. He said that their heathen souls were to be saved, and he was the one chosen to carry out this task . . . armed only with his faith, his silver amulet . . . and a dead snake in a bag, as far as I remember . . ."

He paused at this last thought, laid his hand on the door jamb, grimaced, wiped his hand quickly on his tabard, and continued. *". . . He seemed very committed, a man of singular purpose . . ."*

But Gapp shook his head in befuddlement. "No," he murmured, "that doesn't sound like the Finwald *I* know. Oh, he's certainly committed to his faith, I'll give him that. But he's never, in all the years I've known him, struck me as the missionary type. Not at all. More into studying than preaching."

He thought hard about it. There was something not right at all about this whole business. There had never been any mention of such a mission to the Northlands that *he* had been aware of, and in a town the size of Nordwas, such a thing was unlikely to pass by unnoticed. *What was Finwald up to then? Why had he never mentioned any of this to his quest-mates?* It all seemed very peculiar.

And Wrythe . . . Wasn't that one of the places the company was supposed to be heading for? If he remembered rightly, it was the only settlement in the Far North that lay anywhere near Melhus Island.

Wrythe? Why there, of all places? What was so special, so secret, about it? There had to be a connection, that was clear. But according to the Gyger, that encounter had been two years ago, and Finwald had only had his divine revelation this recent spring . . .

. . . Or so he had told everyone. What did he know that he had kept to himself for two years, possibly longer, to the exclusion of even his fellow questers?

The question hung in Gapp's mind for a long time. It nagged him, it harried him, and it drove him to distraction. Then something Yulfric had just said came back to him.

". . . 'dead snake in a bag'? Did I read that right?"

Yulfric shrugged. *". . . That's what it looked like to me . . . I never found out because he never let me see it . . . A long, thin bag of oiled hessian, strapped to his back . . . bound tightly around something long, thin, and wavy . . . but stiff as a board . . . like I said, it looked as if he was carrying a dead snake . . . never let it out of his sight . . ."*

Gapp stared at the words hard as they appeared on the wheel. He could make no sense of them at all, and wondered again if it was not merely a fault in the translation.

But, when all was said and done, he concluded there was nothing he could do about any of this. It was probably all academic, anyhow; Finwald was dead along with the rest of his companions, and he would never find out.

Gapp was accepted into the household of Yulfric not through kindness, obligation, curiosity, nor even loneliness, but rather through absentmindedness. The Gyger just did not seem to remember the lad was there most of the time, or *why* he was there. Back in Nordwas this had been the norm, but here sometimes even the hounds appeared not to notice him. It felt as if he had somehow disappeared below the threshold of sentient awareness. It was some time before Yulfric stopped looking startled, or vaguely troubled, whenever he came across the boy.

Eventually Gapp became part of the daily routine, the only condition being that he work hard, both in the house and out on the hunt, pull his own weight, and stay there only for as long as it took him to regain his strength and go his own way.

His stay with Yulfric was, as it turned out, only brief. But in the time he spent there, a whole, rich new world was opened up to him. It was a time that, if he were fated to weather the changing fortunes of Fron-Wudu and survive, he would never be able to forget. The secret life of the forest was gradually revealed to his young eyes. He had never believed, in all his fifteen years behind the stockaded walls of Nordwas, that such miracles of nature were happening all the time beneath his very feet.

It was not all wonderment. He was thrust headfirst into a world of pain, hardship, and cruelty that—but for his recent ordeals—he would have found traumatic and hateful. But at the same time it allowed him to experience at first hand a world and a life that he would never have been able to guess at, had he merely passed through as a traveler.

Privation and suffering were really *felt,* here. They were not merely unfortunate experiences occurring now and then. They were constant, and were a central part of the daily routine. If a problem arose, it *had* to be solved. There was no choice. Coming to terms with this was Gapp Radnar's next step in his sudden maturity.

Coming to terms with death, too, was something the young man had to harden himself to. Before, killing had been necessary only when the company had had the misfortune to stumble across a dangerous adversary. Here and now, they actively sought it out: there was no mercy, no fair play, and no natural justice. It was a case of killing for meat. Often that meant very young animals that had hardly even had a glimpse of life yet; or the sick, or aged. All would be ruthlessly taken. Pathos was an unheard-of luxury. Their quarry was simply meat which had not yet been secured.

Forced to adapt to this new way of thinking, Gapp's quaint old notions of "right" or "wrong" quickly fell away, to be replaced by "live" or "die."

Furthermore, though the days he spent with Yulfric were few, they seemed to last longer than any he had ever known. Time took on a new intensity, where day-to-day survival was all that mattered, and what the future might hold was not even a passing consideration. But Gapp soon discovered that there was another side to this coin; the exigencies of survival and the vitality of their lifestyle meant that each day, each hour even, was experienced with a new intensity. They really *lived,* and this gave life a new edge that made his previous existence seem as though he had spent it half-asleep. The years of a hunter might be short, but that did not matter, was never even thought about.

Within several days, Gapp found his senses come really alive for the first time. His reactions quickened, his alertness multiplied many times over, and any debilitation was soon quashed. His whole body now thrilled with a heightened life force as he hunted daily with Yulfric and the pack.

Even his spectacles did not seem to steam up quite so frequently.

If there was one thing that he never quite came to terms with, though, it was Heldered. Nothing had been said about this most unapparent member of the House of Yulfric, and at first Gapp felt that he would rather not know more about it anyway. But there was no avoiding the subject. Things were laid out ready for the giant, meals were cooked and served, plates were cleaned, clothes were picked off the floor. Yulfric had apparently become used to this attention. But it was all done so haphazardly, never with any of the obsequious consistency one would have expected from a servant. If things were done, fine; but if not, well, one could hardly make demands from a domestic helper that, as far as Gapp could tell, was unpaid, unbidden, and unseen.

Only once did Gapp think he caught a glimpse of this "entity." One morning before anyone else had got up, he left his "byre" to fetch a mug of cold water, and upon entering the dining room (for want of a better description) he was sure that he had spotted Heldered. In the half-light of dawn it was difficult to say, but out of the corner of his eye, he could have sworn that he had seen a diminutive figure hovering, fast asleep, above the tabletop.

It had given him quite a start, and he never entered that room again alone. But when he questioned Yulfric, the Gyger would only say that Heldered was a Nisse. This was a new word to the Aescal. Yulfric did not explain it further, and the meditation wheel seemed content to leave it at that. The only conclusion that Gapp could draw was that a Nisse must be similar to the Gardvords and Godbondes back home.

Several households in Nordwas were reputed to have Gardvords. Sightings, however, were rare, and few descriptions existed. As far as anyone could say, they seemed to be household guardian spirits, but much bigger than the floating homunculus Gapp thought he had seen; ogrish, heavyset and naked, some were said to be as big as the house itself, a concept Gapp had always found difficult to warm to. And unlike the Nisse, they expected *payment*. If none was forthcoming, they might charge around the house roaring, stamping, and slamming doors all night, or alternatively the owner might simply wake up one morning to find the pantry bare—or the cat missing.

Either way, Gardvords were decidedly more sinister (not to mention more of a nuisance) than the benevolent little Heldered. And Godbondes, of whom at least three were said to exist in Wintus Hall (though the Peladanes *would* boast this, wouldn't they?), were even worse. These did not exist in corporeal form, and could never be contacted or reasoned with. They did not expect payment, but they were resentful toward guests, hurling things at them if they felt like it, and would even kill unknown intruders.

This did worry Gapp, it had to be said. The thought that a potent Huldre spirit (and all such entities *were* Huldre, no two ways about it) was coexisting in their very house, at liberty to do almost anything, was more than a little unnerving. He could not understand how the Gyger could be so relaxed about it.

But then, Yulfric was Yulfric. . . .

One day, the forest giant called Gapp over to him, and pointed to a door that the boy had never noticed before. There was a look of conspiracy in his eyes which seemed to say: *I have something very special to show you, boy. . . .*

Gapp glanced apprehensively at the Gyger, but allowed himself to be escorted down the short, dark corridor that led to the door. He noticed that it sloped downward somewhat, was perceptibly even more dilapidated than the rest of the house, and smelled of something a bit like freshly baked bread.

Yulfric pushed heavily against the door two or three times before it opened, then stooped under the low lintel to enter.

Gapp paused before following. There was no light whatsoever within, and the smell was appreciably more pungent now that the door was open. Nevertheless, he followed Yulfric down a short flight of creaking steps into the room beyond.

Yulfric struck a light and then lit an oil lamp on one of the shelves, whereupon Gapp stared about in bemusement. Despite the close feel of the room, he could now see that it was a huge cellar with long racks of bottles, jars, amphorae, and kilderkins everywhere. All of them were stoppered securely, but it took little deduction to realize that they all contained some heady alcoholic brew. The meditation wheel was pressed into Gapp's hand.

"*. . . My wine cellar . . .*" Yulfric announced proudly.

Gapp continued to stare in wonderment. But it was the odor that held his attention more than anything. Everything smelled like creosote. There were undertones of baker's yeast, drainage, and old socks, but creosote remained the overriding smell. A halfhearted attempt had been made to dispel (or at least tone down) this olfactory intrusion, as could be seen from the numerous burned-out stubs of perfumed beeswax candles that littered every spare shelf. But forest bees, being what they are, do have a tendency to create somewhat resinous honeycombs, so that any candles made thereof would inevitably smell of creosote.

". . . This, my miniature friend, is where I keep my greatest treasure. For here, in this cellar, is where I make, rack, bottle, and store Skolldhe-Ynggri, the wine of the blackfruit. (Do not go telling anyone, will you, my friend, for this secret is known only to me, Heldered, and yourself.) . . ."

Gapp looked about himself doubtfully, wondering just who else he was supposed to tell. But he nodded in assent; he would tell no one.

". . . Good . . ." Yulfric smiled. *". . . Not even Finwald was let in on this one . . ."*

He went over to the nearest rack, extracted one of the smaller bottles, and blew the dust from it. He held the label up to the lamp's light, then read out the date. He beamed, as if to confirm the excellence of the vintage, and beckoned the boy to follow him, with an encouraging wink.

He carried the bottle over to a small table with two stools beside it, dragging with it the umbilical-cord-like length of yellow cobweb that still clung to it. Several large, hairy spiders had fallen from the web as it was pulled from the rack, and landed with an audible thump on the flagstones before scuttling in alarm back into the darkness. Yulfric set the bottle down and proceeded to rummage about in an old toolbox for a pair of drinking vessels.

As he did so, Gapp's attention was diverted by the stealthy, slithering sound of another bottle sliding out of its rack. Curiously he peered down one aisle between two shelves, and saw to his alarm a bottle now floating in midair. He watched it as it wavered about a little, then heard the soft, careful extrication of its cork. Then it was tilted back, and methodically but relentlessly drained of its entire contents. Gapp called out softly to Yulfric, expecting the precious wine to splash all over the floor, but to the boy's bewilderment, not one drop did so. It simply vanished.

Again Gapp hissed to the giant, but Yulfric was still too preoccupied with searching through the junk for some beakers. Gapp was about to go over and get his attention when he heard a confidential *"Shhh!"* from the emptied aisle, and watched as the bottle was replaced.

Only then did he realize why Heldered chose to work at Yulfric's place.

Eventually Yulfric succeeded in digging out two wooden cups from which they could drink. He handed one to the boy (who held it in two hands, like a bowl) and poured a small measure of Skolldhe-Ynggri into each.

A thin, purple vapor curled up from the neck of the bottle as the wine was poured, which had the same effect on Gapp as snuffing ammonia. But when his eyes and his head cleared, he saw, through a watery haze, the richness of the wine in his bowl, as thick and red-black as the blood they had spilt earlier that day, and instinct overtook him; without thought or prompting, he drank it all down in one.

"*Whoa, steady boy!*" Yulfric laughed in his own tongue. "*That was supposed to last you all night!*"

But Gapp was past caring. In this world of wine he felt a sudden surge of belief in what he was. This mischievous, heady little brew with its fiery strength, fruity taste, and amusing bouquet was *very* much to his liking. Already he could feel it coursing through his veins like molten tin. He held out his bowl once again.

"More, boy?!" Yulfric bellowed indignantly. Then he seemed to remember himself, and poured out a further measure.

"Why not?" he murmured, then directed Gapp over to a stool and carefully sat him down.

"*. . . This . . .*" he explained as Gapp spun the translation wheel with considerably greater speed and robustness than was strictly necessary, "*. . . is the result of many, many generations of love, care, and devotion to the highest ideals of winemaking. This Skolldhe-Ynggri is the crowning glory of the race of the Gygerim, the zenith of our art, the very last word in alcoholic excellence. You may have heard of Hauger ale . . . Truly theirs is a secret worth guarding. But Skolldhe-Ynggri is more than just that; for where the making of Hauger ale is a secret revealed to no other race, the very existence of our brew is concealed, every bit as closely as the recipe for Hauger ale. None but the Gygerim know of it, and we intend to keep it that way.*"

Gapp jabbed a thumb in his chest three times, as though to say, *Except for me. . . .*

Yulfric was momentarily lost, and bit his lip in vexation.

"*. . . Well, you promise not to tell anyone, won't you . . . ?*"

Gapp held out his bowl again, and winked.

"*. . . Good. Anyway, as I was saying, this is our secret. It takes many years in the fermenting, at the correct temperature always, and requires racking at least five times a year. It can only be made with a secret ingredient, and that ingredient is the great hanging blackfruit of Perchtamma-Uinfjoetli, found only in the valley of that name, far to the north—*"

Gapp raised an eyebrow, and put one finger to his lips.

"*. . . Damn! Damn damn damn! Must be the vapors . . . Still, to get to the point, now is the time of year for the harvesting of the blackfruit. In a week's time you and I shall leave for the valley of Perchtamma-Uinfjoetli. It is a round journey of about two weeks, and one which must not be undertaken casually . . .*"

He paused until Gapp managed to get his drunken giggles under control.

"*. . . This journey will take us through dangerous tracts of the forest which I* *would not even consider entering were it not for the reward at the end. It will take us into the very heart of Fron-Wudu. There are very few tracks to follow, and strange creatures and races that are best avoided. Cannibals, I tell you. . . . This time, Gapp Radnar, should you go astray, there will be no one to help you out. Do you understand?"*

But Gapp did not even hear, let alone understand, for he was by now lying sound asleep upon the floor.

What secrets Yulfric had inadvertently let slip did in fact remain secret. The following morning Gapp awoke with the first and worst hangover of his life. And though he tried to rack his marinated brains, he just could not recall how he had got into that state. The previous day was just a blur. All he did know was that in a week's time, he and Yulfric were to leave on "some expedition or other."

And six days later the day for their departure finally came.

<"Awake-Awake-E-oh, small person!"> Yulfric bellowed from the kitchen with unaccustomed buoyancy and frivolity. <"The sun is just up, the sky a cloudless blue, and it's a *beautiful* day for the quest!">

He spoke in his own tongue, without the wheel, and Gapp, still in his byre, had no idea what he was saying. The giant's mood, however, was unmistakable. The boy's hand reached out to drag some more straw over his head like a threatened snail.

How can anyone be so cheerful at this time in the morning? he thought in disgruntlement, and endeavored to ignore his host. But it was the day of departure, and the whole household was buzzing with activity. Yulfric was busy making last-minute preparations, the hounds were leaping about excitedly, and from somewhere Gapp heard the noises—and smelled the smells—of breakfast being cooked. Clearly, Heldered had decided to join in the spirit of the occasion, too.

"Blooding quests!" Gapp muttered irritably. "Who needs them?"

It suddenly struck him that he had heard that line somewhere before, and with the words came also a vague sense of discomfort, and the smell of marsh sedge. But he could not think who it was who had said it.

Probably every sod who's ever had to endure going on one, he concluded miserably, and crawled shakily out of his straw box.

An hour later, their expedition was under way. With Schnorbitz in the lead, the other nine hounds closely following, and Yulfric and Gapp bringing up the rear, the small party issued forth through the gate of the stockade. They paused only long enough to watch the mighty wooden portal being swung shut behind them by its unseen door ward, and then they eagerly plunged into the all-enveloping forest.

It was indeed a beautiful day, as Yulfric had promised. The early mists of a late-summer morning were slowly dissipating. In all but the gloomiest, dankest groves they soon faded into nothingness, like wraiths in the sunlight, and left no trace behind save for a dewy sheen that glistened on every leaf.

Within days the more recognizable tracks that Gapp had by this time become accustomed to were left behind them, and the party began to enter unfamiliar territory. Conversation, such as it was, ceased altogether. The hounds were less inclined to stray, and kept their noses closer to the ground, their hackles twitching on permanent standby. The farther they progressed north, the less obvious became the paths, and much of the time was now spent rerouting, backtracking, and general direction-finding. In spite of his new (if somewhat elementary) knowledge of the forest, Gapp could not understand how anyone, not even the woodcrafty Yulfric, could possibly know for sure where they were. But it seemed the Gyger was as much a part of the forest as the trees, and he knew exactly what signs to look for.

As the days went by, so the forest itself changed. No longer just a wilder, more extensive version of the type of woodland one might find around Nordwas, the territory they were passing through became a totally different world altogether. The trees here were colossal, almost entirely coniferous, and the thick, leafy, brambly undergrowth that choked the forest floor farther south gave way to a spongy carpet of needles and sparse clumps of fern. The air itself became crisper, and smelled deeply resinous.

Different, too, was the game encountered. Boar, hart, and francolin gave way to strange tree-dwelling cats, large rodents with spiny bristles and tiny, almost blind eyes, and bizarre-looking hunting primates that hooted eerily in the forest's gloom. Curious eyes peered at the travelers from every side.

Even the climate grew noticeably cooler the farther north they traveled, and there was already, even at this time of year, a more autumnal fragrance to the air.

A week after their departure, the land began to rise, at first gradually, then steeply, and the trees thinned out. Huge clusters of rock thrust themselves up from the loamy earth, forming little corridors that the party passed along. By day these seemed devoid of life, but during the evening they were host to large numbers of the hooting primates that became part of the travelers' diet. Whenever the giant, the boy, and the hounds passed by, these creatures would immediately cease their hooting and glare silently down at them. Gapp felt extremely ill-at-ease at such times, especially realizing that these watchers would certainly smell the blood of their own kind on the travelers. It was only Yulfric's confident, almost arrogant bearing that reassured the young Aescal somewhat.

That and the ten massive hunting hounds, most of whom did not even bother glancing up at their spectators.

Nevertheless it was a great relief to Gapp to wake up on the morning of the eighth day and hear Yulfric announce that they were now within hours of reaching the valley of Perchtamma-Uinfjoetli. From the crest of the rise just ahead, the giant indicated, they should be able to spot their destination. Gapp noticed a hint of new excitement in the Gyger's gait, and he wondered exactly what he was likely to see. From his own position, at the edge of the tree line, the young Aescal could see nothing beyond the rise but clear blue sky.

But as they ascended closer to the crest, he began to hear something different. At first it seemed little more than a continuous trembling noise, relentless and almost irritating. He could not guess what it meant, and did not dare intrude upon Yulfric's thoughts by asking him. But after half an hour it had gradually increased to a loud rumbling that could be felt running like earth energy through the ground beneath his feet. Gapp was put in mind of the beating of many war drums in the distance.

Then without warning they reached the crest of the rise, and the rumble suddenly became a deafening roar that nearly bowled Gapp over backward.

"Great thundering armholes," he gasped, hardly able to breathe. "Just look at that!"

<"Yes,"> Yulfric replied to himself, guessing Gapp's meaning. <"Look, and marvel. There are not many sights in the world which could compare with that.">

A matter of mere yards before them, the ground dropped away all of a sudden down into an almost sheer abyss, and below them, in front of them, and all around them opened the massive, bowl-shaped valley of Perchtamma-Uinfjoetli. It stretched away for miles all around, its floor at least a mile below them, and almost sheer cliffs hemmed it in on every side except where the valley opened out to the east, way over to their right. Great, towering cliffs soared out of the steeply sloping valley sides, and the light of the golden, early-morning sun streamed all the way through from the eastern end to set the bare rock of these cliffs afire with a deep orange radiance. At the foot of them, a thick wall of trees plunged farther down into the shadowed depths of the huge valley, shimmering and swaying peacefully in the breeze.

The highest cliff at the very head of the valley over to their left must have stood at least a mile above the wooded slopes at its foot. A mile of sheer rock bathed in the full light of the eastern sun, its summit crowned by clouds. And halfway up it was a deep, cavernous hole like a gaping mouth, out of which spewed the great waterfall of Baeldicca the Great, one of the Nineteen Wonders of the World. Out of the rock face looming high above the two awestruck mortals farther along, it spouted and cascaded in a crashing, gushing spray of white, far down into the shadows below.

The air was moist with spray even from this distance. Gapp closed his eyes in exhilaration, and savored the cool blast of droplets it carried. It felt like galloping a horse through an icy winter's morning, and he found himself gasping with the sheer effort of breathing.

It was a sight of such awesomeness that it far surpassed even the great canyons of the Blue Mountains. And way, way below, so far that it was only just visible, a narrow ribbon of silver glinted in the sunlight. It wound like a sparkling thread through a deep green carpet, to disappear from view at the eastern end of the valley, several days' journey away.

The wheel was pushed urgently into his hands, and Gapp reluctantly forced his eyes away from the panorama.

"... *That there is the River Folcfreawaru, the longest river in the whole of the lands of Fron-Wudu, and according to what I've learned, it courses through no less than twelve countries before it finally reaches the sea! It is the only highway of travel that penetrates this deep into the Great Forest, though few outlanders have ever managed to follow it this far.*"

Gapp stared again in awe at all around him.

Yes, he thought, *the Great Forest indeed. Only now do I realize why people name it so. And few outsiders have ever managed to get this far. Yet here I am, Gapp Radnar the esquire, bereft of this companions, lost in the underworld, thrown to the savage mercies of heedless fortune; here, where few men will ever stand! Oh, if only the troubadours could experience this. . . .*

Gapp steadied his feet against the wind, stepped a little closer to the edge, and gazed in wonder at the world below him. He felt prouder than he had ever felt in his life, far prouder even than when he had set off from Nordwas with those funny little men, his erstwhile companions. At this time more than at any other on his wanderings, he was elevated above the ground-level trammels of everyday existence into another plane of being, experiencing the rushing thrill of Life that is denied to all but the greatest adventurers in the world.

Gapp Radnar was now to be counted among the ranks of Heroes.

For long he stood there, on the lip of the precipice, and cast his long shadow over the forest lying below the thundering waterfall of Baeldicca the Great, breathing in the clear mountain air and feeling the refreshing spray on his face.

Yulfric smiled knowingly. He knew by the look on the young Aescal's face what he was feeling, and he was not about to cut short the lad's brief moment of Magnificence. It was something he himself had experienced many years ago when first he too had stood upon this precipice, and he was proud to share it with the little human.

So few ever got to experience this sense of sheer *hugeness,* for so few ever got to stand here on top of the world. Time enough to come down to earth once they reached the valley floor.

It took them two hours to reach the wooded slopes below. A series of goat trails and rock-strewn gullies wound precipitously down the cliff face they began on. Led by the pack leader Schnorbitz, and aided by the forest giant's prior knowledge of the route, the tiny line of hunter-gatherers managed to slip, slide, and scramble down the rocky face of the cliff without serious mishap, until they had safely gained the forested slopes of Perchtamma-Uinfjoetli far below.

Drinking deeply from his waterskin, Gapp was glad to feel the reassuring firmness of rich, needle-matted forest floor beneath his feet. His legs were still shaking from the precarious descent. He pointed to the hounds in incredulity. Had he not witnessed it for himself, he would never have believed dogs could prove such skilled rock-climbers.

"... *Theirs is a race not used to such endeavors, yet luckily they have a good master to teach them. But—now we have more important matters at hand; the blackfruit trees are not very far from here, and hopefully we will have completed the harvest and departed this valley before it gets dark. So we must get to work with haste* ..."

Emboldened by euphoria, Gapp thrust the wheel back into the Gyger's hand and said: "Leave the valley by nightfall? But surely we can stay at least two days here. It is too wonderful by *far* to spend so short a time in—"

The wheel was shoved so hard back into his hands that Gapp was almost bowled over. "... *Listen to me! I have been here for many more years than you have lived—I know something of this valley and its inhabitants. Trust me, Gapp, if you knew them half as well as I do, you would not wish to tarry here for more than an afternoon, let alone overnight! You must understand, this valley is unique, enclosed, isolated—there are races here that do not exist elswhere in the world. Some of them seem to be shy of me and my hounds; they do not know how to deal with anything new; thus they leave us alone. But there are others—half-man, half-beast, Vetterim and Jordiske—that are not so shy. That is why we must stay close, keep our guard up at all times, and not go near the river unless we have to.* ..."

"The river? But you said earlier that the river is wonderful, blackfruit as far as the eye can see, for it's where the greatest concentration of blackfruit trees are to be found ..."

"... *And avoided! The riverbanks are the haunt of the Vetterim. They are a strange race, one that has never bothered me, but one that I have always felt pressing in, their sharp eyes on me all the time. I have never seen more than a fleeting glimpse, or a shadow in the trees, but I am a stranger here just as much as you, and I do not take chances.* ... *These are the cannibals I told you of.* ..."

"Cannibals? But you're a Gyger ..."

"... *Yes* ..."

"And I'm a human ..."

"... *Yes* ..."

"So we've got nothing to worry about."

Yulfric considered this, then ignored it and continued with what he was saying:

"... *Also, I forbid you—absolutely forbid you—to go anywhere near the waterfall, for that is the domain of the Jordiske* ... *Remember what I say to you, and we should both leave this valley in safety.* ..."

And on that cheerful note, the blackfruit harvest began. Yulfric led the boy through the woods until they came upon the trees they were looking for. The blackfruit were large, aubergine-colored, and tasted like fresh figs. For a while the two gatherers contented themselves with just gorging on this delicious fruit, sinking their teeth into the succulent, sun-warmed pulp, and letting the juice trickle down their chins. Then they began cutting the crop down from the trees, and placing it in large sacks. Gapp used a kind of sickle-headed pruner on a long, retractable haft that had been lent to him by the Gyger. He had carried it all this way himself, using it as a kind of walking stick up till now.

But even so, the fruit on these trees was not so plentiful as on those farther down the valley slope, and they had to search carefully.

Eventually, as the hounds had not picked up any scents of danger, but kept larking around frivolously, Yulfric decided that it must be safe for the two of them to split up.

"... *But always stay within earshot* ..." he warned Gapp gravely.

"Of course," the boy replied, rather too glibly for the giant's liking.

The intense feelings aroused in the young man's heart while he had been standing up on the precipice above, however, were not to be subdued so easily, not even by the forest giant's stern warning. For the first time in his life, Gapp Radnar the humble esquire from Wyda-Aescaland felt like a true adventurer, every bit as worthy as the heroes he had long heard praised in the lays of the skalds in Nordwas: for had he not come through the pits of the underworld, faced and overcome horrors unimagined by others, and survived the harsh wilds of Fron-Wudu? And what was more, he had done this all by himself! (Well, Yulfric had helped a little maybe. . . .) Not even Thegne Nibulus could boast as much.

So the Gyger's words sounded more like a challenge than a warning. This was now *his* valley; he alone of all his people had gained ingress here; and he was not about to leave it without a little further exploration.

Peering down through the thickening trees, he listened hard. His ears picked up only the sound of the waterfall, and cautiously he made his way downhill. . . .

Isn't this where I left him?

Yulfric studied the ground. Yes, these were the boy's bootprints, clearly enough, but, judging by the heavier indentations of the toes, the tracks told him that he had been moving stealthily.

Almost as if he doesn't want me following him, he thought in consternation. Little bastard must have sneaked off for a while—and Yulfric did not need to study the tracks further to guess where he had headed for.

He scratched his armpits and belched in frustration. He supposed it was inevitable, really, a young man like that all fired-up with adventure. . . .

He put the back of his hand to his lips, and made a high-pitched squealing sound. Within moments his scattered hounds came bounding into the clearing, and stood eagerly awaiting his command.

"B'khunda gweorna!" he snapped at them, and without waiting, strode off through the bushes in search of his charge.

Gapp emerged from the dense cover of the bushes, and stared up in awe, a broad smile splitting his face.

"Baeldicca the Great," he whispered to himself, smitten by reverence and wonder at the breathtaking torrent of white spray that thundered down from its unseen source somewhere thousands of feet up above, under a rainbow-bedecked blue sky. Though he was still far from its plunge-pool, so mighty was the cascade that still it seemed to tower almost directly above him.

For long moments Gapp contented himself with gazing up at the falls. He tried to contemplate the sheer enormity of it, seeing all those tons of water spewing every second from the river's dark, chthonic source in the cliff face far above. He tried to compare it with anything he had been used to in his life previously, recalling the streams and rivers of his own land; and he could not help but laugh. How small they all seemed now. How paltry, insignificant . . . just as his life had been then; his life in boyhood, now gone forever.

For long moments more he stood there, and he was at peace. Such beauty lay in this verdant glade, untouched by the banal, besmirching hands of civilization. There was an untamable magnificence to it all that, in truth, he never would have been able to appreciate properly had it not been for his time spent with the forest giant.

The giant . . . Yes, where was Yulfric? He should be here too, to witness this sight, to experience all that Gapp was feeling, instead of lurking up there among the stunted blackfruit trees.

Yulfric swiftly forgotten, Gapp returned to his contemplation. How white the spume against the deep blue sky! What beautiful colors dancing around him in the shimmering crystal vapor! So sparkling the fine spray that fell upon his face, even from this distance; cool, caressing, cleansing.

Yes, he was at peace. Though the cascade roared like nothing he had ever heard before, and drowned out all other sound, there was yet a strange, mesmeric tranquility in the oblivion it created. Through its destructive white noise, a beautiful vision of peace was born. . . .

Gapp shook his head, and grinned. He was glad there was no one else to see him like this. What would they think? Not that he cared, really. He drank in one final view of the falls, then turned back along the riverbank.

He stopped dead in his tracks, and stared at what he saw in front of him.

What was it? It looked like some kind of idol, maybe even a scarecrow. He approached it cautiously, half-expecting it to suddenly come alive and lunge at him. As he drew closer, he saw that it was indeed an effigy of some sort . . . but of *what* sort, he dared not think.

Roughly man height, it looked like a log—maybe the lightning-blasted stump of a tree—that had been set up in the middle of a wide circle of stones. It was adorned with garlands of leaves and flowers, and covered in trailers of a thick, poisonous-looking ivy. Although the leaves on the garlands were nearly all dead and the flowers decayed and foul-smelling, the ivy was definitely still alive; it grew out of the ground and swarmed all over the log, strangling it, feeding off it, and yet holding it up in place. Gapp risked peering closer, and saw that its tendrils were lightly flecked in blood.

There also appeared to be the crude likeness of a face on it, made of . . . *Ugh!* He hoped it wasn't *that*!

Gapp backed off, partly in distaste, partly in fear. He had seen things like that before, and it reminded him of drawings he had seen of corn dollies, those pagan effigies found in Ottra, the Blighted Heathlands, and even in the southern marches of his own land. Gapp *loathed* corn dollies.

The words of the forest giant came back to him, about there being "*others . . . half-man, half-beast . . .*" in this valley.

The boy glanced apprehensively about, then moved off. A dark cloud passed across the sun, and he shivered. There was no birdsong, he noticed, and all of a sudden the previous welcome coolness of the fall's spray seemed chilling. This place did not seem so wondrous after all.

He decided to head back to the upper slopes and continue with the harvesting. He had tarried long enough.

"Flippin' weirdos . . ." he cursed, and quickened his pace.

He was just heading back along the riverbank when he heard a movement among the bushes off to his right. Gapp stopped dead and listened closely.

There was the snap of a breaking twig, and he thought he caught a glimpse of something moving in the trees beyond.

"Yulfric?"

There was no answer. Cautiously, he padded over. . . .

Yulfric was half-running now, following the light trail of bootprints that Gapp had left. He noted with growing alarm that they were heading not only for the river, but in the general direction of the giant waterfall as well. He cursed softly and quickened his pace.

Suddenly Schnorbitz gave a growl—a low, dangerous growl that spelled trouble. The other hounds gathered around, and began snuffling noisily at the ground near their pack leader. Yulfric pushed his way through them, and bent close to the earth to study the tracks.

"Krk'ndh! A Guntha Aescalandir fiw-hirnoest toth-t'lah!" he swore, and immediately raced off along the trail as fast as he could.

There, imprinted lightly in the soft earth, running alongside the tracks made earlier by Gapp, were the bipedal prints of long-clawed feet. Several of them.

"Yulfric—is that you?"

Gapp slowly approached the bushes. His mouth had gone dry, and the words were little more than a whisper.

There came no answer. Only a deep silence, a pause even, as though the whole valley were waiting to see what happened next. There was a smell now, he noticed, like from a half-eaten carcass that had been left out in the sun.

Gapp stopped. A loud woman's voice at the back, front, and sides of his mind was warning him: It might be an animal It might be dangerous you might get killed or worse. . . .

But he boldly stepped right up to the bushes and pulled some branches aside. In the gloom of the dense entanglement of foliage he could make out the silhouette of an upright figure, roughly his own height, and staring directly back at him.

His whole body stiffened with fear. Its face was mere inches from his own. The brittle, bony head, far too large for the rest of its skinny body, looked like a reanimated goat's skull, with bristles and long ears that jutted up like horns but dangled limply at the ends. Insectlike eyes stood out from its head in two large creamy hemispheres of matter, featureless save for a thin, pulsating vein that ran down the middle of each.

"UhY-Yu-Yulf—" Gapp stammered, and could only watch paralyzed as the creature raised its oversize, sharp-taloned hands, while coiling itself ready to spring.

But the paralysis of terror that had held him fast so many times before did not take effective hold so readily now. He had already been through too much to succumb to that. There was a short moment of immobility, and then he propelled himself backward with a wild yell of "YULFRIIIC!!"

The creature lunged after him with the speed of a wildcat. At exactly the same time there was movement to either side of it. It was not alone.

In the ensuing struggle, one word Gapp had heard the Gyger use flashed through his mind.

Jordiske!

Three of the devils were on him instantly. Long, sinewy arms of incredible strength shot out to hold him fast, and the undergrowth all around became alive with the whipping of tendrils and the slapping of leaves. Gapp heaved, bucked, and writhed furiously, and kicked out at the face before him with his feet. Both connected with devastating effect.

The kick hurled the Jordiske right back in a spray of whatever it called blood.

"Yulfric!" he howled again, and twisted out of the grip of the two creatures still holding him.

Again they came, long quivering arms reaching out for him. He could not get properly to his feet, and was soon pinned to the ground once more.

Through it all he could hear the sound of feet approaching. Slapping feet— more of them! Still he bucked and heaved, and struck out with his own feet. This time the impact was not so effective, but at least caused one of the devils to back off gurgling in pain and clutching its eye. Gapp briefly sensed something warm and wet trickling over his ankle.

Then they were all over him. He screamed in fury and frustration but could do nothing to save himself. The light of day was blotted out by the melee around him. He could smell the rankness of their sweating bodies, the sweet odor of rotten meat from their mouths. He was beaten, clawed, and nearly throttled, then lifted high above their heads and borne away.

Still struggling madly, Gapp was carried toward the waterfall. Its thundering grew louder with every second he approached it, until soon it filled his head with terror and panic.

By now the spray had increased from a cool shower to a freezing inundation, until suddenly everything went black. It was then Gapp realized with despair that he was being dragged round behind the cascade and down into some terrible cavern.

As he was propelled underground, he was almost sure he could hear the far-off bellowing of the Gyger rising above even the roar of Baeldicca the Great.

Then there was nothing but cold and dark. He had heard the last of his friend Yulfric.

11

"Armholes, Not Again!"

If ever there was a time in young Gapp Radnar's life that might be described as consummate injustice, then this, in his opinion, must surely be it. After all the tribulation that had been heaped upon him, and yet he had forced his way through, there was in some part of his mind a feeling that the world owed him a little reward; or if not a reward, then at least a break. But, now, to be dragged down into the dark pits of the earth by yet more subterranean horrors—this had to be the cruelest kick in the teeth imaginable.

As he struggled vainly for his life in the unyielding grip of his captors, many thoughts and images flashed through his mind. They were like a pictorial diary of all the time he had spent with the forest giant: one blood-drenched page after another, an unending succession of flickering images of young animal lives snatched away in savagery and terror, without mercy or thought. And yet more unrelated pictures followed: the buffalo calf torn to pieces by waiting predators as soon as it slides from the womb; the struggling beetle stuck to the earth by its own insides; the wheel-crushed coney bleating uselessly against the crows that are eating it alive . . .

. . . And, the very final image of this sanguinary picture book of Nature's everyday atrocities, though he had never witnessed it personally, a newly hatched turtle floundering clumsily, comically, upon the strand in that first, desperate race toward the sea, being dragged under the sand by the clicking, snapping claws of crabs . . .

The End.

His end. No, it was not injustice, any more than it was for all the lives he and the Gyger had taken. It was simply Nature. He was the hatchling turtle, clawing desperately but uselessly with his flippers at the sides of the tunnel down which he was being relentlessly dragged.

Fate vomits down my throat once again! he cursed as he fought. But he knew the truth: He had only himself to blame. At least baby turtles do not throw their lives away by loitering around waterfalls that they have been explicitly warned to avoid.

Deeper into the lair of the Jordiske he was carried. He could see nothing of his oppressors in these blacker-than-night tunnels, but he could feel them only too well. Their bony talons gripped him firmly with the strength of giant mandibles, and dug painfully, *mercilessly,* into his tender flesh. Slick with rancid sweat was their oily, bristle-covered hide where it rubbed against him. And the *stench!* It brought to mind a slaughterhouse, or a tannery—maybe even a plague pit.

And all the time they chittered, screeched, and warbled in their strange, alien tongue. Gapp had heard insects make that same noise, he was sure.

Soon a dull red glow began to brighten the tunnels till Gapp could just about make out the grotesque silhouettes of his captors. Wherever it was he was being taken, it might not be far now. But his arms felt constantly as if they were being pulled from their sockets, and he was going limp with the pain. Soon he would have no more strength to fight back. He had to do something fast. Had to wait for exactly the right second to strike. There would be only one chance.

Swinging himself sideways, he managed to briefly press his right hip against one of his carriers. There was an angry flurry of insectoid noises from the Jordiske, followed by a savage rake of claws across the boy's face. He cried out in shock, and began heaving convulsively.

But it had been worth it; for, in pressing himself against the Jordiske, he had felt the reassuring solid length of his sickle-headed fruit-pruner dig into his thigh. In their haste to flee from the Gyger and his hunting pack, they had not had time nor thought to disarm their captive. His jaws clenched hard, and he paced his breathing; perhaps he would get that one chance after all.

Moments later Gapp could feel on his face a cool current of air, moist with the icy vapors of underground streams. He breathed it deep into his lungs, not yet guessing what it might presage. Then suddenly he was released from the sharp grip of his captors, and fell to the ground, where he lay unmoving in a crumpled heap.

He could sense a wide space all around him now, a black void of vast proportions. All around, the sound of running water could be heard echoing. His hand stole down toward the fruit-pruner. . . .

"TCHRRRK! GHRRRTHNNK!" clicked one of the Jordiske in a voice that echoed sharply through the void, and bounced off the rock faces to dwindle into the distance.

"Ygthrrrx! Spfx!" came the disembodied reply from somewhere in the blackness ahead of them.

The sound of hasty shuffling. Talons grasping at him once more. Before he could gather his thoughts, Gapp, still prone, was trussed up in ropes and thongs supporting him under his armpits. From some way up above him came the creaking of wooden beams. It brought to mind a gibbet. From below came the far more distant sound of a stream, rushing and churning through the light-less depths.

Then, for a moment, the Jordiske nearby stopped whatever they were do-ing, and froze in silence. There were no sounds Gapp could hear that gave him a clue as to why they had halted, but in that short pause, he had the distinct im-pression they were keenly sniffing for something. Hurriedly, they continued with their activities, only this time Gapp could tell something was worrying them.

He lay there thinking. His brain raced. Their worry was his boon: Another chance? As his face pressed against the hard, rocky ground, he knew he must not waste that chance. He had to act soon, but he had to get it right. Stealthily his nimble fingers sought out the length of wood still strapped to his hip. His heart beat faster on locating it. Adrenaline streamed through his system and he could feel his entire body tensing. . . .

Abruptly he was yanked to his feet and pushed forward. He could not see a thing, but sensed with alarm that he was standing on the edge of a deep chasm. Something terrible was about to happen. His hand went down again to the cut-ting tool. . . .

Then a howl of demonic fury rent the air of the caverns, froze them like limestone pillars, and echoed far, far into the distance. Every one of them, Gapp included, remained rooted to the spot. Eyes glazed. Hair bristled with dread. Blood hammered.

Then there came the barely audible sound of something large flying through the air, followed by a sickening crunch right next to Gapp. A second later, the body of one of his captors fell, severed in two.

Schnorbitz!

To Gapp's mind that name suddenly seemed the fairest, most melodious and poetic of appellations, chiming triumphantly in his soul. His chance had come! The fruit-pruner momentarily forgotten, Gapp moved back from the chasm's edge and shouted the hound's name above the clangor of babbling voices and liquid growling.

"Schnorbitz! Schnorbitz! It's me, Gapp! Over here, boy!"

Shrieks arose from the Jordiske all about him, and the sound of ripping flesh continued with renewed frenzy. There was a flurry of bewildered shout-ing and warbling from over the other side of the abyss. Pandemonium reigned.

"Schnorbitz!" Gapp called out again, slipping and almost losing his bal-ance in a widening pool of gore at his feet. "Over here! Over here!"

Something collided heavily with him, knocking him to the ground. He leapt back to his feet without hesitation, and again called out.

"Schnorbitz! Over here! Over he-*earrghh*!"

A sharp blow raked across his already lacerated face and his head was wrenched back by the hair. Then, beyond belief, he was thrust violently over the lip of the chasm.

Mouth gaping wide in a scream that could not emerge, Gapp plunged headfirst into the blackness of the void. There was no up, no down; just emptiness, and a rushing of wind that ripped the air out of his lungs. Time stood frozen. The battle above was no more.

A pressure began to build under his armpits, and Gapp realized he was moving through the air in a sweeping arc. He had been attached to some sort of loose harness suspended from the beams far above, and he was now swinging across the abyss to the other side!

He rose to the zenith of his arc and, just as he felt himself reach a point of weightlessness, rough hands snatched him from out of the dark. Once again he was slapped across the face, this time so violently he believed his entire face had been ripped off. For a few seconds he blacked out, then through a morass of pain he heard shrieks of damnation from the other side of the chasm as the lost souls were torn apart.

His chances! Where had his chances gone? As he was hastily unfastened from his bonds and borne off down yet another tunnel, his mind reeled in disorientation. *What of his promised chances?*

Held in sharp pincers by his useless, floundering flippers, he knew that Hope was behind him now, on the far side of a bottomless chasm, and he felt the crushing despair of one realizing he will never see the world of men again.

As Gapp was hauled away deeper into the earth, the Hound of Yulfric finished his grisly work. But too late. Schnorbitz's final howl, an elegiac dirge for the damned, followed turtle-boy down the tunnels, then echoed into silence.

Blood-pounding, hammer-sounding, bounding along tunnels resounding with rasping gasping, mile after mile, sharp bile in the throat, dried throat, dried by noxious air, nightmare-weaving, heaving gulps of air, scorching the lungs, his frail casing of human flesh ready to explode, little boy wandered too far into the woods, pushed along these wormholes of stone, all alone, moan and groan . . .

Barely conscious now, Gapp's mind had been left far behind. There was that dull red glow visible again, and it became all he was aware of. This time, though, it was stronger. Getting stronger with each moment that passed.

Soon Gapp could see a little more clearly. The walls around him were a garish red, and he wondered if this was because they flowed with blood. The Jordiske, too, burned with the scarlet fires of a demon.

Ahead, where the light originated a dull, rhythmic pounding could be heard, its *thump, thump, thump* matching the beat of his heart. Before long the tunnel all around him reverberated strongly. As it thundered through his stomach,

Gapp began to feel very sick. It brought to him primordial, ancestral memories. Tribal memories. Palaeolithic. Old fears laid bare. Was he about to be sacrificed? Eaten? *Alive,* perhaps? Or did they have something even worse in store? The nausea rose up in him, and it would not be held down.

It was warm, now. No, not warm—hot! Ivy creepers of noxious steam snaked up his nostrils from their unraveling garlands below. They smelled of mud; of boiling mud. The corn dollies were coming alive.

Louder than before, the pounding shook the whole tunnel and the red glow waxed into a bright orange glare. A moment later, they emerged from the stifling confines of the vena cava and into the great open atrium of the Heart of Jordiske-Home.

Here, after the darkness of the tunnels, the light was blinding, and the heat insufferable. The pounding reached a climax, and was joined by the roar of a hundred bestial voices echoing deafeningly throughout the cavern. With the feel of lead in his guts and a memory of some dreadful familiarity at the back of his mind, Gapp stared through the swimming in his eyes at his surroundings.

It did not look good. It did not look good at all. He had been dragged down to what must surely be the most enormous cavern in the whole world. At least to his eyes it was, though to be sure his eyes were not up to much at the moment. The various susurrations and distant echoes from all around did suggest an immense space about him. And the air currents—bringing with them the odors of boiling mud, sweat, and meat gone bad—were almost like the wind. As he tried to focus, he began to make out globes of firelight all over the place, near and far. Firepits? Some were near enough for him to see the shapes of the Jordiske within their glow; others, more distant, were mere points of light. There must have been an infinite number of floor levels in this cavern, for the fires were everywhere, up, down and on every side, each suspended in the darkness like an orange star in the sky.

Toward the nearest of these he was dragged: a small group of Jordiske with torches around a flame pit. The fire seemed to give off more smoke than light, and lit up only its immediate surroundings. Beyond that, all was darkness, so that to Gapp it looked like a tiny world of dancing red light, inhabited by only a dozen or so Jordiske, which hung all alone in the vast emptiness of space.

Some of the creatures were leaning or squatting against boulders, picking at their various facial orifices with long, grimy claws, or else combing the teeming insect life out of their matted hair. Gapp was reminded of the spiders in Yulfric's wine cellar. Two were fighting, ignored by the others, butting each other viciously with a sound like a hammer striking an overripe melon; they rolled about the floor, occasionally disappearing from the halo of firelight, until eventually one of them did not come back. Another Jordiske, aided by a smaller assistant, was crouching upon all fours while building up the firepit. Judging from the leathery flaps of hide that hung from its chest to drag along the ash-covered ground, this one must have been an old Jord-hag.

The rest of them watched Gapp approach, and salivated. Claws twitched. Eyes bulged. Lice crawled. And then others began to appear in the circle of firelight.

He was shoved headlong toward them, and instantly they were upon him. Long fingers snatched and grabbed at him from every side, while harsh voices hissed evilly. The horrible little devils were swarming all over him, till he felt his sanity drowning in a murky swamp of death-fear.

He was flung down onto his knees beside the firepit, and once again his head was yanked back by the hair. Skull-like visages leered and spat at him. He could feel their cold saliva running down his face like itchy tears.

Wild-eyed, he was forced to behold the Jord-hag that now approached. In one hand she held a little stone pot, in the other what looked like a painting brush. She grinned insanely at him, and even from here he could smell the slugs that crawled over her cold skin. But what held the young Aescal's attention most was the primitive stone knife slung at her waist. It had that look of painful tearing to its rough, jagged edge, and Gapp's neck felt dreadfully exposed. The blood pumping madly through his arteries had never before seemed as precious as it did now.

The others gathered around. The breath rattled strangely in their throats. Some hissed or growled like cats. All were eager, all expectant, all anticipating. Their stinking exhalations hit the boy's face like a cold, acidic vapor. They watched while the old witch swayed about before the victim, a mantis taking time before the strike, savoring the dish before the meal.

Now she dipped the brush into the pot, and it came out coated in a viscous liquid that glowed toxically and reeked of sulfur. The Jordiske holding him from behind gripped tighter. Gapp knew that he could never break that grip. An involuntary whimper escaped from his throat.

Then the brush came down, and instantly Gapp's entire existence was a world of pure agony. As the vile unguent sought out every laceration on his face and sent geysers of burning agony down each nerve ending, the boy's whole body succumbed to a violent fit of spasms. A seething gale howled through his brain and the only thing he had in his mind was an image of an eel convulsing in a frying pan. The drum beating was now so intense that he thought he was inside one of them, being tossed around like a pea in a whistle.

The madness gradually subsided, but the pain and nausea went on. His head was then forced back up further to behold the Jord-hag now withdrawing the stone knife from its hoop.

She raised it in front of him. Slowly. Everything went still. He stopped breathing. He could not move a muscle. She filled his vision, a ghastly old crone, withered with age, eaten away by malice, disease, and invertebrates, glowing red with fire.

A second ticked by.

Then the knife sprang for his throat. . . .

From somewhere to the right there came a sudden rush of air, and the knife was gone, along with the taloned hand that had held it. There followed a gout of arterial spray, and a stifled squeal.

Another second ticked by, a second of silence so thick one could have choked on it. The Jordiske just stood there, all rooted to the spot, staring in disbelief, each single ocular vein swelling with the cold liquids that churned within it. Had they been capable, they might have gaped.

In the next second, a set of strong teeth with a familiar hot, fishy breath, hooked itself under Gapp's collar, hauled him up off the ground, and launched him like a missile out of the circle of firelight and into the all-enveloping darkness.

"Schnorbitz? How?"

But Schnorbitz's mouth was too full to answer, even if he could. Instead he bounded away through the darkness, madly, unthinkingly, using only instinct to guide him, just as it had led him here.

From behind them went up a shuddering howl. The alarm had gone up, and the hunt was on.

Over crags, fissures, and mud pools Schnorbitz sprinted, the boy dangling from his powerful jaws like a rabbit, never stopping once. In their mad dash, Gapp felt as though he were being shaken to pieces. But he was *free,* and not even for the blood of Pel-Adan was he going to try and struggle out of the forest hound's grip. By the Holy Greatsword, this brute was fast and didn't pause once—it was as if he knew this place like the back of his paw. Boulders he swerved around, chasms he skirted, and all the while Schnorbitz threaded his way easily through the halos of firelight and their leaping inhabitants.

But there was a randomness to his transit that made Gapp now realize that Schnorbitz was picking his way not with any particular direction, but simply keeping moving in order to avoid the growling, spitting shapes that were all around them now, for at home in their enviroment, the Jordiske were already beginning to hem their quarry in.

Suddenly a dark shape sprang out from one side, so suddenly that neither boy nor hound had time to anticipate it. Schnorbitz swerved instantly, without a thought, and succeeded in avoiding it, but he could not avoid the slash of talons that scored deeply across his flank. Feeling neither pain nor fear, he plunged on. There were further looming shapes in the semidarkness all about them, and all the boy could do now was to put his trust in his savior.

After a few terrifying minutes, Gapp became aware that there were no longer any globes of firelight to be seen ahead, and the angry sounds of their pursuers were falling away. Moments later, Schnorbitz slowed down, and finally let go of him.

Gapp lurched to his feet and whirled around in alarm, staring into the cold darkness on all sides. He could see nothing, but could still hear much. Above the rapid *drip-drip-drip-drip* of a nearby pool, the clamor of the enraged multitude of Jordiske was getting closer with every second.

"Schnorbitz, you're incredible!" he gasped "You really—"

But Schnorbitz had no time for this. He tugged at the boy's hand, pulling him on. Whether he knew where he was going, he certainly was not going to hang around here. Pausing only to take firm hold of the animal's tail, Gapp stumbled blindly after him through the lightless tunnels.

It was quiet here. Quiet and close. They had left far behind the vast and echoing cavern, with its stinking smoke and stuffiness, and were plunging down some sort of winding passage. It was cold here, with a continual sprinkle of moisture from above, almost like light winter rain.

Was that why the Jordiske were not following them? Because this was not their territory? That seemed highly unlikely to Gapp—only a few minutes away from their heartland? The thought stole chillingly into his heart that they were only being allowed to proceed this way because it would lead to yet more Jordiske.

No, it was something else. It had to be something about this particular tunnel they had by chance found themselves in. Something that frightened even the Jordiske. . . .

No, best not to start thinking along those lines. He was scared enough already.

It was not long before the blackness again began to give way to a pale light. A moment later, he sighed thankfully as he saw the palest glimmer of daylight reflected off the slick, mossy surface of the tunnel wall.

Not hesitating even for a second, he followed Schnorbitz along the final stretch of the passage. Gapp was exhausted, both physically and mentally, from the horrors of the past few hours, and staggered on through a spray of icy water, no longer caring about what lay ahead.

Then he was out.

For a minute or two he could not see a thing. He just stood there blinking in the blinding daylight, gasping and spluttering, hardly able to keep upright. But he could feel the wide space all around him, hear the low moaning of the wind high in the treetops. He breathed in deeply the fragrance of moss and wet leaf mold that mingled so sweetly with the wind-carried smell of far-off rain clouds. It seemed the most beautiful moment he had ever experienced in his life.

Only now did he remember the pain; his face burned so terribly that he wondered if he still had any of it left. He dropped to his knees and convulsively splashed water from an icy rill repeatedly over his searing lacerations, flushing every last trace of the vile unguent from their raw and ragged pinkness until he was sure they were purged of their corrosive torment.

He still did not know where he was. The brilliance of the unaccustomed light had abated somewhat, and familiar shapes were coming into view, but everything remained blurred, out of focus. . . .

Again his hands went up to his face, and he groaned in dismay. He should have known it. After all that face-raking, the Jordiske may not have torn his features away, but they had succeeded in ripping off his spectacles.

But I'm alive, he breathed. And that was all that mattered.

"Schnorbitz," he croaked, his smile broadening as his watering eyes began to adjust, "you're a miracle—a complete miracle!"

He leaned heavily against the wall of the cave mouth, and paused for a moment to enjoy the warmth of the setting sun upon his chilled body.

"I don't know how you did it, by Scytha I don't . . . but I think I'm in love with you."

The rancid, smoky, sweaty odor from his garments drifted up his nose, and reminded him of the stifling pit from which he had been delivered. He chose to ignore the memory of it, but could not suppress a shiver at the sudden coldness he felt.

Suddenly his eyes snapped open fully, and looked straight into the eyes of the creature in front of him.

It was not a Jordiske.

That he could see at a glance, even with blurred vision. About the same height as he himself, if a little slighter of build, the creature was staring back at him without any movement whatsoever. At first Gapp thought it was a Polg, recalling what he had seen of the few of that race that had passed through Nordwas. But no, it was apparent that this was more animal than person . . . probably.

Though standing on two legs, it did so with a slightly hunched posture, not entirely unlike a Jordiske. Its feet were large and splayed, it had a long prehensile tail that flicked nervously like a hunting cat's, and its hide was sparsely coated in mottled brown, curly hair. Its large and pointed ears moved independently of each other, trembling slightly at the tips. And it met Gapp's stare with eyes as large and green as apples.

In one tiny, clawed fist it held a short spear, little more than a sharpened stick. Other than that, and an ancient leather pouch strapped about its waist, it carried no possessions, nor wore any clothes. Though it did not look as threatening as a cave network full of Jordiske, the Southerner was afforded little assurance.

"Schnorbitz!" he called out. ". . . Schnorbitz?"

But Schnorbitz was not there. Gapp glanced around hurriedly, still trying to focus on the blurred shapes that swam into view. Squinting hard, he saw that he had emerged into a small grove, ringed about by low rocks, but otherwise open to the forest.

"Schnorbitz!" he snapped. "What are you doing? Come here!"

Schnorbitz was sniffing around at the cave mouth still. He was clearly as aware of the newcomer as was Gapp, but hardly gave it a passing glance. The hound seemed more interested in the scuttling movements among the dead leaves than with their new guest.

Cool . . . the boy observed. He turned back to the creature. Both regarded each other in silence, neither prepared to make the first move. Eventually, however, the "half-person" seemed satisfied (after much sniffing and cocking its head) and carefully backed away. It moved with slow, painstaking care, all the while trembling—or rather vibrating—like a bat.

It suddenly raised one hand to its mouth and produced a sharp whistle—some form of signal, presumably—which bounced off the trees and echoed into the distance. As it did so, Gapp was struck by the semitransparent web of skin that joined its raised upper arm to its side. This was not so much like a bat's wing, more like the membrane of a flying squirrel. Gapp stared in fascination; he could not quite bring himself to believe this thing could actually fly. . . .

They both continued to stand there, quietly waiting. Again it put its fingers to its mouth, but this time Gapp did not hear a thing. Schnorbitz, however, whined irritably, and growled at the creature in sharp rebuke.

Moments later, several more of them detached themselves from the surrounding foliage, and moved to stand next to their kin. Gapp stepped back in alarm. They seemed to have materialized out of nowhere. Twelve of them, he now counted, all standing motionlessly before him, watching him guardedly, weapons unraised but at the ready. Some wore ill-fitting tunics of wool and fur, probably taken from humans or Polgs, but most stood "sky-clad." All carried short spears, but some in addition to this held simple bows, blowpipes, and, in one case, a bola.

The oddest thing, though, was that none of them paid any attention to the huge forest hound that had struck such terror into an entire clan of Jordiske. Thoughts of Yulfric and his words earlier that day (was it really only that same day?) suddenly came back to the nervous Aescal youth:

". . . there are others . . . that are not so shy . . . The riverbanks are the haunt of the Vetterim. They are a strange race, one that have never bothered me, but one that I have always felt pressing in . . . a fleeting glimpse . . . a shadow in the trees . . ."

Well, they were certainly more than fleeting glimpses or shadows now, but whether they intended to "bother" Gapp on this occasion, he could only wait and see.

Ah, Yulfric, he sighed, *why can't you be here now? You'd know what to do.* . . .

He wondered then if either he or the dog would ever see Yulfric again, and the thought that they might not sent a chill running through his body. He had grown used to the towering strength of the Gyger these last few weeks, and now without him he felt dismally alone.

Now there was only the dog.

Please, Schnorbitz, he prayed, eyeing the great beast in all its equanimity as it continued snuffling through the dead leaves, *stick with me—you're all I've got now.*

The first Vetter that he had encountered now advanced, and pointed its spear directly at Gapp's chest.

"Schnorbitz!" the boy spat, and finally whipped out the sickle-headed fruit-pruner that he had never had a chance to use on the Jordiske. At the same time he flattened himself back against the rock wall.

But neither the Vetter nor the hound reacted, or seemed in the slightest bit impressed by his defiance. Gapp was beginning to wonder if he were mistaken about Schnorbitz's loyalty to him. In the caves he had seemed a veritable myrmidon, but now, so far away from his master . . .

Judging by the easy they were with each other, he could have sworn Schnorbitz and the Vetters had encountered each other before.

He turned his attention back to the Vetter leader—if this assumption was right. Behind it, the rest of the Vetter brigade drew back slightly and parted, as if to let the boy through.

He gave them all, including the dog, a long, hard stare.

After a while, he felt satisfied that they meant him no immediate harm. If they had, surely they would have done something by now; his fruit-pruner was not, after all, the most terrifying weapon in the world. They looked neither evil nor threatening; it could well be that they were just curious. And they would probably be more favorably inclined toward him if he permitted himself to be led away than if he continued to stand his ground with a weapon in front of him.

Taking a deep breath, he slid the pruner back in place and went with them.

With Schnorbitz following happily behind, Gapp Radnar the esquire from the South was led through the forest into a deepening gloom. Despite this he found that his trepidation was beginning to lessen. Whatever happened, he sensed, the Vetterim could not be anything like as evil as the Jordiske. But still he let his hand rest lightly on the haft of the pruner, for his own assurance more than for any realistic protection, and the Vetters seemed happy to allow it.

The journey lasted well over an hour, taking Gapp through an entirely new territory to that which he had seen on his journey from Yulfric's home. For, though he did not know it yet, his jaunt through the caverns behind the waterfall had not only taken him over to the other side of the river, it had also brought him out on the far side of the mountain and on this northern side the terrain was a different kettle of fish altogether.

The trees here were truly massive. Their trunks measured up to twenty feet in diameter at the base, and soared up to inconceivable heights. Indeed, their tops were nowhere to be seen, lost to sight in a dense canopy, far above, that screened away all daylight. Down below everything was cloaked in darkness like eternal night, and what little light did somehow filter through illumined a dim, eerie, alien world.

This was a world of saucerlike eyes that glowed luminously in the dark; a world where roamed ants large enough to carry off a man, but were too heavy to move as fast; it was a place where spiders built traps large enough to ensnare a buffalo, and hung cobwebs from the higher branches that were long enough to reach the forest floor, swaying like pale phantoms in the gloom; it was the home of worms and beetles large enough to roar, and snakes the size of a small dragon. Invisible fliers—truly invisible, not merely experts at camouflage— silently winged their way through the trees, navigating spaces between the trunks barely wide enough to allow the passage of these ghostly, sylvan manta rays. It was a murky, prehistoric world where Man was not permitted, and even the Vetterim huddled furtively like fugitives.

Even the sound here was not of the world Gapp knew. Roars from many miles away could often be heard as though they were close by; clicks, squeaks, and moans might be amplified, or deadened, seemingly at the whim of the forest, so that it could never be discerned for sure how far away lay their source. There was a Spirit to these woods far more ancient and powerful than anywhere else in Fron-Wudu, and the ghosts were not of humankind.

So it came as a great surprise to Gapp when he heard the sound of music from just up ahead.

Music—jolly and energetic, the kind that immediately made one want to dance and sing. The Vetters visibly brightened, lightened, and stopped looking so nervous; they quickened their pace, eager rather than anxious now, to reach the source of those sprightly tunes. Gapp glanced across at Schnorbitz, and saw that he too seemed to have shaken off the air of grim alertness that had settled on him for the duration of their trek.

It appeared that they had reached the Vetters' lair. A narrow track between the ferns led down a steep bank; in the forest gloom it was difficult to see beyond that. But there did appear to be an intenser patch of darkness up ahead. A wall of darkness, to be more accurate. Gapp again glanced at Schnorbitz, but he could read nothing of the hound's mood.

On reaching this dark barrier he discovered that they had come upon a line of trees growing very close together. These were not in a straight line by any means, and were of all shapes and sizes, some even growing into one another, but there was something in their arrangement that hinted strongly at *purpose,* at conscious design. They were as colossal as any of the mighty trees Gapp had already beheld on his journey here, and were clearly very ancient, so if they *had* been planted as a stockade wall, just how long had the Vetterim been settled here, he wondered.

The gaps between them, such as there were, had been skillfully barricaded by sturdy walls of logs lashed tightly together, and overgrown with a specially cultivated hedge of some unknown variety of creeping plant. Over the centuries these walls had been gradually compressed even tighter by the growth of the massive boles, so they now surely constituted as solid a defensive wall as could be found anywhere in the world.

The party of hunters headed up to one section of this gargantuan sylvan bastion wall from which, Gapp noticed, one of the creepers had been pulled away, and tied around a nearby pine. From this tendril hung a line of drying laundry, and right by the wall itself they could make out a large mat with several pairs of sandals on it.

It was from the total darkness just beyond that two sentinels now emerged. They hailed the returning patrol in low, guttural tones, and beckoned them forward.

"R'rreui htoau auell! Qaeu sss theua!"

"Aanyo goiyou R'rrahdh-Kyinne!"

Gapp regarded these newly encountered Vetters in surprise, as he was led on; the last thing he had expected from these Polg-faced weasels was such goblinesque voices.

One of the two sentinels approached the largest trunk and rapped out a quick message on its bark with the blunt end of his spear. After a brief pause, his signal was answered from within by another rapid message thudding hollowly. The sentinel cocked an ear diligently, then in turn followed it up with a third cipher. A moment later there was a *snik,* and a narrow portal opened up before them. Through it seeped a soft, yellow light, and the joyful music suddenly grew a little louder.

On entering, Gapp was surprised to find not a narrow, roughly hewn tunnel leading through the trunk, but quite a capacious room inside. It was well lit by lanterns, and furnished in an orderly if somewhat spartan manner. Apart from the inner door ward who had let them in, it was currently occupied by three other Vetters, one of whom, judging by the surprisingly ornate footwear, Gapp presumed to be a female, and the other clearly a child. All three came up to the returning party and welcomed them warmly by stroking their underarm webs between their fingers, and alternately patting them rapidly on the head.

As soon as they set eyes on the human at the door, they all froze and simply gaped. The child gave a short, croaky gurgle and scuttled away behind the female's legs. The hunters made a purring noise that could have been a laugh, next indicating to the wayfarer that he should take his sodden boots off, then ushered him inside.

His bare feet fell upon the soft, dry, luxuriantly spongy wood chips that bestrew the floor. They filled the air with a clean, domestic fragrance that induced in the boy a sudden surge of homesickness. (The wood chips, not his feet.) Other items too in this guardhouse reminded him of what he had left behind;

sturdy oaken benches, some with old sandals piled beneath—beeswax candles set in niches around the walls—racks filled with spears, bows, and even the odd clothesline pole—a sheet of pulped inner bark pinned to the wall, crudely adorned in crayon with the image of two big Vetters and one little one, all standing smiling atop a tree with a big yellow sun just above their heads.

Steps carved into the inside wall of the tree-hole gatehouse wound their way up until they disappeared from view through a hole leading to a platform above. On the opposite side of the room were a doorway and two circular windows. The thick door, hung on leather hinges, was propped open by a wedge. It was through there that the music came. Though curious to find out where the little staircase led to, Gapp was escorted through the open doorway instead . . .

. . . Out into a world that might well have come straight from the most fabulous tales of the Herbal Storytellers of Friy.

After the darksome forest, Gapp was about to find himself wandering through a world of light, sound, and movement that grew brighter and noisier with every few steps he progressed. The farther he went, the more he would realize he had not entered some secret lair, but an entire *town*.

From the other side of the trunk, they had emerged on to a stony path that was fenced along both sides by heavy barricades of hedge-grown planking. The Vetters had indicated that he could now put his boots back on before they set off down the lane. A short distance along it reached the base of two great karsts of rock, and thence continued along the narrow cleft running between them.

Down this "street" he was escorted, past the open doorways and windows of the cave houses that had been tunneled into them. Most seemed empty, or at least too dark for a prying stranger to see what exotic things might lie within. Some, however, were lit by oil lamps, and inside them Gapp caught brief, tantalizing glimpses of huddled figures scraping hide, building fires, or scrubbing floors. From other windows the occupants leaned, smoking pipes and scratching their tree-rat pets fondly behind the ears. As Gapp passed, they stared agog at this outlandish creature the hunters had brought back with them.

Then the lane exited the narrow cleft and opened into a world that no living man had ever seen, or heard of, or even dreamt about before.

Gapp felt as if suddenly assailed by a tide of dancing lights and shapes, weird and exotic odors, and a head-spinning array of unguessable noises. Here was a world filled with things that not even the wildest, tallest, most exaggerated tales of the most imaginative soldier of fortune could ever encompass.

Gapp's first impression of the main town was one of bewilderment and confusion; the light was wrong, the dimensions did not make sense, and gravity appeared to have taken a day off. How he wished he had not lost his spectacles! To his dazzled eyes, there appeared to be trees sprouting out of houses, houses sprouting out of trees, houses *within* trees, and jagged rock karsts, pinnacles, knolls, and pillars all covered in trees, covered in houses, or excavated *into* houses. Between all these, Vetters thronged any open spaces, glided through the air from higher places, climbed down tree ladders from their tops to their bases, ran along walkways with gleeful faces, and in all cases put the poor traveler through his paces.

Too much, he thought, *too much.* . . . He just could not take it all in. His eyes went up, and up, and up, and no matter how far up he looked, still there seemed to be yet more up, each hut, tree house, rope bridge, and escarpment house picked out and defined by the multitude of torches, lanterns, candles, and sun-catching crystals that adorned them. He felt that he was standing at the bottom of the world's most enormous, verdant, and overpopulated well. It was astonishing, weird, unreal and dreamlike all once, and within seconds he was forced to lower his gaze right back down to earth, to focus on normal *ground* level, in order to recover some sanity.

Instead of trying to take in everything at once, Gapp concentrated on one thing at a time, disentangling the thousands of images and sensations that were flashing through his brain, until such time as his befuddled senses could sort themselves into some coherent order.

He was eventually brought to a wide open space amid great pillars of rock, wherein Vetters constantly darted this way and that, some across the ground itself and some gliding above. There were fewer trees here, mainly of smaller, deciduous varieties, each supporting a couple of tree houses reached by solid-looking wooden ladders, or sometimes just a single rope. Here and there were much larger trees, wide enough lower down the trunk to be hollowed out to provide dwellings for several families. Though there were merely one or two portals at the base of such giants, lights shone from countless windows as high as fifty feet up the trunk.

Freestanding, there were long, low huts constructed of wood or stone, all glowing inside with candlefire in a rainbow of colors. All with a partial growth of moss covering them, these huts looked almost as ancient as the gargantuan trees that barricaded the town. They had a definite air of permanency to them.

But still, for the most part, the Vetterim appeared to prefer dwelling in the cave houses that had been hollowed out into just about every available rock surface in sight. Everywhere, single conical pinnacles rose like termite mounds, pocked with doors, windows, ledges, and smoke holes. The cliffs of the numerous karsts were even more densely populated, with innumerable abodes occupying the entire surface from top to bottom, some of these only visible as openings in the jungle of vegetation trailing from above. At street level these were clearly the shops and workplaces of tradesmen and artisans.

Many of these trades were instantly recognizable to the young Aescal: builders, brewers, carpenters, coopers, tanners, weavers, potters, fletchers . . . But there were others whose business he could only guess at: mushroom "processors," frog-fat renderers, resin-caulkers, tree-rat trainers, snake-slitters, cane-splitters, bark-oasters, strobile-roasters, and "living-rope" growers.

From the regular sound of metal ringing upon metal that was audible above the general hubbub of music, laughter, shouting, creaking, bubbling, sawing, and seething, it would appear that there was also a blacksmith of sorts operationg somewhere in town. By Gapp's estimation, this unique Vetter smith must surely have just about the highest social standing in the whole community, and a similar recognition that in human towns would have been accorded a great magician.

Each workshop emanated an odor all of its own, but over all, amid this churning cauldron of sights and sounds, wafted the dizzying aroma of Vetter-Home in general, a unique blend of honeycomb, sweat, blossom, urine, broiling, burning, yeast, and dung, and probably a hundred other unidentifiable scents that in Gapp's mind created that very essence of all things "foreign."

Had he realized just how gormless he must appear, standing there gazing at the scene with his mouth open, Gapp might well have felt extremely self-conscious. As it was, as soon as his escort interrupted his trance by goading him on with a pointed stick, he suddenly became aware that a hundred pairs of eyes were now fixed upon him, and he did begin to feel extremely self-conscious.

At every step he took, Gapp was met with instant astonishment from every green-eyed, whiskered face. As soon as the company appeared, whatever the townsfolk were currently engaged in was now completely forgotten. They just dropped everything, including their jaws, and gaped at this freak in utter amazement.

It then occurred to the traveler that he was probably the first human that they had ever seen. He must appear as bizarre to them as a creature from another world would to him. He tried reaching out to some of them gently with an open palm, a gesture he considered to be beyond misinterpretation. This was, however, instantly misinterpreted, and greeted only with swift recoiling, baring of fangs, and, in the most extreme case, screaming headlong flight.

Word spread like wildfire, and soon crowds of onlookers were thronging the narrow streets and marketplaces. Faces peered out of windows, gliders swooped low, and before long there was a steady stream of traffic moving along ledges, walkways, and bridges at every level. Those on the ground, though, kept a respectful but obvious distance, which though at first was welcome to Gapp, soon, oddly enough, he began to find slightly irksome.

During his progress through their town, Gapp was able to get a better look at the Vetterim. (He had already become used to their scent, a musty, meaty odor that seemed both human and animal at the same time.) Now that he could see so many of them all together, he began to notice differences. The ones that had brought him here were mostly fully-grown adults and probably all male, but there were clearly as many types of Vetter as there were types of human. Clothing clearly defined one's standing in this society; some wore short fur capes, with perhaps a belt or pouch; others were almost fully clothed; others still were naked, displaying a full coat of body hair in an infinite variety of color, length, thickness, and style.

(It came as little surprise to Gapp to see that the ones that appeared to be held in the lowest esteem of all were those with patchy curls of red hair. Some things, it seemed, were the same the world over.)

There were even one or two heavier ones wearing a variety of light armor consisting of a leather tabard embellished with crudely fashioned rings and plates of bronze.

He was just starting to get used to the idea of Vetters themselves when Gapp realized that these exotic creatures shared their world with other out-landish races. A group of much taller figures now came pushing through the crowds, bobbing strangely as they proceeded. At first he did not know what he was seeing, but as they drew nearer he could see that these newcomers made the Vetters look almost normal by comparison.

What were they? Gapp screwed up his eyes and halted his escort. *What by Jugg's Udders were those things?*

Taller than any man, these creatures looked more and yet at the same time *less* like humans than did the Vetterim. From the neck upward they were more or less manlike; like a cross between a long-faced Polg and a rat-faced human, they had light brown, hairless skin that was finely needled with tattoos, long, straight black hair, and a fine goatee beard. In addition they had a growth of curly brown hair encircling neck and throat and, strikingly, a single black ivory horn, as long and sharp as a scimitar protruding straight up from the forehead.

Below the neck, though, was where it all started to get really weird. The torso was basically like that of a man, but it sloped out forward from the hips and started to look like some kind of herd animal. Though with only two legs, these resembled closely the hind legs of a deer, long and powerful, with three velvet toes on great, splayed feet. The arms were more human-looking but ter-minated in only three big clumsy fingers, as if they could double up as an extra pair of legs when greater speed was needed.

Finally, they possessed huge, muscular, rodentlike tails that looked as if they could break a man's spine with one flick.

Those creatures peered down upon both the boy and his dog companion through slitted eyes, and began gabbling among themselves like asses. They pounded the ends of their spears upon the ground in agitation, and one or two of them began to push a little too close for comfort.

Gapp was becoming decidedly fraught. He had barely had time to get over his horrifying experience with the Jordiske, and all the weirdness since then, together with this undercurrent of "pointy-spear" violence, had brought him close to the end of his tether. Within the first few minutes of his entering this town, his mind had gradually retreated into some kind of dreamlike state from which he could observe everything in detached safety, as though reading a sto-rybook. But the crowds and the mood was becoming too intense, bringing his

real world sharply back into focus. He put a reassuring hand upon the shoulder of the forest hound at his side, but that reassured neither himself nor
Schnorbitz. The hound, even less used to crowds than he was, and who clearly
hated all the lights, smoke, and congestion, made a few defensive lunges at the
onlookers. It was all snarls, bared teeth, and raised hackles really, intended
only to keep them at arm's length, but it immediately invoked a flurry of hostility, especially among the horn-heads. It was all the boy could do to restrain the
animal before they attacked him.

More than anything, Gapp now wished he had the meditation wheel with
him rather than this great snarling beast.

Just as things were getting ugly, Gapp and Schnorbitz were hurried away,
and after much jostling and growling from their escorts, finally left the
ground—and the bulk of the crowd—below. A narrow, creaking staircase
wound up and around the trunk of a huge tree and took them high up amid its
boughs.

Everywhere around him Gapp could see ledges and platforms, some ringing the entire trunk, others merely jutting out like giant fungal growths. Rope
bridges connected every bough, fragile-looking things that hung precariously.
Huts nestled in the crook of the major boughs, squatted upon sturdy platforms, or hung suspended from "living ropes." There seemed to be no end to
the ways in which the Vetterim had endeavored to create the most ingenious,
elaborate town that their cunning little minds could conceive.

They came eventually to a herbalist's stall located on a small platform, but
hurried on without delay, for its occupants drooled and grinned too widely,
and kept trying to touch not only the newcomers but their escort too. Gapp
was reminded of the more imbecilic Peladanes seen on weekend nights at Wintus Hall.

Out onto a rope bridge they came. Swaying alarmingly, they were led up
and along this, toward the top of a conical "termite-mound" pinnacle, where
the other end of the bridge was anchored. This pinnacle was clearly the hub of
a concourse of walkways, ledges, and other rope bridges that radiated out from
it like strands of silk. It was also taking them, Gapp could not help but notice,
rather high up, and as his weak eyes gazed at the many pathways that fanned
out from its center, all hung with twinkling lamps and torches, it seemed to
him that he was entering an impossible spider's web of dazzling light, while he
was the fly that was plucking its strings upon this bouncing bridge.

The remaining crowd were, as ever, right behind him.

From this focal concourse, they continued along a new bridge, this time a
rigid construction of timber suspended on thick ropes. This rickety and swaying thoroughfare climbed up to a liplike promontory of rock halfway up the
cliff face of an enormous karst, and straight into the cave mouth beyond. Deep
into the karst their route continued, into a labyrinth of passages all brightly lit,
lined with homes and workshops, and thronged with yet more staring Vetters.

Ever upward they went, until finally they came out onto the tabletop plateau crowning the summit of the karst. Gapp breathed in the fresh, fragrant air deeply, and looked around. And stopped breathing.

No, he thought in slow awe, *that pinnacle-concourse is not the center of this world at all. . . .*

He could see that little anthill way below, now no more than a nub of rock amid a web of lights. *This* had to be the center of all things in Vetter-Home, and he stared all around him at the most surreal and wonderful place that any man would ever see.

Right at the bottom and encircling the entire town he could just about make out the great, dark line of the tree-and-fence barricade. Beyond that all was darkness, but within light shone from every house, hut, and highway within the stockade, not just at ground level, or from the trees and knolls rising above them—though still far below—but from the karsts that rose far above even these, and from all around him, and then farther up still toward the enormous trees that grew upon this lofty plateau; and amid these, soaring up to heights that craned the neck painfully, was a single pinnacle of rock that struck upward into the heavens like a spike in a crown: the highest point in Vetter-Home.

Though no book had ever mentioned any place like this, nor any skald or traveler spoken of it, had they tried to do so, their words would have failed utterly to do it justice.

Compared with this fabulous place, Gapp's hometown of Nordwas looked very flat and mundane indeed.

Far above the roof of the forest, the plateau seemed a lonely and verdant garden of celestial tranquility, a world set apart from anything else. Through those enormous trees, the like of which grew nowhere else in Lindormyn, the hunters guided their two charges. Ancient moss hung from gnarled bark pocked with thousands of holes, the homes of squirrels, tree frogs, snakes, and even a black, long-tailed primate that could be seen scuttling all over the higher places of this lofty domain.

The bulk of the crowds had fallen behind them now, or had simply drifted off. The small party was left to continue through the trees, passing under arches formed by huge external roots, until they finally came to the central pinnacle.

There was only one doorway, a great tunnel carved into the base of the rock. Suspended above it was a half-open portcullis-like gate, fabricated from some kind of immensely hard ironwood, and overgrown with tough, fibrous creepers sprouting little pink flowers. A stone ramp led up to it, and there were a few lightly armored hunters sitting around nearby. These all stopped their game of pine-rods when the party approached, and stared at them as they went past, but made no attempt to stop them.

Despite the strength of this place (or perhaps because of it) it was with a definite sense of relief that Gapp passed into the cool, dark sanctuary of the gatehouse. He entered also with that strange feeling of humility and expectancy one might feel when entering the temple of a foreign god. For this was sacred ground he was on, he could tell—the very heart of Vetterdom. Without needing to be asked, he removed his boots as soon as he entered.

The tunnel sloped gradually upward, and echoed pleasantly to the slap of their feet upon the cold, smooth stone. Along its length it was lit by burning stones, little pale-green pebbles that floated in bowls of a sappy liquid, and purred contentedly as they gave off their weird, elder-scented flame. Placed in niches set at intervals along the length of the passage, they illuminated the benches lined against the walls. These settles were of an intricate design that looked totally alien to the Southerner. Above each of them was a kind of living tapestry, woven from the multicolored tendrils of the plants that grew out of cracks in the walls, into images both wonderful and bizarre. Some depicted the Vetters and their "deer" friends, others showed different creatures of the forest, some looking more like demons, or lizards that had died out aeons before the awakening of Man. Gapp quailed just looking at them.

Engravings and statues of wood and stone there were too, farther along the tunnel. Two in particular stood out among the others, positioned on either side of the large doorway to which he was now being directed. They were *big,* bigger than the largest horse Gapp had ever seen, and stood proudly like guardians at their posts. The detail was incredible, the coloring so lifelike. They appeared as some mythical, fabulous beast that possessed the head, torso, and arms of a Gyger, joined onto the main body of a huge and heavyset stag. Staglike too were the antlers sprouting from each head, their forward-pointing tines sharp for ripping, the back ones curving down to protect the back of the neck. Each long tail ended in a macelike cluster of bony spikes.

Gapp gazed in fascination at these effigies, and marveled at the creative imagination of Vetter artists. But as he was conducted between them into the room beyond, he noticed how both glared at him and flicked their tails menacingly.

Quickly he darted on, his heart hammering. Schnorbitz followed more slowly, hackles raised but his eyes focused dead ahead.

This room beyond was an enormous stairwell, with steps, cut into the wall, that wound up to a distant pool of light far above. The treads were broad and, in the light of the burning green stones, Gapp could see how polished and indented they had become under the passing of millions of feet over the centuries.

During the long climb upward, Gapp studied the strange collection of objects fixed with brackets onto the walls. There were ancient iron helmets, possibly even human ones, antique halberds, collections of coins from lands unknown to the Aescal, several enormous skulls of unknowable lizards, and, rather more grimly, a few skins old and brittle as parchment and decorated with Polg war tattoos.

Trophies, he concluded, *museum pieces that form the Vetters' only knowledge of the outside world. . . .*

Landings and chambers branched off the staircase at frequent intervals, but still they climbed and climbed, until finally, slick with a fresh coating of sweat, Gapp emerged from the stairwell, and stood blinking in the evening light.

They had arrived at the very top of the Vetters' world, on a vast wooden platform built around the conical tip of the pinnacle. Here, it seemed miles up in the sky, all was light and breezy. Gentle, beguiling music, in the songs of countless birds. Color, beauty, and enchantment. The sky so close Gapp felt that he could simply reach out and touch it.

The platform itself was supported by the trees immediately surrounding the pinnacle, and the crowns of these trees thrust up through holes in the floor to give the whole platform the appearance of a beautiful park. Scattered all around the main expanse were sun platforms, crystal-hung gazebos, and belvederes of polished, inlaid wood.

Through the veil of golden-green leaves on the uppermost boughs shone the dwindling rays of a glorious sunset, bathing everything in a soft, cleansing light fragmented in the myriad crystals that hung from every branch. Gapp's knees wobbled, as powerful but unidentified emotions began to well up from the prisons where they had been held within him. Willingly now he allowed himself to be guided through this enchanted treetop paradise, marveling at all he saw. The stresses of that terrible day—a day in which he had almost met his death deep inside the earth—blew away upon the soft wind and were forgotten.

They were heading toward a giant tree that protruded through the platform's western edge. One of its massive branches sloped up and away from the platform and a stairway, with handrails fitted, was carved into the bark of its upper side, leading to some place that he could not yet see.

By now they were so high up that Gapp had the impression he was walking out into space. As he leaned over the railing to take a look down, his stomach heaved when he saw just how high up they were. Gleds and gyrs glided above the treetops underneath, yet so far below that they appeared as mere specks. Even farther beneath them the leaves of the forest roof shimmered constantly in the late evening breeze like an unquiet sea.

It was only the railing that kept him safe, and he thrust himself away from it in panic. This whole place suddenly seemed insane, impossible, ready to topple at any minute. Every creak and scrape of ancient wood seemed to presage imminent disaster.

On his hands and knees now, his fingers gripped the wood of the stairway like the toe pads of a gecko. It felt firm, and had the smoothness of antiquity. Breathing deeply, he slowly got a grip on himself, and forced down his panic.

The hunters halted and stood regarding him quizzically, unable to understand what ailed him.

Unimaginative beggars! he thought resentfully, and rose to his feet again.

Now that they were near the end of the branch, he saw there was a kind of pavilion up here. Another of the huge Gyger-stags stood guarding the door, but it let them through with only a slight glimmer of hostility in its eyes.

Inside, though hardly palatial, the pavilion gave the undeniable impression that here lived some kind of royalty. The extensive variety of furs and pelts hanging from every wall, door and furnishing, demonstrated without doubt that this was the abode of, as Gapp put it, "someone very high up."

They passed through to a large room at the back of the structure. Here light streamed in from the open balcony, silhouetting the shape of a solitary Vetter leaning against the balustrade. It was staring out at the magnificent view, as a red sun cast its last light over the great forest of Fron-Wudu. With reluctance, it tore itself away from this vista of unimaginable beauty, and turned to face its guests.

Gapp was surprised to discover that this important Vetter looked just like any other. It was slightly taller than most, with a relaxed and confident bearing, but it did not differ in any drastic way from the rank and file. There was no sign of disdain or arrogance, none of the irony or superciliousness that the young esquire had come to associate with social leaders. Neither were there any outward indications of exceptional wisdom or intellect. The thing Gapp noticed most was the eyes: there was an openness, even friendliness, in them that he instantly warmed to.

"R'rrahdh-Kyinne, aanyo!" it gurgled at the leader of the hunters, then turned to Gapp. "Hal, Mycel-Haug!" it rasped, extending its hand in greeting. "Hal dhu Vetterheime ut Cyne-Tregva!"

It enunciated the words carefully, in a way that made Gapp wonder; either it was not sure the boy would understand, or itself did not speak this language fluently. But it was clear to him that this was a greeting of sorts, so he held his hand out in a similar fashion and, smiling broadly, replied:

"Hal Vetter. Me Gapp Radnar. This Schnorbitz." He next pointed to his mouth, then to the Vetter, and shook his head, as if to say: *I don't speak the language.*

A high-pitched laugh escaped the Vetter's lips, and this was echoed by the hunters (a little more gutturally). The leader repeated Gapp's gestures in reverse in a resigned way, as though saying, *Neither do I very well.* He stepped forward and clasped Gapp's hand warmly. Clearly the boy had made a favorable first impression.

It seemed that this was not the Vetters' tongue after all. Gapp thought it sounded vaguely familiar, though he could not think where he had heard it before. Some trading language employed by the Vetterim, perhaps?

The leader, still clasping Gapp's hand, dragged him out of the pavilion and back down the length of the branch stairway to the platform below. The hunters followed, and Schnorbitz kept close. Gapp was hoping that after this initial friendly encounter he and his companion would receive some hospitality in the form of food and drink. But clearly there were more pressing matters at hand. Gapp could only wonder.

Across the platform they went, and soon arrived at a belvedere positioned on the northwest curve of the platform's outer rim. It was guarded by four sentinels, lightly armored but heavily armed, who were currently relaxing at a foot of the short ladder that led up to an open doorway. They beamed at the company approaching, then stood aside to let them ascend.

Seated at a table all alone was someone that the leader seemed very eager Gapp should meet.

Dressed in soiled white rags and covered in bandages, the stranger slowly, stiffly, turned around. Hands bedecked with antique golden rings reached up and pulled the hood away from his face.

"Hello, Radnar," he said in cool surprise. "I thought you were dead. . . ."

It was Methuselech Xilvafloese.

12

Cyne-Tregva

"You . . ." Gapp breathed.

Gapp's hazy vision swayed, and with it his equilibrium. The entire platform seemed to be moving beneath his feet, lurching as though being tipped over slowly by relentless gust of wind.

No! Not that!

A small hand gripped him by the arm, held him steady, and slowly Gapp's world regained some stability.

He looked into the big, green eyes of the Vetter hunter—R'rrahdh-Kyinne, his name was—and saw no alarm there, only concern for his new charge.

What had happened just then? Had there been a gust of wind? Had the platform really lurched?

A lightness filled Gapp's head. None of this felt real anymore. He could not even be sure what he was seeing now. If only he could *focus* properly again. . . .

Xilvafloese? He did not yet believe it, but . . . it was true. Methuselech Xilvafloese was sitting in front of him, as large as life. A little battered and torn, and all the luster gone out of his raiment, as though he had been used as a rag to slop out a latrine, but alive, and by the look of it, kicking.

"You're here . . ." the boy said with a congested croak to his voice and an asinine gape to his mouth.

In that one moment, all that had gone before—all those tortured miles of suffering, abandonment and fear, all the tribulation that had befallen him along the way, indeed the entire memory of his separation from the company—all was forgotten. He staggered over to his comrade and, to the clear delight of the Vetter chief (and applause from the hunters), embraced him closely.

It was as if he and his former companions had never been sundered.

Methuselech, however, winced in discomfort, and gently eased the boy away from him.

"Oh Shogg, your injuries . . . I forgot," Gapp apologized.

Methuselech merely forced a smile, with hooded eyes. "Take a seat," he ordered, gesturing toward one of the nearby stools, sounding surprisingly calm.

Gapp did as he was told. The Vetter and his hunters did likewise, and watched the scene with undisguised fascination.

Gapp paused a second to appraise his quest-mate. The man looked far worse, now he came to think of it, than when he had last seen him. That beautiful head of hair now looked as though he had spiked it with horse dung, as the barbarians did, and most of the braids once decorating his hood had come off. In all, he resembled a half-plucked, hedge-dragged buzzard.

"But, Methuselech," he said, his voice as small again as it had been before the separation, "I don't understand this at all. . . . How is it you come to be here? Have you been tracking me all this way? That is—"

"Have *I* been tracking *you*? You sure you got that the right way round?"

"What? But that horrible place in the mountains . . ." Gapp was completely at a loss. He half-expected to wake up any moment and discover this was all a dream. "And the others, did you find them? Are they here too?"

Methuselech rose stiffly to his feet—followed by the boy and the Vetters—and laid an untidily bandaged hand upon Gapp's shoulder. "Boy," he said, "I am in as much perplexity on that subject as are you, but our stories will have to wait. There is someone here who would like an explanation."

He pointed to the Vetter chief, who all this time had said not a word. "For the past week now, I have been under the care of Cynen Englarielle Rampunculus," he explained. "As you too are now, and I'd guess he would like a little chat about us."

Gapp had temporarily forgotten that the Vetter and his world existed.

"I'm sorry," he stammered, turning to the chief, and bowing quickly.

Then the leader moved over and joined them. Gapp glanced doubtfully at Englarielle, then whispered, "Xilva, I don't speak his language, I doubt I can make myself understood."

"That is exactly why he brought you to me," the mercenary replied. "I *do* speak his language. Or at least, we share a common tongue. The Vetters' language is unique, unknown to the rest of the world. Not that you could expect otherwise, really, since this is a rather isolated spot. But they do seem to have had some minimal contact with the outside world . . . The Polgrim? It appears those adventurous little wayfarers have paid a few visits to Cyne-Tregva over the centuries, and there is still a certain tie between the two races, albeit a somewhat tenuous one nowadays. The Vetter chiefs—the Cynen—are brought up to speak an elementary form of the Polg's 'Rainflat' dialect. It's a sort of trading language, if you like, but 'court-language' might be more accurate. . . ."

As Methuselech talked on, Gapp began to feel the agitation tighten within him. He had gone almost past the limits of his mind and body today. Why was Methuselech going on about all this stuff when he could just as easily be telling him how he came to be here? The boy was not expecting a detailed account; just one sentence would suffice.

A slight sigh of irritation and impatience escaped him. Why didn't *any*one tell him *any*thing, *ever*? Was he still that unimportant to them? He saw the look in Methuselech's eyes as the mercenary prattled on about what *he* wanted to talk about—oblique, offhand, not even looking at Gapp directly—and realized that in spite of *all* he had gone through to be here, he was still just the esquire. . . .

Images of his siblings' mocking smiles came back to him. A silly little boy. A complete prat. Of course, how could he be so stupid as to think it would ever be otherwise?

". . . Anyway," Methuselech was saying, "it seems I'm to act as your translator. I don't suppose Englarielle even realized that we knew each other, up till now. . . . But then I doubt he has any idea how many humans there are in the world out there, or even the slightest inkling of just how big the world is, for that matter—"

"You don't speak Polgrim," the boy cut in irately.

Methuselech regarded him indignantly. "I speak Aescalandian, do I not? Remember, boy, I am from Qaladmir, the city of a thousand tribes. We speak many tongues."

But Rainflat-Polgrim . . . ?

"Anyway," the mercenary declared, obviously impatient with the lad's wittering, "we mustn't waste time like this. I think the Cynen's getting a little impatient."

So, with the help of Methuselech, Gapp related his story to the royal Vetter. And, in doing so, enlightened his old companion. He began at first to tell tales of a mission to Wrythe, then switched to the truth after Methuselech informed him that he had already disclosed their real mission earlier. (This alarmed Gapp, but he assumed the mercenary must know what he was doing.) He told of Nym, of his fall down the well, and of his subsequent ordeal in the subterranean tunnels, until finally emerging and befriending the forest giant Yulfric. At this, Englarielle smiled and nodded—the Gyger was clearly known to him and his people. Then Gapp went on to describe how he had been waylaid by the Jordiske, and how he finally escaped, only to fall into the hands of the Vetterim. The Cynen showed particular interest in Gapp's description of the lair of the Jordiske, and questioned him at length, wanting to know every detail.

But as the air grew frigid and the night sky rolled over, he seemed satisfied. Making a rasping noise between his fingers, he summoned a flunky, and issued orders for a sleeping pad to be made up for their new guest, and for food and wine to be fetched.

At blinking last, thought Gapp. He was famished.

After finishing a large meal of some shredded, pale, pulpy stuff that smelled like peppery flowers, Gapp washed himself in the wooden basin provided for him, and then begged leave to rest. His sleeping pad was in the same place as his companion's: the wide, roofed veranda of that same belvedere. Several Vetters had been posted in the adjoining room "just in case they needed anything," and Schnorbitz took up his position in the doorway between these two rooms. For the first time since he had left Yulfric's house, the boy felt he could sleep safely.

It felt so good to recline upon clean furs, to be free from clinging dirt, and to be back with his own kind—and, moreover, one of the company—again. He looked about himself through drowsy eyes.

A single, sard-flamed oil lamp sat on the floor planking, and sent up its thread-line of herbal smoke to curl among the sprigs of dried grasses and ericaceous flowers that hung from the crossbeam above. The ocean of trees moaned far below, and a soft wind sighed through the gently creaking frame of the hut. Methuselech was leaning on the railing of the veranda, either gazing out over the lands below or staring up at the stars. The light of the full moon bathed the whole room in a clean white light, and laved the visage of the mercenary in a wash of death-white sharp shadows that shrouded his eyes.

Come to think of it, Gapp considered, here he felt as safe as he had even in the loft of his family's house. Safer, perhaps, for he did not believe the desert warrior would get up in the middle of the night and sprinkle him with urine, or put stag beetles in his socks, as his brothers often did. He looked up at his companion, and studied him.

"Xilva," he said eventually, stifling a yawn, "you still haven't told me anything about the others—why are you here on your own?"

Methuselech was still gazing out at the stars above. He turned away from the balcony, and sat down cross-legged upon his sleeping pad, but remained silent.

"In fact," Gapp persisted, "how are you even here at all? We thought you'd died back there, in that"—*what did Paulus call it?*—"that Sluagh place or something. That sound, that scream, and the awful—"

"I won't talk about it."

Gapp stared at the man in surprise. Methuselech's voice sounded so strange all of a sudden; muted somehow, or "veiled," in a way that passed a cloud over Gapp's soul, though he did not know why. Old Xilva had certainly changed, that was for sure.

But he had to know. "Xilva—what *happened* back there?"

"Are you deaf?" Methuselech cried out shrilly. "I said I won't talk about it, d'you hear? How *dare* you?"

His voice stung Gapp like an acid whiplash of vituperation, and the boy instantly lowered his eyes. He had overstepped the mark, forgotten his rank. But,
beneath his shame, Gapp also shuddered, for he recognized something in his
companion's voice that had never been there before: *hysteria*. It was a tone he
had heard previously among certain war veterans of the Wintus household.
Nibulus had referred to such individuals as half-men, in that they were no
longer wholly of this world, but somewhere between this one and the next. Just
like Paulus's description of the amphibians in the marshes.

Then, as suddenly as he had flared up, Methuselech was back to normal
again, and began relating his story at a point that suited him:

"I followed along the cliff path as soon as there was light enough to see by.
But by the time I reached your camp, you had departed. I tried to catch up, but
my wounds . . . And with each day that passed, the cooler grew your trail. I stumbled on in a daze, trying to find you, any sign at all. I tried for days to find Myst-
Hakel, but in the end I found I had come instead to the marches of Fron-Wudu."

"So you *entered*?" Gapp asked dubiously. "You didn't turn back?"

"By then I'd given up all real hope of finding our companions, alive or
dead. So I continued through the forest. I continued because I *had* to, if I were
ever to get to Melhus."

"What, you went on to Melhus on your *own*?" Gapp exclaimed, not bothering to disguise his incredulity. "In your condition, with no horse or rations?"
His head felt light once more, and there was that lurching feeling beneath him
again. In the silver light of the full moon, his old companion appeared still and
colorless, like those effigies carved on the sarcophagus lids in the vaults of
Wintus Hall.

Methuselech paused for a second, as if reading the esquire's thoughts. Then
he said, "I am not you, young man, remember. I was—still am—driven by great
need. Our quest does not die just because its leaders fall. . . . And, in any case,
there was always the chance of meeting up with the others once again. If I
could reach Wrythe, I might find them there, or be able to wait. . . . or go on after them. There is always *some* hope. I knew how difficult it would be trying to
get through these lands on my own—"

Oh no you didn't, Gapp thought.

"But what choice did I have? Anyway, I stumbled on for several days, the
thought of reaching Wrythe the only thing keeping me going. I traveled along
forest trails guided by instinct alone . . . and of course became hopelessly lost.
Then I met up with a band of hunting Vetters, and the rest you can see for
yourself."

With that, he finished his story, got back to his feet, and went to stare out at
the moonlit forest below.

You gave up trying to find the company at Myst-Hakel, Gapp considered, *to
try and meet up with them at* Wrythe? *No I don't think so, Xilva. . . . You're an*

adventurer, not a zealot—even Wintus told me that, once. The only difference between you and Paulus Flatulus is your loyalty to Nibulus. . . .

"Hmn, perhaps that's it. Maybe it is just loyalty . . ." he muttered to himself. But still he was troubled.

He looked over to the figure of Methuselech again, skull-pale in the cold light of the moon, staring out into the night. The mercenary was gazing northward, and there was a hunger in his eyes.

Despite the overwhelming exhaustion he felt after this longest and most taxing of days, it took Gapp some time to finally drift off. A thousand thoughts and images were still pirouetting around his brain, fizzing and popping like a tubful of wine mulch, and they just would not leave him alone.

Chief among these were his plans. Now that he had become separated from Yulfric, how exactly was he going to get *home*? In some rather weak way, once he had been reunited with his former quest-mate he had felt that these matters were no longer in his hands; Nibulus's friend would be making all the decisions from now. Just as it had been in the beginning. But what the man had been saying about going on to Melhus to complete the quest had troubled Gapp in no small way. He had cast off *that* particular burden during his time with the Gyger, and was not about to take it on again.

Now, however, he did not know what to think.

During the night, Gapp awoke suddenly. He did not know why. There was just some strange presentiment that had jolted him from his slumber. Without getting out of bed he rummaged about in the dark for his spectacles—forgetting they were lost—and had frozen rigid when his searching hand had fallen upon someone's knee, right there by his side. A strange animal gasp had wheezed from his throat, and as he looked up, he made out the unmistakable silhouette of the mercenary, kneeling down over him. The faintest glimmer of moonlight was reflected off the man's sparkling eyes, and they were looking right at him.

Just staring. Without a word.

The following morning, Gapp awoke with only the faintest memory of this strange nocturnal occurrence. To be honest, he was no longer sure it had actually happened.

Methuselech was already up by the time Gapp awoke. He was out on the veranda, checking his bandages and chafing his limbs. There was also a rather unpleasant smell in the air, a bit like burnt meat. As soon as Methuselech realized that the boy was no longer asleep, he spun around and walked toward him.

"Come on you," he said brusquely. "It's late, and we've got plans to make. Come on, *up*!"

Bossy bell-head! the esquire cursed, but dutifully did as he was told.

As they made their way back to the pavilion, they were met by a messenger who seemed anxious that they follow him.

"Ah, Radkin," Methuselech greeted. *"Hail!"*

It was R'rrahdh-Kyinne, the same Vetter whom Gapp had first encountered on escaping from the Jordiske caves. He recognized him instantly.

Following Radkin, they went not to the pavilion this time but to the central pinnacle of rock, and an external stairway that appeared to lead up to the very top of it.

At last! Gapp thought; it looked as if today he would finally reach the very highest point of Cyne-Tregva!

It would be an observatory, he assumed, like the ones Finwald had told him of which stood on the topmost level of Qaladmir: a Chamber of Devices for the augury of the heavens . . . or a throne room in which he would meet the *real* king of Vetter-Home, a sinister leper with spells of undreamed-of potency to control the whole of Fron-Wudu. . . . Or then again, it might be the cage of a giant bird . . . the cell of a seer . . . the altar to an inhuman, multilimbed deity. . . . Was he really ready for this?

Winding around the outer wall of rock, Gapp realized that the burnt-meat stink that he had noticed earlier was stronger here. They continued up, almost to the top, and then came to a wide arch. Through this they passed, and entered a hollowed-out chamber that occupied the top of the pinnacle; they had finally reached the peak of the karst. There was no roof, there were just walls all around, walls of rock breached by four wide arches, each facing one of the four points of the compass. Here the reek was almost overpowering, and now smelled strongly of rose petals being burned on a charcoal fire. It made both the travelers' eyes smart.

Inside the light was poor, despite the open roof, and the low visibility was helped little by the smoke billowing out of the burner by the table. There were many Vetters within, all dressed in long robes made entirely from white bird feathers, and all engaged in some activity around the stone table . . .

. . . Oh.

Gapp halted exactly where he was, and went cold, hot, and numb, all at the same time. For the Vetters seemed to be cutting up and cooking one of their own.

On the slab it lay, an aged Vetter slit open from throat to groin, its skin pulled right back off the bones, and its sternum split in two and wrenched open like the doors of a birdcage. Much of its insides had already been removed, and stood about the place deposited in little pots. The knotted rope that had been used to strangle it still dangled limply from its neck.

There was a sickening, crunching sound as one of the butchers began splitting the victim's skull with a stone knife. Very carefully and with great precision he worked, as did his fellows. There was almost a reverence in the way they moved. One slowly popped the limb bones out of their gristly sockets, while another was efficiently scraping all the flesh from them and placing it also in the pots. Two were involved in the cooking, while an entire team was extracting the marrow. The whole spectacle resembled a production line: a Vetter-processing plant.

A word used by the Gyger now came back to Gapp's semiparalyzed mind: *cannibals.*

"Ah! Hal, Seelva—Hal, R'rrahdnar!" came a familiar voice, and Englarielle stepped out from the midst of the pall of stinking smoke. He too was arrayed in a long feathered robe, as were the group of sullen-faced Vetters with whom he had been conversing. Each held one of the little pots, and was dunking into it what looked like a finger of toast. The Cynen offered a similar pot to each of his guests, and gestured toward a small side table, upon which rested baskets of these toasted "soldiers," together with jars of relish, beakers of fruit juice, and a kind of tree-frog kedgeree.

"Hope you've got an appetite, young Greyboots," Methuselech murmured at Gapp's side. "Looks like breakfast's ready. . . ."

It was their way, Gapp kept reminding himself. Just their way. The Vetter victim had been old, not far from death anyway, and out here only the strong survived. In Fron-Wudu, you pulled your own weight, or you dropped out—or were dropped.

". . . normally killed by members of his own family," Methuselech was translating as he and Gapp partook of the feast. "It's not the most agreeable of deaths, but at least its better to die like this, at the hands of your loved ones, than to be carried off by some wild creature."

The words of the mercenary, though reassuring in some ways, did little for Gapp's appetite as he dunked the toast soldiers into the salty, beetroot-hued slurry in his bowl.

The repast eventually came to an end, and most of the Vetters gradually filed out of the chamber, nodding respectfully to the Cynen as they went. One of them—the eldest son of the deceased, Gapp was told—was presented with the flayed skin of his father as he departed, either to hang upon his wall at home, or to wear during the ritual dance that would be held that night. As he pleased.

It had not been the easiest of killings, it seemed, for the victim had taken some persuading before reluctantly agreeing to be sacrificed. But there was to be a feast of great importance upon this day, and such a sacrifice was vital to propitiate the spirits.

All things considered, both victim and son had taken it quite well, really.

Now only Englarielle and a handful of Vetters—his "higher-ups"—remained with the humans, and they all took their places around the table that moments ago had held the gradually disappearing remains of the sacrifice.

The Cynen now placed upon his own head some kind of helmet. It was at least a size too big for the Vetter; this was compensated for by skilled padding, but still it looked absurdly incongruous. To Gapp it had the basic look of a sallet helm of the style used by Peladanes over a century ago, but it had been elaborated to suit the Vetter's taste, for it now bore the head and upper jaw of a large, crested reptile (with slits for the eyes when the visor was down), and the neck-guard was covered over with snakeskin.

Then Englarielle solemnly brought out an axe, and placed it ceremoniously upon the table.

Oh dear, Gapp thought with trepidation, *this doesn't look good.*

The weapon had clearly traveled far across both time and distance. From an unknowable culture, this hefty axe of some metal that looked more like lead than anything else, was smelted into the shape of a gyag's jawbone, teeth and all. Like the helm, it was antiquated, but it glistened with a fresh coating of bear's fat.

The other Vetters also had their weapons out. Unlike the gyag-axe, theirs were some kind of bizarre and brutal machete, seemingly all blade and no hilt. There was an oval slot at one end for their fingers to go through, the rest forming an entire length of heavy, chopping blade. By the look of them, they had been fashioned with unique skill (and no small amount of relish) not from metal but from bone—namely, the sharpened scapula bones of their enemies, the Jordiske.

This meeting was starting to take on the air of a war council, and Gapp did not like it at all. He had attended many such meetings at Wintus Hall, and knew just how long they could drag on for. At the back of his mind, he wished he had asked for a couple more slices of Vetter to keep him going.

In actual fact, Gapp *did* like it a little, this sudden feeling of importance. Up until now the only role he had played in any of the war councils he had attended was as dogsbody to his master. On this occasion, however, he was actually going to be consulted—maybe even *listened* to—and the novelty was not wasted on him.

Nevertheless, he was not keen to get involved in anything that might hinder his speedy return home, not for any sense of self-importance.

"Tell him we're leaving now, Xilva," he whispered urgently into his companion's ear. "We don't want to get caught up in whatever this is."

Methuselech merely nodded, apparently sharing none of the boy's misgivings.

"Englarielle," he spoke up before the proceedings had a chance to start, and went on to say something to the Cynen in that Polg dialect that Gapp could not interpret at all.

"I'm just explaining that both of us thank the chief with undying gratitude for his hospitality," he clarified after a moment, "and that our stay here has been one of unsurpassed bliss, but on the morrow we shall be departing for Wrythe."

Wrythe! What are you talking about? I'm not going to Wrythe!

Gapp glanced at the Vetters, trying to read their reaction. This was all getting out of hand. Surprisingly, though, Englarielle seemed quite happy about this as he gave his reply.

"What did he say?" Gapp asked.

The other half-smiled. "He says that was what he already thought, and he wants to come with us."

"Ah."

The meeting was a confusing affair. What with Methuselech having to translate everything that Englarielle said, and Englarielle having to translate everything his captains said, and the four other Vetters all talking at the same time, and each seemingly determined to speak louder than the rest, there seemed to be little understanding at all. Besides, Gapp (chiding himself for ever allowing himself to believe it could be otherwise) felt that no one was listening to him anyway. Indeed, Methuselech was clearly not bothering to translate anything the esquire said to the Vetters. And as everybody seemed to be at odds with each other, little was decided on. Before long, tempers became frayed.

The issues were actually quite simple. Englarielle had accepted the idea that Drauglir had now become a genuine threat to all the lands of Lindormyn, including his own, even though neither he nor any of his people had ever even heard of the Rawgr before now. He was all for raising an army of his best guards and hunters, and joining Methuselech on a crusade against Drauglir, now that it appeared unlikely that Nibulus's party was going to make it.

It turned out that Methuselech, during his stay here at Cyne-Tregva, had talked at length with Englarielle about the quest, about Drauglir, and about the ancient battles between the Rawgr and the Fasces. He had also discoursed in great, rousing detail about Melhus and the lands of the Far North. Whatever he had said, it must have been oratory surpassing that of the greatest skalds back home, for the fires of adventure had been kindled in the Vetter's heart to the extent that he was now hell-bent upon raising an army, just like the heroes of old, and himself storming the gates of Vaagenfjord Maw.

Gapp had no way of knowing whether Englarielle genuinely considered this threat a real one, or if he had simply become impassioned with the thought of going forth on an epic adventure. But whatever the Vetter's motivations were, they were clearly not shared by all of his captains, who seemed almost as baffled as to their Cynen's strange notions as Gapp was.

More to the point, Gapp just could not understand why Methuselech—on the whole a sensible man—had told the Vetter of all this heroic stuff. And not just told him, but knowingly stirred him so, filling his impressionable head with things he could not possibly fully appreciate or even comprehend. The Vetterim, from what Gapp had seen of them, were an isolated race, naive, unworldly-wise, and with very simple values. He glared at the mercenary sourly for letting their secret out so readily. But Methuselech seemed quite content with the proceedings.

There was a short recess for refreshments, during which Englarielle took his recalcitrant captains aside and repeatedly slapped them around the heads, and Gapp tried to do the same in a way with his companion.

"Xilva," he began, unsure how exactly to talk with his former master's near-equal, "you can't surely wish to drag the Vetterim into all this. It's got nothing to do with them."

"Nothing to do with them?" Methuselech flared, and Gapp knew he had overstepped the mark again, almost before he had even started. "If you under-stood anything at all, my lad, then you'd know that this has *everything* to do with them. I guess you believe that the Evil from Melhus would simply pass them by and not bother with them, eh?"

"Well, no," Gapp admitted, feeling the full weight of the Asyphe warrior's superiority bear down upon him, "but I don't believe an army of Vetters would be any . . . that is, they don't really . . ."

He trailed off, as he always did when trying to get a point across to his bet-ters. During his time with the forest giant, he had laughed at his former defer-ence and servility, both angry and amused at himself for having been so feeble. But now that he was back among them again . . .

Then he thought of the mines, and the Jord cave, and all he had had to do to survive them . . . and the scornful look that Methuselech was giving him now. His anger flared up.

"They know *nothing* of what lies beyond the forest," Gapp exclaimed, "and when trouble comes—which it will, because *they* are not supported by an en-tire *Toloch* of Peladanes—how are they going to be able to cope with it? Eh? They don't know about the Dead, or Rawgrs, and . . . what about the ice fields, and all?"

He finally plucked up courage enough to look the mercenary straight in the eye. This was real *daring,* no doubt about that. But as soon as he did, he was dismayed to see that Methuselech was neither angry nor impressed. In fact he hardly even seemed aware that the boy had spoken. To Gapp, he looked just like his parents would: that same distracted air, that look that said not only that he did not think it necessary to listen to the boy, but he did not think it neces-sary to even *pretend* to listen to him.

But there was one difference between Methuselech and his parents, Gapp could tell: The mercenary, for some reason that eluded him for the present, actu-ally needed the boy. At length, with a patient but resigned irritation, he turned to the esquire. "I'm sure they're more capable of looking after themselves than you give them credit for," he replied. "You lack confidence in them because you see them for what they appear—"

"Bola-wielding weasels," Gapp agreed.

"But I tell you this," Methuselech went on, ignoring this last remark. "I've got to know them well during my stay; and they're a hardy and resourceful race. Englarielle is a leader of singular ability, and much loved by his people. Look around you! You've witnessed yourself the wonders of Cyne-Tregva, the royal dwelling—is it not a marvel beyond description? Who but the Vetterim could have conceived, let alone actually constructed, this miracle of building? And all without the tools available to other races. I tell you, Radnar, if any people can look after themselves, the Vetterim can."

"That's not the point and you know it!" Gapp snapped. He had started this now, and he was going to finish; it was all the way, no turning back. "Building tree houses and campaigning have got nothing to do with each other. What d'you think they're going to do? Surround the whole of Vaagenfjord Maw with a stockade and shove it all up a tree?"

This is good! thought the esquire. *This I can really get into! Ah, the Liberation! The Justice!* He was experiencing a kind of *soaring* that he could not explain, but that he knew felt *so good, so right.*

"And furthermore," he went on, waxing grandiloquent, "what right have we to drag innocents into the bloody . . . waves of conflict that they would not otherwise be . . . that is, not . . ." *(Keep going! Don't stop!)* ". . . good. And I seriously doubt that any help the Vetterim might avail us" *(Avail? Yes! Yes! Gapp for Warlord! Gapp for Warlord!)* "could exultate the danger into which we are placing them."

There! He had done it. He had spoken up for himself against a warrior. He had risen to their heights.

"Exculpate," Methuselech said.

". . . What?"

"Exculpate. Could *exculpate* the danger," the mercenary corrected him.

Gapp's deflation was almost audible. He was a little boy once again.

Methuselech, however, *was* taken back a little, and for the first time regarded the esquire with his full attention. Now that he did, he was not sure exactly how he was supposed to talk with the lad.

"Look, Radnar," he said, "I know what I said yesterday about hoping to meet up with your master and the rest. And it's true that I am going on to Wrythe. But it isn't with any real hope that I'll be reunited with them. I'm going there simply because it's the last place where we can get any proper food and shelter before the final push. More to the point, its the only place where we stand a hope of finding a boat to get us across the straits."

(We? Us?)

"Even if Nibulus and the others are alive, they probably won't survive the forest as you and I have. They're not blessed as we are; neither with the fortitude that is ours nor the grace of the gods that goes with us . . ."

He's talking to me like Nibulus does with his soldiers, Gapp thought, *like*

Thegnes always do when they want people to follow them into a fight. What's his problem? Has Xilva forgotten how he himself used to speak to people, so he has to imitate others now?

". . . And if that celestial grace chooses to place an army into our hands, well, who are we to throw the gifts of the gods back in their faces?"

The old obliqueness had returned to Methuselech's eyes. He had said all he needed to this boy.

Englarielle and the Vetters started filing back up the steps to resume the meeting, and Methuselech turned toward them.

"You're forgetting one thing, Xilva," Gapp said then. "We don't have any magical weapons. How are we going to do the job, eh?"

Methuselech thought about this detail for a moment. "Magical *or* silver," he reminded the esquire, "that's what Finwald said. And that's even more reason to go to Wrythe; I'm sure we'll have no trouble finding a silversmith there with enough skill to fashion a simple blade. They are renowned for it."

Gapp considered this, never having heard say up till now that the people of Wrythe were "renowned silversmiths." But he was unable to bring his thoughts into any order, for there was something at the back of his mind, something that he had found out during his recent wanderings, that tied in with all this. He could not remember what it was, and now he saw with increasing frustration that the Vetters were waiting for him.

"Come along, then," Methuselech said briskly as he turned to follow them into the chamber. "The council's back on, and don't you worry about magical weapons. Nibulus didn't have any of those things either; they themselves only had a silver blade."

Finwald's silver blade—

"Finwald!" Gapp exclaimed. "Of course!"

Methuselech half-turned, and looked at him blankly. "Pardon?"

"Finwald!" Gapp went on, needing no grandiloquence now. "That's what I was trying to remember. When I was staying at Yulfric's, he explained that two years ago he'd taken in another traveler from Nordwas who'd got lost just as I had, and when I asked what the man's name was, he said it was Finwald!"

". . . !"

"Yes, *our* Finwald! The description fitted exactly, even down to the silver torch amulet, the alchemist's books . . . and a dead snake in a bag."

"Dead *what*?"

"Oh, nothing, I couldn't really make any sense of that last bit. But the point is, he was on his way to Wrythe on his own but he couldn't manage it, so he went back home, and *never* breathed a word of the whole escapade to anyone."

They both stared at each other, their minds in a whirl, the impatient Vetters now forgotten.

"Why would Finwald be going to Wrythe, and on his own . . . and then remain so secretive about it?" Methuselech asked.

"According to Yulfric, he was on some preaching mission, but got lost in the woods on the way. By the time Yulfric found him, he was half-starved and exhausted, with no idea where he was. Apparently, he vowed never to come up this way again and, once he was recovered, he left saying he was returning to Nordwas."

"Finwald on a preaching mission?" Methuselech murmured, every bit as sceptical as Gapp had been.

"That's what I thought, too. And to Wrythe, of all places. Makes you think, doesn't it?"

"Nibulus wasn't in on this, was he?" Methuselech quizzed the esquire. "Or anyone else? *You* didn't know about it, did you?"

"As far as I know, no one but Finwald himself knew. He's definitely up to something, that one, and whatever it is, he's making absolutely sure none of us knows anything he doesn't want us to know."

Suddenly Methuselech whirled round to face Gapp directly. "Tell me about the dead snake," he demanded. "Tell me!"

Gapp hesitated. He would have laughed at such sudden interest in this surely least important detail of his story, but for the desperate intensity he now saw in the desert man's eyes.

". . . I don't know," he replied, trying to remember what the giant had told him, "and neither did Yulfric. He said Finwald never let him see it, never let it out of his sight. It was just something he carried in a bag on his back. Long and thin, stiff as a board . . . but *wavy*."

"Oh hell it . . . it can't be that! It can't! *It can't!* He could not be so . . . Ahh! And just when I am so close . . . !"

"What're you talking about?" Gapp cut in. "You're scaring me."

Methuselech stared at the boy as if suddenly remembering he was there. Then his face set in grim determination. Gapp felt he no longer knew this man.

"We've got to get to Vaagenfjord as soon as possible," Methuselech stated. There was an absoluteness to that statement that would not be questioned, Gapp knew, let alone argued with. It felt to him that by simply uttering those words, Methuselech had already set the two of them inexorably on that path. Even the Vetters sensed that the council had moved on beyond their authority.

"You—"

"*WE!*" Methuselech barked. "We have to get there before the others do! Quick, run and get your stuff together, then meet me back here; I've got to persuade Englarielle to lend us his fastest steeds."

"But . . . hold on, Xilva, I don't think I—"

Methuselech spun round and grasped Gapp by the shoulders.

"Listen to me! We *have* to get to the Maw without a moment's delay—every hour is vital. We'll need to make for Wrythe as planned. There's still a chance we can reach Nibulus and the others before they leave for Melhus. *If* they haven't done so already."

"But I thought you said they didn't possess the fortitude or the grace of the gods to make it."

"And one other thing," Methuselech said, his face just inches from the boy's. "If we do find them, do not, whatever happens, do *not* breathe a word of what we have just discussed. Whatever your giant told you about Finwald, his secret mission, or that 'dead snake' of his must, upon pain of death and everlasting torment in the fires of Hell thereafter, remain *strictly* between me and you. Do you understand?"

"I . . . no I don't . . ."

"Then just trust me!" he cried, shaking the boy by the shoulders. There was a wild glint in his eyes that chilled Gapp. Clearly there was something dreadfully wrong that had to be sorted out before this whole business went any further. But what could he say to those eyes?

He could meekly say, "I trust you," and nothing else.

The mercenary let him go. "Good boy. Now go and fetch your stuff. And fetch mine while you're at it; we need to be away within the hour."

Just as if he were still floating along that underground stream, Gapp was borne along upon a current that would not be defied. The events occurring all around him had been taken out of his hands yet again, and yet again he had lost his hold on that slick and most treacherous handrail of his own destiny. The whole of Cyne-Tregva was suddenly in an upheaval, like a breached termite nest, and Methuselech Xilvafloese was the one who was poking it with a stick.

Messengers had come in earlier announcing that the Gyger and his hounds had left the valley. With that news, Gapp felt, the road to Vaagenfjord Maw had suddenly opened ahead of him as wide as the smile of a skull. It did mean that he would be keeping the forest hound, true, but the world now seemed a much more dangerous place than it had an hour ago.

Whatever happened in the days to come, Gapp reflected with that familiar helpless, sinking feeling, it did not look as if he would be going back home for a while.

True to his word, Methuselech ensured that within the hour they departed Cyne-Tregva. The boy had given up trying to question him, as the mercenary was clearly determined not to explain a thing. Englarielle, too, was bewildered at what was happening; it transpired that he and his army were to follow on, and meet them later. The Cynen had apparently agreed to this, though he could not quite remember how this had happened. His brigade was to meet up with Methuselech on the Last Shore, the narrow strip of land between the mountains and the Jagt Straits, before crossing the sea to the island of Melhus itself. Methuselech gave no reasons for this plan, saying that he had no time to explain, and that he did not know the correct words in Polg, and that "all would be revealed" in the days to come. So they would just have to trust him.

The whole of Cyne-Tregva was for the next hour, and indeed long after the stick-stirring Methuselech and his henchman had ridden out, in a state of confusion and hasty preparation. Englarielle did not have a clue how long it would take to organize a war party of fifty Vetters for a journey of such epic proportions, not having any previous experience in such matters. Aided by Gapp, Methuselech had advised him as best he could, for this was something they *were* used to.

It was decided that the Vetters would ride on the Cervulice, those scimitar-horned, deer-legged creatures that Gapp had taken such a dislike to the previous day. Despite the fact that they were bipedal, the curvature of their spine meant that their prominent posterior provided a comfortable seat for the Vetters, and this was why they were so welcome in Cyne-Tregva. Indeed, the name Cervulus meant "Vettersteed."

When Gapp had found out what they would be using as mounts, his current anguish was redoubled. He was aware that he and Xilva needed something to ride, but he truly did not want to spend the next few weeks bouncing up and down on one of *those* things. He was back in the belvedere gathering up what few possessions still remained to them, when one of the Vetter captains brought him this unwelcome news, by pointing to a line of Cervulice currently issuing from the main doorway of the pinnacle to deliberate with the Cynen.

Gapp broke off from his chore to look out of the window at them. He instantly recognized that strange, bobbing gait that he had noted the day before, almost like a swagger that was anchored down by that enormous tail of theirs. Their three-toed velvety hooves could be heard rapping in agitation upon the wooden platform as they emerged from the doorway one by one, demanding to know what this was all about.

He turned back to the Vetter, a wiry, tough-looking character with a distinctly sharp, severe face and pitch-black, penetrating eyes, and realized he was now holding out a knife for Gapp.

"Of course," said the boy gratefully (having spent all this time since he had fallen down the well without a proper weapon). "Thank you!"

It was, he saw, not just a knife, but one of those extraordinary, hiltless machetes the captains had produced at the meeting. But unlike theirs, this was made from some type of bronze. It was about the same length as his old short-sword, but considerably heftier.

He had never wielded anything like it before, and did not know if he would be able to manage it with any real proficiency, but it was at least a considerable improvement on his sickle-headed fruit-pruner.

The Vetter pointed out a series of scratches etched into the surface of the blade. That they were in Vetter script, Gapp was in no doubt; but he was not sure what it meant. The captain pointed to the markings again, and simultaneously indicated himself.

"You made this?" Gapp finally concluded. The Vetter nodded proudly.

"Then you must be the . . ." He imitated someone working bellows and striking metal. ". . . blacksmith?"

The Vetter nodded enthusiastically. Again he pointed to the markings and then to himself, this time adding: "Illuei-floie aiunglla Mo'eu Tedhe."

" 'Ted'?" Gapp repeated, having only caught the last word. "Your name's 'Ted'?"

The Vetter continued nodding, though it was not clear if he understood the boy either.

After "Englarielle" and "R'rrahdh-Kyinne," Gapp had expected something a little more impressive as a name for the community blacksmith, but . . .

"Thank you, anyway, Ted," he said, bowing low. "I shall . . . treasure it. Really."

This must be one of the few metal weapons in the whole of Cyne-Tregva, he decided, and suddenly felt rather ashamed of his selfish feelings of anguish up till now. The honor of receiving this blade did not escape the Aescal one bit.

His selfish feelings of anguish did, however, return with a vengeance, when he was finally brought face-to-face with the steeds that Englarielle had chosen for him and Methuselech. He was at first greatly relieved when his companion informed him that they would not be riding upon Vettersteed after all, but when Methuselech pointed over to where their mounts stood waiting, Gapp physically sagged with dismay.

"Parandus," Xilva announced. "The Treegard of Vetter-Home: Cyne-Tregva's finest!"

At least as large as the two antler-headed door guardians he had slithered past the previous day, this pair of Paranduzes were quite definitely something special. They had about them what Gapp could only describe as an "air of excellence." Beneath coverings of beautifully inlaid leather trimmed with the finest sable, their bodies were as sleek and muscular as thoroughbred racing stallions, and their faces long and noble. Wide, ornate silver torcs adorned their necks, and, secured by hoops along their flank, they bore the most enormous poleaxes Gapp had ever seen. The business end of each appeared to be one great, solid crescent moon of highly lacquered, viciously sharp flint, three-quarters of which extended from one side of the haft to serve as an axe head, the remaining quarter sticking out the other side in a spike.

"Hwald and Finan will bear us well, I am assured," Methuselech informed him. "Englarielle tells me they are the swiftest there are, and fearsome in a fight. Communication with them will be a problem, but they have been told what is expected of them. I'm taking Hwald, Finan can be yours. Questions?"

For a second or two, two pairs of large, black eyes returned the boy's stare with an enigmatic, detached amusement, before Hwald and Finan returned to their current occupation of popping slices of marinated pear into each other's mouths.

"Just one," Gapp replied, after finally tearing his eyes away from the Tree-gard. "What about Schnorbitz?"

Methuselech waved an irritable hand and turned away to attend to more important matters.

"I suppose he'll have to run along beside. If he can't keep up, that's just too bad."

Thus did Gapp's brief time in Vetter-Home come to an end. Just as Methuselech had announced, within the hour the two of them had mounted upon the enormous Paranduzes, ridden out of Cyne-Tregva, Schnorbitz running alongside, and headed north.

13

Meanwhile . . .

Evening found Bolldhe, Nibulus, Finwald, Appa, Wodeman, and Paulus camped on the edge of the forest. Zhang had wandered some way off, enthusiastically partaking of the lush grass that this new part of the world was furnished with, and the smell of cooking now mingled with the unsavory odor of damp sedge that drifted in from the marshes they had just left.

It was only twelve hours ago that they had bidden farewell to Myst-Hakel, and they had done so with great relief. For several days they had been trying to leave that place, but no matter how hard they tried, there seemed to be one delay after another to keep them there.

There were two main reasons for this. Firstly, Zhang had refused to budge unless he was reshoed, and there ensured much haggling between Bolldhe and the Tusse blacksmith about what constituted a fair price. The Tusse, a now-sedentary member of the notoriously proud Mammoth Caste who went by the name of Ted, was not used to having his prices questioned, even though he did charge in sardonyx rather than zlats (about eight times the going rate) simply because Bolldhe's group looked rich. There consequently was a fair amount of bad feeling, which led to Ted not doing a very good job. So within half a day's journey, Zhang had thrown a shoe and was limping badly.

The company had been forced to return to Myst-Hakel to get the job done properly (and this time for free). This would not have delayed them long if it had not been for Appa suddenly going down with a bout of swamp fever. Wodeman tried hard to cure him, but swamp fever was a little out of his experience. The others had been all for leaving him behind, but the old man would have none of it. It was only an incredible stubbornness that bordered on fanaticism (not to mention the fact that he was a healer himself) that got him over the worst of it, to the extent that he could now rejoin them on the road.

Nevertheless, it did begin to look at times as if they would never leave Myst-Hakel, and they all became very jaded with the place. Bolldhe could not help feeling that this all had a very familiar ring to it.

That should have been the last of their delays, but it just so happened that, on the very morning of their second departure, there came from the north a long, slow rumbling sound. This began at dawn as a low rumor, as of the passing of a giant cart. But it did *not* pass, and instead continued without cessation, gradually growing throughout the morning until, by the time the travelers had set out, it had waxed to a thundering of seismic proportions that shook the whole land.

Hours later, many miles to the north of Myst-Hakel and out upon higher, drier ground, the travelers found themselves sitting, stranded upon a rocky knoll, whilest below and all around them the entire corridor of land between the marshes and Fron-Wudu rolled westward as a mighty river of monstrous brown bodies, flicking tails and tossing heads.

The baluchitherium were on the move, and there would be no passage northward until they passed.

Of all their company, only Bolldhe had ever seen baluchitherium, those massive herd beasts of the Tusse that stood at the shoulder fully three times the height of their proud herders. But even he had never seen them in such numbers; there must have been thousands of them, stretching as far as the eye could see in any direction. And the herd-giant Tusse, glancing disdainfully up at the little huddle of humans on the knoll as they passed, were in no hurry to be on their way. They carried massive spears that doubled as goads, resting across their shoulders on the rawhide dolmans they wore over their ankle-length, berry-dyed kirtles; and across their chests they wore an entire bandoleer of throwing axes.

They were a rough lot, these Tusse, some might even say fierce. All over the known lands they could be found, herding their beasts, whether reindeer, saiga, camel, red bison, mammoth, or even Bonacon. In this part of the world it was not uncommon to find Polgs, or even humans, living among the Tusse, sharing their lives. As was the case here, in fact, for one or two human women could just be discerned amid the dust and the hordes of insects, trudging along in the traditional hooded domino cloak and shouldering heavy panniers. Usually from aristocratic families, these renegade females would throw in their lot with the Tusse for a season or two, deigning to forgo their finery and status for the chance to "be free." Often they ended up marrying their Tusse swains, and though no offspring were possible, it never seemed to stop them trying.

And so the baluchitherium herd passed on. Beneath their elephantine feet the ground had been compacted into something harder than rock, and was piled with veritable hillocks of their excrement, through which the company now had to weave their way, with towels wrapped tightly over mouth and nose.

———————

Eventually, however, they did succeed in leaving this wasteland well and truly behind them, and later that day they arrived at what could reasonably be considered the outer fringes of Fron-Wudu.

Despite their relief at leaving Myst-Hakel, their mood had been somewhat subdued all day. Even the Peladane's whistling had a sparse, forlorn quality to it. The thought that they would be entering the Great Forest the very next day was enough to sober even Nibulus. As the day's march wore on they all began to get a little tetchy, more aware now that none of them had ever passed beneath the forest's forbidding boughs. (At least, that was what Finwald claimed.) This terrain would almost certainly prove to be their greatest test before they reached Melhus Island itself.

Now, as the pale light in the western sky gradually faded to deepest blue, Bolldhe sat wrapped on his bedroll, and studied his new sword. It was a curious blade, there was no denying. In all his travels he had never before seen its like. With that blade undulating out of the hilt like a writhing snake, there could not have been many other weapons like it in the whole world. Not these days, anyhow. He could not see what practical purpose it might serve; it was not a fighting blade, for sure. More decorative, really—or ceremonial?

It was then that he remembered having seen such an instrument before. Not a sword, mind, but a dagger—a Kh'is, the necromancers called it—a ceremonial knife used to sacrifice people on the altars of the temples of Olchor. Yes, he had once seen such daggers when he had traveled through the evil land of Rhelma-Find, many, many years ago now. The memory brought a troubled cloud of darkness with it, one on which Bolldhe did not care to dwell on this their first night in Fron-Wudu.

Trying to ease himself into a lighter frame of mind, he considered the blade's advantages. It was a heavy, out-of-date weapon, to be sure, but it was one that suited an axeman well. Bolldhe had never been keen on swords, partly owing to their association with his old Peladane cult, but also for the more pragmatic reason that he was simply not very good with them. Though he could defend himself well enough if the need arose, he was not a highly trained warrior, and as such he lacked the skill needed to handle lighter swords; but neither was he strong enough to wield the huge two-handers like Nibulus's greatsword or Methuselech's shamsheer. What Bolldhe preferred was a weapon with a bit of weight and requiring little skill to wield, like a club or an axe—but nothing too hefty.

This flamberge was neither too heavy nor too light, and its long grip meant that he could use it either one- or two-handed. It was not so different to his old broadaxe, really.

He studied the sword again, his curiosity growing with every passing minute. It seemed to possess an almost chameleon quality; by day it shone the color of burnished copper, but in the dark it took on a deep, igneous blue, the color of volcanic rock. Even in the dead of night it could be seen shining, as if some secret power churned within.

He held the blade closer to his eyes now, and stared deep beneath its mirrored surface, beyond its changing hues, down, down, into the very heart of its magic, where lay the source of its potency. . . .

With a start Bolldhe recoiled—there were two eyes staring back at him! They studied him with a curiosity equal to his own. His heart beat faster, and he glanced over to where his companions lay sleeping, wondering if he should wake them.

He decided to take another look, cautiously this time, but steadily, reassuring himself that it had been merely a trick of the light. Suddenly he laughed in relief, as he realized that it was merely a reflection of his own eyes staring back at him.

With a quiet, nervous laugh, he wrapped the flamberge in his deerskin tunic, placed it carefully by his side, and rolled over to go to sleep. It had been a long day and, beneath the boughs of Fron-Wudu, the whispering leaves could weave the strangest thoughts into a tired traveler's mind.

They were not alone in the woods that night. From the darkness of the trees, mere yards away, a pair of eyes glittered brightly, regarding the sleeping travelers with interest; two pale eyes that caught the stray moonbeam that found its way through the forest canopy, and glinted coldly in the dark. They were keen, but old, and had the look of eyes that have seen too much coldness and cruelty in the world.

Slowly they came forward, toward the company that slept, blissfully unaware of their new visitor. Not a sound could be heard as the prowler stalked forward, not the slightest crunch of a leaf underfoot nor the merest breath of air stirring.

Closer it crept, until it was only paces from the unmoving figures that huddled within their bedrolls at its feet. One of them was snoring, while another whimpered slightly in his sleep. But from the rest came only the sounds of heavy, regular breathing; dreamless, untroubled sleep.

A sardonic smile spread across its face as it stared down at them. Casually it fingered the hilt of a broadsword slung at its side, while with its other hand it loosely held a large dirk that gleamed dully in the moonlight.

Just then a snorting from nearby snapped the prowler's gaze away from the sleeping men. Swiftly, silently, it made its way over to the slough horse, and stroked his snout soothingly. Zhang did not know what to make of the stranger, but for some reason that he could not fathom, let it continue in its stroking, a privilege normally reserved for his rider only.

Smiling broadly now with strong, white teeth, the prowler slunk back into the shadows, and sat there. It never took its eyes from the sleeping company for a second.

The following morning dawned bright and sunny, despite the covering of ground mist that drifted into the forest from the marshes. The air was filled with the joyous sound of birdsong, and the adventurers all awoke with lightness in their hearts and eagerness for whatever the new day might hold in store for them. Breakfast was cooked with enthusiasm and eaten with gusto, and before long everything was packed away, and they were ready for the off.

"Gather round, men, gather round," Nibulus hailed them as soon as he had finished securing the last piece of his armor across Zhang's back. Now that they had left the torpor of the swamp town behind them, the world had become once again the "domain of the Peladane," and the night spent out in the woods had clearly rekindled the spirit of adventure in him.

"Now, as you are all aware," he began, enjoying the sound of his own voice more than ever, "this next phase of the journey is more likely to cause us trouble than anywhere else. Gwyllch writes that in his day a branch of the trade route extended from Myst-Hakel right the way through the forest up to Wrythe itself, and the roads were clear and well maintained, with posthouses every twenty-five miles! Wonderful, eh? Who could ask for more? Well, the answer is, of course, that *we* could, for nowadays there simply *is* no road, not even the faintest trace of one, and no other known trails. How times change. . . ."

He paused to look around, then continued.

"The one thing in our favor is that, according to the little information Wintus Hall managed to glean from the trappers who have ventured this way, the forest directly north of the marshes is not quite as dense as the rest; the trees are widely spaced, and there is little undergrowth to slow us down. But we have to keep going in a reasonably straight line northwards, so we are going to have to steer ourselves by the sun, the stars, and any other method that presents itself. Well, lads?"

"No problem," stated Wodeman.

"No problem," repeated Bolldhe.

"Heading due north, then," the Peladane continued, satisfied, "we should, in *phnmnm* days' time, reach the lower foothills of the Giant Mountains, and thence come out of the forest. From there we can travel along the higher ground, above the level of the trees, and follow the mountains that will take us west, then swing round north again. Once we get into the northerly regions it will become colder, even at this time of year, so I do not want any delays, all right? Remember, we don't want to have to make our return journey in winter, so I will not tolerate any slacking, any feebleness, nor any . . ." He tried to think of the requisite third word. ". . . weakness. *Appa.*"

But Appa was not listening. He was looking at their leader, but he was concentrating his attention upon anything other than what the man was saying. For if he listened to *that,* he knew, his resolve would simply collapse into the emptiness within his frail heart, and he along with it. *One day at a time,* he repeated to himself over and over in his head, just like the mantras he counted off on his prayer beads. *One day at a time. . . .*

"Continuing further north will bring us to the coastline," Nibulus went on, "which we can follow west until we come to Wrythe. And there the length of our stay will depend on how we are greeted by the townsfolk—"

"Ha!" came a voice from somewhere. The Peladane looked around to see who had spoken, but he could not tell. Frowning, he continued:

"Wrythe," he said, as if savoring the word, "what are your people like nowadays, I wonder? Word has not come to us out of that place for time out of mind, which in itself is not very encouraging. But, for myself, I see little point in being worried before we have even got there, since there is no obvious reason to suppose they should be hostile. But we must still take every precaution not to offend them. All we want there is to get ourselves a small boat and replenish our supplies. *And* a chance to get warmed up a little, eh? Failing the whole package, just the boat will do. Failing *that,* we either steal one, which I would not recommend, or turn round and head straight back home. Which we're not going to do, of course. We *are* going to get across the sea, and Wrythe is the only way across. The Jagt Straits offer no other route across to Melhus Island, and—"

"You could always cross from the Last Shore to Stromm Peninsula, where the sea freezes over."

All six men spun round in alarm and immediately drew their weapons. Who had said that? They stared toward the trees in the direction from which the voice had come, but there was nothing to be seen.

"Who's there?" barked the Peladane. "Come on, show yourself!"

Nothing.

They quickly spread out, weapons at the ready, and searched the surrounding area. But not even Wodeman could find a single trace of anyone. It was as if the forest itself had spoken.

"Spriggans," Paulus suggested, his pale eye narrowing in hatred.

"Come, men," Nibulus ordered at length, glancing nervously over his shoulder. "The sooner we leave these woods, the better I'll like it. Follow me!"

For three days the company trod the needle-carpeted floor of Fron-Wudu in silence, wending their way steadily through the somber, lancet-arched vaults of the forest in constant wariness. The woods were, as Nibulus's trappers had promised, not as dense as they had feared, and the going was not particularly difficult. But this comforted them little, for though the way ahead was clear, unhindered by any real undergrowth, it was this very deadness that unnerved the Aescals. The thick, spongy layer of brown needles that covered the ground yielded no vegetation at all. The trees, too, seemed devoid of life, rising as they did like great iron poleaxes into the sky, bristling at the top with sharp, dark-green needles. No birds sang, no animals scurried, and there was not the slightest sound of insects. Even the light that fell down through the treetops was grey and cheerless.

Wodeman stared about himself in disbelief; these woods were more alien to him than any place he had traveled through yet. Dismayed, he began to wonder if the Earth Spirit dwelled anywhere outside the forests of Wyda-Aescaland at all.

The voice in the woods had had an extremely unsettling effect upon the company. It had spoken their language, giving them advice; but then it had disappeared. Paulus's suggestion that it was the voice of Spriggans was met with skepticism; he was always imagining fey spirits wherever they went. Appa's suggestion that it was the voice of an angel was rejected even more contemptuously.

That voice had sounded human. . . .

Daytime saw the company glancing nervously around at every distant snap of a twig, though the cold mist that hemmed them in restricted their vision to only thirty yards or so. By night there would always be two of their number keeping watch as the others slept. None of them was in any doubt that some time soon, something was going to happen.

On their fourth night in the forest, it did.

"Nibulus! Finwald! Everybody, wake up! Quickly!"

The Peladane immediately threw his covers aside and grabbed for his sword. "Whassup? What is it?" he said foggily. "Wha's going on?"

He looked up to see the dark shape of Bolldhe staring down at him. The two priests at his side groaned cantankerously as they stirred from their slumber. Wodeman, though still and silent, appeared to be fully awake already.

"Shh!" Bolldhe hissed, then pointed. "Over there . . ."

Nibulus's gaze followed his finger, and he tried to peer through the dark. The moon had not even reached its hemisphere yet, but the first glimmers of dawn rendered at least a hint of light. As he continued to stare, he could just about make out the silhouetted figure of Paulus, some way off, frozen into immobility. Judging by the way the crows' feathers were angled, the Nahovian was facing away from them, staring out into the mist with his sword held out in front of him.

"What is it, Bolldhe?" Nibulus whispered. "What's he seen?"

"I don't know," came the hushed reply. "He didn't say—just leapt up all of a sudden and whipped out his sword. I know he's very superstitious, but he must have sensed something more than Huldres to act like that."

Noiselessly, the company hefted their weapons and crept over to where the mercenary stood.

Then they heard it, something blundering through the woods not far off. Something very large and heavy, which sounded as though it was coming their way.

"Quick," hissed Nibulus, "find some cover, but stay close! Bolldhe, mount your horse. Everybody, be prepared to run if need be."

He need not have bothered. Everybody knew exactly what to do. With a silent efficiency the company took up positions and waited, the mist dripping off their faces like cold sweat.

Now they could hear it clearly. The crunch of living wood as branches were splintered asunder. The hoarse breathing of some large animal gulping in great lungfuls of air and rasping them out again. Heavy footsteps pounding upon the carpet of needles, getting nearer with every step.

Whatever it was, it moved on two feet, but was far heavier than any human. Step by purposeful step it came closer.

Suddenly there was a sound off to their right, and they swung around in time to see a figure emerge from the trees, bow in hand.

But then from in front of them again, a thunderous animal bellow echoing through the silent forest snapped their heads back around. Just beyond the crouching shadow of Paulus they saw a huge shape approach. They had only enough time to register it before it crashed into the clearing and was upon them: great, lumbering arms that swung heavily at its sides, a trail of shaggy hair that streamed behind it, and from within its dark head two points of light that gleamed at them malevolently.

"HIT IT FROM EVERY SIDE!" roared Nibulus in fury, and hurled himself into battle—just as Paulus flung himself out of its path and dealt it a ferocious backslash with his hand-and-a-half sword.

Arms spread wide, the beast set about itself in a fit of berserk savagery. Cries arose from the elder mage as he cowered in fear upon the ground. War cries and roars and screaming echoed through the trees. . . .

Suddenly the monster flung up its arms and clutched its face in agony. It screamed horribly, thrashed about at its unseen attackers, and desperately tried to claw the arrow out of its eye. The company leapt back, and watched in complete bewilderment as the beast staggered away from them, still howling in pain.

The arrow, wherever it had come from, was embedded deep in its eyeball. With only the flights and the last two inches of the shaft visible, it had gone straight through and lodged in the brain.

With a final shriek of utter despair echoing after it, the monster fled back into the trees, and was gone.

Barely recovered from their shock, the travelers spun around to face the newcomer with the bow. Four sharp blades and two staves were aimed toward it, and six pairs of legs were coiled ready to spring.

"Just who the hell are you, creeping round the woods on this night?" demanded Nibulus. "Speak up quick, or bleed profusely!"

"Now, now," the man said in a placatory tone, "is that any way for the son of the great warlord Artibulus Wintus to speak to me?"

The deep voice conveyed a strong sense of pride and authority, and possessed an accent very similar to Bolldhe's.

"Who *are* you?" Bolldhe repeated the Peladane's inquiry, advancing upon the stranger with the flamberge ready. "How do you know so much about us? Was it you spying on us in the woods the other day—and telling us about the sea freezing over?"

"Put away your sword, Pendonian," the stranger replied in a calm, almost bored tone. "I am not your enemy—my treatment of yon beast can attest to that. But to answer your question, yes, it was me you heard the other morning, though I was certainly not spying on you."

"Then what *were* you doing?" Nibulus ranted on. "You neither showed yourself nor answered my challenge. We are on a mission of great import, and do not take kindly to being toyed with!"

"Oh, for Nokk's sake," the newcomer sighed, "if I'd known what a bunch of mewling infants you were I'd have left you to deal with that Beast by yourselves. But . . . I can sympathize; I used to get pretty shaken up by that sort of thing when *I* was a novice."

"Novice!"

"It's all right, Nibulus," an unsteady voice said at his side. "This stranger means us no harm. I have read his soul."

Nibulus halted in midstrop, and turned to look at Appa. The old man, still looking half-asleep, was even now wrapping himself up in his bedroll again against the chill of the night.

"Really?" the Peladane said. "You can do that?"

"I can and I just have," replied the old priest, "as can young Finwald here."

The younger priest nodded, and set about lighting the kindling they had prepared earlier.

"So, perhaps we could help Finwald with the fire, and shed a little light on our friend here. Then maybe he could introduce himself."

The fire was soon burning brightly, and the travelers gathered round it, glad to huddle within the golden glow that was for a time pushing back the terrors of the night. Only Paulus remained on his feet, standing apart from the company, still on his guard. He continued to scan the night shadows uneasily.

In the light of the campfire, the stranger was revealed to be a man of about fifty years. Weathered skin, creased and pocked with infinite detail like a map of his life, stretched over a sharp-boned face that was unshaven and ungentle, hard as Ogre hide. Only around the eyes was it soft; though they themselves were cold and hooded, refusing to give anything away, the skin surrounding them could not so easily disguise the man's life story, and it was lined by an entire world of sorrow and care.

A high brow gave him a look of considerable intelligence, confirmed by the fact that he seemed to be reasonably fluent in several languages including Aescalandian and possess a working knowledge of many other language groups.

This cosmopolitan air was evident in his raiment, too. He was dressed in a garish mix of garments from diverse (and in most cases, unknown) cultures, that conflicted not only with each other but also with the man himself: military tunic of faded green sendal with brass buttons and mandarin collar, "barbarian" rawhide saiga skin thrown loosely over this, khaki cavalry boots of scuffed and patched cordwain, violet-and-gold cummerbund that had seen better days. The whole ensemble gave the immediate impression that he had done his shopping in a very badly lit secondhand clothes bazaar.

It was only when one took a closer look that their quality became apparent: Gold embroidery of the most exquisite detail could occasionally be seen glinting dully in the firelight as he shifted himself. Though faded and more than a little threadbare, it was still there under the grime of the years.

The sheen from various items about his person continued to attract glances from his audience; whalebone ice skates slung at his belt on one side, an ivory-handled elk-gut whip coiled on the other, two dirks (one in each boot), in his cummerbund a strange, heavy dagger with notches down the side that he called a swordbreaker, and a broadsword (an Aggedonian temple sword, he informed them later) that came from a land so remote not even Bolldhe had heard of it.

Whatever he was wearing on his head, they could not identify in this light. It might have been a cap of sorts, maybe even a crested helmet of some peculiar design. In any case it looked as though it were made of a lobster shell or possibly a whole crab, with the legs still attached . . . and still *moving*. But they could never quite see, for with his each movement it appeared to alter somehow, as if not quite sure what it was itself.

But above everything, it was their visitor's eyes that their attention kept going back to. These regarded the company with a casual interest as cool as it was transient. There was a measure of affability there, but carefully guarded. This was a man who could like others (sort of) and be liked himself (sort of) but had seen far too much of the world to set any real store by such feelings nowadays.

Even as he spoke, his voice gave the impression that there was little in this world he cared about.

"I must apologize for my little joke the other day," he began, "but it really was too good an opportunity to miss. There you were, six travelers from the South on their first day in the great Fron-Wudu, obviously on some sort of *desperately* important mission, never imagining for a moment there could be anyone else in these woods, let alone a dozen yards away. *Heh heh heh.* I just couldn't resist a little prank."

He trailed off, chuckling to himself, plainly amused by the memory.

The company sat regarding him in stony silence.

"How long have you been spying on us?" Nibulus asked quietly. Normally he would have been in favor of beating the truth out of the man with an iron bar, but this one had followed them for at least three days without any of them realizing it. Nibulus therefore opted for a more cautious approach. "I would like to know how much you heard. What do you know of our quest?"

"Quest, is it?" the man smirked. "How utterly riveting. No wonder you're all so—"

"Now listen, old man," Nibulus snapped suddenly, "I'm getting a little tired of all this! I want to know *now* exactly what you heard."

The stranger rolled his eyes with boredom. "Yes, quests," he replied. "Terribly, terribly important things, quests; part of the very fabric of our being. And do you know what? Whether they succeed or fail, still, it seems the world goes on just the same. But to answer your questions, I have not been 'spying' on you," he promised, taking out a telescope and peering at the Peladane through it, "merely taking an interest in fellow travelers. And what I've heard and how much I know of your business is hardly enough to blow the lid off anything significant, even if I cared to tell anyone else, which I don't. Most of what I know is merely what I see here: a Peladane from Nordwas bearing the badge of the Wintus household, leading two mage-priests and a sorcerer, all from Wyda-Aescaland, a vagrant who speaks Aescalandian with a Pendonian accent, and a Nahovian mercenary. Such an odd mixture, and in so few numbers . . . it doesn't take a genius to deduce that something unusual is up. Naturally, therefore, I was intrigued."

"And that's really all you know, eh?" Nibulus asked skeptically.

"That, and the fact that you are headed for Melhus, via Wrythe, and that presumably means you're after some relic—holy or unholy—in Vaagenfjord Maw."

He scanned their faces in quick succession, reading their eyes, then guessed again. "Well, perhaps not a relic, but it does have something to do with priestly matters, or you wouldn't have brought this wrinkled old prune along." He gestured at Appa. "In any case, it's obvious that if you're going to Melhus, it's to plunder the old Rawgr keep. There's bugger-all else to do there, I can tell you.

"I'll give you some advice for free: Anything worth looting from that place was taken long ago. It's been the biggest draw for tomb raiders for five hundred years. Not that the Peladanes left much after their siege, but then they never do, do they?"

Nibulus should have been enraged at this. It was his duty to be enraged. This was the gravest insult to all that his kind stood for—even if his kind were all perfectly aware that it was the truth—and for most Peladanes it would have been met with instant retribution involving (at the very least) a heavy wooden club. But Nibulus had never been the zealous type, and there was still the matter of this man's putting an arrow directly into the eye of that howling beast in almost near-darkness. Instead he contented himself with a snort of contempt. That was so much easier.

"So how do you know—I mean, what makes you think I'm Warlord Artibulus's son?" he asked, ignoring the stranger's impudent smirk. "I'm sure none of us mentioned *him* at any stage."

"Oh, come come, you sell yourself short!" the other chided. "The son of Artibulus is well known throughout the North. How many other people do you know with the name Nibulus?"

Fair point, Nibulus conceded.

"Yes," the man continued, "Nibulus Wintus: only child of the Warlord of Wyda-Aescaland. No brothers, no *sisters* . . . married, yet *still* no children."

"So who are you?" the Peladane interrupted. "You still haven't told us your name!"

"Kuthy," the man stated simply. "Kuthy Tivor."

There was a stunned silence broken only by the sound of the stranger adding more wood to the fire.

Kuthy Tivor! It was a name known to all of them; a name spoken of in stories from one end of the continent to the other, from the westernmost isles of Pendonium to the Brunamara Mountains that formed the eastern frontier of Vregh-Nahov, and throughout all the lands between. Even in Qaladmir they had heard the name. Stories were told of him in a hundred different languages, lays were sung of his deeds, and there was not one race in all the lands of Lindormyn that did not speak of his adventures (with the possible exception of the Gjoeger, who had never taken to his ostentation, and considered him a bit of a show-off, if truth were to be told).

He was a warrior, a traveler, an adventurer, a bounty hunter, a soldier of fortune; even an accomplished flautist, some said, though he himself hotly denied this defamatory slur. Kuthy was a true legend in his own time, the last of the living heroes.

But was this grizzled, irksome old wanderer that now sat among them truly the hero of a hundred songs? Their skepticism was voiced most eloquently by their leader:

"Bollocks!" Nibulus scowled.

"No, it's true," Appa chipped in, though there was reluctance in his voice, "I've read his soul; and this, at least, isn't a lie."

Again they stared at him in wonder. Kuthy merely smiled back, and nodded, inclining his head toward the aged priest. Then he got up and squatted with his backside to the fire, steaming dry his damp patches.

"So are all those stories about you true, then?" asked Finwald, trying to mask any traces of admiration that might be peeping out from under their mantle of indifference.

Kuthy continued to warm his rear end over the flames and wood smoke without response. Eventually, just as Nibulus started to say something, he cut him short, replying: "Oh, I very much doubt it; people have a habit of elaborating on the truth. Makes what they say sound so much more interesting, makes it worth a story. To be honest, I could go to relieve myself in the gutter and a few weeks later it would've become exaggerated into an entire saga. No, you don't want to believe what people say. It's mostly rubbish."

This, at least, they could believe.

"So what brings you here, then?" Appa asked in a conversational tone. He had not forgiven the man for calling him a wrinkled old prune, but he was determined not to show it.

"Just got down from the North," Kuthy replied. "Had some business up at Trollbotn, in the Ildjern Mountains, you know? And was on my way to Godtha to collect my wages. I was going by the northern coast way, aiming to go all the way to Wrythe, as a matter of fact: going to sell my sledge and dog team there before heading down the Dragon Coast to Ghouhlem"—he held his moose-gut whip up for them to see—"but the dogs got killed by Jotuns, so I've had to leg it all the way down here. Been traveling weeks now, what with having to hunt along the way and everything. . . . I was going to stop off at Edgemarsh—Myst-Hakel—to get myself sorted out a bit before heading west to Ghouhlem. . . . But then I came across you lot, sleeping in the woods like a bunch of militia-reserve squaddies. Thought then I'd tag along a bit, see if there was anything in it for me, you know. . . ."

The implications of what he had just told them were not lost on the company. "Business at Trollbotn" was open to a wide variety of interpretations, but all of them unbelievably dangerous. If he had gone there alone, then either he was a fool or the songs and stories greatly underestimated him. And Jotuns? Those terrible slayers of the frozen wastes, the ice giants . . . to have escaped them must have been worthy of a saga in its own right.

But at the mention of Ghouhlem, Bolldhe and Nibulus exchanged knowing glances across the fire. As far as they were concerned, anyone in the pay of the Dhracus must have few reservations, if any at all, about whom they worked for. The Dhracus were a race regarded with both awe and fear by all others, but mercifully kept themselves to themselves in their isolated lands of Godtha and Ghouhlem.

They shifted uneasily, not sure what to say after that. This man clearly had even fewer scruples than he was letting on.

It might have been the wind, or their own tiredness, but to the onlookers it really did seem that the "legs" of his hat seemed to unfold themselves, and wave in a macabre way about his head.

Bolldhe called to mind one of the stories he had heard of the Tivor. He was said to have a terrible secret, some unspeakable aberration that afflicted his head, and that was why he wore this hat, this strange helm that he would never remove in public.

Nibulus looked as if he were mulling over something important in his head. At length, he seemed to inwardly shrug, as though he had just made a decision. "I suppose it remains for us to thank you for helping out just then," he admitted. "I don't know what that visitant was, but I'm glad you gave it one in the eye. And I don't mind admitting I'm impressed; that was a marvelous shot, especially in the dark. A man of your talents could be a useful ally in these uncertain lands. . . ."

He paused. Now that he had said it, he was not sure he ought to have. The words had sounded better in his head than they did out in the open. All around him eyes were cast down, and someone coughed. No one said anything more for quite a while.

Eventually, however, the silence altered, very gradually, from one of discomfort to one of expectancy. Perhaps their leader's idea was not so bad after all. They had already lost two of their number, and that was before the really dangerous part had even begun. And obviously Kuthy knew these lands better than any of them. . . .

The idea was just beginning to take on a more solid form in their heads when Nibulus continued: "You *do* know what that thing was back there, don't you?"

Kuthy Tivor hesitated. It was a hesitation that told them that no, actually, he didn't. "Whatever it was, I would not like to meet it again. That arrow went straight into the brain, and yet it could still run away. Whatever it was—is—it isn't going to die in the normal way . . . so we'll have to have a care. It could easily return, and I can't guarantee to manage such a lucky shot next time."

"*We* will have to have a care?" Paulus echoed. "Who said anything about you coming along?"

"Nobody, Long Lad," Kuthy replied, "but I reckon it'd be wise for us to stick together till sunup at least, for all our sakes. You swiped the biggie a good un yourself, and it won't forget either of us."

They settled down for what remained of the night, and did not speak further. Paulus, however, remained standing, eyeing the newcomer with enmity. His gaunt form appeared like Death itself, standing there in the night, surrounded by mist, the long sword extending out from his black coat.

Eventually, he turned back to watch the trees, keeping his solitary vigil.

Paulus's vigil did not end when it got light, however, or as the company broke camp later that morning. For, much to his disgust, it now seemed that the newcomer had decided to take as an outright invitation what the Peladane had surely only hinted at. There he was, rolling up what scant baggage he had and, by all appearances, preparing to set off with them. What was more, nobody seemed to be raising any objection. In fact, they seemed reluctant to say anything at all.

"This is the way to Godtha, then, is it?" the mercenary questioned him finally as they began their day's trek northward. "Or to Ghouhlem, or even Myst-Hakel?"

"By a slightly more circuitous route," Kuthy replied, not bothering even to look up at the mercenary who walked by his side, glaring down at him.

"Of course," Paulus clicked his tongue, "I was forgetting—you know these lands so much better than we do. It's just that, last time I looked, I'm sure the Dhracus lands lay distinctly west, or southwest . . . And I'm even more sure that Myst-Hakel lies to the south, seeing as that's the place we've just come from."

"I don't mind helping out for one more day," Kuthy informed him without stopping. "These woods are likely to be more dangerous for you now, and I can take you by quick ways that are out of harm's way. . . ."

"You've been following us for three days at least already," Paulus stated coldly, "heading *northwards*."

But it seemed that any question marks hanging over their new companion's head were, for the present, going to go unanswered. The priests were not now quite so forthcoming with their affirmations of trust in Kuthy but, with a beast abroad, everyone appeared to prefer the risk of the Tivor's presence to his absence, no matter how untrustworthy he might otherwise seem.

Everyone except the Nahovian, he himself mused with rancor, as he resumed his position at the rear.

"I have a suggestion to make, if you don't mind," Kuthy informed them as they made camp at the end of that day's march.

The air was noticeably colder nowadays, the warmth of the late summer wanting to have nothing to do with this place. These woods were more dreadful and fear-laden than any of them had previously imagined and, to cap it all, Wodeman had done another of his disappearing acts sometime during the morning. It was his way, they all knew, but *now* . . . ?

Everybody was edgy and, deep in their hearts, they had to admit they wished they had never entered Fron-Wudu at all. An uncomfortable pause now followed Kuthy's comment, loud with the unspoken thought from everybody: *Oh no, here it comes. . . .*

"It occurred to me earlier on today that, now I've come this far, it seems hardly worth my while going all the way back south just to reach Myst-Hakel, and *then* to proceed all the way through the Herdlands to Godtha. No, if you like, I can take you northwest through the woods from here, right through the forest, and bring you out near the Seter Heights. There you'd be almost within sight of Wrythe, and I myself wouldn't be far from the Dragon Coast; it'd work out favorably on all sides."

They had spent a whole day with Kuthy Tivor, and though none of them now would totally trust him, the thought of his protection and guidance in this cold, hostile land, where they had expected to find none, did seem more than a little tempting.

"So we'd part company at the Seter Heights, then," Nibulus stated, wondering where the catch lay.

"That would be the obvious place," Kuthy confirmed.

"And nobody need make any diversions for anyone else's sake," Finwald cut in. "Sounds all right to me."

"If it's a shortcut," Appa opined, "it gets my vote."

No one said it in so many words, but there was a general feeling among them that they would like to get this part of their journey over with as quickly as possible.

"Good," said Nibulus. "Then it's decided, we—"

"But, before we make any hasty decisions," Kunthy interrupted him, "I do have an alternative suggestion . . ."

Oh no, it has *come.*

". . . One that would halve your journey."

They all eyed one another doubtfully. "And that is?" Nibulus asked.

Kuthy grinned. "Why do you need to go all the way west, through all that treacherous forest, only to cut back east again as soon as you reach the northern coast? Let's face it, Melhus Island is as directly north of us as you could hope, from here. As the crow flies, it cannot be more than half the distance."

"I take it you use the term 'as the crow flies' metaphorically," Finwald put in, "or is that your intended mode of travel? For if we're to do as you suggest, it'd have to be that way."

"What?"

"Well, far be it for me to gainsay one who claims to know these lands better than we do, but your plan does appear to neglect the small matter of the intervening mountains."

"He's right," Nibulus admitted ruefully. "According to our seers back home, not to mention dear Gwyllch, the Giant Mountains are the largest and highest range in the entire continent, and one which has never been breached by man. *Never.* Not even the Gwyllch's Paladins managed to get back home that way."

"I thought they all went back to Pendonium by ship, the same way they came?" Appa asked.

"Not Gwyllch's company," Finwald informed him. "His lot had never come that way in the first place. Gwyllch's reward for all his loyal service and bravery was the long march south: back the way he'd come."

Nibulus smiled fondly at the Lightbearer and his knowledge of this history, even with such a cynical take on it. "It was his *duty,*" he pointed out, "and I'm sure he didn't raise any objection."

"Oh, I'm sure he absolutely loved it."

"Months earlier," Nibulus continued, ignoring the priest, "Gwyllch had been despatched to Nordwas to lead the Aescal battalion from there— overland—to meet up with Bloodnose and the main force at Wrythe."

"And once the job was done," Finwald cut in, "that was where his *'duty'* took him: to lead the Aescal contingent—or what was left of it—back to Nordwas. While Bloodnose meanwhile took the easy way home."

"Due south?" Appa asked, "Through the mountains? But why? They didn't take that way on their journey north. They went *around* the mountains—the way *we're* going. . . ."

"No choice," Nibulus informed him sadly. "After all the time they'd spent at the maw, there simply weren't enough rations to go round—"

"And Bloodnose wasn't exactly the sharing type. So for Gwyllch's company it was either walk home the long, circuitous way—and starve—or try a short cut."

"And that was the last the world ever heard of Gwyllch," the Peladane finished sadly.

Kuthy eyed them all carefully before continuing. "Well, there you go, maybe if you take up this once-in-a-lifetime offer, you might find out what became of them all, for Kuthy can take you by passages known only to him, not *over* the mountains, but *through* them—or, rather, *under* them."

His words were met with a silence that was almost embarrassing. Neither of the priests bothered with the effort of searching the man's soul, for there was not one amongst the company who did not now believe the old rogue was being somewhat economical with the truth.

Or as Nibulus put it: "You lying little shite."

"True!" Kuthy protested, visibly offended. "I assure you. There is a secret tunnel that leads right down and under the mountains, and comes out the other side—"

"A tunnel that passes under the entire range of the Giant Mountains!" Finwald laughed, wondering why they were even bothering to have this conversation. "A tunnel that runs for over a hundred miles?"

"He lies," agreed Paulus. "I say we kill him—he is not to be trusted."

Ignoring this last suggestion, Nibulus said, "Mr. Tivor, it would appear that you are trying to lead us out of our way. Please would you explain."

"And why should you bother going that way anyway?" Bolldhe added, "It might halve our journey, but it would take you right out of *your* way. What's in it for you?"

"So why, if I'm lying, would Gwyllch have ever attempted to cross that terrible barrier?" Kuthy protested. "Was there not an easier way for him and his exhausted and battle-scarred warriors to get home?"

"He does have a point," Nibulus admitted, his curiosity somewhat aroused now, for it had always been a mystery exactly what had become of Gwyllch after the siege.

"And your priests have a skill which they don't appear to be using," Kuthy went on. "Well, boys, am I lying?"

It appeared not, the mage-priests eventually conceded with incredulity—though Appa still seemed troubled by something.

"Thank you," Kuthy breathed. "Now if you'll let me explain, the tunnel I speak of runs only for about half a day's march beneath the mountains. It starts high up in a cleft that can be reached by a minimal amount of climbing; it bores through the mountain, and emerges above the foothills of the land that lies beyond."

"Land that lies beyond?" Nibulus asked dubiously.

"Of course! The mountains don't stretch all the way to the Last Shore; they merely *ring* around an isolated country that hardly anyone knows about. It shouldn't take us more than five or six days to cross the intervening basin, and there at the foot of the northern perimeter, we'll reach another tunnel, leading out of the mountain girdle."

They looked round at each other doubtfully. Then at last, Bolldhe inclined his head to look Kuthy directly in the eyes. "You are talking about Eotunlandt, aren't you?"

"Ah!" Kuthy responded, eyeing the wanderer shrewdly. "Another Asker of Questions. Yes, Bolldhe, I am talking about Eotunlandt."

Tales of Eotunlandt had been told for centuries. It was claimed that within the fastnesses of some distant mountains at the Edge of the World, there lay a strange and marvellous realm that was locked away from the rest of the world: "*. . . a lost horizon, an Elysian Field, an undying land forever sealed . . .*" If any story seemed too fantastical to be true even by the skalds' standards, it was attributed to that mythical land. But even the stories purporting to have originated from there were considered by most to be mere fables. In any case, there was no firm record of anyone actually climbing those mountains to find out.

Eotunlandt. Was it truly a fairy story? Did it truly exist? Did anyone truly care?

"It is said to be a land closed to mortals," Paulus commented. Everyone turned to him. " 'Tis the land of the elder spirits, and . . . *Huldres,*" he went on, almost disgorging the last word.

Nibulus was less impressed. "Well I never," he said, "all these years I've lived in Wyda-Aescaland, and I never realized the Land of Dreams lay so close to our home. And there was me under the impression that it supposedly lay on the very edge of the world."

Kuthy's "hat" bristled, and slid forward a touch. "It *is* on the edge of the world. Where do you think the name 'the Last Shore' comes from?"

Nibulus frowned, then stared at the hat and asked, "What d'you feed that thing on, anyway?"

"Stupid questions, usually," Kuthy replied, "but in the absence of that, cowardice will do."

Bristling in turn, Nibulus decided to bring the matters at hand forward. "And how would you know of this secret tunnel, Tivor? What does it, and this Eotunlandt of yours, have to do with *you*? Are *you* a Huldre? Or an Elder Spirit?"

"And who constructed this passageway?" Finwald demanded, in more practical tenor.

"The truth of the matter is," Kuthy replied, somewhat sheepishly, "that I don't really know. In fact, to be perfectly honest, I haven't got the foggiest idea. It certainly wasn't the spirits, whoever or whatever they are—for theirs is a secret land shut away from the rest of the world, and they intend to keep it that way. It is however possible that Huldres built it, maybe as a way into mortal lands—"

"To plague us with their deviant ways!" Paulus seethed.

"I suppose so," Kuthy went on, glancing at the Nahovian curiously, "but the fact is, it is there. You have my oath on it."

"Hmn, very convincing, I'm sure," Nibulus commented, "but you still neglect to answer my question: how do *you* know about it?"

"I'm an adventurer," he answered. "It's my job to know about such things. There are so many stories about Eotunlandt all over the Far North, more than anywhere else I've been to, and when I first came here, I was naturally intrigued. If such a land existed, imagine what treasures might lie within. And all as untouched as your mage-priests' maidenhood."

Appa coughed, and gave Finwald a knowing look that said: *Friend Kuthy here obviously hasn't met Aluine. . . .*

No, Finwald nodded back, *nor Marla, come to that. . . .*

"So," Kuthy continued, "I kept my ears open. For many years I made it my business to research the legend. I'd listen to the stories of the greybeards, the lays of the *akyns;* I'd ask questions, consult seers, even read books on the subject. In the end, whilst on a little jaunt through the ice caves of Hoc-Valdrea, I came upon an old inscription. It was *extremely* old, too—a whole wall covered in petroglyphs of some ancient script. Fascinating stuff. Well, I was . . . preoccupied with other more pressing matters, as you might say, but in my line of work one doesn't simply walk away from an entire wall of ancient inscriptions without doing anything, so I copied them down.

"Anyway, months passed, then years, and I all but forgot about them. But one day, as I was selling some old scrolls to a theurgist in Drachrastaland, the parchment I'd written the inscriptions down on fell out of the pile, and before I knew it the old fellow was reading it—translating it for me, if you please! He said it was an ancient hieroglyphic system used by the stone-dwellers who had lived in the area around Wyrld's Point, and that it described a legend, something about the 'Land of the Second Ones.' So, for a fee he translated the whole of it for me, and it was then I realized it was a set of instructions on how to get into Eotunlandt!

"Within weeks I was searching the mountains. The legend was vague, obscure, open to all sorts of misinterpretations; but with a little help from some friends of mine"—he spread his arms, as if to imitate a bird—"within months I found it: the entrance to Eotunlandt!"

"So?" prompted Bolldhe. "What happened then?" He was stirred by this tale, and did not care who knew it. In all his own travels he had never come across any legends carved in stone leading to hidden kingdoms. *Some people have all the luck!*

"What happened then," Kuthy continued, noting the glint in Bolldhe's eye, "was that I followed the passage, and it did indeed usher me through to a land beyond. I tell you, it was the fairest, most wonderful realm that has ever beglammered my eyes: blue skies, soft, rich grass, and all within it—trees, beasts, birds, insects—unique. And it was bright and sunny almost every day; the rain, when it did fall, was sweet as dew—"

"But what of those that dwelt there?" demanded Paulus. "Were there no Huldres?"

"Oh yes," Kuthy replied, sensing the Nahovian's anxiety, "Huldres aplenty; small, sweet, and charming; inquisitive and . . . trusting."

Paulus's sword arm twitched with anticipation. He could almost feel a fit coming on.

"I traveled through without mishap, heading north, right across the land. Eventually, I reached the mouth of a second tunnel. This one led steeply upwards until it came out high up in the northern foothills. All below, for miles around, I could see spread out before me like a map: the Last Shore, the Jagt Straits, and Melhus Island just nigh, like a smoky, black patch of tar, all fiery, steaming and turbulent. It was a magnificent sight!"

With that, Kuthy reclined back on one elbow and stared into the flames of the campfire, his pitch complete.

It was all up to them, now.

Nibulus looked around at his company. Finwald was clearly at a loss, and merely returned his regard with a shrug. Appa seemed deep in thought. Bolldhe, however, actually looked enthusiastic for once. And Paulus was almost salivating at the thought of all those Huldres, "small, sweet, charming, inquisitive . . . and *trusting.*"

"Appa?" the Peladane asked, interrupting the man from his rumination and drawing him aside. "I've trusted your 'sight' up till now; what do you think? Is he telling the truth?"

Appa breathed out slowly, dreading the implications of what he was about to say. He looked troubled, as if somehow torn between two great evils. "I believe he *is* telling the truth," he replied eventually, "and he means us no harm . . . exactly. Though there is something, some small something, that he is holding back from us."

"But do you trust him?"

Appa, however, remained strangely noncommittal, and would say no more, even when the Peladane twisted his ears painfully.

The company did not discuss it further. They just sat around their fire and thought their thoughts: thoughts of a man that nobody really believed in—of a *land* that nobody really believed in—did not want to believe in—yet *had* to believe in—a land of Huldres, so hated, so against everything they stood for, and yet so desired—a land where the sun always shone and the grass was so rich.

A shortcut.

And then this forest—its unrelenting miles of dreariness, of cold, of evil . . . and the beast that would be back for them, maybe not that night, maybe not the next, but sometime during their long trek through Fron-Wudu, on some dark night when they were not expecting it.

Five days later they emerged from the cover of the forest, and gazed at last upon the magnificence of the Giant Mountains.

Whilst still beneath the forest canopy they had slowly worked their way up the lower foothills. Soon the trees had begun thinning out sufficiently to allow the company their first brief glimpses of the mountains' ice-capped peaks between the gaps in the treetops. It was a land of boulders and rock pillars; strange, mace-shaped flowers of brilliant amethyst that imbued the forest with the fragrance of aniseed; and twisted conifers hung with immense, hairy vines. Tumultuous streams of clearest water surged down deep-cut troughs to their side, and the air was alive with the croaking and screeching of frenetic birds.

The mood of the travelers had thereupon transformed from one of desperation and flight to an urgent hunger for adventure. The spirit of the soldier of fortune was clearly rubbing off on them.

Now as they stood atop the foothills, with the vast, dark sprawl of Fron-Wudu close behind them, the company gazed up in breathless awe at the dazzling white splendor of the fabled Giant Mountains before them. Cliffs, slopes, promontories, and couloirs filled their vision, climbing up, up, and up, farther and farther, piling one on top of the other until finally attaining heights that none of the Southerners would ever have believed possible.

A chill wind blew down from the icy heights above, swept on past them, and moaned eerily through the treetops behind. The boom and slither of an avalanche echoed down through the valleys and passes high above. Circling in the grey sky, a mere speck against the light, a lone bird of prey called out its plaintive cry.

"Look!" Kuthy called out to them. "This valley to the left—it's at the top of that we'll find the gateway to Eotunlandt. See, follow the line of darker rock as it reaches up that ridge there; you get to that odd-shaped stack of boulders at the summit, and beyond that, that's where the cleft is, the one that leads to the gate."

They stared hard through the tears the icy wind brought to their eyes, following the directions of their new guide, but they could only guess where he was pointing to. Wodeman had still not turned up, even after all this time, and though they all tried not to think about him, they could not help but wish he were here now, to use the evidence of his superior eyes to tell them whether or not Kuthy were bluffing.

Eventually, though, they found that they could spot it, that steep arête with its distant pinnacle, just barely visible if one concentrated hard enough.

"But . . . it's miles!" Finwald exclaimed in genuine shock. "You didn't mention anything about that!"

Appa, too, gaped in disbelief, positively cowering beneath the frown of the slope before him. "You surely can't expect us to climb all the way up there? *Pech!* I'm an old man, not a mountain goat!"

Kuthy completely ignored the pair of them. Even the others appeared unconcerned at their priests' carping. Bolldhe, in fact, was wide-eyed with eagerness.

"Nobody's doing any climbing this evening," Kuthy informed them. "We need a full day's light to ascend by, so we're setting off at first light tomorrow. Right, Peladane?"

"That's the plan," Nibulus confirmed with a slight smile. "For now, men, get what rest you can. We camp here for the night."

That night the company made camp beneath the sparse shelter of a few trees atop a hillock. The light of the waxing moon reflected off the snowy slopes of the mountains to cast a cold, silver sheen over the forest below. Just beneath the treetops hung a mist, giving the forest the appearance of a swampy marsh, but up here at the foot of the mountains where the frigid wind came in fits and gusts, it was clear. A man could see far on this night.

They would have to proceed, they knew, though Wodeman had still not shown up. If he did not return to them within the next few hours, that would be it. None there understood exactly how the shaman managed to find them again in the wilds after those long absences of his, or indeed why he disappeared off like that in the first place. But this time he did not even know where, or in which direction, they were heading; the idea of coming this way had been discussed *after* he had last vanished. Once they were inside the tunnel, they would surely be beyond even his perception.

Well, just in case, they had lit a campfire that, on this high place, would be visible for many miles around. But it was not only the shaman that might be drawn to this beacon; during the previous night, strange noises had been heard in the distance, like sounds of something big moving about in the trees, something on the hunt. . . .

Bolldhe's teeth kept rattling in his mouth, but he hardly even noticed. He sat with his back against the bole of a mossy tree, surveying the mist-shrouded forest thoughtfully. The night sky was cloudless, and he could already see the stars. Apart from a low chattering of wind in the treetops, there was little sound to disturb his thoughts that night. Zhang was champing the grass nearby, but everybody else had turned in for the night.

Appa had taken on the first watch that night. Bolldhe could hear him now, muttering to himself in that mad, fussy way of his, tapping his ring against his torch amulet with one hand and scratching his belly with the other.

Tired after the day's grueling march, Bolldhe's eyes closed without him realizing it. Soon he was drifting in semiconsciousness, the old priest's muttering
threading indistinct images of his companions through his thoughts; his companions, and all that had brought him here to this strange, unknown land.
How bizarre they all were, he thought lazily. What an odd bunch he had fallen
in with, to be sure: a ragtag crew of experts and amateurs, all from completely
different worlds and walks of life, all with completely different beliefs, all motivated by completely different purposes.

And the two priests, they alone of all the party who should be united, even
they were as opposed to each other as any of the rest. One would have thought
that they at least would share the same ideas. But, no, it was as if they were
fighting separate battles.

There was Finwald: he of the keen intellect, the good looks, the affable
manner; a man who could have anything, be anything, he desired, and yet had
elected to become a mage-priest, of all things. And not only a mage-priest, but
one with such unshakable beliefs, so uniquely devoted to his calling, as to
abandon his betrothed, Aluine, for a terrible quest in the Far North. A man of
understanding, a Cunnan, he knew exactly what he believed in and exactly
what he must do.

Then there was Appa: a specter of a man as empty of life as the dogma he
preached. Yet he too was a baffling enigma. For he, more than any other, knew
what it was to suffer for what he believed in. He was old and frail and, though
he possessed a constitution that was surprising in one so elderly, his health was
deteriorating with every passing day. They were all aware of just how hoarse his
coughing had become lately, and his skin seemed more ashen every time
Bolldhe looked at him. How long he could last in the frozen wastes of Melhus,
Bolldhe did not care to think. But there was something deep inside Appa, too,
that was driving him on, forcing his aged bones northwards mile by mile, every
painful step of the way.

A wrinkled old prune, ha! That was a good one.

So what drove an old man to such efforts? What indeed drove Finwald? Or
any of their company, for that matter, even its newest member? Yes, a ragtag
bunch of strangers that Fate had thrown together for a quest that none of them
truly understood.

Story of my life, Bolldhe considered, *never knowing what I'm doing, where
I'm going to end up, or why. . . .*

Within moments he was asleep, and the forest's murmurings followed him.

There was now only silence. A deep silence that numbed the brain and deadened the nerves. Silence, and darkness. Bolldhe was asleep with his companions, he knew, but it had been so long since he had heard them that he was
beginning to doubt they were there anymore.

Had they left him? Was he really on his own? It started to feel as if everyone had died and he was the only person in the world. Fear crept into his heart, and with it a black despair that could only be the work of nightmares.

His hand stole from the warmth of his bedroll and reached out into the cold, dark air. Tentatively he felt about himself, but there was nothing except cold rock, and at once he withdrew his hand.

Again there was that familiar nagging at the back of his mind, and he was worried about something. What it might be, though, he knew not. His unease felt just like it had a month ago, in the Blue Mountain cave as he had listened to the words of Finwald, Appa, and Wodeman. Their words came back to him now, twisting and turning in his mind like coiled serpents: Appa's muttering, Finwald's rhythmic enunciation, Wodeman's chanting. But above all it was that chant, which droned on, deep and insistent.

Bolldhe could not even decide where he was. It indeed felt as if he were back in the Blue Mountains, but that had been weeks ago, surely? He could not still be there, could he? And if he was, that would mean he would have to do all that traveling again . . . once more he would have to defend himself against the wolves and the Leucrota, leave the mountains, leave the company, and then all that stuff with the Huldre, and then the swamp town, and, and . . .

And the horror that awaited him down the silver mine!

Suddenly two pale hands reached out for him from the darkness. They were the same ones as had come out of the darkness of the side shaft and slapped him across the face. Instantly he recoiled, and almost gagged in terror.

But they did not strike him. This time they held something in their grasp. Their bony, thievish grasp. It was a little wolf! A tiny wolf cub, all grey fur and needle-sharp teeth.

Still frightened, but desperate to overcome his fear, Bolldhe reached out and took the cub. It wriggled in his grasp like a worm, and laughed with the voice of a demented child. Grinning, for what reason he could not say, for he was as terrified as ever, Bolldhe began stroking the wolf cub. He stroked and stroked until before long its fur began to slough off in great, sodden clumps, and he was left with a raw, bleeding lump of lupine meat that still laughed in its shrill, childlike voice.

He gagged in nausea, longing to thrust this vile obscenity from him. But he somehow could not let go. The air grew heavy about him, and he realized that he was paralyzed in this darkness. All he could see was this wolf carcass that should have been dead but was very much alive. It glared at him with eyes that were as red as burning embers.

Then the full horror bore down upon him from all sides, a deep, instinctive terror that assailed his every sense.

The wolves were coming to get him.

He broke into a run, and he ran and ran and ran, still clinging on to the jabbering monstrosity that dripped its lifeblood down his arms. The whole pack was after him, led by the cub's mother, the Leucrota, getting closer with each second. Her feet pounded upon the ground behind him like a quake, her mane flew about insanely, and the hoarse rattle of her hot breath grew louder and louder; even now he could smell its carrion fetor heavy in the night air. Even as he could feel the agony from the arrow embedded in her eye.

He could not hope to outrun them. His friends were now running with him too, crying out desperately for him to drop the howling bundle of meat.

Then the pack was upon them. Within seconds, Bolldhe and all the company would be devoured. But the seconds seemed to last for an eternity—

Suddenly he sat bolt upright, and fully awake. Dripping with sweat, he looked about himself. It was still nighttime, but he was back in the foothills of the Giant Mountains, above Fron-Wudu. His companions were all sleeping peacefully, and the comforting smell of wood smoke drifted up his nose, but still the scent of beast was heavy in the air.

Looking across at the campfire, he caught sight of the wolflike figure that crouched just beyond the dying embers. Glowing like a demon's in the darkness, its eyes glinted wickedly, and its teeth were bared.

"Dreaming?" it said in a voice loaded with meaning.

It was the sorcerer, and his smile was wider and sharper even than a Leucrota's.

"Pel's Bells!" the Wanderer breathed in anguish. "I wish you'd send me some pleasant dreams for a change!"

14

Entering Eotunlandt

Bolldhe was still dwelling on his dream when the company finally reached the gateway to Eotunlandt.

"What?" he said vaguely. "Were you talking to me?"

Nibulus sighed. It was already two hours to noon, and Bolldhe had not said a single word to anyone all morning. Everyone else had worked their way up the slopes with steady determination, yet also with an uncharacteristic buoyancy in his step. The thought that they would soon be entering the fabled Land of the Second Ones was like a hand on their backs, both lifting and driving them upward to the promised gateway. Bolldhe, however, had remained aloof from them, guiding the nimble-footed Adt-T'man upward with one hand permanently gripped on the beast's shaggy withers, intractable as ever. Something was clearly preoccupying his thoughts, something that had caused him to brood sullenly all morning.

"Have you been listening to a word I've said?" Nibulus demanded impatiently. "We've been awake for over four hours now, and you still don't seem to be with us. Something bothering you, is there?"

Bolldhe stared at him dumbly. "No. No, it's all right, I've just been feeling a bit restless lately—haven't had much *sleep*." This last word he directed toward the shaman nearby.

"I was just saying," Nibulus went on, "that Kuthy's going to be off scouting about for this gateway of his for a while, and would you like to share a tot of sloe gin with me?"

Bolldhe glanced at the pewter hip flask extended toward him, with its strange burn marks and metallic "growths," and shook his head. He allowed himself to be led by Zhang over to a small pool of spring water nearby, and went back to his thoughts.

Nibulus let him go without a word. He himself was red-faced and sweating from the effort of the climb, and enjoyed a good swig of the gin. Though the lower slopes had only a light patching of snow, the ascent had been steep in places, and the gullies that had taken them far into the mountains had been choked with thorny bushes, boulders, and scree. There were no visible paths to be seen, not even a goat trod, and the whole company had been forced to back-track several times before the Tivor decided that he knew where he was. The only breaks in this grueling climb had been when Appa's coughing fits had forced them to pause for a rest.

But the Peladane's flustered exterior belied the excitement that churned within him. For they had finally found the cleft in the rocks that would lead to Kuthy's secret doorway. Not only that, but Wodeman had returned to them, and also they were about to leave the dreaded Fron-Wudu well behind them. In addition to all this, it appeared that they had managed to escape that beast, whatever it had been. Things appeared to be looking up for a change, and he was as happy as he could be.

They could now all afford to take a well-earned breather. Nibulus looked away from the grumpy old wanderer, and instead viewed the lands stretched out below. He breathed in deeply the mountain air, and stretched his arms wide to embrace the vast wildlands below him. In various shades of grey, green, and brown, the whole terrain stretched before him as far as his eye could see, not a cloud nor any mist to obscure his view. He could see right the way across to the Blue Mountains, now no more than a thin line of jagged peaks on the very edge of the horizon.

The rest of the company preferred to take it easy in this last opportunity before journeying down into the depths of the mountains. While their guide scouted ahead, they started to prepare a hot meal. Only Appa did not join in. He was flat on his back, staring up at the empty sky, a look of pain on his face and pleading in his eyes.

After only a few minutes Kuthy returned to them from the far end of the cleft, and summoned the men around him. There was a slight consternation on his face as he spoke, whether genuine or not, they could not tell.

"Well," he announced, "I've found the portal."

There was a general buzz of guarded satisfaction at this news.

". . . And?"

"And there is something else I feel I ought to tell you. It may not be of any consequence, in fact I'm sure it isn't, but you may as well be warned, just in case."

"Well, what is it?" Nibulus prompted irascibly. "Come on, man, spit it out."

"It's probably nothing," Kuthy went on, "but the last time I was here, the door was locked. It's like a great millstone, you see, and you roll it aside to gain entry to the passage beyond. There's a mechanism that holds it in place, actually draws it into the rock face, and then holds it there. And, once inside, there's a similar device for locking the door. But . . . now it seems to be unsecured. Anybody could get in there if they wanted."

They looked at one another doubtfully, not sure what this could imply.

"What are you saying?" Finwald asked apprehensively. "Did you fail to lock it the last time you used it? Or is there something else?"

"I don't know, it may be just that; I could well have forgotten—or just not bothered—to resecure the door on the inside once I'd got in. At the time, that would have been the least of my concerns. Or, it may be that others have used the doorway since . . ."

"When was the last time you used it?" asked Nibulus.

"A fair few years ago," Kuthy informed them, "but there's something that tells me the door's been used a bit more recently than that."

A sigh of disappointment whispered around the company.

"So it would appear that this hidden tunnel of yours isn't quite as secret after all," Nibulus concluded, regarding the adventurer with annoyance. "I do hope you realize what you're leading us into, here."

Kuthy looked genuinely uncomfortable. He clearly was not used to his secrets being discovered by others, and thoughts of wringing the neck of that bloody Drachrastalandic theurgist were now uppermost in his mind.

"Yes, so do I," he replied to Nibulus's question, "but I'm sure it'll be all right."

"It had better be," Finwald remarked. "We've come too far to turn back now."

They ate their meal in silence after that. Half an hour later, after washing their bowls and refilling their waterskins from the spring, the company followed Kuthy down the high-sided cleft, and disappeared from sight.

Taking one last backward glance at the world of light behind him, Bolldhe followed.

"Here we are," Kuthy announced, pointing at the rock face. "The portal."

Had it been secured, they could see, the door would have been very nearly undetectable; it would have appeared nothing more than a cracked seam in the rock (even if a distinctly millstone-shaped cracked seam). But, now it was unsecured, it stood out clearly from the rest of the rock face, and could have been easily rolled aside by anyone who might have sought shelter in this cleft over the intervening years.

Both Kuthy and Wodeman searched the ground for signs of anyone passing that way recently. After a while, Wodeman spoke up:

"There are some tracks over here," he confirmed, "and they're not that old. Could be that a few people came by in the last month, even two weeks ago."

"Two weeks?" Nibulus exclaimed. "Then they could still be in Eotunlandt right now. We'll have to be extremely cautious. Kuthy, roll back the door. We're going in."

Kuthy leaned his temple sword against the rocks, so he could give the great
granite door a firm push. Surprisingly for something the size and general appearance of a millstone, it rolled back easily. Immediately a cold blast of air
howled out of the dark cavity beyond, causing those standing immediately in
front of it to back away and shield their faces. There was a damp smell with an
unmistakable undercurrent of decay. Around the edge of the ancient stonework
hung trailing growths of semicrystallized moss, which now glistened like dead
elvers as they swayed gently in the air currents.

Appa gagged and held a hand over his mouth. "Cuna preserve us all," he
jabbered. "We're not going in there, are we?" His watery eyes bulged as he
stared down into the blackness. There was no sound other than the shrill
whistling of the wind, but his hand instinctively groped for the talisman around
his neck.

"Don't fret, Appa," said a quiet voice at his shoulder. "It's only a hole. Finwald'll see you're all right."

"Fetch the torches, men," the Peladane ordered abruptly. "Finwald, Appa,
Kuthy, you get 'em lit. We may as well get this over with as soon as possible."

They did as instructed but, just as they were about to enter, Kuthy grabbed
Nibulus by the arm and placed his torch firmly in the Peladane's hand. Eyeing
him hard, Kuthy said, "I'd rather you held the torch, if you don't mind. I may
be your guide for the present, but I am *not* your link boy."

Nibulus glared back at him through narrowed eyes. Then he merely responded, "Just make sure you stay in front, then, hero. Whatever happens, I'd
rather it happened to you first."

"And good luck to you too," the adventurer replied dryly.

One by one, they passed through the portal, and into the darkness beyond.
Kuthy led the way, followed closely by Nibulus, who was determined not to let
this slippery customer out of his sight. Then came Bolldhe, sword in one hand,
Zhang's rein in the other.

The sword had now faded to a midnight blue with just the faintest corona
of silver. Zhang, too, had darkened; at least, his mood had. The horse was none
too happy about this strange new place his friend was leading him into. None
too happy at all. He sensed by the smell of the air what lay down there, and
could not understand why they did not continue traveling the beautiful
foothills instead. Head forward and nose to the ground, he picked his way forward, and felt even more alarmed when the tunnel began to slope downward.
To make matters worse, Bolldhe had wedged his lantern under the saddle's
girth strap, where it was beginning to get uncomfortably warm. This was not
the first time his master had done this, and Zhang felt like having a quiet word
with him about it—but then, he thought ruefully, the human never seemed to
understand a word he was saying. Maybe the man was a bit slow.

At least in one thing the slough horse had an advantage: he was more
nimble-footed than most of the others. But the clatter of his hooves did cost

them any advantage of stealth they might otherwise have had. Nibulus cursed softly, and considered he might as well have donned his clanking armor after all.

Behind the horse came the two mage-priests, torches held aloft and weapons gripped tightly. Wodeman followed, his eyes wide as an owl's, his nose twitching like a shrew's. Paulus took up the rear, a position he assumed out of habit now, and no one seemed particularly inclined to object. As he stepped through and over the threshold, he turned and heaved the door back into place. It rolled to with a dull thud, and the now dim torchlight was barely able to hold back the darkness that crowded in upon them now.

"Have you set the catch, Paulus?" Nibulus called back from somewhere further down the sloping tunnel.

"Of course," the Nahovian lied. (He was happy to be let loose upon Huldres like a terrier in a barrel of rats, but he would *not* pull the lid shut over him.)

They descended.

Though high-ceilinged enough, the tunnel was narrow and crudely fashioned. It soon began to slope down even more steeply through the granite, forcing the company to pick their way forward with even greater care, and sent a scattering of loose stones slithering down the passage ahead of them.

"Kuthy," Nibulus hissed, "how far down does this damn hole go?"

"Not far, not far," Kuthy replied with infuriating equanimity. "Just a few more minutes and we should reach the bottom."

"And then?"

"And then, the chamber . . . I think."

"Chamber?"

"Yes, like a room, only bigger."

"Tivor!"

"Sorry; it's a wide space linking this entrance tunnel with the tunnel proper. No idea what it's for, but from there on the passage is fairly level, and better-constructed."

"But what's in the chamber?"

"Nothing, as far as I know. Least, there wasn't anything last time. I wouldn't worry, really."

Nibulus grumbled. "Better be on your guard, men," he called back. "Tivor here says there's nothing to worry about."

Suit yourself, Kuthy sighed to himself.

They descended with extreme caution, even though their torches—which none of them had any intention of extinguishing—and the din they were making precluded any possibility of avoiding notice.

"Keep close, and have your weapons ready," Nibulus instructed. "And, Bolldhe, take your horse to the back of the line. I don't want him suddenly panicking down here."

"Don't you worry about Zhang," Bolldhe replied. "He'll be the last one to panic, I assure you. Besides, if there's any trouble, I wouldn't mind finding out what this sword is capable of."

As soon as he said it he chided himself; there was no need for Kuthy to know anything about the flamberge, or their mission.

"I'd be careful, Bolldhe," Finwald whispered in his left ear. "You don't want to risk damaging it unnecessarily."

"For Jugg's sake, preacher," Bolldhe hissed, "it's a bloody sword! What in hell's name am I supposed to do with it? Skin rabbits?"

"He's right, Bolldhe," Appa cautioned. "Don't be too quick to solve all your problems with the sword. Only death lies down that road."

I thought that was the whole idea of this quest, Bolldhe reflected, but did not bother to share this thought with his uninvited counselors.

There was a little whispering from ahead, and soon Kuthy appeared beside him. "If you do want to try out your new sword," he whispered, "why not go on ahead? I'll stay and mind your horse."

"Oh really," Bolldhe replied, "I suppose you'd like to hold my coat while you're at it?"

"Pardon?"

"Doesn't matter. Anyway, I thought you said there was nothing dangerous down there?"

"That's right," the shadowed face before him replied smoothly. "There wasn't, last time. But you saw the unlocked door—something may have wandered in since I was last here. And you're the one with the big sword. . . . What's so special about it anyway? Haven't you ever used it?"

Bolldhe cut him off swiftly. "Just shut up and go away! Look, take the damn horse if you must, and get him to the back of the line." He handed the reins to Kuthy and pushed his way past him and Nibulus, before the soldier of fortune could ask any more difficult questions. Kuthy hung back and let the rest of the line pass by. He grinned, and followed at a distance.

Minutes later, the company emerged one by one into the chamber. It was dank and freezing, and here the stench of decay was almost overwhelming. All eyes strained to see beyond the feeble radius of torchlight, until the Zhang-borne lantern arrived.

"Ugh!" Finwald whispered in disgust. "What is this place?"

They paired off and carefully explored the chamber. The sound of their boots upon the stone mingled with the sputtering of torches and the occasional sharp intake of breath.

"I don't like it," the Peladane stated flatly. "It reeks of death."

He cast his torch about and surveyed the walls. They were simple and undecorated, carved out of the mountain to form a roughly rectangular chamber. From somewhere beyond the light of his torch, the cold wind still blew.

Just then the glow of his torch fell upon a pile of rags on the floor. Nibulus went over to look closer, holding one hand over his mouth and nose against the growing stink. Yes, as he had suspected, they were corpses, partly rotted and crumpled in a heap against one wall.

"*Hsss!*" he called out. "Over here!"

The rest of the company moved over and stood around the two cadavers at a respectful distance, inspecting them with distaste.

"Two weeks old, I'd guess," Nibulus said, "judging by the state of the skin."

"Two months, I'd guess," Bolldhe commented, "judging by the smell."

"Yes," Finwald agreed, "not very nice at all."

With the tip of his sword, Bolldhe poked one of the corpses. It shifted a little, crumpling slightly, and there was a brief buzz from inside it. Then its head fell off. Paulus laughed.

"Who do you think they are?" Nibulus asked Kuthy, who had now come up from behind. "And what happened to them?" There was no mistaking his meaning.

"They're nobody *I* know, if that's what you mean," Kuthy replied defensively, "It's been a long time since I was here last. . . . Let's have a closer look."

He went over and prodded them roughly with his own sword, causing a further angry humming noise from within. There was a popping sound, followed by the hiss of escaping gases; then the rib cage of one of them collapsed. The others stepped right back in distaste, save for Paulus.

"Oh look!" Kuthy exclaimed with a smile, lifting a small drawstring leather bag from the crumpled debris on the floor. He undid the strings, and poured out a small collection of shiny emeralds into his palm.

"Jackpot," he breathed in excitement. "This should make up for my sledge and dog team, and more besides!"

Appa spat in repugnance. "Surely you're not going to rob the dead! Have you no respect?"

"Er, no, don't think so," Kuthy responded absently, and fingered through the gleaming little gems in his hand.

"Well, *we* have," Nibulus stated, "and we're not having anything to do with these corpses. No good can ever come of robbing the dead."

"Possibly less harm than robbing the living," Kuthy chuckled, clearly very pleased with himself. "Anybody else want to have a look? They're bound to have something else on them besides."

"No we do not," Nibulus growled. "Now, please would you put away your precious little jewels and let's move on. Whatever killed these two might still be hanging around here somewhere."

"I wouldn't say no," Paulus replied to Kuthy's suggestion, and promptly set about searching the corpses. The others wrinkled their faces as they watched the mercenary delve his hands into each bundle of rags and bones. "Many of these adventurer types have gold teeth." He prized open their traplike mouths and peered inside.

They left him to his necrophile preoccupations, and went off to search the rest of the chamber. Suddenly Appa noticed a series of scratches etched upon the stone.

"Finwald, over here! I've found some writing on the wall."

He beckoned his brother-in-faith over, and pointed to the characters with trembling fingers.

Finwald stared at them curiously, and read: " 'Fahscheia ul ichnaia Cerddu-Sungnir,' and 'Bolca og Yngstre Kvascna uilldacht okkin-veik Pericciu' . . ."

"What does it mean?"

"How should I know? I'm just a priest, not a bloody linguist."

" 'Cerddu-Sungnir the Supreme was here,' and 'Death to the scum of Pericciu Thieves Guild,' " a voice behind them translated. It was Kuthy, speaking from the safety of the entrance tunnel. "Either these two were thieves belonging to that guild, or just a pair of treasure hunters who stopped here for a rest, and got themselves killed by something lurking in the passage beyond."

For a moment there was a pensive silence. "Enemies of the Pericciu Thieves Guild," Finwald muttered, "or guild members themselves . . . ? I wonder why either would be trying to get into Eotunlandt."

"They left enough litter behind them," Wodeman commented. "I can't believe there was only two of them. There must have been more."

"I don't think we should stay any longer," Nibulus announced, unfastening his armor from Zhang's back and putting it on. "I think there is a guardian down here."

Just then they were distracted by a shout from Paulus. He was holding something shiny in his hand. It appeared to be a kind of punch-dagger, the sort used by foot soldiers or assassins for piercing armor, and more especially the spinal column that lay beneath. Its squat, V-shaped blade glinted sharply in the torchlight.

"Diamond-tipped katar," the mercenary proclaimed with elation. "That'll do nicely."

Nibulus cursed to himself as he tried to fasten the straps on his plastron. "Some secret tunnel!" he swore under his breath. "I'd wager every thief in Lindormyn knows about it."

Bolldhe was not listening to any of this. He was studying Wodeman, whose bearing had gone suddenly taut and poised. Something in the way he sniffed the air told Bolldhe that they were not alone here in the chamber.

Then all of a sudden there was a terrific beating of wings, and a piercing squawk shivered the air to pieces. Immediately both mage-priests dropped their torches and went for their weapons, while someone backing into Paulus knocked the torch from his grasp. There was a brief flare of orange light as the burning brand arced through the air, trailing a streamer of acrid smoke behind it. Then the chamber was plunged into near darkness, lit only by the diminishing glow of the torches dropped on the floor.

For the next minute the whole place rang with the din of battle. Everybody was shouting in confusion and swinging about wildly, not knowing what it was they were fighting against, or where or how many there were. Above the metallic clash of arms, the dull thuds, the cries of pain, and the curses rose the furious flapping of feathered wings and that terrible squawking cry.

A blade hummed through the air and embedded itself into something soft. "Uurghh! Get off me! That's my arm—*Aargh!*"

Something was hurled across the room to shatter against the far wall. "It's over there!"

"What is it? Bolldhe, is that you?"

"Stay back! I've got it by the—*Ocht, my leg! My bloody leg!*"

"Where are those stupid priests? Finwald! Appa! Someone, just grab those torches!"

From somewhere nearby, Bolldhe heard Zhang neighing in alarm. He dived over to where the horse was, sweeping up a torch from the floor just before it went out. Then he tripped over somebody lying on the floor and went plummeting. The last thing he saw in the light of the brand as it went spinning from his grasp was the frightened, staring face of Zhang. Then his head somersaulted in a chaos of bilious colors, and Bolldhe knew no more.

When he came to, Bolldhe felt as if his head had split open and spilled its viscous contents upon the ground for all to tread in and slip on, then poured back in and the skull repaired with rusty nails. All around him he could hear the shuffling of booted feet upon stone, and voices mumbling in hushed tones. Tentatively he lifted his head and risked opening his eyes.

Straightaway the light from a thousand suns penetrated his fragile corneas and the jellied brain that cowered behind them. He shut his eyes instantly and groaned. His head swam in the deepest throes of nausea, and he clutched it tightly in his hands as if to hold it in one piece.

"Whatappn'd?" he croaked. "Wherem'I?"

Nearby, one of the disembodied voices hesitated, then snorted contemptuously. "Too much Hauger ale," it chided. "Typical Pendonians—never could hold their drink."

Bolldhe gingerly reopened his eyes, then propped himself up on his elbow. "Do be quiet, Wintus," he moaned. "I'm not in the mood for your weak attempts at humor. Anyway, what *did* happen? What attacked us, and where is it now? Is it dead?"

Nibulus did not answer at once. But when he did, his voice sounded sick. "It's not here anymore. It flew away. And we'd better be off too if we're to—"

"Flew away? You mean you drove it off? The Guardian?"

"Not exactly. We—that is, Wodeman—let it go. He said it wasn't right for a creature of the air to be imprisoned here in the earth."

Bolldhe was already in too much pain to raise either his voice or his blood pressure, so he simply repeated: "Let it go? The Guardian of the Tunnel that slew those two thieves there, and nearly destroyed us too, and you let it go?"

"That's just the point. It wasn't the Guardian, and it didn't kill the thieves. It was just a crow."

". . . A crow."

"Yes. It must have got trapped down here when the portal was last opened. It didn't almost destroy us . . . we did that to ourselves."

Still clutching his head, Bolldhe lurched to his feet and stared around in disbelief. The Peladane stood in front of him, and Bolldhe could now see that look of utter failure and bitter self-recrimination on his face that he had worn that day in the Rainflats. He decided not to press the point.

Behind Nibulus stood Finwald; both appeared relatively unharmed, though the priest was bleeding from a light cut across the forehead. Appa, however, was on the ground clasping his head and shaking violently. Blood seeped between the fingers pressing a wad of cloth against his temple, and his grey face looked even more haggard than usual. He was muttering to himself in a worryingly slurred manner, and did not appear to be at all aware of what was going on around him. Their chief healer, it seemed, would not be doing much healing for quite some time.

Paulus too was upon the floor, sporting a deep gash across his thigh that was bleeding badly. Bolldhe watched him as with trembling hands, the mercenary prepared a brand with which to cauterize his wound. Not one of the company made any attempt to aid him, but the hard line of his mouth suggested to Bolldhe that he had already savagely refused their help.

Wodeman also was counted among the wounded. His arm was bandaged tightly, and hung limply at his side. He must have been in some pain, but none showed in his ruddy face.

A crow! A bloody crow! What hope do we stand when—if—we reach the Maw? Bolldhe shook his head in dumbfounded silence.

Of all of them, only Kuthy was completely unhurt. Bolldhe watched him closely as the adventurer walked about offering token assistance. He was obviously impatient to get on, and was masking this only thinly. Bolldhe seethed inside. Kuthy had known there was something down here; this was probably the reason he had persuaded them to come this way. Yet they were the ones who had overreacted, and brought about their own injuries.

Bolldhe glared at the man with a contempt that bordered on loathing. He wished so passionately to have any excuse to kick him in the ribs. He felt as if he had been used, manipulated, and if there was one thing Bolldhe hated more than anything else in the world, it was being manipulated. More than lies, treachery, and double-dealing, being used was the very worst.

Just then a sizzling sound could be heard, followed immediately by an anguished grunting. The sickening smell of burning skin rose into the air. Bolldhe whipped around, only to see Paulus clutching his leg as if trying to squeeze the very life out of it. The brand lay by his side, sputtering out its last breaths on the floor. He had finally succeeded in cauterizing the wound. Shaking with spasmodic agony, the Nahovian looked as though he might be suffering another of his fits. Even now there was blood on his lips. As Bolldhe stared, Paulus slowly rocked back and forth in his suffering, uttering not a sound. His cowled head turned up to stare glassy-eyed at the wall and, as he did so, Bolldhe caught the expression on his face. It was one of such torment and pride and hate, all at the same time. And there was also a hint of pleading. . . .

Bolldhe did him the courtesy of averting his gaze, and turned it instead on Kuthy. *I just hope that before we leave this tunnel,* he swore to himself, *you taste the suffering that you so casually bring on others.*

Wearily he turned away and prepared to set off again.

Guardedly, but with a sense of grim determination, the company trod the next dark highway that their quest had brought them to. As Kuthy had promised, this new section of the tunnel did indeed run fairly level, but it was also narrower and lower and, now that the portal was closed, the chill wind from ahead had nowhere to escape. The result was that the tunnel now seemed utterly claustrophobic, it forced everyone (bar Appa) to stoop, yet was even colder than before.

The air was as dank as air could be without actually becoming water, and after just a few minutes of breathing it, their lungs felt saturated, icy and rattling. And it was *freezing*. It felt as if they were a troop of dead souls marching along the endless underworld corridor of eternal night.

The going was anything but easy. The floor surface was slick and uneven, and frequently the explorers would curse sharply as their feet trod on jags of icy, diamond-hard rock that jutted up painfully into the soles of their boots, or land ankle-deep in pools of icy water. To make matters worse, their progress was hampered further by the sorry condition of Paulus and Appa. Neither could manage more than a painfully protracted stagger or limp.

Paulus's maimed leg was causing him agony, and it was only his hate that drove him on. He would reach Eotunlandt no matter what—the thought of plunging his weapon in the soft bodies of those lovely little Huldres was so delicious he salivated at the thought.

But for Appa, this journey was no less than a waking nightmare. Though, with Finwald's support, he was somehow managing to keep up with the others, his strength, already sapped by the previous punishing weeks of journeying, was almost at its uttermost end. He was no longer fully aware of where he was or what he was doing. Neither food nor rest could render him the sustenance and healing he so badly needed, and everyone knew that it was only a matter of time before he simply collapsed and never got up again. The hardships of Melhus were irrelevant now; even with his innate old man's stubbornness, he would be lucky to reach the other side of Eotunlandt.

Wodeman, whose thoughts were usually hidden behind that bramble hedge of inscrutability, was for once manifesting clear signs of unease. Bolldhe sensed this early on, and immediately felt better himself.

"What's the matter, Wodeman?" he chided. "Arm giving you gyp?"

The shaman glanced down at his bandaged arm, but shook his head. "It hurts, if that's what you mean, but that is not my problem. My arm is nothing compared with this . . ." He regarded the torchlit tunnel walls around him— mere inches from his face on either side—with dread. "This closeness; this . . . unnaturalness—have you ever felt anything so terrible before, Bolldhe? It feels like I'm buried alive. Cut off from the universal whole!"

Bolldhe bit his lip, and inwardly smirked. After that dream the sorcerer had given him the previous night, he was not going to feel any sympathy for the old sod.

"Really?" he answered. "I quite like it—it's exciting. And I'd have thought this is a great opportunity for you too, a man like yourself."

"Eh? How's that, then?"

"Always you're saying to me how close to the earth you are. Well, you don't get much closer than this—you're practically buried in it."

Wodeman looked away. "Get lost, Bolldhe," he replied caustically. "You're not funny."

Ha! Bolldhe thought. *"Cut off from the universal whole"? I'll have to remember that one.*

The Wanderer, despite his splitting headache, felt elevated once more, and marched on with a new spring in his step.

Hour after hour passed, with no change in the tunnel. The company plodded on like automatons. No one talked, each one of them preoccupied with his own thoughts, until eventually even those were numbed out of them by the unending, unchanging march. Time lost all meaning.

Eventually, Nibulus called a halt. No one, not even Wodeman, had any idea how long they had been down here, or what time it was in the world above. The passage of time was now measured only by the increasing exhaustion of their bodies. And now their bodies told them it was time to stop.

"Right, that'll do for today," he suddenly announced. "This will do as nighttime. We're stopping here."

Nobody argued. At least the tunnel floor was smoother here, and there were no puddles. Within minutes a fire had been lit, and the weary travelers collapsed upon the ground for the "night." The crackling and popping of dry pinecones greeted their ears, and they crowded around the welcome fire as best they could, trying to warm some life back into their aching bodies. Rations were devoured, and not long after, the fire burned itself out. Appa and Paulus fell immediately asleep, and the others soon followed.

As it happened, Kuthy's claim that it would take them but half a day to get through the tunnel did not prove quite as ludicrously exaggerated as the company assumed. In fact, had it not been for the wounded members of the party, they might have left the tunnel the previous night. For now, within an hour of setting off for the second day's march, they finally saw daylight ahead, and with it the heaven-sent fragrance of warm, loamy soil, sweet rain, and cherry blossom greeted their senses.

Moments later, far too suddenly for them to adjust, they emerged from the foul blackness of the pit to stand blinking in the sunlight, shielding their eyes against the blinding glare, dizzy with the cornucopia of colors, sounds, and smells that was suddenly poured over them to assault their senses. They could only stand there transfixed at the mouth of the tunnel, swaying in the breeze, and then, when their eyes finally adjusted, stare in wonderment at this fabled land before them.

What had they emerged into? How was it possible? For this was no less than a land of dreams that they had entered; never in all their lives had the men from the South beheld a vista of such unearthly beauty. Great mountains of the most brilliant sapphire and lapis lazuli reached up to staggeringly unreal heights all around them. High cascades, fed by countless rillets from sun-melted glaciers far above or from springs bubbling up from sources deep within the mountains, fell like a billion diamonds in the morning light. They fountained along stony flumes; they filled the air with the finest spray of heavenly coolness; and through the rainbows with which they were festooned, blue birds swooped madly. Forests of pine, spruce, and never-before-seen varieties of conifer clung to the lofty slopes above, plummeting down steeply toward the terrain below wherein lay woodlands of deodar, tamarind, and oak. From these trees came the constant drone of insect life, the shrill call of large birds flapping noisily amongst the branches, and the susurration of a million leafy voices whispering in hidden, sylvan tongues.

And beyond the forested slopes, lay the rest of Eotunlandt. Sparkling lakes of crystal-clear water dotted the undulating land all about; strangely shaped hills poked their craggy heads out of the carpet of trees, from which arose the haunting wail of far-off, unknown beasts; here and there, an enigmatic line of smoke could be seen rising out of the forest's canopy. Who could guess what dwelled beneath its boughs?

Meadows there were, too, both near and far, rolling meadows of emerald green, with fresh, fragrant grasses that shone with dewy luster. Cherry trees abounded, bedecked in a virgin-white mantle of blossom in this land of perpetual spring.

And there, right on the very edge of sight, could be seen the jagged white teeth of the northernmost rim of the encircling Giant Mountains. Above them, lines of wispy clouds floated against a pale blue sky.

From this high place, the whole of Eotunlandt appeared to them, a vision too beautiful to be real.

Amid laughter and cheers of relief, the company had arrived in Eotunlandt. They ran or staggered out into the land before them, eager to gorge themselves on the new sensations that were pouring into them. New life pumped through their veins until it made them dizzy, and their hearts pounded with excitement. It was like being transported from a dismal and benighted land, in which people wrapped up in coats drift coughing and grumbling through dimly lit, foggy streets like lost souls, to a holiday world of color, sunshine, bustling activity, and overwhelming joyousness. Never before had they felt the like of it.

This surely was the fabled Land of the Second Ones.

15

The Thieves of Tyvenborg

How could Eotunlandt be described? What poetic expressions could do any justice to such a place? What words of lyrical eloquence might one use to give even the vaguest impression of what it was like for the travelers during their sojourn there? For, out of all the languages that the various members of the company spoke, almost immediately it became apparent that their adjectives describing beauty were quickly exhausted.

It is enough here to say simply that their journey through Eotunlandt in those first few days was one of unequaled strangeness and beguiling joy, where bewilderment, fiery exuberance, and unearthly enchantment were their constant companions. They had spent so long in the dismal Rainflats and frigid forestland of Fron-Wudu, where skies were grey and lifeless. And now, stumbling in from the cold, they found themselves all of a sudden wandering through this realm of unimaginable beauty. It felt as if they had rediscovered life itself, and their senses, substance, and souls were atingle with the thrill of it all.

Down into the hanging valley that nestled between pristine blue mountains they went, and were swallowed up by the swaying, whispering trees. Along fair woodland tracks bordered with random scatterings of red-and-white toad-stools, bluebells, and snowdrops they strolled; into the sun-dappled, verdant gloom of hidden sylvan glades; along softly chattering rills of the purest spring water; through tunnels of trees heavily laden with white blossom. It was another world, every bit as far removed from their notions of reality as had been the dungeons of the Huldre woman. It occurred to each one of them that it was all too beautiful. Yet it was real.

The effect it had on them was deep, too deep for description, prose, or verbiage; too deep even for them to understand properly. Upon Appa, of all of them, it was most apparent. As soon as he had beheld Eotunlandt, his dull, watery eyes had cleared; they now shone brightly, and darted here, there and everywhere, taking it all in. His usual sickly, leathery old face was now flushed with new life, the lines of pain and sickness turned now into the creases of a smile. And the farther he walked, the more energy he seemed to gain; it was as if he were drawing in strength from the very air, and the years fell away from him.

Noticing this, Nibulus at one point remarked to his quest-brother: "What's up, old'un? You don't look so bad. Spring fever making you randy?"

Appa laughed out loud more heartily than any of the company had ever heard him do before. "I don't know," he replied. "Could be. All I know is, I feel forty years younger!"

"Really? And what about Melhus? Feel ready for that yet?"

But the priest simply waved a dismissive hand, and continued smiling at the land around him.

Even Paulus, the Huldre-hater himself, had taken on a new air. His perpetual scowl was absent, and his single eye stared hungrily about him. At every squeak of a bough or rustle in the undergrowth his head would snap around. His entire frame was taut, poised to pounce, like a fox a-prowl in a rabbit warren. Being let loose in a land full of Huldres, with a massive sword in his hand: this was the closest to heaven he had ever known.

(Well, perhaps he was not so different after all.)

The effect it was having upon Wodeman, however, was a mystery. For the moment, this priest of nature was walking in an utter trance, seeing all but unable to say or do anything. Whatever was going on behind those sparkling green-brown eyes was far too overwhelming for him to express.

From morn to dusk they walked, nobody even beginning to tire. All were reluctant to tarry for even a short while, for at each passing step there was always something new to see, some new wonder to greet their eyes. In this way they wandered without ceasing, yet made little progress northward, for always there was some new distraction to keep them from their path, some new way to be explored.

As their first long day in Eotunlandt finally drew to a close, still their fervor to continue was undiminished. For, as the sun set in a radiant wash of ardent colors, turning the snowy peaks of the eastern mountains peach-pink and jacinth, there was new spellbinding to be discovered in this twilit world.

Kuthy, of all of them the only one who had been here before, was actually growing a little bored. He decided that if he did not call a halt, they would in all likelihood still be walking ceaselessly by tomorrow morning, and still no farther on their way. But he could guess what his companions were feeling, for he had experienced it himself, a long time ago. So he played along with them.

"My, my!" he trilled. "What a beautiful glade over there! Just the kind of place where one could watch the moonlight reflected off the glassy surface of that little lake, and all."

This suggestion was enthusiastically taken up, and the travelers cast themselves down upon the cool grass and stared at the aforementioned glassy moonlight, and all. Within minutes, weapons, packs, and outer garments had been tossed upon the ground, and the travelers were finally still.

Bolldhe, alone of them, stripped off his grimy clothes and dived into the icy pool. He disappeared beneath the water leaving hardly a ripple, as if he had fallen into a black mirror. Two minutes passed without a sign of him, though no one made a move to help, or even showed a care. Then he reappeared at the far end of the pool, and began languidly sculling toward them, staring up at the nearly full moon peeping between the boughs, and breathing deeply.

The others watched him half-interestedly, lying on the sward or preparing food. Their dried rations were left utterly untouched, for this land provided an abundance of sustenance wherever they looked: delicious, succulent fruit, edible fungus, clear spring water, and wild game that almost *wanted* to be caught. It was the best food any of them had eaten in their lives, and was just there for the taking.

Talking lightly, the company stretched out for the night, only Wodeman being now absent—again. Nibulus broke wind with a deep grunt of satisfaction, and rolled over onto his stomach.

"I've got to hand it to you, Mr. Tivor," he announced, stretching luxuriantly in the long, soft grass, "this certainly beats a monthlong trek through forest and tundra. Is it like this all the way to the other side? I can hardly believe our luck! And the food couldn't be better. . . ." He delved into a clump of undergrowth at his side, and pulled away a handful of big, succulent strawberries.

Kuthy grinned without looking up. "There you go, see? Just put your trust in old Kuthy Tivor; he'll see you all right." He nibbled at a wedge of honeycomb, and strained its gluey sweetness out of his beard.

Nibulus nodded contentedly, reached into another clump of undergrowth, and this time brought forth a jug of cream and a bowl of sugar.

The only sound now was the lascivious gorging of the Peladane, the lapping of water as Bolldhe bathed his feet in its inky coolness, and the steady, purposeful *shink-shink-shink* of Paulus sharpening his blade.

"I could live here forever," Nibulus announced at last in a hushed, tranquil tone. "This place has got everything."

Kuthy snorted. "Except women . . . and tourneys. And troubadours, mead, weed . . . civilization, in fact. No, believe me, Mr. Wintus, you'd soon get bored. This land is not for such as us. Best leave it to the sprites."

"No, I honestly don't think so," Nibulus went on quietly. There was an uncharacteristically contemplative, serene tenor to his voice that stirred his companions from their wandering thoughts. Even Paulus paused in his blade-sharpening, and fixed his eye on the leader.

"Something's awoken in my soul," he explained to them, not caring what he said. "Something that was never there before . . . or maybe something that's been sleeping so long that I'd forgotten it was there. It's like all day I've been walking through the land of my earliest childhood memories, all those fantastic stories of myth told to me by my wet nurse, tales of foreign lands with strange names; hidden tunnels and secret gardens; strange, fey woodlands ringing with unearthly laughter; mysterious flower circles in alluring grottoes. And sud- denly it's all here and now. . . . I really didn't believe this sort of thing could happen to you till you'd died."

Kuthy made a mental note of the Peladane's words, so he could mock him later, once they were out of this land.

Eotunlandt was affecting them all in different ways, but for each of them it was a personal journey of rediscovery, a reawakening. The trials of the previous day were now no more than the distant memory of a bad dream. The unending march through the confines of that black, freezing passage, in which each painful second seemed to drag on for an eternity, had no place in their thoughts now. The dark of this world was the dark of a twilit wonderland where the troubles of the outside world, of even their quest, were of little con- cern to the company now. As they relaxed by the moonbeam-spangled pool beneath trailing fronds of willow and whispering boughs above, it felt as if that previous day had never happened, and if it had, well, it was no more than an- other fleeting instant in the World of Man, too transient to hold onto.

This night, this world, however, had the air of permanency to it. It had all the essence of a recurring dream that one has experienced as far back as one can remember, a place to which the dreamer can return time and again, yet which never changes, never ages, no matter how many years pass within the waking world.

This surely was the more real of the two.

Within scant moments, it seemed, of drifting off, they awoke to a cacophony of birdsong. They peered, blinking, from their dew-frosted bedrolls to look with new wonder at the world around them. The sun was just rising above the east- ern mountains, and another day in Eotunlandt was beginning.

Their second day in the Land of the Second Ones was every bit as joyous as their first. Not even bothering with breakfast, they hurriedly broke camp and dived out into the new day. The morning air was delightfully chilly, and their breath curled out of their mouths in frosted swirls. But already the sun was be- ginning to warm them. With hearts full of childlike animation, they strode from the glade and out over the meadows that led toward the distant line of purple mountains in the north. Chatting lightheartedly, they rambled over field and dale, field and dale, leaving an undulating line of dark emerald green against the silvery sheen of the sunlit, dew-spangled grass to mark their passage.

Again, much like the previous one, this day was one of ease, and plenty, and no small amount of wonderment. Nature was in full bloom, the weather was nothing less than radiant, and the land offered up its bounty at every step. Appa's sickness had all but disappeared, and the wounds they had received in the tunnel, though still colorful and not yet fully healed, no longer seemed to be causing them any pain.

The continuing absence of their shaman was of even less concern to them than usual. He was his own master, and came and went on little more than a whim, it seemed. If this time he chose not to come back to them at all, well, nobody had asked him along in the first place.

So it was with a certain amount of surprise when he did finally return. It was at the end of the day, and they were reclining in the deep, fragrant grass of a low hillock, gazing at the setting sun as it bathed the whole land in a sea of gold. They felt no movement nor footfall, they heard no sound—save for a sudden snort from Zhang—and, despite the open terrain and their high vantage point, they had seen nothing for half an hour. Then without warning, the wolf-man pounced into their midst and landed on all fours.

Appa leapt back and choked on the sour pear he had been eating. Paulus immediately swept out his blade. But the others merely looked up in mild surprise, and regarded Wodeman in silence. He remained as he had landed, crouching on his haunches, fingers splayed on the ground, and a wild look in his eyes. He said nothing, just stared at them intensely, breathing hard. From the vegetation still clinging to his garments, and the powerful smell of his "musk," they could tell he had been running hard.

Not for a moment taking his eyes off them, he reached inside his clothes and whipped out the leg of some animal. His white teeth sank through mottled fur and crunched through sinew and bone. He tore off a large chunk of raw, red flesh and chewed on it enthusiastically.

Appa's hand went unconsciously to his amulet, then down to his crow's-beak staff, and he edged closer to the Peladane. Even so he stared in awe at the shaman, who, in contrast to the company's almost apathetic contentment, burned fiercely with life in every particle of his being.

"Having fun?" Nibulus inquired, and tossed a waterskin over to their returned friend. Wodeman caught it in his free hand, and gratefully emptied it down his throat.

"So tell us, Wode," Nibulus went on, "what've you been up to these last two days? We thought we'd offended you somehow—maybe our coarse dining etiquette or something."

Irony was only vaguely recognized by Wodeman, but these words of the Southerner caused him to hesitate a second. Mulling them over in his head for a moment, he seemed to remember who he was, or had been, for the past eight weeks. The wildness ebbed away from him, and he relaxed a little.

"Ach, what have I been doing, you ask. What haven't I been doing! Having fun, yes—but oh what fun! I've been *living*, boy, *living* like I've never done before: I've never felt so *alive. . . .*"

The others looked at him with a mixture of curiosity, caution, even discomfort, but also with a touch of amusement. He came over and sat down among them, and took another bite of meat.

"What a place, though, eh?" he continued fervently. "Have you ever known the like of it? Could we ever even have guessed such a place existed? I tell you, in these past two days I've done more living than in all the long years of my life put together! I've sprinted fleet with the beasts of the field, the wind on my face and grass whipping about my ankles. For hours did I run, yet there was no tiring. I've sung to the moon shining bright 'twixt the soughing branches of benighted woodlands. Through the icy waters of lakes have I swum like an arrow; spiraled joyously through shoals of brilliantly colored fish that move this way and that as one; stroked the backs of huge silver carp that sang to me in haunting melodies. I've explored deep grottoes of quartz filled with unearthly inhabitants—whether plant or animal I know not—that I would never have believed possible outside a dream. I've sung with the birds, and talked with the beasts of the forest that came to my call—"

"Oh yes, and what about?" Kuthy cut in, nodding toward the haunch of meat in Wodeman's hand. "Dinner arrangements?"

"—and drunk deep of the salty red blood of this land!" the sorcerer rejoined lustily. "Oh yes, for that is Life! And I'll continue to drink of it till I'm sated! From earth that grinds in the crystalline deeps to air that spirals in vortices above the clouds, this land fills me up till I'm as giddy as a sot. I swear, never will I leave this place!"

At this last remark, there was a buzz of surprise—but little concern. The company's wanderings here had been for the most part an exploration of this land, their quest all but forgotten; and it was only in a vague way that they were still heading north. Appa, however, visibly brightened.

Then Kuthy spoke up: "Yes," he said, gazing over the red-gold country about him, while propped up on one elbow, "I may even join you. Since I was last here, I've often wondered what it would be like, or even if it would be possible, to colonize Eotunlandt."

"What!" exclaimed Wodeman, alarmed for the first time since entering this realm, and horrified even more than he had been at the house of Nym-Cadog. "You cannot be serious—not even you!"

"Why not?" Kuthy smirked. "Just picture it: A huge country hitherto untouched by people, teeming with innumerable unheard of species of beast and bird, abounding with delicious, exotic, unheard-of fruits, vegetables untasted by any outsider, timber in countless new varieties. A land where the sun always shines. Everything here just waiting to be plundered. The natural resources are unequaled anywhere upon the face of Lindormyn. I'd be the first to delve my hands into its plenty. By the gods, I wouldn't know what to do with it all.

"Just think, here grow unique commodities of the highest quality. Imagine what I could charge for them! And all in such endless supply—especially the hardwoods. Well, I say *endless,* but I bet I could give it a damn good try, heh-heh.

"Then there's the countless thousands of square miles of fertile land just itching to be farmed—pastures of the richest grass stretching as far as the eye can see . . . wild game in abundance, with no shyness of Man nor any natural defense against him. They'd simply walk into my traps . . . stare inquisitively at the spear-tip about to be embedded in their skulls. Ha, what a picture! And who can guess at the potential for mining? In a land as bountiful on the surface, what must lie beneath? Rich minerals, precious metals, jewels even—and probably much more besides. I'd have mines belching out smoke across this land twenty-four hours a day.

"What couldn't we do, men such as ourselves? Practical men, hard-nosed, worldly-wise bastards like us, with a good head for business and the guts to go out and grab it; men unburdened by any thoughts of sanctity or respect." These last words he almost spat out, like a poison from his system, and stared around at his speechless audience.

"Of course, I'd have to start small-time at first. That's the problem in these parts—such huge distances. But with a little initial capital," he gloated, patting the pouch of emeralds at his side, "I'm sure I could get a small workforce together—plenty of slaves to be had from the Dhracus this time of year. A hundred or so? Yes, just grab as much as I could initially, then see what interest the merchants show on my return.

"And then . . . then, once I'd got a whole damn army of slaves, I'd build a trade route, road and all, right through Fron-Wudu, up to the very entrance of the tunnel itself. Start a trading post there, build it up to a whole town, with me as Big Boss holding all the rights . . . jack up prices because folk'd have nowhere else to go. Expand the tunnel, cut out space for a few underground staging posts along it at intervals . . . hostelries, even a few whorehouses, especially if we can round up a few dozen Huldre girls. Who knows what unique pleasures *they* could give a man, eh Paulus?"

A brief sound of whimpering could be heard from the mercenary's lips.

"Yes, the Tunnel of Love, I'd call it—nice and dark, just right for the ambience. And then—and then I'd simply ravish this land! Ravish it like the virgin it is, a virgin on its knees. I'd log the forests bare, farm the land till it bled, charge top prices in rent, then just sit back and do nothing, and I'd still make more money in a year than the High Warlord of Pendonium makes in a lifetime!

"I'd be the richest man that ever lived!"

He turned to the company to check their reactions, and was not disappointed. As one, they just sat there gaping at him in horror.

Quietly, he laughed. "Don't worry," he said, "the dwellers of Eotunlandt would never allow that to happen, unfortunately."

Then Paulus drew closer. Of all of them, he was the only one to show no aversion to these ideas. "Huldres are no problem," he assured Kuthy, "I could even start an arena here. . . ."

"Really?" Kuthy replied. "Sounds good to me (you sicko)." Then he added softly to himself. "I wasn't referring to the Huldres. . . ."

He turned away from them, fished in one of his pouches, and drew out a small whetstone.

Only Wodeman's keen hearing had picked up these last cryptic words, but he was still too upset by the soldier of fortune's mercenary homily to ponder them. "I feel so sorry for your sort, Tivor," he began. "To dwell in these lands and yet remain so unmoved by it all. You're no different from the Peladanes!"

"Whoa, hold on there!" Nibulus protested, not sure whether to be offended or amused by this unexpected comment.

"Hold on, nothing!" the Torca ranted. "This is no different from what it was like in my forefathers' time. When your ancestors first came to our lands, they acted exactly like this Rawgr who sits among us now. They forced my people to exploit their own land to ruination; they exacted a terrible tribute from every man, woman and child; and if one died, his quota was passed on to his kin. And they corrupted us to our very soul. Hired us as runners, scouts, guards—even miners. . . . Why do you think I hold your sort in such low esteem?"

"What's so bad about mining?" Nibulus asked, not sure why he was even having this argument, but joining in anyway. "Metal is the hallmark of civilization; it's what raises us above the level of the Animal."

"Och, it makes my gorge rise just to hear you say that, Master Wintus," Wodeman replied in genuine pain. "The only iron my forefathers ever wore were the manacles your household bound them with, and the only gold was the pennies they placed on their dead eyes."

The wildfire in him was dimmed now, and he had returned somewhat to his old self. Kuthy had that sort of effect on people.

"You walk in the light of the sun, you people," Wodeman persevered, "but its warmth never reaches your heart. You are like the stone of the crypt."

"Maybe so," Kuthy responded. "I've trod the paths of this world and others, and if there's one thing I've learnt, it's that after a while, once you've seen one nice tree, you've seen them all. And after that you see only firewood."

At this, all the others looked hard and meaningfully at Kuthy. The Tree was one of the most sacred symbols of Wodeman's belief, and to refer to it as "firewood" (or, even worse, "nice") was akin to likening the Sword of Pel-Adan to a bread knife, or the Torch of Cuna to a matchstick.

Wodeman, however, had by now decided that mere words were beneath him. They were the stuff of "civilization," and he wanted nothing more to do with them.

"Marauders," he muttered to himself, and turned his back on them all.

Perhaps it was Wodeman's mention of marauders, spell-woven into reality by this land of fey magic and dreams, but just as the sun was setting, the company did spy some people that evening.

It was not easy to see clearly, for the light had now fled the lower grasslands, robbing them of their many shades of green. Now, save for the peach-gold blush of the snowy peaks that ringed the horizon against the deep azure of the sky, the whole of Eotunlandt had turned grey. Not a flat, lifeless city-grey, but an infinite variety of profoundly rich, living greys: the shadow hues of grass green, earth brown, sunset red, sky blue, and all between. Thousands of tiny points of light were opening, and bobbed and wove among the trees and grasses all around. Far from signaling an end to the day, the dusk heralded the overture of a million tiny awakenings. The faerie night was just beginning, and a thin silver mist crept across the ground.

And there, away to the north, could be discerned a line of figures. It was as impossible to gauge their distance as it was their race; in this twilight world of shifting grey shadows and roving pinpricks of light, dimensions were unsure, and the Old Magic ever tricked the eye. Maybe it was only illusion, but, if so, it was illusion that was shared by the whole company. Moving purposefully from southeast to northwest, a line of about a dozen figures, maybe more, could be seen. They were just black shades against the grey-green of the misty grass-lands, and no details could be made out. But some appeared to be carrying poles over their shoulders, and many had large, misshapen heads. Possibly horned. The occasional red spark, whether fire or reflected sunlight, glinted from them.

Paulus was on his feet in an instant. "Huldres?" he inquired of the keen-sighted Wodeman, stroking his blade and sniffing the air as if there were a bad smell upon it. The sorcerer held up a hand to silence them all, and focused all his senses in the direction of the diminishing figures.

From the north a wind was blowing. All heard its steady approach. First the rustle of leaves and groan of ancient boughs, then the eerie whistling of the high grass just below them. And finally the sudden patter of rain against their faces. It was not a strong wind, but it bore a brief, flurried scatter of distant noises: the sudden call of birds; voices, harsh and mean; stony laughter; the ring of metal.

Then the wind passed, and with it the sounds. The darkness deepened, and the vision was lost.

"Any ideas?" Appa asked nervously as the others sat back down.

"Yes," their leader replied cheerfully, "let's have dinner!"

To this the others readily agreed, and set to building up a large fire, the marching newcomers now forgotten. Appa stared at their activity, then glanced back worriedly to the darkling Northlands. A sudden hiss of hatred at his side caused him to spin around in fright; he looked up to see the gaunt shadow of the Nahovian towering over him. The pale light of his one eye glimmered coldly from his cowled face as he spoke low to the priest.

"Huldres," Paulus confirmed, and gave Appa a meaningful look before he departed. "Be on your guard tonight."

Appa shook his head in bewilderment. *Complete fruitcake,* he thought to himself, and unstrapped his pack.

For the first time since he had entered Eotunlandt, the beginnings of a cloud began to form on Appa's horizon. It could have been the group of strangers earlier that was causing this, but more likely it was the disturbingly neglectful attitude of his companions just now. In any case, it went some way to reminding the old man of his Purpose—their Purpose. He would kick their arses into gear again on the morrow. And with this timely reminder came the memory of who he was, or rather, what he was.

For he was a Lightbearer, and had been neglectful of one of his main duties, namely healing. Their injuries, though mending with marvelous speed, had still not been properly treated, and as he began seeing to the deep gashes, bruises and crudely cauterized wounds that colorfully adorned his companions' bodies, he wondered just how long they might have all languished in this land of enchantment, had not that mysterious line of figures begun to shake a little of the glammer from him.

He waddled over to Paulus first, possibly the least spellbound of the party, and certainly the most grievously hurt. The Nahovian stretched out his leg and let Appa get on with it, while he himself continued glaring northward and sharpening his blade. To the rhythm of the Lightbearer's elegiac mumblings was added the *shink-shink-shink* of whetstone against blade. Paulus could not seem to stop himself doing this, and was at it seven or eight times a day.

Other sounds there were too, that seemed to rise in protest at Appa's priestly incantations: the hiss of a colder wind through rasping grasses, the rattle of drier twigs in the treetops, the cawing of harsher birds. Those bobbing points of silver light began moving up the hillock toward them, and then trembled just beyond the radius of the fire, as if in indignation. There was a dark cloud of resentment building over their heads that was growing with each minute. Appa did not stop his ministrations, but he was aware of just how coarse and alien his chanting must sound in this Huldre world.

By the time he had finished, the fresh sparkle that had brightened his eyes had dimmed somewhat, till Appa began to look more like his tired old self. He settled himself down into a hollow, and remained very quiet and reflective.

Up until recently his world had been a steady, unchanging one, in which Good was Good, and Evil was Evil. But Eotunlandt? Where did that lie? Though not exactly Evil in the way Olchor and his followers were, the land of the Huldres was hardly Good either—he had only to think of Nym-Cadog to remind himself of that fact. It was a "middle place," a twilight world trapped between Nordwas to the south and Melhus to the north. Yet it had healed him when he was on the point of death, and sustained him where his faith had not.

Back home, he recalled with growing unease, fey had seemed the unwelcome intruder, warded off with chants, curses, and crudely fashioned "turning" devices manufactured by the hands and hearts of superstitious, sterile old men. Here, however, fey ruled supreme. It was *their* land, and he the intruder. He was defenseless in the realm of the foreigner, and he began to feel afraid.

Appa drew his grey woollen cloak tightly about him, curled up against the night, and, with one hand clutched around his stone talisman, he drifted off to sleep.

Through the pathless woods to the north, a lone hunter prowled. Old eyes the color of glaciers pierced keenly through the dark; predator's ears twitched at every sound; feet fell softly as a cat's. Yet despite its stealth, it was well aware of the countless eyes watching it go by. *Intruders!* they seemed to spit. *Get out! Get out! Get out!*

A new infection had entered the land, and it had to be cut out.

The hunter emerged from the deepest heart of the forest into more open woodland, and stared around. Suddenly it froze. Through the mesh of branch and twig, a red beacon-bright fire glared. Without a second's hesitation, the prowler sprinted through the trees toward it.

The fire reflected like blood upon the dirk it carried as it ran. Rapidly, noiselessly, it approached the men as they reclined, chattering idly around the fire. It was scant yards away now, and still they were dumbly unaware of its presence. Only a second before it leapt into their midst did the tallest one cry out in alarm. Then it was among them, kicking a million orange sparks into the sky and scattering fiery brands asunder.

The group of campers, stunned for a second by Paulus's sudden warning, instinctively fell back with their hands before their faces. Then Paulus lowered his sword.

"Idiots!" the newcomer cursed as he stamped out the embers. "I could see your fire for miles."

It was Kuthy, and for the first time since they had known him, he was livid with anger.

Appa gibbered slightly, and pulled his bedroll about his head. Nibulus bellowed with sudden laughter, while the rest glared at their visitor in silence.

Kuthy glared back at them. "I could've slit your throats as easily as slicing bread while you lay around gossiping," he spat. "This is no rambling holiday, you know!"

Nibulus continued to chuckle. "Do you know how long it takes me to slice just one round of bread?" he asked. The others lay back down to rest, muttering. Kuthy regarded them with eyes poisoned with contempt.

Laugh away, Southerners, he said to himself, *while you can. We'll see how funny you find it tomorrow. . . .*

After the commotion of the sudden intrusion had died down, the travelers, all together at last, had lain down to get some sleep. Wodeman, though, felt far from tired. An unending succession of feelings kept washing over him, and for the first time since entering Eotunlandt, he was jittery. Chief among these feelings was the sense of being *watched*. It seemed to him that, below their hillock, an entire legion of hostile, spiteful creatures was closing in. He could hear a constant multitude of strange sounds all around: hoots, hisses, croaks, snuffles, and the unfamiliar calls of many other unguessable beings. He could feel their watchfulness, their resentment. The wind, too, was cold, and Wodeman felt uncomfortably exposed to this open country.

But there was something else besides. For on this night, he sensed, a new infection had indeed entered the land, and it seemed to the sorcerer that it was an infection wholly more pernicious than any they themselves represented.

Into Wodeman's mind came a presentiment: Something else had just blundered into Eotunlandt, and it was contaminating the very air that went before it. Flowers wilted as it passed, leaves turned brown, and forest berries lost their sheen, turned rancid, and dropped off. The creatures of the earth went to ground at its approach, birds veered away and cried shrilly as if stung, and insects, their wings crisped, simply fell from the air. At the touch of its feet, grass blackened and smoked, vines recoiled, and the crystal water of streams turned jaundiced and feculent.

Wodeman shivered. He pulled his wolf skin closely around him, and looked around. As he did so, he saw that Kuthy was gazing back at him. The soldier of fortune, he noticed, seemed as wary as he was, and his strange cap was keeping its filaments very much confined to itself. Both men nodded to each other, then stared about them into the night.

The following day they met the thieves.

As blithe and ebullient as before, the company had risen and journeyed out into another glorious day in Eotunlandt. The thought of the strangers the previous night was no more than another of this land's manifold jokes, and in imitation Nibulus had whimsically donned his great helm, wearing absolutely nothing else below that. Paulus had been on the lookout for Huldres to slice, as usual, and Wodeman had, unusually, decided to tag along with the merry company once more.

All morning they walked, encouraged—rather than guided—northward by Kuthy, Wodeman, and Appa now. The day was as vibrant as any in this land, and Bolldhe, like most of his companions, once again allowed himself to be possessed by the intoxicating spell of Eotunlandt. Since emerging from the tunnel, he had shed a large weight from his mind and, after a huge breakfast, all that remained for him to do was shed a large weight from his bowels.

"I catch up with you in a while," he called out to them, and dodged into the woods.

At once the green gloom and secret stillness of the trees swallowed him up. It had been windy out on the heath, a gentle, buffeting breeze that whistled musically and brought with it the sweet-sour perfume of elderflower and the joyful chorus of birdsong. But, in here, all was hushed. Bolldhe picked his way through the tangled undergrowth, and all he could hear was the sad moan of the wind in the high treetops, sounding down here so immensely distant.

Farther into the woods he went. Here he felt no danger, and was heedless to the noisy crunch of his own footsteps that echoed throughout the trees. Soon he emerged into a small, beautiful glade. High, soft grass reached up to his knees, and an unseen rill chattered on its course. Great, red-hatted toadstools the size of umbrellas stood around in clusters, as did creamy-white ones of a rather ruder shape. Bolldhe could smell the fresh green leaves of beshadowed bluebells, and hear the sweet, chirping soliloquy of a single blackbird that was eyeing him carefully from its nearby perch.

"Perfect," he breathed, and dropped his breeches.

The soft blades of grass tickled his bottom playfully as he squatted down and hugged his knees. He instantly relaxed.

Bolldhe took his time. His companions would not get far, and he saw no reason to rush this, one of life's real little pleasures. Instead he harkened to the gentle, muted woodland sounds about him. There were secret voices in that stream, he was certain, and once or twice he thought he heard what might have been an eerie yet beautiful singing far off in the depths of the woods. He looked up and saw that the blackbird was still staring at him. Now, however, he noted it was no longer singing, and in the absence of birdsong he was almost sure he could hear a soft, low chuckling somewhere behind him.

Better wipe up, he thought, and tore off a good clump of grass. *Don't want to get caught like this by any Huld—*

He stopped dead as he felt the cold, razor-sharp edge of a blade pressing against his throat.

The glammer of the past few days instantly fled from him, and was replaced by that familiar "hot" feeling.

No thoughts of death yet, though; he had been waylaid and robbed many times before. *Just do whatever he, or she, or they, want. . . .*

"*Feuirigo binaenenu oememaevf anunsmapama,*" came a voice from not too far in front of him, and was immediately followed by a chorus of harsh laughter from all around. Bolldhe's eyes swiveled frantically from side to side, but he could see no one.

Hvitakrist! he thought in panic. *They were quiet! How . . . ?*

Then several figures stepped out into view.

If there was any comfort in the fact that they spoke Bolldhe's native tongue, then it was swiftly shattered when he beheld his captors. Suddenly Bolldhe felt even hotter, and thoughts of death were now very much on the agenda indeed.

There were five—no, six—of them, not including the one behind him holding the blade at his throat. And in all Bolldhe's years of traveling, he had never encountered such a motley collection of menacing, lawless, internecine, lowlife dross as these that stood before him now. Only two were human, the rest being a mixed bag of other races from all corners of Lindormyn. With wide, darting eyes, Bolldhe quickly scanned the line of footpads in front of him, and counted two men, a Hauger, a Boggart, and (more worryingly) a Grell. But the one that most riveted his stare was the monolithic bulk of the armored Tusse that loomed behind the men, at least three feet higher than they.

Hard as nails and casually murderous of eye, they all bore vicious weapons of war; and all of these were pointed directly at Bolldhe. He swallowed hard.

"Afternoon," he greeted them in a small, croaky voice.

One of the men twisted his mouth in what may have been a smile, and the Grell's mouth split into a wide, fang-filled leer that was definitely not. It was accompanied by a catlike hiss, and Bolldhe could smell its rank breath above even his own excrement.

Hell-Adan, I hate Grell! was all Bolldhe could think as he stared in transfixed loathing at the blue-black hide and long, acid-green, spiked hair of this particular member of that odious race.

It was true; wherever he had traveled, Bolldhe had always steered well clear of the stockaded villages of that particular race. Like all "self-respecting" folk, he had an aversion to close association with other peoples, having contact with them only when he had to. But in the case of the Grell, he would go a full day's travel or more just to avoid them. There were many men, he knew, who did seek them out for their own various dubious purposes, but in Bolldhe's opinion, the only humans that mixed with their sort were those who were every bit as bad as the Grell themselves: pimps, racketeers, bootleggers, mercenaries, and—yes, once again—Olchorians. These last might find use in them as temple guards, bodysnatchers, or even torturers—for the Grell had a reputation for brutality. They also had a reputation for profligacy, which many found particularly gratifying. Their females were too loathsome, fetid, and "sticky" for even the most desperate, but the male bawds had of late become very popular with well-heeled ladies who had too much time and money on their hands.

This one in front of him bore three throwing axes of the variety popular among the sea wolves of the Crimson Sea for indulging in live target practice. But Bolldhe guessed this one was not a pirate; judging by the net he carried

and the pole-flail with its three spiked balls, he was probably used to working
as hired muscle in a bawdy house.

Bolldhe suddenly felt the blade at his neck pressing closer against his
pounding jugular, and all such thoughts immediately froze. The next instant,
strong little fingers were enmeshed in his hair and his head was wrenched back
painfully. A muted cry escaped his throat, and he stiffened even further. Then
a sharp kick in the spine shot a red fire of pain throughout his body. Almost
falling backward, while still squatting with his breeches around his ankles, he
was held thus by cruel hands, and forced to stare upward.

He heard the thieves advance.

"*Janenu, ichva bebana, peqquci nunapena?*" one of the humans demanded.

It was the language of his home country, Pendonium, though tainted with
an outlandish accent and in a dialect he had never heard before. *Janenu* meant
"where," and *peqquci nunapena* denoted "your precious" or "your beloved."
This could mean either "Where is your money?" or "Where are your friends?"
(*Ichva bebana* was the term used to describe a bowel disorder that dogs picked
up from scavenging in latrines. Bolldhe dismissed this as irrelevant.)

"*Kinasema oevf-laet doerst!*" he jabbered frantically, using the most basic
register of Pendonian he could manage, and hoped for the best. Whether they
knew of his companions or not was unimportant. At all costs he could not be
seen as a lone traveler, without allies.

Bolldhe trembled with fear, and felt horribly vulnerable in his debagged
state. Still he was forced to stare skyward. Then a circle of faces appeared on
the perimeter of his vision, cutting out the sunlight. One in particular regarded
him closely. It was a hard, cruel face seemingly designed to convey a dread
sense of sanguinary malice. Thickset and brutal with pale, clammy skin, it was
framed by black hair that was long and lank, and clung wetly to the neck and
shoulders. The lips were like thick slugs, and the tiny eyes were like those of a
pig, and black as a sharks'—soulless. Lice and maggots crawled about this apparition's clothing.

"So," it said in Pendonian, "you're a Peladane. Well well, interesting. We'll
have to introduce you to Eggledawc; he'll like that . . ." (Bolldhe whimpered as
he felt gloved hands run over his kneecaps.) ". . . and I'm sure he'd like to introduce his war hammer to these here."

"I'm *not* a Peladane!" Bolldhe blurted out, again in Pendonian. "I'm from
Hrefna!"

Hrefna was a huge, wild, and largely forested region of northeast Pendonium. Farthest away from the capital Ymla-Eligiad (in terms of influence, if
not distance), it had always been a dark and ungovernable place, and was by
and large abandoned by the Peladanes. Over the years it had become the
haunt of outcasts, thieves, disillusioned ex-Peladanes, and the darker presence of the Dhracus from neighboring Godtha. As far as High Warlord Godwin Morocar of Ymla-Eligiad was concerned, Hrefna was pariah, but it did

serve as a convenient, self-ruled buffer zone against Godtha. Otherwise, the less he had to do with it, the better.

But if Bolldhe had hoped to curry some favor by claiming he was from this place, he was soon brought face-to-face with the reality of the situation when his inquisitor cried "Liar!" and smote him.

Bolldhe's mind exploded with unbelievable agony, and his legs buckled beneath him. For several seconds his world turned white. When finally, as he gasped and retched, his sight returned, sickly colors writhed before his eyes, and he could see his fingers twitching horribly. His lips tingled, and the left side of his face felt numb. Then he heard a soft bubbling, and could smell burnt skin.

Oh gods! he thought in disorientation and nausea. *What the hell was that?*

With his mouth very close to Bolldhe's ear, his tormentor said softly, "And I only rapped you lightly that time." The grinning man then held the weapon in front of Bolldhe's face, and he knew he had spoken the truth. It was a heavy miter of black iron. Such macelike scepters were usually little more than a spiked ball on the end of a stick, but this one was more antique and intricately wrought. It radiated menace and power like a wizard's staff.

The man continued: "Lie to me again, and I will strike a little harder, and boil the skin from your bones. You're not from the forest, for you talk like a Westerner, or a Southerner from Arturan perhaps. When you meet Eggledawc, then you will hear a true Hrefna accent."

He gave a nod, and Bolldhe was released, to collapse to the ground. Though various points, blades, and clubs were being pressed into him, he savored the cool, soft grass against his burnt face, felt the freshness and life in it, breathed in its vibrant pungency, and tried to bury himself in it.

Then he was yanked back up, and stood staring about himself. In the next few seconds, he appraised the outlaws.

The tormentor with the miter was a big hard bastard, that was for sure. Death hung about him like a shroud. It was in the pits of his eyes, the lines and scars of his heavy face, even in his swagger. And those big hands looked as if, without any need of weapons, they had ripped the life from many a screaming victim, while he had chuckled.

More worrying still, Bolldhe recognized something unmistakably "ceremonial," almost religious, in both the raiment and the arrogance of this beast, which was borne out by the Kh'is that he now saw sheathed at his belt, that distinctive Olchorian sacrificial dagger with its undulating blade. Were these cutthroats servants of Olchor, then? Just thinking about that brought the choking taste of vomit to Bolldhe's mouth. For if they were, his death would be a heinous one.

He looked closer at the man's garb for any sign, any badge, of the Evil One. About his shoulders the oppressor wore a navy-blue mantle, and beneath it a leather doublet of deep purple, hung with bright iron scales. Neither garment

bore any device or token of Olchor. But when he turned around to say something to the Tusse, Bolldhe saw embroidered upon the back of his mantle three
characters. He stared closer, and was astonished to realize these were not Olchorian sigils, but runes of the Torca!

Olchor's *Death's-Head*, the rune of *Erce*, and Cuna's *Torch*. All together.
What in the world could that mean?

And what was the big man doing traveling with all these non-humans? Why
would he choose such brutish, bestial company? It seemed perverse.

Whilst ostensibly keeping his eyes upon the ground as if in deference,
Bolldhe did manage a few swift glances in their direction, surreptitiously eyeing each of them up and down. His trembling legs could hardly hold him up,
and his dread was such that he could feel his gorge rising inexorably. But he
was well aware that if he were to stand any chance of getting out of this one, he
had to know (or at least begin to guess something of) his enemy. He compelled
himself to concentrate.

The Tusse, at nine feet, was at least a foot taller than the blacksmith back in
Myst-Hakel, and much bulkier. He was encased entirely in an enormous suit of
plated mail, which was surmounted by a sturdy little helm that sat atop his
small head like a mead bowl. In one hand he held a bhuj, a massive meat
cleaver of notched, blackened iron. In the other, he gripped a maul: the five-
foot-long mace that was wielded two-handed by humans. He looked, frankly,
unstoppable; more like a Jutul, one of the fire-giant smiths of the underworld.
Unmoving, he simply stared at Bolldhe, without hint of expression or thought.

If this was really a band of thieves, then this one presumably was not the
one sent to shin up drainpipes.

In the same hand that held the bhuj, the Tusse gripped a leash, at the other
end of which was tethered the Boggart. It was as stunted and hirsute as any
Boggart the world over but, unlike the bulk of his race that were normally to be
seen scavenging on the periphery of civilization like pariah curs, this one had
attitude. The small, tusklike teeth that thrust up from its lower jaw were gold-
capped, and on its hands it wore a pair of bagh-nakh, or spiked knuckle-
dusters. It glared at Bolldhe ferally, and salivated.

"Careful, Peladane," the miter-bearer warned. "The males of their species
don't like being stared at in the eye. Think on, or Grini here might decide to
search for the future in your entrails."

Grini. Yes, that was the name inscribed on his collar. Bolldhe quickly turned
away. The Boggarts' shamanistic rites were well known; they would pull out the
innards of their victims, and in them try to divine the future. (Their futures

invariably turned out to be red and steaming, which perhaps was not so inaccurate, after all.)

And then they would eat them.

The hunched-up Grini was passed back to his master, the one who had been holding the knife against Bolldhe's throat. Unsurprisingly, this one turned out to be a Polg. This cocky little shit sauntered over to take the leash, and as he did so, treated their prisoner to his best intimidating sneer. It always amazed Bolldhe how the Polgrim found it so easy to look down at races that were at least a foot taller than they. Was it practice, he wondered, or were they genuinely and inherently the most arrogant little vermin on the face of Lindormyn?

As ostentatious as the worst of his breed, this Polg was arrayed in clothes of deep red, green, and brown, all hung about with silver and gold, and he sported a mustache that was almost long enough to hold his trousers up. An assegai spear with a leaf-shaped tip was strapped across his back, and a haladie was stuffed into his belt. Both weapons were typical hunting tools of the Polg elite. The haladie, had Bolldhe been in a better position to appreciate such things, was especially impressive: a kind of "double dagger," it had two long, gracefully curved blades, each extending from either end of the grip, and by the aura he had felt as it was held to his artery, Bolldhe guessed this one was magical, possibly the kind that could return to its wielder like a boomerang.

This is bad, Bolldhe thought, *this is terrible. Such weapons . . . !* These lot were far better equipped than any group of mere thieves should be; they were more like an expeditionary task force than wandering rogues. Bolldhe's thoughts reached out for his quest-mates, wherever they might be now. But there was little comfort in any notions of a rescue from them. What could they do against adversaries such as these?

At a word from the leader, the only other human in the group stepped up to Bolldhe. Though this one had blond hair tied into a very long and greasy horsetail, the two men were sufficiently alike to be brothers; both were large and muscular, with brutish, pig-eyed faces. But unlike his funereally clothed brother, this one preferred to show off his physique. His jacket had been removed and was tied about his waist, so his knotted torso was bare.

As he approached, he made a sudden lunge at Bolldhe with his voulge. The heavy, spiked blade sang past Bolldhe's face, missing his nose by a scant fraction of an inch. Bolldhe jerked back and fell on his backside, and the thieves roared with laughter.

The blond man grinned like an idiot, and Bolldhe forced a similar smile through his dread, though by now he was on the verge of tears.

"An inch closer and you'd be dead on your feet, fucker," the voulge man breathed. He glared psychotically at his prey, then thrust the long haft of the weapon into his ground. Bolldhe peered at the blade with wide eyes; it was coated with some old stain that stank unbelievably. Was it poisoned?

But before he had a chance to ponder further, the man had placed a brawny hand on Flametongue's hilt and snatched it away from him.

Immediately the light dimmed as the sun went behind a cloud, and high, screeching voices sang in a wind that suddenly sprang up from nowhere, bending the treetops. Everyone, Bolldhe included, looked up in alarm.

Then the cloud passed, and the wind died.

The thief shrugged, and turned his attention back to the sword. "Do for starters," he assessed, and tossed it over to his brother. Still staring up at the trees, the other caught it by the hilt, then lowered his perturbed eyes to the flamberge. He turned it this way and that, thoughtfully, while the first one continued searching Bolldhe for any items of worth.

He swiftly pocketed Bolldhe's shark-tooth necklace with its beautiful pearl, and handed out the other items of worth to his accomplices: the scimitar brooch-pin, the garnet-studded leather belt, those heavy jade bracelets, even Bolldhe's prized lizard-hide waterskin—all those beloved souvenirs of lands he had traveled through, places which were farther distant than anyone save he himself even had the wit to imagine! He burned at the loss of these dear possessions.

But not at the loss of Flametongue; for all he could care, they were welcome to that horrible thing.

The leader finally tore his gaze from the flamberge, and looked over to his brother. "Right, that's everything, is it, Cuthwulf?" he asked, still slightly preoccupied. "Fine, let's get back to the others, then; they should be finished by now. Flekki, bind the citizen and bring him along."

The Hauger, cloaked, hooded, and robed almost like a monk, waddled across to Bolldhe, unstrung a length of rusty copper wire from her belt, and, while the Grell held their prisoner's hands behind his back, bound him painfully by the wrists. She was a River Hauger, Bolldhe could tell as clearly from her garb as from her odor. For the clothes smelled permanently musty with river mist, and had the hue of pond scum; even the array of brass tools at her belt were green with damp. As she made fast her flesh-cutting bonds, Flekki eyed Bolldhe with a face as grey, hard, and calculating as any of her kin, but with an additional hint of the swagger-and-leer of her present company. Gods, she was ugly.

> "Bind him tight with copper wire,
> Blind his sight with drop o' fire,
> Bake him, break him, never tire,
> Make his aching proper dire."

Thus she sang as she went about her work. When she was done, she pulled a pata onto her hand, and with it prodded Bolldhe to get moving.

He stared down at her in disbelief. The pata was similar to Paulus's punch-dagger, though it was attached to a gauntlet and was as long as a shortsword. Bolldhe was well aware that it was a favorite tool of the assassin's trade. Just what under the sun *were* these people?

Just as they were about to leave the glade, the leader paused for a second and turned back to Bolldhe. "And, friend," he called out to him, "pull your breeches up, there's a good chap."

Eotunlandt may not have altered in any real way since his capture, but to Bolldhe's eyes the whole land had now been drained of all its beauty and enchantment. It was as cold, hard, and lifeless as any rocky wilderness, and as grey as ash; if there were to be any warmth or color now, it would be in a hot splash of red.

The burn on his face was by now shooting needles of intense pain deep into his head, causing him to feel acutely nauseated. He was also sweating freely, but this was not just with fear. The air had changed, had become clammy as the jungle, close as hay fields on a late summer evening. And this, he was sure, was not just down to his own imagination.

From somewhere far up ahead, voices now came to him upon the sluggish currents of air. Voices thick with rage, sour with violence. One voice in particular. As they got closer, Bolldhe could hear that it was Nibulus's voice; he was spewing forth a seemingly inexhaustible gush of highly imaginative double-barreled profanities, though to whom, and for what reason, Bolldhe dared not allow himself to think just yet.

It was, then, with a truly sinking heart that Bolldhe beheld his travel companions. In a bluebell-hazed meadow that sloped down from a copse of ancient and twisted oaks, they stood. In a circle around Zhang. Facing out. Weapons before them.

Encircled by the rest of the thieves.

Bolldhe looked with dismay at this additional bunch. Again there were seven of them, four men, a woman, another Hauger, and something he had never seen before in his life, a Dhracus. Like Bolldhe's captors, they also had that air of deranged, gleeful bloodletting about them.

There was no fighting as yet, but a cacophony of heated dialogue that clogged the air with a veritable tephra-fall of fury. Nibulus's salient diatribe, from what Bolldhe could make out at this distance, seemed to be aimed not at the marauders ranged before him, but at the two priests, both of whom were clearly refusing to obey his orders to "get stuck in." He was unarmored, as he had been ever since they had entered Eotunlandt, but from the manner in which he gripped Unferth, it was clear his defiance was undiminished.

"What's the matter with you both? I've been outnumbered by far worse odds than this before! Just fight, will you!"

But they would not. Wodeman was on the ground, trying groggily to get up while still clutching at a deep gash across his forehead. Paulus was clearly waiting for Bolldhe to come back and even things up a little, and so he stood poised but unmoving. With his bastard sword held at half-guard, he stared expressionlessly back at the masked thief before him who was trying to menace him with an assortment of weird weapons.

And Kuthy, well, he'd buggered off ages ago.

Bolldhe was shoved on roughly, then shoved again harder so that he staggered and almost lost his footing. Finally he was kicked in the back so hard that he flew forward, failed to recover his balance, and pitched toward the ground. Though at the last moment he managed to twist his head round to avoid hitting the ground with the burnt side of his face, still the impact almost knocked him senseless, and he cried out in agony as sharp tips of grass nearly punctured his crisped skin.

Powerful hands wrenched him back to his feet, and again he was propelled onward. This time he needed no encouragement to hurry.

Whoops of jubilation passed between the two groups of thieves as they were reunited, and a volley of coarse, derisory bawls and obscene gestures were launched at the beleaguered travelers. If there had been any stalemate previously, it was now over.

Nibulus, who had also been hoping for Bolldhe to return, now looked up and saw him. He also saw the company he had brought back with him, saw his hands tied behind his back, and saw the Hauger's pata held at his neck. His jaw slackened.

"Bolldhe, you stupid prat!" he roared. "What are you doing?" He was so angry he did not know which leg to stand on.

"I've just come back to rescue you all," Bolldhe cried between gasps. "Isn't it obvious?"

One of the men from the second group called out something in an unknown tongue to the leader of Bolldhe's captors as they approached. He was a short, stocky man in his late thirties, who stood out from the rest of his bizarre companions simply because he looked so ordinary. His short hair, heavy red face, and mundane clothing gave him the appearance of a builder rather than a thief.

He did however (and this was the absolutely pivotal detail) have a huge morning star at his belt, and moreover he was currently pointing a large blunderbuss directly at Nibulus.

As the two groups came together again, they outnumbered their prey fourteen to four, not counting the incapacitated Bolldhe and Wodeman. Surrender, it seemed to Bolldhe, was inevitable, further debate a formality, and resistance was suicide.

So why, in all that was sacred, was Nibulus still standing there waving his sword about? Bolldhe's insides began to churn and twist anew, and a black weight descended upon his soul; he could almost hear his last seconds of life ticking away.

Whatever it was the blunderbuss man had said, though, caused the leader of Bolldhe's thieves to shake his head in disagreement. He jerked his thumb at Bolldhe, and replied in the same language. This, however, was met with an unequivocally curt response from the smaller man, and surprisingly the miterbearer backed down. Sneering in rancor, he turned back to Bolldhe and spoke again.

"Tell your fellows to yield. They have no chance now. Just give us your valuables, your weapons, your horse, and go!"

All eyes were now on Bolldhe. He cleared his dry throat, and translated what he had been told. From the Aescals there came a buzz of relief that communication was now possible. There was also a hint of admiration for their failed rescuer, though Bolldhe was too scared to feel any pride.

"You understand them, Bolldhe?" Nibulus asked with hope in his voice. Then he added, "What the hell's happened to your face?"

"Shaving accident," Bolldhe replied. "And yes, I do—it's my own language, sort of. And I strongly urge you to do as he says."

"No secret messages," the pig-eyed brute warned, and held the needle-sharp point of his Kh'is to Bolldhe's eyeball.

Just then there was movement within the circle, and all faces turned to see Wodeman heaving himself back to his feet. Not dazedly, as might be supposed from his wound, but staunchly, and with his staff gripped in firm hands. It was as if he had deliberately remained upon the ground in order to draw strength from the earth, in preparation for the Antaean task ahead. And there he stood now, meeting with calm, steady eyes the glare of the enemy, looking a formidable adversary, an imposing presence, his heroic stance only slightly lessened by the wolf's-head cowl that, with its snout now sliced off, lolled down one side of his head looking more like a very sick cat.

"That's the spirit!" breathed Nibulus to his weird comrade with a grin.

Bolldhe, however, merely adjusted in his mind the odds to fourteen-to-five.

"Just do as they say," he croaked to Nibulus. "Now, please?" He waited for the Peladane's response, while rillets of sweat poured down his brow. The air truly was growing stifling now.

Nibulus's eyes never left those of the man with the blunderbuss. The Peladane did not recognize what was being pointed at him, but he knew well the ways of war, and there was something undeniably unnerving about staring down a huge, flanged barrel aimed directly at one's head by a boar-faced, red-eyed maniac with a body like a Jutul's, bracing his legs as if against some potential force. With the rapidity of a heart's fibrillation, words now flickered through his mind: half-recalled, half-heard words spoken in hushed tones around the campfires of the bivouac on the eve of battle in some distant, eucalyptus-scented land: Mascot? Mess kit? Miss cut? Moss cat . . . ?

But the word eluded him, and so did its rumor. A second or two passed, and something in the lines around Nibulus's mouth told Bolldhe he had now made a decision.

"Get ready to elbow that bastard in the guts as soon as I strike, Bolldhe," he said levelly. Bolldhe's eyes widened.

"I'm sorry," Nibulus added with genuine regret in his voice, "but they'll slaughter us as soon as we stand down."

"No!" hissed Appa, and grasped the Peladane's Ulleanh. The thieves meanwhile readied their weapons.

"Yes," Finwald interjected. "They will kill us. Haven't you guessed yet? They're from Tyvenborg."

Appa's face faded rapidly from its usual xanthic yellow to a pumice grey.

Tyvenborg. That name was a byword for ruthlessness and knavery throughout the Northwest. For time out of mind the malefactors of the "Thieves' Mountain" had festered within their fortress like a swollen pustule, to regularly leak down into the unhappy lands around. Situated deep within the wild mountains situated in Pendonium's easternmost reaches, it had over the years attracted all the maggots of the surrounding area to it like an open sore.

The language Bolldhe now translated (though it was only now he realized it) was the Cant of Tyven, a bastardized, simplified version of Pendonian, cross-bred with the tongues of its neighbors. The presence here of the dwellers of Hrefna and Godtha, too—it all fell into place. Only a dive like Tyvenborg could spew forth such a mixed bag of lepers as this.

And the followers of the robber-baron Mordra-Culver shared no love for any man associated with the High Warlord Godwin Morocar, bitter enemies as they were.

The man with the blunderbuss, apparently the leader, stared hard at Nibulus. Never before had he met with such defiance in the face of such odds. His large, sad eyes glared at the Peladane's, and he guessed what was going on. He shuffled uncomfortably.

"Dolen!" he shouted at the Dhracus. "*Tdap-dhna hwic' oichnidz?*"

The Dhracus cocked her head oddly, and tipped back the peak of her legionnaire's cap, and her hitherto veiled eyes now glistened intensely as they probed those of the Peladane. Nibulus wavered uncertainly, strangely beguiled by those coal-black eyes, set as they were in a face that was too white to be alive, yet too perfect to be a ghoul's.

Then her blue lips parted with a hiss:

"*Nycweh luwkou koiu nadh h'diw!*" she growled, and immediately the thieves prepared to attack. Bolldhe clenched his eyes uselessly against the Kh'is. One thief, a man in colorful silks who had been eyeing the baggage—and especially Nibulus's armor which was strapped on to the horse—made a grab for Zhang's reins, and was unceremoniously kicked back several yards for his efforts. As shouts rose into the air, Bolldhe drew back his elbow in preparation for the required jab.

"THAT'S ENOUGH!" bellowed a voice suddenly, and everyone immediately halted.

It was the leader. He had lowered his blunderbuss, and spoke now to Bolldhe in Cant.

"So maybe we will kill you if you disarm," he said, "and maybe we won't; it's a chance you'll have to take. 'Cause if you don't obey, you will certainly die. . . ."

Not waiting for a response, he laid his blunderbuss upon the grass, and followed it with his morning star. Bolldhe hurriedly began to translate, hoping that the urgency in his voice might delay the slaughter to come.

"Take a look around you," the leader said. "We're thieves. We steal. But we only kill if needs be."

It seemed to be working. For the moment.

The leader left his weapons where he had laid them, and walked around, introducing his band of cutthroats.

"I am Eorcenwold, and I give the orders. And this," he said, placing his hand on the mantled shoulder of the miter-bearer, "is Brother Oswiu Garoticca, priest-assassin of the Order of Cardinal Saloth. He is my brother, too, brother number one as it were. I can see by your face that you are already aware of what his miter is capable of, and don't underestimate that blade at your eye, either. It sucks souls: a very useful tool for his cult."

Bolldhe was translating as best he could, but he hesitated at this last. *Does my eye have a soul?* he wondered.

"Brother number two," Eorcenwold went on, indicating the blond horse-tailed rogue with the voulge, "once visited the Caves of Aggedon, where that poleaxe of his slew a Fossegrim. And he has never wiped its poison from the blade, have you, Cuthwulf?"

The blood of the sea wyrms of Aggedon was reputed to be worse than the vilest man-made toxin in the world.

"And my sister, Aelldrye," he continued, but did not elaborate on her prowess. Like him, Aelldrye was short and of unremarkable appearance, unthreatening save for the two-handed glaive she held in trembling hands.

"The Little People: Khurghan, Flekki, and Brecca." Eorcenwold pointed out the Polg and two Haugers. "Don't judge them by their size; Khurghan's accuracy is second to none throughout the Hunting Grounds, and even his tribe cast him out for being too barbaric!"

Bolldhe avoided the gaze of the belligerent little thug who toyed with his weapons like a feral child.

"Flekki, too, has some interesting missiles," Eorcenwold said of the River Hauger's tiny metal throwing rings. "There are some intriguing substances coated on those chakrams. You never know what you'll get from them—quick-killing poison, crippling agony, paralysis, impotence, or any other imaginative effect her cunning little alchemical brain can devise."

The thief-sergeant for some reason neglected to detail the skills of Brecca, the second, rather innocuous Hauger. Certainly this thin, slightly hunched Stone Hauger held no apparent threat, or even any real weapons unless one counted the piton hammer and adze, the only two of many tools at his belt that might cause even modest harm. He was a solemn, careful, even timid-looking Hauger, who seemed to favor means of defense rather than offense; he held a large shield of iron-banded wood on one arm, another strapped to his back, and wore an iron cap beneath his hood.

Instead Eorcenwold moved on to introduce the masked man who was facing up to Paulus. Little of his lithe, greasy frame was hidden by his sleeveless tunic, but what his face looked like beneath that large helmet, none of the company could guess. Only a pair of cold, red-rimmed eyes could be seen behind the heavy face shield. In fact, had it not been for the long strands of igneous-blue hair that trailed down his back, the fact that he was a half-Grell would have gone unnoticed.

What was of more immediate concern to Bolldhe though, was the veritable arsenal of weaponry he carried. A two-headed battle-axe was strapped across his back, and an ornate scimitar was sheathed at his side. In each hand he held extraordinary weapons:

"Cerddu-Sungnir's manople may look wicked enough . . ." Eorcenwold warned of the sword that was attached to the iron gauntlet in the half-Grell's left hand.

"Preying Mortis," the half-breed hissed, introducing his favorite toy, "will eat your heart, and leave the rest for me."

". . . but that crossbow is the real danger; it can fire five quarrels at a time. And the scimitar is a Dancing Sword, that can fight on its own."

Cerddu-Sungnir's eyes widened in malign expectancy. Like the other thieves, he was enjoying every bit of this. The leader's roll call of their weaponry was as sweet to him as the gloating of a torturer before his ghastly job commences.

"I won't bother to detail the various skills of Hlessi." The leader nodded toward the Grell. "I'm sure you've all heard enough stories about his kind, and let me just say that at two weeks he holds the current record for keeping a torture victim alive. . . ."

("Only because I get paid by the hour," Hlessi demurred, in his own tongue.)

Others still were introduced, one by one. Dolen Catscaul, the Dhracus, a knife in each hand. Raedgifu from Rhelma-Find, a vainglorious young man with a taste for fine silks, baggy leather trousers, and flesh-ripping flails. Also, Eggledawc Clagfast, the Hrefna-dwelling ex-Peladane with the huge war hammer. (Bolldhe's knees involuntarily recoiled.)

And finally . . .

"Meet Klijjver!" Eorcenwold announced with relish.

Everyone turned to look at the colossal, armored figure of the Tusse herd giant. He did not speak, snarl, glare, or even move, come to that. He did not have to.

Bolldhe wavered, unsure of the translation. "Meat Cleaver?" he asked, interrupting Eorcenwold's flow. "You mean the bhuj?"

"Klijjver is his name," Eorcenwold snarled, not pleased at the interruption. "Meet him."

". . . Right, I see," Bolldhe replied, and finished the translation.

"All in all," the thief-sergeant summed up, "you have about thirty weapons—some of them missiles, some poisonous, some magical, and some just bloody big—all pointing at your worthless hides, all wielded by fourteen of the most savage and lethal thieves in the whole of Tyvenborg. And if you don't hand over your stuff right now, then don't bother drawing another breath, because you won't be needing it."

He returned to his own weapons, picked them up as calmly as a gardener might collect his tools, and waited.

So there it was, Nibulus's choice. They could risk almost certain death by trying to fight it out, or they could risk almost certain death by laying down their arms. All eyes were on the Peladane.

Surprisingly, Nibulus appeared calm. Yes, there was a slight sheen of sweat on his face, but that was nothing new. His eyes, however, were rock-steady, and they never left those of Eorcenwold, studying, appraising the man.

Then he made his decision.

"He doesn't want to attack us," Nibulus announced in Aescalandian. "I've read it in his eyes."

Bolldhe's hopes vanished. *Great!* he thought. *Now try reading his followers' eyes. . . .*

"He says that sounds reasonable," Bolldhe quickly translated for Eorcenwold, loud enough for all the thieves to hear, "and could he have just a moment to put it to his men."

"Finwald!" Nibulus called out at the same time. "What kind of magic do you have against them?"

"Remember the last time we were outnumbered?" Finwald said by way of reply. "The wolves? That kind of magic."

"No," Appa stuttered, trying to keep his voice as neutral as possible whilst leaving out none of the urgency. "I have a sleep spell, you have a friendship spell; if we both act togeth—"

"Don't. Be. A. Cretin," Finwald replied to his brother-in-faith, smiling and nodding amicably at the increasingly impatient thieves. "We need strength, pure and simple. Wodeman? You with us? When in the Wild, follow the Law of the Wild, yes?"

"Actually," Wodeman responded, making a show of laying down his staff, "in the Wild, the weak always run from the strong. I say we break out at the weakest point in the circle and make a run for it."

My giddy aunt! Bolldhe gaped, realizing that the words of the three magic-users were intended for his ears just as much as for each other's. *They're doing it again! Even here! Don't they ever stop trying to lecture me?*

Finwald moved closer to the Peladane. "These bitch-born scum only respect what they fear," he said, sheathing his sword into its cane, but surreptitiously feeling for a pouch of special powder inside his cloak, "and like all dogs, what they fear is strength. We have more magic than they."

Despite Bolldhe's lack of faith in all things Cuna, he had to admit that he was impressed by the mage-priest's confidence. And if it was only an act, then it was an act that was worthy of praise from Luttra's greatest stage-histrios. Few could have appeared so cool with the weapons of fourteen Tyvenborgers pointed directly at them.

But he was also fuming with a sudden rage at the continuing attempts of his would-be mentors to manipulate him, even here at the point of death. It was a rage that welled up from some deep, deep reservoir, and its intensity caught him quite off his guard. But it also channeled his thoughts in the only way they could go. If he was not going to employ Power, Peace, or Escape, there was only one alternative.

"Eorcenwold!" he called out all of a sudden. "How do you fancy taking on a new recruit?"

A brief scatter of laughter was shared among the thieves. Also, much to Bolldhe's regret, both Nibulus and Paulus snapped their heads around to stare him straight in the eye.

He cursed. Had they actually understood what he had just said? Both of them had spent time among the armies of Pendonium, he knew, so was their word for "recruit" known to them? Bolldhe had little care for conscience in his life, loyalty being a disposable commodity to him, but now, with the glare of the two veterans fixed upon him, his proposed treachery burned hotly in his face.

But the tip of Brother Oswiu's Kh'is was now again touching his eyeball, and he was held fast. "I hardly know them!" he cried, in Cant of Tyven. "I'm just a sword for hire . . . and the horse is mine!"

Oswiu held up a hand sharply. While the others paused, he purred into Bolldhe's ear: "Just how loyal are you likely to be? We keep together fairly tight in this team."

A few sniggers played around the assembled thieves, and Bolldhe could smell the rank breath of Oswiu's sudden laugh in his face.

There is no honor among thieves, he reasoned, then said: "As loyal as each of you; I side with the strongest."

"Not good enough!" Eorcenwold exclaimed, but was interrupted by his brother.

" 'Through the blood of his kin will the Infidel be cleansed,' " he quoted. "Let him prove his loyalty by slaying one of his own."

Whoops of exultation arose from the thieves; the party had begun! Hlessi's long, purple tongue flicked out in anticipation, and Grini strained at his leash, eyes bulging.

Eorcenwold, however, looked slyly at his brother. "You just made that up, didn't you?" he asked in his native Venna tongue.

But Oswiu was undeterred. "Better they attack one another than us," he replied, smiling at Bolldhe's uncomprehending face.

Eorcenwold hesitated. It was clear to all that he was reluctant to let this continue.

"What are you waiting for?" his brother number one challenged. "Are we not Tyvenborgers? Let the blood flow, I say!"

His words were taken up as a chant by the increasingly excitable thieves: "Let the blood flow! Let the blood flow! Let the blood flow!"

Nibulus and Paulus were also shouting; this war chant was known to them.

Then, without warning, Bolldhe was shoved into the midst of his companions. "Choose your sacrifice," Oswiu commanded. Eorcenwold stepped forward to intervene, and Appa, clueless as ever to what was going on around him, approached Bolldhe to offer comfort.

It was for Bolldhe one of those panic-fueled moments of self-preservation. He grabbed the priest by his amulet and yanked him back toward the waiting thieves.

"Bolldhe!?" cried Nibulus, and started forward, but was immediately checked by the blunderbuss that was swung up into his face again. In the same instant Oswiu whistled to his brother Cuthwulf, who tossed over his voulge, which Oswiu caught in one hand, and pushed into Bolldhe's grip.

Appa was suddenly punched in the stomach by the vicious Khurghan so that he doubled over in pain and surprise, then dropped retching to his knees. Hlessi grabbed the priest's arms and wrenched them painfully behind his back till he was forced to kneel helplessly before Bolldhe with his neck extended.

Pech! Bolldhe thought, his head spinning at their sheer speed. *They don't mess about, do they?*

"Bolldhe . . ." Nibulus warned darkly, but Bolldhe did not hear. His quest companions, the thieves, the strange land around him, everything in fact faded until he was in a tiny world all of his own. Time ground to a shuddering halt. The only sounds that he could hear were the wheezing sobs of the old man, and the pounding of his own heart. All he could see was the scrawny, turkeylike neck beneath him, appearing in a focus of incredible detail: the fine grey hairs, the dirt-encrusted creases of the aged skin, the brown leather thong of the amulet, rubbed glass-smooth and darkened by the sweat of decades. While the only things he could feel were the weight of the hefty, poison-coated voulge in his slick palms, and the almost unbreathable closeness of the air.

A vague part of his mind briefly thought: *How the hell did I get myself into this?* Then there were no thoughts in his mind at all. No strategies, no debates, no conscience. Nothing except the sight of that bare, outstretched neck, and the question: *Could he truly sever it?*

And then the world suddenly came crashing back into his mind, as everything around him exploded in thunder and pandemonium. The ground shook under a series of deafening quakes that almost bowled him off his feet. It was like the approach of some gargantuan beast. A sudden gale howled like a host of furies out of a sky turned black with piling storm clouds and filled with screeching birds. Everyone was wailing in terror, swept up in a tide of uncontrollable panic, trying to run in half a dozen different directions at once. Zhang reared up screaming and flailed the air with his forelegs. And then something huge filled the entire sky.

One of the true inhabitants of Eotunlandt had finally arrived.

Bolldhe stared uncomprehendingly at the vision before him. His gaze went up, and up, and up, until his head craned so far back he almost toppled over.

It was, of course, a giant. What else could one expect to find in a place with a name like "Eotunlandt"? But this was neither a Jotun—those fifteen-foot ice giants that haunted the remote mountains of the Far North—nor even one of the eighteen-foot, two-headed Ettins. This was a True Giant, a two-hundred-foot behemoth that stepped right out of Lindormyn's most ancient myths into a world that no longer even believed in them.

It was now, however, as real as the mountains. Over the canopy of oaks it towered, the treetops barely reaching up to its knees. A long, simple, one-piece tunic of earth brown it wore, that billowed and snapped in the gale like the sails of a great ship. Arms bedecked with primitive bronze bracelets, each big enough to house a sentry tower, hung at its sides. And way, way up there, partly hidden by clouds, was a monstrous head. All that could be dimly seen of it were two yellow eyes that glared down at them like the beams of two lighthouses in a sea fog, framed by a forest of shaggy hair undulating in the sudden wild wind, and mantled by forks of lightning that smote the ground about them.

The bottom dropped out of Bolldhe's world. He stood there gaping, unable to move, to cry out, to even close his eyes to avoid the leaves that whipped around in the air. All he could do was whimper—then empty his bladder down his legs. It was a being from another world, or from the Beginning of Time; like an Elder Spirit from the primal chaos before the world was made; like a god come down to earth to stand before them, to judge them, to damn them all into hell. It filled Bolldhe's whole world and, though all around him seethed in a maelstrom of noise and terror, he could do nothing. He was nothing.

Then vaguely into his overwhelmed mind he began to hear something different: a shrill sound like the wind, but with the order and form of music, so that it cut through the chaos and cacophony that was tearing his mind apart. It sounded familiar somehow, and his fleeing wits desperately clutched onto it,

like a drowning man. It was a sharp whistle, a call, an urgent signal from someone nearby. Somehow Bolldhe managed to wrench his eyes away from the
colossus before him and flail his gaze this way and that, trying to locate its
source.

Over there in the trees! Someone was frantically waving at him, and there
were other figures stumbling madly toward whoever it was. Without thinking,
Bolldhe tore after them. Plunging into the wind as though into powerful break-
ers pounding on the shore, he forced his wobbling legs to propel himself onward. Up the slope he hared, almost blinded by the snowstorm of white seeds
flying around from the tall, wind-whipped summer grasses. As he neared the
tree line, he managed to make out, through tear-fogged eyes, the face of Kuthy
Tivor shouting unheard words and waving him on. Then he was plunging on
through the trees.

Seconds later, an earth-wrecking explosion tore the air apart, and the
ground beneath them lurched. He and several others nearby were tossed from
their feet only to come crashing to the ground.

The giant's foot had landed and, even as they sprang back to their own feet,
earth showered down around them. All that was left of the place where they
had confronted the Tyvenborgers was one large, foot-shaped crater.

No one paused to locate, or even to shout out to, each other. Bolldhe,
Kuthy, and whoever else was with them leapt off through the woods. There was
no plan, no direction, no thought of anything save running as fast as possible
away from that foot.

And for the next hour, under the cover of the trees, this was exactly what
they did.

It is not every day that you come face-to-face with a god. Not while you are still
alive, that is. And sane. And sober, come to that. So when a two-hundred-foot-
tall giant steps out into your daylight, waking world, bringing with it the storm
clouds of Hell, you have to question your sanity. Quite possibly for a long time
thereafter. It did not help any of the company that they had all witnessed the
very same thing. It was all, simply, too big.

Their flight did not in fact consist entirely of running. That first hour was
mainly spent hiding, darting out to move on, then hiding again, and all the time
staring upwards and listening. At first there were just Bolldhe, Kuthy, and
Wodeman. But gradually, and purely by chance as they scampered about like
field mice running from a kestrel, they bumped into others. First Nibulus and
Appa, the Peladane almost dragging the spent form of the priest behind him
like a lame old Boggart; and then later Paulus suddenly appeared among them.
Finally Finwald came running up, wild-eyed and clasping his hat to his head.
But, soon after, the shaman disappeared, and they were six again. At no time
was there ever any sign of Zhang.

Driven by terror and instinct alone, they continued to dart through the cover of the trees. None knew, cared, or even thought about the direction they might be taking. The gods had come down to earth, or risen from its depths, and were trying to destroy them. All they could do was keep fleeing.

It was a terrible flight, one that none of them would ever forget. None of their previous encounters had been even a fraction as awful. Above them, around them, behind and sometimes before them was the giant: unrelenting, omnipresent. At every roar they expected its foot to come crashing down through the treetops to stamp them into the mire of their own blood. Yet this never happened. Sometimes they would see that awesome, terrible face peering at them through the forest canopy, and occasionally a huge hand would pull the upper boughs aside to try to get at them. But in spite of the ease with which it could have rubbed out their lives, it seemed reluctant to push too far. Almost as if something unseen were hindering it.

At other times they heard it move off, drawn by something they could not see. On one or two of these occasions, they heard a distant scream of terror, but whether it was human or horse, they could not tell.

Eventually, as they plowed deeper and deeper into the woods, the stamping and roaring receded. It seemed that, for the present, they had miraculously escaped certain death.

"It was the forest that saved us," Kuthy stated. "They cannot pick their way through the thicker reaches of the woods without harming their sacred trees."

They sat huddled beneath the cover of a large rowan. It was late evening, and the sun would have gone behind the mountains by now. But no sunset could be seen here: in these dense woods it was almost pitch black. A few furtive noises could be heard around them, sometimes a snuffling and a scraping, and as a kind of background hum there was also an almost continuous low moan from Bolldhe as he nursed his burnt face. The fragrances of scented wood and summer flowers were almost overpowering, but still not strong enough to completely mask the smell of his crisped and suppurating skin.

Nibulus, though, had other things on his mind. He leaned closer to Kuthy and, with his face mere inches from the other's, suddenly yelled: "And how the hell would you know that? You've never even seen any of these things before— have you?"

Kuthy stared back at the younger, bigger man. His grey eyes gleamed in the near darkness, but his expression could not be judged.

Then Finwald's weary voice was heard. "There's no point in denying it, Kuthy. You've led us up the pixie path ever since we met you—first the tunnel, now this. You knew what dwelt in this land all along, didn't you?"

There was a pause, then Kuthy admitted with what sounded like genuine repentance: "Alas, I cannot pretend otherwise. I have been through Eotunlandt before, and yes, I have seen the giants. I've never seen them quite so close up, but I did know about them, yes."

"Then why in the gods' own surnames didn't you tell us?" Nibulus asked in exasperation. "Did you want us to get killed?"

"Now, you know that's not true," Kuthy responded levelly. "If it hadn't been for me you'd all probably be nothing more than a stain on the sole of a giant's foot by now."

They thought about this for a moment, and had to admit the truth of it. Had Kuthy not returned to them and cut through their terror with his whistle, they would have run witless in circles or sat paralyzed with fear, and would now be very much "at one with the earth."

"Yes, for that I will be eternally grateful, my friend," Appa wheezed. "By Cuna, never before in all my seventy years have I known terror like that. . . . I still cannot believe it. Just what sort of world do we exist in? All these . . . things! Had I known what the world was like north of our borders, I'd never have ventured further than the Blue Mountains, quest or no."

Indeed, none of the company could bring himself around to fully believe it. In this ancient, fey wood, crouching together in the dark beneath the rowan's boughs, it all did seem more like a horrendous dream. Furthermore, a dream that had not yet run its full course.

Nibulus subsided a little, but was still angry. "Just tell me this," he said to the Tivor. "Why did you then hold back what you knew? Just what are your purposes, eh? We've lost our horse and all our baggage, we've got no idea where Wodeman is, or even if he's still alive. . . . We're trapped in the land of our worst enemy, and we don't even know what that enemy is, for Forn's sake!"

But Kuthy did not answer; he had become absolutely silent, and though he still sat cross-legged upon the ground, his bearing had suddenly tautened. Instantly everyone froze, and they too strained their ears to hear whatever it was that had moved out there in the deepening dusk.

Footsteps, furtive, purposeful, coming their way . . .

A whining snort . . .

A familiar voice: "They are the Elder Spirits. The ghosts of the Great Ones who trod the world before Man awoke. Ancient enemies of the gods."

Wodeman floated toward them through the darkness of the woods, moving strangely, silently, a dreamlike expression upon his visage. Behind him came the slough horse, walking with uncharacteristic quietness, in a way that suggested some great oppression of mind.

The company found themselves unable to move. Still closer the spectral newcomers came.

The spell was broken by Bolldhe. "Zhang!" he breathed, and crawled out from under the roof of branches toward his friend. The horse backed off snorting, and would not allow himself to be touched.

Wodeman slumped to his knees and groggily crawled in among the others. They shied away, not quite sure what it was that had joined them. Paulus's breath rattled in his throat, and his sword was drawn.

"What's going on?" Nibulus asked cautiously. "Wodeman?"

But Wodeman remained as he was, and he did not speak. If it was indeed Wodeman. He looked like the wraith of his normal self.

"Zhang's all right," Bolldhe informed them, though he could not get near enough to lay a hand upon the terrified beast. "And it looks like our baggage is all here. I think."

Nibulus hurriedly crawled away from the silent shaman, and leapt up to check that his armor was all in place. Eventually the two of them managed to calm the troubled horse down, and reined him in. After doing so, they both relaxed a little, and felt a lot more comfortable with their new visitants in the night.

"Make a fire," Nibulus ordered. "This place is scaring our priests."

"No fire," Wodeman mumbled. "Not yet." He was on the point of collapse, but refused to succumb to his exhaustion just yet.

"What happened?" Finwald asked the shaman in a whisper. "Where did you get to? Is the giant still out there?"

". . . Sent earth power through the forest," Wodeman explained. "Shook the treetops a mile away. Drew the giant off, sent it away . . . but only just. Didn't like it. . . . They didn't like it, Erce magic in their realm, the realm of Huldre. . . . Tried to send it off after the thieves, but they got away, headed north. They're good, that lot. . . ."

Again he trailed off, not sure what he was saying, or even what he meant to say. Then he simply stopped, and went to sleep in that same kneeling posture, utterly drained by his recent elemental confrontation.

The others were not sure what to make of any of this.

"The ghosts of the Great Ones . . ." Finwald mused.

"Hmn, didn't look much like a ghost to me," Nibulus opined. "Altogether too substantial, I'd say."

"Mind you, there was something strange, now I come to think about it," Finwald said. "I'm not positive, but I think I could see right through its legs— the trees, I mean. Like a parallactic shift . . . or then again maybe not. But in any case I'm sure I could see the trees through it."

"Almost as if it weren't really there," Kuthy agreed. "I know what you mean. The first time I saw the giants, I experienced an overwhelming feeling of sadness, one that sprang up from nowhere. . . ."

"You're joking!" cried Nibulus.

"I was a fair way off, mind," the old adventurer added. "They knew nothing of my presence. But I remember feeling that somehow it was all wrong. From the sagas we hear that their sort died out at the ending of the first days, and as I watched them march over their domain, I felt that they shouldn't be there— here. And maybe they aren't, really."

"So what are they?" Finwald persisted.

"I can only guess," Kuthy speculated. "A final vestige of the greatness they once were, perhaps—like ghosts, in a way, unable to understand that their time is up."

"Horseshite," the Peladane spat. "Did you see the size of that hole it made in the ground? I could have used it for my own bear pit! Ghosts, you say? I don't think so."

Then Paulus spoke. It was not often he gave his opinions, or indeed said much at all, so whenever he did, it caused the whole company to pause. "I suppose the Giants must be Huldres, then," he said mockingly. (Nibulus groaned.) "After all, this is the land of the Huldre, is it not?"

It was now completely dark, and they could see nothing of the mercenary's face. But his tone was unmistakable.

"Yes," he went on, "as you assured us, plenty of Huldres, small, sweet and charming. . . ." He hacked and spat at the soldier of fortune in loathing. "If I did not need you to get me out of this accursed place, I would push my blade down your throat and into your heart."

Cheated of the sport he had been craving for so long, the Nahovian drew his coat about himself, and gnawed upon his own bile.

For once, the others agreed with him. "You lied to us," Bolldhe put in. "You lied to us about the giants, you lied to us about the Huldres, you lied to us about that tunnel being secret. You just can't stop lying! Hell, I think I'll join Paulus when it comes to carving you up!"

"And why in Cuna's name did you abandon us just before those thieves turned up?" Finwald joined in. "You knew full well something was going to happen, didn't you?"

But Kuthy Tivor was not going to let these whelps talk to him like that. "I go off on my own when it suits me," he said. "Just like your shaman here, just like you, Bolldhe. I didn't know anything was going to happen, though with you lot dancing amongst the daisies and lighting fires in the night, maybe I should have guessed it would. If you think so ill of me, then go and find the northern portal without me.

"But this I will say to you for nothing: The only traitorous deed any of us has witnessed on this day, my friends, is that of our dear Bolldhe. Or were my eyes playing tricks on me when I came out of the woods and saw our noble hero here standing over Appa with a voulge in his hands? What was that all about, Bolldhe, eh? One of those quaint old folk dances you picked up on your travels? Or were you trying to impress them with a conjuring trick?"

It was now Bolldhe's turn to make excuses. Immediately he was conscious of the blood rushing to his face, pinning a rosette of guilt onto his unburnt cheek, and he instinctively put a hand up to his face. *What was that all about, indeed?* he asked himself; he still was not sure what had got into him.

Then he realized that it was too dark here for the others to see him. He hated the fearful darkness of these woods, but he had to admit it was now saving his bacon. He lowered his hand, and instead cleared his throat—several times—before speaking.

"I was playing for time," he mumbled apologetically, then cursed himself for the feebleness of his reply. He cleared his throat again, then continued in a louder voice.

"I had a religious maniac holding a soul-sucking dagger at my face, and it looked like any second you, Nibulus, were going to start a fight! In fact you said so, remember? Damn, I can't believe you did that to me! 'Be prepared to elbow that bastard in the guts, Bolldhe,' you said. Pel's Bells, what a leader! All very well for you to say that in your position . . ."

"Don't talk bollocks," Nibulus sneered. "We saw what happened; there was no knife at your eye *after* that cultist shoved you towards us."

"Absolutely," Finwald agreed with his friend, his voice dark with accusation. "You were back amongst us then, no worse off than we. Why didn't you stand and fight? I can't believe you went and grabbed Appa like that, and dragged him back to your new friends. I told you, Appa, we should never have brought him along in the first place."

Everyone waited to hear what the old priest had to say. But if Bolldhe had expected him to come to his aid, he was disappointed.

"I'm afraid," Appa began gravely, "that I have to agree with you, my dear brother. He is unreliable, and not to be trusted. I have stood up for you all along, Bolldhe, and tried so very hard to understand you. But time and time again you have failed us. I really feel sorry for you, I do. What aching loneliness there must be in your existence. For that is how your life will always be: a long and empty road towards death, without partner, lover, family or friend.

"But any choice in this matter is out of my hands. I'm duty-bound by my god to see that you do this task, and that's what I'll do, even if I can't understand for the life of me why the Lord Cuna would choose you of all people. Finwald, Bolldhe must continue with us."

There was a long, stifling pause. A lonely wind sighed through the higher branches, and a pinecone thudded dully onto the needle-carpeted ground a short way off. This really was serious, they all knew, if even Appa had turned against Bolldhe.

Then Wodeman suddenly breathed in sharply and spoke up. His voice was still frail and distant, so they were not sure if he was talking to them in his sleep. "Bolldhe alone saved all our hides back in Nym-Cadog's prison. Strange, such is the way of those favored by the gods: sometimes they're true, sometimes not. But the skalds tell us that a hero is made not by the way he has lived, but only in the manner of his death. Bolldhe may fail us again and again, but if he's true right at the end, then he's true forever."

He was right of course, they could not deny it—even if he was still asleep. As Appa put it: "In all the old sagas, the heroes only become heroes by a great

and noble death. They can be the lowest type of rat all their life, but if at the
end they die a glorious death, the bards will sing their praises till the end of
time. Maybe that is all that is left to you, Bolldhe."

"Well, at least you're all still alive," Kuthy went on, on a lighter note. "If
Bolldhe had fought alongside you, I imagine you'd all be glutting the ravens by
now. Maybe Fate took a hand, and maybe Bolldhe was doing his will."

(*Like hell!* Bolldhe thought.)

Then Nibulus spoke.

"I can't prove anything, Bolldhe, and I don't give a toss about what the
skalds say. But I'll tell you this: In my opinion, you're not even up to the standard of a traitor. I do not want you at my back any longer. As far as I'm concerned, you're faithless. We cannot trust you any more than the Tivor here—"

"Thank you very much!" Kuthy exclaimed indignantly.

"You're both birds of a feather. Rotten apples. From now until we leave this
accursed land, you walk up ahead, where I can see you. And when we are on
the other side of the mountains, you can leave with Kuthy, not us."

There was absolute silence now in the woods: no wind, no furtive rustling,
and even Bolldhe's skin had ceased its snap, crackle, and pop. It felt as if even
the gods were listening. Bolldhe could say no more. He curled up into a tight
ball, and cursed everything in his life. True, the Peladane was young, and apt to
change his mind; maybe Bolldhe would be forgiven. Certainly the old priest
would not let it go that easily. But for now, Bolldhe just cursed; cursed the
night, cursed Eotunlandt, and cursed himself. He hated this place. It was close,
and dark, and fey. Anything could be lurking out there. They could not leave
the forest because of the giants, and he was stuck here under this tree with a
group of people who hated him. And if they ever made it out of Eotunlandt,
what then? Could he survive on his own in the frozen North?

It was one of Bolldhe's darkest hours. He envied Nibulus for his sense of
honor, loyalty and camaraderie, even if he himself did hate "all that."

"Anyway," he muttered to anyone who cared, "I couldn't have fought alongside you against the thieves; they stole my sword."

A second of even deeper silence passed, then Finwald yelled, "They
WHAT?"

16

Eotun Steps Are What You Take

"It's them, I tell you! No doubt about it; I can practically smell them, even from this distance."

Finwald's eyes were out on stalks, glassy with concentration as he peered through the undergrowth. He and the company were lying belly-down in a patch of wood sorrel, hidden from view by the bracken and stinging nettles. Though the trees were spread much more thinly in this part of the woods, the dense undergrowth afforded them the cover they needed to spy out the open terrain around about. About a hundred yards in front of them, the last of the trees petered out completely, and from there on a thick carpet of bracken sloped upward to the hill country beyond. The grass up there was thinner and coarser than the lush woodland fronds in which they were lying now, and from a few miles away they could hear sheep yelling to each other.

Finwald crawled forward on his belly, catlike, and reached the cover of an ancient, moss-coated ash with cuckoo-pint and fungus growing at its base. He glanced skyward nervously, before daring to raise himself from the cover of the bracken for a better view. Quickly he ducked down again, and scuttled back to his companions.

"It's them," he repeated excitedly. "There's a line of smoke rising from behind one of those rocky knolls on the lower slopes of the hills, over to the left there. Someone's cooking breakfast. We can surprise them if—"

"But did you definitely *see* them?" Nibulus asked.

"Who else can it be?" Finwald demanded shrilly. There was a wild look in his eyes that they were not used to seeing. Nibulus said nothing, but frowned; in doubt maybe, but more likely in consternation at the priest. He looked terrible. His customary neatness, style, and cool dignity seemed to have been gradually torn away by the grasping, animated plant life of Eotunlandt's forests, to be replaced by mud smears, burrs, thorny twigs, and slug slime. To Finwald now, of all of them, there looked to be more of Eotunlandt than Wyda-Aescaland.

They had been traveling for seven days since their encounter with the giant, fearfully picking their way through the thickest parts of the forest. Uppermost in their minds was the fear of being spotted by a giant again, and the strain was taking its toll like never before. Yet always Finwald, the only one of them who looked around himself rather than up, urged them on with greater speed. Down in the permanent gloom beneath the dense forest canopy, there had not been much in the way of undergrowth to hinder them, and they had actually made good speed. None of them knew where the thieves had got to after the incident with the giant, or even if they had survived, but they all had the feeling their enemy had escaped for the most part, and would be heading for the only exit out of Eotunlandt, as they themselves were. Finwald seemed convinced that only if they could reach this secret gateway out of Eotunlandt first would they find the thieves.

But it was a constant battle between his urgency and his companions' fear.

"Perhaps it *is* them," Appa admitted, "but we cannot risk leaving these woods—we'd be seen for sure."

True enough, it was open land out there, and none of them was willing to leave the sanctuary of the sacred trees. And even if Finwald were right, no one was too keen on the idea of a reunion with the Tyvenborgers. But for days that was all the priest could talk about. "We must get Flametongue back," he murmured. "It's a gift from Cuna, I swear it!"

The others were less convinced about the flamberge's importance. They already had a silver blade and, as Finwald himself had assured them at the outset, that was surely enough to do the job.

"Appa," Finwald said slowly and deliberately, holding his senior's gaze, "believe me, it *is* them. It just is, all right? And if they—or anyone, come to that—can risk starting a fire out in the open, then how likely d'you think it is there are any giants nearby? That smoke can be seen for miles!"

Appa gave his former protégé a somewhat hurt look that seemed to say *Calm down. No need to get tetchy.* Then he said, "All right, all right, but what about the Tyvenborgers? They'll have sentries, and they'd spot us a mile off out there in the open."

Finwald paused at this. He paused long. Then he realized that he really had no answer.

For a week, a whole damn week, he had driven the company on as hard as he could with his various devices: every persuasive argument that came to him, every line of oratory, flattery, or cajolery he could think of, every threat he thought he could get away with, all delivered with every ounce of passion within him. Yet with each second that passed, each moment one of the company might delay for whatever reason, each hindrance that happenstance threw in their way, his desperation grew that little bit more intense.

He had so much to contend with. There was the terrain, to start with. In these deep woodlands it was very difficult for Kuthy, their guide, to judge where they were exactly, yet none of them would risk open country for fear of the giants. Then there were the inadequacies of the various members of the company, too: Appa's slowness, Bolldhe's sulkiness, and, worst of all, Kuthy's lack of interest in hurrying and his outright refusal to be told what to do by anyone. And after all was said and done, Finwald was not even the leader, so there was only so much he could achieve. He just thanked Cuna that Nibulus was his friend, and on his side.

The closer they came to the northern rim of the mountains, the more fretful Finwald became. He had begun to despair of ever seeing Flametongue again, and in his darker moments had considered the possibility of using some spell of persuasion on them all, something to put the wind at their heels. But, even in his state, he would not sink to that level. Not with his friends.

But then Kuthy had reminded him that there was only one portal out of Eotunlandt, and if the thieves were headed north, as it was plain they were, they would have to pass through it, too. Thus Finwald had turned his despair into a single-minded determination to reach the portal before they did, redoubling his efforts to drive the company on as fast as possible and so cut them off. It was the only point at which he was sure of encountering them again, and thus the only chance of regaining the sword.

It was a race to the gate.

Now finally, after a week of cursing fretfulness, they were surely within a day's march from the portal, and it was here at last that they had spotted their first sign of the thieves. Finwald's heart had leapt. He was within an inch of regaining Flametongue, and he was not going to take any risks. But neither was he about to let this godsent fortune slip through his fingers.

"We've no choice," he insisted. "We must catch them. It's now, or it's never."

"*Never* suits me fine . . ." Bolldhe mumbled, but no one was listening to him anymore, even if they did silently agree.

They all instead turned to the Peladane. It was clear how some of them felt: Why risk so much for just a sword? Not even its last owner, Bolldhe, was particularly inclined to recover it. In fact he seemed glad to be rid of it.

"Actually," Nibulus said, "I don't believe those Tyvenborgers are that dangerous. I saw the look in their eyes, and the way they held themselves. They're not real fighters."

"Agreed," Paulus said. "Thieves are maggots to be squashed beneath the Boot of Righteousness. I saw them, too, and they are cowards."

Paulus had been itching for a fight all week. Skulking here in the woods was not to his liking. He may have been many things, but nobody could ever accuse the Nahovian of being a coward. Furthermore, he had a score to settle; he hated thieves with a loathing that bordered on the unholy in its intensity. But it was not just the Tyvenborgers that had infuriated him so; he still had not forgiven Kuthy for leading him on with tales of Huldres. Paulus Flatulus wanted blood, and he was not too particular whose blood it was.

Bolldhe sighed. He could see where this was heading. But his opinion counted for nothing here. It was up to the other three to try to talk the Peladane out of this madness.

"What do we actually know of Tyvenborg, then?" inquired Wodeman. "How dangerous can they be?"

"It's the single largest collection of thieving scum on the face of Lindormyn," Nibulus replied. "Bandits, picaroons, freebooters, plunderers, cracksmen, and cutpurses . . . Men, Haugers, Grells. Venna, Rhelma-Find, Pendonium, wherever there are people, of any race, if they're lowlife arse-pickings, chances are they'll end up in the Thieves' Mountain. They're strong, but that strength comes from numbers, not courage or skill at arms."

"Though they can be handy with a blade, at a pinch," Paulus pointed out.

"And they often have magic," Kuthy added. "The very laxity—no, carelessness—they show towards new members is their great advantage. No entrance exam for them; they'll take anybody. No cult is barred, nor race nor gender. They are without rules, who knows what magic they may have?"

"But I still say they are no match for true fighters," Nibulus insisted. "If we can just surprise them . . ."

Bolldhe regarded the leader as he drew a gauntleted finger down the edge of his greatsword. *The old sod's starting to believe in his own myth,* he thought. *He's never talked like this before.*

He delicately probed the scabbed blisters on his face. "There is one magic I know for sure they have," he said softly, unsure whether they were allowing him to speak yet, "and I really don't wish to feel its touch again."

Nibulus gave Bolldhe's burns a perfunctory inspection. Though he was still unwilling to allow this faithless coward to remain with them once they had left Eotunlandt, his anger at Bolldhe had subsided somewhat these seven days past. Nibulus had seen cowardice many times before; he had had to do unpleasant things about it, cut it out. But he had never had to cut out one sixth of his troop; a Toloch, after all, consisted of fifty thousand men—and eight thousand, four hundred men was not something he would discard lightly.

"Looks almost healed to me," he commented. "I'd be more wary of the weapon itself than its magic."

"He only tapped me with it," Bolldhe reminded him. "And there are more magical and poisonous weapons in their arsenal."

"Poison, yes," Nibulus agreed. "I could smell the Fossegrim-stench of that voulge from twenty paces."

"I concur," Appa muttered darkly. "I was considerably closer to it."

"And River Haugers were ever devious, alchemical disease-ridden little bastards," Paulus put in, recalling Flekki's chakrams.

"But what magic did we see?" Nibulus continued. "Bolldhe's boiled face with its crumbly scabs, granted. But as for the rest of the supposedly magic stuff that bloke was going on about, well, we only have his word for it . . . and that being the word of a thief, mind you."

"But what about that 'pipe thing' he was pointing at you?" Wodeman asked. "Looking at it, I couldn't see any way it could work, but he looked fairly sure of it."

"Don't know, don't care," the Peladane replied blithely.

"Pipe thing?" Kuthy repeated. "What d'you mean?"

"You didn't see it?" asked Nibulus. "Oh no, of course, silly me, I was forgetting; you were too far away by then." He gave the Tivor a look. "No, it's something I've heard of before, years ago up near Trondaran way, but I can't think what the word is. Sounds a little like 'mascot,' or 'mess kit' . . ."

Kuthy thought for a minute. "Mascot? Musket? No, not one of them! Not a *blunderbuss*! Ah, I hate blunderbi! Ach, Nibulus, I'm afraid you're right about Trondaran; they make them up in the mountains there—something to do with dragonfire, I think, but I've never managed to get hold of one to see how it works. In any case, that's not something you'd want going off in your face, believe me." He looked genuinely worried. "And that half-Grell's Dancing Sword, those are things I *have* come across myself, and I never want to experience another demonstration of their powers."

"And there is the small matter of the Dhracus," Bolldhe pointed out. "She seemed to read your mind well enough."

"Getting very chatty, aren't we?" Nibulus scowled at Bolldhe without even looking at him. "Anyway, she didn't read my mind, only guessed it. That's no skill. Anyone with a pair of eyes could tell that I'm not the kind of man to surrender."

"Be that as it may," Appa remarked with a shudder, "she is a Dhracus, and they have powers. . . ."

"A Dhracus from Godtha, though," Kuthy observed. "I've had enough dealings with that people to know it's their cousins in Ghouhlem that possess the psionic art. Those from Godtha are mere apprentices. We needn't worry too much about her. No, it's that big bugger—Oswiu something-or-other. He's the one that concerns me. He's the one with the power."

"Brother Oswiu Garoticca," Appa reminded him, "Yes, I agree, there was a potency I felt in that one that I've never before known in a man. He is a true Rawgr of Olchor. I doubt not for one second that he has much dark enchantment to hand." He then clutched his amulet, and started rapping his ring against it fretfully.

Nibulus snorted, and drew himself up to his full height. "He's a thief! Any power he has can, and should, be purged by the sword. Just like any other spineless Olchorian."

"I don't think he is an Olchorian," Bolldhe essayed. "Not exactly. Did anyone see the runes on his mantle? Olchor, Erce, and Cuna. What d'you make of that?"

"The Order of Cardinal Saloth, wasn't it?" Finwald asked. "Yes, I'd forgotten about that. Anyone got any ideas? Kuthy?"

But for once, Kuthy had no suggestions. To everyone's surprise, it was Wodeman who now spoke up to elucidate them, Wodeman the uneducated coppice priest, he who hardly ever left his woods. "Cardinal Saloth Alchwych," he explained with unaccustomed venom, and then spat. "To all my people, his name is like the dung they use to spike their hair."

"So who is he then," asked Finwald, "if not a follower of Olchor?"

Wodeman deigned to avert his eyes from his companions'. "A Torca," he confessed.

A very pregnant pause followed. Then Appa said, "You're joking!"

"A Torca," Wodeman repeated. "Yes, one of my own. But one who long ago left the path of Erce. Down dark forest paths known to none but himself has he gone; paths haunted by forest wraiths that howl out gibberish madness, paths spun with the tangling webs of Falsehood, drawn ever on by the sweet stench of nightsoil, into lightless, trackless Chaos that broods at the heart of the Great Wood."

Kuthy smirked at the shaman's articulations. "You mean he was a sorcerer who got a bit lost in the woods one day?"

"That is the absolute truth of it, Tivor," the shaman replied tersely. "Got lost in the woods for sure. And there he founders to this day."

"But why the runes of Olchor and Cuna?" Appa asked.

"The three runes do not stand side by side as equals," Wodeman explained, "rather Erce stands at the center of all, with the other two flanking it. The Scales of Balance pivot on the head of Erce. The other two sit in the pans on either side. Thus Erce ever strives to balance the opposing forces of Good and Evil, that would tear the world apart if they could."

Finwald scoffed in derision and sat down upon the grass, his sword cane across his lap. Appa joined him, sighing heavily and plucking the dead brown holly leaves off the hem of his woollen robe. It was clear they were in for a long lecture. Bolldhe pointedly decided to join them.

"I hardly think that acts of kindness to help each other along life's difficult path are going to tear the world apart," Appa chided. "But do go on."

"I completely agree, Appa," Wodeman went on, "and isn't that exactly what I've been doing all my life? Don't tell me you know nothing of your brothers skulking off to the woods at night to petition my help when their own resources have dried up. I don't have the skill of counting, as you learned men have, but even if I had, I doubt I'd be able to tally the total number of

Lightbearers and Peladanes who've come to me over the years. Oh, it's not much I do, I know; divining for wells, purifying water, petitioning the earth spirits at sowing time, thanking them at harvest . . . locating game for a hungry family; and there are many ills I can heal that are beyond the wit of your herbalists. No great Acts of Good, I know, but I dare say they help where help is most needed."

("Don't worry, Finwald," Appa assured the impatient priest in a whispered aside, "I'm sure the Tyvenborgers will still be there for a while yet.")

"And the Scales of Balance?" Nibulus inquired, guessing where all this was leading to.

"The Scales of Balance remain steady," Wodeman confirmed. "My help is small, mundane, and pragmatic. It goes unnoticed by kings and high priests, and more importantly, by gods. I believe my works help the ordinary man far more than any damn crusade would—"

"Without our swords you would have no life, no land," Nibulus growled. "Who d'you think holds back the forces of Evil? You can't do that with twigs and herbs!"

"Without your swords we wouldn't have an enemy in the first place!" Wodeman cried. "You think Olchor cares about farmers, do you? I hear the Evil One's servants take little interest in those lands free of both your cults." This last was directed at the mage-priests also.

"Limp, peace-loving woman!" Nibulus spat.

"Dung-headed lemming!" Wodeman rejoined.

"Oh, bollocks!"

"Arseholes!"

"Ah, just like my days in the Quiravian debating society," Kuthy observed, "and if any of you lot care to shout any louder, I'm sure we'll soon be hearing what the Tyvenborgers have to say on the subject too."

Both parties quieted into a sullen silence. Then Finwald, wondering whether he should prolong this debate any longer than was absolutely necessary, rose to his feet. "Evil must always be fought," he stated. "That's what life is: the perpetual struggle between Good and Evil."

Wodeman settled back down on his haunches, and drew out his clay pipe. "We are all of us men," he said, calmer now. "We live in the world between the Yttrium Chapel and Hell. We are the pivot. I do acts of good that help ordinary people, not Acts of Good that disturb the Balance. For every supposedly 'holy' Act of Good, the Scales tip in favor of Evil, and vice versa."

"It all makes what we're doing here pretty bloody pointless, then, doesn't it?" Bolldhe commented. This time he felt entitled to speak up, seeing as all this was so obviously for his own elucidation.

But Wodeman was not to be put off. "What *who* is trying to do, Bolldhe? We know what Finwald wants, but as for the rest of us, I'm sure you'll agree we're still in the dark. Do *you* know what we're doing?"

"Haven't got a clue," replied Bolldhe, then added, "as usual."

"Quite. We, the Torca, believe that the Balance must be kept. Helping each other out, as we all do, adds no weight to the scale pan of Good. But every time a temple of Olchor is razed, or some other such act of holiness is committed, you can be sure that the exact opposite will happen to balance it out. We ourselves have all committed acts of revenge now and then, so we should understand. This is nothing too difficult: night and day, winter and summer, death and birth; it's all part of the ineffable Cycle of the Cosmos—"

A loud yawn interrupted the sorcerer's speech as Kuthy stretched himself out on the dewy grass and stared up at the morning sun slanting through the leaves.

"And the Cardinal?" Nibulus reminded the Torca. "Where does he fit into all this?"

"Just as the Torca refuse to take sides in the endless squabble between Good and Evil, so too do most people—only not in the way we believe in," Wodeman explained.

"Ah, indeed," Finwald concurred, eager to get this over with as soon as possible, "the neutrality inherent in such a belief system is readily accepted by many people. They develop it to suit themselves, looking after number one and ignoring everyone else."

"Exactly what you'd expect from the thievish element in *their* part of the world," Wodeman resumed, jerking a thumb in the direction of the rocky knoll with its line of smoke. "And then Saloth Alchwych came along, a Torca who 'got lost in the woods.' He was a Torca like any, but he expanded the ideology of his followers in Hrefna Forest. They were always a thievish, self-centered lot, so close to Tyvenborg, so it wasn't hard to gain a following. Their perverted idea is to bring Good into the world by deliberately causing Evil. For every gold zlat they steal, somebody profits—when they spend it. For every child they slay, new life comes into the world. And when they assassinate a Good, Holy Man, then surely it is the best, easiest way to ensure that an Evil, Unholy Man dies.

"It's difficult to gainsay the logic in their thinking, but we all know the truth. Just try telling it to our friend Oswiu out there. . . ."

"True enough," Kuthy agreed, "you'd have to be a fast Torca to make him see sense."

"So what do we do?" asked Bolldhe. "Kill him? Or would that tip the Scales against us?"

"We avoid them," stated Wodeman, "though I confess that I'd dearly like to feed him to the earth. 'From death springs new life,' we say, and so honor the fungus that grows on the decaying wood of a dead tree, or the blood of the animals we kill. But they sleep with the bodies of their victims, make puddings from their blood, and feast upon the maggots that crawl from their putrescent flesh. Cardinal Saloth's murderous brotherhood have taken all that we hold sacred, and turned it on its head."

"Yes, right, this is all very fascinating," Finwald commented, "but do you think we could just go now and actually *do* something about our necrophilic friends out there? Or were you planning on simply talking them to death from here?"

Wodeman's face bristled with sudden anger. "How *dare* you mock everything that I stand for! *How dare you!* I don't remember you ever deriding my magic back in Nordwas, on your secret little midnight trips into the woods. You seemed quite happy to accept the help of a servant of Erce back then."

What's this? Bolldhe thought, his ears pricking up. The others, too, paused, looking from Wodeman to Finwald.

"Wodeman . . ." the Lightbearer murmured.

"Wodeman nothing, you hypocrite. I've covered for you long enough. If this is the way you're going to treat me, then when we return to Nordwas you can just go and locate your *own* earth crystals and powders and whatnot. You and your weird little experiments!"

Of all of them, only Appa seemed unsurprised. "Is this true, Finwald? You haven't been getting up to your old tricks again, have you?"

"Of course he has," Wodeman replied, filling Finwald's silence. "Don't tell me you didn't already know?"

"What're you all talking about?" Nibulus cut in, feeling rather left out in all this.

Appa sighed, the sadness and disappointment evident in his voice. "You can take the alchemist out of Qaladmir," he said, almost to himself, "but the alchemy still remains in the heart. Isn't that right, *Nipah*?"

"Nipah?" Nibulus demanded. "Finwald, is there something you haven't told us?"

"There's a lot I haven't told you, as I'm sure is the case of every living soul on the face of Lindormyn," Finwald retorted. Then, somewhat sullenly: "Nipah was my old name—Nipah Glemp. It's a name I left—along with everything else in my old life—back in Qaladmir when I quit that seamy place."

"So Finwald's not your real name?"

"Finwald's the name I took when I joined Appa, twelve years ago. I took it as a testament to my conversion—"

"So you were originally an *alchemist*?" Nibulus inquired, unsure what to make of this, and more than a little suspicious that his friend had never even mentioned this before.

"An apprentice only," Finwald replied. "To a sorry little excuse of a man called Pashta-Maeva."

"Yet you still sneak off into the forest to ask Wodeman for crystals and powders and whatnot?"

"My spells," Finwald retorted defensively, "require certain substances that are not readily available in the marketplaces of Nordwas. Like those I used for the firewall that saved our lives back in the Blue Mountains, remember? There are many tools that can be legitimately used in the service of the Lord Cuna."

But a choice had to be determined, and swiftly. The Peladane stepped forward, and planted his sword before him in the earth. "*I* lead," he declared, "and what I say, we do. But I'm not going to lead a group of seven against fourteen (especially when most of that seven aren't even soldiers) unless I'm sure I have their full support. I believe a united party is a strong party, and if we are strong, we can beat them. So we must vote: Do we fight them and win back the flamberge and our pride, or do we skulk around them like a pack of sick, craven dogs?"

If the son of Artibulus had ever harbored dreams of becoming an orator, Kuthy reflected, then it was probably for the best that he had never given up his day job. "Let's skulk, I say," he declared blithely.

"Agreed!" came Appa's response. "I like dogs."

Wodeman had already given his opinion. But against these three were Nibulus and Paulus, eager for a fight, and of course Finwald, who would not go without Flametongue. So the casting vote fell to the least among them, Bolldhe, and he wasted no time in giving his response.

"It seems to me," he deliberated, "that the only thing we have to counter their superiority in arms"—Nibulus scowled—"is our superiority in magic."

Appa, Finwald, and Wodeman beamed at Bolldhe's acknowledgment of their powers, at last.

"So before I vote, I want to see what their gods have to say."

Thus, in a thicket of ash and beech on the northern edge of the forests of Eotunlandt, the tournament between the gods commenced. All three of the magic-users cast their various scrying spells.

Appa looked to the heavens and closed his eyes in concentration. He mumbled prayers through dry lips until his eyes were wet with tears.

Finwald tried something less direct. He brought forth a tiny crystal on a delicate silver chain, and sang to it in a clear voice that set vibrations in the air. It was a pleasing chant, but its sole purpose was to stir the crystal to its task of divining. This was Finwald's *locate* spell, and it would make the crystal incline toward the presence of Flametongue.

And Wodeman, ever the earthy one, promptly cut the palm of Bolldhe's hand with his little pocket knife, and watched carefully as the blood dripped onto the soil.

"Many things can be seen of the past, present, and future when your blood mingles with the elements," he claimed, and stared hard at the earth as small droplets of Bolldhe's blood sprinkled upon the soil. The shaman was softly chanting now, sounding like bees in foxgloves; his eyes fluttered as his mind reached farther into realms that were closed to ordinary men.

Bolldhe himself was troubled. How unlikely it all seemed. Was he really to make a life decision based on the muddled rantings of these three wise men? Could they really see into the future by such means? As Bolldhe watched his lifeblood slowly sink into the ground and disappear, the only vision of his future it brought to his mind was of a violent and bloody end followed by cold oblivion. He shivered. He could feel that old, familiar heaviness in his gut again. Bolldhe was frightened.

He wiped the grime from his face with the back of his hand, and walked back into the forest a short way. And when he turned back to observe his companions, he froze in astonishment, for a most extraordinary thing had just occurred.

Was it a vision? Bolldhe squinted hard at the image before him. Or was he dreaming again? All the sounds of the woodland around him, his companions' murmuring voices, even the gentle breeze above them, all faded until a numbing silence enveloped his senses.

There before him was the forest, the same as it had been before, but now it was blurred, pushed into the background somehow; marginalized, perhaps, to focus on the center of his vision where the three magicians were. At the center stood Wodeman, his arms held out straight on each side of him. To either side of him were the mage-priests, chanting their theurgy, unaware that they were being watched so intently. And they were floating! At one time Finwald would rise a few inches off the ground, while simultaneously Appa would descend into the earth. Then the opposite would happen, Appa rising and Finwald descending.

Bolldhe averted his eyes in fear, and he felt sick. He breathed in deeply several times and shook his head, then he looked back. Still the vision was there: two priests slowly floating up and down, and the sorcerer rock-steady between them, unmoving. Like the pivot of a set of scales.

Then Wodeman's eyes snapped open, and Bolldhe's world was enveloped by them. Those green and brown eyes, all earth-lore-wise and demanding.

"So," they seemed to say, "which is it to be?"

Though there was no overt malice in those eyes, Bolldhe felt an overwhelming need to just turn and run as fast as he could. He did not like this one bit. Why could he not wake up from this vision?

Then the sorcerer's voice came to him again, deep and resonant as if it traveled through the very earth and up into the tops of the trees. "Very well," it said, "ignore me then—but you will have to choose at the end."

The voice trailed off into a whisper that became the rustling of the leaves, and Bolldhe's vision began to fade.

"Wait!" he called out urgently. "I don't understand—'at the end'? D'you mean deciding about the thieves, now, or are you talking about . . . you know, the real end?"

But Wodeman merely raised one bushy eyebrow and wagged a finger. "Ah no, no clues," he smirked. "That's for you to decide."

Bolldhe cursed. Then he looked at the priests, first one, then the other. Both were still wrapped up in their spells, oblivious of all else in the world. First there was Appa—always counseling caution, always fearful. Well, that was something Bolldhe could readily understand; his entire life had been one long headlong flight, always running away, or putting things off. And that, to be honest, was exactly what he wanted to do now. But the old man seemed, somehow, so devoid of vitality, so lacking in sincerity. So damn dogmatic. Was Bolldhe to follow him, and run away all his life? End up like that dried-up, scrawny little cadaver? *"At the end"* he would have to face up to things.

Somehow, it seemed so much easier to follow Finwald's advice. Well, not easier, but more . . . wholesome. Now there was a man who knew his own mind. No vacillation or self-doubt for that one. He would follow his faith even if it led him down a Carrog's throat. His faith burned in him like a fire, not like Appa's porridgy procrastination. Finwald's dark eyes were steady and true, and he alone of the "nonfighters" was committed to the fight. In a way, he was "in with the big boys," "one of the lads." He made Bolldhe feel so lame.

He turned and faced Wodeman squarely. "So, who would you choose?" he demanded. "About the thieves, I mean."

Wodeman shrugged. "You already know which way I'm voting."

And as soon as he had said those words, Bolldhe heard the low, shuddering howl of a wolf, rising from the woods up into the heavens, greeting the sky.

His dream-vision flickered for a second, then winked out. He was back amongst his companions once more.

What on earth was that last bit? he asked himself, *Did I really hear a wolf, or was that just part of the dream?*

"You all right, Bolldhe?" Nibulus asked, looking at the blinking wayfarer curiously.

"Uh, yes, fine thanks," Bolldhe stuttered. "Just . . . getting a bit bored with all this magic stuff. I don't really believe in it anyway."

A chorus of "Oh, fine!," "Now he tells us!," and "You asked for it in the first place" went up from the assembled spellcasters, followed by various disgruntled mutterings of ". . . waste of my good time . . . ," ". . . waste of his good blood . . . ," ". . . ingrate . . . ," and ". . . oaf . . ."

"Come on, Bolldhe," Finwald sighed irritably, "we're supposed to be working together on this. Remember what we agreed at the Moot: the more methods we have at our disposal when we reach the Chamber of Drauglir, the better chance we stand of destroying him."

He turned from Bolldhe's sulky, scabby face in contempt, and muttered into his friend Nibulus's ear, "I know he's under a lot of pressure on this quest and, as a Lightbearer I've always been taught to be patient, but sometimes I really feel like smacking him in the face."

"Well, I'm sorry about wasting your time," Bolldhe cut in sarcastically, "but I've made my decision anyway."

They waited. "And . . . ?" said Nibulus.

"No maggot-breath threatens to suck the soul out of *my* eyeball. Let's go and get that sword back."

After a brief and levelheaded discussion in which each of the company had their say, gave their point of view, and made their suggestions, it was decided that the raid should consist of a careful blend of catlike stealth, lightning speed, and savage, merciless brutality.

The terrain between the edge of the woods and the smoking hillock was far too open to provide them with any cover, so they opted to keep under the screen of the trees until it led to a low spur that would shield them from view; this same spur led to a point within two or three hundred yards of the knoll. After that, they would have to see. It would take about an hour to reach the thieves, Kuthy estimated—"if that's who they are, of course."

As they marched through the sparse woodland, Bolldhe began to wonder why exactly he had voted to retrieve the sword. It was, he had to admit now, hardly the obvious choice. There was pride, of course; nobody could forgive the Tyvenborgers for the humiliation they had heaped upon him. And there was the matter of the treasures that they had purloined from him. (Actually, he was keener to retrieve those particular items than he was the sword; give him fandangles over flamberges any day. Though he had to admit that, short of slaying them all, this was unlikely.)

There was also the matter of his current unarmed state. At the moment he was borrowing one of Kuthy's dirks. Nice thick blade and easy to use. But he would need something a little more effective in the days ahead.

"But of course, that's not the reason either, is it, Bolldhe?" he whispered to himself, as he kicked through the dense fern leaves underfoot. No, it was all really a knee-jerk reaction against the magicians. He was so fervidly sick of their machinations.

I wonder what their scrying spells actually revealed, though, he found himself pondering. In his haste to scorn them, he had not given them the chance to reveal to him their results. Not that it mattered one bit, of course; it probably would have been all lies, anyway. No matter what the spells actually told them, the three magic-users would only give the version that suited their purpose. Just as he himself always did when auguring for those ridiculous women who had paid him so well over the years—his purpose being to tell them exactly what they wanted to hear.

But now, marching toward a fearful and quite possibly fatal situation, purely on the whim of his own casting vote, Bolldhe began to wonder. He looked around at his companions. No use asking Wodeman or the priests. Or the two warriors, come to that; they hated all that stuff. Kuthy, on the other hand . . .

"Tivor," he said in a low voice as they walked side by side, "I don't suppose you know anything about scrying for the future, do you?"

"I don't suppose I do," the soldier of fortune replied unhelpfully. But then he looked around at the trees and seemed to change his attitude. "There was an occasion, though; many years ago when I was on a job in Trondaran. Some nutcase tried to discern my future in the trees."

"The trees?"

"Yes, she sat down on the hill we were on, knees above her head like a frog, and chewed on this black tree gum that smelt terrible. Then she just stared for ages down at the forest below. Trancing. Trying to see patterns in the trees."

"And did it work?"

"Who can tell? All I know is that, up till now at least, my life hasn't featured leaves particularly heavily, dogs don't use me to mark out their territory, and I don't go brown in the autumn. I don't know, perhaps she wasn't the imaginative type. Still, it could have been worse, I suppose—at least she didn't try scrying for my future in the latrine."

"Yes," Bolldhe interrupted, laughing. "Then you'd really be in the shit."

Kuthy turned and looked at him, unsmiling. "Actually, *I* was about to say that."

Bolldhe's smile vanished, and he fell back to walk on his own again. He should have known better. Despite the fact that Kuthy was older than Bolldhe, and so much better in so many ways, he seemed undeniably and almost determinedly childish. *All those years on the move,* Bolldhe reflected, *no home, no job, no family, not even any long-term friends; it's hardly the type of life to instill any responsibility in a man. . . .*

Then the obvious struck him. *That's me, in ten or twenty years' time,* he thought gloomily. *Take away the hero stuff, the legends, the adventures, and what have you got? Yes, me! I'm a lesser Kuthy, a Tivor-in-training. In fact, I'm not even that much.*

Bolldhe briefly wondered if Kuthy ever stared up at ceilings, as he himself did. He pondered on this for a moment, then dismissed the idea; someone like Kuthy Tivor would not have enough time. He would more likely stare up at the skies, the stars . . . and farther even beyond. Whereas Bolldhe might be found supine upon a dingy, sweat-stained bedroll in some lowlife caravanserai, musing on the swirls of knotted wood or patches of fungus above him and trying to make patterns out of them, the Tivor would be doing the same with the clouds, the constellations, and the moving tides of the universe itself. That was the difference between them: Bolldhe's horizon was about eight feet away, whereas Kuthy's was literally limitless.

It was a depressing thought. It was true that Bolldhe reluctantly admired Kuthy, but it was admiration for Kuthy the legend, not Kuthy the man. He was well aware that he could never become anything like the legend, but did he even want to end up like the man?

Yet everything he was doing in his life so far was pointing exactly to that. Just like Kuthy, he had not grown beyond the stage of being a young bachelor;

was still treating life like a game, even when others his age had moved on to the next stage. Even when the game was no fun anymore. Even when younger people seemed much more mature. It was embarrassing.

Bolldhe smiled sadly. People often admired him, looked up to him for what he did and all the places he had been to. Much in the way he himself did with Kuthy. But, in truth, Bolldhe looked up to ordinary people more. Raising a family, keeping the wolf from the door—it took courage and skill to stay put, to see things through. People like that did not just walk away whenever hard times befell them. Whereas he merely played at life, they knew it was real; they dealt with what seemed to Bolldhe insurmountable hardships, simply because they had no choice. And the ones who seemed to have taken the greatest knocks in life—drought, destitution, disaster—well, it hardened them, matured them. Even if it soured some of them in the process.

Kuthy, on the other hand, was the biggest player at life Bolldhe had ever met, and he really irritated him sometimes. The hero seemed to think he was clever when he joked about serious matters, especially death; much in the way an adolescent thinks it is clever to swear. He almost seemed to expect them to congratulate him for his wit and perspicacity in this.

Bolldhe stared at the back of Kuthy's multiappendaged headgear as he strode before him. Though he could not see his face, by his gait (and by the playful way the "liripipes" of that hat were stroking his unseen face) he guessed the man was smiling. Why on earth was the old soldier here with them? Not even Appa, with his almost supernatural powers of empathy, could guess his real purposes.

Bolldhe continued to stare at the hat that covered Kuthy's head. In the fortnight or so since they had known him, none of the company had seen him without that damn headgear; he had not taken it off once, not even to scratch his scalp. What was he trying to hide? Bolldhe could only speculate.

Then, as he studied its glistening surface, Bolldhe thought for a second he could see his own reflection.

The sun was climbing high in the sky as they finally emerged from the cover of the trees. Beyond the woodland's threshold the land sloped gently upward. Now, quite clearly, they could see the distinctive buffalo-horn pinnacle of the rocky knoll peeping over the crest of the spur. There was no immediate sign of anyone, but the few wisps of smoke every so often that drifted vaguely up from behind the ridge showed that someone had been here at least recently, if no longer.

Wodeman scouted ahead. For a moment or two they watched his nimble frame leaping in an almost anuran manner up the hill. Then he seemed to fade, or blend in, and was soon lost to them.

They waited, fidgeting silently. Several minutes later, he was suddenly back among them.

"It's them," he breathed excitedly, and Bolldhe's body flooded with adrenaline. "They're still eating, but it looks like they'll be breaking camp soon."

"We'll have to move fast," Nibulus said, leaving his armor strapped to Zhang for the moment. "Is there any way of getting down to them unseen?"

"It's thick bracken all the way down to the knoll," Wodeman replied. "I could crawl through it right up under their noses, but you lot'd be extremely lucky to manage the same."

"Perhaps a swift charge from the top of the hill, then," Nibulus suggested, a gleam of relish in his eyes.

"I think I can do better," the sorcerer replied. "There's a bit of a breeze up here now; if the bracken's already swaying a fair bit and the wind's good and loud, any blundering about you all do shouldn't be noticed. All it needs is a little push."

"A push?"

But Wodeman did not explain. With a wink and a grin as if to say *Just leave it to me,* he leapt away back up the slope, and once again melted from sight.

Nibulus turned back to his men. "Whatever he's doing," he said hurriedly, "we can't hang about. Appa, you stay here with the horse. The rest of us—"

"If you need someone to hold the horse out of sight," Kuthy cut in, "I can do that."

"Appa can do that!" Nibulus corrected him, thrusting his face into Kuthy's.

"Absolutely," Bolldhe agreed, staring at Kuthy through narrowed eyes. "Your skills will be more useful with us, hero."

Bolldhe had made up his mind that he really did not like Kuthy Tivor one little bit. Ever since they had met, the man had not been able to take his greedy, thievish eyes off Zhang.

And, as Paulus took a certain pleasure in pointing out, "Appa's as slow, puny and scrawny as an old deshelled tortoise left out in the sun to dry."

"I am as Cuna made me," Appa responded defensively, visibly wounded by this remark, though he did admit rather sadly that he would only be a burden out there.

"Suit yourselves," Kuthy replied with a shrug. "Both of us can hold the horse, then. I have absolutely no intention of risking my skin for somebody else's sword, no matter how you lot voted. I told you before, my only commitment is guiding you through these lands."

He looked around at them, and from their faces it was clear their feelings ranged from disenchanted to absolutely sickened. It was not just disappointment in the man himself, but also in the legend. Nibulus in particular—ever the competitive one—was hoping to witness some of the Tivor's much-vaunted expertise with the sword, and see if he really was as good as he was reputed to be. Besides, to fight alongside a legend such as this was ever the dream of warriors.

But there was not a thing they could do about it. Not a thing.

"Besides," Kuthy went on, "by rights you shouldn't have escaped those maniacs last time. We've already pushed Chance's goodwill to breaking point. It'd be churlish to ask any more of her."

"Thank Pel we'll be leaving you soon," Nibulus muttered, "you little git."

"I can follow you to the top of the ridge," Kuthy offered helpfully. "My bow is quicker than any of their missiles."

"This will make a great song for the bards," Finwald said. " 'The Lay of Brave, Brave Tivor.' "

But Kuthy just smiled, and took his bow from his back. "I wouldn't believe everything you hear in the stories," he said. "Bards don't get paid for singing about cowards."

Without another word, the five raiders loped off up the hill to rejoin Wodeman. They found him just below the crest of the ridge. There he knelt on one knee, eyes clamped shut and deep striae lining his leathery brow. He was squeezing one of his runes tightly between finger and thumb. It was almost certainly the elemental rune of Air, but this was difficult to see as there was blood on it. Wodeman's blood. As usual.

Bolldhe could not help but wonder at the Torca, a people so close to nature, yet so ready to spill the contents of their own bodies; in his experience, one of the preoccupations of nature was to keep one's blood inside one's veins.

Whether Wodeman's "little push" was working, Bolldhe did not know, but up here the wind was undeniably stronger. It did not come from any particular direction, rather it flew about in fitful gusts, spiraled through the tall grasses, and whistled shrilly like an unquiet elemental spirit. Wodeman's red curls flew up to dance to the music of the air, and his wolf-skin cloak bristled.

Nibulus and Paulus pricked up their ears at the familiar sound, hesitant for a moment. They had heard the same back in the Blue Mountains when Wodeman had conjured his Air Elemental against the Leucrota and its company. But now it was rather different; last time they had heard exultant shrieks of uncontrolled elemental frenzy, but this time the sound was remote, and troubled, as if it were being summoned to this alien land contrary to its will. There was chaos in that wind, yet it wavered, unsure as to whither it should go.

Disquiet in their souls, the company flattened themselves on their fronts, and crawled up to the very top of the ridge. There at last, they peered down at the land below.

Sloping down to the rocky hillock, the hillside was, as Wodeman had reported, a thick carpet of bracken. The bright green fronds were whipping this way and that, and swallows darted and swooped in exuberance.

And lurking at the shadowed base of the knoll were the thieves.

By the look of it, and much to the dismay of the Aescals, few if any had perished at the hands (or rather feet) of the giant. Twelve of them could now be seen moving around their messy camp. The hulking figure of Meat Cleaver was easiest to recognize, but so too could be discerned the shock of acid-green hair belonging to Hlessi, and the brightly colored silks of Raedgifu. Four diminutive figures sat off to one side, still eating by the looks of it. And halfway up the slope, only fifty or so yards away from Bolldhe and the others, was a lone sentry. It was Eggledawc Clagfast, the former Peladane with the huge, double-pointed war hammer. He was still chewing upon the last of his food, and was facing vaguely southwards, away from them.

"We'll pull him down first," Nibulus whispered, readying himself.

"Might be better as a hostage," Paulus suggested, with uncharacteristic humanity. "Yes, we can always torture him to death when we've got what we want."

"Bolldhe," the Peladane hissed, "think you can do it? As soon as you take him, that can be the signal for the rest of us—"

"We're almost here!" a sudden voice interrupted. They turned, to see Kuthy staring off up to the north somewhere.

"What?"

"The tunnel entrance—the way out of Eotunlandt. It's just over there, see? I recognize the shape of the valley. Just over there, no doubt about it."

"Are you sure?" Nibulus asked uncertainly. He was trembling with adrenaline, and did not like being sidetracked like this.

"About a mile or two that way, honest. I'd never forget a valley that distinctive. I'm just surprised we came out of the woods as far north as this. Last time I came from another direction."

Bolldhe gritted his chattering teeth. "Yes, you're full of surprises, aren't you? You sure this isn't another way of avoiding the fight?"

"I already am avoiding it, dear boy," Kuthy replied. "Remember?"

Nibulus crawled over to Kuthy. With his face just inches from the adventurer's, he stared hard into his eyes. "Tell me honestly, Kuthy, are you telling the truth this time? No more of your bullshite, mind. I'll know if you're lying. And if you are, I will kill you."

Those cold blue eyes, hard as tengriite, pale as a timber wolf's, met the honest brown eyes of the Peladane, and held them. Then he grinned, unable to keep a straight face. "You can trust old Mr. Tivor, even if he is a little git."

Nibulus's eyes narrowed; then he shrugged. "In that case, there's no longer any doubt that the Tyvenborgers are indeed heading the same way as we are. Only two portals leading into or out of Eotunlandt, right?"

"That's what the inscriptions said," confirmed Kuthy.

"Bugger!" Nibulus swore. "What is the probability of two separate groups of travelers both journeying through this hidden land at exactly the same time?"

"Perhaps not such a coincidence at all," Finwald broke in. "Now that I come to think of it, one or two of those Tyvenborgers looked somewhat familiar. Perhaps they were present at the Moot. Perhaps they're heading for the same destination as we are. . . ."

"If they are heading for Melhus," Nibulus said carefully and deliberately, "then this changes everything. They have already made us their enemies; but now they are a real threat. We must eliminate them, kill them all. Dismember their foul carcasses, and burn the remains, then sow the blood-soaked ground with salt."

The others looked in puzzlement at their leader.

"It's the only way to be sure," he said by way of explanation.

Despite the wind, it was uncomfortably warm, and none of them could hear anything except his own heartbeat.

"Bolldhe," Nibulus instructed, "better stick to your job. Pull that sentry down, but try not to alert the rest of them. Then kill him quick. If he's allowed to cry out or struggle, the game's up, and we have to immediately attack. If you do your job properly, that'll give us more time to get a bit closer. In any case, when you've done that, we four—me, Paulus, Wodeman, and yourself—must dispatch the enemy as quickly as possible. Kuthy, I want you to rain down arrows on the ones farther away. And Finwald . . . do some of your fire tricks, anything that will kill them or drive them away. As I said earlier, they're cowards, and even if we only kill half their number, the survivors won't bother us again. I promise you."

"You really think my sword is that important?" Bolldhe asked, not feeling good about this at all. "Is it really worth fourteen lives?"

"Yes!" Finwald hissed.

"No," Nibulus declared, "I don't. I'm not talking about some enchanted ironmongery here—I'm talking about our survival. If Finwald's right, and they're on their way to Vaagenfjord Maw, we will meet again. And next time *they* might be in our current position. This might be our best chance."

A voice growled behind them: "Then we'd better go right now." It was Wodeman. He had finished his evocation of the spirits of the air, and had come to join them. The fire that they had seen in his eyes over a week ago—on his return from his lone wanderings—was back now, and fiercer than ever. "I don't know how long the Elementals will help us. They're ever fickle, and this land is not to their liking at all. Can you not hear them bickering?"

Thus did Bolldhe find himself once again in a position over which he had no control. He was used to being master of his own destiny, but ever since meeting Appa back in Nordwas, he had been thrown into one bad situation after another. Up here in the Far North, the concept of Fate infused everything. The gods laughed at puny mortals who believed that they were in control of their own lives. He could hear their shrieks of mirth in the chaotic wind around them.

Now here he was, belly almost to the ground, inching his way through the bracken toward a man he had been ordered to kill. It was all wrong, of course.

He believed in that flamberge no more than Nibulus did. Yet it was Bolldhe's own vote that had got him into this whole mess.

The sweat from his palm had already soaked into the elk-hide-bound hilt of the dirk he gripped so clumsily. The blade felt so heavy at this moment in time; heavy, brutish, and repugnant. Far heavier, in fact, than his old broadaxe had ever felt. Could he really ram that thick length of cold, hard metal into the soft, pumping flesh of the Tyvenborger's neck? Could he kill this human being who had, like Bolldhe himself, turned aside from the path of the war god? This man who was in all probability no worse than a thief? Yet the half-second of savagery it would take to commit the deed would transform Bolldhe irrevocably into both thief and murderer.

As each frond of bracken parted before him, as each crunch of vegetation beneath knee or forearm brought Bolldhe closer to poor, heedless Eggledawc Clagfast, the certainty and immutability of Bolldhe's imminent transformation summoned ever more bile to his throat. It was simply murder.

The air was becoming warmer and stickier by the minute, and there was a pulsing charge of electricity in it that tingled through Bolldhe's teeth. He paused for a moment, and squinted through the swaying green leaves at the back of Eggledawc's head, now only yards away. So much like Appa's neck, he reflected. He almost wished the man would turn around and spot him.

Do I really want to be a murderer for the rest of my life? Bolldhe wondered. He thought forward to imagine what that would be like, but he could not; there was a black barrier before him. He thought back to what his life had been like previously, and that was not much better. Oh, he had killed men before, he was almost sure of that. But then it had been different. He had fought many times over the past few years, but it had always been in self-defense. And in all cases, he had been spared the certainty of knowing if his opponents had subsequently died. His method was simple: Hack, slash, and put the boot in, then leg it as fast as possible. Never go back to check whether they survived. Too dangerous, and if they were dead, that was their fault for attacking him in the first place. Bolldhe himself never provoked fights.

But going back farther in his memory, had he ever started hostilities? As aide to that mercenary guarding the caravan heading to the Crimson Sea, when Bolldhe was just fourteen, he had sometimes been called upon to help repel attacks by brigands. He had stabbed his weapons out of the windows of the wagons into anything that moved, and often his blade had come back stained red. Had he ever killed, though? He had fired off arrow after arrow into the night, but always at distant, half-seen, enemies. Again, had he killed?

He stretched his mind back even farther, deeper into his past. And suddenly it became very humid indeed, and the electricity in the air made his head spin sickeningly with vertigo. There was a black barrier in his past, too; something in his own mind that was too strong even for him to reach through. What in the name of Pel-Adan . . . ?

An engram. A memory too dark and too terrible to behold. Turn back! Look away! Madness and blood, designed and directed by . . .

Bolldhe was eight years old.

Child. Beast.

Terror and fury as primal as it gets. Unfettered by adult mind-blocks. Limitless. Bottomless.

His eyes snapped open, baby-blue and cold as a reptile's. Glared with hatred through the grass. Grass that soughed with the song of the waves. Saw Eggledawc. Foe! Forsaker of the One True God! He must stab, rip flesh, eviscerate, bathe in hot blood!

He gripped his wonderful new dirk, felt for a second the orgiastic intoxication of carnage fill his brain. Then he pounced. . . .

Dolen Catscaul was not happy. She sat upon a large rock at the base of the knoll, somewhat apart from her new "cohorts," and was idly scraping the dirt from under her fingernails with the tip of her misericord. Hardly a fitting use for such an ancient and magical knife, she knew, but it seemed to sum up her life at the moment. As the only Dhracus in the party, she was experiencing the full gamut of prejudice and mistrust that was the inevitable lot of one such as her.

Is it my skin? she wondered, and splayed her twelve long fingers to regard their immaculate whiteness. It was no great secret that the other females in the party begrudged her this, but Dolen could not begin to understand why. Take the leader's sister Aelldryc, for example; Dolen greatly admired that "freckled beetroot" complexion of hers. The reward for a healthy outdoor life, in her opinion. And as for the mottled greyness of Flekki's face, to Dolen, it was as the sheen of a fair silver birch in the crepuscular moonlight. Admiration was fitting, not envy.

The very concept of jealousy was ludicrous to the Dhracus. They did not complain about, nor even concern themselves with such trivial, superficial irrelevancies. But those others were not Dhracus, and they appeared to embrace an inexhaustible supply of the most ridiculous and illogical sensibilities, half-truths, and pseudovalues. It was as though they needed such things to distract them from the real things in life. Why could they not simply focus on what mattered?

How they ever managed to invent the wheel, I'll never know, she thought. They seemed too busy obsessing over the size of various parts of their body, especially the females, or picking lice out of each other's hair, to ever get important things done.

Or maybe they just don't like my forked tongue?

"No," she said softly to herself, with the ghost of a smile on her silver-grey lips. "Eggledawc doesn't seem to mind that one bit. . . ."

Eggledawc Clagfast. The mere thought of the name warmed her heart and

exorcised her current gloomy preoccupations. Those five syllables, from the
initial sweet and playful opening vowel, through the luxuriant dark "*l*" con-
sonant clusters, to the final whispered promises of the closing sibilance, encapsulated all that she so loved about humans: the passion and tragedy of
their poetic lays, the haunting beauty of their music that could slay the soul or
raise the dead, and their sense of humor that was as uproarious as it was inexplicable.

She was glad that she had met Eggledawc. He was different from the others.
Never made any demands. Never grew angry. And, like her, he was a free spirit.
When she had first met him in the dark of a forest glade in Hrefna, neither had
been afraid though they had both had good cause to be, for sure. For both of
them, it had been the first time either had seen one of the other's race. It was
the firelight, she believed; in its sanguine illumination, the skin of both human
and Dhracus had glowed the same color. And over the following few weeks,
both had delighted in their similarities as well as their differences. It had been
a time of joy, new feelings, and sharing; especially for her, so blessedly gifted
with the empathy of her race.

Where is he anyway? She looked up from her nail-picking, tilted back the
peak of her cap, and scanned the surrounding area with keen eyes. Almost instantly she located him, still standing guard up the slope. It was getting rather
windy, she noticed also; the bracken was whipping this way and that most
oddly, and her swain's hair was flying up around his head in a chaotic jig. But in
spite of the wind up there, down here it was becoming uncomfortably hot. She
had not felt like this since the giant had materialized—*Sluagh's Devils, that had
been terrifying!*—and the air felt charged with the presage of blood. . . .

She turned back to her thoughts. Ah, these Tyvenborgers! Why did she
ever let Eggledawc talk her into joining them? It was not even as if he himself
was a thief by nature. But then, there was not much difference between the
terms "outcast" and "outlaw" in most people's minds. And to lump all the
denizens of the Thieves' Mountain into one word, that was just as nonsensical
as categorizing the pygmy shrew and the baluchitherium as just "animal." In this
band of fourteen alone could be seen the entire spectrum of people, from the
maggoty Oswiu Garoticca, to superior beings such as herself and Eggledawc . . .
and perhaps Eorcenwold. Dolen liked Eorcenwold.

One group, a million differences, and she perhaps the most different of all.
She knew what they said about her behind her back, of course. Every negative
thought within their brains crackled out upon waves of empathy to the re-
ceivers in her own mind. Chief among these was, as ever, distrust and fear.
They, like all other non-Dhracus, believed she was too perfect, "the ultimate
being." But in truth, all Dolen Catscaul cared about was how best to get on
with her friends.

Needless to say, she knew the real reason why the Dhracus were so shunned
by other races; that singular, undeniable fact, that terrible secret of her kind,

that underlay every single mean little thought, opinion, or negative reaction of the non-Dhracus, and gave shape to all their—

What the Frigg was that? "EGGLEDAWC!" she cried as her brain was engulfed in terror and blood, and her stomach lurched with a leaden weight of nausea. Instantly the entire camp leapt to its feet as the Dhracus's screech split the air.

During the first few seconds that followed, many things happened at once. The wind-tossed bracken appeared to sprout several howling warriors that charged down upon the camp with cries that stopped the heart. In his shock Brecca the Stone Hauger stumbled and knocked over the kettle, sending a hissing plume of steam right into the faces of his three companions. An arrow thudded into Klijjver's huge pauldron, throwing him staggering back with its force. Weapons were snatched up, orders were bellowed. The enemy warriors leapt into the camp, and another arrow struck Klijjver, this time directly on his iron cap, snapping the giant's head back and sending him sprawling upon his back.

Then, during the next few seconds, other things followed. Khurghan's double-bladed haladie spun through the air toward the tallest attacker, struck his bastard sword with a steely ringing that echoed around the valley, and showered orange sparks down upon his black hood before wheeling around in an erratic arc and returning to the gloved hand of its wielder. Hlessi meanwhile tripped over his net in his haste to flee from the largest warrior. Cerddu-Sungnir threw down his crossbow in frustration, and stood his ground with his battle-axe. By now, Dolen had both her knives out, and was still screaming relentlessly.

Then Eorcenwold planted his feet firmly on the ground and brought up his blunderbuss. "THAT'S ENOUGH!" he roared, and everything went silent, as quickly and as suddenly as it had started.

Finwald hesitated, as next did Wodeman. Then all was still. Nobody moved. Not a word was uttered. Even the conjured-up wind lost its force and died; the voices within it echoed off into the distance with a final sputtering cackle, and, as it went, so the unnatural closeness and humidity descended in full upon the land. Nibulus, once again, found himself staring down the bore of Eorcenwold's musket.

His eyes bulged madly in his meaty face, glaring in hatred at the thief before him. As sweat poured down his neck under the increasing heat, he cursed vehemently at another standoff. Again, *again,* it had all gone wrong. The Dhracus woman's warning call had robbed him of the element of surprise; the thieves' panic had been cut through by their leader's voice, and they now held their ground. Bolldhe, for some reason, was still holding on to his prisoner; and the natural reluctance and tardiness of the nonwarriors in the band of Aescals had helped lose them the initiative. They had once again failed him.

Damn the day I ever brought them! he cursed to himself. *Why couldn't I*

*have had a company of real soldiers? Men I could order! Pel's Balls, even this
ragged band of brigands obey their lord with instant obedience! What wouldn't I
do for a voice like that. . . .*

"Right," he whispered to himself. "Decision now. Fight or run?"

He glanced around him for a second. Cerddu-Sungnir had gone back to furiously reloading his crossbow; Hlessi had regained his net, and was moving forward slowly, growling horribly; Cuthwulf and Aelldryc had taken up position on either side of their brother.

Then the twang of Kuthy's bow could be heard from the top of the hill behind him. But by the time the sound reached them all, the arrow had already been casually deflected by Dolen's left-hander parrying dagger, as she slowly advanced upon Bolldhe.

Finally, a deep wheezing noise could be heard, like a bison coughing in the chill of early morning. Klijjver hauled his metal-shod bulk unsteadily to his feet, blinked dumbly, then noticed the two arrows embedded in his shoulder plate and helm. He took hold of them firmly, and yanked them free. There was no trace of blood. He then came on with maul and bhuj in hand, and his comrades laughed evilly.

Again, Nibulus deliberated: fight or run? He had not quite decided which one it might be, but at least he now knew it was not going to be *fight*. Paulus and Wodeman drew closer to the Peladane, waiting for his signal. Nibulus opened his mouth to give the order, but unexpectedly it was Finwald's voice that cut through the silence:

"The sword!" he cried. "Give us the sword you stole! Give it to us, and we will trouble you no more."

The thieves muttered together in incomprehension, then Bolldhe's voice came down from the slope. Still holding on to the frozen form of his captive, he translated Finwald's words into the thieves' own cant. His voice, however, sounded strange—croaking weakly, tremulously, almost as though on the point of hysteria.

Only the Dhracus was close enough to hear what he said. Without even a split-second's vacillation she sprang away from Bolldhe, wove through the thieves in a blur and, before anyone could stop her, had snatched the flamberge from a pile of baggage lying at the base of the knoll. Oswiu roared in fury and lunged after her, but Flametongue was back in the hands of a very startled Finwald before she could be halted.

"*Zikih oi'dhnap, Egeildehwc-kiewha!*" she demanded, now striding back toward Bolldhe with both knives in her hands. Finwald, meanwhile, sprinted back up the slope without so much as a backward glance. Oswiu started to leap after him but, at a word from Eorcenwold, Cuthwulf barred his way with his poison voulge. The two brothers glared at each other, but made no further move.

Nibulus very swiftly appraised the situation, then wordlessly bade Paulus and Wodeman to back off alongside him.

Dolen, meanwhile, had approached Bolldhe and stopped just a few yards from him. Her face was like murder: an inhuman, alabaster mask of iron will and domination, her eyes fixing Bolldhe's like a snake's. He was still holding Eggledawc before him like a shield, the dirk held to his throat. Eggledawc kept absolutely rigid, not daring to move even his eyes.

"Egeildehwc-kiewha!" she repeated her order, and a red halo began to glow around her black irises like a poker thrust into a fire, or an eclipsed supernova. Bolldhe appeared transfixed, unable to release his prisoner to her. Choking amid shuddering breaths, he kept staring with insane fear at the Dhracus, as though she were the Angel of his Death.

But despite his terror (which was only in part due to the fear-effect of Dolen's magical misericord) Bolldhe was himself once again, no longer that child.

Suddenly the mask of Dolen's menace melted into an expression of utter puzzlement. She cocked her head to one side, and was still. Her breathing faltered. One trembling white hand reached tentatively forward. Then her whole mind went forth with it and entered Eggledawc's.

Searching. Feeling.

Nothing.

There was no mind. Eggledawc had left her. Her dear human swain was . . .

" . . . dead . . ."

The word whispered through her slightly parted lips like a sigh from the crypt.

Now the wind, a real wind this time, began to blow. Bolldhe stared glassily at the Dhracus before him. The redness had faded from her eyes, and they were now as black as coffin-nails. Her hair writhed out from under her legionnaire's cap, danced wildly in the waxing wind, shadow black against the dark-grey storm clouds that were piling up and rolling in from the South with unnatural speed.

Bolldhe made a strange gurgling noise in his throat, and backed away. As he did so, the body of Eggledawc slipped from his grasp, and landed in a kneeling position before Dolen, his eyes staring vacantly through her. His throat was covered in blood, and the blade that had slashed it now lay next to him, abandoned. The engram in Bolldhe's mind had now faded. Under its thrall, through a red mist he had staggered, and now that it had dissipated, he saw with disbelieving eyes that he had finally stepped over that terrible threshold.

The skies turned as dark as twilight, and thunder rolled throughout Eotunlandt. Behind clouds huge and black, like the sails of a pirate ship, lightning flashed. They could taste it in the air. The wind, still building up, as yet held back its full fury.

By now the other thieves at the bottom of the hill had worked out what had happened. Amid screams of rage and injustice they surged forward. To Bolldhe's stricken mind, it was a vision of hell itself, as a thousand Rawgrs with glowing eyes, saber-toothed jaws and butcher's blades flowing with blood now screamed toward him. The clash of metal upon metal heralded the onset of Chaos, as Nibulus and his men launched themselves into battle.

Then one voice rose above all others: "ENOUGH IS ENOUGH!" Only the Tyvenborgers fully understood it, but even to the Aescals the meaning was plain. Into the fray the stocky figure of Eorcenwold strode. His blunderbuss forsaken, he now whipped out his morning star and flailed it above his head, ceasing for the moment all hostilities. All eyes were upon him.

"This is too much!" he cried in cant. "I demand a life for a life. Yon cut-throat must die!"

His stubby, outstretched finger pointed directly at Bolldhe, who, before he could gather his wits together, found himself in the middle of a ring of scream-ing, spitting bandits. Outside this circle, both Nibulus and Wodeman were bellowing in protest, but neither was making any move to save Bolldhe. Kuthy could just be seen, a small silhouette at the top of the hill, his bow hanging at his side; Finwald was long gone; and Appa did not even know what was hap-pening. Bolldhe was utterly alone amidst this screaming mob. Facing him was the Dhracus.

He leapt for the bloodied dirk that lay upon the trampled bracken where he had dropped it, and snatched it up in his trembling red right hand. There he crouched, readying himself, facing the avenging angel before him. And then, as if in a dream, all else drew back from his sight, and all sound faded into the background, save for the gathering wind that flailed the tops of the bracken, and fluttered the neck cover of Dolen's cap.

Then his soul fell into her eyes. *Oh god,* he thought as he stared into their solemn depths, *what have I done to her?*

Such aching sorrow there was in those eyes, such wounding, such loss—too much to be contained within her head alone. Perhaps it was due to her psychic ability, or perhaps because that fair head had simply not been built to hold such hurt, but it seemed to be overflowing, pouring out, wave upon wave, un-til all those around her were as stricken as she was. All there could sense the vi-sion that was playing over and over in her mind: a vision of her and Eggledawc thundering on horseback over high, purple-hazed moorland, smiling a bright, eternal smile at each other as they rode, a cold scatter of rain in their faces. To-gether they had found a perfect happiness in this hostile, miserable world—something beautiful and unique.

But now that had been so cruelly ripped out and destroyed, and her special love curdled and broiled into a poisonous rage. Like a black viper, it uncurled its coils within her soul, poised ready to unleash its venom.

Then she sprang, and there upon the heath of Eotunlandt, amid the scream-ing wind of the approaching storm and the vengeful howls of the Tyvenborg-ers, Bolldhe and Dolen Catscaul did battle. It was a fight like no other that had been seen in that land before, one to tear the hearts of Bolldhe's company, or slake the blood-thirst of the thieves. Blow after blow after blow hammered down upon Bolldhe in the seething heat of Dolen's ire. Tears of blood poured from her eyes, streaking her stark white face into a deathly mask of infernal hatred. Grey lips peeled back from her gritted teeth, and with every blow she screamed, driving Bolldhe farther and farther to the ground.

It was no equal fight. The speed and dexterity of her race could not be matched by even the greatest warrior of mankind in Lindormyn—and Bolldhe was not even a warrior. Even without her anguish she could have slain him with but one stroke. But consuming love turned to hate had poisoned her, and the cruelty that was the reputation of her kind spewed forth. She was playing with Bolldhe as a cat does with a mouse. With her parrying knife she smote him, each stroke placed with absolute precision to extract the maximum pain whilst administering the minimum injury, and with her misericorde held aloft, she poured surge after surge of hellish nightmare into his brain.

How long he would endure, she did not know, but she meant to prolong it, and watch him die in shock and unspeakable, screaming agony.

Suddenly, a terrible sound pierced through the din of yelling voices and the swelling tempest. It was a shrill, whistling screech, like an animal or bird in its death throes. All—the Dhracus included—looked up in alarm toward the top of the slope whence it came.

There, Kuthy could be seen, blowing hard on his flute and gesticulating maniacally. He then cupped his hands to his mouth, and shouted as loud as he could. At first nobody could hear anything more than a pathetic bleating. But during the sudden lull in the fighting, the storm also abated slightly. In this brief pause his voice could just be heard—and with it a message that froze them to the soul:

"The giants are coming! The giants!"

Though his message was delivered in Aescalandian, the word "Jotun" was universally understood. As one, every head snapped around to look in the same direction Kuthy was pointing. Then all eyes widened, and all hearts stopped dead. Sure enough, many miles to the south but rapidly approaching, the towering shapes of no less than ten giants could be seen. All courage that any there might have possessed now vanished utterly.

All except Bolldhe. For him, the exact opposite happened. Up until now his whole being had been focused upon the terrible misericord brandished before his eyes, that stiletto-straight blade that filled his mind with a dread he had never imagined possible. He alone had heard nothing of Kuthy's warning. But now, in those few seconds of hesitation as the misericord-wielder glanced southward, the fear effect wavered. Suddenly freed from its spell, Bolldhe, still lying on his back, lashed out with his feet in desperation. One boot swept round and knocked the Dhracus's legs from under her. She cried out in surprise and, as she fell, Bolldhe brought the pommel of his dirk smashing up into the side of her head. With a grunt, she collapsed, both her daggers still clasped tight, one in each hand.

But if any of her group had noticed her fall, it made no difference to them. As little thought was spared their fallen comrade as was given to the pile of baggage dumped at the base of the knoll. No one even thought to try and hide. Just like the last time a giant had appeared, mindless panic possessed them all; it was every man for himself.

Unlike last time, however, when the giant was already upon them, now there was an obvious clear direction in which to flee: *northward*. And this they did with a single-minded determination. Bolldhe's companions, too.

Now the full fury of the storm broke over them and, wailing, they ran to the hills with eyes full of dread. Rain lashed down from the heavens to blind them, and it seemed a satanic choir of harpies screeched amid the elemental madness of the tempest to confound their senses.

Still reeling with physical agony, unbearable guilt, and mental aftershock, Bolldhe was not as quick to react as the others. Now he too had been abandoned by his companions. As the leviathans thundered ever closer, bringing with them the chaos of the accompanying storm, all he could do was stand there panting, and staring down at the pair of pathetic crumpled bodies at his feet.

Eggledawc's eyes, still glazed in fear and pain, stared up at nothing, the blood from his ripped throat now washed by the rain over his skin. Next to him lay Dolen. Her face was drawn tight with an inner agony that Bolldhe could only guess at. Hurt beyond belief by Bolldhe's unforgivable act of murder, abandoned by her own companions, and now totally unable to save herself from certain death.

A wave of utter despair swept over Bolldhe, and he pitched forward, almost retching in nausea. What had he just done?

But almost as soon as it descended upon him, Bolldhe's despair was thrust aside by a sudden fierce resolve: She would not die. Bolldhe swore it: If any were to fall this day, it would be him. But not before he had saved the woman.

Though not knowing exactly why he did so, he laid Eggledawc's war hammer reverentially upon the dead man's chest (much in the way Peladanes' bodies were graced with their swords as they lay on the funeral pyre), and tenderly closed his eyelids. Then he snatched up the limp form of the Dhracus—man, she was light!—and ran off almost blindly through the driving rain, through the wet bracken that slapped at his thighs, and up to the summit of the slope.

At the crest, blinking back the stinging rain, he stared down beyond to where he had earlier left Zhang in the care of the priest. Above the howling tempest and the ever-increasing thunder of the approaching giants, he called out: "Zhang! Appa!" But he could see nothing of them through the rain. In rage, he screamed at the top of his voice. Passion filled him. Through her sodden clothes, Bolldhe became aware of feeling something of the warmth and softness of Dolen's body in his arms. His heart almost broke in pain of love for this total stranger, not even a human. . . .

All pain and guilt put aside for the moment, he allowed his soul to soar at the thought of what he was doing, this, his atonement. With that, he let the full power of the storm surge into his wounded heart and pour through his veins.

Then, beyond any hope, he caught sight of the blurry shape of a horse galloping toward him.

"Zhang!" he cried out, in utter delight. A second later Appa was out of the saddle and standing beside him. The priest's grey woollen robe clung about him like wet paper, and he was gasping for air.

"Bolldhe!" he cried in relief. "Thank Cuna you're still alive. I thought I heard you call."

"Take her!" Bolldhe yelled into his ear, then heaved the slumped and sodden form of the female thief over Zhang's withers. "Get yourself back on now, and don't stop till you reach the gate! Whatever happens, don't let go of her!"

Ignoring the priest's stammering protests, Bolldhe hoisted Appa roughly into the saddle. "Tivor knows the way. Now GO!"

For a second, Appa's eyes met Bolldhe's inquiringly. The old man may not have known the reason for Bolldhe's strange actions, but he did realize one thing: he, for once, was doing the right thing.

Perhaps the old rogue, Appa's last and only hope, would die today. But "Whatever happens, don't let go of her"—Bolldhe had clearly come a long way.

So, with a hoarse cry, Appa galloped off toward the hills, and was swallowed up by the storm.

Then began his flight to the portal, and Bolldhe wasted no time. Even as Zhang disappeared from sight, he was already plunging headlong in the same direction the horse had taken. Instinct now took over; though Bolldhe may not have been the most athletic of men, his single-minded attitude to self-preservation could not be rivaled, and running away from danger was one of his most practiced skills. Across the heathland he sprinted, legs pumping like engines, eyes and nostrils flared wide.

Over some bushes he leapt in an arc that was gazelle-like in its perfection; under a low-hanging bough he ducked, snapping his head aside lightning-fast to avoid having his eye gouged out by a protruding twig; down the side of a steep, stream-cut defile, over the churning water in one huge bound, and up the other side all in one single momentum of speed.

On and on he ran, toward the mountains that reared up before him, though only dimly visible behind the screen of rain. He did not precisely know where he was heading, but he had to keep going as fast as he could; any doubts would only slow him down.

Doubts, nevertheless, were clawing at his mind in their hundreds. He realized that only Kuthy knew the portal's exact location, but he had no idea how to pinpoint the man in this storm, for he could barely see twenty paces in front of him. And what if Kuthy had abandoned them? Maybe he had been lying again when he said the portal was at hand? Perhaps he should forget Kuthy and follow the Tyvenborgers instead; they must surely know where the gate lay.

By now the rumbling of giant steps had grown into a huge booming as of great drums beating underground. It felt as if the whole of Eotunlandt were moving to this beat, rivaling the commotion of the storm. Yet the storm itself was escalating; bullets of hail now joined the bombardment, stricken birds came tumbling and screeching out of the sky, and whole branches went flying through the screaming air.

Yet, amid all this, men's voices could be heard: one coarse bellow from somewhere in front, quickly answered by several hysterical cries from somewhere nearby.

His heart leapt. He had caught up with them already! Despite the delay caused by carrying the Dhracus to his horse, he had actually managed to close the gap between himself and the others. What a runner! Pride gave him an additional surge of adrenaline.

Now he could see figures running on either side of him. Close by on his left was the vast charging bulk of the Tusse, head down, thundering along in full armor like a steam train. Gods, he looked as unstoppable in flight as he did in battle. How could such a heavyweight achieve a speed like that?

On his right were others, too far off in the rain to recognize. But they were veering off to the right now . . . following the lead of the bellowing voice out in front.

That must be the way. Bolldhe immediately hared off after them. But as he went, he called out, between heaving gasps, to the herd giant. Whether Klijjver heard him or not, he had no time to check.

Steeper now the ground rose. Bolldhe cursed, and doggedly pumped on. Within seconds he could see another figure just ahead of him, running desperately. Skidding in the mud and flailing its arms, it was evidently on its last legs. As Bolldhe gradually narrowed the distance, he could hear it gulping in great lungfuls of air between each sobbing exhalation.

This one was small and ungainly. Hauger? Yes, there was that unmistakable iron cap on its head. The shield on its back had come partway loose, and was now bouncing this way and that erratically, making it more difficult for its wearer to run smoothly. Yet there was no time to stop and tear it off. For this little bloke it was an encumbrance that might cost him his life; he knew he was likely to die. Bolldhe could hear it in his sobs.

Seconds later he had overtaken the stumbling, rasping little morsel of giant-fodder, and left him to his fate. Then, as if in answer to a prayer, the ground suddenly leveled out. He had reached a low plateau, and at last, *at last,* Bolldhe

beheld the gate leading out of Eotunlandt. Perhaps half a mile away, but unmistakable even in the pelting cascade of rain, the black shadow of a cave
mouth could just be discerned against the pale grey of the rock face. Already
various running figures were approaching it.

Then the first of the giants reached the foot of the valley. A monstrous roar
shivered the air as the ten behemoths surged up toward them. As they came,
they brought the heart of the storm with them. For, as truly as they had been
summoned by the Spirit of Battle between mortals in their land, the tempest
heralded their coming and tore about them as they charged. More birds still
were forced to the ground or broken apart in the sky. Beasts cowered in yammering terror in their hiding places, or went running wildly for any cover available.

Only the Huldres showed no fear. They went shrieking through the air in
unconstrained delight, tossed high by the gale and then swept around again to
plunge toward the ground with ecstatic glee.

The hysteria of the storm and the pounding of the giants now resonated so
loudly in Bolldhe's ears that sound had lost all meaning. He could feel his wits
nigh departing: the world around him, his memories, his life, his death, these
meant nothing to Bolldhe anymore. All he knew now was the chase; he had
never run so fast in his life, and never would again. He felt that he had been
running forever, had never known aught else but this terrible flight through the
madness of the storm, with the stampeding giants at his back gaining on him
with world-striding ease.

Suddenly he was aware that yet another was running by his side. He
glanced over uncomprehendingly, then realized that it was Nibulus. As he recognized his companion, Bolldhe saw that there was laughter in the other man's
eyes—*laughter*!

Then he realized that a second runner was keeping pace with him, on his
other side. This one was Eorcenwold, also wearing an inane grin on his wide,
florid face.

With the gale tearing at their clothes and the rain lashing every exposed
inch of their skin, the three men sprinted in one final burst of insane speed toward the looming cave mouth. Bolldhe's head went back and he shrieked with
laughter, and the madness of exhilaration consumed him. Together, the three
of them would run to the world's ending.

Then Bolldhe tripped and fell flat on his face. Of course.

He skidded along the rain-slicked grass for several yards before coming to a
dazed halt. Meanwhile, the other two pounded off into the rain, but just as
Bolldhe was hauling himself to his feet, a foot planted itself firmly on his back,
and he was slammed onto the ground again. It belonged to none other than
Brecca the Stunted One, who had thus leapt over Bolldhe and was now the last
of them all—save Bolldhe—to try for the safety of gate. Still bleating in mortal
terror, the Hauger quickly disappeared from sight.

Blood in his eyes, unable to stand, lungs red-hot and feeling about to explode, Bolldhe flailed about himself in utter insanity. The ground kept bouncing him up and down like a pea on a drum skin, each approaching giant's footfall causing a stronger tremor than the last. Bolldhe had only moments left, but the gate was still a few hundred yards off. Dimly he was aware of the three shapes of Paulus, Khurghan the Polg, and Grini the Boggart, leaping nimbly toward the cave mouth from another direction.

Into his fractured mind flashed the vague thought: *Who's going to look after Zhang now?*

Followed immediately by: *No, not that bastard Tivor!*

In a sudden snarl of rage, Bolldhe catapulted himself forward in a final surge toward the gate. Just then it seemed to him that, oddly, the whole of Eotunlandt held its breath. Everything somehow faded away; the frenzied storm, the earth-wrecking stampede, the screeching exultation of the Huldres. All, for a second, still.

And then, from out of nowhere, the colossus came crashing down right in front of him. The earth heaved beneath the massive impact, and Bolldhe was thrown clean off his feet, jarred to the bone. Where it had landed, all plant life withered, and the ground was desiccated, cracked and split with long fissures. Bolldhe lurched to his feet with a choking cry, and stared at what stood before him.

No! his mind screamed. *Not now! Just when I'm this close!*

There it stood, barring his way: the sickest phantasm, the "Loathly Denizen of Darkness," a warped and mutated abomination to poison the entire world.

The Afanc.

It had grown immeasurably since that last encounter in Fron-Wudu, until it was now a thing that appeared too heavy to remain upright, and must surely collapse beneath its own weight. Taller than five men it stood, a gargantuan tower of convoluted flesh from which serrated bones thrust out like branches. New appendages flailed loosely about it, and once the rain hit its deformed, furnace-hot body, it hissed rapidly away into steam. The old wounds gaped yet further: the Unferth-slice to the gut, the bastard-stab in the back, and the broadaxe hew across the face. In addition, the heavy, lumpen head lolled cumbersomely from side to side, weighted down by an eye that had swollen so hugely around the arrow that Kuthy had set there that it appeared to be giving birth to a new monster even viler than itself.

But the worst injury by far was the burning it had received from Bolldhe's oil flask. Indeed, the monster's entire face and throat had not so much transformed as *shifted* into another form, perhaps even into another plane of reality. It was a slid visage, a melted countenance, a facial glissando. And for this most offensive transgression, it would now deal with Bolldhe first.

Crying out in fury and frustration, Bolldhe swung away from the monstrosity before him, and headed back the way he had come—back toward the giants. With a beserk shriek that echoed throughout Eotunlandt, the Afanc tore after him. As ever, it could do nothing else but follow the vengeance that was its very quiddity, having no care at all for the approaching giants.

Someone, Bolldhe knew not who, cried out from the safety of the tunnel: "NO!" But there was nothing else he could do. Whether for the sake of the quest, or even for himself, Bollde knew he could no longer take that path northward to rejoin his companions. He was Bolldhe, the survivor, the changer of directions, the one who could take a new road without a second's notice. He needed a new way, right now.

They watched him go, those in the tunnel mouth, watched as the tiny grey man slithered about upon rain-slick ground, the rapidly gaining Afanc hot in pursuit. And then he was lost to them in the blinding curtain of the tempest.

A great shape, loftier than the hightest bastion of Wintus Hall, emerged from the deluge, a black shape materializing from the grey. The first of the giants was upon them. Bolldhe needed no other cue. With a nimbleness that was almost magical in its celerity, like the ragged hare he was, the Wanderer doubled back on the spot. The Afanc, however, too huge and lumbering to veer or even slow its headlong charge, carried on straight into the path of the giant.

The foot came down.

There was a sound like a siege hammer pulverizing a basketful of rotten shellfish, and an aftershock that sent Bolldhe once again tumbling to the ground. A purulent gout of matter the color and stench of a blood blister was followed by a cyclonic eruption of furious, agonized bellowing from somewhere up there in the sky—as the great jagged bones of the Afanc pierced the giant's foot, and sent fountains of the creature's poison into its bloodstream.

But the Afanc, finally, was done, dissolved into nothing more than a massive puddle of venomous effluvium.

Bolldhe, too, was done. Spent. Could not rise from this one. In a second the next giant footfall would descend, this time with himself under it. And the gate, even farther away now, might as well be on the other side of the world. He would never make it.

Then out of a dream, or nightmare, there came a flurry of sound and movement, and rough hands wrenched him off the ground and onto the back of his horse.

In his ear he heard a voice, not of Kuthy, but of Wodeman, and it cried:

"So you really thought I'd leave you dying? When there's room on this horse for—?"

"Just shut up and ride!" Bolldhe screamed, and Zhang was propelled toward the cave mouth like a quarrel from a crossbow.

A huge foot slammed into the ground less than fifty yards behind. It drove into the earth with such force that Zhang was bounced off the ground and flew several yards through the air, dislodging both riders from the saddle; Wodeman held on by the horse's mane with just one hand, and Bolldhe had both his hands enmeshed in Wodeman's hair. In a fountain of muddy water the trio landed again, both riders slamming down onto the horse's spinal column, Zhang's knees crumpling beneath him. In a second or two the next foot would be upon them, and all three would be blended as one on the sole of the giant's foot.

But Zhang was from the Tabernacle Plains, and there were few horses in the world tougher or surer-footed. Staggering madly, he slid on for a few yards more, then miraculously succeeded in righting himself, and without an instant's delay was off again.

Those last two seconds stretched out to last a lifetime, and in that same lifetime Bolldhe's senses expanded to take in the whole world: the smell of rain-soaked upland turf; the feel of Zhang's iron-hard muscles beneath him; the sight of Brecca, still wailing in terror, limping just ahead of them, with that bloody shield hanging from just one strap and swinging about all over the place; various faces—Nibulus, Kuthy, Eorcenwold, Aelldryc, Flekki, and Klijjver—just within the cave mouth and screaming their comrades onward . . .

. . . then the Peladane's eyes flicking upward, dilated and aghast; the sudden cessation of rain immediately around them as a giant's descending foot provided temporary shelter; the gasp of Wodeman's final breath . . .

Then complete darkness as the foot came down.

They were through, into the cave, and the whole world exploded. All five senses merged into an awful semireality of Hell. Bolldhe, Wodeman, Zhang, the others, even the very stone and the air, all were thrown into space and scattered into a billion particles, swirling without form or meaning through the vortices of nil-space to sink finally, mercifully, into some place the other side of oblivion.

Glossary

A. *The Races of Lindormyn*

1. DEMIHUMANS

Boggarts—Diminutive, downtrodden and hairy, these are normally found scavenging on the peripheries of "civilization," and get used as slaves by Polgs. They do, however, possess limited shamanistic powers.

Dhracus—A strange, isolated race with superb dexterity, high intelligence, and psionic powers. Very rarely encountered, and universally feared.

Grells—A thuglike, brutish race of strikingly ugly appearance and demeanor. Found all over Lindormyn, they live either in their own stockade towns, or scattered through the territories of other races.

Half-Grells—Owing to the general licentiousness of the Grell, their half-breed offspring can be found in all parts of the world of Lindormyn.

Haugers—A short, slightly built, flat-faced people that dwell in well-ordered communities, usually apart from other races. Highly civilized, intelligent, and inventive, they are excellent craftsmen and make shrewd merchants. They fall into two types:

(1) **River Haugers**—More gregarious and interactive with other races than their "Stone" cousins, owing to their control over large stretches of Lindormyn's waterways. Apart from their obvious river-based skills, they are noted also for their expertise in herbalism and alchemy.

(2) **Stone Haugers**—Living in upland escarpment villages or plateau towns, and providing Lindormyn's most skilled engineers, they have a wealth of inventions that other races, even their "River" cousins, rarely get to see. Though quiet by nature, their kings employ sizable armies of highly skilled and uniquely equipped soldiers.

Jordiske—A disgusting and animalistic race so far only encountered in Fron-Wudu. They have hairy, slug-infested skin, long filthy nails, and a head much like a goat's skull but with long limp ears and bulbous eyes. Archenemies of the Vetterym.

Polg—Hunter-nomads of Lindormyn, short, lithe, and extremely tough. They are proud, fierce, and contemptuous of other races. They dress somewhat ostentatiously, and affect a permanent swagger.

Vetter—The short, almost ratlike Vetterim live only in the deepest reaches of Fron-Wudu.

Though bestial in appearance, they have developed a unique and highly inventive culture. They are nimble, and owing to "arm membranes" have a limited gliding capability. The only outside race they have had contact with is the Polgrim, and even this has been very sporadic.

2. GIANTS

Ettin (mountain giant)—At eighteen feet tall, the two-headed Ettin is the tallest of the giants. Found only in northerly regions, Ettins are hardly ever encountered by other races, though they sometimes raid the northern part of Vregh-Nahov. They are considered barbaric and evil by most races, and are greatly feared by all.

Gjoeger (swamp giant)—Twelve-foot-tall cousins of the Gygers, the Gjoegers are probably the rarest of all giants, and are shy not only of other races, but even of their own kind. They are highly intelligent, and possess a certain limited magic unique to their species.

Gyger (forest giant)—Also twelve feet tall, but extremely skinny, Gygers are nevertheless immensely tough and strong. Apart from their build, they are similar in appearance to the Gjoegers but instead live in large communities. They are excellent hunters and trappers.

Jotun (ice giant)—Fifteen feet tall, wholly evil, and covered in thick white fur, Jotuns are the most northerly of giants, and the most animalistic. Encounters with them are, fortunately, extremely rare.

Jutul (fire giant)—Ten feet tall but extremely broad, the black-skinned Jutul are best known for their skill at metalwork, especially in the making of bizarre and potent weapons, some of which they trade with other races for magic purposes. Apart from this trade, they live out their strange, subterranean lives by successfully ignoring the rest of the world.

Ogre (hill giant)—Nine feet tall, the "stone age" Ogres are the most primitive of giants after the Jotuns and Ettins. With limited intellect, they live tough lives in isolated uplands, shy and fearful of—while despised by—other races. Their cultures and religions are unique, as is their shamanistic tradition.

Tusse (herd giant)—Eight feet tall, these are the most common of all giants, and the closest to humans in appearance and culture. They live mainly apart from other races, roaming the wide-open spaces as nomadic herders. Their society is divided into strict castes depending upon which type of animal they herd.

3. HULDRES

Afanc—Strictly speaking, not a true Huldre, the Afanc is the result of cross-breeding between Huldre and non-Huldre species. On the rare occasions they are brought into existence, the resulting offspring depends upon the original nature of both Huldre and non-Huldre parent, but it is always unpredictable and frequently chaotic.

Bucca—Though it is the tiniest of fey creatures, the Bucca nevertheless possesses powers both awesome and frightening. It can be found only in the most sacred depths of the most ancient woodlands, and appears to most races as a mauve daisy, though in truth this is merely an illusion.

Ganferd—The most lamentable and malevolent of Huldres, the Ganferd appears as a lone, cloaked figure haunting the most desolate of places, and it will lure unwary wayfarers into some kind of trap in order to feed off their draining life force.

Knockers—Otherwise known as fairy miners. Often heard, rarely seen, they have a reputation for spite and mockery.

Kobold—Extremely foul, lumbering, monstrous Huldres, unintelligent and evil.

Nisse—The smallest and most benign of household guardians, the Nisse appears as simply a little old man, but even then only rarely, as they much prefer to remain invisible.

Spriggan—Small unseen Huldres of the hills, forests, and marshes. Inquisitive in the affairs of mortal races, they can be mischievous, at times even harmful.

Vardogr—The Nahovian name for the banshee, the wailing harbinger of a man's death.

B. The Creatures of Lindormyn

Adt-T'man (slough horse)—A small, tough, independent, and agile horse that lives free upon the Tabernacle Plains. Their Eastern name means "friend horse," but Westerners call them slough horses because of their molting.

Baluchitherium—This herd beast is one of the biggest animals to be found in Lindormyn, reaching twenty feet high at the shoulder. Its leathery hide is extremely tough, and it is heavily muscled.

Bonacon—Living singly or in small herds, bonacons are bizarre-looking animals notable mainly for a foul, geyserlike anal secretion they use for self-defense, which is said to be noxious beyond belief.

Cervulus (pl. Cervulice)/"Vettersteed"—Weird, bipedal creature of Fron-Wudu, part humanoid, part cervid (deer). Quarrelsome and aggressive, they fight with both horn and sword.

Fossegrim—The dreaded sea wyrms of Aggedon, whose blood is reputedly the most poisonous substance in the world.

Jaculus—An extremely venomous, arboreal snakelike creature with potent magical properties.

Knostus ("The Faithful"/"Loef")—Warhorses of the Peladanes.

Leucrota—A huge, hyena-like carrion-eater that prowls cemeteries.

Nycra—A boneless mass that can take on many forms.

Parandus (pl. Paranduzes)/"Treegard"—One of Fron-Wudu's larger "multipart" creatures; part deer and part Gyger.

C. Other-dimensional Beings

Air/Wind Elemental—Exists in the elemental plane of Air, but can be invited into the everyday world by those with the art of summoning it.

D'Archangels—Most powerful servants of Olchor.

Fyr-Draikke—Dragons.

Rawgr—Demons, the most ancient of all beings, having existed before the world was formed.

The Skela (Syr)—The Guardians of Balance.

True Giant ("Second One")—Two hundred feet tall, after the Rawgrs these are the most ancient beings on Lindormyn. Extinct now, but can still be summoned into corporeal existence by the "Spirit of Battle."

D. Races and Religions

Aescals—Predominant inhabitants of Wyda-Aescaland.

Akynn—Bards, storytellers, the keepers of history.

Asyphe—Desert warrior people living in the Asyphe Mountains to the south of Qaladmir.

Cynen—Polg title meaning "king"; also used by Vetters.

Lightbearers—Any followers of Cuna, including:

   Elder—High priest of Cuna.

   Mage Priest—Priest of Cuna.

Nahovians—People of Vregh-Nahov.

Oghain—People of Wrythe, including:

   Oghain-Yddiaw—The fighting corps of the Oghain.

Olchorians—Any followers of Olchor, including:

   Necromancers—Priests of Olchor.

Peladanes—Followers of Pel-Adan cult, a racial religion, including:

   High Warlord—Supreme leader of all Peladanes on Lindormyn.

   Warlord—Leader of a Toloch.

   Thegne—Leader of a Manass-Uilloch.

   Sergeant—Leader of an Oloch.

Skalds—Bards.

Stroda—Men or Haugers resident in Myst-Hakel.

Torca—Pagan people of the north.

E. Deities and Demigods

Cuna—The "god" of Truth and Light, ostensibly.

Drauglir (variously known as Daemon/Fiend/Hell Hound/Night-Stalker/Sea Wolf)—The most powerful of Olchor's Rawgrs, and the head of the Unholy Trinity of D'Archangels.

Erce—The Earth-Spirit.

Gruddna—Second most powerful of the D'Archangels. A great dragon.

Olchor—Lord of Darkness.

Pel-Adan—War god of the Peladanes.

Scathur—Third of the D'Archangels; a Rawgr in man form.

Skela—The Guardians of Balance, of which Chance, Fate, and Time are but three.

F. Places

Arturan—A town in south Pendonium.

Ben-Attan—A desert town.

Bhergallia—Small forested country west of Venna.

Blighted Heathlands—Desolate and uninhabited land to the west of Wyda-Aescaland.

Blue Mountains—A wild, uninhabited range that separates Wyda-Aescaland from the Rainflats lying to the north.

Crimson Sea—Large inland sea in the west.

Crouagh Forest—Huge forest extending from Grendalin into Quiravia far to the southwest.

Cyne-Tregva—Vetter town in Fron-Wudu.

Dragon Coast—The wild, sparsely inhabited northwest edge of the continent, extending north from Ghouhlem to the Seter Heights.

Eotunlandt—Fabled "Land of the Second Ones."

Folcfreawaru River—The small river, issuing from a cliff face, that runs west-to-east through Fron-Wudu.

Fram Peninsula—Large peninsula southwest of the Herdlands of the Tusse, and extending northwest into Linnormen's Sea; the southwesternmost point is the country of Friy.

Fron-Wudu—Huge northern forest, running from the Seter Heights in the west to the Ildjern Mountains in the east; to the north of it are the Giant Mountains; to the southwest are the Herdlands of the Tusse; to the south-center the Rainflats; to the southeast the Polgrim Hunting Grounds.

Ghouhlem—The northernmost country of the Dhracus: a horn-shaped peninsula extending west from the Herdlands of the Tusse.

Giant Mountains—A range of huge arctic mountains encircling Eotunlandt.

Godtha—Southernmost of the Dhracus lands, it is a peninsula north of Hrefna.

Grendalin—Forest country of the Gygers, running along Quiravia's northwestern marches. The Nail Mountains lie to the north, the Crimson Sea to the west.

Herdlands of the Tusse—Massive expanse of plain and scrubland extending to the Seter Heights in the north, the Nail and Speinstieth Mountains to the south, the Blue Mountains to the east, and to the western continental coast.

Hrefna Forest—Wild, lawless region of northeast Pendonium. Tyvenborg lies to the east, Godtha to the north.

Ildjern Mountains—Range of massive grey mountains beyond the northeast edge of civilization; Fron-Wudu lies to the west.

Jagt Straits—Arctic sea that separates Wrythe and the Last Shore from Melhus Island.

Last Shore—Northernmost coastline of continental Lindormyn.

Lindormyn—The world (a name meaning "Dragon").

Lubang-Nagar—The "Drake Tunnel" of Vaagenfjord Maw, which connects the Hall of Fire to the Inner Keep.

Melhus Island—Large, volcanic island, most northerly in the world.

Moel-Bryn—Small town in western Pendonium; Bolldhe's birthplace.

Moghol—The Trough of the Dead; deep subterranean chasm separating Vaagenfjord's outer reaches from the inner.

Myst-Hakel (Edgemarsh)—Small swamp town in the northern Rainflats. Its name means "Cloak of Mist."

Nordwas—Stockade town in the north of Wyda-Aescaland.

Old Kingdom—Largely uninhabited forest-and-river country to the west of Wyda-Aescaland, south of the Blue Mountains. No longer a kingdom, but home now to a few scattered communities of Torca, though largely given over to Huldres.

Pendonium—Huge country in the extreme west; homeland of the Peladanes.

Perchtamma-Uinfjoetli—Huge, bowl-shaped, steep-sided valley in Fron-Wudu; source of the River Folcfreawaru.

Polgrim Hunting Grounds—Wide plains between Wyda-Aescaland and Vregh-Nahov.

Qaladmir—Desert city.

Quiravia—Massive southern country, forested and temperate in the north, arid in the south. The much-vaunted "seat of culture and learning." Largely peaceful and prosperous, but with an undercurrent of corruption.

Rainflats—Largely uninhabited stretch of wetlands between the Blue Mountains and Fron-Wudu.

Ravenscairn—Cat's-tooth-shaped pinnacle above Vaagenfjord.

Rhelma-Find—Small, corrupt country lying between the Crimson Sea to the northeast, Bhergallia to the northwest, Pendonium to the southwest, and Jeithrir to the southeast.

Seter Heights—Small offshoot of the western Giant Mountains, in the northwest corner of Lindormyn; formerly inhabited by Torca.

Sluagh Valley—Largely unknown haunted cleft in the Blue Mountains.

Smaulka-Degernerth—Vaagenfjord Maw's "Hall of Fire," a huge tunnel that almost entirely encircles the Inner Keep of Ymla-Myrrdhain.

Trondaran—Tiny, isolated mountain country of Jyblitt the Hauger king, between Volg's kingdom and the Hallow Hills.

Tyvenborg—"Thieves' Fortress," on the border of Pendonium and Bhergallia.

Vaagenfjord Maw—The fastness of Drauglir on Melhus Island.

Venna—Semibarbaric, corrupt country occupying the narrow strip of land between the Crimson Sea to the south and the Nail Mountains to the north.

Vregh-Nahov—Forested country east of the Polgrim Hunting Grounds.

Wrythe—Most northerly town on the continent, home to the Oghain.

Wyda-Aescaland—Midsize country south of the Blue Mountains; home originally to Torca, now inhabited predominantly by Aescals, but ruled by Peladanes.

Ymla-Eligiad—Capital of Pendonium.

G. Weapons and Warfare

Assegai—Short Polg spear with a leaf-shaped blade.

Bagh-nakh—Spiked "knuckle-duster"; a favorite weapon of assassins.

Bachame—A special insulating fabric made by Peladanes.

Bhuj—Meat cleaver.

Chakram—Small Hauger-made disks of metal, usually poison-coated.

Crow's Beak staff—Short, hefty staff with a sharp "beak" at the business end.

Fasces—The old alliance between Peladanes, Nahovians, and Oghain that defeated Drauglir five hundred years ago.

Flamberge—Ancient, heavy sword with an undulating blade.

Haladie—Polg "double dagger."

Katar—A short, V-shaped punch-dagger designed to pierce heavy armor.

Kh'is—Mainly Olchorian sacrificial dagger with an undulating blade.

Left-hander—Heavy, wide-bladed parrying dagger.

Manass-Uilloch—A company of twenty-five hundred Peladanes, or fifty Oloch, under the command of a Thegne.

Maul—Very heavy two-handed mace, about five feet long.

Manople—Long blade attached to an iron gauntlet.

Misericord—A long, thin, stiletto-like dagger, especially useful for delivering the final blow to a fallen armored enemy.

Miter—Long, macelike weapon, with a heavy, spiked ball as its head.

Oloch—A company of fifty Peladanes, under the command of a sergeant.

Pata—A short punch-dagger attached to an iron gauntlet. Assassin's knife.

Shamsheer—The curved, five-foot-long, two-handed sword of the Asyphe.

Sword-breaker—A hefty, notch-bladed knife used to parry, twist, and snap opponents' blades.

Tengriite—A very strong, lightweight metal used by Peladanes in making armor and weapons.

Toloch—A company of fifty thousand Peladanes, or twenty Manass-Uilloch, under the command of a Warlord.

Ulleanh—The green cloak of a Peladane.

"Unferth"—The legendary greatsword of Pel-Adan himself; also the name given to the greatsword carried by all Warlords.

Voulge—A pole weapon with a spike extending at right angles from the main spear tip.

And now for a sneak peek at

A Fire in the North

BOOK II OF THE ANNALS OF LINDORMYN

The keening of the Children could be heard even within the deepest fastness of the keep. The victim slumped against the wall in the schoolhouse heard it, even above the wailing of the imprisoned child-souls and the rasping protests of the embittered dead that seeped from the very walls into his head. Manacled, his eyes staring vacantly ahead, and a thin line of discolored drool hanging from his lip, Methuselech had undoubtedly seen better days. But there was no reaction in him to that dire screeching that subdued every man and beast for miles around in cowering dread, no recognition in his eyes of its portent. Methuselech's mind had fled, run screaming to a far realm beyond this awful reality.

Even when he heard footsteps softly pattering across the flagstones outside—those soft, little children's feet; even when he heard the bar lifting from the door—such tiny hands, such unearthly strength—still he did not respond. Their work had been interrupted, but Methuselech knew it made no difference; they would be back soon enough to finish what they had started on him.

It was only when that voice—urgent, fearful, *human*—finally penetrated his brain like an astral harpoon setting its barb into the floating leviathan of his soul, that he slowly drifted back into the real world. Still bewildered and idiot-faced, he looked up, and saw Gapp Radnar staring back at him.

"Radnar..." he breathed hoarsely. "So they killed you too?"

"What?" the boy replied.

Gapp was regarding him intensely. Methuselech could see the terror in his eyes, the barely checked panic. There was also a presage of despair and an abundance of doubt. These were things the necromancer recognized so well, had centuries of experience of. But, for the first time in his long existence, he also saw concern. Care and concern for him.

He shook his head. This was doing nothing to alleviate his confusion.

"Methuselech," Gapp whispered, "are you all right?"

"All. Write..." Methuselech repeated distantly, not understanding the question.

"Listen to me! Can you walk?" Gapp went on urgently, unwilling or afraid to touch Methuselech's body, or even inspect it too closely.

Xilva's lower jaw started moving, albeit a little too loosely, but no words came out.

"That is, could you walk if you weren't manacled to the wall?" Gapp continued, half to himself. He clicked his tongue, at a loss what to do.

He could not complain too much, though; the first part had, after all, been easy. The time of day could not have proved more fortuitous. Few of the Oghain had risen yet, and those who had went about heavily attired against the freezing early morning fog, hooded and cloaked like shambling monks. It had been easy for the boy's light fingers to acquire such raiment. Thus clothed, he had smoothly infiltrated Wrythe's murky depths and arrived without incident at the keep itself, which, due to his own actions at the stabbur, he found unguarded. Slipping nonchalantly through the main door he had to choke back a scream when he found Schnorbitz already waiting for him there. How the animal had guessed his intentions, or managed to arrive without raising the alarm, Gapp did not have time to speculate. They had both arrived at the heart of darkness, and had swift work to do.

"Listen, Xilva," he hissed, "we're got to get you out of here now—those things could be back any minute. Hwald and Finan have drawn them off into the forest, and Schnorbitz's acting as watchdog at the front door, but we've got to act fast. Is there any way I can get you out of these manacles?"

"They removed his bones, you know," said Methuselech dreamily.

"Beg pardon?"

"Him over there. With special knives. Inserted them into his skin, dislocated his joints, separated the flesh, then drew out the bones, one by one. Hardly left a mark. What they couldn't remove, they just dissolved with vibrating tools. Turned his whole body into a boneless lump. We used to try that when we were kids, but could never get it right. They must have perfected the process—that one's still alive."

Gapp had no idea what he was babbling on about, and no time to care. He yanked furiously on the chains, but to no avail.

"The other one they tied to a stake," Methuselech went on, an abstracted look further clouding his eyes. "They tore pieces off him, and threw them to the Wire-Faces. He was still alive as they chewed his flesh."

Ignoring him, Gapp looked about the chamber for something to help him. If this was a true keep, a donjon, he assumed there would be some kind of tool he could use.

"And the last one." The prisoner smirked inanely. "They decided to cook. They heated him up in that suit of armor till he bubbled and smoked. Screamed like a lobster, he did!"

"Just shut up!" Gapp cursed, "Shut the flipp up!"

The boy was on the point of just giving up and leaving. If this really was, as Xilva suggested, a torture chamber, then it was surprisingly lacking in metal implements. Not even an axe or a jimmy to be found. The man was obviously raving.

Then he went cold all over—as the spirit of the Children entered him.

"Did you just say 'suit of armor'?" he asked, dreading Methuselech's answer.

"Over there," the prisoner confirmed, nodding to one corner. Though he had not really registered it at the time, his attention being somewhat diverted by the orgy of blood witnessed last night, Gapp now recalled that he had indeed seen a suit of armor in this room. There it stood, blackened and threatening. Even from here he could smell burnt...something. He had to find out for sure.

"...for weeks encased in a shell of iron," Methuselech was droning, "a metal cocoon..."

Gapp drew closer, closer still, until he could feel the heat radiating from it. Ignoring the revulsion that stuck in his throat, he grabbed the helm's visor and wrenched it open.

"Oh for the love of..."

He trailed off. It was like being struck full in the stomach with a flange-headed maul. The poor man's face was now a glistening lump of charred meat, mouth gaping in an eternal scream, looking through him with eyes as dead and white as those of a boiled fish.

Gasping, the youth staggered back. He turned and looked at Methuselech with eyes aged far beyond his years, his face clammy and drained of blood.

"Who *were* those people?" he demanded in disbelief.

Methuselech looked up at him and squinted like a psychotic, then giggled. "The Children have such monstrous appetites."

Gapp took another step back. "They eat them?" he breathed. "All of them?"

"No, not all of them. They usually leave the spines—give them to the Oga to wear. Like jewelry."

"But who were they?"

"Just people like you," Methuselech replied, a little more coherently now. "Adventurers to the Maw. But they never get further than here. Merchants might pass through unhindered; they're no threat. Your sort, on the other hand..."

"*My* sort?" Gapp was on the point of bolting from this place and leaving Xilvafloese alone with all its horrors. But he had to find out.

"I always felt there was something familiar about this place, ever since we arrived. And now I think I know what it reminds me of. You!" He leaned closer. "Who *are* you?"

"I'm the Black Sheep." Methuselech replied. "And I should never have come back."

Gapp ignored this babble. "What business is it of the Majestic Head if people want to go to Melhus anyway?" he demanded. "And how do *you* fit into all this, eh?"

"Yggr and I, we're in the same business. Or rather, we were. I'm the Black

Sheep, but he's the Caretaker. We've both been around here for a very long time. In fact, he's always been here…And his name's not Yggr; it's Scathur."

Finally, Gapp's legs gave way completely, and he sank to the ground, smitten by the full weight of despair and dread that that name brought upon him.

"We're dead," he whimpered.

"He's an artist," Methuselech murmured, "an artist who wears his victims' blood upon his raiment as a badge of honor, and encourages his wire-faced protégés to do likewise. I once saw him create such a masterpiece out of a man's body that his weeping could be heard throughout the lower levels, mingling in ecstatic rhapsody with the man's screams. He doesn't hate them; he exalts them…An artist in rapture, who's even been known to fall in love with his subjects."

Staring deep into Methuselech's eyes, Gapp was suddenly aware of two pairs of eyes looking back at him. There were the eyes of this present persona, this Black Sheep who was talking to him. But there were also the eyes of Methuselech Xilvafloese, that happy-go-lucky friend of Peladanes who (he now had to admit) Gapp had always found one of the more pleasant members of the little band from Nordwas. Either way, Scathur had no love for *him,* either of him. And against every instinct in the boy, Gapp had now come to save him. Pity, and that embryonic spark of loyalty that Hwald and Finan had engendered in him, overcame his misgivings.

"What did they do to you, Xilva?" he whispered.

"They forced me to watch all of it—that atrocity exhibition. Then they gave me a choice: either I gouge out my own eyes, or they burn them out with hot pokers. I have to decide before they return."

Gapp lurched up from the floor with a cry and lunged at the manacles, trying to wrench them off the wall.

"But it's too late!" Methuselech hissed, looking up at the boy in supplication. "I told them everything! Everything! Scathur knows as much about the Quest as do I. About Nibulus, Finwald, *everything*!"

"I really haven't time to worry about any of that at the moment," Gapp said, as he tugged on the manacles. "All I know is that your caretaker and his little friends will be back for their dinner very soon, and I don't intend to end up as pudding."

He gave up pulling on the manacles, and leapt over to a trough where he had noticed some cutlery. He grabbed one of the knives, the nearest one, and was just about to return to his task when something caught his eye. He hopped over to another of the dining implements, and snatched it up.

"My sword!" he gasped.

It was true. The blade they had taken from him, that sturdy little hiltless machete given to him by Ted the Vetter, was once again in his hands. These Children clearly had good taste when it came to stylish kitchenware.

Buoyed by this sudden upturn in his fortunes, Gapp set to working on the irons with renewed vigor. He inserted the pointed tip beneath the metal plate, and levered for all he was worth.

But it was useless: those manacles would never give. And now time had almost run out. Instead, and as a measure of his desperation, Gapp frantically began hauling on Methuselech's arms. He pulled, heaved and twisted, like a maddened terrier with a badger's hind leg, until finally, with a sound like a boiled chicken's carcass being pulled apart, Methuselech's hands came off.

The older man struggled to his feet and lurched off towards the door, the boy still staring in open-mouthed horror at the dismembered hands on the floor.

"Don't worry about them," Methuselech panted. "Let's go!"

Half in a dream, Gapp reeled after him. *Maybe he really is dead, after all,* he thought, as they caught up with Schnorbitz and fled the town.

That was the thing about Methuselech: you never could tell.